Be

Book one in the 'Fading Mirror' series

For Ayinke Moon

◐

Contents

Beyond The Mirror

Beyond The Mirror

This is a work of fiction. All of the characters, organizations, and events portrayed in this novel either are products of the author's imagination or are used fictitiously. Any resemblance to actual persons, living or dead is purely coincidental.

Preface

Dhukai are secretive organizations composed of spies, assassins, and mercenaries. Although their activities are often deemed illegal, they remain in high demand by affluent and influential families, including noble houses and monarchies. Many Dhukai serve one specific house or family for generations, establishing a legacy of loyalty and service. Additionally, some lower-level Dhukai offer protection services to middle-class peasants who can afford their fees, ensuring a wider range of clientele and influence.

The Dancing Swans

Shumaiyuki always found delight in the music of her own laughter, so she laughed often. And today she was a symphony of sweet-sounding giggles, whose melodic notes wafted behind her like incense smoke on a soft breeze

Running, she navigated Odahni Castle's mind-boggling maze of long, copper-green corridors. The pitter-patter of her rose velvet slippers atop the soft, iridescent gold runners played like a quiet metronome flowing with the tempo of her mirth. She ran faster and farther away from the gaggle of nursemaids who gave chase.

"They won't catch me this time," she turned onto another hallway indistinguishable from the last

"Come on then!" calling back with a big pearly grin.

Her bright, green gold eyes watered ever so slightly from the gust of her flight. Wow! They were so slow to keep up. She continued down the tedious stretch, warmly lit overhead by flat angular paper lamps.

Farther ahead she could see the corridors divide. What was it again? The right turn, or left? Her eyes darted back and forth for confirmation. Left, right, right… half turn, wall! she counted out the steps on one hand as she sped up and took the left corridor upon reaching the intersection.

Then came a desperate call from her rear.

"Princess! Princess! Please child, it's enough!" This from a soaring, wilted woman who struggled to keep up, her meager frame made fuller by the heavy layers of her jade and beige silk robes.

Shumaiyuki laughed even louder. "You have to catch me, Nami!"

"Little beast! I am your Obánā! My given name has no place on your tongue!"

"Just because you're my Obánā doesn't mean I have to listen to you all the time!" Shumaiyuki quickly wiped away a wisp of saliva which trailed from her mouth to cheek.

"Why? Why must you be so troublesome of late when once so obedient?"

"Why were there men up here the other day? And what was that sliding wall they were closing?" Shumaiyuki shot back. "I'm going to see what's behind it!"

She was certain of what she had seen.

"They all pretended to not know what I was talking about!" Lies! She stopped to catch her breath, tapped her foot out of habit, and waited several seconds.

"I don't want to get too far ahead of them in case those men are there again," she braced the underside of her thumbnail against the back of her two front teeth and nibbled. *"There could even be a monster, or demon hiding behind that wall."*

"Shumaiyuki!" Nami's grating voice was closer now and brought a curl to the girl's upper right lip. *Obánā is getting worried*, she thought. "She never calls me Shumaiyuki," and took off down the hall again, made a right turn and called back, "Why are you so slow?" Her voice was both angelic and naughty.

"You are a terror!" responded the governess. "End this lark now and all will be forgiven! Please, princess."

Shumaiyuki continued running, laughing loud enough to ensure that she was heard. "This is what you get for lying to me."

She knew that men, mainly soldiers, came and went on the ground floors of Odahni Castle. But no man, aside from her uncle, was allowed to enter its upper apartments. Thus, when she wandered onto two men sliding an ornamental wall back into place, her curiosity was set aflame.

"You told me it was just a dream, Obánā!" she shouted. "It wasn't a dream," she thought.

She took a deep breath and broke into a sprint, found the half turn previously envisioned, and stumbled forward through a rectangular opening into an empty room where the wall stood.

Victorious, she placed the balls of her hands on her hips, cocked her head to the side and smiled.

Shumaiyuki glanced around. The room was heavily shrouded in shadows, and the warm light of dusk filtered in from a large window to her left. The small space was empty, save for three large, reeded tatami mats laid atop a honey-colored placard floor, and a fanciful gold paper lantern overhead decorated with flying swans and peonies.

Every apartment the princess had visited in the castle was generously adorned with the essentials of leisure and domesticity. She thought it strange that this tearoom was so sparse. But she was not drawn into mischief by its lack of decor as much as she was by the dominant three-paneled wall she stood across from, or rather, its middle 8-foot by 12-foot section.

"Doesn't look like a dream to me," she whispered as she let her eyes drink in the dazzling scene before her. Painted in the center panel of the wall, beneath a persimmon sky with gold-dusted clouds, were two elongated opaline swans dancing together in a shallow pool of water surrounded by polychromatic stalks of thin bamboo.

Shumaiyuki slowly walked closer as she considered the image. Then came a pause as she studied it further. With wings outstretched to the heavens, she saw the swans were conjoined at the gut, with one's neck violently caught between the other's beak.

A single eye from either, locked in an eternal glare with the other.

Shumaiyuki balled her fist and shook her head back and forth as if to ward off the sudden uneasiness that had settled over her. Determined to sate her curiosity, she marched over to the image and placed both her small hands on the breast of the swans and gave a heavy push. The wall gave a springy push back, and then sunk inwards several inches.

"Princess!"

It was Nami, much closer now, so Shumaiyuki quickly slid the wall along its inner metal track until it was hidden behind its outer wall. Inside revealed another space, much smaller than the room. It housed a parched, splintery staircase that ascended to the uppermost reaches of the castle in a stacked box pattern.

"Wow!"

Shumaiyuki's eyes grew larger, and a smile made its way back to her face as the apprehension she felt from the swan dance abated, and the excitement of adventure returned.

"Shumaiyuki!" The girl jumped at the exasperated voice of Nami and turned to see the old governess standing in the room's doorway panting, a sharp look on her face. Behind her were several more maids of varying ages, all wearing a mix of concerned and vexed expressions.

"You get back over here right now! Do you understand me? You should not be here!"

"You said there was no room with a swan wall! But look. Here it is, and you've all been hiding it from me!"

"You are not to play in this part of Odhani!"

"I can play wherever I want, Obánā! This is my castle! All mine," she pointed at the old woman. "I'm only eight now, but uncle says one day I'm going to marry the emperor, and then every castle in Behrani will be mine too!"

She stuck out her tongue and slid the wall closed, encasing herself in darkness, though she could just perceive a distant source of light above which she took to be the top of the staircase.

"Sure is a long way up," she sighed. "But I can do it! I can do anything because I'll be an empress!"

She ran up the first stretch of the first flight, seven steps in all. She turned left, seven more steps, and then another, 1-2-3-4-5-6-7 up. Another left and seven more stairs cleared her of the first hurdle.

“That wasn’t so bad,” she said, slightly out of breath. “But there’s a lot more to go.”

“Shumaiyuki!” Several feet below her, Nami stood at the foot of the stairs, bathed in a soft palette of light from the outer room. Shumaiyuki noticed a pleading in the old woman’s voice she had never heard before.

“Dear child, don’t make me climb these stairs.”

The thought delighted Shumayuki. “If you want me, you’re going to have to come get me, Obánā,” she said and took off to clear the second flight.

The old woman struck the air with a gnarled fist and turned to her subordinates.

“You, and you! Quickly! Up after her,” she ordered two nervous-looking youths, adding wearily, “I will tail along presently.”

“This must lead to a secret tower!” Shumaiyuki’s voice echoed off the walls of the dark, cramped space as she maneuvered into the first turn of the third flight, climbing ever upward.

“Come back down, child, or your lord uncle will be terribly upset with you! Is that what you want? To disappoint the lord of your house?”

Nami struggled to speak, still catching her breath. Her thin veil, a soft green embroidered thing, stuck to a mist of perspiration dappled across the wrinkles of her brow.

“When I marry the emperor, uncle should fear ever disappointing me!”

“Oh saucy! You’ll catch an early nap for that one!”

“Not if you don’t catch me first!”

Shumaiyuki gathered her coral, rose, and peach robes at her waist to quicken her gait. To her chagrin, the two maids were already into the third turn of the second flight. She would have to make a sprint of it.

Adding something between a hop and a jump, she pushed forward off the rickety banister with her arm, adding to her forward momentum. Her tiny legs began to cover two steps in every single stride, determined to win the race. For her, the prize would be solving a spectacular mystery. To lose now would mean her being dragged back to her chambers in defeat, never to be allowed anywhere in the vicinity of the swan wall again.

When Shumaiyuki finally did reach the top of the stairwell, thirteen flights of creaking timber lay beneath her. She winced when she glimpsed the two maids navigating the ninth and tenth.

“They’re too fast,” she said, out of breath.

Hot beneath her heavy robes, she stood before a simple woodgrain door not much taller than her, noting an adult would have to bend down to pass through. She quickly slid it aside and stepped into a brightly lit, ornate corridor whose long narrow walls were embellished with an expansive mural illustrated with scenes of life and leisure.

There were maidens lounging, the delightful greenery of tea gardens, distant mountains in varying shades of indigo, and multicolored skies. Each image sparkled and shined with a life of its own.

“Am I dreaming?” Shumaiyuki skipped gaily down the hallway, a look of joyous wonder on her face.

The mural was cool to the touch. Shumaiyuki ran her hand along a panel replete with curved-roofed architecture, street vendors, horse-drawn carts, and extravagant palanquins. The people in the town seemed to move as she passed them, an illusion of light and the metallic-infused paints used to render them. However, her quiet revelry was abruptly interrupted by the soft screech of the splintery door sliding back open.

Shumaiyuki glanced back down the hall to see one of the teenage maids crouching and pulling her way through the door, quickly followed by the other. “Princess,” she scolded in a harsh whisper.

Shumaiyuki burst out laughing. “Isn’t it wonderful?” she sang, spinning around in a circle with outstretched arms. “It’s like we stepped into a treasure chest! Look at the ceiling! Even the clouds sparkle like diamonds!”

Panicked looks seized the maids’ faces as they both made quick, clunky gestures covering their mouths and waving their hands, a clear warning for Shumaiyuki to keep her voice down or not to speak at all.

She laughed louder. “If you want me to be quiet, come and get me then.” She turned around and barreled down the hallway at her top speed. As she neared its end, she heard a voice float from around the bend ahead of her.

“Princess, please calm down and come back to your chambers,” the craggy voice of an older woman, but not Nami’s, thought Shumaiyuki.

This was immediately followed by a defiant and emphatic, “No! Leave me alone! I hate all of you.”

Shumaiyuki turned the corner onto the adjoining corridor, attempted but failed miserably to halt her forward momentum as she ran head-on into what appeared to be a mirror image of herself.

The other girl leaned heavily on her left side, supporting herself with a wooden crutch stuffed underneath her armpit. Her green-gold robes swayed as she hobbled in gold velvet slippers. A thick, scarlet obi made her waist, the opposite of Shumaiyuki’s soft yellow obi laced with red threads. The girl too wore a decorative hairpin, a gold swan in flight, an exact match to Shumaiyuki’s silver hairpin.

The two collided face to face, and Shumaiyuki was thrown backwards, followed by a bright flash of light, darkness, and then the ceiling’s painted shimmering clouds as she lay on her back. The other girl let out a little yelp and flew back into the pillowy legs of an older, lumpy woman stuffed into drab gray and blue linen robes.

“You should watch where you are running!” the girl snapped as she rubbed her sore nose.

Shumaiyuki rose from the floor and stepped back, her nose and lips sore from the collision. She tried to form the words for an apology but found a lump in her throat prevented her from speaking.

"Wait… it's you," said the girl, as she peered into Shumaiyuki's red face. She pointed at Shumaiyuki with a rigid finger, turned back to the older woman, and screamed, "It's her! Yuyuki!"

The woman, pumpkin-like with a wrinkled, heavy round face, bulging eyes, and sagging lips, scowled. She covered the lower half of her face with the sleeve of her robe.

"What is it doing up here?" she pointed accusingly at Shumaiyuki as the princess's maids rounded the corner.

Tears welled up in Shumaiyuki's eyes as she covered her ears, dampening the sound of the woman's voice. Both maids lowered their own tear-filled eyes to the floor, stammering unintelligible excuses when they were cut short by the girl.

"You are not me!" she screamed; her face contorted into a horrid, scary mask. Her hazel, almost golden-green eyes were two orbs of enraged fire, aimed at Shumaiyuki like daggers. She was panting furiously, her thin chest heaving, her head whipped left and right.

Shumaiyuki backed away, instinctually raising her arms in defense. Yet she hadn't sufficient time to let the horror of the accusation sink in, for the girl had already dropped her crutch and nimbly hopped forward on her right leg, wildly swinging her arms.

Shumaiyuki screamed as the girl grabbed the frontal bun of her hair and pulled her face down to the floor. The young maids shrieked and held one another, unsure of what to do. Shumaiyuki, face pressed roughly against the green runner, felt like she was being stoned from above, and wailed as the girl pummeled her with her balled fist.

"Shumai!"

The old woman, with a gait tilted to the right and round about the hips, waddled over to the girls. She found it a challenge to fully bend over and intervene and called out again, "Shumai, that's enough! Stop beating the thing!"

"You are not me!"

The girl, Shumai, maneuvered her entire weight onto Shumaiyuki's back, and with both arms drove the poor girl's face harder against the floor, ignoring the repeated calls of "Shumai!"

"Ouch!" Shumai hastily drew back her hand, finding a tiny prick of blood on her palm.

Shumaiyuki's swan hairpin was to blame. Her face twisted into a growl, with teeth bared, as she snatched the silver swan from Shumaiyuki's tattered bun, ripping out several strands, and with a mighty downward thrust, screamed, "Die!"

The girl let out a stifled scream as Nami's withered hand caught her at the wrist, preventing the deadly strike. The old maid delivered the murderous cherub a severe slap to the face that sent her flying back into the arms of the old, round-faced woman.

"You dare strike the princess Shumaiyuki! You will be beheaded for this!" cried the round woman.

"And you would stand there and watch her murder our future empress?" Nami glared at the girl, Shumai, then back to the maid, "You are well aware that your charge is now Yuyuki and should be addressed as so. This is Shumaiyuki," Nami pointed to the crying princess, a crumpled mess of silk robes trembling on the floor.

"Recognize your disrespect and repent." Nami knelt down and took the shaken girl into her arms.

The princess's nose leaked a stream of blood and snot mix, as sweat and tears stained her face, which she promptly hid in the old woman's withered breast. Shumai buried her face in the plump woman's waist. She patted the girl's back and shouted, "You may have the Lord's ear. But once he finds out you allowed it up here…"

"It!" Nami spat the word back at the woman. "Vile hag! Hold your tongue lest I remove it myself," she took the hairpin and deftly spun it around in her hand, aiming it at her rival.

The old pumpkin gave a deflated welp and backed away, clutching onto Shumai as the child cried and mumbled, "She's not me…"

"This will not be forgotten, Obánā Ehpthebi Nami."

"Tend to your ward, Obánā Te-Tae, and I will tend to mine," said Nami, and lifted Shumaiyuki up with her as she stood.

She waved away the two weeping maids' offers to carry the child instead. Shumaiyuki looked up from the safe nest of her nurse's arms, her voice a fragmented whisper, "Obánā? Who…who was that girl?"

Nami leaned down and laid a soft kiss on Shumaiyuki's damp forehead.

"A dream, my love. Just a very bad dream," as warm tears fell from her eyes onto Shumaiyuki's bruised cheek. She carried the shaken child down the gilded corridor back to the sliding door, repeating, "A dream. Just a very bad dream."

Emily Heart

"Shu-mai-, Shu-mai-yu…ki. Yu-yu-ki. Yuki?"

Lost in thought, Emily Heart slowly played with the name's syllables just under her breath. Japanese? Maybe? She wasn't certain but could swear one was at least a delicacy she had enjoyed, once or twice with Rebecca, and thus continued to explore their pronunciation.

It was the abrupt clang of a plastic bowl being placed atop a worn formica table in front of her, that wrenched her from her hazy reflection.

"Eat! You slept late. You have to do double-time to get to class," said a tiny twig of a woman handing Emily a dulled silver soup spoon.

"Morning Dolores."

"Excuse me, you little smart mouth?"

"Jeez grams, just kidding." Emily rolled her eyes.

"Great! Cream-of-wheat again," she looked down and frowned at the steaming contents of mush inside the faded pinkish bowel.

"Wow. Instant at that!"

"How can you tell the difference?"

The older woman with a slight hunchback, subtlety lurched forward as she walked over to the kitchen sink and filled a mug with boiling water from an electric kettle.

"I can't ever tell."

"Oh, I can tell the difference, grandma."

"Sorry kiddo, it's rent week. You know how it is. A day late and Mr. Reid plasters our door with eviction notices."

"Oh god that means instant ramen and fried eggs for dinner all week."

“Or boiled,” Dolores shrugged. She gave Emily a curious once over, “You look a little worse for wear this morning. What’s up?”

Emily sighed, “Up late working on that dumb ‘Through the looking glass’ assignment.”

“Through the looking glass? You used to love that book. Though I was a little concerned, the Queen of Hearts was your favorite character.”

“Yeah! But the assignment is on the essential parallelism in Carol’s narrative blah blah blah, whatever. It barely makes sense! I swear Mrs. Temple has checked out and is just giving us busy work until graduation. It’s eleventh grade all over again when Mrs. Sheldon had us reading stupid Narnia witch and the wardrobe!”

“But she did give you a separate reading assignment once you complained about it.”

“It was about Ernest Becker’s ruminations on dying grams.”

Dolores placed the mug of steaming Lipton tea next to the bowl and handed Emily a quart of half and half; a white carton decorated with a lavender cow jumping over a pink daisy sun.

“Well, I thought it had an interesting blurb.”

She walked back over to the small, heavily enameled metal sink. A powder blue tub, rust chipped here and there along its curved rectangular hull. And attended to the dishes within. She looked back over her shoulder as she sponged a chipped plate.

“Don’t get yourself all worked up this early in the morning Emily. Your grades are fine. Plus, I’m working closely with Mr. Green on college admissions.”

“Don’t know why. I already told you I’m not even sure I’m going,” Emily mumbled the words as she navigated a mouthful of hot cereal.

“You said you were thinking about taking a gap year. Not forgoing attending altogether. I’m personally against it. Especially with that brain of yours, the scholarships will come pouring in.

You're going to college straight away kiddo, and no liberal arts bull either."

"I told you I wanted to take a year off to look for work first!"

"Don't worry so much about the money. It'll come when it's needed."

"Somebody has to worry, grams. It's not like you put away a nest egg for my future!"

"Hey that's not fair Emily. You know I've worked myself close to an early grave to keep a roof over our heads."

"Off the books grams! We don't even have savings for god sake."

"Suddenly you're worried about savings?"

"Suddenly? This is like our daily conversation. What are you talking about suddenly?"

"Wow! You're in a mood this morning. What are you still upset over Darren Toliver?

"He's a fucking jerk!"

"Emily! Language!"

"What! Are you upset we might lose our PG13 rating? It was you who said I could curse when I turned sixteen. Well, I turned seventeen two months ago ma'am."

"Doesn't mean I like it. And maybe you shouldn't be dating someone you think is an 'effin' jerk. Especially if it's going to make you so moody."

"You wouldn't call a man moody!"

"You kids call everything sexism nowadays. You've been moping around the apartment all weekend now, and for what? A boy. Not sexist. Facts!"

"Honestly Darren is like number nine out of the top ten things on my mind. My number one is more concerned with how we're keeping the lights and wifi on this month?" said Emily.

"Probably wouldn't be so strapped had you let me do that modeling thing at the mall. Which when I graduate I will pursue whether you want me to or not."

"You watch your mouth young lady,"

Emily noticed a sudden sharpness in her grandmother's tone and rolled her eyes to the ceiling.

"What! What did I say that was so wrong?"

"I told you the whole idea of you modeling after you graduate is ridiculous. The last thing we need is your picture pasted up all over the place Emily."

"Why because of our immigration status or lack thereof?"

"You're cutting it real close with me Emily."

"But I was approached, grams. That lady said I have a look. And you saw the pictures Beck took of me! As self-conscious as I am, I thought they were great."

"That lady?" frowned Dolores. "The so-called agent you met on the street who brought you to tears? That one? You think I want to watch you go through the pain of questioning yourself to fit someone else's standards of beauty?

It's hard enough watching you try to keep up in your daily school life. You think I don't notice."

It's not like I cried in front of her."

"But she made you cry, nonetheless. What was it she said? You have a weird, but workable face."

"I think in retrospect it was supposed to be a compliment."

"And it wasn't just that! She kept pressing you for what race you were too. That's what sent you over the edge."

"Why'd you open that door grams? I bet no one ever kept asking you, what race you were mixed with like you weren't even human?"

"That is my point, lovely." Dolores softened her tone and stroked Emily's hair with the back of her veiny hand. "It broke my heart to scc you crying like that."

"And do you remember the first thing I asked you?"

"Oh, dear Emily don't. Not this early in the morning."

"What am I? That's what I asked you, and you just brushed the question off like you always do."

"Emily you're being…."

"What? What am I being? Am I being black or white? Spanish, Asian? Arab blend? Little bit of South American in there? I ask you and you tell me it doesn't matter! It matters grandma! It matters to me when I have to lie and say I have an African mom and Asian dad just to get people off my back. And then I have to make up which countries in Africa and Asia. It's exhausting."

"It's because you're overthinking it."

"And you have the nerve to tell me race doesn't matter because we're all God's children."

"That we are indeed my love."

"We are frigging atheists grandma!"

"Ok! That is enough Emily. I'll hear no more of this. Humph, gap year. What was the point of that MIT summer camp if you're going to just waste your genius?"

"It's never enough, is it! No parents, or grandparents. You can forget about cousins, aunts, and uncles. I bet a few of them had to be pretty genius too! Guess I'll never know, will I?"

"This again! So let's do it. We lost all our documents and family pictures in the fire."

"The classic 'we lost everything in the fire' cliche. Ding!"

"Cut it out with your CinemaSins crap. You can be such a smart ass sometimes Emily."

"Must've got it from my dad…oh wait."

"I'm done with this!" Dolores ran a handful of cutlery under a piping stream of water to clear them of suds. "We lost everything in that fire. Your parents…You know they…"

"Sacrificed themselves to get us out of the house. I know grandma. It's your go to story to guilt me into shutting up."

"Your being really mean Emily. Hurtful even, and I don't know why. But I wish you'd stop and think about what you're saying."

"So dramatic, grams? It's like we're in witness protection. You think immigration is going to see my photo on a billboard at the mall, and what? Kick down our door and march us off to jail? You sure you didn't kidnap me from a birthing ward or something?"

"What a rotten thing to say, Emily!"

"But…"

"And you hear how all these celebrities have stalkers. They have to get restraining orders, bodyguards, all kinds of stuff. Look at what happened to that actress in the eighties. Guy just shows up at her door and then.." she clutched at her chest, "just horrible."

"The job was just some local print stuff." Emily dipped into the bowl of what appeared, hot, damp sand and choked down a spoonful, sulking.

"I know you're worried about money kiddo, but I've got it handled. I always do. Don't I?"

Emily remained silent as Dolores busied herself with drying a glass that seemed to Emily, already perfectly dry. Several minutes of silence followed as she alternated between spoonfuls of hot cereal and tea, the latter helping her swallow the clumpy mixture of butter, sugar, cinnamon and…sand?

After several strained moments Dolores realized she had been holding her breath. "O.k wants going on with you?" she exhaled and placed a glass on the counter, a little too close to the edge for Emily's liking.

Emily didn't like the tension in Dolores's face either, particularly because she was the cause. "Nothing grams, I'm just… I don't want to really bother you with it. It's hard to explain."

"I'm all ears."

Emily hesitated, she stared at the spoon as she slowly swirled it in the mush, and then cautiously,

"Remember what happened to me after my drink was spiked at that party."

"Of course, I remember."

"Back then I was imagining all that crazy stuff…we just never really talked about it, you know."

"We're talking now," Dolores sat down next to her and placed her hand on the girl's shoulder.

Emily quickly turned away so that their eyes didn't meet and focused on the kitchen's butter creme colored walls, stained a tannish hue from frying grease and lack of proper ventilation.

"Emily," Dolores quietly coxed.

Emily ran her eyes over the kitchenette, cramped with rotund, oval shaped mid-century appliances and faux wooden cabinetry. A wave of phantom soreness passed over her nose and cheeks, vestiges of her dream.

"I've just been having a lot of those weird thoughts again. I don't know. On and off."

Emily felt ashamed in the shadow of her grandmother's pained expression. Coupled with the nervous unsteadiness of her own voice, she felt all the more uncomfortable.

"And my dreams lately. They're sometimes too real to be just dreams. Like I'm awake but still dreaming at the same time. Got me thinking. Maybe it's true. Maybe we are in a simulation and we don't even know it."

Emily detested the hint of vulnerability she displayed. It embarrassed her as she always thought of herself as self reliant and able to work independently through any challenge, mental or otherwise. But even she had to admit her current preoccupation with her dreams, which were growing in frequency, excited within her an increasing anxiety of impending doom.

"How long? Why didn't you tell me about it the minute it started happening?'' The sudden urgency in Dolores's voice highlighted wrinkles in her muscular face Emily had never noticed before.

"Because I didn't want you to get all freaked out like you are now! I'm o.k. I don't want you to worry…really," Emily attempted a chuckle that somehow sounded to her, like an admission of guilt.

"We cannot have a repeat of that."

"You make it sound like it was my fault."

"I'm not saying it was Emily, but you could have suffered serious brain damage. And now you're telling me you're slipping back into…"

"I'm not slipping back into anything. It's nothing like I was then. Just a weird dream or two. So calm down. I'm ok."

"What kind of dreams? I need you to tell me everything."

Dolores took Emily by the shoulders and forced the girl to face her. Emily found the desperateness in her voice unnerving and wished she hadn't said anything.

"Look at me! See, I'm smiling. Happy." Emily forced a grin.

"Sorry, my love I don't mean to freak out, but I was just so scared for you. I thought we had put all that behind us."

"And we have grams. Like I said just a dream," Emily took Dolores's hands into her own and gave them a squeeze.

"I can call Dr. Feldman at the office today," Dolores stood and massaged Emily's shoulders.

"Um. Please don't, grams!"

"I'll be discreet. Trust me, more than half the people in the city are on the couch. Who knows? I could probably use some couch time myself."

"You telling me," Emily stood, towering over the diminutive woman, and hugged then kissed her on the cheek.

"O.k, I gotta like, get ready to bounce so…I'm gonna brush my teeth and stuff, but nice talk Dolores," she winked.

"Don't be a smartass! Miss food waster," Dolores pointed to the half eaten Cream-of-Wheat.

"I'll have the rest for dinner. Save us some dough." Emily left the kitchen and turned to her immediate left and entered their bathroom, half the size of the kitchen, with a powder blue commode and sink, and a narrow standing only shower. It oddly enough had a lower ceiling than the rest of the apartment which always made her feel somewhat claustrophobic while inside. But in the moment it served as a quick escape to quiet her nerves.

She braced her hands on the sink, regarded her reflection in the spotty mirror/medicine cabinet hung above it, and took a deep breath. Emily studied her buttery apricot complexion and what she saw as the odd symmetry of her face.

"Why is my chin so pointy and sharp?" She frowned and poked at a tiny red pimple right at its base, then ran the back of hand over her impossibly high cheekbones, often commented on, usually positive.

However, she thought they made her look chipmunk-like. She squinted her narrow slits for eyes and then attempted to make them wider, and stared into two green gold discs and smiled.

She counted a light spray of freckles over her flared nose with its pert tip, then pursed her heart shaped lips into a kiss and laughed quietly.

After she splashed her face with several handfuls of warm water, she pulled back her auburn hair; each strand held a subtle metallic sheen akin to that of a raven's feather. She secured a crooked ponytail that was closer to the nape of her neck than the intended, center back, of the head.

"Hey, don't forget your cash card. I transferred enough for your lunch and an after-school snack." Dolores called out. She was still at the kitchen sink drying off the surrounding counter.

"Got it! Thanks."

Emily squeezed out of the bathroom and stuck her arm back into the kitchen waving the small white piece of plastic in the air so that her grandmother could indeed see that she had the card.

She shimmied her way through a narrow, dimly lit hallway that opened onto a tiny obstacle course that served as their living room. It was packed with large cardboard boxes marked in all caps, with titles like, 'LINENS', 'VHS' and 'BABY STUFF'.

The boxes competed for space with a confusing arrangement of worn-down mid-century furniture, two full clothes racks, and an old floor model, vacuum tube television.

Emily deftly navigated the maze to the apartment's front door with her grandmother close behind and retrieved her backpack off the floor at the door's base before she swung it over her shoulder.

"Emily. Are you sure you're ok?" Dolores smoothed a damp, silvery strand of Emily's hair from her eyes as Emily knelt back down so that they were at eye level with one another.

"Should I be worried?"

"The 'should I be worried, but don't really want to discuss the matter too deeply cliche!' Wow grams, you're really knocking ' em outta the park this morning."

"That's not fair Emily. You always try to turn a serious matter into some kind of joke. We'll talk tonight. I mean it, ok."

Dolores leaned in and kissed Emily on both cheeks followed by a quick I love you. Emily attempted a smile, then trotted down a wide hallway lined with the same metal doors painted over in thick coats of hunter green as their apartment.

She made her way down a chipped granite stairwell badly in need of a once over with a mop. Outside she was immediately misted over with tiny beads of sweat as she stepped out into the overcast but humid air. Her nose wrinkled at the familiar musky blend of sulfur and cinnamon rot, courtesy of a nearby baking factory, and an energy plant several blocks south, at the edge of the river bank.

She turned around and regarded the dull oak colored, pre war building she was raised in. It had seen better days, pock marked with a red brick here, a gray one there, signaling years of band aid repair.

Pre-war buildings in varying states of disrepair were indicative of her working-class neighborhood whereas its surrounding town of multileveled apartment complexes and businesses were more modern and austere in appearance. Emily appreciated the mix, with hopes of one day living in her own doorman building.

She pulled the extra-large hood up over her head, casting her face in shadow, and began her morning walk to school.

She only got a few steps before she noticed a little scrap of thin white and yellow paper neatly tucked beneath the wiper blades of her grandmother's car and called back up to her apartment in a braying yell that affected a depression era, Brooklyn accent.

"Hey ma! Hey ma! You got a ticket!"

After several seconds Dolores appeared and rested her elbows on the inner ceiling of the living room window.

"What are you carrying on about?" she asked.

Emily pointed to the ticket on the nicked windshield of the faded, butter creme hatchback and repeated,

“Hey grams, you got a ticket! Looks like you forgot to switch sides of the street for trash pickup!” and blew her grandmother a kiss. Dolores caught the kiss and crushed it in her hands with a frown and called back,

“That was your job last night”

“Yeah but I don’t have a license, so…” Emily shrugged then skipped down the street.

Seitogi

Emily yawned and stretched as she stood by the intersection. Waiting for the traffic light to change, she caught a side eye from the well-dressed woman standing next to her, and immediately felt a little self conscious.

She looked over her khaki, high rise capris, oversized, pink plaid hoodie, and scuffed boat shoes and wondered how she had ever decided that would be an appropriate outfit to wear.

Both offered the other awkward smiles, with Emily scurrying across the street the moment the light switched to green. Her hands stuffed in the papoose of her sweatshirt; her face obscured by its hood.

She crossed over to the sidewalk parallel with the woman, and continued on without looking back. A moment later, she froze and let out a little yelp as her world went dark. She felt a pair of moist hands covering her eyes and instinctually struck backwards with her elbow, connecting with her assailant's ribcage.

The hands were quickly withdrawn, and then she heard,

"Oww Ems what gives?" a freckle-faced girl with a bouncy mass of curly red hair that swept beneath her ears and fell down her shoulders, quickly pulled away and grabbed her gut laughing.

"Bro! What's up with you? Why are you all jumpy?"

"Oh, it's you Beck! Not cool," Emily hung her head and took a deep breath.

Beck, Rebecca wore wide red-rimmed circular glasses with blue banded braces. Her arched eyebrows and slender nose gave her an uncommon beauty. Her wide eyes flashed a cool blue and her rose pink lips turned up in a perfect smile.

"You o.k?" she asked Emily with a hint of concern.

"Fine, you just scared me, that's all."

“You were supposed to pick me up so we could go over notes for Mrs. Temple’s quiz. Remember?”

“Damn! Sorry Beck, I forgot. My mind has just been all over the place this morning…I was up studying all night and woke up really late.”

“Because you’re a neurotic STEMMY. I blame you if I get an F.”

“I’d blame that dorky cinema society newsletter I bet you were working on instead of studying, and you know I hate being called a STEM girl. It’s so sexist.”

“As president of our school’s prestigious film organization, Emily. It is up to me to preserve the wondrous legacy of the silver screen. And seeing how my best friend is a genius, it’s up to me to get good grades off her homework.”

“God, you sound just like grams this morning, going on about college. So did you get the newsletter finished?”

“Yes, but not that you care, STEMMY.”

“For God’s sake Beck! Including us, we only have five members,” Emily laughed. “Sorry to tell you sis, but no one watches old Elizabeth Taylor movies anymore.”

“jeez Ems! We still watch. And what kind of talk is that from the friggin vice president? Bette Davis would turn in her grave!”

“I only agreed to be your veep as a favor. I barely know who Bette Davis is.”

“Oh my god Emily. Jezebel!”

“What! Jezebel? Oh dear lord, of course! The lady who was ostracized for daring to wear a red dress to the ball.”

“And we can’t forget, ‘All About Eve’ can we?”

“But can’t we tho?”

“Gawd you’re breaking my heart here, Heart.”

"Sorry." Emily made a sad face, "You know you're my favorite person right."

"Coffees on you," Rebecca sighed, and then, "Oh my god sexy alert, sexy alert!"

"Wha..?" Emily looked up ahead, where approached a tall young man dressed in a sun bleached, navy yukata and pants. He wore a ratty blue top knot atop his head, of which was tilted back sniffing the air. Seemingly unaware he was about to walk right into her.

"Watch where you're going jerk!" Emily gave him a hard shove as they passed but kept walking without looking back.

"Why'd you have to yell at him Ems? He was hot. Like, brand me with a scarlet letter, hot!" said Rebecca.

"Oh girl, put it back in your pants. He was a total weirdo. Walking around sniffing the air like a bloodhound? And what in the hell was he wearing? "

"Granted it was a little cosplay-ish with the light blue hair and all, but you gotta admit he was hella cute."

Emily sighed, turned back to give him another look, and grimaced,

"Oh my god Beck! He's just standing back there staring at us."

"See Ems! You pissed him off. Why'd you have to push him?"

'Oh shit I think...Yes he's walking back towards us Beck! Do something!"

Giggling, Rebecca grabbed Emily's hand and pulled her along with her in a sprint down the street. Emily gave into the scary hilarity of the moment and laughed too as they ran.

Being raised in the city, she was no stranger to the lewd looks and unwanted attention she received from men much older than she, and had already at her young age built up a mental callous in order to carry on through her day without screaming.

It was second nature for her to glance back every few steps when she walked alone, day or night, and she kept a small tube of pepper spray on her keychain just in case. Looking over her shoulder, she was relieved she wouldn't be needing it, as the man didn't chase, but just stared at their retreating figures with a look of confusion on his face.

Two blocks later, they stopped in a bodega where Emily used her lunch card to purchase her and Rebecca's coffee. After making sure the coast was clear of Mr. Blue haired cosplay, they made their way over to Victory Park where on the playground a group of older people were going through the motions of their morning Tai-chi.

Emily and Rebecca took a bench directly across from the elders, and quietly watched for several seconds before Rebecca reached into the front pocket of her shoulder bag and produced what appeared at first to Emily, a short thick twig.

"Look at what I swiped from Ari's ashtray."

"Your brother's such a pothead."

"Yeah. Lucky for us," Rebecca lit the blunt with a flameless lighter, took a pull, and then passed it to Emily. "He probably won't even notice it's gone."

Emily inhaled, silently following the slow graceful movements of the seniors with her eyes, a warm smile on her face. Gone were the days she and her grandmother would join in.

She was much younger then. But she stopped by almost daily before class, as she found it a calming experience.

"You alright Ems? Thinking about D Man."

"No, not anymore. I actually have other things on my mind."

"More important than Darren! Share?"

Emily took another pull followed with some light coughing and passed the smoking blunt back.

"I'm having those weird dreams again and it's screwing with my head."

"Oh cool! It's been a while," Rebecca dug into her backpack and pulled out a notebook, "Remember this? It's been a few months, but."

"Why are you carrying that around with you?"

"For an occasion like this. Now tell me everything."

Rebecca flipped past several pages of text where Emily's name appeared repeatedly and landed on an empty sheet. She quickly scribbled down: Emily Denice Heart / Dream 13.

"You're ridiculous. You know that?"

"Come on Ems. You have to admit this is some great stuff. With all the detail you give. I'm telling you it'd be a money-making screenplay. If you're not going to document them, I'm sure as hell am. Besides, you said it was like therapy the last time we talked about your dreams."

"Money making. You are literally the most unethical therapist I've ever met."

"You're welcome," Rebecca took a pull from the blunt and handed it back to Emily.

Emily rested her eyes back on the tai chi.

"I was a little girl again. But this time not in that village, but a castle. I was a princess known as the Pearl Swan."

"See! Pearl Swan. So cool!"

"I lived in this castle, where I found a secret door that led to a tower where another girl who looked just like me lived. We even had the same name. But she tried to kill me."

"Do you mean she tried to kill you like, metaphorically? Like when Luke Skywalker fought and killed himself in The Empire Strikes Back?"

"I don't know. Maybe? Or twins? The other me walked with a crutch, and accused me of trying to like, be her."

Emily looked down as Rebecca's hand quickly wrote down her words verbatim and smiled. Though she was moderately social with many friendly associates, she considered Rebecca her only true friend.

They met on Emily's first day of third grade. With Emily barely able to speak English at the time, Rebecca had befriended her when no one else would.

"I appreciate you letting me get some of this madness out of my head Beck." She handed Rebecca the blunt once her hands stopped moving and had sat down the pen.

"I'll go into detail later," she continued, "We need to head to class."

"You're stalling," Rebecca sang.

"Oh great! Shidia Moffit 12 o'clock," Emily rolled her eyes.

"Oh she's not so bad."

"You just think she's sexy.

"I know," Rebecca covered her mouth coughing, "I think everyone is sexy though. But Shidia has her good side."

"I'm so mad at how you can even find good in the devil."

"Bro. She looks like a classic Veronica Lodge!"

"So what! She told me right to my face I look like an Alaskan Aboriginal, which doesn't even exist!"

"I think it was supposed to be a compliment."

"Really? Beck. Shh, here she comes."

Tall, raven haired with porcelain skin and steel blue eyes, Shidia Moffit did indeed look like the Archie comics Veronica. With a questionable smile on her face, she marched over to Emily and Rebecca and gave them both a once over while tossing her long hair over the shoulder of her crested blazer.

"Getting stoned before class ladies? Classy." she said. "How lovely of you to share," she reached forward, taking the blunt from Rebecca, and pulled heavily. After holding the smoke in her chest for several seconds. She dramatically tilted her head back and released it straight up into the air.

"So, Heart," addressing Emily. "How devastated are you over Tolliver playing kissy face with Micmara at the game Friday night?"

"Hardly devastated," Emily reached for the blunt, but Shidia held it back and took another long, pronounced pull.

"Oh, but he's so bad to embarrass you like that in front of everyone. So lucky you weren't there to suffer it in person. Am I right Shaw?" turning to Rebecca, but Emily spoke up before her friend could answer,

"We're running late and walking that way. You should walk in the opposite direction," clearly fuming, Emily snatched the blunt out of the girl's hands more aggressively than she had intended.

"Oh my god, Heart. So combative. Word of advice. I'd tone it down some. Ever since your, (air quotes) incident, you're so quick to get pissed off. It's all anyone is talking about. Am I right Shaw?"

"Leave Beck out of this! You say people are talking about me?"

"Oh my god! See what I mean. So not chill, Heart," air kissing Rebecca, "Later Shaw." She cut her eyes at Emily and strutted away shaking her head.

"Hey at least she didn't say anything about how you're dressed," Rebecca said, sighing.

"What's wrong with the way I'm dressed?"

"Nothing! Nothing, you're fine. Hey, don't let Moffit rile you up, Ems. You know she's just jealous of you and Darren."

"I don't care! She's such a biotch. Only calling people by their last name? Who does that?" She stomped off towards the Tai-chi group with Rebecca close on her heels.

"You know how she can be. Just ignore her."

"But you heard what she said! Everyone is still talking about me being roofied. It was over a frigging year ago!"

"No one is talking about that anymore, except her."

Rebecca caught up and locked arms with Emily as they passed the elderly group and continued up a short hill at the edge of the playground; it led to a small, crumbling stone stairway.

Up the stairs, they passed through a rusted fence and took a brisk pace across a worn baseball field overgrown with weeds and patches of grass. Emily could see the top floor of their high school just beyond a fence of trees which boarded the whole of the field.

"So, what are you going to do about Darren?"

"We spoke on the phone yesterday afternoon. Asshole was too scared to even FaceTime me. I should have broken up with him right then and there, but I am going to do it as soon as we get to school."

"Oh no Ems! You can't break up with him! We're talking about Darren Tolliver here. Captain of the football team!"

"He's a running back and his stats suck."

Rebecca shrugged, "Well, o.k…whatever. He's super fine though!"

"You do know, I don't define my worth by dating Darren, right?"

"I know, but that's what you have me for. You're the school's star couple."

"We are not a star couple! You can't imagine how insecure you're making me feel right now."

"Insecure. What do you have to be insecure about? Your long legs? Or your tiny waist?"

"There's more to life than my mediocre looks Beck. Just ask my grams, she'll tell you."

"Says the girlfriend of the captain…sorry, running ball, guy, to the girl who's still trying to lose her baby fat," Rebecca, pinched her fairly average stomach through a thin ribbed blue knit sweater for reference.

"You don't have baby fat!"

"Girl, stop playing. I have a Baby Heuy belly, and full body freckles that make me look like I have measles, while you have cute anime ones perfectly accented on your nose."

"Anime freckles Beck?"

"Just saying. You're fine girl. Wear it with pride."

Emily placed her arm around the bunchy redhead's shoulder and nuzzled her face against her cheek,

"Well, you'll always be beautiful to me Ms. Shaw"

"Gee, thanks mom."

Once through the frail thicket of trees, and another rusted fence, they crossed the street over to Elmhurst High's Monument Mew, as the school was previously known as Monument High.

They walked up the mew already littered with students hanging out as the bell rang and hurried towards the four-story gothic structure that was Elmhurst.

"Ms. Shaw, Ms. Heart, mind the bell," warned a red bearded man in a loose gray suit and greasy hair as he hurriedly made his way past them, up the massive stairs and on through the school's church-like doors.

"Looks like you're running late yourself Mr. Shaw!" Emily shouted after him.

"Don't tease my dad bro! You know what an A-hole he can be." Rebecca nudged her in the ribs.

They both laughed their way up the stairs and entered into a long, student packed hallway. Arriving to a class half full and made their way to their respective desks with Emily slipping Rebecca a purple post-it sheet on the way.

"Some crib notes, better cram quick."

"You could have given this to me outside Ems."

"Sorry. You distracted me with the weed."

"So now it's my fault?"

"Tell you later, Temple's giving us the eye."

"Sucks, she made us move our desks apart." Rebecca sighed.

Emily sat down at her desk and began sifting through her book bag until she produced a blue, composition notebook skinned tablet and began immediately swiping through its pages.

"I'm going to need you to help me out on this one babe," the shy baritone of his voice vibrated in Emily's ear like the annoying buzz of a bee.

"Mosquito," she said, and turned around and looked into the subjectively handsome face of a smiling sand colored boy with hazy, gray eyes and a sharply tapered crew cut hair.

"Mosquito?" he asked.

"Yeah, they're blood suckers. Remind you of anyone?"

"Bro! Are you still in a mood?"

"Do I look like your frigging lifeline Darren? That's a no in case you were wondering, and I'm not your damned babe or bro!"

"Oh, come on Ems, how long you gonna act like this? How many times I gotta tell you Sara kissed me. Not the other way around."

"Well, you weren't trying to stop her were you. I saw the video! In fact, you looked like you were having the time of your life."

"Give me a break babe. I told you; it was nothing…anyway what's up with you today. I mean your hair is a mess and your clothes are all wrinkled. You're not even wearing any makeup?"

"You are really pushing it."

"My fault. I'm just used to my girl dressing the part you know. We are in contention for prom king and queen, wouldn't hurt to…"

"Ok Darren! You know what? I don't care about being prom Queen. I don't care about wearing cute little outfits or hair and makeup just to please you!"

"Yo Emily dial it back some. You're the one who…"

"The one who what?"

"Wow! You can be so stubborn sometimes. But it's part of what makes me love you," he reached for her, but Emily was quick to brush his hand away.

"I've got a lot of things on my mind. Right now, you aren't one of them. Now leave me alone or I'm going to call old lady Temple over."

"For fuck sakes! Help me out here Emily. I can't fail this test!"

"Ok. I will help you," Emily took a deep breath and affected a pleasant smile which to her delight caused Darren's to flip into a frown.

"We are over. Done, finito. Leave me alone. Don't talk to me in the hallways, don't call my phone, don't visit my home. I want absolutely nothing to do with you Darren Toliver."

"Nope! You're just upset about a stupid misunderstanding and don't know what you're saying."

"Screw you Darren! Don't tell me I don't know what I am saying!"

"You don't! You'd have to be crazy to break up with me."

"You know, you're such a user. I have been nothing but a brain bank for you these last two years."

"Whoa –the hypocrisy? No one even knew your name before I plucked you of obscurity. Bro, you rode my coattails to be one of the hottest girls in school now. So I'd be careful of who you call a user."

"What? Are you saying I used you? Oh for god's sake stop talking to me. You're such a goddamned idiot! I'm so glad I never gave you any!"

"That's because you're a tease. You barely even give me any over the clothes action and I still rock with you. Now you wanna dump me?"

Emily turned towards the front of the class and thrust her hand up into the air.

"Mrs Temple! Darren Tolliver is harassing me because I won't let him cheat off my homework!"

A quick hush silenced the morning buzz of the classroom as all eyes turned on Darren.

"No…no," stammered Darren raising his own hand.

Mrs. Temple, a dry timbered witches broom turned upside down and clothed, rose from her seat and slammed her hands down on her desk.

"Alright Tolliver I warned you!" Croaked the woman, clearly somewhere in her mid to late thirties, yet somehow she affected sixty plus.

"Lunchtime detention in Mr. Miller's room, and if you keep it up, it will be for the rest of the week."

"I didn't even do anything Ms. T."

"You showed up to class today didn't you," the woman mumbled, eliciting muted laughter from the twenty or so students.

"That will be enough then. Tablets out." she demanded as she returned to her seat.

"Nice work Ems," whispered Darren.

"Take one for the team Tolliver and go fuck yourself." Emily stuck out her tongue and then focused back on the tablet, rapidly tapping her foot on the worn linoleum floor.

Hours later, the first thing Emily saw when she stepped out of school for lunch was Rebecca waving to her from Monument Mew.

She waved back and skipped down the curved steps past other students and trotted over the grass, still moist, for the sun had yet to make a full appearance in the overcast sky, and the two girls hugged.

"So, I spoke to Darren." Rebecca began.

"Really Beck?"

"Hey, listen, he's really bummed out you've avoided him all morning. He wanted me to tell you he's sorry. And I personally think you should hear him out."

"Why because he's cute and on the football team?"

"He's also a shoo-in for the prom king. You could be his queen."

"Totally failing the Bechdel test here sis," said Emily.

"Bechdel, smechtdel! I refuse to let you turn down a crown! Not everyone gets to be PQ in her senior year Ems."

"You don't even care about any of this crap, Beck! You hate Americana BS."

"But I can't ignore an actual, cinematic teen romance involving my best friend happening right before my eyes either."

“The last thing I want is to be anybody’s queen!”

“Any girl would be lucky to have a boyfriend like him.”

“He is a selfish conceited jerk,” said Emily “Like, right out of a movie or something. I can’t believe I put up with it for so long.”

“I thought that’s what attracted you to him,” Rebecca laughed. “And you know Sara Micmara has had it in for you since junior high. She’s just trying to make you jealous.”

“Well, I’m not jealous. In fact, I don’t care. I mean what are people our age doing shacking up like we’re going to get married for anyway? Once high school is over I’ll never see either of them again. Shouldn’t we focus on our own personal growth first?”

“Girl what has gotten into you? You sound like one of my aunts! You know, the three-shut ins.”

I don’t know Beck. I feel like I’m already having a midlife, oh shit!…Oh no, oh no, oh no!”

Emily clutched onto Rebecca’s arm and began to drag them both back towards the building. Her shaking eyes fixed on the blue haired man she had shoved earlier as he boldly walked across the field towards them draped in his tattered foreign clothes.

“What’s come over you? Why are you…oh it’s him!” Rebecca followed Emily’s gaze to the approaching man.

“I’m not imagining him. You see him too Beck?”

“Of course, I see him! You must have made quite an impression on him earlier!”

“I’ll scream!” Emily called out as he shortened the distance between them in quick long strides. The intense look in his tight, jade colored eyes both frightened and intrigued her. His strong jawed narrow face, almost effeminate in its prettiness was eerily familiar; he was reaching for her.

“Enoshi…” he began but she frantically cut him off.

“Get the hell away from us!”

“Oh my God Ems, do you know him?” Rebecca purred while she playfully pawed at Emily’s cheek, like a cat.

“Ouiet!” Emily covered Rebecca’s mouth with her hand and pointed a rigid finger at the man, “And you. You get out of here or I’ll call the police!”

“Why are you acting this way?” he asked, “You are in danger here. The wizened woman tasked me with returning you to Behra.”

“Whoa! What language are you two speaking Ems?” Rebecca’s smile grew larger.

Emily let go of Rebecca, her thoughts were scattered as she realized the blue haired man hadn’t been speaking English at all, nor was she. But, how she could so easily speak and understand a foreign language was a mystery she hadn’t the time to pursue.

“Enoshi! Come with me.”

He moved Rebecca aside and took Emily by the wrist while digging in the breast of his dingy, slate colored yukata and fumbled about for something. But Emily dug her heels into the grass causing him to stop with an odd expression on his face.

“Enoshi! It’s me, Seitogi! Don’t you want to go home?”

Seitogi! The name sent Emily into a mental tailspin. Suddenly her mind was filled with dark images of large, scary men chasing her, a child, through falling snow, and a blue haired boy, streaked with blood as he cut through them with a short blade, while calling out to her, “Run Enoshi, run!”

“Seita…” Emily breathed his name out, barely audible.

Back inside the school, Darren, still reeling from his argument with Emily, sat at his desk, face down attempting to doze in order to clear his mind.

“Hey Darren,” Helix Foster’s nasally voice snapped him out of slipping further into an oncoming nap.

“Who’s the weird cosplay dude spitting at your girl out there on the grass?”

Darren shot up from his desk and joined the tiny, fox-faced boy with glasses too big for his head at the gated window and looked down onto Monument Mew. Both boys ignored Mr. Miller’s entreaties for them to return to their desk.

“Who the heck is that guy?” asked Darren.

“Don’t know! But body language says he’s pushing up and she’s not with it.”

“Or he’s the real reason she’s trying to break up with me!”

“And then there’s that way of looking at it,” Helix sounded skeptical.

“Well, we’re about to find out what’s really up! Getting all pissy with me because I gave Sara a little slip of the tongue and she’s running around with an extra from Bleach!”

“Or she’s shit scared,” added Helix, “because she looks shit scared to me bro.”

“I’ll get to the bottom of it.”

“Tolliver! Foster!,” Mr. Miller stood, “Back in your seats or you’ll be seeing me the entire week! Including after school!”

“It’s a date then!” Darren winked and darted out of the class, down the hall, passed the elevator and ran down a massive stairwell.

He brushed past several groups of students lingering about and burst through the school’s front doors just about out of breath. He growled at the sight of Emily attempting to shoo away the cosplay man like one would a feral cat.

“Hey babe! This dildo, fanboy bothering you?” he called out as he ran up to meet them.

“Oh, not now Darren.” Emily held up her hands to stall his advance as several students began to gather around them, forming a substantial crowd.

"What? He escape a movie set or something? What's with his gear? And that hair?" Darren stepped up to Seitogi, chin to chin. "I think you better get lost bro if you know what's good for you."

Seitogi looked to Emily confused,

"What is this boy?"

Emily puffed out her chest, feeling a smidge of confidence in Darren's presence, and repeated the threat to Seitogi in their shared language. But what Darren heard was:

"Leise-yu fuy khen."

He cocked his head to the side, swung it in Emily's direction and said:

"What's with the gobbledygook Ems?"

"They both speak some kind of language," with stars in her eyes, Rebecca bounced on her tippy toes behind Emily, clutching onto the back of her shoulders.

"The Wizened woman sent me. She is waiting for us on the other side of the mirror."

"That's enough talking, big guy." Darren took a few steps back and squared his shoulders affecting a fighting stance. The confused look on Seitogi's face grew stern as he too squared off.

"I'm uncertain of what this boy is doing," he spoke to Emily though his eyes never left Darren, "But you should warn him of the imminent harm he faces should he continue this play."

This isn't a game Darren! Emily whipped her head back and forth between the two men and the ever-growing crowd, but a lump in her throat quelled her voice.

Seitogi will kill him! Her legs were frozen in place, her hands shook. With her eyes tightly squeezed shut, she saw Seitogi, the boy not the man. She saw him standing in pure white snow, bathed red in the blood of five men who lay at his feet. Breathing hard, the boy offered her his grisly hand as the snow lightly fell around them.

“Enoshi.”

“So, this is the guy huh?” Darren’s tone was accusatory. It shook Emily back into the present.

“Sara said she knew there was another guy!” he continued.

“So, you have been seeing her!” Emily gave him a hard shove, effectively placing herself in-between he and Seitogi.

“He’s nothing! Don’t bother wasting your time on him,” Emily said to Seitogi in a quick rush of sounds and syllables only he could decipher, and then in English.

“I know I sure as hell have wasted enough of mine on him!” Emily’s eyes filled with tears as she turned away and ran down the lawn to the main road.

Seitogi made to go after her, but Darren jumped back in front of him to block his way, saying,

“Step off bro! Ems is my girl!”

Seitogi emitted a strange sound caught somewhere between a groan and a sigh, stepped to Darren’s side, and in one swift move swept the boy’s feet out from under him.

Darren was suspended in the air for a moment, and then landed flat on his back in the grass with a loud thump, forcing him to belch out a sound many debated afterwards was more a forced deflation of air rather than a loud passing of wind.

“Stay down,” warned Seitogi as he took to a quick gallop after Emily. Seconds later he was running with her side by side where he forcibly grabbed her by her upper arm to halt her gait.

Emily jerked back almost falling to the ground, gritted her teeth and quickly turned around delivering him a crisp slap across his face.

“Enoshi!” he shrieked and released his hold of her.

“Oh no Sei I’m sorry,” Emily reached out to him, but drew back, “Seita,” she repeated softly.

"Don't you remember me?" he felt a pain in his chest as his eyes filled with tears. Emily looked away as though she were ashamed.

"Seitogi I…" she began but found herself falling backwards as he stumbled forward into her.

He cursed himself for letting down his guard as Darren sacked him like he was taking down a defenseless quarterback. All three fell to the concrete. Emily scurried from under Seitogi as Darren took to pummeling him in the face and upper body.

"No Darren! Stop! You don't understand what you are doing!" Emily knelt to pull Darren off of Seitogi and received a sharp impact to her gut from his elbow. The blow sent her flying backwards with the back of her head colliding with the concrete, only slightly buffered by the cushion of her hair.

Despite the cushioning, Emily felt a sharp pain ricochet through her skull as the world temporarily went black. When she opened her eyes the gray clouds above were replaced with an ornate ceiling painted with clouds that sparkled like the finest of diamond tiaras.

"Enoshi," the sparkling clouds dissolved into Seitogi's sad eyes as he held her in his arms. Kneeling, he slowly helped her sit up. Darren scampered from the ground regaining his footing and rushed forward throwing a kick aimed at Seitogi's head.

Seitogi blocked the blow with his forearm and sprung back to his feet, still holding Emily as though she were the weight of a fallen leaf. Before Darren could rush him again, Seitogi landed on one foot, leaned back and delivered the boy a kick to his ribs, sending Darren back several feet to the ground.

Darren spat up a small amount of blood into his hand. Fear, rage, and embarrassment rippled through his psyche. Who was this man, this strangely dressed foreigner who seemed to know Emily so intimately? He rallied to his feet and roared, beating his chest like he would on the field after taking a rough hit during a game.

Seitogi shook his head, and once again warned, "Stay down!"

Unperturbed, Darren charged forward with a volley of wild thrust and jabs, forcing Seitogi to swing Emily behind him in order to defend against the series of ferocious, but ineffective punches.

"I haven't the time for this!" he yelled in his foreign tongue, caught Darren's arm at the wrist and pulled until it was straight and rigid. Darren screamed a terrified 'No!' as he tried to pull away with all his strength to avoid the inevitable.

No amount of struggle could stop the momentum of Seitogi's free hand, where in a reverse guillotine, he snapped the boy's elbow upwards, forcing white bone and cartilage to break clear through the skin like sharp shards of timber peeking up from the forest floor.

A hushed silence fell over the crowd save a few audible gasps as the ghostly echo of the cracked bone hung in the air. This was followed by a chorus of horrified screams in an array of pitches and tones as the crowd of students dispersed in all directions.

With his lower arm dangling loose from the elbow break, Darren howled like a fox caught in a bear trap and collapsed into Rebecca's arms; a wisp of his blood grazed her cheek as she lost consciousness and fell to the ground.

Emily cried out something inaudible and ran over to her fallen friends. She attempted shaking Rebecca back to her senses, but the sight of Darren's jagged, bloody bone, shredded muscle and ripped tendons was too much for her stomach and she vomited violently and fell back onto her hands and knees.

Seitogi reached into his yukata and produced a palm sized mirror encased in a thin frame of intricate bronze filigree, and with an outstretched hand, reached for Emily.

"Come with me, Enoshi."

Her response was a heavy, guttural sort of grunt, as she protectively wrapped her arms around Rebecca and held her tightly. Darren trashed back and forth in the unconscious girl's lap screaming loudly.

"Come Enoshi! We must leave. Now!"

"Get away from us you psycho!"

Seitogi looked at her impatiently, sighed deeply, then grabbed her arm, with his other hand he held the mirror up and stared into it.

Emily clawed at his grip, and with a feral scream that drowned out Darren's loud wails of pain, she cried,

"Let go of me!'' She tried pulling away, but Seitogi was not letting go. He reached down to stop her from scratching him, when Emily caught a glimpse of her eyes reflected in the mirror.

First she felt a kinetic rush of energy flow through her body. It vibrated right down to the core of her very being. She felt herself unfolding. Layers upon layers of herself were being stripped away, melting into the ether.

The physical became a blank slate. The concrete ground, the giant mew and towering gothic structure. They all disappeared along with the sky, and for one long, never-ending second, her world dissolved into a bright, white nothingness.

The scent of pine filled the air, crisp and lush with a rich green hue. It was an intoxicating aroma, infused with the refreshing and natural scents of grapefruit and tangerine, and delicate undertones of vanilla. Unlike the overpowering smell of cleaning chemicals her grandmother used to use in their small apartment, this pine scent was familiar and evocative, stirring up distant feelings of both yearning and serenity within Emily.

With each inhale, she was taken back to her childhood home in a quaint forest village. It felt like an eternity had passed since she had been there, but now she was back where she belonged and a sense of tranquility enveloped her. The rustling of leaves and the soothing songs of birds only enhanced the peaceful ambiance, and she took a deep, grounding breath, fully immersing herself in the moment.

However, the peace was short-lived and deceptive. The sudden darkness of an early morning sky shattered the serenity, as the rustling leaves transformed into loud, percussive flapping sounds, whipped about by the wind. Darren's gut-wrenching screams added to the chaos, as he thrashed about in the dirt, kicking and tossing in an apparent state of distress. The once peaceful atmosphere was now filled with fear and agitation, making it clear that something was very wrong.

"What the hell?" Emily shuddered as she sat up, her skin covered in goosebumps. Despite trying to make out her surroundings, all she could see were dark shapes in the pitch black. The starlit sky was devoid of any moon, and the dark canopy of trees above her only added to the eerie atmosphere.

The air had grown cooler, and she wondered why it felt like late fall. She shifted uneasily on the damp, grassy dirt, which was littered with stinging pine cones of various sizes, twigs, and dull sharps that poked her backside and the palms of her hands.

Along with Darren's wailing and the clatter of creaking branches, Emily could hear what sounded like ghostly human voices in the distance.

“What is this?” she whispered to herself. “Some kind of haunted forest?”

“Shut him up, or he’ll get us killed,” Seitogi warned, his voice barely above a whisper.

Killed! The thought sent a jolt of panic through Emily. She blindly reached for Darren and clumsily tried to cover his mouth, but his thrashing movements made it nearly impossible to keep his cries muffled. Desperately, she tried to calm him, begging him to lower his voice, but to no avail.

“Where are we?” Emily asked, trying to ignore the nagging feeling in the back of her mind that she already knew the answer.

Seitogi pulled her to her feet. “We have to move. We came out at the wrong location.”

“Get your damn hands off me,” Emily snapped, pulling away from him and dropping back down to the ground. She frantically searched for Rebecca in the darkness, finally locating her and pulling the unconscious girl up. “Wake up, Beck! Wake up!” she whispered urgently, shaking Rebecca vigorously.

“We are not alone,” Seitogi warned. “See the torches?”

“What have you done to us?” Emily demanded, her voice shaking. “Why is it nighttime?”

“We are back home in Behra, Enoshi,” Seitogi said, his voice heavy with the weight of their situation.

Emily didn’t want to accept it, but deep down she knew it was true. They were back in Behra, and she had no idea what dangers lay ahead.

“My name is Emily Heart!” she screamed, her voice filled with anger and fear. “You kidnapping pervert! Son of a bitch!”

“The boy is too loud,” Seitogi warned. “We must leave him and find the Wizened woman.”

“We are not going anywhere with you,” Emily protested, her voice trembling as she burst into tears. She glanced around, trying to see deeper into the surrounding darkness.

As she looked, she realized that Seitogi was right. Among the trees, she could see the flickering lights of live torches, accompanied by the varied shouts of men. Her heart raced with fear, and she clutched Rebecca close, not knowing what to do. The situation was rapidly spiraling out of control, and she felt completely helpless.

“Who are they? What do they want?” Emily asked, her voice filled with fear.

“Your head, Enoshi,” Seitogi replied urgently. “Now let us go, before they capture you and take it.”

With that, he grabbed her wrist and pulled her along, trying to lead her away. But Emily wasn’t having it. She screamed, slapping and punching Seitogi with her free hand as she tried to pull away.

Seitogi, however, was quick to react. He lifted her from the ground, tossing her over his shoulder like a sack of potatoes. Ignoring her protests of “We can’t leave them!” he took off running into the dark.

Emily swung back and forth like a broken pendulum and had to grab onto the back of Seitogi’s pants to steady herself. In a desperate attempt to make him stop, she clamped onto one of his buttocks with her hand, pinching down as hard as she could.

“Take me back! Take me back!” she screamed, tears streaming down her face as she was carried further and further away from the safety of her friends.

“Damnit!” Seitogi swore, wincing from the sharp pain caused by Emily’s pinch. But he didn’t have time to dwell on it, as he quickly pivoted to avoid the pointed end of an extended staff. The sudden stop caused both him and Emily to crash to the ground.

Two men stood over them, laughing. One held a flaming cloth-wrapped stick, while the other wielded the sharpened staff. Both wore rippling, brown body suits made of a rough material that also covered the lower half of their faces, giving them a sinister appearance.

"Enoshi, stay down," Seitogi commanded as he took to the air, as if pulled by a theatrical rigging system. He gained sufficient altitude, then darted back downwards, dispatching both men with swift kicks to their necks. One fell to the ground, his head bobbing from his shoulders like a ball on a string. The other fell on his torch and was consumed in flames.

Emily stumbled to her feet, her knees scraped and her hand throbbing with pain. The acrid stench of burning flesh filled her nostrils, and she covered her ears, trying to block out the ear-piercing screams of the man writhing on the ground.

"What's happening?" she cried, as Seitogi pulled her close and held her tight, trying to calm her shaking. She looked down at the burning man and felt her stomach turn, horrified by the sight of his contorting, smoldering body.

"More are coming," Seitogi warned. "Climb on my back and hold on tight. These men want to kill you."

"Why me?" Emily asked, her voice trembling. "Who are they? Why do they want to kill me?"

"On my back, Enoshi!" Seitogi urged, his voice urgent and low.

Emily hesitated, glancing between Seitogi and her friends lying on the ground. "But, but Rebecca…Darren!" she protested, before crying out in horror as several more men emerged from the shadows. She counted nine, catching the eye of one. She hid her face behind Seitogi's sleeve, trembling with fear.

Leading the group was a tall, lanky man, dressed in the same rough, brown jumpers as the rest of his men, but wearing a heavy black cloak as well. He wrinkled his nose beneath his mask and barked out orders to end the misery of his burning comrade. "Secure the other two," he said, pointing to Rebecca and Darren.

Emily cried out, but was held back by Seitogi, who wouldn't let go. With a raised hand, the lanky man cautiously approached, followed by his men, who slowly encircled them.

"Yoh Seitogi!" the man called out.

"Reyer," Seitogi replied, his voice tense. "What business do you have with me? Why is Chua's Dhukai even here?"

"The boss wants your head along with the girls too!" Reyer answered, his voice cold and menacing.

"We need to keep the girls intact," added another man, who was shorter with a thick neck and raspy voice.

"What does Chua want with my head or Enoshi's?" Seitogi asked.

"It's mainly business," said Reyer. "And you went behind the boss's pup's back to do this job for the witch."

"I don't work for Chua or The Laughing Lark, and I don't owe them anything," Seitogi stated as he grabbed Emily and swung her around to his back. She quickly climbed on, clinging to him for dear life.

Reyer raised a hand to signal his men to stop their approach. "You're a good kid, Seitogi. I don't want to have to gut you. It would really upset Ms. Ary. But you have to work with me here. Your life for hers. What do you say, boy? Give us the girl, and we might let you live."

"Make way for me and Enoshi, Reyer, or find your life forfeit as your comrade's have already suffered. The stench of his flesh should serve as proper warning."

"Let him burn, you cocky little shit!" Reyer cursed. "Take them!"

Seitogi growled, as the group of men pounced on him and Emily all at once. Breaking through before they could be trapped under a shell formation, he rushed forward with a leap, climbing up Reyer's body, from torso to chest, leaving a dirty footprint on his face mask as he launched into the air, off the top of his head.

Reyer's body hit the ground, and his men collided head first as Seitogi landed behind them and ran.

"Get up you fools!" Reyer bellowed, his voice ringing through the forest as he dusted off his black cloak and mask. The other men groaned and stumbled to their feet, rubbing their heads and wincing in pain. "Get after them! We can't let them get away!"

Seitogi ran as fast as he could, his heart pounding in his chest. Emily clung tightly to him, her arms wrapped around his neck and her legs around his waist. They left Rebecca and Darren behind as they plunged deeper into the forest.

The sound of Darren's cries faded into the distance as Seitogi pushed himself harder and harder. His breathing became strained as he carried both his own weight and Emily's, but he didn't stop. The glow of the torches faded behind them, and he knew they were putting some distance between themselves and their pursuers.

But he couldn't let his guard down. Reyer was not one to be underestimated, and he was sure that the man would not give up the chase easily. He needed to find a safe place to hide and regroup, and quickly.

"What is this?" A woman, tall and imposing with a sturdy build, emerged from the dense underbrush, tapping the tip of her dagger against her palm. Behind her, an army of rough and masked men, all wielding flaming torches, followed suit.

She displayed a wide, gap-toothed grin as she approached a screeching Darren. Knitting her brows, she nudged him with the tip of her suede boot.

"Boy! Why make such a racket?" she said, as she fingered a raisin-like mole on her right cheek. She gestured to one of her minions, who stepped forward with a torch, illuminating the scene.

"Oh. It looks as though he's injured. And what hair on this one," she said, admiring Rebecca's tresses. "She will fetch a handsome price. But she doesn't look anything like the Golden Swan."

Reyer knelt before the imposing figure of the woman, almost as tall as he, twirling the dagger in her hand. "Arymaitei's pet has taken flight with another girl," he reported. "It was too dark to make out her face, but it seems that he is intent on protecting her."

The woman motioned towards Rebecca and Darren, "Bind them." she commanded. "And you four, go after Seitogi and bring me the girl. But beware of my daughter's pet. As you can see, he has no home training, and he bites," she added, gesturing towards the two dead men.

The thick-necked man spoke up, "Reyer told Seitogi that you wanted his head!"

Reyer delivered a quick slap to the man's jaw, "Bloody tell all! It was just a negotiating tactic, Lady Chua. I would never take the boy's head."

"I don't think he would offer it so easily either," she laughed, wiping the remaining dust from Seitogi's footprint off the lower half of his mask.

* * *

"I have to stop for a moment and catch my breath," Seitogi stumbled forward, almost dropping Emily.

He had been running nonstop, carrying her for several minutes. He felt like his heart was going to burst. Emily appreciated the pause too. She just wanted to stand still and breathe, to take it all in and figure out where she was, and what was going on.

This was definitely not a flashback or hallucination, she figured, which made it the most undesirable of realities.

She thought back to sitting in the park with Rebecca just that morning and suddenly her ears began to ring, she cupped her hands over them pushing inwards, squeezing.

"It's o.k., I'm ok," she told herself in a shaky voice. "I'm just, I'm having some kinda weird day. Nothing is really happening. Nothing happened…oh my god Rebecca! I left Rebecca," she began to hyperventilate, "We have to go back! We have to go back Seitogi!"

"It would be suicide to do so. I'm sworn to protect you and I won't allow it."

"She's my best friend! She'll be killed right? I mean…"

"Awei Chua and her Inouei were not supposed to be here. I'm sorry Enoshi. We were supposed to be meeting the wizened woman who sent me to collect you."

"Ino…what? Duka? I don't know who, or what you are talking about! But we just can't leave my best friend in the hands of a bunch of dollar store ninja's!"

"We have to find the Wizened woman," Seitogi took out the mirror he produced earlier, near the mew. He held it up, turning it at different angles.

"This is serious! What the hell are you doing with that stupid mirror?"

"I'm trying to catch enough light for a proper reflection so I can reach her! Find her somehow."

"Don't play the pronoun game with me! Who!"

"The Wizened woman. The mirror belongs to her," Seitogi handed Emily the mirror, "It was how I was able to bring you home. Somehow the mirror changes the world around you."

"Are you telling me we got here, from my school, through this?"

"Yes. The Wizened woman's magic is very powerful."

"So, you're telling me we literally stepped through the looking glass? Well, this sure as hells not Wonderland," Emily could barely see herself in the mirror as she held it to her face. And what in the hell is a Wizened woman?"

"They are healers! Um, mostly traveling medicine women, but Maishae is different. She is a powerful one who knows the ways of magic."

"Christ sake! So we've got magicians, magic mirrors, men on fire and a haunted forest. Ok, I am hallucinating again."

"We have to find her. Now is the hour of the stag, it will be sunrise soon. We can make it to her hovel safely if we stay off the main roads."

Seitogi reached out expecting Emily to return the mirror, but she was quick to snatch back her hand.

"I'll be holding on to this for the time being."

"Enoshi. It belongs to the Wizened woman."

"Then I guess I'll return it to her when we find her. And my name is Emily! Emily Heart!"

"You always were stubborn," he sighed.

"Don't act like you know me!"

"I could take it back by force if I wanted."

"Yeah! Go for it, big guy. I may not look it! But I can be a bit of a badass, man!" she made clenched fists, thinking: My god. Aside from the cops, I've never even been in a tussle, let alone a street fight.

"What do you mean you're a bad man? You're being silly, we have to go," Seitogi walked off in a huff, "And don't lose that mirror!

"What about Beck? My friends?"

"Can you rescue them alone, Enoshi? Or would you just join them in captivity? Knowing Awei Chua, she will seek to fetch the best price for them, so for the time being their lives are not in immediate danger. The sooner we find the Wizened woman, the sooner we can focus on your friends. Now come along before we are captured too."

The two walked for the next hour or so, both seemingly sore with the other. Emily hated it. In essence she was on a major hike, with no socks, sweating in a pair of leather boat shoes of which she had to keep stopping every few minutes to empty of dirt, rocks and debris.

It made walking an excruciatingly slow affair. They passed through a field of tall, sharp grasses that scratched her ankles and stuck to her pants, and hoody. Later, they navigated a steep downward hill where fallen trees and hidden stumps threatened their every step.

At one-point Seitogi stopped abruptly and ducked down into a thicket of nettles. He pulled Emily down with him and covered her mouth. Silently, he pointed out a small patrol of armored men trudging through a mess of swampy grasses several yards ahead of them.

Emily suffered through the prickly husk as fear of being captured numbed her inside out. It was an excruciating half hour wait watching the group slog their way through the marsh. But both breathed easy as soon the men were out of sight.

"They were different from the other guys from earlier," said Emily.

"We are in Kue prefecture, Aiyo territory."

"Aiyo!" Emily shuddered, her heart racing with fear and anxiety. She had a vague feeling of recognition towards the Aiyo soldiers, but she couldn't quite put her finger on why. She had memories of a village and Seitogi, but they were distant and hazy, and she only remembered him as a boy. But despite her uncertainty, the mere sight of the soldiers filled her with dread.

“Atem,” she whispered the name, and a shiver ran down her spine. Her heart was pounding in her chest, and she felt like she had spoken a curse.

“They must have lost their way in the dark and wandered into the marsh. Damned thing is like quicksand. Do you remember? I had to pull you out of a similar one near our village when we were kids.” Seitogi reached out and nervously picked a leaf out of her hair then fell silent as they walked side by side.

“What’s with that dumb look on your face?” Emily asked.

“I was just thinking of how you fell in and grabbed my leg and pulled me in too.”

“O.k…”

“I just remember my strong connection with you, and how I vowed to always protect you. Even all the way back then.”

“I don’t…I can’t remember any of that,” Emily felt her face get warm and looked down at the ground.

“Do you remember anything about us?”

“Us? As in me and you?”

“Yes! Me. Behra, Daiye village? Anything?”

“I’m sorry! I…I don’t,” Emily dared not look up as her heart pounded.

Why was he talking about ‘strong connections’ all of a sudden? Plus, she wasn’t being completely honest with him. Seitogi was recognizable to her, but only in a far off distant way. Like trying to remember a character from a childhood television show one had long since forgotten.

But she couldn’t deny his essence. She knew him, and his shy earnestness, she just didn’t know how, or rather when.

He seemed so serious, but somewhat boyish too. It wasn’t something she could put a finger on, she just knew it. And it frustrated her immensely.

"You're embarrassing me."

"I don't mean to. Just give it some time, but rest assured I'm only here to protect you. I've missed you terribly, Enoshi and I'm glad you're home."

"I don't want to be here! I'm sorry if you think…I don't know what you were thinking, but if you cared about me you wouldn't have kidnapped me or hurt my boyfriend!"

"Boyfriend?"

"I mean we're not together anymore. Broke up this morning as a matter of fact, but that's besides the point. You broke his damn arm in two, bro. You took us against our will."

"Ahh, the boy! You're upset about the boy!" Seitogi seemed relieved. "Once we find The Wizened woman, she can use her magic to heal him. You'll see. So don't worry too much about it. The sooner we find her the better for us all."

'You must be some kind of special idiot! Magic? You expect some sorceress to fix him with magic!" Emily's teeth began to chatter forcing her to lightly bite down on her tongue to stop the clicking.

Seitogi frowned at the insult "Let's keep moving. We've wasted enough time waiting for those Aiyo men to pass."

"I can't. I'm freezing, and my feet are wet from this gross marsh. I need to rest and collect my thoughts."

"Movement will warm you up."

They trekked in stoney silence with Emily periodically attempting to call Rebecca's phone despite the lack of a signal. *"This is miserable,"* she thought, as she stomped through the brush, several feet behind Seitogi while holding the phone and shaking it several times.

"What are you doing? Put that away before its light draws attention!"

"Shut up and don't worry about what I'm doing back here!"

Emily felt like she was at the end of her rope. The physical and emotional toll of the last few hours had taken a heavy toll on her, and she was feeling the effects in every part of her body. Her skin was sore and itchy from being damp, and her ankles were red and swollen from the numerous scratches and insect bites she had suffered. The mosquitos, midges, or gnats - she couldn't even be sure which one - had been relentless, tormenting her for what felt like an eternity.

As she walked alongside Seitogi, she was consumed by fear and paranoia. Every rustling in the bushes and every snap of a twig made her heart race.

She was certain that they were being followed by the Aiyo soldiers and that they would be ambushed at any moment.

After all, Seitogi had already killed two of them, and she was sure that the rest would be seeking revenge.

Her thoughts were interrupted as Seitogi grabbed her hand and pulled her closer, whispering, "Stay alert and keep moving." She nodded, taking a deep breath, and trying to calm her racing heart. But she couldn't shake the feeling that they were being watched and that danger was just around the corner.

"Stupid Seitogi," she muttered, stumbling as she followed.

As the first light of dawn started to stretch across the sky, Emily felt herself becoming increasingly exhausted. Her legs felt like they had turned to jelly, and it was becoming a struggle to keep her eyes open. She had lost all sense of time and couldn't even begin to guess how long they had been walking.

Her thoughts turned to her grandmother, and the thought of Delores collapsing with grief at the news of her disappearance was too much to bear. She could see the old woman surrounded by kindhearted strangers, who were weeping for her. Had anyone started searching for them yet? Had their disappearance made the news? The thought of becoming a headline, with reporters scrambling to uncover the truth, filled her with uncertainty.

Tears flowed down her cheeks as she struggled to process her thoughts. The morning air was crisp, and her body shivered as she felt dizzy and unsteady. Despite her exhaustion, she couldn't shake off her feelings of unease and apprehension.

"You o.k. back there?" Seitogi turned his head slightly and called out to Emily. "You look exhausted. We're not too far from her cabin. I can carry you the rest of the way."

"No thank you," Emily replied, sounding more alert than she felt. "I've never felt better rested."

Seitogi shrugged and continued on, with Emily trailing behind him. "It's only just up ahead," he said, sounding nonchalant.

After a mile or so, Seitogi suddenly lowered himself, signaling for Emily to do the same. She quickly snapped out of her daze and followed suit, lowering herself to a crouch and pulling up closer behind him.

"Who are we hiding from now?" she asked in a hushed tone. Seitogi pointed ahead and whispered,

"The wizened woman's cabin is just beyond the marsh, located on the other side of that ridge. I need to be cautious and assess the situation before we approach. I don't want to be caught off guard," Seitogi explained in a hushed tone.

"But what about me?" Emily protested, fear evident in her voice. "You can't just leave me here alone!"

"It's safer for you to stay hidden here among the bushes," Seitogi replied, his tone lacking any warmth. "Stay put. I need to gather information before we proceed. I'm going now."

As he started to stand up, Emily threw her arms around his waist and dug her heels into the ground, refusing to let go.

"I'll scream at the top of my lungs if you don't take me with you," she warned, determination in her voice.

Seitogi's expression turned hard and unyielding. Emily searched his eyes, looking for any hint of compassion, but found none.

"I told you to stay here," he repeated firmly.

"Please, you have to take me with you!" she begged.

Seitogi roughly pushed her arms away and repeated his earlier order, "I said stay put!"

Emily let out a pained cry and collapsed onto the ground, her hands and nails covered in fresh mud. She gazed out at the horizon with tears streaming down her face.

"What happened to protecting me?" she sobbed. The hopelessness in her voice was palpable.

Emily took several deep breaths to calm her nerves, when she heard a strange rustling from a nearby bush. Instantly, she sat up, holding her breath as she listened intently.

Suddenly, two small deer emerged from the bushes, a doe and her fawn. Their gentle eyes met Emily's for a moment, before they disappeared as quickly as they had appeared.

Emily turned to where Seitogi had been standing, but to her surprise, he too had vanished without a trace. She searched the area frantically, her heart pounding in fear as she called out his name. But there was no response.

As the minutes ticked by, her fear grew, wondering what could have happened to Seitogi and where he could have gone. She felt vulnerable and exposed without him, and she hated how that made her feel.

The snapping of a twig made her heart race as she quickly sought refuge behind a nearby bush. As she peered through the hedge, she was greeted by the sight of a massive, lumbering beast. Its fur was a deep, rich brown, matted and unkempt, with tufts of fur sprouting from its broad, muscular shoulders.

Its snout was long and pointed, with two formidable tusks jutting out from either side. The creature moved with an almost feline grace, sniffing the air as it walked from tree to tree in determined strides, searching for its next meal.

As it moved, it would take short drops and long grabs at the branches it moved under, using its powerful elbows as feet in its pursuit of a plump rodent. Emily watched in awe as the beast gracefully navigated the forest floor, its massive size making it a formidable hunter.

Despite its intimidating appearance, she couldn't help but feel a sense of wonder at the sheer beauty and power of the beast.

She breathed a sigh of relief as the animal passed her by, but her heart jumped again at the sound of a quiet laugh. She spun around, searching for the source of the sound, her mind racing

"Were you afraid?" Seitogi's voice startled her, causing Emily to jump and look up at him. "Don't worry," he continued, "they're territorial creatures, but they won't bite unless they're provoked."

He reached out and offered her his hand, his touch gentle and warm as he helped her up from the ground. She didn't have the energy to resist or pull away, as she was just relieved that he had come back for her. Seitogi then took a step closer and used his thumb to wipe away some of the tears and dirt that had accumulated on her face. Despite her initial instinct to push him away, she found herself leaning into his touch, grateful for his comfort.

"Are you ready to move on? I've checked the cabin. It looks abandoned and ransacked, but I think we'll be able to find some ointment and cloth to treat your wounds."

Emily hesitated, "Are you sure it's safe?"

Seitogi smiled reassuringly, "I'm sure. Now, let's get you on my back. Climb up and hold on tight."

Kneeling down, he made it easy for her to climb onto his back, and once she was securely in place, he stood up and started down the path towards the cabin.

* * *

As they approached the wizened woman's cottage, the trees grew denser, and the sunlight became increasingly scarce casting a mysterious and eerie shadow over the area. Seitogi was sweating profusely from the effort of carrying her, and Emily could feel his exhaustion as well.

She had been on the verge of falling asleep when just before they reached the cottage, Seitogi suddenly stopped and shook her off of his back, causing her to stumble. Her legs felt like lead and she needed to use his shoulder to steady herself. The sudden movement had made her dizzy and she couldn't help but feel a twinge of annoyance at being so unceremoniously jolted awake.

The sight of the wizened woman's cottage filled Emily with a sense of unease. The door had clearly been kicked in and the window was shattered, and she was not sure if it was safe to enter. Despite her reservations, Seitogi strode confidently inside, leaving Emily standing alone. She followed him hesitantly, into the dim interior, and was surprised by how unassuming the cottage was. Made from scraps of metal and wood held together by packed mud or clay, the squat, mushroom-shaped structure was far from the grand and mystical lair she had imagined a magical abode to be.

As she stepped onto the cabin's littered floor, she was struck by its circular shape and the stark contrast to the lush, green forest outside.

The room was cluttered with debris, with an upturned bed, a broken wardrobe, and a chair lying in disarray in the center. A straw effigy of a crow sat atop a dusty, old porcelain doll, adding to the eerie atmosphere of the place.

The walls were adorned with various objects and symbols, including a flat piece of wood etched with an ancient language that seemed to jump out at Emily. As she gazed at the text, she felt a strange tingling in her brain and was able to translate the words "Bless this Home" into English. Along one wall, there were a few books with torn pages scattered about, and a jar filled with coins and other mysterious trinkets sat on a nearby shelf. The overall effect was creepy and unsettling, making Emily feel as though she was stepping into a place long forgotten by time.

The interior of the cabin was filled with a pungent aroma that was a mixture of lavender and a rancid, decomposed odor. The latter was so overpowering that it made Emily feel nauseous. As she stumbled across the room, she noticed a corner that seemed to be the source of the foul stench.

"I smell it too," Seitogi commented, "It's called pom pom, it's a plant you boil with lavender to make medicine."

"I don't understand why anyone would want to make medicine out of something that smells so putrid," she commented, still trying to shake the scent from her nostrils.

"The wizened Women have their ways," Seitogi explained, "They believe in the power of natural remedies and use pom pom to treat a variety of ailments. It may not smell great, but it's effective."

"Well, this smell is making me sick. I need some fresh air," Emily said, feeling the need to step outside and get away from the overpowering odor. She stumbled towards the broken door, her hand covering her nose and mouth. The pungent odor of the pom pom was overwhelming, and she felt lightheaded.

"Stay close to me and be quiet," Seitogi instructed, placing a finger over his lips.

"What's going on?" Emily asked, her voice trembling.

Seitogi listened intently, his eyes closed. He slowly made his way to the damaged door and whispered, "Enemies. They're coming. Quick, hide behind the wardrobe!" He stepped outside and saw three men approaching the cottage.

With a sneer, he called out, "You call yourself Dhukai, but you're so loud you're embarrassing! I told you to hide, Emily," he scolded as he stepped back inside the cabin.

A hulking man with a rough face and bald head entered the cottage, leering at the two of them. "Well, well, what have we here?" he growled, his tongue lolling from his mouth.

"Why are you here?" Seitogi demanded of the man who had entered the cottage.

"Lady Chua instructed us to keep watch over this place," he replied.

Seitogi was ready for a fight as the man suddenly swung at him with a spiked mace, narrowly missing his face. Emily screamed in fear as the man advanced on Seitogi, driving him deeper into the cottage.

But Seitogi was not one to be easily defeated. In a quick move, he feigned a collapse, only to quickly jump back up and dodge another swing of the mace. With remarkable speed and agility, he grabbed the man by the back of the neck and used it as leverage to launch himself forward, chest to chest in a reverse piggyback position. Wrapping his legs around the man's waist, Seitogi used his dagger to repeatedly stab him in the throat in quick successive jabs, taking him down in a matter of seconds.

The man emitted a loud gurgling sound and fell face down atop the overturned furniture as Seitogi flipped backwards. He landed, picked up the mace and in one hefty strike, smashed the back of the man's head in, painting the floor, surrounding area, and Emily's lower half with blood and skull offal.

Emily was filled with a mix of terror and disbelief as she screamed at the top of her lungs, her hands clasped tightly over her mouth. Seitogi shot her a quick, annoyed look, before shouting a command to remain where she was. Without a moment's hesitation, he bolted out of the shattered entrance of the cabin, facing off against three more of Awei Chua's menacing henchmen.

He sprang into action, his movements fluid and graceful as he dodged and weaved between the three attackers.

With a quick twist and turn, he avoided a swipe aimed at his midsection and a heavy sword swung in his direction. He then launched himself into the air, delivering a powerful kick to the face of one of the attackers, sending him crashing into a tree where his skull was impaled on a sharp jagged branch.

He deftly dodged a swing from a second attacker and bent down and retrieved the first man's sword. He swiftly regained his footing, twisting his body around in a semi-circle as he rose from a crouched position, while shoving the wide blade through the man's eye until it protruded from the back of his skull.

In a fluid motion, he lifted his knee and used it to push off the man's torso, freeing his blade from the man's cranium. With lightning speed, he ducked under an attack from the third man, narrowly avoiding a dangerous strike, and sliced clean through both the man's legs, separating the upper third of his body from the thigh down.

Standing, he pressed the blade through the downed man's throat. Effectively decapitating him.

Emily was consumed by a feeling of dread as she considered the dangerous predicament she was in. She had started the day as a normal high school student, hanging out at the park with her friend Rebecca. But now she found herself in the middle of a dangerous sword fight, with her friends potentially in danger as well.

The thought of Rebecca and Darren being hurt or worse, dead and never found, was too much for her to bear.

A chill ran down her spine as she imagined them being slowly consumed by the earth, lost forever. The guilt of her actions weighed heavily on her, and she couldn't shake the feeling that this was all her fault.

The sound of combat had come to a halt. Emily, anticipating the worst, prepared herself for the final blow and remembered her grandmother fondly.

She regretfully thought about the troubles she must have caused her, and hoped Delores knew that she always had good intentions.

Seitogi reached down and tried to get her to stand up, but she remained motionless. There was a strange smile on her face and her eyes were glassy. Seitogi's voice seemed distant, as if he were speaking from underwater, and she let out a small giggle before screaming, "No!"

She jumped to her feet and bolted. Her heart was pounding in her chest as she stumbled out of the cottage, her mind filled with thoughts of danger and escape. She felt as though she was running for her life, fueled by a primal instinct for survival.

Just as she thought she had outrun the danger, a strong hand reached out and grabbed her shoulder, halting her in her tracks. She spun around to face Seitogi, her breathing ragged and her eyes wide with fear.

"No!" she cried out, struggling to break free from his grip.

Seitogi tightened his grip, his eyes burning with intensity as he spoke. "You have to trust me, Enoshi. Those men would have taken you to your enemies at Odahni, where surely the Golden Swan would have you beheaded. That is why I was sent to retrieve you. The wizened woman told me that House Aiyo wants you dead."

Emily felt a shiver run down her spine as she remembered the towering fortress of Odahni Castle. The fear and familiarity of the place was overwhelming. She turned to Seitogi, her voice shaking.

"Who is the Golden Swan and why would they want me beheaded?"

Seitogi looked at her with a mixture of confusion and frustration. "You don't know who the Golden Swan is?" he asked.

"She is Princess Shumaiyuki, of course. She's the reason you had to leave in the first place, or at least that's what I was told."

Emily's mind raced as she tried to piece together the memories of the girl with the golden hairpin and the crutch from her dream. "Shumai? Shumaiyuki," she whispered to herself. "Why does she still want me dead? What's her problem?"

"It's far too dangerous to be out in the open like this. We need to find a safe place, and fast," Seitogi said, gripping Emily's hand tightly. "I've been racking my brain trying to come up with a solution, but I'm out of options.

"I think it's best if we seek the help of Dou Dadachi. I have no doubt that he'll know exactly what to do in this situation."

"Dou Dadachi?" Emily repeated, furrowing her brow. "I think I remember that name."

"You should. He's the priest who brought you to our village when you were just a baby," Seitogi replied. "He's well-known for his wisdom and knowledge."

"How do we find him?" Emily asked, her curiosity piqued.

"His compound is east of here, about two days journey," Seitogi said matter-of-factly.

"What? Wait! Two days on foot?" Emily exclaimed, aghast at the thought.

Seitogi chuckled. "Relax, Enoshi. I added an extra day because you walk so slowly."

Emily scowled but couldn't help but smile at Seitogi's playful teasing. It reminded her of their youth, when they used to roam the forest together, searching for truffles and getting into all sorts of mischief. They had been inseparable back then, but as they grew older, their paths had diverged. Emily had been taken from Daiye village, but why? Now, as they set out on their journey to find Dou Dadachi, she couldn't help but feel a sense of nostalgia for those simpler times.

As she followed Seitogi down the path, Emily felt a renewed sense of purpose and determination.

She was eager to discover more about her past and her connection to the enigmatic priest and wondered if she could ever recapture that sense of closeness she and Seitogi had once shared.

The Golden Swan

Odahni castle was a breathtaking sight to behold. The grandiose structures elegant white and umber towers were a shining example of the architectural brilliance and sophistication of Berahnian ingenuity. Its sweeping rooflines evoked the feeling of a flowing river, while the intricate wooden carvings and latticework added to the castle's tranquil aesthetic. Built of natural wood and stone, the central courtyard, rooms, and hallways fanned outwards creating a sense of balance and harmony between the man-made structures and the natural world.

The grounds were a magnificent display of horticultural prowess, with every inch of the verdant land dotted with blooms of every color and variety. The lush gardens were a feast for the eyes, with intricate water features and beautifully crafted pagodas, each one a work of art in its own right. The castle was surrounded by tall walls and fortifications made of interlocking bamboo, a reminder of Berahni's feudal past and encircled by a moat, further enhancing its grandeur.

Inside was a stunning display of decorative mastery. From the moment one stepped through its gates, they were transported to a world of beauty, where every surface was adorned with the finest materials and embellished with intricate patterns of gold and white lattice. Each room was a masterpiece, showcasing the skills of the finest craftsmen and artisans of Berahni.

Unlike traditional castles with their cold and oppressive spaces, here they were bright, airy, and filled with natural light. This allowed one to fully appreciate its beauty, from the soaring ceilings to the intricate carvings that graced the walls and pillars. The interiors were designed to evoke a sense of balance and harmony, with a focus on creating an atmosphere that was warm, and welcoming.

Princess Shumaiyuki was in her element as she took advantage of the afternoon light that was illuminating her painting in progress. With the utmost care and attention to detail, she worked on a beautiful depiction of a cherry blossom in full bloom.

The sun's rays were reflecting off the petals and stems, creating a vibrant, shimmering effect that made the painting come to life. Shumaiyuki's delicate brush was guided by a steady hand and an eye for detail, as she used it to blend the colors ever so softly.

Her long brown hair was styled in two thick braids that were fashioned atop her head in intricate S-patterns, adding to her regal appearance. As she examined the image on the thin slab of wood that served as her canvas, she was lost in her own world, absorbed in the beauty of her creation.

She took a momentary break and cast her gaze towards a regally dressed man who was occupied with fishing in a small pond in the garden. She sighed and looked to the ceiling.

"These disputes have been going on for some time now," said a short, melon-faced man kneeling outside on the warm grass. He wore a purple vest featuring the distinctive persimmon crest of House Rihtzkaya.

"And why have you allowed things to fester to this point?" Shumaiyuki asked, her gaze returning to her painting. "What is your explanation, Inashata?"

"I've requested the groom's family to return the dowry after they backed out of the marriage. But, Jiyuka Shomba refuses to do so."

"How boring. That scandal was months ago. Everyone in society has moved on. Are they really willing to go to war over this?" Shumaiyuki glanced over at the man who was completely focused on his fishing.

"No, Highness," he began, "I don't believe that Jiyuka Shomba is truly willing to go to war over this matter. It seems more like a reckless act, a ploy to gain political power and support from some of his allies."

The princess nodded as she considered the situation, taking in the information with a critical eye.

"However," Inashata continued, "the Tambo are currently amassing their troops along Jiyuka's border, and he is now requesting the support of House Aiyo."

Shumaiyuki gazed down at the painting in front of her, lost in thought as she attempted to make sense of the complex situation.

And then, "We Aiyo are known for our diplomatic approach," she replied. "Is Jiyuka Shomba truly seeking our assistance in this matter?"

"Indeed, your Highness," replied Inashata with a deep bow. "He is requesting the support of the Aiyo Tabaiken, the most skilled and respected soldiers in all of Berahni. Their presence alone would be enough to bring an end to the conflict without a single weapon being drawn."

"The gall of Shomba to presume that we would waste our Aiyo soldiers on his petty conflicts," the princess sneered with disdain. "Does he truly think his sullied reputation is worth the blood of the world's finest warriors?"

"Your Highness, as one of your devoted subjects, I implore you to rethink your stance," the vassal spoke up, his voice growing stronger.

"Inashata Rihtz! Do you not have any sense of dignity? How dare you ask us to be dragged into Shomba's trivial disputes with his neighbors."

"Please forgive my previous omission, Your Highness. I do not wish for the Aiyo to become embroiled in this conflict, but if Jiyuka and the Tambo engage in battle, it would take place directly on Rihtzkaya borders!"

Shumaiyuki sighed and delicately added a drop of red paint to her canvas, her gaze fixed on her work. She spoke softly as she continued to paint.

"Jiyuka Shomba is a weak and ineffective leader. If the Tambo were to remove him from power, it would not be a significant loss.

It may be better to allow them to fight amongst themselves and then seize their territory as our own. What do you think, Uncle?" she said, turning to the man with a questioning gaze.

Ayio Yulori observed that Inashata Rihtzkaya's demeanor had changed, and he appeared desperately in need of support.

"I am Tehshio, not you, Shumaiyuki. And as the clan leader, any decision regarding military aid will be made by me." Yulori let the fishing line fall back into the water, observing the ripples that distorted its surface. He remained silent, while Shumaiyuki sighed and took one more look at her painting before quickly blending the colors with a swift brush stroke.

"My lord," Inashata attempted to speak, but a piercing gaze from the man he was trying to persuade left him at a loss for words.

"Why are you so interested in this conflict, Inashata?" Yulori asked, his deep baritone voice ringing gently throughout the yard. He dropped his fishing branch on the grass and stepped up onto the veranda to enter the wide sitting room, where he took a seat on a waiting pillow across from his niece.

"You've managed to avoid the skirmish for months. Why now?" he continued. "I fail to see what is at stake for the Rihtzkaya Clan to involve themselves in this dispute?"

As Inashata scooted forward towards the veranda, he could feel the tension rising between he and Yulori. He was determined to make his case, however.

"Your Highness, I fear that you are not fully comprehending the situation," he said, trying to keep his voice calm. Shumaiyuki's eyes narrowed, as she noticed his approach. She paused in her painting, the sound of the brush against the canvas suddenly silenced.

"Plese do not forget your place Lord Rihtz," she warned, her voice cold and unwelcoming. "It's clear that your fear of the Rihtzkaya being drawn into this conflict is clouding your judgment."

“That’s enough, Shumaiyuki,” Yulori interjected, but she silenced him with a flick of her wrist and returned her focus to her artwork. Despite the anger that seethed within him, Yulori remained silent, choosing instead to recline on the floor, laying his head on his arm and simply observing the situation.

Odahni Castle was home to many powerful figures, but none so imposing as its lord, Aiyo Yulori. With his striking appearance, he was a true embodiment of wealth, power, and prestige. His muscular physique was perfectly complemented by the rich robes of a high-ranking noble, and his thick black hair was held in place by two elegant swan-shaped bone clasps.

Yulori relished his position of power. Not a single word escaped his lips that he thought wasn’t profound, wise, or clever, and he was not afraid to bend the rules when he deemed it necessary for the greater good of his house, and by extension, the country. He was revered by his Tehshio peers as a man of great guile, and was widely known for his wisdom, and cunning wit.

Yet, within the Aiyo clan, Yulori faced a formidable rival in the form of Princess Shumaiyuki. Despite being twenty years younger and a woman, she was seen as a direct competitor to Yulori’s position, and her intelligence and cunning were not to be underestimated. Despite their differences, however, the two were bound by their shared ambition and the desire to serve the greater good of their house and country.

“You’re aware of the fact that the Tambo hold their annual military exercises near, not on, Junko’s border, right?” asked Shumaiyuki, fixing her uncle with a piercing gaze. “Shombo has been complaining about it for years. Don’t you think he’s just overreacting due to his own guilt?” she said.

“But what about the dowry?” Inashata looked as if he would cry.

“Yes, that’s another confusing aspect,” Shumaiyuki said, her expression showing her frustration. “Why would they even accept a dowry for a baby girl? It’s absurd.”

"Well, my lady, the children were betrothed at birth before Shombo's scandal took place," replied Inashata.

"However, tradition dictates that the dowry be exchanged when they reach marrying age," Shumaiyuki pointed out, her frown deepening.

"The nation stands on the brink of war with Seizhone," Yulori declared, "and with our pacifist emperor sequestered in his meditations, it's up to me to keep the country from collapsing. I cannot afford to be sidetracked by petty squabbles and distractions. We must not revert back to a time of internal conflict. Send a message to both houses, informing them to resolve their disagreement, or face the consequences of having our Tabaikin intervene and settle the matter."

Shumaiyuki turned to her uncle and stated confidently, "Why bother sending terms, Uncle? Regardless of the outcome, we will end up annexing their territory and expanding our own, just as Grandfather would have wanted."

Yulori, raised an eyebrow. "I would advise caution in speaking for what Father would have wanted, Shumaiyuki," he said.

Shumaiyuki shrugged her shoulders and asked, "Why is that, Uncle? Who are you to dictate what Grandfather might have wanted? If only he were still with us to guide our way."

"You speak of father as if he were dead and it was you, not I, who inherited his position as Tehshio."

"Well, as long as he remains under house arrest in Nyongoyuchi Palace, he might as well be dead," Shumaiyuki replied matter-of-factly. She was about to continue speaking but was interrupted by a loud cry of pain that echoed from deeper within the building.

"What is all that commotion? Who is making all of that noise?" Shumaiyuki asked, turning her head towards the room's entrance as she heard heavy footsteps approaching.

A runner dressed in flared green and gray linen robes rushed into the room, knelt down, and called out, "I have a report!"

Yulori sat up from his lounging position and held up his hand, signaling the runner to wait. He then turned to Inashata and said, "Have the letters sent to both houses as is my will. You are dismissed."

Inashata, with a deep bow, retreated through the garden exit. Once he was gone, Yulori regarded the runner and simply said, "Speak."

"Awei Chua has arrived," the runner reported, panting slightly. "She has captured two foreigners in Minka forest."

"Foreigners?" Shumaiyuki repeated, pausing as she considered the term. "I see…and who are they?"

"We don't know for certain," the runner replied. "Neither does Chua. But they are a boy and a girl, mid-youths, my lady."

Shumaiyuki gazed intently at the runner. "And you say they are foreigners. How can you be sure?" she asked.

"Yes, my lady. Their attire, the way they communicate, everything about them is unusual. The boy is currently suffering from a severe injury and cries in pain as we speak, and the girl is peculiar, with speckled skin as pale as snow and hair like flames."

"That doesn't sound like Yuyuki at all," Yulori muttered softly. He then commanded, "Bring Chua and the captives to the garden." After the runner had left, he turned his gaze towards Shumaiyuki.

"My dear Shumai," he said in a soft voice, using her pet name, "it would be best if you went to your quarters and let me handle this."

"I would very much like to stay, thank you."

"It's crucial, as our future empress you maintain plausible deniability in the inner workings and political maneuverings of our House," Yulori warned.

"I'm not asking for your permission, uncle," Shumaiyuki replied coldly. "I am informing you of my intentions."

“Your naivety is charming, my dear niece,” Yulori chuckled. “But let us not forget that the affairs of the House are my domain. It is not appropriate for a young woman like yourself to be involved.”

“I respectfully disagree with you, uncle,” Shumaiyuki countered. “Obánā,” she called out to an elderly maid sitting quietly in the corner of the room, “prepare my float. If these foreigners are the ones the old witch sent that boy to retrieve, then I should be here to receive them. Particularly if one of them seeks my crown.”

Yulori stood tall over Shumaiyuki, his expression serious. “You have a tendency to act without careful consideration, Shumai,” he said. “It’s also time for your physical therapy, isn’t it? You have an engagement ceremony in a few months. Remember, you wanted to walk on your own two feet during the festivities. That won’t happen if you continue to use that floating couch given to you by the witch.”

“My disability must be frustrating for you but imagine how I feel being labeled as ‘crippled’ behind my back,” Shumaiyuki replied with a hint of bitterness in her voice. “I use the float because it exudes power!”

“Power? You look ridiculous floating on that thing.”

“We are wasting time here uncle.”

“I will handle this situation with Chua on my own.”

“What would you have me do? Sit idly by and watch as someone tries to take what is rightfully mine?”

“We have only just learned Yuyuki still lives, and we have no idea what her intentions are. It would be wise for you to exercise caution and restraint.”

“I regret that I cannot blindly follow the path of caution,” Shumaiyuki said quietly, mostly to herself.

Yulori sighed and looked down at her frowning. “You must understand the gravity of the situation we are in, Shumai. If the Aiyo are to seize control of the nation from the Anele, it is essential that our clan remains untainted by any actions that could be considered treasonous.”

"I may be young and a woman, but to underestimate my abilities is to misjudge me, Uncle," she countered. "If you believe that my skills would be better suited to a life of leisure, then by all means, continue to question my competency. But the elders of our clan recognize and support my capabilities."

"Shumaiyuki, you are a precious asset to The Aiyo," Yulori declared, his tone resolute. "It is crucial that you are shielded from any involvement in political intrigue or scandal. If an Aiyo woman ventures into treacherous territories, then it will set a precedent for all women of Kue to follow."

"But I have said what I needed to say, uncle," Shumaiyuki replied firmly. "As a member of the Aiyo, I will not be confined to the sidelines while the future of our house and our nation is at stake. I will not be protected from intrigue or scandal at the cost of my own agency."

"But, Shumaiyuki, the path to power is not always straightforward. You must be careful not to get caught up in any scandals or controversies that could tarnish our family's reputation."

"I understand the stakes, Uncle," Shumaiyuki said, her voice steady. "But I also understand that there is no growth or progress without risk. I am willing to take the risk that you aren't, and I will do what is necessary to ensure the success of our house and our nation."

"Your youth and your gender put you at risk, Shumaiyuki," Yulori warned with a stern voice. "The Aiyo's reputation and power are in my hands, and I will not allow you to compromise it."

"And yet you invite criminal Dhukai into our gardens," Shumaiyuki countered. "That is where the true scandal lies, Uncle."

"A necessary evil," Yulori conceded, holding up a hand. "But let us not argue further. We have guests arriving and it is not the time for this conversation. We must put aside our differences and extend the proper Aiyo hospitality."

"Of course," Shumaiyuki replied coolly. "Let us put aside our differences and welcome our guests with the respect they deserve."

***

Moments later, Shumaiyuki lounged leisurely, fanning herself as she reclined on an elegant, low-slung, leg-less chaise lounge. Upholstered with a plush, white fabric and hovering just above the veranda, as if suspended on a cushion of air, the sofa emanated an air of sophistication. Her ivory and green robe cascaded over its sides, and its elongated, sinuous form provided the perfect spot for unwinding.

In stark contrast, Yulori was seated rigidly on a traditional tatami rug, his face scowling as he gazed out into the garden where Awei and her men sat cross-legged on the warm lawn. Behind them, Rebecca's sobs echoed softly, while Darren, whose bleeding, broken arm was now a shade of purple, let out intermittent kicks and screams of pain, a pattern he had been repeating for hours.

"Chua, what is the meaning of this?" Yulori's voice was filled with annoyance as he pointed at Darren. "How dare you show up unannounced, and with that thing making such ruckus in the very center of my residence. I have never been so embarrassed."

"I apologize," Awei said with no hint of contrition. "I had intended to announce myself, but I was caught off guard by the capture of these foreign interlopers. In my rush, I failed to send a messenger ahead."

"You are aware of the proper protocol," Yulori scowled.

"You know that I am here on important business," Awei replied with a smile. "I do not have the time or patience for niceties such as etiquette or polite manners."

Shumaiyuki furrowed her brow upon seeing Darren, and then turned her attention to Awei and asked, "What's wrong with it? Shouldn't we silence it by cutting out its tongue?"

"No, that would be too savage, my dear niece," Yulori replied with a look of disapproval. Shumaiyuki's expression darkened, as if she were about to lash out, and then she glared at Awei, Rebecca, and Darren with disapproval.

“Well, I don’t like it,” she grumbled. “At least stuff a cloth in its mouth to muffle the sound.”

Rebecca, disoriented and struggling with her tied wrists, suddenly rose from the ground and ran towards the veranda, crying out, “Oh my God! Emily, please help us! Where are we? What’s going on? Who are these people?” Awei moved swiftly to intercept her, blocking her path with a harsh slap to the face.

Rebecca fell to the ground as several guards surrounded them. Awei roughly grabbed her by the hair, and she stopped struggling. Her eyes were filled with tears, and she was now trembling with fear. Her initial outburst had faded, replaced by her helplessness.

“Please, don’t let her hurt us anymore.” She addressed Shumaiyuki with her plea, though her gaze was fixed on the ground. Awei sighed heavily, grabbing Rebecca by the collar of her sweater and pulling her back to her spot next to Darren.

“Let the thing be, Chua” Yulori instructed. “I need it to be conscious for questioning.”

“But It’s speaking in a language we don’t understand,” Shumaiyuki complained. “And It’s a mess with all of its carrying on.”

“When addressing someone of higher rank, you should show proper respect,” Yulori said to Rebecca. “This is especially true when addressing royalty.”

“My apologies, your lordship. The girl is frightened, and the boy’s injury is severe. We attempted to treat his, but it may require amputation,” said Awei.

“Give it some beggar’s root to ease it’s pain,” Yulori commanded a maid, before turning his attention back to Awei. “What news do you have of Princess Yuyuki?”

“She has fled with Abete Seitogi, but my men are actively searching Minka forest, and I expect to have them both in custody by the end of the day.”

"How could you let that unsavory creature escape with her?" Shumaiyuki exclaimed with frustration. "I was expecting Yuyuki the imposter, not this unimpressive thing," she gestured towards Rebecca with a slender bamboo stick, similar in size to a scepter. "You've brought us this comical-looking girl, a bawling and useless boy, and a host of questions."

"The Golden Swan is right," Yulori chimed in. "My questions for you are even more pressing now that you have failed to deliver the imposter."

"It's just a temporary setback, my lord, not a failure." Awei responded calmly.

"The situation has become much more complicated than we anticipated," Yulori commented, his tone filled with frustration. "That boy may have already taken Yuyuki to the witch, putting all of us, including The Aiyo and your men, Chua, in danger. I must say, I am disappointed in The Inouei Dhukai's performance."

"My apologies, my lord," Awei spoke up. "We were caught off guard with the unexpected appearance of additional players, but I assure you that everything will be resolved in a matter of days."

"Your cavalier approach to the situation has only added to our troubles," Shumaiyuki interjected, her voice tinged with annoyance. "And to make matters worse, you promised to have them in your possession by nightfall. Now you're telling us it may take days? This is unacceptable."

"I am confident that The Inouei Dhukai is capable of rectifying this situation," Yulori stated firmly. "You will bring the imposter to us. I expect nothing less."

"My lord, please do not mistake the Inouei for inexperienced mercenaries," Awei responded firmly. "My men are the backbone of my entire army, and they cannot be treated as mere servants by anyone, not even the great Golden Swan."

Shumaiyuki sneered, "It appears that you have lost sight of your proper place, Awei. I never thought I would see such a disgraceful display."

"Ha, my place! My lady, I hardly resemble a servant to a lady. But if we had some private time, perhaps I could turn the tables. If it suits Her Grace," Awei said with a suggestive wink.

Shumaiyuki gasped in shock, her face flushing as she covered it with her fan. Awei chuckled in amusement.

Yulori sighed in exasperation, "But you will behave yourself, Chua!" He said. "If you can safely retrieve the imposter, I may overlook your disrespectful remarks towards the Golden Swan."

With a deep bow, Awei stood up, "I won't fail you my lord. The girl will be delivered to you in a matter of days if that."

Rebecca suddenly cried out, "Yuyuki!" causing everyone present to look at her. Yulori's face darkened as he spoke in a low voice,

"Keep it quiet."

But Rebecca was undeterred. "Yuyuki!" she cried out again. "That's what you called yourself when you were roofied that time!"

Yulori's expression became even more severe, and he barked, "Silence!" As he rose to his feet, Rebecca immediately fell quiet, clearly intimidated by his commanding presence.

"It seems that it thinks it knows me," Shumaiyuki's eyes were fixed on Rebecca, as her white and gold lounge ominously rose several feet above the floor. Her ivory and green robes trailed behind her as she floated down from the veranda into the garden, wielding her slender bamboo stick with a sense of authority. The sun glinted off of her golden swan hairpin, adding to her already regal appearance. "Yuyuki is not my name," she said in a cold voice, "It is the imposter's. And once I find her, she will be begging for death."

"I don't know what you are saying!" Rebecca cried out in desperation. "I don't understand your language!"

The sharp end of the bamboo stick struck Rebecca's shoulder, sending her crashing down onto the grass. She let out a heart-wrenching wail and curled up into a ball, embracing herself as she wept. Her head spun in all directions as she tried to figure out where to run, but her fear was overwhelming.

The reality of the situation was settling in and the tears continued to flow down her face. She realized that the girl in front of her was not Emily, despite their striking similarities. This was someone else entirely.

"Where is Princess Yuyuki?" Shumaiyuki demanded, her voice cutting through Darren's cries. Rebecca, however, was unable to respond. She was paralyzed with fear, staring blankly at Shumaiyuki and Yulori, she couldn't believe what was happening to her.

She felt as if she was trapped in a nightmare, and that at any moment she would wake up. Darren, in his desperation, pleaded for their release. Just as he did, the maid returned with the beggar's root and approached him with a saucer of the bitter brown elixir.

"Please stop! What are you doing to him?" Rebecca reached for Darren, but the maid ignored her and with a shaking hand, she held the medicine to his lips, and he took a breath and swallowed it down. He felt its effects almost instantly. He gazed in horror as the world around him began to collapse, sinking into a seemingly bottomless pit. The edges of his vision started to fade, and soon everything was consumed by darkness.

"Darren!" cried Rebecca repeatedly, panic and fear in her voice as she watched the boy succumb to the effects of the medicine. She was terrified that he might not survive and that she would be left alone in this strange and frightening place.

Shumaiyuki, meanwhile, floated back to the veranda, her disdain for the situation apparent in her expression. "Shame," she remarked, "It doesn't speak Bhrenhi, but instead whimpers like a mouse."

Yulori approached Awei and and tossed her a small cloth bag filled with coins.

"My lord!" her tone a mixture of disbelief and anger. "These two are worth far more than this paltry sum. Look at that girl's hair! You could shear it three or four times a year and fetch a king's ransom."

But Yulori was not swayed. "This is not about selling livestock, Chua," he replied sternly. "And I've already wasted the beggar's root on it and now it's useless. The only option we have is to throw it in the moat."

Awei's expression tightened at Yulori's words, and she cautiously spoke up, "My lord, I understand your frustration with the boy, but what about the girl?"

"I'll take the boy, my lord."

"Humph. Huasau Atem." Shumaiyuki turned away in disgust at the sight of the man.

Tall and gaunt Atem entered the garden. His narrow jaw and jagged teeth were accentuated by his deep-set steel eyes. He wore a green and gray jumper that was stained and torn and had been roughly mended in multiple places. His presence seemed to cast a shadow over the area.

"Chua," he said, nodding in Awei's direction as he walked past her and approached Darren, who was still being held by the maid.

His eyes were piercing, and he seemed to exude an aura of menace and power. With each step he took, the tension in the garden seemed to increase, until it was almost palpable. Despite this, he was confident and self-assured, and he stood over Darren with a look of hungry excitement in his eyes.

"I can make excellent use of him."

Shumaiyuki gave Atem a disdainful look, "You mean to use him for your sadistic skinning practices? I thought you liked to hear the screams of your victims while they were still conscious."

Atem lazily turned to the veranda and gave a bow, not showing any fear or discomfort.

“How dare you look me in the eye!” Shumaiyuki slammed her stick against her lounge and turned towards Yulori.

“Lord Aiyo,” she exclaimed, “Why can’t you control your….?”

“That is enough.” Yulori quickly interrupted her, He then turned towards Atem. “What exactly do you plan to do with it?”

“We require a replacement for the relief runner at the sparring grounds,” Atem spoke up. “The previous one seems to have met an unfortunate end involving my blade, my lord.”

“Very well, have it then,” Yulori said dismissively, turning his attention back to Awei.

“What is it worth to you to bring me the imposter?”

Awei clenched her jaw and tightly gripped the bag of coins, “I am confident that I have everything under control, my lord.”

“Remember, your success or failure rests on your ability to bring me Yuyuki,” Yulori warned. “If you don’t bring her to me, the consequences will be dire. My Tabaikin troops are unmatched, and your Dhukai is still growing. Don’t think for a moment that you stand a chance against them in battle.” He gestured towards Atem, who was now carrying the unconscious Darren over his shoulder.

“It’s a shame, really,” Atem added, his voice a gravelly baritone. “I’d hate to have to face you on the battlefield, Chua. I’ve yet to win your hand.”

Awei’s expression was grim as she clutched the bag of coins. “Understood, my lord. We will do everything in our power to retrieve the imposter and bring her to you. If it pleases you, we will take our leave now.”

“It would very much please me,” said Yulori.

Awei respectfully lowered her head as she and her men moved in unison towards the outer gate of the garden.

Rebecca watched as they left, feeling a strong desire to go with them instead of being left with the strange girl who looked like Emily but was not.

She stood up, ready to make a run for it, but then fell back to the ground, tears streaming down her face, overwhelmed by the realization that this bizarre turn of events was really happening.

"She's not Emily! I know she's not! Emily would never let this happen. I can't believe this is all happening for real. I have to wake up!" she cried.

"It's intriguing, don't you think?" Shumaiyuki said with a hint of curiosity as Yulori took his seat once again. "I find its fiery hair quite appealing. It would make a beautiful winter scarf."

Yulori gazed at her with evident displeasure.

"If Maishae was involved in bringing this thing here, then it is certainly not an innocent. I will make it tell me everything it knows about Princess Yuyuki," he declared.

"You seem to have forgotten that it cannot speak our language," said Shumaiyuki, pointing out the obvious.

Yulori, however, remained unfazed. "It could be a ploy," he replied coolly. "You two guards, bring it over here."

Shumaiyuki was quick to interject, "I believe I should handle this."

"For whatever reason? It could be dangerous."

"Please uncle, it looks more frightened of its own shadow," Shumaiyuki argued. "Remember, I have the witch's speaking box. It may allow it to understand us, and us, it."

"That piece of junk Maishae gave father all those years ago? Yulori was less than impressed, "I thought we had gotten rid of the cursed thing after its last outing."

“It works,” Shumaiyuki declared confidently. “One of my maids spoke Sukiha, and the voice from the box repeated the phrase flawlessly in Brenhi.”

Yulori, stroking his thin mustache, appeared skeptical. “You’re telling me it actually worked?” he asked.

“Of course, it did,” Shumaiyuki replied. “If you had been home in Odahni instead of Nyongoyuchi at the time, you would have known. Everyone was talking about it for days.”

Yulori nodded, “Yes, I’ve heard of the talk. But I heard that it was an utter failure, only able to poorly repeat one word which quickly became boring.”

“I will have my girl fetch it,” said Shumaiyuki as she directed the chaise lounge to glide towards the edge of the veranda with a thought. She snapped her fingers and barked at a struggling guard who was dragging Rebecca by the ankle.

“Release it, you imbecile! It has legs for a reason,” Shumaiyuki commanded the guard and spun around to face Yulori. “Do you care to make a wager on the box?” she asked with a mischievous smile.

“I have no interest in gambling with you,” Yulori replied coolly.

“It’s amusing to see it thrash about and scream like a feral creature,” Shumaiyuki commented, referring to Rebecca. “I’ll have Te-Tae give her a dose of the beggar’s root as well.”

“Do what you must, Shumai. I have pressing matters to attend to in Nyongoyuchi. But it must be locked away until you find you speaking box, and Obinari must be present in case it becomes violent during the interrogation.”

Shumaiyuki watched as the guard struggled to control Rebecca, who was thrashing and squirming in an attempt to escape. Despite his efforts, the guard was unable to calm her down, and it took a great deal of effort to bring her to the veranda and get her to kneel. Yulori cast a critical gaze over the young woman before nodding to his niece and departing, leaving Shumaiyuki alone with the guard and the sobbing redhead.

Shumaiyuki hovered gracefully over to Rebecca, who was still struggling in the grip of the guard. With a gentle touch, she reached out and caressed Rebecca's cheek with the tip of her bamboo stick.

A smile spread across her face as she looked into girl's frightened eyes.

"As a woman, I understand the urge to scream at the top of your lungs," she said. "But it's not appropriate for one to show it." She floated away, calling for her trusted Obánā, Te-Tae. The woman appeared moments later, her pumpkin-like face exuding a motherly and proud expression.

Shumaiyuki turned to her and said, "If I am to keep this creature, it must learn to behave. Give it the beggar's root to calm its nerves."

Te-Tae nodded and knelt down beside Rebecca, who was still trembling with fear. The old woman placed a comforting hand on her shoulder and gazed deeply into the frightened girl's teary eyes. As Te-Tae looked at her, she stopped struggling and her eyes softened.

"There you are," Te-Tae turned to her retreating charge, "It won't be needing the root my lady. It is just scared."

"Hmph, who isn't," quipped Shumaiyuki.

"Nevertheless," Te-Tae continued, "I believe it will be more cooperative if we show it a little kindness."

"Very well," Shumaiyuki sighed. "Let's see if we can get it to talk. I would like to know everything it knows about Yuyuki."

Te-Tae smiled down at her Rebecca, "You'll be alright. Just take a deep breath and try to calm yourself."

Rebecca closed her eyes, slowly letting the tension in her shoulders ease. When she opened them again, she was calmer and more collected.

Shumaiyuki watched the exchange with interest, "Well done, Te-Tae. You have a way with it."

Te-Tae nodded, “Thank you, my lady. I have a lot of experience with scared children.”

***

The dark shed was small and cramped, with only a tiny window allowing a sliver of moonlight to filter in. The air was thick with the scent of mold and dirt, and the scratchy bed of hay Darren was lying on provided him little comfort.

His injured arm throbbed with pain as he lay there, feeling lost and alone in a world he couldn’t comprehend. Thoughts of Emily and Rebecca, and whether they were safe, swirled in his mind.

The shed’s door creaked open, and he tensed, unsure of who or what was approaching him. But then he heard a familiar voice, gruff and commanding. “You,” Atem said, entering the shed and looming over him. “Can you understand me?”

Darren shook his head, confused by the unfamiliar language. Atem grunted in frustration and grabbed him roughly by the arm, leading him out of the shed.

As they walked towards the sparring gym, Darren’s head swam with a mix of fear and curiosity. He wondered where Atem was taking him and what he wanted. Darren stumbled along, following the man’s long strides as they walked through several winding corridors. Finally, they came to a small room. Atem gestured for Darren to sit down and motioned towards a dwarf of a man, with a wrinkled face and a long, gray beard. He wore a dark robe and carried a leather bag of tools.

The man spoke in the same language that Darren didn’t understand, but his tone was gentle as he pointed to himself and repeated the word Mizer. Darren slowly said the word along with him and found himself more relaxed. The Mizer’s movements were precise. He examined Darren’s injured arm and rubbed it with a numbing oil, and Darren felt the pain begin to subside.

The man then began to perform a sort of surgery, adjusting the bone fragments and resetting the joint.

As the Mizer worked, Darren felt a glimmer of hope. Perhaps his arm could be saved. He watched as the Mizer deftly manipulated his injured limb, trying to piece together the fragments of bone. His arm ached, but the pain was lessening with each passing moment. Darren knew that he needed to be patient and let the man work.

Atem stood nearby, watching the procedure with a curious expression. "What are you doing?" he asked the Mizer, who responded in the foreign language.

"Applying muck-worm's milk to glue the break. If it holds, it will mend, but never be the same. Luckily, he is a strong youth. He'll get a use from it yet. Though I'm not certain Lord Aiyo would approve I use such expensive methods on a possible foreign spy."

"That is not your concern, the Lord's feelings is it? Fix him, man, and be done with it!"

"No need to be rough about it. Have I not fixed you many a time too?"

"I wouldn't say many," grumbled Atem.

Darren couldn't understand their words, but he thought Atem seemed concerned and that the Mizer knew what he was doing. The surgery continued for what felt like hours, but eventually the Mizer finished his work. He gave Darren some herbs to help with the pain and left the room, nodding to Atem as he went.

Atem turned to Darren and began to speak, his gruff voice now somewhat gentler. "You'll work the pissers and the slop hall until you heal, and then we'll see what to make of you," he said.

Darren shook his head, feeling a mix of confusion and frustration. He didn't understand why Atem was so insistent on speaking to him when he couldn't understand the language. But he felt a sense of gratitude towards the man for helping him, and he knew that he owed him something in return.

"Thank you," he said, bowing his head. "Thank you for helping me."

Atem nodded, looking slightly surprised by the show of gratitude. “You are strong,” he said. “Stronger than I thought. You will need to be, to survive in this world.”

Old Priest Dodachi

Seitogi and Emily trudged through the dense forest, searching for sustenance. As they journeyed deeper, they encountered patches of wild berries, which they eagerly plucked to satisfy their hunger and drank from murky streams to satisfy their thirst. The cool temperature of the night had given way to a sweltering, humid heat, and both were exhausted and in need of rest.

"Dou-Dodachi was once the highly respected head priest of the imperial household." Seitogi explained to Emily as they journeyed through the forest. "However, a scandal erupted when it was revealed that he had a secret child, which resulted in his banishment from the palace. Despite his fall from grace, he remained a kind-hearted individual. During his travels, he would stop at various villages to pray for peace and took it upon himself to bring you to our village when he found you."

As the day turned into night, Emily became increasingly withdrawn and silent, lost in her thoughts. She was concerned for her friends, but despite her growing memories of Seitogi, she still found herself somewhat frightened by him. She couldn't be sure if she could fully trust him.

As they walked, the night dragged on endlessly. The trees blocked out all moonlight, and the air was cold, causing Emily to shiver. Eventually, they stopped for a while, and she was able to sleep, with Seitogi keeping watch over her. But their rest was short-lived.

Seitogi woke her when he felt vibrations from an unknown source in the distance. They quickly hid amongst thickets and tall grasses, their hearts pounding with fear. At one point, they could hear Chua's hunters passing quite close to their hiding spot.

They remained crouched and hidden, waiting patiently for their opportunity to escape. Seitogi was ready to strike if necessary, his eyes fixed on the hunters as they passed by. Finally, when the danger had passed, they cautiously rose and continued to navigate through the darkness, moving as stealthily as possible to avoid detection.

As the sun rose the next morning, Emily and Seitogi were running through the trees when they heard a high-pitched whistle in the distance. "We've been spotted," Seitogi cursed under his breath. He grabbed Emily's hand and they broke into a sprint towards a large bank of trees, hoping to find some cover.

But it was too late. Within minutes, Dhukai hunters burst from the bushes, throwing metal darts in their direction. Emily and Seitogi dodged and weaved, trying to avoid the razor tipped projectiles as they sprinted deeper into the forest. Motivated by the thirst for survival, Emily imitated his movements and jumped over clusters of trees and cut through thick underbrush.

Their hearts pounding with fear, they finally made it to the cover of the trees, panting and out of breath. Emily could feel the adrenaline coursing through her veins as they hid, waiting for their pursuers to give up the chase. She couldn't believe how quickly things had turned. Just a few moments ago, they had been running freely through the forest, and now they were hiding like fugitives from their pursuers.

Seitogi kept a watchful eye on their surroundings, scanning the trees for any signs of danger. Finally, after what felt like an eternity, the sound of their pursuers faded into the distance. Emily and Seitogi breathed a collective sigh of relief, knowing that they had narrowly escaped capture.

As the sun beat down mercilessly, Emily's stomach churned with hunger and her breaths came in ragged gasps. She could barely stand the oppressive heat, and was on the verge of collapse. Suddenly, she came to a halt behind Seitogi as he held up a hand to signal for silence. A second later, he grabbed her hand and pulled her along with him, running at breakneck speed.

They burst out into a clearing just as their would-be killers rounded a thorny mound of bush. Emily's heart sank as she saw that they were completely surrounded. Her eyes, bleary and stinging from sweat, found dark ones, green ones, and light brown ones above masked jawlines, all staring back at her with a menacing glare.

She clung tightly to Seitogi's hand, feeling a sense of dread wash over her. They were outnumbered and outmatched, and there seemed to be no way out. She could feel her heart racing as she tried to think of a plan, but her mind was blank. She could only pray that they would make it out alive.

"Stay back!" Seitogi swung the sword he had acquired back at the wizened woman's cottage. With a warrior's cry, he leapt out at their attackers, brandishing his blade like a mighty thunderbolt. Emily didn't know whether to hide or run, so she grabbed a large stick and held it aloft like a baseball bat, swinging it indiscriminately at anyone who came too close.

The air was filled with the clang of metal on metal, as Seitogi hacked and sliced away at his opponents, four men wielding pointed spears. His sword flashed in the sunlight as he closed in on his targets, his eyes fixed on their every move.

Chua's hunters knew they were in trouble, and fear filled their eyes as they desperately tried to fend off his attacks. But it was no use. Seitogi was too skilled, too fast, too powerful. He lunged forward, his sword singing through the air, and one by one, he dispatched them with ease. As the last of their attackers fell to the ground, Seitogi stood triumphant, his chest heaving with exertion.

As three more hunters appeared, Seitogi dropped his blade and charged towards them at top speed. In one swift motion, he snatched one of the hunters by the neck, crushing it with a satisfying crunch.

He then swiftly toppled the second hunter and finished him off with a lethally skilled spine twist.

Immediately after the kill, Seitogi jumped up and landed on a large boulder, ready to take on the last man standing. He crouched menacingly on the rock above him, his gaze locked on his prey. The hunter looked up at him with fear in his eyes, knowing that he was facing a deadly foe.

But before Seitogi could strike, the man suddenly threw down his staff, defeated. As if on cue, another hunter arrived, panting and out of breath. The two Dhukai men looked at each other, their slain colleagues, then back at Seitogi.

Without a word, they both bowed their heads in his presence and then turned around, running in the direction from which they came.

Seitogi watched them go, his body still tense with the adrenaline of battle. Emily approached him cautiously,

"Why are they leaving?" she asked, throwing her stick aside.

"Because they're the smart ones," said Seitogi.

After another restless night of shivering in the cold, and a grueling half-day of sweltering hiking, they finally reached their destination. Dou-Dodachi's lair was a veritable fortress carved into the side of a mountain. Very few knew where it was, but its cold gleaming natural structure could be seen for miles.

It was a stronghold to protect its dwellers of reformed transients, vagrants and the like who now dedicated their life to prayer. Emily's mouth was dry and her stomach was empty, her body begging for sustenance. But despite all of that, she felt a rush of excitement as she gazed upon the imposing structure before her. She hoped that this was the place she had been searching for, the place where she would find the answers she had been seeking for so long.

Seitogi walked beside her, his eyes fixed on the path ahead. His face was set in a determined expression, his body tense with the exhaustion of their journey. Emily could sense his urgency, as he led her towards the hidden entrance of the fortress, his eyes darting back and forth, scanning for any signs of danger. The trail was treacherous, and Emily struggled to keep up with his brisk pace. Her legs ached with exhaustion, and she could feel the beads of sweat trickling down her back in the scorching heat. It was a boiling hot summer day, and their discomfort from the intense heat of the sun was causing both of them to feel a little woozy.

The two finally reached a brownish green, moss-covered wall, overhung with a thick tangle of dry vines, branches and leaves. Pushing through the hanging brush, they felt a huge breeze coming from a cavernous opening.

"I wonder what's down there?" Emily whispered, reaching out and placing her hand on Seitogi's shoulder.

"It's been a while since I was last here. This is the way."

Emily followed Seitogi as he stepped into the deep, dark recesses of a domed tunnel. Their footsteps echoed as they slowly walked into what appeared nothingness. Further ahead Emily saw a flickering lantern, its light, a ghostly orb dancing on the warm breeze.

"Do you offer peace or war friend?" A deep, spine-chilling voice resounded in the darkness.

Seitogi stopped dead in his tracks, ears stretched as far as they would reach to hear the shrouded figure in front of him.

"Peace or war?" it came again.

"I offer only peace," he called back.

"Yet you reek of fresh blood."

Emily clung to Seitogi's arm until she found her courage and stepped up beside him.

"We have come to seek the protection of Dou-Dodachi. Please let us in."

"Yes, I see," answered the disjointed voice, "Follow the light."

After some consideration, the two hastened their steps until they were at the end of the tunnel standing before a large wooden door guarded by a dower looking man dressed in a beige tunic that stopped just above his bloated ankles.

He handed Seitogi his paper lantern attached to a stick, and gave a great heave as he pushed the heavy doors outwards. The door creaked as he struggled to push it open. Seitogi offered to help, but he refused the service with a hiss. Once he managed an opening large enough for them to fit through, he ushered them into a large ceremonial arena of colossal size.

Emily could hear the faint ringing of chimes and chanting through the wind rippled mountain walls. The door swung close behind them, as two armed priests, weapons at the ready, quickly walked over.

The men never spoke an audible word to the gatekeeper, they just performed a series of head nods that seemed to convey their wishes. Emily was unsure of what awaited them but after several more nods and acknowledgments, the two men politely invited her and Setogi to follow them.

They crossed a small bridge into the stone fortress and were led up several flights of stairs to the priest's chambers where he met them at the door.

"Seitogi dear boy! It has been a terribly long time since we last met," the priest was not a tall man, but not short either, portly with plump jowls, close set, brow-less eyes, and a bald head.

"And who are we here? You've brought a guest too?"

"She is Enoshi, Master. The very same one you rescued all those years ago."

The old man looked Emily over, his smile stretched across his face displaying a few missing teeth.

"My word. So it is Princess Yuyuki, or should I say Shumaiyuki." Dou-Dodachi couldn't help but bow to her.

"Please, come inside and rest."

The priest welcomed Emily and Seitogi into a sunken, cylindrical room with a domed stained-glass ceiling that cascaded the room with colorful shadows. Emily was speechless as they descended stairs that spiraled down into the spacious interior. All of the curved walls were lined with stacked bookshelves, and in the center of the room was a cherry wood block surrounded by log shaped pillows.

"Well," said Seitogi, "This is it." He smiled at Emily as she took in their new surroundings.

“So, what do you think?”

“This place is amazing,” she replied softly.

Dou-Dodachi ushered Emily over to a tall paper screen and called over a young woman arranging tea along with another maid.

“Prepare a hot bath for the princess and outfit her with a fresh robe and moccasins. And you bring gruel, and sardines to go along with the tea.”

“I want my clothes back! I can wash the blood and brain out later on,” she gave Seitogi the side eye as the maid looked at Dou-Dodachi.

“Please have her clothes washed immediately as well, before the blood sets in,” he said.

“You change too. You reek of blood.”

Dou-Dodachi handed Seitogi a robe and directed him over to a separate screen. The old man wore a plain robe of beige linen himself and straw sandals. He took up the service of the tea abandoned by the maids and laid out cups and the kettle still fresh from the hearth. Emily was first to join him and sat on her knees as he poured for her.

“How’s that feeling? Better?” he asked. “You are safe here princess. So, relax and take meal until your bath is ready.”

“But mister you don’t understand! He kidnapped me and my friends and now we’ve gotten separated, and I don’t know where they are and it’s all his fault!”

“Seitogi did? You don’t say.”

“And he kills people right in front of you like we’re in a movie! He should be arrested for what he put me through!”

“I just spent the last two days defending us against hunters from the Inoue Dhukai,” Seitogi joined them at the table and held out his cup to Dou-Dodachi.

“She wouldn’t be alive if it weren’t for me.”

“I wouldn’t be here if it weren’t for you!”

“I know! You’d still be out there wandering around Minka forest being chased.”

“No! That’s not what I meant… he kidnapped me from my world! Earth, it’s like a different planet. You have to help me get home.”

“I will offer you as much help as I can princess but look here is the food. See there is savory rice gruel and mushrooms with skewered sardines.”

“It smells delicious, Master Dou-Dodachi, doesn’t it, Enoshi?”

“I’m too sick to eat after watching you kill all those people!” said Emily, but her growling stomach betrayed the validity of her statement.

“Sick or not, you’d better suffer a hot meal while we have the chance.”

Emily accepted a bowl of the gruel and took a few exploratory sips before greedily gulping down its entire contents. Seitogi and Dou-Dodachi smiled as the priest dipped the wooden ladle back into the clay pot and served her another helping. After three bowls and four sardines, Emily politely belched behind her hand and offered her appreciation.

“Seitogi told me you brought me to his village? I don’t know what that means, exactly,” she looked to the priest who seemed somewhat uncomfortable with the question. But Emily pressed. This was the safest she had felt since arriving in Behrani and needed to start putting the story together.

“It was when you were a child, a baby really,” the priest poured himself another cup of tea as he spoke.

“You lay in a patch of grass off the side of a road crying, wrapped in cloth. There were signs that an altercation of some sort had taken place; some scattered footprints in the dirt and significant droplets of blood on the road, but no one else was around.

I was on my praying pilgrimage and wasn't far from Daiye Village of which I frequented, and so took you there. The magistrate was Abete Syinta, Seitogi's father. He and his wife Demai adopted you and raised you as their own."

Emily didn't know how to feel but was too embarrassed to even look in Seitogi's direction. She did remember their close childhood connection, she vaguely remembered Syinta and Demai, but none of that mattered. She wanted to go home and blamed him for her current danger.

"That sounds like quite a story, but are you sure I'm the baby you found? I mean, I seem to have two memories. One was raised from childhood on the planet Earth. So, I couldn't have been raised in his village. Though the memory of Daiye kinda exist."

"Oh, I am certain, princess. I could never forget your face, or your emerald eyes. Yet, you do appear much younger than I would have expected you to be. For you are the Golden Swans elder by a year, but you seem junior to her in appearance."

"I noticed it too," Seitogi chimed in. "I figured the wizened woman would be able to explain it, or at least fix her."

"I don't need to be fixed; you bum! I just turned 17! What's the big deal?"

"How very interesting. You see princess, you should be well approaching your twentieth year in life."

"Twenty? I don't know! Maybe there is a time difference between our two worlds or something."

"Perhaps princess, but…"

"Please just call me Emily, and look. I just want to go home, and his stupid mirror isn't working. I can't get a signal on my phone either."

Emily couldn't stop talking despite being exhausted. "My grandmother raised me alone! She would never lie to me about my age or being from another world!" fresh tears fell from her eyes.

"I'm sure your grandmother was only protecting you if she kept the truth of Behrani hidden."

"Yeah. He says he's protecting me too," she flicked her chin in Seitogi's direction. "Is he going to pay for the years of therapy I'm going to need after spending a few days with him?"

"I assure you princess, Seitogi did what was necessary to ensure your safety."

"There's no way my grandmother knew about this place. She wouldn't have kept me in the dark," Emily was adamant, yet her inner voice questioned her own self assuredness of Dolores's innocence. After all, her family history, at least per Dolores Heart, was murky at best, outright baffling at worst.

"You shouldn't concern yourself with such things right now," said Dou-Dodachi.

A maid entered the room from behind a large tapestry depicting a map of the country and helped Emily to her feet. Her body ached in ways she didn't know a body could and she felt the itches and stings to an even greater extent now that she wasn't running on pure adrenaline.

She thanked the old priest and hobbled away supporting herself on the maid's shoulder. No sooner had the two women left the room when Dou-Dodachi looked Seitogi directly in the eyes and asked,

"Why would Maishae task you with bringing the princess back to this world?"

Seitogi noticed red, blue, and orange shadows shifting on the walls as day sunk into evening, the air in the room seemed stuffy.

"Enoshi's life was in danger. The wizened woman said the Aiyo had discovered a way to find and kill her."

"What nonsense," said the priest, "And you believed her?"

"Outside these walls the forest is crawling with Awei Chua's Dhukai. We also came across Aiyo men. They are seeking her head as we sit here."

"That woman is a witch with powers beyond our understanding and not to be trusted. Unless the Aiyo has mastered sorcery, surely she has deceived you."

"She wouldn't, and why should she?"

"What has she promised you in the deal?"

"I have always protected Enoshi."

"Evasive, and a frail answer. Does her father know she is here?"

"I…" Seitogi hesitated, and then remained silent.

"Don't you know who her father really is? Of course, you do, you served as his ward once, and so then you must know how her appearance could stop a coming war."

"We've been on the brink of war with Seizhone since before I was born. I won't let her be used!"

"Ah-ha, then I ask again, and it will be the last time. What has the witch promised you?"

"The three of us would be going to Dhreesh. Away from this place to a peaceful country."

"So, she has promised you her hand. Tsk, tsk. Was the princess not also promised to you by your father? Back when you were a boy? When we were all ignorant of her bloodline? Is it that silly promise that has led you to indulge in this fantasy that you are owed the hand of an Aiyo Princess meant to be your empress? Boy! The witch is using you, as does she use everyone, who crosses her path. I don't know what scheme she is planning for the princess, but I will not allow it. She will be taken under her father's protection."

"You can't master! Lord Yienguoi-Jin is…"

"Her father! And the one who should be making decisions for her. I consult with him regularly and even he is ready to come out of the shadows and sue for peace with Seizhone. Now, with the princess by his side, surely peace will be had for all."

"She isn't someone to be traded away! You see her. She is a foreign girl. And her friends, weak, crying things. They are not built for this world. I regret bringing her here now and with the wizened woman gone."

"Gone you say? Tell me all about it."

Seitogi cleared his throat, "There is not much to say. I was to retrieve Enoshi, and meet the wizened woman near the border. From there we would set out for Dhreesh. But we arrived in Minka forest instead. We went to her cabin. When we got there it had been thrown about. Shortly after we were attacked by Chua's Dhukai."

"Did it feel like a trap?"

"No…I believe they followed us. Look I understand you think turning Enoshi over,"

"Shumaiyuki," the priest's voice echoed off the walls as he stared into Seitogi's eyes, "Her name is Nham Aiyo Shumaiyuki."

"We can't stay here. I'm sorry master but I am going to get Enoshi now. Please don't try to stop me."

"I've watched you milk at your mother's breast, you will remain respectful. Sit back down. No need to alarm the princess anymore than she already is. I suspect her memories of old will find their way back to her soon enough. Then she will know her place, and her duty. I will forgive the fact today that you have forgotten yours."

Seitogi felt lightheaded and his mouth was rapidly filling with saliva the way it does when one is about to vomit.

"Sit, you don't look so well."

"You've poisoned me. Dou-Dodachi…"

"Just a harmless dose. It won't even put you to sleep, but it will stop you from taking any rash actions."

Seitogi plopped to the floor landing upright, slobber dribbled from one side of his mouth onto his robe.

"I gather you thought you would eventually escape the witch's clutches and take the princess off on your own. But you must think of what is good for Behrani. Even now there are daily skirmishes at the border with Seizhone. Imagine what a full-blown war with our neighbors to the east would look like. Almost all the men in your village would be sent to the front lines. Don't you think it dishonors them to put them in harm's way? All because you think you are owed a girl who was but a mere child you once knew."

"You can't…use her like that."

"We all have a use. The princess is to reign alongside the crown prince. Our countries, united." Dou-Dodachi stood and walked over to Seitogi and gave his shoulder a squeeze, "But you did the right thing bringing her to me. I have already sent a pigeon to alert Minister Djowobb of her presence."

"Djowobb can change his name and pretend to be a bureaucrat all he wants! But he will always be Lord Yienguoi-Jin of the Taisehsai Dhukai! You know it as well as I do. I wouldn't put him past turning her over to the Aiyo and collecting the bounty himself."

"All men deserve a chance to reform as proved by all the saved souls that roam this very compound. Until Minister Djowobb arrives, I shall have to keep you restrained,"

Dou-Dodachi clapped his hands, some seconds later two armed priests entered with blank looks on their faces.

"Take him to a room where he can rest, bind his arms and legs. Be wary of him."

"Master, I would never behave violently in your compound!"

"One can never be too careful when it's the fate of the country at stake now can they."

The priest pulled Seitogi's limp body to his feet and dragged him from the chamber. Once he was alone, Dou-Dodachi began clearing the table while humming under his breath. He rearranged the pillows and laid down blankets.

He lit candles all over, creating a veil of flickering light just as the maid led a refreshed Emily back into the room. Where is Seitogi were the first words out of her mouth. Dou-Dodachi and the maid laid her down on the pillows.

"He is currently bathing princess. Rest for the time being, I'm sure you could use some."

"I am tired, but I'm just too worried about Rebecca and Darren to sleep."

"Try it. Close your eyes and regain your strength."

* * *

Emily didn't know how long she had slept but she was awakened by the heavy creaking of the door at the top of the spiral stairwell as the priest closed it and guided several men in hooded cloaks down its lengthy twist. They were a gregarious bunch, laughing and talking loudly the whole way down.

"Enoshi," to her side, Seitogi groggily came to. The tallest of the group, a man wearing a wooden demon's mask framed in a mane of wild horse hair, walked over clapping his hands,

"Ah Seitogi! My little traitor is here too!" he said and slapped the boy hard across the top of his head. He looked at Emily and she was immediately taken aback as he removed his mask.

Her heart swelled at the sight of his hideously scarred, yet handsome face. A sharp indent of once carved flesh formed a deep line from the corner of his right chin, and jutted diagonally upwards and across, cutting a jagged path through his lips, nose, left eye, permanently welded shut, and forehead.

His one good eye shined, bright with emotion. Without thinking Emily was up on her feet running to him with tears in her eyes calling out,

"Dad!"

"Yuyuki!" he took her into his arms and hugged her tightly, making cooing sounds over her. Emily reached up and felt the deep scar slashed diagonally across the whole of his face and called him "Bakyu!"

"Bakyu? Minister Djowobb?" asked the confused priest.

"It's her nickname for me because I reminded her of a monster when she was a girl," answered Yeinguoi grinning ear to ear.

"You still do," Emily giggled."

Yienguoi-Jin rubbed his chin and tilted his head, a curious look in his eye. "Something is off though?" He looked to the priest for answers.

"She appears to be a few years younger than she should be my lord. Perhaps she's been enchanted by the witch."

"Wait! Don't tell him that! I haven't been enchanted by anyone!" Emily said in Brenhi, and then unknowingly switching to English she clutched onto Yeinguoi's cloak beneath his neck and looked into his eyes pleading,

"This can't be real. Please tell me I'm strapped down to a bed in the psychiatric ward right now. Because. You see, about a year ago I snuck out to this party and someone slipped something in my drink. I started imagining all this crazy stuff, and now! Now it's happening again!"

Yienguoi-Jin looked over to Dou-Dodachi, "What is happening to her? Why is she suddenly talking gibberish?"

"It's the language of her world she calls Arth" offered Seitogi, "and she is obviously frightened and confused."

Yienguoi-Jin took Emily by the shoulders and gave her a little shake.

"Daughter, you are home now. Speak in your native tongue and know that you are safe. There is no need for fear. Now, let's have a look at you."

He gave Emily a little nudge forward and then motioned for her to turn around. Muddled, Emily turned in a small semi circle and then a full twirl of sorts.

It was not too long ago a scout she met on the street had her perform the same actions for all passing by to see.

“She lacks poise,” he commented. “Walk towards me.” He ordered; Emily followed.

“No, that won’t do. She doesn’t at all walk like a princess. Pull your shoulders back and straighten your spine and neck. Good, now tuck your chin into your throat and walk with your hands flat before you.”

“What are you?” Emily tried and failed to get a word in.

“Your voice too. Though it may be music to a father’s ear, it is far to grating for that of a princess. The public will never accept it in its current form.”

“Excuse me! My voice is just fine! And I don’t know what kind of weird ‘Go see’ you think you have going on here, but I am just fine as I am!”

“She’s boyish isn’t she?” he asked Dou-Dodachi.

“She needs time to settle back into herself, Your Grace.”

Yienguoi-Jin reached forward and stroked her cheek. Emily flinched away, uneasy.

“Hum… her skin isn’t at all supple. Much too rough. We will have to have her soak in warm milk and honey for a day or two before presenting her to the empress.”

“I’m sorry? What was that now?”

“He means to marry you off to the emperor’s heir,” said Seitogi.

Emily backed away from her father, “What is he talking about? I’m not marrying anyone! I just want to go home!”

"You are home my daughter! And yes, you will be married as is your duty. We have much to discuss on the matter. For now we must go. Enemies are all around us," and to his men, "Keep the boy bound and bring him along. We may rehabilitate him, yet."

"You can't be serious right!" Emily shrieked in English. She turned and ran towards the tapestry map, but Yienguoi-Jin was quick and caught her about the wrist.

"Girl! What is wrong with you? Behave!"

"Behave!" Emily scrambled to get away from him, and then jumped up and wrapped her legs around his waist, pummeling him with clenched fists screaming,

"I want to go home!" over and over again.

Yienguoi-Jin laughed a good hearty laugh at her bizarre foriegn tongue.

"See. She'll give prince Rilkian a run for his money, eh old priest!"

"She has an exuberant spirit, Your Grace."

"Enough " said Yienguoi-Jin, and delivered her a quick chop to the back of the neck rendering her unconscious.

"We will be on our way, old friend. Thank you for alerting me to her arrival. We shall acclimate her to her role as future empress."

"And what about Your Grace? Once you present her to the emperor the truth of your lineage will be known as well."

"I am prepared to atone for my silence if it ends all the useless bloodshed on the border."

"Then safe journey, Minister Djowobb."

"You must remember to call me Yienguoi-Jin when the mask is on old priest."

"Apologies, Your Grace."

Speaker Box

The spacious interior of the Golden Swan's receiving room was a masterpiece in subtle opulence. Framed by dark wooden columns and screens of dazzlingly intricate carvings of gold filigree, its walls were painted a deep peacock blue accented with tiny flecks of gold leaf.

From the ceiling hung a frosted paper chandelier which had been lit when they entered, and cast sparkles all over the walls. There were two shelves packed with scrolls and books. Porcelain vases held green and white flowers. Framed scrolls with beautiful calligraphy, and gold and red tatami mats covered the floor.

Shumaiyuki sat on her floating chaise lounge in the center of the room, propped up by several pillows with a mesmerized look on her face. Her hair, a deep chestnut with natural metallic highlights complimented her bronzed, amber skin. Her almond shaped eyes, a deep gold green, set in a sea of the purest white, radiated focus and her lips, painted a rich matte chocolate, heightened Her Graceful elegance.

She had never laid eyes on such a peculiar collection of objects in her entire life, and was fascinated by the novelty of it all. It showed in her elegantly expressive features. At 19, her beauty was already legendary throughout Behra.

She, looking down at Rebecca's pair of baggy, high waisted jeans spread out on the floor before her. Next to the jeans was a thin, blue ribbed sweater, pink socks, beige bra and underwear set, and a pair of cream athletic trainers with baby blue stripes.

Rebecca's shoulder bag contained the following items: a red pair of wide rim prescription glasses, a Hello Kitty key chain with attached house keys, a square power block, a small box of disposable contact lenses, a compact digital camera and iPhone, one paper notebook, one pink iPad, a mini pack of Always liners, a Sanrio pencil style cosmetics bag, a black USB lighter, and a coffee table book, Wes Anderson's "Overhead Shots of Marvelous Curiosities". Shumaiyuki took hold of the 12 x 12 book and eagerly turned from one page to the next, intrigued by its gorgeous matte/pastel photos, and soon became absorbed, particularly by one shot.

An overhead of an astonishing stop motion animated set piece of a garbage dump, inhabited by a family of three opossums. The photo was captioned with an illustrated ribbon which read, 'Sweet Home'.

"What is this?" Shumaiyuki wondered out loud.

Forced to wear an unflattering, excessively large burlap robe, Rebecca immediately sprang up when she heard the girl's voice. Shumaiyuki held up the book so that Rebecca could see and pointed to the photo repeating the question and becoming angry when Rebecca stammered in English that she couldn't understand her.

Shumaiyuki glowered, "What is the meaning of this? Are these paintings? Or is it just…hum. How are they rendered?"

Rebecca stared at her frightened and confused. Her tongue felt swollen in her mouth. After being locked alone in a cell for two days, she was paralyzed with fear. Shumaiyuki's frown deepened as she grew frustrated, tapping the 'Sweet Home' with a clear polished nail, and then finally –

"Stick! Where is my stick!" her voice rose as she searched about her lounge growing increasingly irate. She regarded a servant as she looked,

"I will ask you once more, where is my stick?" She then slammed the book down on the floor. "Find it! Be quick!"

The servant fled from the room and then soon returned with the stick in her trembling hands, a thin piece of green bamboo, just over a foot in length. Shumaiyuki snatched it from the girl and struck her several times, warning:

"How many times have I told you to stop hiding it? The more you do! The more severe the beating!"

"That is enough Shumai, leave the girl," Te-Tae slowly toddled into the room carrying a worn and splintered box about the size of a conventional milk crate.

The big woman, in a dark blue robe that complimented the muted colors of her wavy gray hair, moved with lethargy while complaining,

"This box child. It's not as light as it seems."

"Where is the girl I sent? How dare she take two whole days to find it! I will beat her!" she bellowed; her face twisted with anger.

But the old maid stood her ground, unimpressed by her charge's threats. "You'll be beating no one," she retorted, setting the walnut-colored box down on the floor. "I sent her to collect refreshments. The box was buried deep in the treasure room, and much had to be moved about in order to find it."

"But you are too old to be carrying such things! I will beat her as is my duty as her mistress!"

"Its weight is light enough that no one need suffer retribution for my labor. Now let us get on with the exhibition."

Shumaiyuki scowled, but she knew better than to argue with the old maid. Te-Tae was the one person inside Odahni who could stand up to her without fear, and she quietly respected her for it.

"It may not be as heavy as all that, but I'll punish her just the same," the princess mumbled to herself. She leaned forward and turned a rusted metal dial. The box immediately emitted loud sound waves of choppy, kinetic static.

Shumaiyuki spoke into one of two mesh covered holes on the top of the box, and after several seconds of crackling noises, the words translated into a stern, robotic sounding voice -

"Speak into the box."

"What? What - was that English?" Rebecca's whole face contorted into a look of profound confusion as she attempted to process what she had just heard. She scrambled over on her knees to the speaker box and looked at it with uncertainty, pausing before saying,

"Can I? I can talk, and it will translate for you?"

"See it speaks Brenhi now Obánā!" Shumaiyuki enthusiastically waved her stick in the air.

“Say something else!” she clapped. “What is this book? The paintings are bizarrely exquisite?” her eyes wide.

Rebecca took a moment to process, and then said, “Oh? They aren’t paintings at all. These are called photographs.” she stammered.

Just then, another maid entered carrying a tray with tea and flat round cakes. Shumaiyuki’s chaise rose from the floor, and she floated over as the girl set the tray down on a table. Without hesitation, she struck the servant across her back with her stick.

“I asked for the speaking box days ago! You should have had it ready beforehand! And Obánā is old and ragged! How dare you make her work your chores!”

“Leave the bloody girl Shumai! What have I told you about discipling the staff?” Te-Tae weakly protested.

“Please don’t beat her!” Rebecca begged into the box.

Shumaiyuki hesitated, scowled, and floated back over to the red head and glared,

“It will not speak unless It is spoken to first,” and struck Rebecca on the shoulder with a hard slam of the stick, followed by,

“I will do as I see fit! You should have known better than to question me!”

Rebecca looked up and caught the maid’s tearful gaze. She shifted her eyes and looked down at the ground. Tears welled up in her own eyes.

“My god! What is this? The Silence of The Lambs? I’m a human! Not a goddamned it!” She began to wail. Shumaiyuki answered with another slap from the stick.

“Oww! What the hell? Stop it!”

“It seems not to know It’s place Te-Tae.”

“It will learn,” the old woman replied with a half yawn, fanning herself.

"What have you done with Emily and Darren?"

"Emiendarun? What is this thing saying?"

"I don't know, but it has been carrying on about Emily, Darren, these last few days." Te-Tae slowly pronounced the names, sadly shaking her head.

"Yes, Darren! The guy I was with!" Rebecca interrupted, for which she received another strike from the stick, but with less ferocity though it still smarted. "He has a broken arm. He's Emily's, um..Yuyuki's boyfriend!"

"Yuyuki! And, what is this Emily?"

"She's my best friend. She looks exactly, well almost exactly, like you! I mean, you're a little older, and far more sophisticated, and well obviously a better dresser, because you're like, rich I guess? Look! I can show you just please don't hit me again." for this request she immediately received a strike on her shoulder, followed by –

"What is this best friend? We do not have friends!"

Rubbing her sore shoulder and wincing, Rebecca asked, "Are you kidding me? Of course, we're friends! Do you not understand the concept of friends on this planet?"

"We are aware of what a friend is, fool!" Shumaiyuki swung the stick again but Rebecca avoided the blow to the princess's dismay.

"No, no, no! I don't think you truly understand! Emily and I are friends; we have shared goals. We work together, help each other out and share a deep emotional bond. We're like sisters," she sobbed.

"I can show you o.k.! If you'll let me just grab my phone," she carefully reached for her iPhone and slid it over to herself.

Shumaiyuki and Te-Tae stared at each other, puzzled. The guard posted at the entrance slowly moved his hand to his sword. The two maids lined up behind him.

Rebecca held up the phone, she wiped away the tears from her eyes and said,

"This is Emily. She's…we are… *sniff, sniff* are friends. We've known each other since we were nine or ten. *sniff, sniff* Does this mean you still don't understand?" She leaned forward and placed the phone back on the floor and wiped her eyes.

The chaise settled down, landing on the floor, Shumaiyuki timidly picked up the phone and gasped quietly,

"Yuyuki." Turning to Te-Tae and showing her the illuminated lock screen photo of Emily and Rebecca making silly faces.

"What is this? Speak!"

"It's a communication device called a smartphone. If you let me, I can open it and show you more."

"Come then. I won't strike it should it please me," Shumaiyuki waved her over.

Rebecca was quite hesitant on what to do, unsure how to approach someone with such high-status as royalty and wary of receiving another whack. So she crept, slowly and with difficulty; Shumaiyuki felt the need to encourage her by hitting the floor with her stick.

Rebecca opened the phone with the royal princess and her servant forgetting all decorum as both leaned in close as Rebecca tapped the rainbow shutter icon. Thousands of pictures popped up and both Shumaiyuki and Te-Tae exclaimed "Yuyuki!"

"Well, in my world, she's called Emily. Emily Heart. I live around the corner from her. We've been best friends since fourth grade."

Rebecca scrolled past many photographs and stopped on one with Emily and Darren kissing in the school cafeteria. Te-Tae averted her eyes with an audible gasp. Shumaiyuki skipped a breath and covered the lover half of her face with her long sleeve.

“So, she and the boy are betrothed then?” she asked. “Harlot! She wishes to lay claim to my Rilkian, when she has already been married, and had her petals plucked?”

“What! wait, no they aren’t married! I mean my god, we’re just kids!” Rebecca raised her hand so as not to be hit as she reached for the phone.

“But is this not a kiss?” Shumaiyuki’s voice went high. “It’s a scandal! The thought that such an impure thing could wear my crown turns my stomach.” she stared down another photo of Emily stuffing her mouth with a forkful of spaghetti, tomato sauce smeared her chin and cheeks.

“She is ungraceful isn’t she? And see how her face is like that of a child’s. Is she not my senior, Obánā?”

“By a year, or a little more Your Grace,” answered Te-Tae. “But I agree she appears a girl compared to you.”

“It will show me more!” the floating princess slapped the floor again with her stick.

“Um, I know. How about a video,” Rebecca scrolled down some and pressed play on a short video of her and Emily dancing in front of a cafe.

Shumaiyuki drew back in horror, squealing and swinging her stick wildly at the phone as her chaise lifted her towards the ceiling. Te-Tae tried to run and fell over, and the guard was momentarily frozen in place.

“Obinari stop them! Seize them!” she screamed. The guard, Obinari ran over but drew away horrified by the video with the laughing girls.

“It’s not real! It’s not real,” Rebecca cried, “See!” she picked up the phone and turned it towards Shumaiyuki.

“Leave me and save the princess!” Te-Tae admonished the maids helping her to her feet as Rebecca hit record.

Shumaiyuki covered her face in fear and Obinari fell onto his backside, not knowing what form of death to expect from the strange tiny people. After several seconds Rebecca coaxed Shumaiyuki to float down to the floor and showed her the 15 second clip she had just recorded of the princess covering her face.

"Obánā! It's me! She's mystified me!" said Shumaiyuki. "Come look! Hurry and help her over you halfwits! Why do you look so afraid when there is nothing to fear?" She seemed pleased. Obinari looked on curiously and asked what it was as Rebecca replayed the video.

"It's called a video…It's like a moving picture, or painting I guess."

Shumayuki struck the guard harshly on the back of the neck, "Who told you to speak fool! Don't think I didn't notice your display of cowardice just now! I could have been dead, or worse, my beauty maimed while you sat there on your ass!"

She hit him three more times before he returned to his post. She then turned her attention back on the phone and gazed at herself in wonder.

"I can show you larger photos on this," Rebecca picked up her tablet and turned it on. Everyone in the room except Rebecca balked at its opening chime. She opened a file marked 'Shows' and turned on a mythical martial arts drama.

"This is me and Emily's favorite show right now. It's called, 'Love in the time of Ming'."

Shumaiyuki gasped softly, then again more loudly, "This.. this is what we are to believe is a moving painting?"

"Why do the people look just as real as you and I?" asked Te-Tae, "Heavens, and see how that one flies, and has lightning in his palms!"

"It's just special effects," said Rebecca, "Really bad ones at that. They don't have the biggest budget, but still, it's like such a good show," Rebecca nervously eyed her tablet's battery meter,

76%. She was wondering for how long she could keep their attention and maybe have a chance to escape.

"So, the people there have special effects? What powerful gods to harness lighting in the palms of their hands. Oh Obánā, If I had warriors with such might I'd already be empress supreme. I should like to learn everything I can about this world of yours." Shumaiyuki looked at Rebecca waiting.

"Oh! Earth! My world is called Earth."

"Ert," Shumaiyuki tried out the pronunciation and smiled, pleased with her work. "Another!" she demanded.

Rebecca nervously scrolled through the tons of photos and videos when the princess grew impatient and slapped her hand away, taking over the search herself. She stopped on a video of Emily with her arms raised making a horrid face.

"What is this one?" to Rebecca.

"Shit, um…let's go to another one."

"Make it move, or I shall beat you until you are the color of a beet!"

"Um, you just have to tap it with the tip of your finger. Like this," Rebecca reached forward but paused. "I gotta warn you it's kinda crazy."

"Crazy?"

Rebecca tapped the video and the still picture flourished to life with a sweating, snarling Emily breathing heavily while ignoring the various calls of 'Emily stop!' and 'Calm down!' from her terrified peers, all of whom had their phones out recording her. Awash in night and streetlights accompanied by the revolving red flash of two parked squad cars, she stood in the parking lot of a single-story home, with three downed police officers at her feet. Several more surrounded her with batons drawn, slowly approaching.

"Emily please stop! They are going to arrest you!" came Rebecca's terrified voice off camera. Emily replied something in garbled Brenhi, seconds later the speaker box translated:

"I am the Pearl Swan! The daughter of a demon!" She immediately charged the officer closest to her and snatched his baton while sweeping him off his feet. He hit the grass in a loud thump, his comrades, frozen with fear, were like sitting ducks as she wildly swung the baton while kicking and dipping in a wide circular pattern. Her pointed foot and the polished wood connected with knees, skulls and ankles alike.

"Obánā! She is fighting in the style of Klai-Schwuh!" Shumaiyuki touched the old woman's shoulder. "See how she is possessed with the spirit of Yeinguoi-Jin himself! How should she be so skilled in Kill Craft?"

"I know not Her Grace. But has she not just confirmed for us, the rumor of her birth? A Tahseiseh."

"Impossible! She is no Dhukai!" Turning to Rebecca with rage in her eyes.

"It was a house party we went to! This house party!" Rebecca flung herself into a desperate bow, pressing her face into the floor.

"Someone slipped something into Emily's drink and she just lost it! It happened right when the police arrived to break up the joint! No one could stop her. She just kicked ass with no questions asked. We all thought she was babbling nonsense, but I guess it was Brehi?"

"Brenhi you fool!" Shumaiyuki struck the floor next to her with the bamboo stick. "What is a slip drink?"

"A mizer's power potion perhaps," Te-Tae offered.

"No, it was some kind of drug. A roofie, speed? We never found out what it was exactly. But yeah, I had never seen her like that before. She had to be institutionalized for like, almost two weeks. That's when she started with all the demon princess stuff. It was a scary time."

“Demon princess eh,” Shumaiyuki stroked her chin, “Perhaps it does lend itself to some of the gossip surrounding her birth. What say you, Te-Tae?”

“The sooner we have her head on a pike the better, Her Grace.”

“I agree. It seems that our Pearl Swan has sharper talons than one would have thought. But would she be so bold as to return here to Odahni?” she eyed Rebecca in a way that made the girl want to shrink in on herself. And then used the tip of the bamboo stick to lift her freckle laced chin enough for their eyes to meet.

“It shall remain in my apartment for the time being. It will tell me everything It knows about Yuyuki, and we shall have daily discussions on the various intricacies of It’s Ert.” she motioned over a maid who sheepishly approached, “Prepare it a bath and ready it, the autumn room.”

“I’m sorry. What’s happening now?`` Rebecca received another strike of the stick.

“It doesn’t speak unless spoken to!” Shumayuki insisted.

Rebecca broke down into tears again apologizing and nursing a fresh whelp on the side of her arm.

“Nor will It cry!” another strike, but not as hard, more of a stern tap. She turned to the two maids, “Well why are you standing there gawking? Off with you then. It shall remain here with me until the bath is ready. I want detailed explanations for all these items.”

“O.k, Sure.” Rebecca mumbled.

“It is to say, “Yes my lady,” said Te-Tae.

“I understand,” Rebecca mumbled, and pointed to her glasses saying, “Is it okay for me to take out these contacts and put on my glasses… my lady?”

“Here,” Shumaiyuki handed Rebecca the tablet, “Show me the paintings from before.”

Rebecca reopened the photo app and handed the tablet back to Shumaiyuki. She eagerly took it and began swiping through the photos whispering,

"It must be some form of magic." And then suddenly, there was Emily and Darren kissing again.

"Oh, how unheard of," she blushed behind her raised sleeve, but unable to take her eyes off of Darren.

***

Darren woke to the sound of swords clashing and soldiers shouting. He sat up on his makeshift bed, a pile of straw in the corner of the sparring gym and rubbed his eyes. Though braced and bandaged, his arm throbbed with pain, a constant reminder of his fight with Seitogi.

He heard a group of soldiers approaching, their voices growing louder as they neared. "Hey, one arm! You awake?" one of them called out, laughing. Darren couldn't understand their jeers, but he was sure they were no worse than anything he had heard from his coach on the football field.

He knew that he had to find a way to regain his strength and prove them wrong. He got up and made his way to the latrines, carrying a bucket of water and a worn brush in his good hand. The stench was overwhelming, but he tried not to let it bother him.

As he scrubbed at the floors and walls, he thought about his fight with Seitogi. It had been a whole three days since, but it seemed weeks had passed. He thought of the pain of his broken arm and the anger fueled him. He vowed to himself that he would never be weak again. He would get his revenge, even if it meant never returning home.

In the distance, he could hear the soldiers training. He watched them when he could, studying their movements. He couldn't help but admire their camaraderie. The Tabaiken reminded him of his team back on Earth, where he had been a star player and a shoo-in for homecoming king.

But now, in this strange world, he felt he was nothing. He shook off those thoughts and focused on the task at hand.

When he finished with the latrines, Darren moved on to the dining hall. It was a chaotic mess, with plates and cups strewn everywhere. The soldiers ate quickly and sloppily, eager to get back to their training. He and another boy tried to clean up as best they could, but the soldiers didn't make it easy. They would purposely knock over cups or spill food on the floor, laughing as Darren scrambled to clean it up.

Despite their cruelty, Darren remained determined. He refused to let them get the best of him. He saw his duties as a form of training, a way to build up his strength and endurance. And every day, as he worked, he thought about his fight with Seitogi. He thought about the anger and the pain, and he channeled those feelings into his chores

As he finished cleaning up, Darren looked outside to see the Tabaiken sparring in the setting sun. He felt a growing desire to join them, to become a skilled swordsman like them. He knew it wouldn't be easy, but he was determined to try.

He whispered to himself, "You may have left me to die Emily so you could run off with your little boyfriend, but I'll find you both. I'll do whatever it takes to become stronger. I'll do whatever it takes to make you's pay for what you did to me."

A Tragic Love

Emily was jostled awake by a disturbing, up-and-down motion that rocked her body back and forth. A revolving, crunchy, creaking sound grated on her ears and was accompanied by the noisy clippity-clop of hooves striking the ground.

Once again, she was shrouded in darkness, lying on a prickly bed of straw. She ached, mainly in her lower back and legs, but she managed to give them a good stretch, kicking them in the air. Her stomach groaned, *Am I hungry again already?* Where was she, even? What happened to the priest?

“Master Dou-Dodachi?” she yawned.

“You’re finally awake. How are you feeling?”

“Oh, Seitogi. It’s you?”

“You don’t have to sound so disappointed.”

“It’s hardly a cause for celebration. Where are we going?”

“We’re in the back of Master Yienguoi-Jin’s wagon, en route to Domotedai. We’ve been on the road for hours.”

“Domo… what? What is that?”

“Domotedai is the emperor’s Castle town in the center of Nyongoyuchi, the capital. Lord Yienguoi-Jin works as an Imperial minister under the Sowao Clan and lives there.”

“Imperial Minister! That guy? But he’s a crook, isn’t he? I remember him and his gang of bandits… you worked for him, didn’t you?”

“He took me in when I was a boy, after my father disowned and exiled me from Daiye.”

“This sucks! I wouldn’t be in this situation if not for you! ‘Don’t worry, Emily! We’ll be safe with the priest,’ he says!”

“It wasn’t my plan to be betrayed by Dou-Dodachi.”

"Why did you take us there in the first place if it wasn't safe? And why didn't you know you couldn't trust him? We have to get out of here! Can we escape?"

"My arms and legs are bound. Even if I were free, we wouldn't be able to make it far."

"Goddamnit!" Emily's voice broke, and fresh tears crested her eyes.

"You've changed, Enoshi. You never cried so much when you were a girl. How have you become so weak?"

"Weak! Screw you, bro! I'm weak? First, you kidnap me and Beck, no telling where she is! And then you smash a guy's skull right in front of me and expect what? Me to be some kind of boss bitch about it? You damned idiot! I'm traumatized, just like any normal human would be!"

"I had a plan," there was a tinge of sadness in Seitogi's voice. "I just wanted you to be safe… to protect you like I used to, Enoshi."

Emily felt a wave of sadness wash over her too; maybe she was being too harsh. She felt her way over to him in the dark.

"We didn't really get a chance to talk about it over the past few days, being chased and all. But, we were close, at one time, weren't we?" Sitting next to him, she continued, "It was so long ago, Seita."

"Seita," he repeated the word quietly as though it were his own private, cherished mantra.

"No one but you ever called me that," he said. "Well, Ary too, but…"

"I may seem weak to you," she said, wiping her tears. "I can't help it if I'm scared. I've had the rug pulled out right from under me. It's not something you just wake up to every day."

"Forgive me. I didn't mean to offend you."

"It's okay, I guess. Look, I'm going to untie you, but then you have to help me retrace our steps so that we can find Beck and Darren," she choked up again when mentioning Darren. "It's my fault he's hurt," she muttered.

"You can't blame yourself for his reckless actions, Enoshi. The boy shouldn't have interfered."

"He was trying to protect me! Anyway, you owe him. The least you can do is help me find them."

"Sorry, Enoshi. It would be impossible. We are no longer in Kue, far from it. But as I said back in Minka forest, with their strange appearance, they will probably fetch a good price… maybe not the boy. He would be quite useless without his arm. There is a chance he might be put to death."

"Was that an attempt to reassure me?"

"I'm just being honest. But the fact he is foreign may save him. His exotic looks may land him in a pleasure den."

"Pleasure den! My god, I would never be able to face his parents again. What would I tell them? You have to save him, Seita!"

"What responsibility could you possibly have to his parents? Have you two been promised to one another as well?"

"What do you mean, 'promised to one another'?"

"Meaning, have you been matched for marriage? Is that what you meant when you called him your boyfriend?"

"Marriage! No way! Are you crazy? I was his tutor towards the end of ninth grade so he wouldn't have to repeat. Somehow, that summer, we started dating, but that's it. And what did you mean by 'am I promised to him as well?"

"When we were children, a few years after you were brought to Daiye, we were promised to each other, Enoshi. According to village law, all children are matched young. We were matched by my father."

"Wha…what! Are you saying I'm your fiancée?"

"It's complicated, what with all the years we've been apart, but yes. We were meant to be married when we came of age."

"Well, let me help you un-complicate things. I am not marrying anyone! It sounds ridiculous even having to say it! I don't even believe in marriage. It was never in my plans!"

"But the boy…he fought for you?"

"Doesn't mean I'm in love with him! Like I said, we were just dating! Oh, none of that matters anyway. I just want to find them and get us home. And since it's your fault we're here, you are going to help us find our way back."

"You sure do know how to belt out orders, don't you?"

"It's the American in me, but what I say is true, Seita. It's your fault we are here. You did this to me. You fix it!"

"Amerigon?"

"American! America. The country I'm from."

"You are from Behrani, Enoshi, not Amerigo."

"Heart! My name is Emily Heart. Stop calling me Enoshi."

The canvas-covered wagon came to a halt with a hard jerk. A minute later, a masked Yienguoi-Jin opened the canvas's back flap, flooding the dark interior with dull shards of moonlight, and offered Emily his hand. She swatted it away, causing him a considerable amount of mirth as he held his belly and laughed.

"You knocked me out, dammit! Your own child!"

"Ha, you were misbehaving and speaking in tongues!"

"I was upset, and speaking en…en," she realized she had no Brenhi word for English, and so just decided to say English.

The pronunciation made him laugh even harder as he reached in and pulled her struggling figure out into the cool night air.

"Come along," he commanded, "It's late, and it will be morning in a few hours."

"But what about Seitogi?"

"No need to concern yourself with the boy. He will be taken care of."

Yienguoi-Jin handed off the wagon to a waiting servant and walked towards an ivy-covered wall, where two armed men guarded either side.

Both men bowed to Yienguoi-Jin as he passed through, followed by a skeptical Emily.

She followed him down a torch-lit hallway flanked by two rows of kneeling men who called out in unison,

"Heicho-Hieba!" 'crown princess.' Emily remembered the title from her youth and suppressed a smile despite her fear.

Walking towards her and Yienguoi-Jin from the end of the tunnel was an older man. He was taller than her father, but she didn't consider him too imposing. He had thin wrinkles at the sides of his eyes, small signs of age on a face that still had a large amount of tight skin.

He wore a white robe under a casual crimson jacket. His hair was salt-and-pepper gray and wavy, tied into a neat ball atop his head. He walked with a confident step, as if he had all the time in the world to take. In an instant, Emily felt comfortable in his presence.

"Is it really her?" he asked with delight upon reaching them, he held Emily's face in his hands, and smiled. "Ah, indeed it is. These are the eyes of that child I met so long ago. Do you remember me, princess, from Gyonjuin Bridge in Kue?"

"I'm sorry, but I don't, not exactly," Emily could sense fresh tears coming and quickly wiped her face.

"Oh, dear me, my lady, please do not cry. This is a day for celebration!"

“She’s a very emotional girl,” Yienguoi-Jin remarked, his voice suddenly sounding smoother and more elegant to Emily. She shot a quick, sour glance at him and then looked to the older man for support.

“Hello, sir. I’m Emily Heart, and I need your help.”

“Emily Heart… Well, Emily, I am Sowao Daw Phule. You were introduced to me as Heicho-Hieba, Nham Aiyo Des Shumaiyuki.”

“Shumaiyuki?” repeated Emily. She rubbed the sides of her head with the tips of her fingers. “Enoshi. Yuyuki. Shumaiyuki. This is all so ridiculous,” and then, “I’m sorry… I don’t know what’s going on. I think I’m having a nervous breakdown.” Her tears fell anew.

Phule’s face was sad, his eyes kind. He told Emily, “Please don’t cry, princess. I will help you however I can.”

“Do you understand? I don’t belong here!” through sobs and tears.

“Where do you belong if not Behrani?”

Emily shook her head and wondered, ‘Where did she belong?’ She thought she might faint and covered her eyes with her hand, mumbling, “It’s all so confusing.”

“Why are you confused, my dear?”

“It’s a long story.”

“Then please tell me, Emily. I’m listening.”

“I’m an American! Please try to understand, I was kidnapped! Um, please take me back to America! Please. I want to go home…”

Phule stroked Emily’s hand. “I understand that you must have a wealth of questions. And that this is a most peculiar situation. But you will be well taken care of. The hard part is over. You are back home.”

“What home? Are you referring to this place? Behrani!”

"Indeed, princess, you are of Aiyo blood. The most powerful family in all of Behrani aside from the Imperial House Anele. That is the truth of the matter, Emily."

"That's absolutely absurd!"

Lord Phule looked to Yienguoi-Jin and said, "Minister Djowobb will explain it all to you, my dear."

Emily followed his eyes to the masked warrior, "Him! He's a jerk! He attacked me and threw me in the back of a cart!"

"She was hysterical. Not at all what one would expect from someone born of her station," said Yienguoi-Jin.

"What's with all the fancy talk all of a sudden," Emily poked him harshly in the ribs.

"See there. She's prone to violent outbursts. Not at all ladylike. She will have to be retrained."

"Hey! You're not the boss of me!" Emily said. "I'm not training for anything!"

"This girl," Yienguoi-Jin threw his hands up with a chuckle and shook his head, "See how she behaves."

"Well, she has been through some changes, hasn't she, Minister Djowobb? I will help you become reacquainted with us, princess. You will stay here tonight, and we will talk about your past and your future."

"With all due respect, Mr. Phule, I can't stay here. I have friends trapped here too. It's my responsibility to find them."

Phule sighed with a nod towards Emily. "I understand how worried you must be for your friends, and I assure you that we will help with finding them. However, you must understand that there are certain traditions and protocols we must follow here in Behrani. While you are here, you are Heicho-Hieba, and it is important for you to learn about your heritage and your responsibilities."

Emily frowned, feeling conflicted. She liked the looks of Phule, but he was saying nothing better than her father.

"It appears the girl is a touch dense as well," said Yienguoi-Jin.

Emily gave him another sharp jab, but this time he slapped her hand away.

"You don't know anything about me!" she said, "You don't know where I'm from or where I'm going."

"I beg you to forgive Minister Djowobb's words, princess. Please come inside for now. I am sure you must be starving. Come, please, all will be explained."

"Ok, but listen! I have friends… two of my friends!"

"All will be explained," repeated Phule as he led her down the corridor.

Emily nodded nervously and followed the two men, who promptly led her down another long hall filled with kneeling men and turned many corners, going deeper into the compound. She was very confused by the place. Who were all these people calling her 'Heicho-Hieba' as she passed? What were they all doing here? They knew nothing about her. Emily wasn't sure what to think of their adulation.

Through the gate, they proceeded. Lord Phule led them down an emerald lawn, their steps crunching on the gravelly path which stretched on through to a lantern-lit garden.

They made it to the entrance of the three-story residence, the whole of it dark wood, with sliding doors and a tiled roof with curled eaves. Lanterns bordered the veranda, flanked by hardy bushes and all manner of plants which, though nourished by the shade, were still lush.

Lord Phule led them up the veranda steps and through the door, which was flanked by a square of paper lanterns, the wood of which had been shaped and painted to look like a rising sun. Within was a wide hall, with many doors leading off.

To the right, a flight of stairs led up, to another flight which curled along the landing, round a corner, and up to the left.

They were met by a procession of maids chattering about the Heicho-Hieba, who came to attention at the sight of their lord and his guest. Emily, whose face was red from crying, became acutely aware they were all staring at her.

“She is the bride,” Emily heard a whisper. Lord Phule cleared his throat loudly and delivered the group a stern look.

“Please, this way, my lord,” one of the maids stepped forward, her face lightly powdered, her eyes like black polished jade stones, gesturing for them to follow. She took them to a circular chamber with a wide oval door.

The first thing Emily noticed was the sound of a wind chime made of brass and crystal, hanging from the upper curve of an open terrace. The room was empty except for a few lacquer boxes and a circular arrangement of tall, paper screens decorated with cranes, which made the interior seem smaller than it actually was. A serving table carved from jade sat sunk into the center of the floor.

The maid showed them over to the table where they were seated. They were followed by a bevy of young maids, who came in carrying dishes of tea, pastry, cold sausage, and pickles.

“Bring us warm lager!” Yienguoi-Jin commanded, slapping his thigh. Emily glared at him and sipped her tea. She was pleasantly surprised by its wonderful flavor.

“Are you pleased with the tea?” asked Phule.

“It’s delicious. Thank you,” and then to Yienguoi-Jin, “It was pretty rude how you just spoke to that girl! You should be ashamed.”

All the maids, seated away at a respectful distance, stared at Emily in shock, and then back to Yienguoi-Jin, and then immediately pressed their foreheads to the floor. Emily couldn’t tell if it was out of fear or loyalty.

“If you are going to stay here for any time, then you will have to understand the customs of this place. I shall teach you many things you’ll see,” Yienguoi-Jin said as he nibbled a pickled radish through the mouth hole in his mask, “There is a great deal you’ll need to learn to survive here.”

“…you think I want to stay here and watch you have these poor girls bowing to you! Do I have to explain the concept of equality or equity to you? We are made from the same original clay, or whatever! From the beginning of things?”

Yienguoi-Jin lazily waved his hand in the air, “We are above their station. There is no need for honorifics. You’ll never fit into society if you don’t learn to understand this, and you’ll need to improve your Brenhi. You sound like a foreigner,” he said.

Emily looked over at the maids, they were all young girls in their early to mid-teens, and all she saw was fear in their demeanor.

“You can’t convince me these girls are happy with their station in life as slaves serving you. And I am a foreigner, thank you.”

“I assure you, princess, all servants in the Sowao house are from proud households and generously compensated for their service,” said Lord Phule.

“It’s the law of nature. The High Houses have preeminence over the Diminutive clans in all things,” added Yienguoi-Jin.

“And what station does someone like you hold? And how long are you planning to keep that stupid mask on anyway?”

“You injure me, princess.”

“Princess? How did it even come about that I’m a princess with a crap gangster like you as a father? That’s right, I remember you and your lair full of masked freaks counting out your loot.”

“Hah, the princess remembers your former occupation, Lord Minister,” said Phule, forced cheerily.

Yienguoi-Jin laughed, “Yes indeed. I was highly respected in my days in the Dhukai. At least one of my girls inherited my skills.”

"You'll have to remember, princess. Your father is no longer Dead-Eye Yienguoi-Jin of the Taisehsai Dhukai, but Minister Djowobb of the Imperial House," said Phule.

"I'll explain my meaning in simpler terms. This man before you now is Yienguoi-Jin of the Taisehsai. His name is that of legend. For him to be Minister Djowobb of the Imperial House is a tremendous honor, thus Yienguoi-Jin can no longer exist," he motioned for a maid to refill his cup.

"Minister Djowobb is highly respected even among the families of Nobles and The Court."

"Don't worry. I don't plan on sticking around long enough to blow his cover," Emily added, with a little uncertainty, touching the tips of her fingers together.

"Right!" said Yienguoi-Jin, more to himself, "The lager!…ah, thank you."

A maid brought over a large tray. On it was a stone decanter of a very dark, rich frothy liquid, and three stone cups which the maid was careful to delicately pour into one by one. She handed each a foam-crested draft, bowed, and backed away.

Emily took a sip from her cup and smiled with pleasure as the smooth, grounded woody flavor warmed her.

Suddenly, she noticed the light breeze that had been coming from the open terrace; its scented air was filled with the lush green fragrances of the outside garden.

"I thanked our servant, lord lady. Are you pleased, now?"

"Hardly," Emily sipped her beer, and then, "What were the reasons for your sending me and my grandmother away? And where is my mother?"

"Your grandmother?" asked Lord Phule, perplexed.

"Her grandmothers are dead to this world, though one lives in exile," said Yienguoi-Jin, and gulped down his beer followed by a loud belch. Emily felt her insides tighten in disgust. She couldn't believe this was the man she had dreamt of meeting her entire life.

"Dolores Heart is a lot of things, but dead isn't one of them."

"Dolores Heart?" Phule asked again.

"My grandmother," Emily's voice cracked. "She is the only mother I've ever known. Which is why I want answers. I don't know if she was keeping me in the dark or not. Now that I'm here, I don't know if I could blame her. But I want to know who my mother is! Where is she? Why did you send us away?"

"I did not send you anywhere," said Yienguoi-Jin, removing his mask to reveal his hidden agony. "The witch, Maishae, took you away all those years ago. I searched everywhere for you."

"Took me?" Emily saw the pain in his eye, and her mood softened somewhat. "Are you saying I was kidnapped?"

"He's right. The witch made a previous attempt but was thwarted. Even she herself, with all her guile, could not infiltrate Smitemae," added Phule. "She got a hold of you during a rare excursion to the Summer's End Festival."

"But what did she want me for? I was just some kid!"

"That, I do not have an answer for, my lady," said Phule.

"And what about my mother? She must have been sick with worry."

"I loved your mother…very much," said Yienguoi-Jin softly.

Lord Phule made a circular gesture in the air, and the maids bowed and left. When they were alone, Yienguoi-Jin continued.

"Ameiki was the love of my life, your mother. But I was young and very foolish then. Unlike most men, I was born to a high house. Wealthy, arrogant, and adventure-seeking… but."

He closed his eye and rolled his chin towards the ceiling before focusing back on his beer.

"She was a damn good woman. Strong, warm, fair, and faithful. She didn't deserve her fate."

"She was," Emily replied, her voice soft. "What are you saying to me? She's dead?"

"Your mother was Princess Aiyo Oeki Ameiki," said Lord Phule with a sorrowful tone.

"And our Minister Djowobb, your father, is the Seizhone crown prince, Zhon Yeingui Yeit."

"You? Wait, you're a prince too?"

"Was a prince," said Yienguoi-Jin.

Emily's eyes were notably heavy, and her vision blurry; she wanted them to stop talking.

"Ameki should still be alive. Ameki," here Yienguoi-Jin's voice exemplified his pain. "It is my fault she is gone." Emily felt the room spin. Her head felt like there were a thousand gears and machines overloading, making her feel dizzy. So I have the life I had before, so what is the life I have now? She thought.

"My mother was a princess of the Aiyo dynasty? And you are a prince!" She asked again.

"There has been great unrest in Nyongoyuchi since Princess Ameki's death. All eyes have been on House Aiyo. Their power almost rivals that of the Imperial Court," said Phule.

"There is no need for anyone outside these walls to know you are here until we present you at court. And it is in our interests to keep this matter quiet."

The pain in Emily's head was becoming too much for her. She put her hands on her forehead and began massaging, trying to push the pain back down to the pit of her stomach.

"The princess doesn't look too well," said Lord Phule. "Maybe she should rest before night's end."

"It's the beer. She will be fine," replied Yienguoi-Jin. "But maybe we should leave it."

"No!" said Emily, "I want to know everything!"

"That may hurt too much," said Lord Phule. "I am sorry, my lady."

As the two men retreated to the viewing terrace, Emily felt her headache like never before. The room was now slowly spinning. She looked at the large decanter, the smooth frothy brew flowed like water as she refilled her cup and said loud enough to be heard,

"As your princess, I command you to enlighten me on the subject of my troubled lineage, gentlemen. Please take your seats!"

The two men returned their attention to Emily, who chugged the beer and refilled her cup again.

"You don't look like you care for beer," said Yienguoi-Jin. "Careful, or you'll be sick." He sat down, took another gulp of his beer, and wiped his mouth with his sleeve.

"Tell me. What happened to my mother?"

"I loved her. That is what happened and that should be enough."

"What does that even mean?"

"It seems we have always been on the brink of war with Seizhone. Ever since Imperial General Aiyo Aitolori's defeat at Uenzhi," said Phule, rejoining them.

"The Aiyo have wanted the destruction of our neighbor to the east for generations. However, the Imperial House Anele, or rather the emperor, is pacifist and doesn't really care who the Aiyo want to fight. All that matters is that both nations are fueled by their paranoia of one another."

"Whatever the reason, both our countries have never been close. Weak diplomatic relations, no real trade to speak of. No political marriages either," said Yienguoi-Jin, "That was until the emperor suddenly proposed one."

"Such as a marriage between a Seizhone prince, and Ameki, a princess of our highest house," said Lord Phule.

Emily took another gulp. She was sinking more into a fog and found it hard to keep up with all they were saying.

"My father hated Behra and saw the proposal as an underhanded demand for a hostage. Yet he also saw it as a perfect opportunity to banish me from his court," continued Yienguoi-Jin.

"Though I was born crown prince, my father was always adverse to me because he hated my mother's family. He denied me any role in the kingdom's affairs in favor of my younger brothers, products of his second marriage after my mother's exile. He viewed me as irresponsible and foolish. Perhaps true. I got into mischief. I drank and fought a lot. He even accused me of conspiring to overthrow him once. So, he acquiesced to the emperor's demands."

"On the other hand, the Aiyo were vehemently against the proposed marriage. But the emperor vetoed their appeal to the Imperial Court," said Phule. "Ameiki didn't have a choice. The marriage was forced upon her by the Imperial House."

"But you said you loved her?" said Emily.

"It was love at first sight when I met your mother. It was during the signing of our engagement scrolls at the Uenzhi Border that we officially met. I never believed such a thing could exist. But it did for us."

"A date was set for the wedding, but it was months away. It pained my heart to be away from Ameikei, and so I often stole across the border and rode into Kue. We would meet secretly and woo one another with poems and songs," he dabbed at his eye with his sleeve,

"I didn't have to learn to love her. It was instant. She taught me a lot. She taught me to see the truth and the beauty of our similar cultures. She taught me to elevate myself to be a better man.

But in the end, tragedy found us. Anele Riju took her life, and I became the god of death."

A tear streamed down Emily's cheek. She wiped it off with her sleeve.

"I betrayed our love and became Yienguoi-Jin." his voice cracked, and he became inconsolable as the tears flowed from his one good eye.

Emily sat down her cup with loose hands, and the remaining beer spilled out onto the smooth jade tabletop. She was very dizzy and felt that she was slipping. She wanted to get out of there, to go somewhere, anywhere, where she could clear her head to think about things.

Her eyes were now full of sudden tears. She was somehow overcome with despair, like everything in her mind was pouring out with the liquid in her cup. She could feel herself blacking out.

"Please compose yourself, Minister Djowobb," said Phule.

"I'm so sorry, my lady. Maybe you both need rest… it is very late. I am sure this day has been exhausting for you. Let me take care of everything. I need you to rest." He clapped his hands, and two maids appeared from the hallway.

"Show the princess to her room, please."

When they got there, the maids undressed Emily and wrapped her in a feather-light robe. She was exhausted, and the tiny wounds on her limbs hurt like an inferno. "Please," She called out, "Please let me sleep."

"Sleep sounds like a very good idea," said one of the maids as she helped Emily lower herself down onto a large, pillowy futon.

Emily was used to drinking the occasional beer or two at a house party or barbecue, but she was severely underprepared for the impact of the woody lager.

She didn't know what to do with the pain in her head. She wanted to sleep, but she also wanted a long hot bath, her grandmother's pepper soup, and her own twin-sized bed.

She stared at a slice of the moon through a half-open shoji as the maid extinguished the lantern. The cry of a nightingale was the last thing she heard before it all went black.

Yienguoi-Jin

The royal wedding between Seizhone Prince, Zhon Yeingui Yeit, and Aiyo Princess, Oekei Ameiki, was the event of the season. Attendees came from as far south as Dreesh and the northern countries of Tahn and Rhule. However, Seizhone King, Zhon Zoheit Yeitein, only allowed a small delegation of lower nobles to accompany the prince to his nuptials.

"Who could be more suitable for you than she?" The prince's mother, Lady Showa, had beamed with pride when he told her of his engagement. "I admit I am a tad saddened that I haven't had the opportunity to meet her myself. But perhaps His Grace will eventually grant me permission to attend," she said.

"I just don't understand why father won't allow you to relocate with me to Behrani. You two have long since divorced. Why continue to keep you as hostage? Oh, don't frown, Mum, upon your advice, I have not uttered a word of my grievances to him."

"Yet you air them to all else with an ear to listen. Cheyenne. Nami?"

"Yes, but only those two."

"Is she beautiful?" she asked.

Here, Yeingui smiled and told her, "Her smile is like the morning sun after a long, cold night. Her skin is golden and flawless, and her eyes are like jade. Her hair is thick and black, and her lips, the color of ripe plums and full.

She makes me feel like my blood is on fire when she holds my gaze. She is the most beautiful woman in the world, Mother."

"The Fire Nation has gifted you with a jewel of a wife-to-be, Your Highness. You are a lucky man."

Yeingui smiled, thinking about Lady Showa, and whispered, "With all my heart, I truly believe she is the most beautiful woman in the world."

He yawned as his gilded, horse-drawn carriage tore down a half-paved dirt road that stretched through the great Uenzhi Border crossing, a wide buffer zone of deciduous broad-leaved trees separating Seizhone from Behrani.

Of course, the royal carriage was courtesy of the Aiyo's more than ample dowry. The others in his procession, nobles and members of the royal wedding party, were just as excited as he was to visit the capital city, Nyongoyuchi. They were laughing and singing as they traveled—a wondrous sight for the country peasants as they passed through their small towns.

Yein was weary of the long journey; he was impatient to meet the girl whose smile he had been speaking of so fondly to his mother. When his procession finally made it to the halfway point, they stayed at an Aiyo guesthouse in the town of Pueth.

The prince was escorted to a lavish suite, which was to be his for the duration of his stay. The Aiyo had outdone themselves.

The young prince was more than pleased with his suite and his attendants. Fabrics from Seizhone's fabled silk islands were draped over simple elegant furniture. There was an origami chandelier, a marble bathtub that could fit many, and a bed fit for an emperor.

The next day, he dressed as a peasant and stole away from his group to explore the local scenery alone. He hummed as he walked down Pueth's main street. *"The Fire Nation's people are happy; I would like to know how their spirits burn so bright."* He smiled.

After a few minutes of walking, he found himself in front of an inn. He stood and watched, envying the simplicity of the peasants' lives. They all seemed content with their lot in life, and in good weather, everybody seemed to be out in the streets.

He saw children running about under the watchful eye of their parents. Maidens going to and fro carrying market goods. He noticed a very old woman in a wooden sedan arguing with a bald man. "I said take me out of town! You turned your horse the wrong direction! Why did you turn your horse around?"

It appeared that she was heading for the city gates just as he was. He smiled and watched their squabble from afar.

Yien walked for miles, without a care, without a worry. He finally made it to the city's harbor. He looked at the calm, beautiful blue water and smiled.

"It seems that even the water wishes this to be a joyous occasion," he said.

Three Aiyo soldiers who had been following him walked up to the young prince. They told him that he should return to the village, as it wasn't safe for him to be there alone. Yien smiled and looked out into the sea and told them, "The ship you see docked over there is from the southern lands of Azeroth, famous for their herbs and spices."

"My lord?" asked one of the soldiers.

"It is a rare opportunity when I am able to enjoy my own company, sirs. I may be a royal, but today I want to feel like a normal man," Yien told them.

Thinking that the prince was mad, the soldiers left, but nervously. He looked back out at the sea, smiling, and then turned to walk out of the harbor. He saw the Aiyo men hesitate and then linger behind, watching him, and he ran as fast as his legs could carry him.

When he was well out of sight, he heard a bird call behind him and followed with his eyes as it soared towards a forest in the distance. Yein decided he would hike there and have a late lunch. An hour later, he was sitting under a tree in the shade, eating the fine food that was provided to him by his servants.

Soon the shadows of the trees were the only thing that he could see. The sun was slowly setting, and the forest was getting darker.

The air rapidly grew cooler due to the forest's proximity to the water, so he decided to make a small fire to keep warm and keep the wild animals away.

He had never been so comfortable as he was now. Growing sleepy, he stared into the fire, dozing. Suddenly, he heard the sound of hooves and a wagon or carriage. It grew louder and closer, and without warning, something struck the fire with a blinding flash of light.

Yein jumped up and away, as burning pieces of the firewood fell from the air back down to the ground, sizzling as they hit the grass. Someone had initiated an attack and disappeared into the leafy canopy above. Yiengui looked up at the spot where he had seen the figure and cursed.

But the attack wasn't over. He heard the noise of the vehicle. It sounded like it was on top of him now. He grabbed a piece of flaming wood and ran in the direction of the noise, preferring to be proactive rather than reactive.

Finally, he reached a clearing and could see a flatbed cart clearly in the moonlight rumbling towards him. There were several masked men in its cab.

"Dhukai!" Yein's jaw tightened as one of the masked men crouched with a very large bow and let fly an arrow in his direction. Yein swatted the projectile aside with the burning stick as the cart stopped only a few yards away from him.

He watched as the Dhukai leapt off their cart and ran towards him. He turned and ran into the woods in the opposite direction, betting it would be easier to battle them amongst the trees rather than in the clearing.

As he ran, he heard their angry shouts and the sound of their footfalls. Hoping that he would have some luck, he outran another volley of arrows from the archer, if only by seconds.

He took a quick peruse of the surrounding terrain, judged the lay of the land, and ran towards the rushing sound of a stream with the hope of finding somewhere to hide.

His legs felt like they were burning, on fire, a combination of the day's walk and the sudden activity. When he finally reached the stream, he hid among the reeds to catch his breath.

Yien could hear the attackers on the stream bank, cursing and calling out to each other as they searched for their prey. Then, the sound of pursuit. The prince knew that if he didn't move quickly, he might be caught. The woods were extensive, and he assumed he was in their territory, leaving him without much of a chance of escape.

"Out of the frying pan, into the fire! Not on my watch," Yien said to himself as he took off into the woods, trying to find a better place to hide. But he was ambushed by a Dhukai wearing a hairy demon's mask and a rough leather jumper.

The man emerged from behind a tree and delivered a solid kick to the prince's chest.

"Coward! You're the one who attacked me first!" he said, landing on his back. He quickly popped back up as the man came running at him with a dagger.

Yien immediately brought up his hands to block the strike, but the man put all his weight into the stab, sinking the blade into the prince's shoulder.

The blade was long and thin, probably made for throwing as well as stabbing. Yein pushed him off and quickly put his own dagger up and blocked the second blow. The metals clashed; Yein dropped and struck his rival in the rib, drawing blood. This gave the man pause, and Yien took the opportunity to turn around and run at full speed in the direction from which he had come. A chase ensued.

Both men ran as fast as they could, one trying to escape and the other to keep up. The prince could not outrun his pursuer. The wound to his shoulder was slowing him down, and the man pursuing him seemed to be getting faster.

Their chase took them further into the woods, with the sounds of the water behind them, gradually fading out of earshot. The sound of Yein's and his enemy's footfalls were their only company now.

Yein ran until his lungs were fit to burst and then turned around to face his assassin. His breathing was short and ragged.

The Dhukai pulled up to a stop, sweating beneath his wooden demon's mask with its very stern expression, framed in a mane of wild horsehair.

The neighing of a horse alerted Yein that he had run full circle, as the Dhukai's wagon sat yards behind him.

"A powerful person wants you dead, my lord," said the Dhukai.

"I can imagine many would," answered Yein. "On whose orders?"

"That question can't be answered by me."

"Then why mention it altogether?" The prince charged forward and pounced on the masked man, and once again, their blades clashed. Yien knew that the man wanted to kill him, but he also knew that he had to put up a fight and survive for the sake of Ameiki.

The demon-faced warrior's comrades returned and formed a circle around him and Yein as they fought. With both men's short daggers locked, Yein put his leg against the Dhukai's knees and pushed him hard to the ground.

"You're good," the man said, getting back up on his feet. "But let's not forget you are severely outnumbered."

"He is Daewon Iogwoei! Hakurumi of the Taisehsai Dhukai. By their code, his men cannot interfere since it is he who has challenged you!" came a shout from the dark that reminded one of cobwebs in dark places and thick, viscous phlegm.

"Is it true? You are their leader and they can't interfere?"

"As I am Hakurumi, it is so."

"Then it seems your wealth in numbers is a useless threat, Daewon Iogwoei."

"You are afraid and stalling, my lord," Daewon said. "Don't worry, I will deliver you a swift death before you can run away again."

Yien took that as a compliment, but still, his immediate enemy had full use of both his arms, and his wound was hindering his movement. He realized he needed to change the flow of the battle.

He charged forward and knocked Daewon face forward to the ground, but this time, he grabbed Daewon's sword arm and pulled it behind his back, pressing both his knees down to lock it in place. The Dhukai struggled hard, but his chances of escape were very little.

"Now, how do you feel?" asked Yein. "So you said there was someone who wanted me dead?" he asked.

"Yes. A powerful woman. One far more powerful than I," he answered in an angry tone.

"But she should know that murdering a prince of Zhon would unleash a destructive force on both our countries!"

"That is one way of looking at it," said Daewon and twisted his body in such a way that Yein was forced to release his hold of him and roll in the dirt to avoid another stealthy stab.

"The Taisehsai have another way of looking at it," said Daewon and released another blade from beneath his sleeve. Yein popped back up to his feet and parried both blades flying at him, pushing the Dhukai towards the edge of his men.

"We do not enforce the code; we obey it," said Daewon.

"So who does enforce it?" Yein asked as he stumbled back, his hand stained red; he had been stabbed in his abdomen. Daewon seized the opportunity, triggering an all-out flurry of flips and somersaults where his two daggers seemed like twenty.

Yien kept up a ferocious defense, but still felt the sudden burning of multiple razor-thin cuts all over his body. How could the Dhukai move so fast? The circle of men had tightened, giving him no opening for escape.

Out of desperation, he made a lunge for Daewon, but the Dhukai deftly flipped over him and slammed his foot into the prince's ribs. Yein fell to his knees, gripping his side, coughing up blood.

"I'm getting tired of this," said Daewon. "The Taisehsai are an honorable Dhukai following the ancient traditions. We are not simple blades for hire. We abide by the code, the book of laws that uphold all the rules, by the god of death himself, Yienguoi-Jin."

"I never impugned your honor! I know the Dhukai are bound to see a job through when their services are acquired. But this assault on me will start a war! Will you be content counting your gold on a mountain of corpses?"

"Humph. A golden mountain of corpses. You Seizhonese have such a flair with words. We were surprised by the prince's martial skill, were we not, lads?" Daewon asked his men, who, in a moderate mumble of agreement, agreed.

"Ancestors be with you, my lord," Daewon nodded with respect. Then, in a quick forward leap, he slashed Yein across his face, starting from the corner of his bottom left jaw and continuing at an upward angle - diagonally across his nose, and dispatching his right eye. The blade sank deep the whole way and came out of the slice with half the prince's pupil still attached to its tip.

The pain was searing, unfathomable. The ghastly open wound was hot to the cool air, but Yien did not pull back or scream; instead, he seized the moment. He sprung forward and wrapped his arms tightly around Daewon's knees, and simultaneously kicked off the ground, spinning into a tightly tucked backflip. The air was shattered with a loud, inhumane crunch as he pile-drived Daewon head first into the ground.

Yein landed erect, stirring up a small dust storm at his ankles. Daewon lay beside him, his body twisted in the wrong direction in a crumpled mess atop thick fragments of bloody neck-bone that jutted through punctured skin. His head was almost fully decapitated, and his mask lay next to him, a long crack defining its wooden upper left corner from where it impacted with the ground.

A terrible scream shook the prince. It was an instinctive wail of pure terror, in a tone so petrifying in pitch and voice that it vibrated through his very core. It came from one of the Taisehsai men as he ran towards him. To his left, a slash was made at his neck. The dark cover of night became illuminated by the moonlight's reflection on many blades. The silver of drawn swords came into view as the dark became a blur of swift and reckless slashes.

The onslaught of the Taisehsai men triggered a wave of adrenaline in the prince, and in two moves, he grasped two of the blades, one in his right hand and one in his left. He twirled, slicing through two of them, signaling the rest to immediately back off. The strikes ceased, but the surrounding shouts did not. He backed two other swordsmen against the ring of their comrades and held the blades against them.

"My, my boys," came that same voice from earlier, curdled and dry, "According to Dhukai law, he's your new leader now!"

"Who speaks?" Yein addressed one of the men who remained on the other end of his blade.

"The wizened woman, Maishae. There is a price for her paid by one of the high houses," he answered.

"It's the Aiyo's, you dimwit! There is no need to be discreet about it! He is the head of the Taisehsai now!" A miniature, hunched-over old woman with grizzled skin and a beak-like mouth stuck her arm out of the small bear cage tied down in the far corner of the wagon cart and shook her fist.

"You have no choice but to follow his commands now. Master, free me, and I can heal your wounds," she said.

Yein recognized the voice as that of the old woman he had witnessed arguing with her driver earlier that day and felt a tinge of hope seep in.

"If it's true, then free her," said Yein.

One of the men bowed and quickly shuffled over to the wagon, unlocking the cramped cage. He helped the old woman down onto the grass and escorted her over to the prince.

"The young man is hurt; let me see him," she said and walked over to Yein, whose arms were burning from holding the swords at the men's necks.

"Let me help you with those, my dear. I'm Maishae. You can give me the swords."

Yein all but collapsed as he relaxed his stance and allowed her the blades. In a blur, the twig of a woman turned on the remaining Taisehsai men, brandishing the weapons.

As she sliced and hacked through them, the men broke formation. The sheer speed of the old woman's movements left them bewildered. While appealing to their new master was an option, it would have been pure madness. Despite their resistance, they were no match for her exceptional skill.

Maishae helped the wounded Yein staggered past the fallen over to the wagon; his body was crumpled and buckled. He twisted around, and the fear of life and death had made him invective.

He addressed the woman with a quivering voice, "What is this? To what house do you belong?"

She smiled brightly with a creaky yet deep voice, "Here, let's get you into the back of this cart and lay you down."

Yein took her cold, bony hand inside of his own and held it tight as she helped him. Once he was lying down, she returned to the slain men and retrieved Daewon's head and his demon's mask. She put them in the back of the cart with the prince, took up the horse's reins, and spurred it on down the clearing under the moonlight.

As he awoke from his feverish dream, Yein found himself lying under a heavy woolen blanket in the small hovel of the old woman. It was very dark inside, and no one else seemed to be present. He called out for her but still did not hear anything — it took him some time to figure out that he was alone.

He had expected to find her tending his wounds and renewing his hope for surviving, as she had been doing for weeks. It also seemed strange that she would have left without saying anything due to how eager she was to see him healed; apparently, though, it wasn't only an illusion.

The woman was gone, or she never existed at all! In fact, there were many doubts now filling his head. He couldn't rely on them to determine his thoughts because he lacked the strength and clarity to take them into consideration, what with the numerous doses of beggar's root she administered to him to take away the pain of his wounds.

The days of his nobility seemed but a distant dream, 'Your past skin,' as she had called it. He stood up and grimaced as he felt an intense pain on his side. His face was still swollen and ached terribly. He walked towards the back of the cottage and saw Daewon's mask sitting there on a table, the leather binding the horns, the crack in the wood.

He felt sick at the realization that he had killed a man with such brutality. He had been trained to do so since he was a child, necessary for a prince of Zhon, a nation where 'Might is Right' could have been its slogan.

He assembled a few provisions; a hunk of bread, cheese, and water and prepared to leave. He procured a knife and a longsword, one of those Taisehsai men no doubt, and then sealed the door. Soon after, he was on the run. Whether it was for his life or his sanity, he wasn't sure.

The prince wasn't able to get very far, avoiding the predators in the forest. He tried to bathe his wounds with cold water from a pond, but the water was too cold, and the chill rendered him shaken to the ground. That's when he saw it.

The old woman seemed to step before him out of thin air, behind her a rectangular opening displayed a portion of her cottage's interior, now firelit and warm. She was gauntly muscular, and wore a raggedy white tunic. Yein thought she was at least well into her seventies, perhaps eighties.

Her face was tightly wrinkled, and her poor complexion made her look like a nocturnal creature that slept in a hole in the ground.

"You'll freeze to death out here, handsome," she said, and dragged him back through the portal and laid him shivering back in bed.

"Let me get you something hot to drink." She returned shortly and handed him a steaming cup of some plant decoction.

She stood over his pale body and put two blankets over him to help warm him up.

"You must listen to me," she said. "I tried to warn you, I did, but you can no longer live in that world anymore. You must forget everything you knew." The old woman then leaned down and gave him a kiss on the head.

"I will take care of you from now on, my handsome prince."

Yein was shivering with such intensity that he couldn't move. His legs felt like jelly, and his injuries ached so badly he could hardly stand it. He looked up at the old woman who had saved him and whispered, "Ameiki," before the drugs took control of him.

Yein awakened later that evening and opened his eyes only to find the woman quietly standing over him. She seemed so strange; he couldn't remember if he had just been dreaming.

"Where am I?" he asked.

"You're back in the land of Kue, sweet prince," she said reassuringly, "You ask the same question every time you wake up."

"How long have I been here? Am I your hostage?" replied Yein and fell back onto his pillow.

"Just over two months, and you are certainly not my hostage," she smiled.

The old woman then turned and returned to the fireplace, began rubbing the sleeves of her clothing.

"What's the matter?" said Yein, rising to a sitting position, "You have something else in store for me?"

"I'm afraid not," she returned. "I always wanted to give you something for freeing me from those rogues."

She then, very hesitantly, brought out a wooden, circular box and handed it to him.

"What is this?" he asked, accepting it.

"Open it," she told him, "It's for an ancient Dhukai custom you must fulfill."

He cracked the lid and looked in and saw Daewon's head caked in salt with lavender embedded in the hollows of its eye sockets.

"You may have it if you wish," she said. "It is a gesture of appreciation, a gift that you have earned," she told him as she picked up the demon's mask.

"This is also a very precious gift and a symbol of your martial prowess," she said, "When you are ready. Go and claim your trophy. The Taisehsai Dhukai is yours for the taking!"

She handed him the mask, Yein looked at it. The tone and texture of the wood were extraordinary. It was hardened and cracked, and the face appeared somewhat grotesque.

"But how will I?" he asked. "I haven't the skill nor heart to lead a Dhukai."

"You will have to take up arms again. They have a new hakurumi, a man called Hun Yoosnom. He is the only rival you need to focus on defeating."

"I do not know what you speak of," replied Yein, "I have never heard of a man called Yoosnom."

"Aye, but he has heard the rumors of the hideous man who looks like a sun lizard and claims to have taken Daewon Iogwoei's head. They say he roams the wood boasting that he is the true leader of the Taisehsai Dhukai!"

“What nonsense! Who would start such a rumor?”

“I did, of course! Now for weeks, Yoosnom has had to keep one eye looking over his shoulder with his fellow Dhukai Houses, awaiting the day you challenge him, which you must do. You have no other choice.”

“Why would I lead a Dhukai instead of returning to Ameiki?”

“The Aiyo Princess has since been wed to the emperor’s brother. Everyone thinks Yeingui Yeit is dead. He is! And shall remain so.”

The old woman placed a large oval mirror on the table and turned it on him. The image that caught his one eye was monstrous. The scar across his face was like a lightning bolt embedded into his skin. Several bits of hair had sprung out from the crevice, but the rest of it was indeed quite black.

“If looks could kill, I am sure Yoosnom would be dead already,” she said, and then, “Neither Zhon nor Aiyo will have you now. You can’t ever let the princess see you like this.”

Yein began to sob and turned away. The man in the mirror was not he; it couldn’t be. He was terrifying.

“You have no other recourse, my prince. Time does not wait for the weak,” she said, “You need to become stronger, more cunning so as to best him! The herbs I’ve been giving you hasten your healing threefold. Soon you will be able to train.”

The old woman picked up the spices she had used on him, bark, roots, and dried flowers.

“I don’t want to fight again, but I will do whatever I have to. To reclaim my honor,” he said.

“Then stop trying to run away from me, and let me heal you,” she replied, “Then when you are ready. I will teach you how to fight him.”

"If I take up the mantle of hakurumi, what's in it for you? Particularly when you are the only one championing me. Power? Security?"

"The reason I did all these things, I did it all to help you Yeingui Yeit. It's because with my powers, I have seen your future. The great man you become."

"You are a bloody wizened woman! All of you are nothing but charlatans. You've seen no future."

"I am a healer. I may not be able to make you the beautiful man you once were. But I can make you the greatest Dhukai in all of Behra."

Yein looked down at the mask on top of the round box. The demon image stared back. "Yienguoi-Jin," he whispered. He grabbed the mask and put it on. It seemed to fit right. He gazed at his reflection; it was the face of the god of death, Yienguoi-Jin. He sat up and breathed in deeply.

"I understand," he said. "I will go and bring them Daewon's head as proof I am the one due his crown. If Yoosnom refuses me, I will take his head too, but first, let me rest more."

Yein's head pounded, and he felt dizzy from the drugs, but he didn't care anymore. "How far and where can I find them?" he asked.

"They call their mountain lair 'Smitemae' it's south of here hidden in the Shweivord Cliffs, not more than two days journey."

Yein closed his eyes, exhausted. He felt a haunting sense of despondency overcoming his body. He felt like he couldn't resist her anymore. She was correct in that the Zhon Prince and bridegroom to the House Aiyo were no more. He would have to pave a new path forward. Something deeper was calling for his attention now - rediscovering his true self. And then he blacked out.

***

“I’ve lived many lives, young man, and learned a lot in my travels,” the old woman said, “especially about survival and the art of killing.”

The forest was thickly covered with trees. The ground felt spongy under their feet. A strange animal’s cry pierced the night air.

“But I already know how to fight!” Yein shouted back, finding it hard to keep up with her. “It’s not that I don’t want to learn from you, it’s just that -”

“I’m old!” she said, grabbing his arm, “Then come,” Maishae dragged him through the undergrowth so fast that he had to half jog to keep up with her in his leather slippers and loose pant-robe.

“You will do your training before the sun rises, or I will turn you into a real sun lizard!”

“Do you think that’s possible?” he asked half-jokingly.

“Yes. Yes, it is. You haven’t seen a pinch of my true power!”

Yein knew that she was serious. Half-stumbling in an effort to keep up, he couldn’t help but think that he was being too rash in accepting her offer. After all, he argued to himself, there is no way that she can possess authentic magic.

The mere thought of magic was disparaged in Seizhonese societies, but the Behrani people employed the probabilistic in their daily thinking.

Hence, the abundance of citizens in the country who were willing to financially support an industry of so-called wizened Women who traveled from town to town selling their potions and miracle cures.

A loud resounding thud drew his thoughts back to the present.

The old woman had dropped next to a log and lay on the ground, apparently unconscious.

“W-What happened?” stammered Yein.

In a flash, she reached out and slammed him to the ground and stood over him, panting. She slowly tilted her head, one eye squinted, and looked down at Yein.

"You're a fighter, so I am certain you have heard this somewhere along the road," she said, "Never underestimate your adversary."

The old witch's eyes focused on a shard of moonlight reflected from the roof of a small building and pointed to it.

"We'll have to continue our training outside of the academics tower," she mused, "There is open space there. You must build up your strength."

For the rest of the night, Yein trained with the wizened woman. She taught him refined punching and kicking techniques, as well as many fall and roll exercises. They maintained their nightly routine for several weeks.

She kept up with him; most of the time with ease, and on occasion would fall to the ground and lie with sweat pouring down her face. It was the first time she had seen someone able to match her speed in a long time, and even then she had been forced to stop to catch her breath.

"That should do it for now," she rasped one evening, brushing dirt off her bare arms.

"Are we calling it a night already?" Yein frowned.

"You are ready. We will have to get you a new pair of leather boots if we are going to scale the Shweivord Cliffs," she said.

"I feel as ready as I'll ever be," said Yein.

"Good! We'll leave in two nights."

***

After three days and two nights of walking, they stood beside a wall of towering flat rock that stretched for miles on either side of them and shone a dull metallic silver under the cloud-streaked moonlight.

"Remember to stretch and relax your muscles before we begin to climb," she said, "Or else you will wear them down."

"I don't need you to tell me that," said Yein. "Now then, I think I have come up with an idea."

"Oh?"

"I think that we should test your magic. We may need it, don't you think?" he said.

"I don't think you know how powerful I am, young man," she said, cracking her knuckles, "Anyway, I'm much too old to carry on showing off."

"How about a hidden entrance?"

"Not on the map I have, but I've climbed cliff faces many times before. These are much taller and more difficult, but they aren't impossible to scale," she said.

"And how are you going to hold onto that thing?" he pointed at the lacquered box containing Daewon's severed head.

"I have it strapped back there tight enough. Don't you worry about it," Maishae said, patting the box tied to her hunched back.

"I believe I have the stamina for this. I'll be able to climb it despite the height," said Yein, "Or you could…"

"Another idea," Maishae said, and then waited expectantly.

"Use your powers to fly us up there," Yein raised an eyebrow.

"That's enough fun. We have a long climb ahead of us."

The climb was strenuous, and they did not reach the top until after the moon had lowered in the sky. Yein and Maishae stood on top of a plateau that was wraithlike in its endlessness and desolate in its isolation.

The southwestern stretch of cliffs formed a natural border for the whole of the Aiyo territories of Ulduar, Nukua, and Kue and held a great deal of land between them. Such industries as mining, farming, and electrical turbines powered by the air made them the wealthiest family in all of Behrani.

Water and fire elements excited by deep volcanic activity made the surrounding land humid, producing vast deposits of thick, tar-like energy in the form of many narrow, bubbling streams.

Walking along the top of the plateau was treacherous due to the steep drop and sharp falling rocks, but the sky was clearer now, and the remaining moonlight showed their way.

The huge rocks of Shweivord made a natural maze for them to navigate, fraught with peril. The seething heat waves from below made it difficult to spot their hidden lair among them. However, as they approached nearer, Yein noticed a light shining up through a fissure in one of the lower valleys.

"Let us investigate," he eagerly turned to Maishae. "It may be wet; be careful on the way down."

A terrible howling echoed on their side of the cliff, masking the clang of metal and grating on rock.

"Do you hear that?" he asked.

"The Taisehsai are famous for their Ghost-steel. They're the only ones who know how to mine and forge it. They even supply weapons for the Imperial Dhukai with the Aiyo as mediators," she said.

The two carefully navigated down the slippery, steep embankment. The narrow path seemed solid at first but quickly grew slick with smooth stone and unevenness. Maishae fell.

Yein grabbed her by the back, pulling her up and righting her. Maishae groaned, her forearm throbbing.

"Come, there is a narrow ledge here; let us continue," she said.

They both leaped down into a tangle of bushes, hearing the deep clamor of the tinker shop growing louder. Crouching, they pushed the brush aside and saw sparks hit the ground and the legs of men silhouetted against the light of the open sky.

"Blacksmiths' apprentices. I count six of them. We must use stealth to bypass them and gain entry…" Maishae said.

"They are sloppy. Where are their defenses?" asked Yein. "We must make an example out of these ones to motivate the rest."

"What do you mean?"

"We simply announce ourselves with our blades."

"I am willing to risk it," Maishae said.

"Then, let us hurry," Yein said.

Yein and Maishae rushed at the men, surprising them. In the momentary confusion, Yein unsheathed his sword and used a single, well-placed strike to fell one of the Taisehsai. He hit the ground with a clatter of metal and the hiss of a slowly cooling blade.

The remaining men turned to attack with orange-hot unfinished blades and striking mallets, but Yein and Maishae were vicious in their offense and made short work of them.

Grabbing the keys from one of the men's belts, Yein ran ahead and unlocked the door that looked as though it was carved into the very stone of the cliff face.

The compartment inside was torch-lit from large overhead sconces and, though natural, appeared man-made. Inside were hundreds of swords, spears, shields, and the like in stacks of neat rows.

There was a large set of open stairs where there stood a surprised-looking man holding a lit lantern. There were two smaller doors behind him, and another man standing with a spear.

Yein and Maishae stared back and forth between the two men, who simultaneously shouted, "Who goes there?"

The man in the front, with the lantern, bowed his head. His black half mask was striped with red on its profile.

The man beside him sighed and lowered his spear, revealing a pocked face and several stripes down the side of his mask.

"My apologies for the mess we left out there," black-clad and cloaked, Yein stepped forward wearing the cracked Yienguoi-Jin mask, wet with blood, as was the sword he held at the ready.

The pock-faced man peered at him curiously, "Iogwoei?" Then he turned to the man in the red mask. "He's with the witch as well. Tian, go alert the others; we have intruders."

"No, don't go, please," Yein said. "I don't want to hurt you. I am, however, here to take my place as your master and claim Smitemae as my domain."

The pocked-faced man laughed, "I'm afraid we already have a master. Now tell us where you got the mask, and we might spare you your limbs."

"To put it simply, gents. I request an audience with Hun Yoosnom. Be nice and take me to him, or I could hack my way through your ranks until I get to him," Yein said.

The man in the red mask stood quiet, seemingly thinking. Then he said, "Very well. I will take you. He will be curious about the mask, after all. More than likely, he will kill you for it. But if you survive… we both want a raise."

"That sounds appropriate," Yein said.

"Tian? What are you doing?" asked the pock-faced man.

"You yourself said it best, Belfast. Hun is a terrible master and didn't even challenge Iogwoie for the position."

"You don't have to say it in front of strangers," said Belfast. "I'll take them instead," he added.

The man in the red mask, Tian, rolled his eyes, "Are you sure?" Belfast wasn't, "I'll come along anyway," eyeing Maishae nervously.

Yein followed them, with Maishae tittering behind him carrying the lacquered box. Passing several barred doors and avoiding two large wooden constructs operated by ropes, they came to stairs leading down to a wide hallway with numerous rooms and open spaces.

The pock-faced man led them down the hallway, stepping into the rooms, "Most of this structure is for mining. We are responsible for keeping the armory in good condition to store the tools and weapons we make for sale."

"Why are you two men so apt to help me in my conquest of your Dhukai?"

"Because the Yienguoi-Jin mask you wear is authentic. I should know. I polished it for the master on many occasions," said Tian.

"You two were close?"

"We were on his inner council, but when Hun took over, we were demoted down here to oversee the smithies."

They wandered into a large room, the opening into which barely let enough light in to illuminate the space. Inside there was a large, thick door, which was sealed with a lever.

"This is it. I, by my own authority, cannot let you open this door."

"I figured as much," Yein said. "However, don't misread my intentions or stand in my way. I would hate to have to kill you."

“Right then. I’ll go fetch Hun,” Tian said. He opened the door, walked down a few steps, and down a long hallway. The echo of the opening of another doorway was heard; after a minute or so, Yein could hear a rumbling conversation—perhaps, he thought, arguing.

A voice, loud and angry, came through the barred doorway. “You brought him here! I will handle you later.”

“He is coming. Let me speak with him before more blood is shed,” said Belfast.

Hun appeared at the end of the hallway and hurried up the small flight of steps. He took a step out of the doorway with several men behind him, one holding a blade at Tian’s throat. Hun was an older gentleman, weathered and handsome. He wore his hair longer than a man half his age should, neatly combed and tied, and he looked to have some muscle.

He carried a stout metal spear and bowed. “Yes, what is it?” His voice was calm.

“I’ve brought home the man who once led your fabled house,” Yein said.

“You are not Iogwoei. What is your name?”

“Dead-Eye Yienguoi-Jin.”

“Yienguoi-Jin?”

Yienguoi-Jin turned to Maishae, “Show him.”

Maishae stepped forward and opened the box containing the head of Daewon Iogwoie. In the torchlight, Hun’s eyes went wide, both fixed, unblinking. They grew dark, the pupils dilating, and then he reached down and closed it. Concerned murmurs could be heard from his men throughout the chamber.

“That isn’t Iogwoei,” he said.

“But isn’t it?” Yienguoi-Jin asked, tilting his head. “We both know that it is Iogwoei’s head. You accuse me of being a liar because you know the end of your reign over the Taisehsai is near.

Honor yourself and your code. You cannot avoid this fight between us."

"So, you are the eyeless one I have heard about. You could not have defeated Iogwoei. I would know; I trained him."

"I am his heir through defeat," said Yienguoi-Jin, "And your master."

They stood there, staring at each other. Neither spoke. Then Hun took a step forward, his eyes rapidly dilating.

The men behind him kept their hands on their swords. "Tian who is the masked one?" asked one.

"A fascinating fool," he answered.

"I'll give you one chance," Yein said. "Accept me as your master. Or I will kill you where you stand. Now choose."

"Very well, then. We fight. I will take that mask and your head. But if by some chance I lose, I will give you my men. And I will order them not to harm you."

"Your word?" Yein smiled. "Understood. Let us fight."

The men leapt at each other in an instant, drawing their blades and thrusting them towards the other. Yienguoi-Jin backed Hun down the hallway, where they burst into a room, pushing aside tables and chairs.

He threw an overhand slash that Hun parried and countered. Hun's spear punctured the cloth of Yein's suit and scraped the side of his chest. Yienguoi-Jin yanked and drew forth a curved dagger, threw his arms back, and followed through with a slice. Hun's spear point scratched down his arm and nicked his hand. Yein cursed and followed through with another jab.

Both men continued their exchange of blows inside the crowded room. Yienguoi-Jin cut down with his sword in one hand, his dagger in the other. Hun blocked and thrust with his spear, a difficult practice in the cramped space.

His foot landed on a small wooden rod that tripped him up, and he fell backward with Yienguoi-Jin not wasting his moment to move. He threw his fist at the falling man's face. Hun blocked high and spun away. Yienguoi-Jin missed a follow-up as he turned and sliced at Hun's face. But he sidestepped the man's next lunge of the spear and came in low, throwing his hand at his stomach, finally landing a blow and stabbing Hun in the gut several times in quick succession.

The blows slowed Hun but didn't stop him. Yienguoi-Jin saw an opening and followed through with the next sequence of jabs. He saw Hun starting to waver.

"Keep your guard up. Don't get lured into a trap. Remember, you are fighting the God of Death," Yienguoi-Jin said over the loud, stoic shouting of the Taisehsai men. The rapid dance of jabs and blocks repeated again and again. Yienguoi-Jin backed out of the room to avoid getting struck.

Hun followed him in pursuit, Yienguoi-Jin backed away, blocking Hun's thrust from the spear. Then he dropped his dagger and pulled the spear from Hun's hands and swung it at his head.

Hun cursed as the tip of the spear pierced his shoulder. He dropped to his knee and raised a thin dagger. Yienguoi-Jin eyed him for a moment and then swung the spear again, knocking the blade from the man's hand.

He stared Hun in the eyes and said, "An honorable end," and then stuck the metal staff through the man's head, the sharp end embedding itself in the floor.

Through the opening of the doorway, there were glints of sword and clinking metal as the men fought to be the first to get through. Tian and Maishae's eyes went wide; they knew they had little time to react to their intrusion.

Like a mantis, she leapt onto the man's shoulders and called out in a booming vulture's cry,

"It is done! You heard your master's promise! On your honor as Dhukai, you must heed it!" The men came to an abrupt halt and looked at each other, unsure of what to do.

"Master Hun was strong and honorable," said Tian. "He gave his word."

"Fetch the Master's body from the floor," Belfast said, "clean up the mess here." The men did as they were told.

"Also," Yienguoi-Jin said, "there are bodies outside the armory entrance. Collect them and prepare a funeral pyre. We will announce my ascension and honor the dead all at once."

"Yes, my lord," the men bowed and backed away.

"You two come with me." Yienguoi-Jin said. Belfast and Tian fell in line behind him as he walked. "I will keep you as my advisors, assure me of your loyalty, and I can assure you of mine."

***

Just over an hour later, the three, followed by Maishae, made their way down the steps of the smithy. Yienguoi-Jin looked out at the work yard and saw the entire clan at attention. He removed his mask and handed it to Belfast.

"Are you sure, my lord?" He asked.

"Yes. I've released myself from the ties of my birth and taken a new oath; no need to hide my face from my clan."

"This is your House now." Belfast bowed. The entire crowd that gathered talked amongst themselves when they heard the news, but their chatter ceased at the sight of Yienguoi-Jin's mangled, lizard-like face.

"The Taisehsai are weak! You have failed in upholding the honor and nature of being a Dhukai. Your training is weak. I have proven it this very night. You were not prepared. I am your new lord," his voice boomed through the yard. "A new era of our Dhukai has begun. You must be ready for what lies out there when the time comes." He gestured to the side of the yard.

A pyre had been built, with the bodies of the blacksmiths and Hun's beheaded corpse laid atop the wood.

“Then let us begin this new day,” Yienguoi-Jin said as he took the mask from Belfast, placed it back over his face, and flung a torch across the yard, setting the pyre ablaze. “My clan!” He said, finishing. “I am your new master. I am Dead-Eye Yienguoi-Jin, and I will lead the Taisehsai to glory.” He added a roaring cry, a call that resonated through the crowd.

The men repeated his cry in chorus as they touched the ends of their iron staffs to the ground in unison. Their silhouettes looked eerily lit in the moonlight as the fire developed.

The flames of the pyre burned high and bright, casting a ghostly light over the scene. Yienguoi-Jin smiled his grotesque smile beneath his wooden mask and nodded to Maishae. The wizened woman nodded back; her beak-like mouth twisted into a toothy grin. “It is done,” she said.

“Yes. It is done,” he agreed.

Domotedai

Emily awoke the next day just short of noon, her head still throbbing from the previous night's drinking. She looked around her unfamiliar surroundings and yawned. Sunlight streamed in through a half-open shoji covering a large window terrace. The air was already warm, muggy even.

"Where am I?" she asked herself out loud, trying to piece together the events that had led her there.

The room was meticulously neat, ornately designed, and furnished with an elegance and purpose that was obvious to anyone who entered. There was a wardrobe of carved cedar, as was her bed. Next, her eyes found a looking glass, which sat atop a refined vanity.

After regaining some of her senses, she stood up, struggling at first, her head foggy and mouth bitter with traces of beer. She eventually walked over to the terrace for some air.

She could feel the sun warming her bare neck and face, and the breeze—a pleasant surprise—slowly lifted the hair from her shoulders. Though humid, the sun gave off a gentle warmth as compared to the previous day's unforgiving heat.

It shone brightly over the treetops, the sky full of fluffy white clouds. She gazed at the garden below and couldn't believe how vibrant the trees were. All the foliage was a rich, green-blue color, even the grass had hints of blue.

The garden was beautiful and had a strange, other-worldly presence to it. She heard voices and giggling coming from below where maidens walked on narrow, pebbled paths between trees and bushes, pruning and shearing.

Emily lifted her gaze towards the neighboring homes built among the trees that sprawled beyond the garden's stone wall. Beyond the expanse of rooftops, she could see a denser population of buildings, larger, more colorful, and finely detailed. She thought, "So this is Nyongoyuchi."

After a moment, she walked back inside the room and made her way over to the vanity. She looked at herself in the mirror; her eyes had lost some of their luster, but their full radiance was undiminished.

She brushed her auburn hair aside and rested her head on her hand, sighing. *What's that?* She noticed that her Earth clothing had been folded and arranged on a stand in the corner and smiled wryly - a lovely surprise, she thought.

She tousled her hair, stretched, and turned away from the vanity when a soft rap on the door caught her ear. She whirled around,

"Come in," she breathed. Her voice rose softly.

A young maiden entered, carrying a cup of hot tea on a silver tray. She nodded her head politely, a soft smile on her lips.

"Princess, you are awake." She walked over to a table and set the tray down, "Tea, my lady?"

Emily smiled, "Thank you. I'm not used to being waited on," She took the cup, tasting the warm brew. "But I am not a princess, please just call me Emily. I dislike such titles."

The maid nodded her head again, "As you wish, Emily."

Emily smiled and nodded, "Thank you…" She sipped again at the steaming tea, the fragrances wafting up around her made her smile.

"This is nice. Is it peroppy tea?"

"Yes, it is, my lad—Emily?"

"It's been since forever. I can already feel it easing my brain fog."

"Minister Dwjoeb thought you would find it soothing."

"I see," Emily set the cup down on the vanity and walked over to her clothes. Atop them was her phone, wallet, and the mirror she had taken from Seitogi. She set these items aside and inspected her chinos.

She was stunned at how Dou-Dodachi's maids were able to clean the bloodstains out of the freshly washed pants and hoodie. "What exquisite work," she said, and then - "jeez. Exquisite? Who am I?" she laughed.

"Do you want help dressing, prin—forgive me, Emily?"

"No, thank you. I can do it by myself, but thanks for the offer. I think I'll get dressed, and then I should go find Minister Dwjoeb. I have a lot of questions."

Emily took her robe off and 'hop jumped' into her pants. She was pleasantly surprised to find that she still smelled like the oil the servants had rubbed underneath her arms.

"I need to purchase some of this and take it back home with me. Wait a minute! My money is no good here…" *but there is that princess thing. I should be able to at least get a freebie. Hah! Some princess swag.*

She put on her shirt and her hoodie. She didn't have any socks, but she found her shoes, the leather stained dark where they were smothered in blood. She pictured Seitogi again, bashing in the Inouei man's skull, and a shudder ran up her back.

"Damned lunatic. Where is he anyway?" she whispered, and then, "My god, I have to pee!" she turned to the maiden, "Where is the bathroom?"

"Bathroom, my lady?"

"I need to pee. You know, I feel like I'm going to burst," she rubbed her belly and made a hissing noise.

The maid smiled and bowed, the look on her face signaled to Emily that she understood, and then walked backward while kneeling until she reached a wall. She then slid open a small opening and retrieved a large porcelain bowl and placed it at Emily's feet.

Emily arched one of her brows at the strange bowl and said, "I thought it was it just the priest's place. Does no one here have indoor plumbing?"

The maiden was already attempting to unfasten Emily's pants, but Emily gently pushed her hands away, saying, "It's okay! I can do it myself!" She then pulled down her pants and relieved herself.

The maid averted her eyes, focusing on a blank spot on the wall. "I need tissue, or whatever you use to, you know," Emily spoke, and the maiden bowed her head, taking folded rice paper from the breast of her robe. She handed Emily a sheet, then held the bowl and turned around to leave the room, presumably to empty it.

"You didn't have to sit there the whole time and wait!" said Emily, looking quite annoyed. "Where are you going? Take me to Lord Phule!"

"Pardon me, Emily. But the Lord is outside at the Imperial Palace now."

"Then I need to see Yien…Minister Djowobb."

"He has accompanied Lord Phule."

Emily rubbed the tiny pimple on her chin, "What about Seitogi?" she wondered aloud, and then, "Take me to the dungeons! I want to speak to the prisoner that was brought in last night."

"Forgive me, Emily. I do not know?"

"Oh give me a break!" Emily tensed and glared down at the girl, "Is there no one here that is allowed to speak the truth?"

The maid bowed her head, saying nothing, and turned to leave the room.

Emily's cheeks flushed with anger, "Wait just a minute!"

"Forgive me, but I do not understand the meaning of your words."

"I mean the 'truth' of things - be truthful with me," she said.

The maid tilted her head, puzzled.

"Where do you detain the prisoners? I want to see the guy that came in with me last night. You know, tall, blue hair, really cute?"

“Seitogi is off-limits to you, you rotten child!”

The churlish voice sent an unexpected thrill up Emily’s spine as she turned and regarded its owner, who stood proudly in the room’s doorway with a crooked smile on her face.

Emily’s eyebrows raised, and her mind spun. She stared at the woman’s linen robe, thinking to herself, “My goodness, she looks exactly the same!” And then she squealed, “Obánā!” With a little hop that turned into a sprint, she ran past the chambermaid right into the arms of the statuesque woman.

“You’re real! My god, you’re not just a dream!” she whimpered.

“Of course, I’m not a dream, silly child. And you are as beautiful as ever. Taller, and with some nice” - she squeezed Emily tightly - “curves,” she looked Emily over.

“My beautiful Pearl Swan. You have grown. Remember when I would sing you to sleep?”

The thought of Nami’s voice sent a warm fluttering feeling through Emily’s mind. She had always loved her singing. She thought of her voice as one of the most beautiful sounds she had ever heard, and even now was realizing she had heard it often in her dreams.

“Just look at you…oh, my beautiful dear,” she took Emily’s face into her withered hands and delivered several kisses on both cheeks.

“You are finally back where you belong.”

“I’m not so sure about that,” Emily brushed away a tear, “It’s all so confusing, but”

“But no, my heart. You are home, and that’s all that matters to me.”

“But see, I don’t feel like that at all! Aside from the casual murder, women are clearly second-class citizens here! I mean, it’s not like we’ve met the measure of full equality back on Earth, but this is insane!”

“You should not concern yourself with such things, my love,” Nami took Emily by the hand and led her over to a basin of water where she helped Emily wash her face and rinse her mouth.

“It’s alright, Nami, I can wash up myself. I always was pretty independent.”

Nami reached out and caressed Emily’s hair, “It’s my duty and my honor to take care of you,” she said softly and gently wiped away a few stray tears from Emily’s face.

Emily smiled, “It’s just been so long since back then. I don’t know if I could ever see this place as home. I miss Earth, I miss my grandma most of all, but I don’t know how to go about finding my way back.”

“Don’t fret about that, dear. I’m sure once Minister Djowobb gets back, he will explain everything.”

Nami led her from the room. Emily instinctually wanted to pull her hand away from the old woman, but the familiar warmth she felt towards her former nurse stayed the action.

“Min…Minister Djowobb?” Emily asked with a hint of suspicion in her voice.

“Always respect your elders. Even when they are wrong,” her grandmother’s words echoed through her mind as she forced a smile and managed,

“I’m not sure he is at all interested in helping me get back to Earth.”

“Earth?”

“Yes! The planet I was sent to…or I don’t even get how this is supposed to work. Like, am I still on Earth but in a different dimension, or am I altogether on another planet? Or is it the more than likely choice, that I never left Earth at all and I’m strapped down to a gurney foaming at the mouth right about now?”

Nami smiled, “I do not know, my love.”

They stood in silence for a moment until Emily said, “Where are we going?”

“To take a meal, and then getting you bathed and into proper dress befitting your station.”

“Oh no, this is fine,” Emily attempted to make light, “My street clothes are super comfortable and…”

“Street clothes?” Nami wrinkled her already wrinkled face in dismay.

“A lady does not dress for the streets, my dear. No, no, not at all. I wanted the rubbish burned to ash, but the Lord of the House insisted they be kept. Nevertheless, you are a princess of House Aiyo, and you will maintain the appropriate appearance.”

Emily snatched her hand away and stopped walking.

“Can’t you see I’m not the same little girl under your charge? I have my own thoughts! My own wants and desires!”

“Duty, princess.” Nami’s voice was dry and serious, “You have a duty to your title and your clan.”

“Well, then maybe I don’t want to be a princess in this world you call home.”

Emily held her head high and defiantly ventured forward. Nami remained quiet and seemed unfazed by her declaration as they walked. She took Emily to the same room the reluctant princess had drank in the night before. They were nearly at the table when Emily became aware of a presence behind her.

She looked back, and a large woman with twinkling eyes and skin the color of polished onyx approached Nami, lowered her head, and spoke too quietly for Emily to hear.

"Are you certain he came here?" Nami looked from the woman to face Emily. "Forgive me, my lady, but an urgent matter calls. I will soon rejoin you, but for now, please eat." And with that, Nami departed the room with the woman in tow.

Emily watched her go and then turned back around to the table. A platter of sliced meats, cheeses, breads, and fruit lay waiting to be eaten. Suddenly ravenous, Emily reached for a plate and began to hastily load it up.

"Forgive me, my lady, but I must serve your plate to you," a servant bowed.

"I'm fine, whatever," Emily said, and resumed filling her plate.

For the moment, she concentrated on the rich flavors of the food and forgot all her problems, but Nami arrived in the room not more than five minutes after she had begun to eat.

"Good, you are eating. I won't be able to join you after all," she said, "When you are done, Ohna here will take you to the baths."

Emily nodded and continued to eat, "Sounds like a plan."

"Very good," Nami, uncertain if the girl was being dismissive, then turned to leave.

"Wait!" Emily called out.

"Yes, dear?" Nami turned around.

"Will I see you again today?"

"Most certainly, my lady." And with that, she left.

Emily rolled her eyes and quickly finished, took a deep sip from a bowl of savory broth at her elbow, and pushed the plate away. For a moment, the servant stood in silence until she cleared her throat,

“You should bathe and dress now, princess,” said Ohna.

“I was thinking of taking a walk around the grounds,” Emily said as she followed Ohna out of the room.

“But I was told you should relax today after your long journey. The bath will be good for you.” Ohna was a round girl with big, bright eyes, and a quiet voice. She seemed very diligent in her duties.

“It would be refreshing to just walk around the gardens,” Emily continued. “I’m sure the guards will do a fabulous job at keeping me from escaping, so you can relax.”

“There are no guards, but I will be happy to accompany you, my lady.”

“No thank you. I don’t need a chaperone.”

“As you wish, I will be waiting nearby if you decide you do want any company,” Ohna bowed, flashed a quick smile, and walked off.

Emily walked around the house and out into the gardens. It was summer, and to her, everything seemed so alien, but also more alive and, at the same time, more colorful. She found a path that wound around the mansion, and she followed it for a time before entering a large clearing and stopped.

On the other side of the clearing in the shade of a large tree, leaned a boy against its trunk. His curly marine blue hair was tied into three, free-standing top knots atop his head. He raised his hand and waved as Emily walked towards him.

Emily fired up a smile and returned the wave, “Hey!” she said.

“Good morning!” the boy smiled. “You look pretty,” he added.

“Thank you?” Emily returned, still smiling, “That’s very kind of you to say, but aren’t we a little forward? I don’t think we’ve met.”

“I’m not just talking about physical beauty,” he smiled, “You radiate a uniquely beautiful aura. It’s pretty and makes me smile.”

“Oh. Are you a mystic?”

“Stable hand. My master allowed me the day, so I’m relaxing before the heat sets in. I’m Gléhson. It’s nice to meet you.”

Despite the fact that his hair was messy and unkempt, he looked a little disheveled, but Emily found him quite handsome. He had a friendly face with amethyst-colored eyes and a wide smile. His straight teeth were like mother-of-pearl, his sorrel skin was smooth and flawless.

Emily detected an earnestness in his gaze that made her blush.

“It’s nice to meet you, Gléhson. I’m Emily. Emily Heart.” She bowed politely. He returned the gesture.

“Would you like to sit and chat?” he asked.

“Well, that depends,” Emily hesitated, “I think the grounds here are lovely. I would love to chat and trot around on a horse. Seeing that you work in the stables, maybe you could hook me up with a ride?”

“I’m sorry?”

“A horse! I would like to ride around the gardens on a horse,”

“Oh! I see. That sounds nice,” agreed Gléhson, “Have you ever ridden a horse?”

“Oh, all the time. I’m a regular National Velvet.”

“Are you being completely honest with me, Emily Heart?”

“The stables, please,” said Emily.

“We don’t have to go so far as there,” Gléhson whistled, and several seconds later, a fine steed promenaded up a slope of grass along a man-made waterway that meandered throughout the property.

“Emily, this is Wind-spear.”

“Wind-spear. He’s a very handsome horse. I can tell he has spirit,” said Emily.

Gléhson helped her mount and remained standing on the grass as he took its reins and guided them around the gardens. They were vast and beautiful. Emily loved every moment of him acting as a tour guide, pointing out and naming all the unfamiliar flowers in bloom. Her only regret was not having Rebecca there too.

“My lady!” Nami’s voice boomed from somewhere behind her. Standing on one of the manor’s many balconies was Nami, Ohna, and the elegant woman with the onyx skin.

“Damn, Madame Nanda is here too,” said Gléhson.

“Who is she? She’s stunning?”

“A very mean and bossy person,” Gléhson said, and in a single leap, hopped onto the horse and landed in the saddle behind Emily.

“I’m afraid I have to go now, Emily, but it was a pleasure meeting you. If you wouldn’t mind dismounting now.”

Emily swiveled her body around his in a quick, smooth motion that even surprised her and positioned herself behind him.

“Sorry, that’s not going to happen. You’re taking me with you. I’m being held hostage here, and you’re going to get me past those gates.” She poked him in the back with the tip of a paring knife she swiped from the breakfast table.

“It looks like I’m the hostage now. I guess I have no choice but to act as the princess commands,” he smiled.

“So, you did know who I was!” she smacked him lightly in the back of his head, “I’m not your goddamned princess either! My name is Heart! Emily Heart, and don’t you forget it! Now go, or I’ll gut you like a fish.”

“You don’t seem the gutting type, my lady.”

“You see that woman back there? Nami may look frail, but she’s stronger than me, you, and the horse combined! And trust me, she is the gutting type!”

“Sounds good enough for me,” Glehson squeezed his thighs and gave a gentle kick, and Wind-spear bolted down the narrow path, kicking up pebbles and dust.

“Hold on tight and don’t drop your knife,” he said as Emily wrapped her arms around his waist.

“Oh my,” Nami said in a hushed voice.

“We have to follow them. Quickly, Ohna. Call the guard!” rushed Madame Nanda.

“I disagree,” said Nami.

“Why?” asked Madame Nanda. She had a very high voice that Nami never did care for and found all the more annoying at the moment.

“To involve the guard would invite scandal! We can’t very well tell them the princess is out on a jaunt with a strange boy now, can we? No, we must collect them ourselves.”

“How would you propose to ride then? We cannot take my carriage. As you say, it would invite scandal.” said Madame Nanda.

“We have a carriage, one used by the kitchen staff to go to market. We can give chase in that. You’ll ride at a distance behind us in your sedan.”

“Very well then. Once again, I beg you to forgive me for this intrusion,” said Madame Nanda, her beautiful face soft and tender, but etched with concern.

“Then let us be quick. They already have a head start. Quickly, Ohna, go fetch the wagon!”

Gléhson spurred Wind-spear on through a maze of hedges and shrubs, scattering birds and tiny animals as they galloped. Emily held on very tightly, afraid of falling.

Nearing the gate, she could hear the hollow clank of Wind-spear's hooves and men shouting in the distance.

Galloping at full speed, Wind-spear darted through two open iron gates built into the stone wall and shot past a pair of guards unsure as to what was happening.

They rode between two thick decorative columns bearing the Sowao family crest—a crescent moon just above three wavy lines—and just beyond that, they continued down a tree-lined, gravelly path. At the end of the path, they sprinted off into the woods, leaving a trail of dust behind them.

Emily watched as the neat row of trees leading from the manor melded into a dense wall of trees on either side of the path. They passed other stately mansions shrouded in the leafy shadows of daylight, and further in the distance, she could see thicker forestry sat atop rolling hills like osteoderms on a stegosaurus's back.

"I think we are far enough from the mansion now. Let's stop for a bit." Gléhson eased Wind-spear to a gentle stop in a small clearing surrounded by tall trees. Next to them was a small, trickling stream of crystal-clear water that fed into a river that was coursing around a bend in the distance.

"You were brilliant back there! I didn't know a stableman could be such a good rider!" Emily dismounted with his assistance and fell into his arms, which he wrapped around her and held her tightly.

"Careful there," he said. "So where am I taking you, my lady?" he asked.

"The palace town isn't far, is it?"

"About twenty miles, if you follow the Abbiole river," he said, smiling at her. He took the reins and tied them to a tree. "He will be alright here."

"The Abbiole, sounds lovely. What's the furthest it goes?" Emily gazed at the trickling water for another moment.

"It leads to the capital. The water is clean," he said. "It flows around the city in a circle, keeping it lush and green. A few miles in, you come to the heart of the empire, Nyongoyuchi Palace. It's surrounded by the river on its own separate lands. I hear they are beautiful, but no one from my station is allowed there."

"It sounds beautiful," replied Emily. "Can you take me? I have to get back home, and maybe the emperor can help me - my grandmother must be worried sick."

"The palace is quite a distance," said Gléhson. "And it's highly doubtful you would be granted an audience with the emperor. He notoriously keeps to his meditation and sees no one."

"Nonsense," said Emily, "I'm a traveler from another planet. He'll want to see me."

"What is that now!" laughed Gléhson, "This is not how I expected this day to turn out."

"You don't have to believe me," Emily sighed.

"I do not mean to doubt your word, Emily. It's just you must understand, travel between worlds is impossible."

"I'm living proof that not only is it possible, it has happened."

"It appears that I have no choice but to believe you." He pointed to the knife loosely held in her hand.

"Oh, I wasn't going to cut you!" she said and put the short blade away into her hoodie's pocket. "See. All gone."

"We will probably not be let anywhere near the palace. But I'm game."

"Then it's agreed," Emily held out her hand and said, "let's shake on it!"

They walked side by side along the bank of the stream. The sun was high over the landscape, and the shadows were becoming less defined.

Emily could see people working in the fields, tending to their animals, hauling things in little carts. The scenery was quite beautiful, and she felt a sort of tranquility she hadn't felt since she arrived.

"Are you going to be in loads of trouble because of me? Even though it's your day off as a servant?"

"I am a stable hand, my lady. I have worked in the heart of the Sowao estate since I was a young boy. The stable master has always looked out for me. I count myself lucky."

"Well…thank you again. For everything," She turned to him, and as she did, his face inched closer. He looked directly in her eyes, lip quivering. Emily noticed him and looked to the ground, stepping back, blushing.

"What is it?" she asked, "Something weird on my face?"

"There is nothing weird about your face, my lady," he stuttered. "But we should make our way before the day gets away from us. I would like to show you the capital."

"All right," she replied, then looked down at the ground feeling nervous again.

After a few moments, he broke the awkward silence. "If I may ask, I admit I've been curious too. How did you really come to travel to Behra?"

"It is simple, really. I was raised on an alien planet, and stepped through a looking glass."

"I…see," answered Gléhson. Emily paused, then a smile crept across her face, and she shrugged.

"You don't believe me!" she said. "All right. Fine! I will show you." She took out the mirror from her pocket.

Gléhson's eyes widened, "You mean to tell me, you traveled here through the mirror?"

"Just like I said."

“But is it possible to leave from this side?”

“I suppose we’ll have to find out. After you,” Emily said, holding the mirror out to him.

Gléhson took hold of the mirror but seemed fearful of entering. “I don’t know if I should,” he mumbled, looking back at the forest.

“It’s safe,” assured Emily. Gléhson stared into the mirror intensely for several seconds before Emily burst out laughing. He blinked in confusion,

“I’m sorry,” she said, “I don’t mean to make fun of you.”

“No, go ahead, my lady,” He said, laughing too. Emily laughed again, then nodded and took a deep breath. She closed her eyes and spoke to the mirror.

“Mirror, Mirror.” Emily couldn’t help but laugh again.

They remounted Wind-spear and rode off, following the stream which was a few feet from the road. The sun was high, and the skies were clear; it was a perfect day. They passed many lovely places and friendly people going about their way.

Children would point at them and beam, while some adults would wave and say hello. Emily waved back and smiled, and said hello too. Gléhson seemed nervous at first but quickly warmed up.

They entered thicker woodland, and the sky became somewhat darker. The sound of the wind and the feather-like leaves on the trees was more prominent here. Emily’s mind was off again. She was thinking about Rebecca and Darren. How would they get home? She stopped her mind from spiraling and gazed at the road for a moment.

“It’s so pretty,” she said. She took a deep breath and smiled warmly.

“Yes,” replied Gléhson. “It’s even more beautiful in the capital, though.”

“Is it?,” she said quietly. She felt sad again and leaned her head against his back, holding him tightly around the waist. He seemed to tense up for a second but soon relaxed. A few minutes passed before he broke the silence,

“It seems we have almost disappeared into the forest,” he said.

It was true. They were at a point where all signs of society seemed left behind. Gléhson slowed the horse down and stopped. Emily sat up, wondering what was wrong, then looked up to see the forest thinning and so did the land bordering the stream as it gushed into the open river.

It was a small plateau, all by itself. There, the flowers were in bloom, and all around the river was an open field. A steady, cool breeze swept over its edge.

“This place is beautiful,” she said.

“It is,” Gléhson looked towards the plateau as if he was staring at something. “But the ground is dangerous; you will have to hold on as we are going to sprint through.”

He lurched Wind-spear into a strong jolt, and immediately cantered off alongside the rapids. Emily grabbed him and held tightly as the horse rapidly picked up speed.

She looked back to see that the land was sloping down and that the woodsy area was now running parallel to them. She looked ahead to see the river rushing around the bend. A cheer escaped her lips, even though no one was around to hear it. An unconscious reaction from seeing such a beautiful sight.

Ahead, Gléhson could see the horizon, and there was no more woodland on either side. He spurred Wind-spear up a steep incline to a large wooden bridge and a cobblestone path a few meters beyond it.

“Hold on!” he shouted as they closed in on the end of the road. Wind-spear snorted, and Emily gasped as he broke into a full run. The wind was harsh now, and Emily squinted, her eyes tearing.

On approach, the horse jumped off the plateau and ran along the road. The two were very close to the edge, and Emily's heart skipped a beat. As they neared the bridge,

"Step on it!" shouted Gléhson.

They drew close to the edge, and in one final, mighty bound, jumped over a crag onto the bridge. Below, the river raged and roiled, the thundering waters sent up a wake of frothy white mist, sparkling in the sunlight.

"WHHHOOOOAAA!" gasped Emily. She had not been expecting the trail to be so bumpy, and her heart was still pounding from the sudden jump over the crag. She sat down on the back of the horse, eyes watering as she stared at the bridge.

Gléhson tightened his grip on the reins and looked straight ahead intently. They took several minutes to cross, as the rivulets of water splashed up beneath them. As they approached the end of the bridge, the water split off, falling over the side right in front of them.

They crossed the bridge and stood atop a slight rise. Gléhson gazed down at the Abbiole flowing into a valley, with a reasonably large city embedded in its center.

"There's the palace town Domotedai," he pointed, "That's Mount Giyun there in the center of it all, on top of that is Nyongoyuchi Palace."

"I'm looking forward to getting down there," said Emily. She looked back at the landscape, watching a fresh reflection of the sun shining on the water. "It's beautiful."

It was a moderately steep climb down into the valley. After navigating it, they followed the river another mile to the city's outer wall. It was a crowded affair. Outside of the wall stood several barkers, shouting. Various soldiers, merchants, and peasants all seemed to be milling around as they entered the town.

"It is a busy place during the daytime," he said. Emily nodded and marveled at the structure's majesty. It spanned for miles and was covered in a pale orange brick. There were gaps between its stones, which were lit by windows on each dimension.

They rode past the guards and dismounted. He took the reins, and they joined the crowd, heading through the city's entrance.

"The palace is the most massive structure in this city; it's a sort of visible sign of the empire. The city is used to put on glorious spectacles to represent the wealth and prestige of the country.

He looked down at Emily and smiled, then pointed as they passed through, "Nyongoyuchi Palace is a thirteen-story structure, which reaches a height of forty-five meters."

They entered the city. Emily paused as she observed the architecture. The plan was laid out as a grid. Homes, stores, and market stalls lined the streets.

Some had their names painted on their roofs in small, white letters. It reminded her of the mural painted in the tower of Odahni Castle. "It's even more beautiful in person," she whispered.

"Whoa, so this is the capital," she said in awe. "It's much larger than I thought it would be."

Gléhson chuckled, "Yes, I suppose it is." He nodded. "It is a bustling thing. The people of the country travel here with great haste, it seems. It is a good thing."

They walked along a cobblestone road over to a watering hole where he tied Wind-Spear's reins to a post and let him drink from a metal trough. Emily leaned against a tree that stood beside the watering post, enjoying the sounds of people going about their business. She was watching something off to the side when suddenly a group of people came tumbling through the street.

She gasped at their crazed dancing accompanied by a playful melody. It was almost a fluid, random moving routine. They twisted and bowed, kicking up dust from the road as they passed on by.

Gléhson laughed as he patted his steed. "They are called the Yamishet. They create daily festivals for donations," he explained.

Emily walked back over to him, and his eyes met hers, he smiled and looked down and back up at her face.

“You have such a wonderful smile,” he said. Emily blushed and turned away.

“Thank you.” She answered. They went over to a nearby food cart, where a lady was serving a line of people. Gléhson joined the line and motioned for Emily to stand beside him.

“We deserve some refreshment too,” he said.

Emily was excited to try some of the dishes. She picked up a drink from the back of the cart and took a sip. It had a slightly tart taste and a very light, sweet aftertaste. The woman working there served a line of about four people and warned Emily to get back in the queue.

Emily went back to Gléhson. When it was their turn, she peered into a bowl of steaming broth with doughy dumplings, delighted by the smell of the creamy, spiced lemongrass. The woman serving food took a few bowls off a nearby shelf, placing them in front of Gléhson.

Emily’s stomach rumbled, and she looked over the steaming broth. The server, a stout woman with a pleasant, wrinkled face and a gentle smile, patted Emily’s hand reassuringly. Her dusty black hair was tied back in a long ponytail. A few strands of silver crept in, matching her eyebrows. She looked back at Emily and smiled warmly.

“Do you see anything else that interests you?” Gléhson asked. Emily nodded. She took the bowls, and the woman served him a plate of dried fish.

As they ate, Gléhson pointed to a tall, stone building and explained the city’s original founder and the Anele Imperial legacy. They passed by many other vendors selling food, clothes, shoes, and household items.

There were a number of buildings where garlands of silver hung commemorating the thirteen noble families that had governed the country since its unification.

"Each Imperial sigil represents one of the families, though different from the families' personal crest. I had to learn them all when I was a child. It was torturous."

"Can you name them all now?" Emily teased.

"Hum," he scratched his head, "The Aiyo's are the half moon. The Anele's, a righteous sun. Other families represent: a cruel night, a perfect day, a violent storm, a forgiving sunrise, a wonderful morning, a furious evening, an inexorable night, a passionate sunset, an eternal dawn, a natural dusk, and a dour midnight."

"Something about all that is eerily familiar."

"The buildings here are the offices for the executives of those noble families," he said. "The families are the country's executive branches and are the overseers of the fourteen baronies. They have served the Nyongoyuchi Anele Imperial family for generations."

Fearing he was boring her, the stable hand switched the topic and asked Emily about herself. It paid off.

The two shared stories of their lives as they walked through the crowded streets, guiding Winds-spear by his reins. They laughed and talked for hours. Emily could not remember a day that had gone so well. It was like a dream.

"My first year in school, I would always be labeled a 'weird girl' for whatever reason. I was slightly different; English was a second language. Teachers would make comments about how my hair was too shiny, or my clothes were weird. One day they even hauled my grandmother into the principal's office for giving me metallic highlights. She had to prove to them it was my natural color.

Whereas everyone here has the same thing with their hair. I noticed it on the maids this morning, and I see it on you too."

She ran her hand through his rich mane of tightly packed marine blue curls, from which three rope-like locks dangled from the top of his head and rested at the nape of his neck.

"It's something I've never really taken into account," he said.

“Hey, you know, I apologize for forcing you to take me with you. I just really wanted to get out of that place.”

“Then are you really in danger?

“That’s the thing. Like yes, but I don’t know who to trust. You know what! I’m fine. It’s probably nothing. But thank you! You’ve been really sweet. It’s been such fun hanging out with you,” she kissed him on both cheeks; “We’ll totally have to do it again, like in some other lifetime.”

“Oh, um, I,” Gléhson stammered.

“You’re blushing,” said Emily, still holding his arm.

“You just kissed…you just kissed me,” he said softly, then he turned away. Emily’s face flushed with joy and warmth.

“But you’ve got to be at least a year or two older than me. What? Am I your first kiss?” Emily drew back in surprise. “And that wasn’t even on the lips. Here’s a proper one.”

She leaned forward and gave him a quick peck on the lips. Once again, he turned away, blushing, and she noticed a few townspeople had stopped their activities to watch.

“You kissed me,” he said with a shaky voice

“It’s a well-known Earth custom, not a wedding proposal, silly.” She gently stroked his warm cheek.

“People take that type of thing really seriously here. Not me… just, people,” his voice trailed off, embarrassed.

“We must get to the palace,” she said, gazing off in the distance at the towering mountain that served as its foundation. “Why would they build it all the way up there? We can’t afford to waste time. We have to go. I need to know my friends are safe.”

A young boy in a colorful costume with sandy-brown hair and deep-set eyes approached and asked for a copper coin. Emily hesitated and smiled with a hint of embarrassment.

“Yamishet,” whispered Gléhson as he handed the boy the coin.

“Thank you, m’lady.” The boy performed a little flip and then disappeared into the street traffic.

The air was filled with the rich smell of cooking meat and various foods. Emily grinned before reaching out and grabbing a paper cone filled with fried potato wedges.

“Oh my god! French fries! They have French fries!” she giggled, stepping back to let Gléhson pay. He caught Emily’s eye and looked back at her as they walked.

“What is it?” he reached for a wedge and stood a few feet back. “You’re giving me a look.”

A group of musicians started playing on a nearby corner, warbling to the tune of a somber refrain.

“So be honest with me, Glehs. You’re really like Lord Phule’s kid or something, right? His son?” she patted Wind-spear’s side as she spoke.

“I can assure you I’m not.”

“Well, you’re sure as hell not a servant. You’re too confident, and you stole a horse without fear of reprisal, or the horse belongs to you,” she leaned in close to him, peering into his eyes.

“You are far too educated and speak with a forced common accent. Plus, you’ve been spending money on me left and right since we got here. And lastly, you’re much too comfortable around a royal, even if I don’t identify as one. No servant, or sorry, stable hand would ever just reach over and pick from their superior’s meal like you just did. Either way, there’s more to you than meets the eye.”

“I could say the same about you, Emily Heart,” said Gléhson.

“Oh no! I’m an open book. Just an Earth girl stuck on the Moon.”

“What if I told you I was a dashing assassin sent to lure you away from Phule’s mansion?”

“Nah, you’re too handsome and charming to be an assassin,” Emily dismissed the idea. “I don’t know about dashing, though.”

“I’ve been told I’m dashing.”

“Sure you have, by your servants, Mr. Phule junior.”

“I am not Phule’s kin. Look at me. Do you see any resemblance?” he asked.

“I just assumed you got your good looks from your mother.”

He gave a faint smile.

“My question is, if you’re not who you say you are, then who are you?” Emily stared at him intently as they walked down the street.

“I am a hand in Lord Phule’s stable,” said Gléhson. Then he smiled and added, “Here, we’re leaving the street. We’ll head up this way.” He pulled Wind-spear along and turned up a quieter path.

“Where are you taking me?” Emily asked, stopping in place. That was when she saw them. Across the street were two of the men who had accompanied her father the previous evening, she was sure of it. She looked at Gléhson with rage in her eyes,

“Please tell me you’re not with them!”

“Who? No, I’m with you.” Gléhson stopped and looked around. “I recognize them,” he said, and helped her onto Wind-spear. “We’ll stay off the main streets and simply head parallel to them. I think we can lose them that way.”

He hopped into the saddle and trotted into an alley, following a side road, carefully avoiding the main thoroughfare. Ahead of them, Emily watched the bustling crowd and saw the men again, just a few yards ahead.

Due to the narrowness of the side street and its small side yards filled with trash and carts, they hoped they would not be spotted.

“They’re all over the place,” he said. “Quick! Look for an open stable, a manger, tack room—some place we can hide.”

Emily made a face, then looked around herself. Suddenly, a look of crazed realization came upon her face.

“Where am I supposed to look? I’m not from here!” she said.

“Come on,” Gléhson pulled the reins and galloped further down the street. They were two houses down when he noticed a man standing, looking right at them. He slowed but kept her behind him. Just then, the man turned and walked away with his head down.

“Behind that house,” whispered Gléhson. There was a tree, shrub, and a large wooden barn sat adjacent. It was unlocked; they went inside and closed it shut. “We’ll wait here.”

“Do you think they’ve seen us?” Emily asked, her face now ashen.

“I don’t know. We may have lost them back there. I’m going to look,” he said, keeping his eyes on the entrance to the barn. “You and Wind-spear hide behind those crates near the back.”

Emily nodded and took Wind-spear with her towards the back of the barn. She crouched in the shadows, her breath raspy. A mouse ran across the floor. Wind-spear raised his head and licked her face.

“Oh! Gross,” Emily whispered. She reached out and petted his neck. “Can you understand me?” she asked, eyes wide as the horse bowed its neck and rubbed his head against her. He nudged her again, snorted, and lowered his powerful head to snack from a nest of hay.

Gléhson looked up at the ceiling, listening to what sounded like multiple footsteps on the rooftop. He retreated to the back of the barn and hid with Wind-spear and Emily. The footsteps moved on.

After a long pause, they heard a loud thump against the side of the barn. They both froze. Emily’s heart raced. Wind-spear licked at the straw on the floor, then whinnied and pawed the ground.

Emily’s pulse pounded in her ears. After a few more moments, she heard the muted sounds of men talking. Gléhson grabbed her hand, crouched by her side, and whispered gruffly,

“I want you to mount Wind-spear and be prepared to charge after I undo the latch and open the doors. Do you understand?”

“Yes, but what about you?” Emily asked.

“I’ll hop on when you pass,” he paused, quickly scanning the barn, “Don’t be afraid. We can outrun them.”

“Outrun them?” Emily grimaced.

“We’ll stay off the main road until we get to the city gate,” he said quietly.

“But…the palace?” Emily began.

“You have shown me your strength, princess. You can do it.” He helped her mount Wind-spear and then crept to the front of the barn, placing his hands on the heavy metal latch.

He paused, looked back inside the barn, and flattened himself against the entryway. Then, quickly, he threw the latch, releasing it with a flourish. Gléhson’s eyes went wide.

“Go, Wind-spear! Go!” he shouted.

Within a blink, he jumped onto the back of Wind-spear as the horse charged through the entrance. He could hear the voices of the men above him. Four of them, masked and crouched on the roof of the barn like nesting spiders.

The fifth was on the ground, holding onto the lead to Wind-spear’s breast collar and running alongside the horse in what should have been an impossible feat for any man. He twisted the lead in his hand and pulled back, making the horse buck and neigh against the pressure. Gléhson remained calm, watching the masked man try to control the horse.

“Let go you knave!” he demanded.

The masked man tightened his grip on Wind-spear’s bridle in response. Bending over, he did his best to hold on as the huge beast fought him.

"Oh no, you don't!" he cackled. Emily whirled around in the saddle and glared down at the man.

"Let go!" she screamed as Wind-spear reared and pawed the air. The masked man seemed to enjoy the show.

"You're scaring him!" Emily yelled.

The masked man laughed. "I like you, Wind-spear!" he said, tugging the bridle. "But I'll take you down if I have to."

Gléhson grew impatient. "I'm going to warn you one last time."

"Father, stop it! What do you want?" Emily yelled, sounding more annoyed than frightened. Yienguoi-Jin, hesitated, and a look of pride hid behind his mask.

"You're scaring him," she repeated.

Gléhson nearly lost his grip as the horse practically bucked him off. "Leave Wind-spear alone!" he said.

"Demon!" yelled Emily. She lunged toward Wind-spear's bridle, but Yienguoi-Jin caught her arm and ripped her from the saddle.

"Get off me!" she screamed. Wind-spear reared once more and smashed his hooves down on the ground. Gléhson fell backward, landing on his rear end. White dust billowed down on top of him.

"Stop!" he said, incredulous. He stood and began to dust himself off. Yienguoi-Jin held onto Emily's arm, grinning as he turned around and flung her onto his back as if she were a rag doll. He then dashed down the side street to a waiting carriage. Inside sat Nami and Ohna, the former frowning with her arms crossed.

Yienguoi-Jin dumped her inside and shut the door, pointing to the driver.

"Take them," he commanded. The driver whipped the horse, and the carriage raced off down the street. Gléhson stood behind him in the haze of dust, watching the carriage drive off into the distance. He blinked as the vision began to fade.

"She was beautiful, truly special."

He dreamingly felt like he had just lived out something from a fairy tale. And if it was a fairytale, Yienguoi-Jin was the troll under the bridge.

"Beautiful," he whispered again, brushing himself off completely. Gléhson was lost in thought, so he didn't notice the figures moving in around him.

They could have killed him if that was their intent. Instead, Yienguoi-Jin grabbed him by the shoulders and turned him around to face the imposing figure of Madame Nanda, her proud face etched in frowning wrinkles.

"My lord," she said. Her high-pitched voice was heavy with disappointment.

"Obánā," he bowed.

"Wipe that bloody silly smile off of your face!" she stomped her foot. With the wave of her hand, Yienguoi-Jin dragged him over to and roughly tossed him inside a waiting carriage etched with the sigil of an encircled flame, the Anele family crest.

The Engagement

The Sowao residences were nestled in the river hills of Domotedai's western suburbs. The mansion, though impressive, was not extravagant or ornate, and considerably smaller than some of its less prestigous neighbors. The mansion's most striking feature was a tower situated at the back of the property, which housed a prayer room for its Lord.

Emily's eyes were red from crying as she stared ahead at the sand-colored building growing larger in front of her as the carriage drew nearer. They came to a stop just before its front gate, where a lone Sowaon soldier stood guard. A footman opened the carriage door and helped her step down the runner. The soldier guarding the gate lowered his eyes and stepped aside, bowing.

Nami and Ohna followed her, their faces grim and backs straight. The trio passed through the imposing gate and walked silently along a pebbled path that led them to the main house. Lord Phule and a very displeased-looking Minister Djowobb greeted them at the entrance.

Lord Phule wore a calm expression, though his eyes twinkled. "I am glad to see you are safe, princess," he said.

"Madame Nami, Ohna, how nice to see you all again," Minister Djowobb offered a polite bow, noticeably ignoring his daughter. "Minister," they bowed in return.

"What is this nonsense you are all on?" Emily asked. "You two know very well who he is."

"Who might that be, my lady?" Lord Phule asked.

"You know exactly who I mean," she growled, glaring at the man.

"Princess, if you will allow me," said Lord Phule, "we have prepared your bath in our gjo."

"Gjo?"

"Yes, Your Highness, a gjo is a bathing room."

"Good. Anything to get away from you two!" she said. "Now, can you both get out of my way?"

"Princess," Lord Phule began to speak again.

"Enough!" yelled Emily. "Step aside! Both of you!"

"But princess –"

"No buts!" She stormed through the entrance.

Lord Phule turned to Nami, "Ensure she is bathed and ready for this evening. This incident has forced us to move up the schedule."

"Yes, my lord." Nami bowed, then turned to Ohna, "Take her to the Gjo. I will join you shortly."

After the two left, Phule turned to Minister Djowobb.

"The empress has scheduled the ceremony for this evening. I shall go and prepare the marriage contracts."

"I appreciate your help, my lord," Minister Djowobb nodded with a smile.

Meanwhile, Emily realized she was wandering aimlessly when Ohna caught up with her.

"I don't know where I'm going," she huffed, hating the helplessness her voice betrayed. She felt small and alone. Ohna gazed at her as Emily's eyes began to water. Pulling herself to her full height, she managed –

"It's not that easy," she spoke quietly. "I'm not happy being here," she said, drawing her arms to her side.

Ohna took the lead, walking with her eyes lowered but not speaking. She guided Emily through a labyrinth of hallways, staircases, and doors before they reached the Gjo. Ohna stopped, slid open its door, and escorted Emily into a large sauna-esque bathing room that smelled of fresh eucalyptus. A bath, sunk in the middle of the cedar-wood room floor, had steam rising from its surface.

It was a long rectangular pool, big enough to fit three or four people, with crystal clear water and a few decorative leaves. Two maids on either side stood up, undressed Emily, and doused her with a bucket of cold water before helping her into the steaming bath. Once she was settled in, they bowed and left.

Ohna folded Emily's clothes, placing them onto a wooden box off to the side. Emily eyed her with some irritation but decided, for the moment, to relax and let go. She closed her eyes and exhaled loudly, letting the heat seep into her sore body.

"Wow, this feels amazing. I haven't had a real bath since grams and I stopped going to Spa Castle! We just have a crappy shower at home that always clogs, and that little dip at the priest's doesn't count."

Ohna handed her a tray of soaps, and after a few unwelcome attempts at lathering and fussing with her hair, Emily told her she was content to wash her own body. The maid bowed and sat by the doorway.

Emily washed the sweat and dirt off her face and limbs, feeling relaxed and weary. She cleaned the rest of her body, washed her hair, and then ran her hands through her smooth locks. She glanced at Ohna, and before long, she felt very sleepy. She leaned back and closed her eyes, smiling.

"You are to be soaked in milk and honey next," Emily jolted up with a start. Nami stood in the doorway, fingers laced before her abdomen, wearing a grim expression on her face.

Ohna walked over and slid aside the wall behind Emily on the far side of the tub, revealing another Gjo, identical in size and layout, only its tub was filled with what looked like steaming milk.

"What? Wait! You were serious about that?" Emily asked.

"There are also herbs and essential oils blended into the soak," said Nami. "The honey and milk will smooth your skin back to its newborn state. The mint, lavender, and bergamot oils will stimulate your senses and help you relax."

She escorted Emily over to the milk-filled tub and helped her step down into the warm, rich substance. Emily sunk in and exhaled loudly.

“Oh, it’s just heaven!” She let her arms and legs float freely beneath the warm liquid. “What’s this?” She asked, touching one of the many wooden bottles sitting on the side of the tub.

Ohna turned, looking at the bottle. “It is a blend of plants and oils.”

“Leave us,” said Nami, kneeling beside the pool and taking up Emily’s hair into her hands.

Ohna bowed and left, closing the screen door behind her.

“That was a little abrupt,” Emily frowned. “What’s going on?”

Nami picked up the bottle and began pouring some of its contents into Emily’s hair. She felt a warm sensation spread over her scalp.

“Your father is not the bad man you think he is. He is only looking out for your best interest,” Nami said.

“Oh. You want to talk about him. Humph! Talk about a disa-fucking-pointment.”

“His intentions are noble, my lady.”

“I’m not so certain of that. He hasn’t seen me in years, and already he’s trying to marry me off. He won’t even tell me how my mother died.”

“It is painful for him to speak of Lady Ameiki’s death. I would not press him on the subject,” she said softly. She closed the bottle and reached for another one.

“Wait, did you know my mother too?” Emily asked.

“Yes, I spent the better part of my early years here in Behra working in her house. She was a very strong-willed woman. She was as lively as you are.”

"Why didn't you tell me about this earlier?"

"We spoke only briefly this morning. That is before you went gallivanting off to the capital."

"Oh, forget about that! You must tell me everything about her? I want to know what happened between her and my father. Why did she die? How, and when?" Emily asked.

"My lady, please don't push. He does not wish to talk about it," Nami collected the girl's hair into her saturated hands and began to massage her scalp.

"I have to know," Emily said, turning her face to the side. "I'm not a child anymore, Obánā. At the very least, I deserve the truth."

Nami looked down and wrung the water out of her hair. "You are aware of the terrible fate that befell Prince Yeingui Yeit?" she asked.

Emily nodded, "Only somewhat. I know he and my mother were supposed to marry, but he became the God of Death instead?"

"It was a tragic fate, him becoming Yienguoi-Jin, an ominous omen. He took on a very dangerous role, being sent alone into the far reaches of the empire to wed the enemy. He was expected to forge a truce between two great warring nations. To say this was difficult would be an understatement."

"It sounds like you knew him too."

"I did," the suggestion of a smile shifted the shadows on her face. "I was his Obánā too, though in Seizhone we are called Bhronthise."

"Oh," said Emily, sitting up. "So that means you knew him when he was a boy?"

"Yes, since birth, in fact."

"Wow. I never would've imagined…since he was a baby?"

“Yes, from birth well into his teenage years,” Nami said. “He was a good boy, and an even better man to me and all of the house staff. He made many sacrifices out of misplaced faith, and the diplomatic mission he was sent on was like walking towards certain death. But he was very much in love, and brave, and foolish. But in the end, he was marked by the God of Death and became consumed by him.”

“Since you knew him as a baby,” Emily paused and looked over at Nami, “how did you come to work in Odahni as my Obánā?”

“Oh, it’s a long story,” Nami said, sitting up a little bit more.

“I’m all ears,” Emily said.

“Excuse me, my lady?”

“Please, tell me the story.”

“Where do I begin, child,” Nami said, “I was part of the original wedding procession from Seizhone meant to relocate and serve your father here in Behra. I arrived beforehand to prepare for him, but after his death, Princess Ameiki kept me as a servant in her house. I shared in her pain and told her everything I knew about him. Stories from his childhood and the like. She was a very sweet, proud, and beautiful woman. Just wonderful. Even though she was from a powerful family, she was one of the most gracious and kind people I ever knew. We grew very close, and I miss her every day. You would have adored her, and she, you.”

“Then why is she dead, Obánā?”

“After your father, Prince Yeingui, died, Princess Ameiki was married off to the emperor’s brother, Duke Anele Sahyuh, commander of the Drizien knights and widely known for his cruelty. He took her away from Odahni to live in the capital. Once here, she was forced to live in a different world from her sheltered circumstances.

I came here with her and watched as her flame died out.” Nami picked up a small jar and palmed a greenish cream into Emily’s hair.

“She began to rely on the cups to cope with the pressures of her newly married life.”

“But why? Was it depression? What was the issue?”

“Yes, she was depressed. We all were after your father passed away. And her marriage only exacerbated things. Riju, that’s Duke Sahyuh, knew Ameiki didn’t love him. This wasn’t unusual, as love is rarely a factor in noble marriages. But he wanted at least a marriage of duty and respect. He hoped she would become his perfect wife and bear him many children. However, she refused to let him touch her. She was still heartbroken over Yeingui, and the marriage was never consummated.

“That’s a lot of pressure for a marriage,” said Emily.

“Any marriage, my love, but especially one where neither party has affection for the other,” Nami said kindly. “To make matters worse, Riju couldn’t stand that your mother loved a ghost. He couldn’t compete with Yeingui, even in death, and it infuriated him. He resorted to other means to make her comply with his demands, threatening her and her servants. When she didn’t budge, he took it a step further.”

“What?” Emily said in disbelief.

“He locked her in her apartments, allowing her to interact only with her handmaidens. He believed that she needed to adjust to her new life and should only have contact with people he trusted.”

“That’s horrible!” Emily looked away.

“Indeed, it was,” Nami replied. “And it had the opposite effect he intended.”

Emily furrowed her eyebrows.

“Being forced to stay in her apartments all the time, without contact with anyone, only made her think of your father more. Ameiki, who had always loved Yeingui when he was alive, became bitter and started drinking after his death.

She grew to hate Riju for what he had done and soon became paranoid of everyone and everything. I was the only one whose counsel she sought. I loved her like she was my own daughter."

"That's awful," Emily frowned.

Nami nodded. "In two years, she became a shell of her former self, barely functioning. Her soul had been shattered, and she lost her sense of direction. And then, he appeared."

"Who? My father?"

"No, not at all, child. Are you listening? I am talking about Yienguoi-Jin!"

"Yeah, I know. They're the same person! You keep saying he died, but the jerk is very much alive! Ouch! Did you just pull my hair?"

"Always respect your father, even if he is detestable," said Nami and continued her tale –

"At first, he sneaked into her garden and watched her from afar. He knew if he came any closer, she would see him, so every night he stayed back, observing her pain. He grew more and more enamored with her all over again."

"He saw the goodness in her and loved her more than ever before. She quickly became his obsession, and he would visit her often. One night, she noticed him watching her and went inside. He was shocked at her state. She was a mere husk, completely alone and helpless."

"He knew he had to help her. She was his hope. So, he followed her and removed his mask. They needed each other, and it was a mutual understanding. They both had what the other needed, and it was love."

"Were you a fly on the wall or what?" Emily asked.

"She confided in me. I was her only confidant aside from your father. She trusted me and knew I could keep her secrets. She loved him with her whole heart and soul and dreamed of a life with him."

"And she told you she still loved him?" Emily asked.

"She did. During that time, they grew to depend on each other. When Riju found out about Yienguoi-Jin, he was enraged and tried to have him killed. But Yienguoi-Jin easily defeated the Duke's guard and escaped."

"But how did he find out? Who would've told him?" Emily asked.

"Your mother did! Or rather, her body did the talking for her. She had become pregnant and didn't even try to hide it. I dare say she flaunted it, and Riju was furious. He was a particularly cruel and violent man."

"The servants who whispered about the scandal amongst themselves were beheaded. He sent out many searchers and commanded soldiers to hunt and kill Yienguoi-Jin, but they came up against the force of the Taisehsai Dhukai."

"Duke Sahyuh knew if he started a war with the Taisehsai, he would have to involve the emperor, who, mind you, knew nothing of what his brother was doing. But Yienguoi-Jin disappeared, and Ameiki fell into despair. She felt she couldn't carry the baby alone."

"She wanted him to know he was going to be a father and see you born. Throughout her pregnancy, I was the only one she trusted. I would rub her back and sing to her late into the night, easing her pain and soothing her mind with the same songs I sang to you when you were in my care."

"Shortly before you were born, Yienguoi-Jin returned, and she begged him, pleaded with him to take her away. I told him they had to do something to escape the madness and make a new life for themselves. He agreed, and they began to plan their escape."

"He must have been worried about her," Emily said.

"Yes, he was, but that wasn't all. He was afraid Duke Sahyuh would kill both of you despite the potential of a civil war with the Aiyo.

In the end, the Duke placed an iron guard around his castle, and there was no way for your father to free her. Upon your birth, she named you Yuyuki, but the Duke had you taken away from her after a few hours, and days later, gave you over to the Jyoshi Sisterhood."

"The Jyoshi?"

"But he sent assassins to kill you and the nuns. Years later, I met one of the surviving sisters. She told me how they defeated the assassins, hid their bodies, and left you on the side of the road as they saw you as a bad omen."

"And that's where the priest Dou-Dodachi found me and took me to Daiye Village," said Emily, connecting the dots.

"Yes. He did, in fact, save your life."

"And with a demon as a father, maybe I am a bad omen."

"Yienguoi-Jin never found out. He was simply told you had died. He never knew he'd been denied the chance to learn you were alive," Nami sighed and retrieved a stack of neatly folded towels. Emily stayed silent, digesting the shocking revelation.

"Not long after you were born, Duke Sahyuh forced himself onto the princess, an event which led to the birth of your sister, Shumaiyuki. But Ameiki refused the child her breast, convinced the baby was the spawn of a monster. She sought to escape back to Kue."

"I agreed to help her, but only if she took the child with her. She was convinced Shumaiyuki was too weak and would slow her down. She feared the Duke would seek retribution, but I assured her she was strong and would live."

Nami opened a large towel for Emily, "Out you come now." She helped her out of the milky soup and began to pat her dry.

"The journey back to Kue was a long and tiring one. We were forced to travel only at night and use concealment during the day to avoid notice. We eventually made it back to Odahni Palace, and your grandfather welcomed her and Shumaiyuki with open arms."

"Days later, Duke Sahyuh arrived angry and demanded an explanation for the disappearances of his wife and daughter. Lord Aiyo told him they'd left him because he lost his way and they would not be returning to the capital. Shocked by the news, Riju flew into a rage."

"To prevent Kue from becoming embroiled in an indefinable conflict, Lord Aiyo and his noblemen demanded Sahyuh leave. Riju refused and accused the lord of treason to the crown. So, Lady Ameiki stepped in and spoke with him in private."

"Lady Ameiki thought she could reason with him, but an argument ensued." Tears were falling down Nami's cheek as she dumped a bucket of fresh water over Emily, rinsing off the remaining milk and honey.

"He killed her as they spoke," Nami covered her eyes with both hands and could not continue, beginning to sway a little.

Emily was about to ask Nami what happened when Minister Djowobb opened the screen and stomped into the room, making them both jump.

"How dare you walk in on a lady's toilet!" said Nami.

"You're taking far too long, Obánā."

"I-I was in the middle of telling the princess about Lady Ameiki!" she objected.

"I'm here to inform the lady that we have an appointment at Gah Temple this evening. Leave the past where it belongs, Obánā—in the past."

"I will do no such thing. The lady has every right to know the truth."

"Do your job and get her dressed, old woman." The minister scoffed and turned to leave. "Dry her and see that she's oiled and perfumed."

"Thank you, Obánā," Emily looked up at her after Minister Djowobb had left.

“It was my pleasure, my lady. Now, if you’ll excuse me, I must get back to my duties and go prepare your dress.” Nami left the enclosure, leaving Emily with a mute Ohna and the two maids who welcomed her earlier.

She closed her eyes as the three toweled her off and felt very much alone again. She wasn’t exactly sure what she wanted to do or think about her conversation with Nami. It took a moment for her to decide she would confront her father head-on.

***

Emily didn’t know what the event was, but she knew she looked radiant, and was dressed for more than a night out on the town. Her scarlet and gray silk robes were light and had a flowing, easy grace about them and were richly embroidered.

Her thick obi, exquisite in design, was a dark blue color, so dark it almost looked black. Her crown was ornate, made from polished, crescent-shaped black ore encrusted with tiny gems. Diamonds of all sizes and shapes could be seen, along with jade and marble stones.

Around her neck was a golden circlet, also decorated with tiny diamonds. Her shoulders were covered with a rich blue silk cape, lined with a layer of gold muslin. She wore a rich amber bracelet with an emerald dangling from it, and a solid gold ring with an oval-shaped red stone.

As she sat in a bamboo chair waiting for her father and Lord Phule to arrive, she sipped tea and tried to control her anxiety. Five minutes passed. Seven minutes. Her heart was pounding, she was falling apart inside, but she’d be damned if she showed it.

After waiting ten minutes, Emily saw their tall shadows pass by the shoji, and they finally entered the room. She smiled and put her tea down as they sat opposite her on tiny cushions with Phule pouring he and Djowobb a cup. She waited patiently for her father to speak, to fill the silence, but it was Phule who spoke first, apologizing for their tardiness.

Emily spoke before either could get out another word, saying, "Minister Djowobb, a word in the garden. I have certain questions I need answered before we even consider carrying on with tonight's activities, festivities, or whatever the hell it is you have planned."

Emily made her way over to an open archway that led outside. The night was warm and slightly humid. Djowobb huffed and followed her out under the growing moonlight. Emily turned to face the scarred man; he was much taller than she was. Although she felt slightly intimidated, she spoke with a forced confidence.

"When did you find out I was alive?"

"Seven days ago, from my spy in Arymaitei's Dhukai. I was informed Seitogi had taken on a job from the witch against the Larks' wishes and that the two had a falling out. It was over returning you to this world."

Emily repeated the name Arymaitei, and then said, "I'm not talking about a couple of days ago! I'm reffering to when I was Abete Enoshi!"

Djowobb took a step backward, unsure of how to answer. He stared down at the stone path. His eye narrowed in thought.

"I found out shortly after your fifth birthday. I was on my way to Daiye to retrieve you when I happened upon you and Seitogi in the snow. He had killed assassins sent by those who remained loyal to Duke Sahyuh. I admired the boy's courage but took you anyway. He followed us, and later that night rescued you. I allowed you two to escape."

"It would appear then, I owe Seitogi my gratitude," Emily said with a dark smirk. "He pretty much saved my life and kept Sahyuh from finishing me off."

"That is what I meant to say," Djowobb said. "The boy was interesting. I allowed you to return to Daiye with him because he was honorable and skilled. He declared you two were already matched. I guess I thought life would be better for you in a small farming village. His uncle ran an old dojo. I thought you deserved a simple life.

Never would I have imagined the Aiyo would ever recognize you. But only days later, you were whisked off to Odahni and put behind an iron curtain."

"But why was I brought back in the first place? Obánā just told me Duke Sahyuh tried to have me killed as a baby too. Why would he order me to be brought back and act in my sister's place?"

"Duke Sahyuh is dead," Djowobb said after a moment of hesitation. "He was slain by Lord Aiyo Teiyulori, your grandfather." He fumbled on his words, "Your mother left him and returned home to Odahni, but Sahyuh followed her, and when he arrived, they argued, and he strangled her to death. Right in front of the baby."

He gave a small sad laugh followed by silence in the darkness of the garden. Emily's head swam from all the lies and horrible truths of the matter. Djowobb was telling her what she wanted to hear, and she wasn't sure if she could trust the man; he obviously had an agenda. But she needed answers about herself and her sister.

"Your grandfather immediately slew him in a rage. For Sahyuh had murdered his daughter. He sent the Anele soldiers back to the capital with their lord's head. The Aiyo and the Aneles were on the verge of a civil war, but the emperor was a pacifist and offered a solution."

"Lord Aiyo was forced to abdicate his lordship to his son, Yulori, and enter the palace where he would live out his days under house arrest. In exchange, the Aiyo stipulated with the secret hand of the empress that Ameiki's daughter would marry her son, the heir to the throne, therefore solidifying the renewed alliance of the country's two most powerful families. Without the Aiyo military and industrial strength, the country is nothing. Even the ruling family knows that. Do you understand what I am getting at, princess?" he turned to face Emily, the tension between them palpable.

She took a step backward. "I'm afraid not, you have a penchant for monologuing instead of getting to the point! Why me? Why wasn't I left to live a simple peasant life?"

"Because Shumayuki became ill. Months before your sister was to be matched with the emperor's son, she was bitten by a beetle and became feverish, and was left paralyzed on one side of her body. The girl was no longer fit to be Heicho-Hieba. But Aiyo Yumeiko knew of your story from Dou-Dodachi and formed her plot to replace Shumaiyuki with you."

"Though a year older, you and the girl were almost identical. At the time, even as lord of the house, Yulori did whatever his aunt told him, and he went along with the empress's plot. Together they locked Shumaiyuki away, and you assumed her name and status."

"That girl locked away in the dream tower," Emily placed her hand over her heart, "It's no wonder she wanted to kill me. So we are sisters after all," she shook her head.

"And she wants to kill me now! That's what Seitogi was talking about!"

"Yes and No," Djowobb said calmly, he turned to face the night sky. The stars were pinpricks, and the moon a bulbous globe illuminating the garden faithfully.

"What do you mean?" Emily replied.

"The majority of the Aiyo back the Golden Swan over your uncle. If she were to come into power at court, we are certain she would make a play for the throne itself and then march on Seizhone."

"Hell. I think I liked it better when my life was just one giant MacGuffin," Emily fanned herself. "If I've been gone all these years and Yuyuki never really existed? Who am I supposed to be then?"

"You are Heicho-Hieba, Nham Aiyo Des Shumaiyuki."

"Heicho Hieba," Emily repeated, "Crown Princess… oh my god, that ceremony. When I was a girl, shortly after I was brought back from Daiye…"

"You were matched with Crown Prince Rilkian in an official ceremony at Nyongoyuchi Palace." Djowobb smiled with pride, creasing his already distracting scar.

"Matched..." Emily turned and stomped back into the tea room, where Phule attempted a smile.

Emily felt a rush of blood to her face, "Where are we going tonight? Why am I all dolled up like this? Tell me!"

Djowobb followed her in and spoke before Phule could form a response – "The Empress Anele has invited you to a ceremony with the high council, members who still support the unification of our nation with Seizhone through marriage. They have the authority to restore your name and the title Crown Princess. The decree was made and signed by the empress herself, so it is not negotiable."

It was at this point that the ground seemed to fall out from beneath Emily. Lurching forward, she did a double take of her father who continued to force a hideous smile.

"What? What are you talking about?" Emily turned away, covering her face in her hands. She tried breathing deeply to steady herself. But the more she thought about it, the clearer it became.

"How could Yumeiko replace Shumaiyuki with...me?" she whispered. "I was never the princess, she was. Shumai."

"This is a matter of utmost importance," Phule said as he took a sip of tea. "With the assistance of your great-aunt, and a few others in the court, the matter of succession has been solved." He reached into his robes, took out a folded parchment, and handed it to her. She opened it and looked over the foreign charters.

"As if I could actually read this! What does it say?"

"It is the statement announcing that you are to become Crown Princess to the future emperor," said Phule. He huffed a little as he waited for Emily's response.

"I will be a queen? That's marriage, right? I thought I made it clear I'm not marrying anyone!"

"Well..." said Phule, nervously, "I believe the Minister had something to say. Yes, what are your feelings on this Minister?"

"Before my father and you get too involved in all this wedding nonsense, I need to make it clear this marriage is not to my wishes, nor was it ever decided by me!" Emily said with a mixture of scorn and anxiety.

"Listen! I'm not getting married, and I have no plans to marry anyone in the near future. Jeezus, I'm only 17! I barely know who I am! The last thing I'm doing is getting hitched to some guy I don't know!"

"You are a 20-year-old woman whose clock is ticking. You are to become empress! It has been settled. You should be overjoyed at the prospect." Minister Djowobb took a seat.

"You already have a Shumaiyuki to marry your stupid prince!"

"I just explained to you outside that she is just as rotten as her father was."

"She is quite capable and ambitious," said Phule. "If she were born a male, I fear she would have already usurped Lord Aiyo and challenged the emperor for his throne."

"She is a maniac! She tried to kill me when we were children… I thought it was all a dream. But it was real! Look, I have no interest in challenging her. If she is supposed to marry into the imperial house, what does that have to do with me?"

"You are an Aiyo princess," said Phule, "The Aiyo is the most powerful family below the imperial house. They have more soldiers than the top five families combined and serve as the vanguard for both the imperial army and its navy. Aiyo women have supplied heirs for the Imperial house since your great-grandmother, Aiyo Mikoe. None have been more powerful than the current empress, Yumeiko. And she herself has chosen you as her successor."

"That doesn't explain…" Emily began, but Djowobb cut her off impatiently.

"You are the firstborn of Ameiki, and my heir, which also makes you heir to the throne of Seizhone, as my brothers below me have died!

Do you understand now, daughter? Your marriage to the crown prince will unite both countries and protect us from future wars. Even now, the messengers have already been sent to Seizhone to alert my father of your presence."

"And once you produce an heir, the peace will be solidified," added Phule.

"I've never heard a bigger load of crap in my life! I am not marrying some guy I don't know, let alone giving birth to a peace baby! I don't care who my father or grandfather is," Emily stood, fists balled. "Don't women have rights here?"

"We are right, of course," said Minister Djowobb.

"No! I mean, rights! Like the right to make our own decisions about who we marry, who we love. Having agency over our own bodies?"

"Hmph! These decisions are made by your father," said Djowobb.

"My father died in a make-believe fire," Emily glared at the minister, and then turned back to Phule. "And I've seen all the movies. A marriage of convenience never works out for the couple involved or the country that relies on it to unify. I'd kill myself first."

"You'll do no such thing," laughed Djowobb and sipped from his tea.

"Won't I?"

"Here then. Show me," he tossed her a bejeweled dagger with a smile. Emily took the blade and placed it in her obi.

"I'd just as soon use it on you," she said, eliciting an eruption of laughter from him.

"Do you see Phule? This girl has no respect for her father," he laughed while he leaned forward and patted her on her shoulder.

"I have a report," a came voice from the garden.

"Speak," said Lord Phule.

"Rihtzkaya Inashata entered Odahni on behalf of the Shomba to seek Aiyo's backing in their effort against the Tambo."

"The Aiyo would gain nothing backing either house," Phule told Djowobb, who nodded in agreement.

The messenger continued, "Awei Chua entered Odahni with two foreign spies of neither Dreesh nor Seizhone blood."

"And the witch?" asked Phule.

"Nothing as of yet my lord."

"We don't know why the witch brought you back," said Minister Djowobb, "And we are not going to let her get her hands on you again. I don't believe she has just disappeared. She had some plans for you. She'll be back." He pointed to Emily who looked at Phule.

"It is imperative we find her to stave off any future mischief." Phule ordered, "Find her, the sooner the better!"

"It will be done, my lord," The messenger bowed then rose to go, but Emily stood suddenly.

"Foreign, spies! Tell me. What did they look like?" Emily immediately thought of Darren and Rebecca and decided to see if she could gain any new info on their whereabouts.

However, the messenger hesitated and looked to his lord. Lord Phule nodded slowly. "You may answer her."

"I did not see them myself, my lady."

"But…"

"We have a complicated network of spies that cover vast ranges. Odahni is a three-day journey. Thus, information trickles down the network and arrives at his ear," answered Phule.

Emily nodded that she understood but decided to press.

"Did you at least get a description of them?"

"Only that one was injured, and the other had hair of fire."

Emily played his words over in her head. Surely he meant a redhead. Everything else was so upside down in this world; describing a redhead as "hair of fire" seemed pretty on brand.

"It's them!" She turned to Lord Phule. "I'm sure of it! He's talking about my friends! Rebecca and Darren!"

"What is this?" said Phule with a raised eyebrow.

Emily moved towards Minister Djowobb and grabbed his hands, "You have to send someone to get them!"

"It's not as simple as that."

"What do you mean? They aren't prisoners, are they?"

"That is precisely what they are, my dear," said Phule in a gentle tone. "The Aiyo are our enemy. If they have captured anyone associated with you, surely they will be used as bait to draw you out."

"No way." Emily's mind raced; what could she possibly do? She looked into her father's eyes. "I'll do it! I'll marry whoever you want me to if you rescue them!"

"You don't have much choice in the matter," he patted her hand.

"The hell I don't," she moved quickly and snatched her father's dagger from his waist and placed it at his throat, "If you don't help them, I'll kill everyone in this damned castle! Starting with you!"

"I'm sorry, princess," said Phule with a touch of embarrassment in his voice, "but you have the smooth side of the blade on his neck. I'm afraid you won't be able to make the cut."

Minister Djowobb merely laughed, and then with one quick motion slapped the blade out of her hand with such force that it stuck in the wall across the room. Emily retreated back to her chair, holding her smarting hand and whimpered,

"Please help them."

“We will,” he said, looking over at his daughter.

“Don’t make promises you can’t keep,” she said.

“We will make every effort,” he said, “and if necessary, I may seek help from Yienguoi-Jin.”

“The Minister will do nothing of the sort,” said Phule, “But I understand your apprehension.”

Emily looked up to father and then to her Phule.

“I have my sources in Odahni. Your friends will be safe, I promise,” Phule said.“Now we must go to Gah Temple, where destiny awaits,” he stood.

“Will my aunt be there?”

“The empress will attend and looks forward to meeting you.” Djowobb raised himself from his seat and clapped his hands.

“Come along, dear princess we have very little time,” he said, motioning her towards the exit.

Bonfire Rave

Gah Temple was a marvel to behold. Constructed nearly seven centuries ago at the heart of a picturesque glen, the imposing edifice occupied a low isthmus of land that bridged Domotedai city's core to Mount Giyun, upon which the Imperial Palace resided.

From atop the nearby hill, one could enjoy an expansive view of the city on the other side of the river. The sandstone and marble chapel, a slender pillar stretching towards the heavens, boasted elaborate carvings on its exterior that narrated scenes of ancient battles between gods, demigods, and demons amidst celestial objects.

Serving various purposes, the temple housed servants, accommodated guests, and facilitated administration. However, its most significant function was as the primary place of worship for the imperial family.

Emily felt overwhelmed, as events seemed to transpire at a breakneck pace. She was guided through a dim, narrow corridor that sharply contrasted with the vibrantly adorned walls and ceilings.

A monk in modest robes led them to a small room, where an elderly priest was meditating in front of a grand statue of Guoiyien-Jee, the Goddess of Life. The deity appeared to be attentively listening to the old man's prayers.

"Dou-Dodachi!" Emily exclaimed in surprise. She couldn't fathom why he was present.

Upon standing and bowing, the priest addressed Emily, Lord Sowao, and Minister Djowobb. Dou-Dodachi carried himself with grace and confidence, his wrinkled tunic a soothing shade of blue adorned with red embroidery and gold thread. His eyes sparkled with enthusiasm.

"Why are you here this evening?" Emily inquired, unable to contain her curiosity.

The priest smiled at them and replied, "I am here to attest to the authenticity of your lineage. You are an Aiyo princess." He retrieved a lengthy, folded silk cloth from his tunic and presented it to her.

As she unfolded the fragrant fabric, Emily was overcome with emotion. Clutched in her hand was a silver hairpin shaped like a swan. She glanced up at her father, whose face bore a pained expression.

"This was a gift from my mother."

"Yes, it is known as The Pearl Swan. Your mother had a trusted servant place it in your bassinet before you were given over to the Jyoshi. I found it with you on the side of the road that day. It is an Aiyo heirloom, forged from platinum and ghost steel—a one of a kind," explained the priest.

"And why do you have it?" inquired Emily.

"I gave it to him," interjected Minister Djowobb. "After you disappeared, I entrusted it to the priest to use as a means of praying for your safe return."

"Now that the true Aiyo princess has returned," declared the priest, "we can complete the unification and end all wars."

Emily's skepticism was evident. "I'll be frank with you. You sound like idealistic kids. I'm the only teenager in this room, and I don't think that marriage will end any, let alone all wars. Moreover, I'm beginning to see through the nonsense you're trying to feed me." She glanced back and forth between the three men.

"As I understand it, both of you—the priest and my father—are more or less disgraced! Aren't you just using me to regain your lost power? You were exiled from the palace because you couldn't keep it in your pants, right?" Emily directed this at a mortified Dou-Dodachi, then turned to Minister Djowobb, "And technically, you're dead. But Prince Yeingui can have a triumphant return to life if he delivers his father…"

"That's enough!" interrupted Djowobb. "The girl has no understanding of what is at stake here."

"You're right; I don't. But I know this much—I'm not staying here. My friends are out there, and they must be worried sick about me."

"You have a duty to your house and country!"

"Hypocrite, you abandoned your house to become a dookie or whatever you call yourselves! All you are is a killer for hire. That's why you look like the monster you are. You don't care one iota for my well-being, so long as it paves a path for you to take your father's throne. Both brothers died—did you kill them yourself, or did you have one of your goons do it?"

"Princess, please," Lord Phule attempted to interject, but—

"And what's in it for the Sowao Clan? Power, position? You may try to play the good cop, but you're just as bad as him! All bad—all of you!"

"Please, my lady. You are working yourself into a sweat, and your makeup is starting to run," said Phule.

"That's because you people don't have friggin' air conditioning!" the girl practically screamed. Then, after a deep breath, her voice dropped to a normal tone as she added,

"Point is, I don't seem to have a choice in the matter. But if I am going to play along with your little game, I want something in return."

"And what would that be, my daughter?"

"Your oath, that you'll really rescue my friends and bring them back here to the city. I know what Phule said back at his place, but I want your oath."

"We already discussed that. Its redundant," said Djowobb.

"You're asking the world of me damnit." Emily looked up at her father.

Djowobb sighed. "It seems this girl is intent on wearing me down with her challenges. Very well, if this is the only way to gain your cooperation, my men and I will depart for Odahni at dawn.

In the meantime, Priest Dou-Dodachi will escort you to the Dawn Room. Your mother will look down from the heavens and be proud."

"I highly doubt my mother would be proud to see the child ripped away from her milking breast being forced into a similar servitude with the nephew of the man who murdered her." Emily muttered in reply.

She hid her face in her hands and sobbed. The sound of her weeping filled the room. Her father drew her into an embrace and held her tightly. She could not push him away.

"Come now. Dry your tears. You are the daughter of a great people."

The priest and Lord Phule left the room, leaving father and daughter alone.

"Father…" her voice was muffled by her hands and the magnitude of the betrayal she felt.

"You will see, things will work out, your mother will guide you. The nation needs you."

***

The Dawn Room was massive, with a high ceiling and ornate columns. It looked like something out of a grand theater. Its walls were red and orange marble with gold inlay that sparkled when it caught the light.

The panels and beams in the ceiling were painted in the warm hues of sunrise, and gold-plated skylights allowed the moon to shine through. Evenly spaced between the columns were twelve marble statues, each representing one of Guoiyieni-Jee's priestly disciples.

At the far end of the room, a very toad-like, grim-looking priest sat before a large silk screen image depicting the battle for creation between Guoiyien-Jee and Yienguoi-Jin.

Next to him sat a small dais with a green velvet pillow at its center. Somehow, Emily knew she was meant to sit there. Walking with Dou-Dodachi towards the dais, she felt a prickle of anxiety kick in.

After what seemed like an hour of walking, the grandfatherly priest turned to her and nodded toward the pillow. Unsure, she did as she was told.

"Princess Aiyo," said the toad priest, motioning to the dais with a sweeping gesture. "Please come and sit. This pillow is the center of the Behranian destiny. Here, all the major decisions of generations past were made."

"So, you're saying in a few minutes, I will decide the fate of this country?" said Emily.

"Well, no. Not in a few minutes," said the priest, "but you will make an irrevocable decision. It will create a chain of events that will determine the course of Behranian history for generations to come. Just as it did ten thousand years ago. One of the many legendary heroes that adorn our walls was the first person to sit on this when Guoiyien-Jee established the Ruling Hierarchy."

"Guoiyien-Jee?" said Emily. The toad priest quickly corrected her and turned her around to face a screen.

"Who are you?" she asked.

"I am Kem, the official scribe of the Dawn Room," he said in a voice thick with the royal tones of his caste. "I have been ordered to scribe this document and will do so to the best of my ability."

Emily gazed in wonder at the towering silk screen. It was adorned with trillions of threads in a dazzling array of colors and depicted a fierce battle between two figures: a man and a woman. The man, who was nearly ten times larger than the woman, breathed out a stream of fire from his mouth, aimed directly at her. The smaller figure on the right, dressed in a white robe with long pigtails, countered with a powerful gust of wind from her hands.

Emily immediately recognized the figure as Guoiyien-Jee, and the larger figure as Yienguoi-Jin, whose face was that of a demon.

Suddenly, the screen split down the center, with each side receding into the outermost walls.

Emily's heart raced as the opening screens revealed a woman, elegantly dressed in scarlet silk robes, seated on a small, elevated platform with a retinue of attendants sitting behind her.

The woman radiated power, and her amaranth eyes sparkled with an inner fire. The priest halted and lowered his head in respect.

"This is our lady, Empress Aiyo Yumeiko," said Kem.

Emily's eyes hardly noticed the beautiful woman because she was instantly drawn to the sad-looking boy who sat next to her on a lower platform. He wore fine robes, but his head was bowed, and he stared at the floor.

Emily's mind was a whirling dervish as he and the chamber's occupants came into focus. The young man's right cheek was tinged red as though he had been slapped, and his downcast eyes were puffy, suggesting tears had fallen. He rubbed his eyes and gazed up at Emily with a quick, devilish smirk.

"It's you!" she gasped.

"Shhhhhh," said Kem, "We are not to speak. We are meant to simply listen to the decisions which will determine your fate."

Emily dismissed him with a quick glare and then said,

"Glehson, what's the meaning of this?"

"I see you have already met the crown prince," said the empress. She was known for her strong and strict demeanor and carried a stiff and regal air, as if every word from her lips might have bearing on Emily's fate. Her face, like her son's, bore the unmistakable trademark of her royal clan.

"I was not aware the stable boy was also the emperor's kid," said Emily, staring at Glehson.

The Empress Yumeiko looked unamused by her niece's bravado. The priest behind her glowered with displeasure, and it was all Djowobb could do to stifle a laugh. Glehson, on the other hand, wore an embarrassed smile and kept his head lowered.

"Hey, stable boy! Is Glehson even your real name?"

The chamber erupted into quiet murmurs as Glehson looked up at Emily. "I'm afraid not," he said.

Hushed gasps and whispers came from the empress's retinue of courtiers, some averting their eyes, others hiding behind their fans. Emily was upset by the nobles' response. If it weren't for their status, she would have screamed at them all.

The empress, however, seemed to enjoy this reaction, a pleased smile playing over her lips.

"You are a very spirited girl, princess. But here we do not address our superiors with such familiarity, nor do we speak out of turn, particularly in such a place of great reverence as this."

"Apologies esteemed empress," said Emily, somewhat sarcastically with a cut of her eyes at the woman. She looked back at Glehson. "But I was speaking to the stable boy, and he's proven himself to be far beneath me."

"Silence!" Djowobb exclaimed, standing from his sitting position at the far-right side of the screen. "The empress is right. We are here in a place of reverence. It is your first time in the Dawn Room, and you are not allowed to speak."

Emily slapped the floor, gritted her teeth, and stood. "Sit there! Shut down! Wear this! Don't speak! You're not the boss of me, scarface!"

Kem and Djowobb looked at each other in consternation. They had no idea how to respond. The empress, on the other hand, seemed slightly amused, perhaps Emily reminded her of her younger self.

"Guoiyien-Jee's light shines strongly through you, but dear princess, please," she said warningly while directing her gaze at the priest. "This is a serious matter. You are not allowed to speak unless you have special permission. And the crown prince is your superior. You must not insult him in any manner."

"Yeah, well your son likes to play games, and I'm not one for being played! I just dealt with that bullshit from Darren the other day, and I won't accept it from him!" pointing to the crown prince.

"Please sit, princess," said Kem. "This is our way of doing things," he said, "You could cast a void over the entire proceedings. You mustn't leave the pillow again. Would the general abandon his men on the battlefield?"

"Yes, princess," Minister Djowobb pleaded, "Sit down. You risk causing great damage to your family and the empire with your rash actions."

Emily looked at them both and then angrily sat back down on the pillow. She folded her arms in front of her as a different set of priests entered the chamber, chanting behind faceless, wooden masks.

"Let's get on with the ceremony," said Yumeiko as she fanned herself.

"Please be seated. Brother Kem will perform the reunification blessing," Dou-Dodachi addressed the chanters.

Kem took his position and began to recite ancient verses while reading from a great scroll. Yumeiko stared at Emily while remaining completely expressionless, causing the girl to feel even more self-conscious and angrier than what she already felt.

"Before them was she who brings the dawn. At least that was what she called herself. Her skin was as dark and rich as the soil, and her eyes were deep clear pools," the priest droned on, "The light of her skin glowed like the sun. Her hair cascaded and billowed behind her."

Glehson kept his eyes on the floor as Emily glared at him with a fixed stare. He feared making eye contact and focused on the maze-like lines of the floor's polished wood grain. The chanters transitioned into a faint humming sound before landing on a melodic, quiet chorus.

Emily turned away from the prince and studied the latecomers who Dou-Dodachi had seated on the left side of the room. Behind them, she spied two wide doorways.

"And as she stood amongst the downtrodden and wretched, there came a great wind from the four directions, followed by a tremendous gale, and the roar of thunder."

Emily could feel the empress's eyes burning into her and turned to meet them head-on with her own icy glare. To her chagrin, she saw an easy resemblance in her aunt's face with her own. They were indeed blood related.

"And her naked body was clothed by the rays of the sun, and she wore a crown of light with twelve spires upon her head, and the wicked wailed while the wretched rejoiced." The chorus of chanting priests' voices rose with Kem's monotonous delivery.

Their musical accompaniment to his tiring recital was the only thing keeping everyone from falling into slumber.

After nearly twenty more minutes of reading, Kem set down the heavy scroll and bowed to the empress, the dozen courtiers, and the crown prince.

Among them, a small, slender man in rich gold and green brocade stood and, speaking in a ceremoniously performative voice, said –

"And what proof confirms this child is the firstborn to the Oeki Ameiki of House Aiyo?"

A murmur spread throughout the room, even among the singing priests. Yet again, Emily thought it all seemed quite performative, as though they had prepared through hours of rehearsals and practiced this very event in case she ever reappeared in their world.

Dou-Dodachi stood, "I bear witness to the matter that this Shumaiyuki is the true Aiyo princess, daughter of our dear departed Oeki Ameiki and her husband in spirit, our own Minister Djowobb, first son of the House Zhon."

This revelation was followed by another round of performative murmuring and questions, to which Emily was certain everyone gathered already knew the identity of her father.

"And what proof do you offer aside from your word, good brother?" asked the slender man again, his silver-capped teeth glinting as he spoke.

"It is I who rescued her from certain death as she lay helpless and discarded on a winter road, not even a full month old."

Here, Dou-Dodachi approached Emily and held out his hand. She instinctively gave him the hairpin. The priest then bowed and presented it to the empress for inspection, saying, "This Aiyo heirloom was wrapped in the child's swaddling cloth when I found her."

"Why, this is truly the Pearl Swan. It was given to me by my mother, and I passed it on to Oeki when she was a girl," said Yumeiko.

The room erupted in excited whisperings and muted movements as the empress turned the hairpin over in her hands. She turned, only slightly, to regard the grouping seated behind her. "This is certainly the Shumaiyuki who was matched with the crown prince in this very room all those years ago."

Emily lightly cleared her throat and bowed, "I'm sorry, but I was born as Yu…"

"Silence!" Minister Djowobb slapped the floor.

Emily once again rallied to her feet and shouted, "You be silent! This is all a big shell game, isn't it? Obviously none of you are thinking about my interests! And you, sitting there acting all emo-boy, not saying a word!" She pointed an accusing finger at Glehson.

"That is because he knows the proper conduct when at temple," the empress's voice was like liquid nitrogen as she wrinkled her face.

"You know what? About an hour ago, I thought I could do this! At least for the sake of Becks and D! But you will all have me dead just like my mother! Who, by the way, named me Yuyuki! Not Shumaiyuki! And what's more," glaring at the prince, "I would never even date a jerk-off like you! Let alone marry you! We're cousins, you duplicitous asshole!"

The empress considered Emily with narrowed eyes and a cold smile. She was very serious, as if she had more important things to do than waste her time with a girl who rolled around on the floor and screamed obscenities at her.

"I'm not sure what game you are playing, but the time for games is over. You are an Aiyo princess and have a duty to…"

"Rilkian! My name is Rilkian. I'm sorry, Emily. I'm not as rotten as all that!" Glehson stood suddenly, his voice shaking as he dared to speak out over the empress. Even Minister Djowobb silently winced, holding his breath with his hands clasped before himself as he regarded the emperor's heir.

"Mother, please don't be angry with me. You are the empress, and I am but a mere vassal. But I wronged Emily through deception. I promise you, Emily, it wasn't for a lark." Rilkian bowed to Emily. "I hope someday you can forgive me."

The empress looked at her son as if he had sprouted antlers.

"Rilkian, don't you dare!" she said in an alarmed whisper.

"I'm sorry, Mother. Something must be done. I think it's only fair we let Emily share her thoughts on this too," he said.

The nobles gasped in shock and dismay. Emily looked at him curiously. Her cheeks warmed, and her heart pounded in her chest. She felt a small spark of excitement and fear. Nervous but exhilarated at the tension that was growing in the room.

The empress's eyes narrowed. She again silently gazed at Emily for what seemed a very long moment and then, with a disgusted look, she looked back at her son, who averted his eyes.

"Trust your own counsel, Your Highness. This is your birthright. But understand you have a duty to uphold the rules of the crown. Hardly anyone has ever been allowed to speak in the Dawn Room!" The empress's voice was icy cold. She then turned her eyes to Emily and continued.

"So please, princess, be very respectful and reverent. And choose carefully what you say next."

Emily looked at the empress's sharp, cold, and intimidating eyes. She felt small, as if made of doll parts, and that the woman could destroy her in a moment.

"Is that a threat?" she asked in a growling voice she hadn't ever heard come from her mouth. In a blinking moment, Djowobb had moved from his spot and stood directly in front of her, placing a hand on each of her shoulders.

Emily loathed his glare - malevolent and sharp. Like a tiger's eyes. She struggled to free herself of his grip. She could feel her cheeks burn. She felt her hands prickle and her palms sweat. She could feel herself becoming flushed, as well as hot and cold currents of anger and fear, resentment and excitement rushing through her.

She was being held hostage. An uninvited and unexpected party had hijacked her life and was forcing her to do something she didn't want to do. It was a horrible feeling. But she was determined she wasn't going to play their game.

"How dare you!" Yumeiko slapped her closed fan against the floor, but Emily persisted, struggling to free herself of Djowobb's grip.

"Oh, I do dare, Lady Macbeth! You don't scare me! Hah, empress! I didn't vote for you!" Emily said defiantly.

"My word, Minister Djowobb. She is just as wild as that other woodland urchin of yours," Yumeiko said in a low voice.

Emily looked in her father's face and saw that he was nearly as red as she must be; his ghastly scar and eyepatch didn't help.

He was angry, his lips were twisted in a frown of frustration, and his one eye was screaming at her.

"That's it! I'm out!" she said. And ripped herself from his arms and turned on her heels. "I won't do this!" Storming across the room, she pushed her way through the row of chanting priests, and, ignoring her father's calls, rushed out of the Dawn Room, almost tripping on her opulent robes.

The nobles placed their hands on their cheeks and sighed in silent dismay. Aiyo Yumeiko's eyes widened in surprise, and she again slapped her fan against the floor.

"Give me the room!" she ordered. The priests and courtiers began to amble out, but she cursed and slammed her fan again.

"Not you three! Stay," she said, pointing out Minister Djowobb, Lord Phule, and Dou-Dodachi, who seemed intent on blending in with the retreating monks.

When the room was clear, they all sat in silence for a long time, the three men gazing at the grainy wood on the floor. The prince looked irritated in his heavy robes. In contrast, Yumeiko was composed, simmering and serene.

When the silence had become unbearable, she finally spoke.

"I know these things are uncomfortable, but you must better control your seed, minister. The girl is utterly wild, isn't she? Perhaps I shall take her into my personal care and iron the savage out of her myself."

"If you'd been more understanding and flexible, maybe you could have helped her out. Maybe she would've stayed," said Rilkian.

The empress narrowed her eyes and snorted.

"She didn't run away from me. I was perfectly charming. She is clearly averse to her father." She looked at the prince's face and started to laugh.

"Don't laugh at me!" Rilkian stood. "You all think toying with people's lives is your right! It isn't!"

"You would have no life if not for me! Sit down before I have Madame Nanda deliver you another slap!"

"I'm going after Emily! We all owe her an apology!" Rilkian glided past them and left through the same door Emily had escaped through only moments before.

The empress's cold smile sank, and she sighed in shame. "I've done everything for that boy, and see how he behaves. The emperor feels I have crushed his spirit with procedure and rules. The rules of level and rank can be stupid. But they are the rules."

She stood and began pacing in front of the dais.

"He is overly emotional and acts as if he despises me, just like the noble houses do. But I have gone too far in trying to appease them. I have lost the love and respect of my only son," she said, dabbing beneath her eyes with a silk cloth, despite the absence of tears.

"I will live many more years, but I'm certain Rilkian will celebrate when I'm gone… Oh, Phule, have I failed? Have I failed in my duty? Have failed him?"

"Please, Your Highness, you are being much too hard on yourself," Phule offered halfheartedly. He knew the young prince's lack of respect went beyond any rules. The boy simply wanted to be left alone.

"You have been his mentor while the emperor has had little influence. Why haven't you better prepared him for his duty?"

"I am sorry, Your Grace, but," Phule stammered.

"And Yuyuki! She has been in your charge for days! Why haven't you instilled in her the knowledge of her place? It was as if you unleashed a wild beast in the room!"

"She will need some time to know herself, Your Grace."

"Oh, bloody details," Yumeiko sighed, slumping back onto the dais.

***

Emily roamed the temple's corridors, utterly lost and ignoring the beautiful carvings, furnishings, and decorations she was not used to seeing.

Out of frustration, she tore down her sculpted hair and began to scream. When she finished, she caught a glimpse of herself reflected off of a tall window.

She looked at her self, a mess of smeared dark makeup and tears, and then leaned into the image, letting her body slide down the cool glass surface until she was sitting on the floor.

She sat there with her knees to her chest, leaning against the glass, and cried. She cried until there were no tears left, until she was breathing heavily, and only a small wheezing sob escaped her thin, dark lips.

Rilkian came around a bend and looked relieved when he saw her. His relief quickly turned to concern when he noticed she was crying. As crown prince, he wasn't used to such high emotion in his presence. Then again, he had little experience with humans outside the imperial palace. Even when he occasionally escaped to wander the city, he felt alone in its crowded streets.

"Emily, are you well?" he inquired, kneeling beside her. He reached for her shoulder to offer comfort. She slapped his hand away and made a strange barking sound.

"Don't touch me! Just don't."

"I'm sorry. I only thought you'd like some company," Rilkian sighed and looked at the ground. "I was just worried and wanted to talk with you.I didn't mean to…" He trailed off as he felt his heart sink and his voice falter. "I'm sorry…Emily."

"I don't need anyone's sympathy, least of all from you! I'm leaving this crazy planet! Starting with finding my way out of this godforsaken temple!" she said.

“What? You can’t leave! It’s dangerous at night, and you don’t know your way around,” Rilkian’s eyes widened. Emily looked at her feet.

He was right; she had no idea where to go if she were to leave the temple.

“I’ll find my way; I know I will.”

Rilkian opened his mouth to speak, but she cut him off.

“Don’t bother. You don’t care, I know you don’t. You lied to me all day. I’m going to be alright. I just need to get out of here.”

“I want to leave sometimes too,” Rilkian said. “But this is my home, and my life is here.” He looked at her with wide eyes as he knelt in front of her. “I only approached you this morning under pretense because I wanted to meet the woman I was told I am to marry. I just wanted it to feel like I had some say in the matter. I’m sorry I hurt you. But today was the most special day of my life… spending it with you.”

He looked at her with half-closed eyes and his lips turned upwards in a semi-smile. He appeared as if he was about to kiss her. As he did so, she burst into tears and leaned forward to kiss him.

Rilkian pulled back, aghast. “What are you doing? Why would you do that again?!”

“Because you’re gaslighting me, and I know it freaks you out!” she said.

“Wait, what? No, I don’t know what that is.” He replied as he stood up and backed away from her.

“Oh, don’t be like that.” Emily sighed as she got to her feet and then wiped her tears from her face. “Gaslighting means you’re manipulating, lying to me. It’s not cool. Can’t you see that we’re in a similar situation? Clearly, you don’t like being told who to marry either!”

“Shouldn’t we talk, seriously? There’s a lot that needs to be said, and I feel like you are in denial,” Rilkian pleaded.

Emily pursed her lips and looked off into the distance at nothing.

"Okay, you're right. But I don't want to marry you. Apparently we are cousins. And aside from that! I don't want to be the wife of some pompous prince. When I marry, if I marry, I want it to be for love. Do you understand? I want to marry someone I can trust."

"Our blood ties are what bind us," he said. "You can trust me, Emily."

"I'm sorry. Am I speaking to Glehson or Rilycan?"

"It's pronounced Rilkian, and I'm not an untrustworthy pompous prince! I would love to escape my life and be Glehson every day if I could.

I just got up the nerve to talk to you because I wanted to be someone straightforward and noble for you. That's why I'm here now. I wanted you to know the truth."

"More gaslighting," said Emily.

"Come on, I'm not."

"Then why are you still here? If you really want to pursue a different life, you're in a better position to make it happen than I am… But instead, you're here in your fine and expensive clothes, moaning about how difficult your lavish life is."

She walked out onto a balcony that wrapped the temple in an elaborate exterior U shape. She looked out across the water, and stars filled the sky. She leaned her back against the wall and slid down to the floor where she sat under the dim light of a crescent moon.

Rilkian came over and sat beside her.

"What do you want?" Her tone was icy.

"I want to live in a shanty in the wilderness. I want to be a peasant," he smiled.

"No, you don't."

"Sometimes I do, but today…" He broke off and sighed.

"What?"

An awkward silence enveloped them. Rilkian looked up and pointed at a star.

"Do you see that star?" he asked. "It's Fulaiye."

"The one that burns twice as bright as the sun?" Emily asked.

"Yes, exactly," he smiled.

"I remember it," she replied. "That star burns bright because it was born very near a supernova. It was just formed from the remains of the parent star. It's like me," she said.

"What are you saying?" asked Rilkian. "What is a supernova?"

"A supernova is a star that violently explodes and then forms a black hole."

"It must be knowledge from your world?"

"Yeah, I get pretty good grades in science, but I'm not like a super STEM chick or anything."

Rilkian looked at Emily, and then his face dimmed as he turned to look at the bright star in the sky.

"Want to see something else? Come on." He grabbed her hand and helped her back to her feet. They walked back into the tower, but Emily winced and pulled away.

"Can't you see I want some time to myself?"

"I'm sorry, I shouldn't have grabbed your hand like that. But please, can you just trust me?" he asked.

He led her down a hallway and into a room that, with its domed ceiling, looked like an observatory. There were boxes of scrolls, tables with drawings, and instruments of various forms.

“See the markings here on the wall? They tell us the route the stars take across the sky,” Rilkian pointed out tiny markings in the dim light. “The priest etched them in. But that is not why I brought you here.”

He walked over to where the etched wall met the floor and leaned into the stone, and it gave way, revealing a hole in the floor beneath it. He jumped down into darkness.

Emily followed but paused when the edge vanished, and she looked down into pitch black.

“Just jump? I’m not sure if that’s a good move for me to make.”

“It’s not very deep at all. Don’t worry, I will catch you. I would never let you fall,” Rilkian’s voice echoed from the void.

Emily approached the opening with caution and perched herself on the edge. Rilkian assisted her as she carefully descended, holding her securely around the waist. Once they were both safely inside, Emily heard Rilkian moving about and the sound of two stones being struck together. In the next instant, the darkness was dispelled by the warm glow of a lit candle.

The room was tight and small with a stone floor, a wooden table, and a chair. In the corner was a cot set up with white sheets, a thick bolster, and a pillow. Next to the cot was a chest.

Another candle was set in an iron sconce that jutted from the wall. There was a spiral staircase cut into the stone which led downwards.

“What’s down there?” asked Emily.

Rilkian leaned in close and said, “The stairs lead down to the sewers, but we can navigate them to the city undetected.”

“The sewers?” Emily asked. “I’m not so sure about this.”

Rilkian smiled. “I escape the palace through the sewers all the time. Well, not just the sewers, but some sewer tunnels. It’s our way out.”

"What if it floods?"

Rilkian shook his head. "Nothing will flood. We are fine."

"How do you know? Maybe a flood will rise, and we will be washed away."

"Listen, I know what I'm doing. Trust me."

Emily gave a coy smile and said, "Trust you? For all I know, you're trying to kidnap me."

"I kinda am," Rilkian said. Emily recoiled, and he quickly added, "But I mean it differently. I mean I might kidnap you to rescue you."

"Really? You would rescue me if I was kidnapped?" She sounded skeptical.

"I'm trying to rescue you now," he said.

"Emily, you're the most beautiful girl. Every movement of yours is graceful, even when it isn't. You're intelligent and direct and…" he said as he threw his hands into the air.

"I cannot abide you being forced into marrying me or anyone else."

He took Emily by the hand and led her to the chest. He opened its lid and pulled out a clean shirt and a pair of loose-fitting pants with a flourish. He immediately began removing his clothes, moving quickly. Emily felt a warm flush rise to her face at his lack of modesty and the sight of his smooth, bronzed body.

He then grabbed another pair of pants and a shirt and pulled her over to the cot.

"These clothes will help you hide. They're men's clothes, but they are easier to maneuver in than women's robes," he said.

Emily looked over her shoulder, then back at Rilkian.

"I'm not getting undressed in front of you."

"I'll turn around if you like?"

"No! I don't even know you. I don't know if you are nice and are trying to save me or whether you are some kind of perv trying to get alone with me…"

"What do your instincts tell you?" He asked sternly.

Emily looked into his eyes. She felt a magnetic pull drawing her in. Her memories from Behra were spotty but she did have them, distant memories of the boy who stood before her as a now a man. There was something peculiar about him that stirred in her a sense of wanting to belong to his world.

She tried to reason with herself but, maybe this was a good thing. She knew he wasn't a bad or evil man. Whatever was going on inside her head. Whatever was happening, he felt right. He seemed genuine, and she didn't feel nearly as threatened as she let on. She decided to give it a shot.

"Let's do this."

"Great! Please get dressed. Or do you need help with your robes?"

"They are a bit cumbersome," said Emily, "It took five maids to dress me. So, are we really doing this? All of a sudden, you're going to help me?"

"I owe you, don't I?"

"But where will we go? I don't have anyone here. Plus, my friends are…"

"Let's take it one step at a time," said Rilkian. "First, we get you out of here. Then we can decide where to go from there. Earlier, Dodachi mentioned the wizened woman to my mother. If she's responsible for bringing you here, then perhaps I can help you find her, and she can send you back home."

"And what about you? What will happen to you?"

"They can live without me for a few days, or however long it takes to find her."

"You'll have to marry the real Shumaiyuki then. And I hear she's a real piece of work."

"You have such a way with words, Emily," he said, smiling. He began to help her take off her obi and outer robe. She wore a short silk gown underneath and smiled awkwardly, feeling suddenly exposed. She shyly stepped around her discarded robes, watching his eyes follow her every movement.

"I need you to remember you are a boy?"

"A very handsome one," Rilkian said with a wink.

Emily blushed. "You're completely hopeless!"

It took several minutes to get Emily out of her robes and dressed in the local attire. But once ready, they started down the stairs in silence as they descended into the smells of the sewer.

He took a torch that was affixed to the wall of the stairwell and lit it. As they descended, its light danced flickering shadows across his face.

"The others are probably already looking for us. It is well past midnight," he said.

The stairs went down the length of the temple, terminating at a locked iron gate. He removed a needle like rod from his belt and pushed it into the small keyhole on the grate. It clicked and the grate swung open.

They squeezed through the opening and moved along a narrow ledge to a larger tunnel beyond. Although they were beneath a tower, Emily could see a stream of water flowing through the cavern. Brightly colored stalactites and stalagmites dotted the ceiling of the strange underground landscape.

"It's so dark," Emily said. "It's good we have the torch."

"Don't worry, I know where we are going," said Rilkian. "Careful of your step or you'll get stuck. This path can be tricky, but it will lead us back to the surface."

Emily followed, nervously placing her hand on his shoulder. The only sounds were their footsteps, a trickling of the water, and the crackling of the torch. The stench of the sewer seemed to grow in intensity with each step they took. Emily wrinkled her nose, and Rilkian said,

"It's horrid, but you'll get used to the smell."

"It's more than just the smell. I can taste it in my mouth." She gagged.

"But can you breathe ok?" Rilkian asked, his voice muted by the tunnel.

"Yeah, fine," Emily said. He looked back, and their eyes met across the darkness. She felt a warm sensation in her chest, but the heat was also making her sweat beneath her clothes.

As they walked through the winding tunnels, Emily began to lose her sense of direction. Eventually, they came to a bend where the path split. Rilkian stopped and put his hands on his hips, letting out a long sigh.

"We're not too far now," he said.

They continued until they found an old, cramped pump room with rusted metal cogs and pistons. Rilkian pointed to a stairway in the corner of the room that led up to the street. They climbed the stairs and emerged onto a quiet, cobbled road at the edge of the city.

Emily took a deep breath, savoring the clean air. "It's good to breathe fresh air," Rilkian commented.

"Yeah, it is," Emily replied, grateful to have escaped the suffocating atmosphere of the tunnels.

They resumed walking, and Rilkian led the way back towards the city. They passed by wooden buildings that looked old and derelict and crumbling stone walls, but as they walked further, Emily sensed something unsettling about the area. The fresh air she had breathed earlier was replaced by the smell of decay and rotting food. Despite her uneasiness, she tried to push the feeling away.

They passed several people on the street who seemed intent on minding their own business. Emily could hear their voices speaking in strange dialects, but they barely glanced at her and Rilkian as they passed by.

As they walked, they passed a woman carrying a small child on her hip. The child looked up at Emily and grimaced before they continued on. Suddenly, Emily began to feel spooked. She heard growling in the distance, perhaps two dogs fighting. She also heard a baby crying, followed by high-pitched screaming and the sound of something heavy hitting the ground. The noises were out of place, too loud to be outside noises at that late hour. Rilkian's hand on her shoulder brought her back to reality, and she looked up at him.

"Are you okay?" he asked, noticing the distressed look on Emily's face.

"Huh?" she asked, her mind still reeling from the strange noises and unsettling atmosphere.

"You looked like you were going to be sick," Rilkian said, concern etched on his face.

"I'm okay," Emily replied, trying to shake off the feeling of unease. "Just a little freaked out. Where are we?"

"We're in Toren Town, the slummiest area of the city," Rilkian explained. "It's the last place anyone looking for us would think to look."

He led her down a vague off-road path, and after a few blocks, the buildings began to thin out. They turned onto a crumbled road that was not the same one they had come on.

After another block, the road was completely overgrown with rough patches of browning weeds.

Emily glanced behind them and saw four shadowy figures wearing hooded robes and masks milling about. “Rilkian, look behind us!” she exclaimed. “We have to run!” She pulled him to the right down a disintegrated sidewalk, and they jolted through a dark alley without looking back.

Emily’s heart pounded, and she gasped for breath. Ahead of them, the walls were jagged and black, but between them, they caught the light from a distant fire.

Without a word, Emily and Rilkian jumped over a fence and sprinted down the road towards a large crowd dancing around a bonfire. The thick, smoky air was easier to breathe here, and the sounds of music, laughter, and footsteps engulfed them.

Emily looked back once again but saw that the hooded figures were gone. “Who were they?” she shouted over the heavy percussion of a tribal beat.

“I don’t know,” Rilkian replied. “There are all sorts of bandits and gangs in these parts. But let’s lose ourselves in the crowd just in case.”

The happy, tipsy partygoers approached Emily and Rilkian with smiles, offering them drinks and urging them to join in the festivities. After much coaxing, the two youths shook off the feeling of being pursued and joined in on the fun.

They plunged into the festivity, dancing and drinking with the crowd. They lost themselves to the dim thumping bass and the heat of the fire. Soon, they were resting by the bonfire, breathing heavily. Talking had become difficult, but they managed to catch their breath.

“Thanks for bringing me here,” Emily said, smiling at Rilkian.

“The pleasure is mine,” Rilkian replied, grinning back. “I figured you needed to unwind.”

Emily wasn’t sure where she stood with Glehson, or Rilkian, as she now knew was his real name, but she was enjoying his company much more than she wanted. She could go on dancing with him, away from her troubles and the mystery of tomorrow that was beyond their reach.

A girl caught Emily's eye and Emily smiled back at her. "This is great!" she exclaimed. "It's like what we call a rave where I'm from."

Rilkian was slightly inebriated, with a wide smile plastered across his face. The night's events were swirling in his head and he was enjoying every moment of it.

"Even better than a rave," Emily continued, but she realized that he was starting to drift off. She gave him a few shakes, not yet ready to end the night but becoming concerned about where they would sleep.

"Hey, maybe we should get out of here and figure out where we're going to spend the night," she suggested.

"Yeah, you're right," Rilkian replied, glancing around. "I'm sure there are plenty of cheap accommodations here in Toren." His words slurred a bit, and he grinned sheepishly.

"You don't get out much, do you?" Emily asked.

"This isn't my first bonfire! I came once before, alone," he replied.

"I bet you did!" she said, laughing. "Well, it's a first for me, and it's been fab!"

"If that's what you call it," he said with a smile.

Emily gazed into the fire's reflection in his eyes, feeling a magnetic pull towards him. He wrapped his muscular arms around her, and she felt the heat flowing through her from his touch.

She could feel the world around her softening and melting away, and she wanted his lips on hers as she looked into his eyes. She pulled away, fighting her rising blush.

"We should go," she said.

Taking his hand, she led them back out into the smoky air through the festive crowd.

After some time, they came upon a smaller group gathered around a woman serving a burgundy punch from a large wooden canteen.

"… And the Sprocket folk have been throwing parties in this very mew for forty years," she heard a gray-haired man say. Behind them, musicians slapped djembe skins, and people danced. Emily smiled and drank a cup of punch from a wooden cup. She found the warm elixir was pleasant .

"I wonder how much longer this will go on." Rilkian said, taking another swig.

"I guess the it will be over when we all pass out. That may not be too long from now," Emily giggled and leaned into him. He put his arm around her as they strolled.

She felt a bit light-headed, but she didn't mind. It was a nice feeling, not heavy like the beer from the previous night. Plus, it had been a long time since she had been to a big party, and none had been like the bonfire rave.

"I don't know," Rilkian said, slurring a bit. "The fire doesn't look like it's dying out, and more people seem to be arriving. I'm just lucky I get to dance with the prettiest girl here," he pulled her in for another hug.

"Ah," Emily said, "Well, before the night is over, despite how it began, I'm glad it happened. I mean… I guess I'm happy we met even though it was under false pretenses."

"This night can never end," Rilkian said. He looked so happy it broke Emily's heart, for she knew it would have to.

"Well, tonight might be the last night that either of us will indulge ourselves so much," she said.

"Perhaps… maybe, but that doesn't mean we can't enjoy it now."

Emily considered his words for a moment, as if it were possible for the night to go on indefinitely.

“I don’t want to go back home to the palace,” Rilkian said softly into her ear.

They rejoined the swaying crowd and danced to the percussive beat, as it transitioned into a slow rhythm. Emily forgot everything else. As they danced, the fire roared.

Before she realized what was happening, Rilkian pulled her close, leaned in, and kissed her. The sensation of his lips touching her’s was electric. Rilkian’s full lips were soft and warm and sent chills throughout her whole body. His tongue pulled her lips into him and massaged them, and she felt her arms go limp.

She could smell the leather of his vest, the scent of woodsmoke, and the sweat of the masses. Her head swirled from the sweet taste of the punch. Their kiss lingered, and for a moment, the world around them melted away.

“Won’t people think we’re scandalous?”

Rilkian looked around but saw only happy faces.“I don’t think anyone cares here! I know I don’t!”

“I think that’s because you’re drunk.”

“I’ve had my first, second, and third kiss all in one day, and they were all with you!” he exclaimed as he leaned in for another.

“I think it’s made me a little barmy!” The excitement and intensity of the moment were palpable, and he seemed eager to experience more.

Emily found the pace of events overwhelming. Despite her growing attraction to Rilkian, she felt that things were moving too quickly. The truth was, she barely knew him.

They had been betrothed as children, but she couldn’t shake the feeling that they were only using each other as a distraction from their own pain.

This realization doused the flames of her feelings, and she pulled away, pretending to sneeze as a pretext for breaking the moment.

Rilkian brought his hand up and caressed her cheek, softly running his fingers through her hair. "You're quite lovely," he said. "Very, very lovely."

"And you're very charming," she giggled, feeling the world spin. She leaned into him, and they stood like that for some time as the music and laughter danced around them.

After another hour of festivities, both had to admit they were tired and hungry. They walked toward a line of revelers munching away at cart foods. The smell of roasted meat had never been so enticing. Emily chose a kebab of grilled pheasant and a hunk of sourdough toast with butter.

After eating and feeling satiated, they began to exit the party towards a dark cobbled alleyway heading to the center of town.

"Where are we going?" she asked.

"The square," he said. "To find a room for the night."

They turned down an alley, the light of the bonfire casting long shadows between the dark, narrow streets. Emily was suddenly anxious. She didn't know if it was the excitement of the night or the fear of what was to come.

"I had a great time with you tonight, Emily. Honestly, I am quite taken with you," Rilkian said, taking her hand.

"Yeah, I think I'm falling for you too, but… It's just… I don't think its right," she said and sighed, "I mean, we're family, right? Oh, things are just happening too fast. Whoa!" she said as she stumbled.

He steadied her and held her close. "Let's find proper lodging first. Then we'll…" Rilkian glanced around them. Two hooded figures entered the alley. Two other figures blocked the exit to the street.

"Emily, get behind me!" Rilkian drew a dagger.

He turned to the men. They wore tattered rags and long black hoods. It was dark out, and the light from the bonfire had dimmed. Rilkian felt panic race through his veins.

"What do you want?" he demanded, waving the dagger in front of him.

"Hmm, a delicious mistake…." one said in a deep voice. The two separated; one man walked toward them tossing a short blade from hand to hand. The other circled Rilkian to his left in an attempt to outflank him. Rilkian's eyes grew wide. He was not ready for this.

The tension grew. Emily's heart thudded in her chest. What would these men do to them? She turned back and looked down the alley. The others hadn't moved.

"I don't want any trouble," her voice quavered, "We don't have anything of value."

"I'm not here for possessions, pretty lass. I'm here for that sweet head of yours."

"Woah!" Rilkian shouted as the man rushed him. He brought the dagger up, but the man was faster.

Rilkian swung his knife but missed his mark while his attacker threw a punch, clipping him on the side of his head. Emily screamed as the other man grabbed her from behind and wrapped her in a bear hug.

Rilkian kicked at the man in front of him and tried to grab him but missed again. With a swift swing of his arm, he recovered and swiped at the man's throat but was punched in his upper chest and knocked back to the ground.

"What are you gonna do, little girl?" the other man said, squeezing Emily. I will deliver your pretty head to my mistress," he said as he secured an arm around her throat.

Emily screamed, kicking, struggling, and scratching at the man's arm. "No!" she screamed again, tugging, and pulling at his arm.

Rilkian brought himself up, dagger in hand, and slashed at the man's shoulder. Then came a low but distinctive whistle, "Ka-kuwa-koo," it elicited a strange familiarity in Emily. It was a sound like that of a griffon sphinx, a sound she had often heard when she was a little girl.

The attacker who had circled around Rilkian lunged forward as the whistling started up again. Rilkian took a step back, his position impaired. The man slammed into him, flinging his arms out and causing Rilkian to fall back, the dagger flying from his hands.

"On the roof!" the man blocking their exit from the alley shouted, pointing overhead.

Emily looked up to see a solitary figure silhouetted against the thin sliver of crescent moon. His loose robes looked like those of a monk, and he held a small, pointed staff. A hooded cloak cast a concealing shadow across his face, revealing only pale eyes and a sharp nose outlined against the night sky.

"What are you doing up there? We were here first; these are our bounty!" the man holding Emily said.

"I think not. Release her. Give me the girl, or you will all die here."

"Friend," the man tightened his grip on Emily, "I have a knife at her throat."

As the man spoke, the shadows on the roof seemed to stir. Suddenly, the cloaked figure appeared behind him with extraordinary speed, driving the pointed end of their staff into his head. The man's body crumpled to the ground as the figure withdrew the staff; the moonlight illuminated the bright blood as it dripped from the blunt metal.

Free from the fallen man's grip, Emily ran to Rilkian and grabbed his hand. The attackers quickly gathered around their fallen comrade before disappearing, leaving behind only a few broken bricks and streaks of blood as evidence of their presence. The cloaked figure made no attempt to pursue them.

"Thanks. Um, I'm Glehson, and this is Emily," he bowed, but the man failed to return the gesture.

"You don't have to be grateful," he said. "I do not work for you. I do not need your thanks."

"Seitogi. How long have you been following us?" Emily asked shyly.

"Long enough," he replied. He knelt down and picked up Glehson's dagger. He stood up and walked towards them, handing it to him.

"Come, Glehson. You're bleeding," he said as he walked towards the end of the alleyway.They followed him slowly. Seitogi stopped at a narrow and dark passage that led to a squat building.

"In here."

They entered the building and sat on clay bricks as Seitogi attended to the prince's wound, a light gash on his forearm.

"You must not purposefully put yourself or others in harm's way. You are weak in the ways of kill craft."

"The man was skilled beyond that of a common thug," Glehson replied as Seitogi pulled out a clean strip of cloth.

"But I fought him off still."

"Is it a bad cut?" Emily asked. Her face stained with tears.

"A puncture wound. It'll heal." Glehson kept his arm out as Seitogi took another strip of cloth and wrapped it around.

"So, what was the plan here?" Seitogi asked and tightened a knot. "Why would you be wandering the city, intoxicated around vagrants? Enoshi could have been harmed!"

"I have no idea who you're referring to," Glehson replied coolly. Just then, a low and powerful horn echoed through the alleyways, its source seemingly far off.

"It seems like your little gathering is coming to a close," Seitogi noted, changing the subject. "Glehson, how do you know Enoshi?" The tone of the conversation had shifted, and Seitogi was now focused on the prince.

"Enoshi?" Glehson appeared puzzled, and Seitogi gestured towards Emily and repeated the name. "Enoshi."

"He works at Phule's house," Emily explained. "In the stables." She stood protectively between the two men.

"How would a stable hand come to possess a ghost steel dagger? Are you a thief as well?"

"I could ask the same of you," Glehson countered.

Seitogi leaned in, nose to nose, staring at the prince. "What possessed you to take her from the safety of Gah?"

"While I am indebted to you, sir, that business is none of yours to question."

"Your stable-hand," Seitogi cut his eyes back to Emily. "Enoshi. Come with me. Let the stable-hand be on his way and return to his master."

"But?" She looked at Glehson.

"Look, I owe Emily! I helped her escape so that we could find the wizened woman and return her home. With your commendable skill, I would pay handsomely should you escort us in our endeavor."

"You are a fool," said Seitogi as he turned to walk back outside. "You'll think much better of it when you sober up."

"Wait," he took out a pouch of coins, "Take my purse." He handed it to Seitogi.

"You may keep your money, but she will come with me."

"I'm not leaving her side," Glehson forced the purse into Seitogi's hand.

"I am not going to be responsible for protecting you too," Seitogi opened his palm and dropped the purse to the ground. "You would only slow us down."

"Slow us down! Where are we going?" asked Emily. "Because I'm not going anywhere without Glehson! He's risking a lot to help me! What are you doing?"

"I just saved your life right now!"

"O.k. fine. 15-love to you! But that doesn't mean I would just ghost my friend! Look at him! He's hurt!"

"Looks like you're the one responsible for his injuries. He was protecting you, right?"

"What's with all the shade?"

"He could've gotten you killed back there! If I hadn't got there in time! Now I have a job to do, and I don't have time for this! You're coming with me, and that's all there is to it!" said Seitogi as he walked back into the passageway.

Glehson and Emily hurried after him. The passage opened back onto an alley lined on one side with empty crates, stacked up in neat rows. They ran through the maze-like corridors as Seitogi led the way.

"What job?" Emily repeated, her voice rising in frustration. "Seitogi, slow down, where are we going?"

"Will you both just shut up?" Seitogi stopped in his tracks and faced them, holding out his arm. "The job is to get you back to Arth. The only person I could think of that would offer us safe sanctuary and a lead on the wizened woman's whereabouts is your sister."

"My sister? But you said yourself that she wants me dead!" Emily exclaimed; her face twisted in confusion.

"I am not talking about the Golden Swan. I'm referring to the Laughing Lark," Seitogi replied.

"Laughing Lark?"

"My former boss, Arymaitei," said Seitogi.

Emily involuntarily shuddered at the mention of the name Arymaitei.

Seitogi shrugged. "She's brash, mean, and petty, but she would welcome and protect you."

"What about my friends?" Emily asked anxiously.

"We'll discuss them when we arrive at Meriwall, her compound about a day and a half north of here," Seitogi replied. "But first, we need to find horses. So kindly hand back over that purse, stable boy."

The Laughing Lark

Emily woke up drenched in sweat as early evening light streamed through the windows. She had no idea how long she had slept. She sat up and blinked a few times, then looked around.

She was lying in a plain room with white walls, a small mattress under her, and a few odd pieces of furniture to her left and right. She turned back to the window. It had bars, which she assumed were to keep someone from breaking in.

She yawned and stretched her body to get it moving. The past two days she had been lost in a daze, but she grinned all the same, remembering the thrill and excitement of the journey rather than concentrating on particulars.

She paused, taking another look around the room, like a child in an unfamiliar place.

"What was that dream I was having? Who the hell is Eleanor?"

Haunted by the dream, she had a sense of being out of her body and playing an observer in another person's life. She looked toward the window. The sun was setting. Its orange glow filled the entire space, like a painter had placed it there as a backdrop.

The citrus hue faded slightly as the sunset took over. She sat for a moment, almost meditative. She got up and made her way over to the far wall.

There was a wooden board with hooks and hangers. To her delight hung her capris, t-shirt, and hoodie.

She began undressing, throwing her Behranian clothes onto the floor. Her body reeked of stale sweat, and she sighed alongside a yawn while absently humming a pop tune. She began to dress when she heard –

"Did you sleep well? You don't look all that refreshed."

Emily swung around, stumbling as her eyes settled on a young woman sitting across from her. She was comely in appearance, draped in a finely threaded, peach colored silk gown, sheer enough to expose her nude body underneath.

She sat cross-legged, her hands resting on her inner thighs. Her eyes were a sapphire green, which contrasted beautifully with her dark, terracotta skin. Her fiery auburn hair, however, was cut short, pixie-like, and with a ratty top knot for a crown, in direct contradiction with her elegance.

She looked Emily over, a long glance down and then back up that made Emily feel self-conscious.

"Relax, no one here will ask anything of you," she said lazily, a mischievous look in her eyes. She remained motionless next to a small wooden table with a vase of dry flowers sitting on it, and a large door to her right.

"You look like you could use a meal. You were pretty smacked when you arrived last night, and now you've slept right through the day. You need something to soak up all that alcohol."

"Oh, I wasn't drunk at all, I just had a few sips." Emily took a step back, slightly confused. She was having trouble shaking her hangover and absorbing the shock of her new surroundings. She looked from the girl to the door, to the window, then back with a confused frown.

"I'm sorry. Would you mind if I freshen up?"

"Of course not. If you need assistance, you need only ask. I'll be right here."

"Have you been sitting there watching me all night?" Emily asked while looking around the room.

The girl laughed and replied, "I'm usually the one keeping an eye on things around here, particularly my guests."

Her response bothered Emily a little. The girl didn't look bothered at all, and it seemed like she enjoyed having the upper hand, which made Emily especially uneasy.

"Don't worry about what I do," the girl said, smiling. "It's my job to make sure nobody goes anywhere they shouldn't."

Emily didn't catch what she meant, but it unsettled her to a degree. The young woman seemed too at ease and comfortable, as if this room was her home. Each passing moment made her more and more uncomfortable.

Emily took her time, partly to calm her nerves. She walked over to the vase of flowers and looked at them.

"They've been dying since the sun's descent," the girl said, offering an explanation. "They'd be much more beautiful if they lived forever. But this particular species dies every night and rises again at dawn."

"I've never heard of such a thing."

"I do hate things that return from the dead when they shouldn't," she continued. "But then they are so beautiful. It would be a shame to snuff them out before they've had a chance to fulfill their purpose. What's your purpose, sister?" she asked with a deep ear-to-ear smile.

"Oh – fug, Arymaitei." Emily sighed, recalling her arrival at Meriwall the night before with Seitogi and Glehson. She held onto the table with one hand and massaged her temple with the other. It was as if she suddenly felt the effects of the ale more than ever.

Arymaitei laughed, a loud, cackling sort of tone that seemed to be mocking Emily, though in a playful manner. Emily's eyes narrowed, and she looked at her sister, dumbstruck.

Arymaitei rose from the table. She was a tall girl, perhaps 5'9", and started to walk towards the door, with Emily following her.

"Wait. I must talk to you," she said.

"Let us go find Seita and get you fed," Arymaitei replied with a short laugh. She gave a slight nod in the direction of the door. "I'm glad you are finally awake. We have so much catching up to do."

Emily walked as if in a fog, desperately searching her mind for the memory of how they arrived in this new place. After departing Domotedai, she, Glehson, and Seitogi traveled a variety of terrain, ranging from the edge of a cliff to a large meadow, to the forest floor. It was exhausting, to say the least, but they trudged on.

Having secured the horses, Seitogi took on the role of their unofficial leader despite being upset that Emily refused to ride with him. He rode ahead, constantly checking his compass and remaining vigilant for any sounds or movements.

Glehson and Emily shared an old taupe-colored horse for their journey with Emily sitting front saddle and he behind her holding the reins. As soon as Seitogi was out of sight, he cleared his throat and took a deep breath to hold back the heat creeping up his cheek. He wished he wasn't sitting so close to her; she smelled like flowers, grass, and dew. It was intoxicating.

"I had no idea you had another sister. Were you two close?" he asked as he gently leaned over to grip the reins. Emily scowled, nearly forgetting the question until Glehson repeated, "Another sister?"

"Oh, sorry. It's all been coming back to me in a rush since reconnecting with my…Minister Djowob, Yienguoi-Jin, whatever. But, from what I can remember, I was only with her for five or six months.

I didn't know her very well," Emily said, and then, "You are aware of who my father really is, or perhaps, who he was is the better way to put it?"

"I admit I found out recently from Lord Phule himself. I have to say I was shocked that Minister Djowobb was the famed Yienguoi-Jin."

"I only have a few memories," said Emily. Glehson looked at her skeptically.

"I don't know how much you know about the circumstances of my birth, but according to my Obánā, when I was eight, she caught wind of a plot conceived by those loyal to Duke Sahyuh to murder me so that his daughter, Shumaiyuki, would be the one who married you. Shortly after, my father infiltrated Odahni and rescued me from certain death. From there, we traveled many days until we reached his mountain lair."

"You must have been terrified."

"Funny thing, I wasn't. I remember being excited to be away from the castle. I saw so many interesting things and people along the way. Plus, I knew Yienguoi-Jin was my real father. I had met him a few years before with Seitogi."

"Seitogi?"

"Seitogi…he and I were reunited at Yienguoi-Jin's lair," Emily blushed, "I was so happy to see him, but I'll never forget the frowning little girl standing right behind him. Arymaitei, about a year younger than me. My father's daughter with his wife, that gap-toothed woman. Awei Chua, she and Ary hated me."

"Hated? Arymaitei hated you? Why?"

"Sorry, hate is probably too strong a word to use, but I remember, no, they definitely weren't happy I was there. It was an awkward situation." Emily laughed, "Yienguoi-Jin spent a lot of time with me, so did Seita. We'd train together, hunt."

"I think he had plans for me to become a Dhukai and join the Taisehsai. Ary and her mother felt neglected. I remember the two of them…Awei, I remember her and my dad arguing about me. It didn't help that until I reappeared in Seitogi's life, Ary was always by his side."

"I am sorry you had to go through that. You certainly didn't ask for it though, did you?"

"No, I didn't," Emily said, smiling, "But I suppose I did get to know her some, and we even became friends…kind of. We were kids, you know."

"You did. Must've been nice," Glehson replied. Emily could tell he was trying to hold back a smile.

"My sisters and I are raised in different parts of the palace. We only see each other on birthdays and holidays."

"I'm sorry to hear that. I feel so bad for you."

"Please don't. We are good friends just the same."

"Lucky you. It's better than having one sister trying to kill you."

"It sounds like you've had a very interesting life, Emily."

"It's gotten more interesting since I've met you."

The two continued their conversation as the day wore on. Glehson learned that Emily considered herself a hard worker, but socially awkward and not very good with people in general, yet he found her kind and understanding.

Emily learned he was studious and emotional, and perhaps a little too brave for his own good. By the time Seitogi returned from scouting ahead, both of them were deep in conversation, one that reminded Emily of conversations with Darren back when they first began dating. He had been so open back then.

Seitogi noticed and frowned. "Are you two enjoying yourselves?"

"You seem troubled," Glehson looked at him, confused.

"You two are talking so much you'll call attention to us. I could hear every word." He paused and looked up at the sky as if trying to figure out what was missing.

"A few miles ahead, we'll be passing through some sketchy places. I need you two to be alert."

"What do you mean 'sketchy places'?" Emily asked, not trying to hide her unease.

"We're leaving the realm of the emperor's guard and entering the bandit lands. Anything goes. That's why it's called the land of vengeful spirits. Out here, gangs are everywhere. We must be careful and aware of what's going on around us."

They continued south through small towns and villages that were once living and prosperous but now occupied by hundreds of lost souls. Each village they passed through the streets were mostly empty, and the only sound was from their horses' trotting hooves.

Emily thought it would not be a good idea to walk in those areas at night. She could not shake the uneasy feeling in her stomach; she imagined they were being watched by unseen eyes.

Later they stopped to take a short break in an open field, eating savory rice balls and ale. It was midday, and they were exhausted. Emily would have liked to spend more time there, but Seitogi was anxious to reach Meriwall. She looked to the sky and sighed, "A couple more hours." She looked over to Glehson and smiled; he smiled back.

"Everything will be fine. At least I hope so," she thought.

As evening fell, the towering trees became thicker, as did the fog. They passed common folks here and there, the roads busy with travelers. The sun was beginning to set. Emily and the two continued on riding until the trees grew so close together they had to dismount and walk their steeds.

Darkness fell and an eerie fog pressed down around them as they searched for the right road. Fatigue and cold set in as they passed the remainder of the ale between them to keep warm.

Seitogi was exhausted, but he led them the right way, "A few miles more," he said.

And several miles later out of nowhere, a large pack of ragged men brandishing weapons appeared, blocking the path and making their intentions known. Glehson yelled out for them to back off, but Seitogi raised his hand and said,

“Stand down, it’s me! And I have guests who are cold and hungry.” Seitogi dismounted and stretched his limbs.

“Oh, Seita! You’ve finally come back! I was so worried about you!”

Arymaitei sprung from within the group of men like a jack-in-the-box and flung herself into Seitogi’s arms, sending them both sprawling to the ground.

“I’ve missed you so much, Seita, um, darling.” She wrapped her arms around him, pulled his face into her breast, and groaned with pleasure. Emily dropped her head to look away, and Glehson stared on, flabbergasted.

“So, she’s Arymaitei?” he whispered. “She’s a bundle of energy, isn’t she?”

“More like a ‘jump scare’ in the flesh,” Emily looked up and rolled her eyes as the men made fun and laughed at the humiliating sight of their leader embracing one of their own.

Arymaitei straightened up, wiped the dirt from Seitogi’s clothes, and with a smile on her face, said,

“You’re in a lot of trouble. My mother has put a bounty on your head. Says you killed over half a dozen of her men.”

“Tell Chua I didn’t kill anyone who wasn’t trying to kill me.” Seitogi tried to get up, but she pushed him back down and chuckled lightly,

“That’s a good one. You think she’ll buy that, even if it’s true?”

Seitogi stared into Arymaitei’s eyes, “You know I’m telling the truth, don’t you?”

“Of course, I do, Seita,” she answered, pulling him to a standing position and leaning in to whisper in his ear.

“I can see that you are going to be honest, even to the bitter end, Seita. That’s good. Too many liars nowadays,” she said. “I won’t turn you in, but I’m afraid my mother won’t forgive you so easily, and neither will anyone else in her Dhukai. I cannot change your destiny. Not this time.”

Scitogi frowned and tried to collect his thoughts. He began to explain, “Let them come then. I have more important matters to attend to,” he said, stretching his legs with a few slow kicks.

Arymaitei shrugged her shoulders, “And I see you’ve brought along a familiar stranger,” she nudged her chin at Emily.

“I beg your pardon, Arymaitei. You remember Enoshi, uh, Yuyuki. We need your help.” He gestured towards Emily and Glehson.

“Ah.” Arymaitei smirked, taking her time to look the pair over. Glancing towards Seitogi, she added,

“You look a mess, by the way. Have you been sick?”

“I’ve been fine.”

“I think not. You must be suffering from some kind of fever to bring Awei’s stolen bounty here to Meriwell. And who is this boy with such fine features?”

Her tone annoyed Emily, and she began to wonder how Seitogi could ever think she would help them.

“It’s been a long time, Yuyu,” she brushed past Seitogi and walked up to Emily, who was shorter than her by an inch.

“Well, you’re the talk of the town, aren’t you?” she added.

“Stop calling me Yuyu,” Emily said, slurring her words just a bit.

Arymaitei smiled, “I’m sorry. Have you been in the cups? And in the company of men?” she took Emily’s chin in her hand.

“You are a bold one, aren’t you, princess?”

Emily tried to brush away from her sister's grasp, but Arymaitei held her chin tight.

"Ahh. And a feisty one. I like that. You haven't changed much either."

"Stop teasing me, Ary! I don't feel well, and I want to lie down," Emily slapped the girl's hand away and moved in for a hug. Arymaitei pulled her into her arms, and Emily laid her limp head on her sister's shoulder.

"You spoiled brat!" she stroked Emily's hair. "It seems you've been getting into places you shouldn't have been lately!" said Arymaitei. "What happened to you? How have you been?" She stood back some to inspect Emily.

"Never been better…" Emily suddenly felt exposed under the gaze of her sister. She remembered Arymaitei as a snaggle-toothed girl, not this womanly figure whose height and curves made her feel like a skinny child in comparison.

Arymaitei simply nodded and pulled back, "Hmm, I see…that bad, huh?" she held both Emily's hands in hers. "I'm going to get you cleaned up. You need to eat, put some warmth in your body. We'll talk later."

She turned back to Seitogi with a serious look on her face, "We must talk more about you not obeying me and working for that witch. She must have promised you something you couldn't resist."

Seitogi remained silent; he simply shrugged his shoulders. Arymaitei went about issuing orders to her men about guest accommodations and where their horses would be kept. She motioned for Seitogi to follow her, and he did.

Emily turned her head to speak to Glehson and found him staring at her nervously. She tried to smile, but she was so tired she could barely move a muscle in her face.

"Are you really daydreaming just after waking up?" Arymaitei stood by the door, waiting. Emily shook herself out of her thoughts and apologized.

“Come along then. Let us take a meal.”

Arymaitei led Emily down a warmly lit hall; her flowing robe billowed softly behind her, and her steps made barely any sound.

“Hey, are you just going to walk around in public wearing that?” Emily asked, embarrassed. “I shouldn’t even have to ask, but don’t you have any other clothes?”

“My evening gown is fine,” Arymaitei answered, suddenly stopping. “The night holds on to the humidity of the day in these parts, and I prefer comfort over modesty. Do you not like it? I had it made in Domotedai.”

Emily rolled her eyes, “Well, it is a nice color,” she said. “You look pretty in it and all. But, honey, I can see all your bits. And so can anyone else.”

“My bits,” Arymaitei responded. “Well then, you shouldn’t look. Here in Behrani, we do not trifle over such things,” she said with a little smile.

With that, Arymaitei glided back towards her, “Come. I want to get to know you a little better,” she placed her arm around Emily’s shoulders. Emily was tired and didn’t resist.

“Seitogi tells me the witch Maishea sent you to another world and that he went there to visit you. I had no idea he could do such a thing. Is it true?” She asked as they walked. More memories began coursing through Emily’s mind; she warned herself that Arymaitei was a crafty one.

“Yes. To both. Just as Seitogi told you.”

“Oh, he is such a chatterbox. We talked in my chambers all night. I barely got any sleep if you can imagine.” Arymaitei raised an eyebrow and tilted her head a little.

“Were you wearing that little see-through get-up the whole time you two were talking?” Emily suspected Arymaitei was being petty and was in no mood for it.

“Oh well. As I said, I like to be comfortable in my own home. Relax. It’s just a gown, after all.”

The two walked past several sets of doors. One of them was left open, revealing a large bedchamber. There Emily caught a glimpse of Seitogi’s cloak laid atop a bed that had yet to be made, and for a moment felt an animalistic urge to barge in and confront him. Instead, she stopped walking, causing Arymaitei to jerk back on her forward momentum.

“What is it?”

“You sure you don’t want to step into your bedroom and cover yourself up? Maybe with Seitogi’s cape?”

“Oh, my bedroom is back at the main house. I suppose Seita found some time to rest his eyes after he returned here in the early hours.” Arymaitei pointed ahead, “Beyond there is a very nice hall where we all take evening meals together. It’s very communal.”

Emily thought back to when they were younger. Arymaitei always insisted they eat with their father and the men. She remembered how Arymaitei often took on what she considered traditional male roles. Ary was always the first to dive off the cliff into the lake or jump a boar while hunting. Ary leading her own Dhukai was somehow a natural progression of the girl she remembered.

“Do women and men eat together? Do they do that here?”

Arymaitei laughed. “Yes. My Dhukai is nothing like how father ran his. Here we are all equals. Except, I’m the boss!”

She flung open the doors onto a large domed hall, warm and thick with the smell of wood burning in a large fireplace. Emily could almost taste the wood and the smoke in her nostrils and inhaled as deep and quickly as she could, as it seemed to clear her head some.

The hall was filled with men eating at rows of long wooden tables. The noise was apparent as they rose to their feet and stood at attention, and called in unison,

"LADY LARK!"

"Listen up lads, this is Yuyuki!" Arymaitei announced, taking Emily by the arm, and leading her to the center of the room.

"She is my sister and will be staying with us for some time. So show her proper respect! Got it!"

The hall erupted into applause and cheers with the men repeating the name 'Yuyuki! Yuyuki!" over and over again. Emily smiled nervously as Arymaitei walked her over to a long table where Seitogi easily blended in with the host of brutes, Glehson seemed comfortable in their company as well. She was relieved to see him though. Seitogi, not so much.

Seeming to sense this, Arymaitei sat her directly opposite Seitogi with a smile,

"Take the chair, please," she said.

Emily thought Seitogi looked uneasy and kept her eyes lowered for fear they would shoot flames at him.

"Did you sleep alright?" He asked with what she perceived as a nervous tinge to his voice.

"It seems I got a hell of a lot more sleep than you!" Emily said as she sat awkwardly at the table with her sister sitting next to her.

"I see you found your clothes. I took them from Phule's compound when I escaped. I thought you would be more comfortable in them," he smiled.

"It was very thoughtful of you," Emily kept her hands folded in her lap, her stomach roiling.

She wanted to go back home to her old life. She was in a room presumably full of killers. However, she had to put on a brave face, and so she simply sat and waited to be served.

After a minute or two, a gruff, troll of a man came along and presented her with a delectable feast of stewed vegetables mixed with doughy yeast rolls alongside baked quail, and roasted duck.

There were plenty of sliced cured meats, fragrant rice, and large flagons of thick mead with other seemingly tasty treats she didn't recognize.

Seitogi's gaze did not leave her, and she couldn't help but glance at him. He now wore thin black armor over his coat and arms. It was impressive. She thought he looked strong, but still couldn't believe he had spent the night with Arymaitei. Why did that upset her so much?

Another stolen glance across the table and he caught her eyes and wouldn't let them go. Emily looked away and took a sip of mead and focused on Glehson, who was involved in a lively conversation with a number of the other men, his back to her.

Arymaitei leaned into Emily's ear, "You know he's just a little boy in a grown man's body," she said.

Emily bit her lip looking down, "Glehson? He's not—"

"Isn't he a doll, though?" Arymaitei interrupted with a sweet little laugh. "I love the way he's afraid to look at me."

"It's probably because you're practically naked," Emily replied, earning a gasp and a blush from her sister.

She had a feeling that Arymaitei might just be showing off a little and watched her sister's eyes move on to Seitogi.

"Are you and Seita having trouble? I mean, you are his bridal match flaunting another man right in front of him." She giggled.

Emily blushed but stayed quiet. Arymaitei just smiled and continued -

"Do you think Seita still loves you? You can never tell with some men. Though he and I have grown so much closer since you've been gone."

Glehson turned to look at Emily and they made eye contact before he turned away.

"Ohh. He is a beautiful one, isn't he? And he has eyes for you, Yuyu. Doesn't he? It must burn Seita up inside. Humph, I wonder how long before he kills him. You know how he gets."

Emily turned to her sister with a look of horror on her face. This was a dangerous game to play.

Arymaitei smiled at her, "I'm just having a little fun with you, sis." she whispered.

Emily swallowed and glanced over at Seitogi who was sitting upright, his eyes now closed. Was he angry? She didn't think so. But was he upset? He really had no right to be, she thought, but was still concerned somewhat with how he felt. She thought he looked pained. What did she do?

"You should eat, Yuyu."

But Emily's mind was racing, and she could barely take a bite. At the far end of the table, a group of men stood up and gathered in a circle. All jolly and bellowing, they began to recite a ballad dedicated to Arymaitei.

"Oh, here we go," Arymaitei groaned. "Every night that lot serenades me with hopes I grant one of them my hand and thus leadership of my Dhukai."

She stared at the men with a look of utter disdain. "They are all such …savages." she yawned.

One of the men had decided it was his day to have a try at reciting a poem, but it was more of a chant than anything else.

"Lady Lark, when will you marry? And why not me? We are comrades and all, you know!"

Arymaitei rolled her eyes as the men throughout the hall stomped the floor matching the rhythm of his words.

She turned to Emily, "The only reason they do it is to have a chance at bedding me," she said as she draped her arm around Emily's shoulder.

The man continued his poem, and now began his second verse,

"Lady Lark, never mind all that stuff about your father's ball and chain," he laughed, "I know how you like the wild life! You're young and vibrant, like me.

I know you like what I like, the lands, the waters, the hunt, the kill. I know the look on your face, I know the sound of your voice, Lady Lark's laughter, it's music to my ears."

The men stomped and sang as they continued to encourage, "Lady Lark, I swear to you, if you'll marry me, I'll give you all the lands and possessions of my kin, all the glory, all the trophies of the hunt."

"Your kin?" Arymaitei stood up, "What kin?" she called across the table. "I know of no kin of yours," she made her way toward the men, and in a moment she was in their circle, the silky translucence of her peach robe rounded on her figure like petals curled around a bud.

"Were you not disowned by that very kin of which you speak? Thus, you are disqualified from any claims to their lands, or treasures?" Arymaitei stood before the man and put her hands on his shoulders. The hall fell quiet as he pondered her words.

"Lady Lark, I swear to you, my exile was the craft of my vile brother. I alone am the rightful heir to the lands and possessions of my father!" he exclaimed, the men roaring in his support.

"I see," she purred, "And do you have any proof of this? Such as a letter written in blood? The date, the time, the location? The names, signers of the parchment? How can you prove your story? And whose blood are you willing to spill to prove your claim?" she pushed the man back a step, and the hall was silent.

Seitogi turned to look at Emily with a dark look in his eyes. She was stunned. His face seemed drawn into shadow where none existed. But why? This was all so confusing. Arymaitei paused for a moment that felt like an age.

“Any suitor of mine, disowned or not, will have to fight me for my hand.” She turned to the men in the circle,

“Any of you men wish to prove their worth, you may step outside and enter into a duel with me. I will accept nothing less than a full round. And your life.”

She turned to walk away when suddenly a man burst from the other side of the gathering.

“I’ll take you up on that offer, Lady Lark! Step outside and let’s settle this like real men and women, hand to hand!”

Arymaitei sighed, “Gworushen. You are a rough man. A hard man. You have quite the reputation with the maidens. You parade it often, and loudly.”

She turned her head aside with a disgusted look, “Yet I continue to elude your charms. How many times have I let you live despite defeat by my hand? Isn’t it pathetic by now?” she tilted her head, offering him a smile.

He hurriedly stepped across the hall, “Yes, yes, Lark! But the past is not present, and today your defeat by my hand is guaranteed. Thus, we will wed and let the matter be settled,” he smiled.

“Seitogi, come with me!” Arymaitei dismissively looked over her shoulder. “We need to talk.” And then to Gworushen, “Ten times. Ten times I’ve put you down. The thirteenth I will snap your neck, and then the matter will really be settled.”

Seitogi glanced at Emily, bowed, and then followed after Arymaitei. The men parted to let them pass. The hall door swung shut behind them, leaving Emily feeling isolated and afraid. Her mind swirled with confusion as she was suddenly conscious of all the faces in the hall staring at her. A small shiver ran down her spine as she realized that her resemblance to her sister was unmistakable.

Feeling instantly uncomfortable and overwhelmed, Emily looked quickly at the faces of the men before returning her attention to her plate. Glehson walked over and gave her a reassuring pat on the back.

“How are you finding the meal?” he asked.

“I’m doing well,” Emily replied. “But I’m just a little bit lost.”

Glehson smiled. “Don’t worry,” he said, trying to reassure her.

Emily smiled and began to feel somewhat better. Everything was just too much to comprehend at once. She let the murmuring of voices wash over her as she continued to eat. Her head began to clear, her stomach settled, and her fears faded.

Shaking her head to herself, she realized she needed to get herself together. She stood up, asked Glehson if he wanted to explore the compound, and then walked to the door Seitogi and Arymaitei had left through.

Meriwall was enormous. One could easily get the impression that a walled city had fallen and been selected to be rebuilt. The structures, streets, and buildings were of a mixture of white stone, gray brick, and polished wood, enclosed by a solid, ancient-looking stone outer wall.

The entire compound was surrounded by forest on all sides, the only path held by a higher section of the compound’s wall, its actual boundary veiled by overgrown mixed brush. Strewn with heavy trees drawn along the southern perimeter of Belan’s Moatiteii lands, it was laid out in a way to maximize its defensive strength. It was surrounded by acres of dense forest that seemed to lead down to the distant horizon.

It was as impressive from inside as from outside. Nothing about it seemed to stand out, yet everything about it stood out. The streets were clean, the men disciplined, and everything about the area seemed to have order and structure.

The buildings were large, a series of connected dwellings each containing one main room, a kitchen, and a number of smaller rooms in which the Dhukai men slept. They were small but large enough to house around forty people.

Emily roamed the paved streets with Glehson aimlessly as evening set in, letting the world around her slowly seep into her consciousness. There was even art adorning some of the buildings and music played through windows as they passed.

"Wow, look at everyone. And to think they all work for her," Emily said. "It's so amazing. So many people, so much land."

Glehson nodded, as he allowed his eyes to explore the compound. "Maybe if this place is so big," he began, "She'd give me a job."

Emily jumped. "You're not thinking of working for her, are you?" Emily asked. She hesitated for a moment, then continued, "You're no good at stealth and all that stuff."

Glehson grinned. "Stealth?"

"Yes, stealth. You're no good in the woods, you know, like climbing, hiding. Ninja stuff."

Glehson just smiled, "That's one of my best skills, if you haven't noticed. Anyway, I would only petition her after we've gotten you home."

"What about the crown? You're meant to be emperor one day."

Glehson laughed, a large, proud sort of laugh then shrugged, "There is no way I will be emperor," he said. "I've never wanted to be."

He looked around the compound, and then at Emily again, "But, I might find a good place here."

"Oh, I get it." Emily said, suddenly. "You like her, don't you? Prancing around here wearing next to nothing in front of a room full of everyone."

Glehson stared at her, not sure if she was serious or not. Emily broke into laughter,

"I'm just yanking your chain, relax!"

"Emily," Glehson wore a serious look on his face. "I want to take you home."

Emily just looked at him, a silent question plastered on her face, then smiled weakly, "Then… let's do this."

As they walked up a trail, they found themselves very quickly at a junction. One way led from the Fort into the dense woods, the other two were intersecting trails, one led across to a grassy hill and the other to a gray, stone house, enclosed in tall walls with an uneven walkway leading up to its porch.

It wasn't a striking place. Plain, orderly, and incredibly exclusive in size. A wide, wrap-around veranda stretched along the entire front of the house; The windows, like the doors, all had delicate wooden shutters below them, with an elegant square of elaborate, custom-designed knots and circles in the center. Above each wooden shutter and door was a green pot filled with bright flowers.

Emily could just make out a man in the dimming light, who seemed to be waiting for someone. He sat casually on a large bench placed in the corner along one of the outward-facing walls.

"He is familiar," she said. "I'm sure I've seen him before. But… where?"

"Who do you think he is?" Glehson asked.

"Belfast. Oh my god! It's Belfast!" said Emily, running off towards the house.

Glehson followed behind calling, "Wait, what's the matter?" By the time he caught up with her, she had already sprinted over to the man who was intently reading a scroll. With a huge smile on her face, she shouted out,

"Belfast! Belfast, I didn't know you were here!"

Her voice echoed around as her feet hit the wooden floor. The pock-faced man labored to stand but managed to do so just as she reached him.

"Yuyuki! Is it really you?" he said, his face breaking into a smile, a smile Emily returned.

"It is, good sir! How have you been?" she said, glancing around the man from head to toe. "You don't work for her too, do you?"

A look of confusion filled his face. "Work for who?"

"Ary!"

"No. No, I don't," he said, looking her over. "It's just business between Dhukais. I've been here for about two weeks now. It's really nice though. You've grown, haven't you, little sprite!"

"I have," Emily looked around and then whispered, "Look, Belfast, I need your help," putting her hands on his shoulders.

"What do you need help with?" he asked her, eyeing Glehson, who stood on the grass looking up at them.

"We've got to get back to Earth. Me and two of my friends! Do you know anything about the wise witch Masha?"

Belfast shook his head to the side. "I'm sorry, but I've not heard of the wise witch Masha."

"Are you sure? I desperately need to know where we can find her."

"She means Maishae, uncle," Arymaitei stepped from inside the house. Behind her stood Seitogi, stoic and hard-faced.

"The wizened woman, Maishae."

"Maishae?" Belfast bristled at the name. "Sorry, I don't work for Maishae, never have."

"She wasn't asking if you worked for her, uncle. You must forgive that his hearing has gone in one ear," Arymaitei apologized.

"I don't need you telling her about that," the old man chuckled. "Why didn't you tell me the princess was returned? Does your father know?"

Arymaitei leaned back against a support beam "I didn't tell you? Huh, she only arrived last night, old man."

"You have sauce for a tongue, girl," he wagged a finger.

"We need to leave," Seitogi said.

"Seita's right. My eyes on the road tell me Lord Sowao has an Imperial host en route here. They'll be here in a couple of hours."

"But what's so big about Lord Sowao?" Emily asked. "What's he got to do with us?"

"He is a very powerful man," Belfast said, laughing a little. "He controls the Imperial House's finances."

"And it looks like he and Minister Djowobb want their investment back," Arymaitei said.

"Well, maybe," Emily said, rubbing her chin, "But they don't even know we're here."

"I think you're forgetting something," Glehson said, stepping to the doorway, "It's not just you they're after."

"And that's why we need your help," Emily turned to Arymaitei and looked back to Belfast. "We need you to help us."

The old man's face shifted, "What do you need me to do?"

Arymaitei looked at the two of them, a smile on her face. "We need you to leave Meriwall, uncle. The Taisehsai can't become involved in the Merry-Larks conflicts. You've got your own people to think about. I will send you off with a worthy escort until you reach Smitemae."

"You're a good woman, Arymaitei," Belfast grumbled in disappointment.

"Yes, I am," she said, leaving the veranda and stretching her arms.

"You two. Glehson, Yuyu. Tonight, we set out for the Raven Temple, off the river. With this fog, we have to move quickly."

"How do you know where to go?" Glehson asked, "What's at the Raven Temple?"

Seitogi stepped forward, "It's a thieves' inn, run by Raven Master, White Eyes, a retired imperial spy. Anything you want to know about anyone, or any place. You are bound to find it out there."

"The birdman!" Arymaitei scoffed. "Is the reason Seitogi's involved in this mess in the first place."

"What is that supposed to mean?" asked Emily.

"He convinced Seitogi to go against my order and work for that witch."

"It was only one job and it was worth it," said Seitogi. "The Raven Master is a good person, Ary. Plus, he owes me."

"Ary, I don't like the thought of you wasting your time conversing with that scallywag, White Eyes," Belfast said.

"Trust me, I've met worse." She then turned to Seitogi, "I will grab a few brothers to escort us. You all saddle up."

Seitogi nodded, "Enoshi, Glehson. Please come with me. It's time to go."

"Shouldn't we wait for the morning to leave?" asked Emily.

"What part of Phule's host is on its way to Meriwell do you not understand?" asked Arymaitei.

"It would be safer to leave under the cloak of night," said Seitogi.

Emily and Glehson followed Seitogi down through the house and out into the back where an old man tended the horses.

"Good evening, Bron. We need these beasts saddled up quickly. Imperials are headed our way," Seitogi called to the man.

He cursed and spat, then threw some hay at the trio of horses who were munching on it.

"Shouldn't be more than an hour. Poor things galloped here almost a whole day straight, but I'll get 'em saddled up."

"Come," Seitogi said, "Let's pack some provisions while we have the chance."

"I haven't even bathed yet," said Emily.

"You will have to manage without," said Seitogi.

"Bro! I walked through the sewers and danced all night! I'm not going anywhere smelling like I do."

Seitogi sighed, defeated, "Come on," he motioned towards the house, "I'll take you in to get cleaned up, but no bath. We don't have the time to heat water."

Emily turned and smiled at Glehson. "I'll be right back," she said and then followed Seitogi inside.

***

An hour later, they were off in the saddle, rushing through the fog along the river's edge underneath a somber moon. Seitogi led Arymaitei and Emily who shared a steed, with Glehson and four Merry-Lark men making up their rear.

It began raining, and it picked up quickly. Emily wanted to take shelter, but Seitogi refused, stating the squall was their best chance at staying invisible to potential pursuers. So, they pulled on their long cloaks with the hoods up and rode on as a hiss and crack sounded in the sky.

As the storm intensified, the ground shook, and the air charged. Water inundated the road, and the sky cracked into thousands of volts. Trees and branches swung wildly; in the sensory chaos thatemerged, they had veered too close to the river, its current threatened to pull them downstream.

Seitogi managed to steer them onto a side path just in time as the river flooded over the road. Lightning struck a tree beside them, and the thunder followed immediately, the boom so loud Emily felt dizzy. She kept her eyes shut tight; her arms wrapped around Arymaitei's waist as Ary drew alongside Seitogi and called out.

"We need to pick up the pace. It's going to be a long night!"

Crossing The Line

The night sky was dark and cloudless, and the air was cool against Darren's skin as he slipped out of the sparring gym. He clutched a wooden sword in his good hand, his injured arm still bandaged and in a sling. It had been several days since his fight with Seitogi, but the pain was still there, a constant reminder of what he saw as his weakness.

He made his way to the arena, his footsteps silent on the cobblestone path. The arena was a vast, open space, surrounded by stone walls that rose up to the sky. It was usually used for training during the day, but at night it was abandoned.

Darren stepped into the wide-open space and took a deep breath. He raised the wooden sword in his hand and began to move. It was difficult, practicing with one arm, but he refused to let his injury hold him back. He moved with a fluid grace, each step precise and deliberate. He had been watching the soldiers since his arrival, studying their movements, and now he was putting that knowledge into practice.

The wooden sword was heavy in his hand, making it feel like a real weapon. He swung it in wide arcs, his body following each movement. He felt a sense of satisfaction as he moved, knowing that he was getting stronger with each passing day.

But the pain in his arm was still there, a constant ache that threatened to derail him. He gritted his teeth and pushed through it, determined to become stronger.

He felt sweat on his brow and his heart beating in his chest, but he didn't stop. He knew that he had to keep moving if he wanted to achieve his goal.

As he moved, he felt a sense of freedom that he had never felt before. He was alone in the arena, with only the night sky and the cool air to keep him company. It was a feeling of pure joy, of being in the moment and doing something that he was coming to love.

He practiced for hours, crisscrossing the arena, his movements becoming more natural and direct. And as the night wore on, his muscles ached and his sweat stung his eyes, but he pressed on. He was lost in the moment, lost in the joy of training, when suddenly he heard a voice behind him.

“What arc you doing here?”

Darren spun around, his wooden sword at the ready. It was one of the night watchmen, a tall man with a stern face. He grabbed Darren by the arm and marched him out of the arena and towards Atem’s quarters.

“What is going on here?” Atem demanded as the night watchman pushed Darren into his chambers.

“I found him training in the pitch,” the night watchman said, his voice harsh. “He stole a sword, see.”

Atem raised an eyebrow, his eyes flickering to the wooden sword in Darren’s hand. “Is that so?”

Darren couldn’t understand what was being said, but he could sense the tension in the air. He bowed his head and waited, unsure of what would happen next.

But then Atem surprised him. “I’ve been watching him train every night,” he said. “And I have to say, I’m impressed.”

The night watchman looked surprised, but Atem ignored him. “You’ve been performing your cleaning duties during the day and training at night?” Atem said, addressing Darren. “Good endurance. You’re a hard worker. I underestimated you.”

Darren didn’t know the language, but he felt he understood the meaning behind Atem’s words. He bowed respectfully and tried to form a response with the few words he had picked up, but it came out as a jumbled mess.

The next morning, Darren was woken by a boy not much older than him. The boy led him to the baths, where he was cleaned and given a fresh sparring robe. It felt strange to be treated so well, to be given new clothes and a clean bath. But he tried to focus on the task at hand.

He was led to a large training hall, where a group of young men were gathered. They were all dressed in the same short, gray hemp sparring robes, their faces serious and determined.

Darren felt a surge of excitement as he looked around. This was what he had been wishing for. He was actually going to receive official training.

The instructor stepped forward, a tall, muscular man with a shaved head. He barked out orders in that foreign language, but Darren did his best to keep up. The other students looked serious and focused, and Darren tried to match their intensity.

As they began their training, he felt a sense of pride and determination. He vowed to himself that he would get revenge on Seitogi and Emily. He would become the best swordsman in the castle, no matter what it took. And with that thought in mind, he threw himself into his training with everything he had.

The following day, Shumaiyuki sat in her receiving room, a stern expression etched on her face. She wore a regal purple robe adorned with intricate gold patterns, and her hair was pulled back in a tight bun. Behind her sat Rebecca, wearing a scarlet robe with pink lotus flowers, her red hair done up in a ridiculous fanned-out tower cinched with a large gold clasp at the scalp.

"Explain to me, Atem," Shumaiyuki said sharply, "what you mean by allowing this foreigner to train with the cadets. Lord Aiyo is away, and I will not have you taking advantage in his absence."

She raised a metal spike to eye level and thrust it towards a wooden slab set six feet away on the floor. With a little concentration and a clean strike, the spike hit the target dead center.

Atem stood tall and proud; his arms crossed over his chest. "The lord gave me permission before he left," he said firmly. "And the boy is of sound build and a quick study in swordplay."

Shumaiyuki raised an eyebrow, looking skeptical, and launched another dart at the target, another dead center strike. “And what of his loyalty? How do we know he won’t turn on us?”

“The Lord and I interrogated him with your little box,” Atem replied. “He has proven himself to be trustworthy.”

“Why wasn’t I informed about this, Obánā? Who gave them permission to touch my speaker box?” Shumaiyuki turned her attention to Te-Tae.

“I have eyes, but don’t see all under the sun, my lady,” the old woman bowed as she spoke.

Shumaiyuki nodded, her gaze shifting to Darren who stood nervously beside Atem. “Speak into the box,” she commanded.

Darren hesitated for a moment before complying. “Yes, ma’am?”

“Why are you here in Behrani?” Shumaiyuki asked.

Darren shifted uncomfortably. “It was some kind of weird magic that I can’t understand. All I know is that it was Emily’s fault.”

Shumaiyuki held up Rebecca’s tablet, displaying a picture of Darren and Emily kissing. “But do you not love her?”

Atem nudged Darren in the ribs approvingly, but Shumaiyuki demanded his silence. “Answer the question,” she said sharply.

Darren shook his head. “No, I was never in love with her. I broke up with her the day we came here.”

Shumaiyuki studied him for a moment, then spoke again. “You are lying. I can still see a passion for her in your eyes.”

Darren frowned. “You must be seeing my passion for revenge,” he said. “Seitogi hurt me, and I want to make him pay.”

Shumaiyuki raised an eyebrow. “That attitude is suited for a mercenary, not a Tabaiken.”

Darren retorted, “Whatever it takes.”

“And you, Atem,” Shumaiyuki said, turning her gaze back to him. “How do you feel about your experiment’s thirst for revenge? Sounds more scoundrel than soldier.”

Atem was taken aback by Shumaiyuki’s words. He had not expected her to be so harsh in her assessment of his ward. He smiled coldly.

“If a thirst for blood through vengeance is what motivates him, then I have made the right choice, my lady.”

“I see. But then, you would say something like that, being something of a scoundrel yourself.”

“I don’t think you understand, my lady,” Atem said, trying to explain himself. “This boy has been through a lot. He’s lost everything he knows, and he’s trying to find his way in this world. Revenge may not be the best motivator, but it’s all he has right now. I think he has potential. If not as a Tabaiken, then surely as you say, a mercenary,” he smiled teasingly, displaying his ghastly crooked teeth.

As he finished speaking, there was a moment of tense silence in the room. Then, unexpectedly, Rebecca spoke up.

“Excuse me, Lady Shumaiyuki,” she said, her voice soft but firm. Shumaiyuki turned to face her, surprised at her sudden interjection.

“Revenge can be a powerful motivator, but it can also consume one’s thoughts and actions, leading them down a dangerous path,” Rebecca continued. “I may not know much about the life of a soldier, but I do know that Darren has suffered a traumatic experience and is going to wind up getting himself killed if you let him continue on with this soldier fantasy.”

Darren bristled at the accusation, his mind flashing back to the trauma of his broken arm and the intense pain that followed. “I’m not some fragile flower, Beck,” he snapped. “You should speak for yourself and your own mental health! I can take care of myself.”

"But can you?" Rebecca countered; her voice steady but gentle. "We're in a foreign land, surrounded by people you don't know, and training with soldiers who don't seem to care whether you live or die. Is this really what you want?"

Darren hesitated, feeling the weight of her words. He had been so focused on revenge that he had forgotten to consider the bigger picture. He knew that he couldn't go back to his old life, but he didn't know if he was ready to commit to this new one either.

Shumaiyuki watched the exchange between the two with a furrowed brow. She sensed a shift in the dynamic between them and wondered if their disagreement would escalate further. "What do you think of what my pet has to say, Atem?" she asked, raising her voice in order to steer the conversation back on track.

Atem shifted slightly, his eyes flicking towards Darren. "I believe the boy has the potential to become a valuable asset to us," he said, his voice gruff but confident. "Don't be swayed by the words of this… silly girl," he added with a dismissive wave of his hand.

"I have learned these past few days that my pet, Lady Ribiki, is quite knowledgeable about many things. Though she cries incessantly, silly she is not," Shumaiyuki corrected him, her voice crisp.

Darren shifted uneasily, "Pet, Lady Ribiki?" he repeated in disbelief.

"We're still working on my title," Rebecca added, looking dejected.

"Look," Darren said. "I may be from another world, but I know what I want," his voice firm. "I want to train and become a skilled swordsman. Revenge may be what motivates me, but it's not all I'm after."

I want to prove to myself that I'm not weak, and that I can overcome any challenge."

Shumaiyuki watched him with interest, studying his determined expression before nodding. "Very well. Dorin will continue to train with the cadets, but under close supervision. And Atem, you will oversee his progress and ensure he does not stray from the path of a true Tabaiken."

"Certainly, my lady, as Lord Yulori has already decreed," Atem said with a bow. Shumaiyuki wrinkled her nose and was about to reprimand the man when a low whistle interrupted her.

"Both of you, be gone!" she waved Atem and Darren away with her hand. "I have other business to attend to."

Once the room was empty except for Te-Tae, Rebecca, and herself, she approached the speaker box and turned it off.

"Teje, what do you have for me?" she asked into the air.

"Lord Aiyo is waiting for Awei Chua in his private gardens, my lady," a disembodied female voice replied.

"But uncle is in the capital," Shumaiyuki said in surprise.

"He returned from his travels this morning, my lady, cloaked in stealth," the voice explained.

"What is he up to?" Shumaiyuki wondered. "Obánā, come with me and let us join this private meeting."

"It would anger the lord, my lady," Te-Tae warned her.

"When has that ever stopped me?" Shumaiyuki replied. "Now, come along."

* * *

Awei Chua was a tall, athletic woman with pronounced features. More handsome than beautiful, she was striking all the same. Her hair, a crown of tightly coiled curls in shades of rich, dark copper, had a single strand of white woven through. The curls expanded out from her head in every direction, adding height and breadth to her already impressive stature.

Her dark eyes were very wide, and she never seemed to blink, giving her a watchful and regal appearance.

Dressed in a padded leather vest over a fitted canvas bodysuit and black thigh-high boots, she patted her forehead with a cloth, leaving traces of her thickly applied brown make-up on its fibers. A gap in her front upper teeth was as distinct as the mole she often toyed with on her chin.

Shumaiyuki studied her strong features from an upper terrace as the massive woman paced back and forth in the lower courtyard. There was a haughty crispness to Chua's voice as she angrily addressed two of her men.

"I told you this was to be kept under wraps. I'm now no longer sure it was the right course to take. Damn it! This is just too big to cover up now!"

"She is a loud one, isn't she, Obánā?" said Shumaiyuki.

"And her face is so full of expression. It almost seems as if she is acting out a scene in a play. Watch her now. She has taken off her ring and is twisting it between her fingers."

"Excellent observation, my lady," Te-Tae said with a tired smile.

"She is not just a loud woman. She is really a very controlling one. You see how furiously she is berating her men."

"Yes, very controlling."

Awei sat down on the sidestep of the courtyard, her eyes still looking up at her two guards. She fiddled with the ring, put it back on her finger, then stood up and stalked off towards a small stone bench.

The two guards stood looking at each other. Their body language suggested they were properly chastened. Both bulky and heavily muscled, their faces were inscrutable beneath their masks. Their eyes, however, were cast down.

"She awaits uncle. No doubt with news of the imposter," Shumaiyuki continued.

"Where did he find such a rogue to handle his intrigues? Could he not have used a more respectable Dhukai?"

"She is the descendant of a wealthy dynasty," Te-Tae began. "I knew a servant who worked in her father's house. She said Chua once lived a life of comfort."

"You don't say. She does have a certain arrogance about her that would denote a lower noble."

"Oh, hardly a noble, my lady. Her father, and grandfather before him, imported cloth from various regions."

"Oh my. A family of merchants. And you said she was from a wealthy dynasty," Shumaiyuki scoffed.

"Merchant or not, she was always bigger than her peers and came to her martial abilities naturally."

"Oh, how I envy that you are privy to such gossip in the servants' wing," Shumaiyuki pouted.

Te-Tae rolled her eyes and continued, "But I hear she grew up naive and sheltered. She had never seen the ugliness and brutality of the world. She spent her money and all of her time indulging in fighting tournaments. It made her a nuisance in her father's life. She refused marriage and was driven from his estate. After some desperate times, she turned to a lifestyle of absolute ruthlessness and spent years devoting all her efforts and energy to becoming a Dhukai…" Here the old maid abruptly stopped speaking and covered her mouth with her fan.

Awei was looking up at the two from the courtyard and frowned.

"My lady, we must speak no more on this matter. I am afraid my lips are being read." With her eyes, the old woman pointed to the far side of the courtyard, "And now, we must display some decorum. See, your lord uncle approaches."

“Yes, how dare he return from the capital without stopping by my apartments to pay his respects.”

“He is lord of the house, my princess. He need not address you as though you are,” said Te-Tae.

“You may go, Obánā,” Shumaiyuki said as she rode her floating chais from her poorly hidden spot on the terrace. Te-Tae bowed and left in a hurry as Shumaiyuki glided into the garden, lounging gracefully as she came into full view. Her white robes were smooth and fluid. Her flowing hair quivered in the gentle breeze, her green eyes serene.

Awei rose up from the stone bench to greet her as Yulori slowly walked up the path through the grove from the opposite direction. Shumaiyuki noticed that a distinctly colder look came into Awei’s eyes as he approached them.

“Your old servant has a tongue dipped in salt, my lady,” she said.

“If not for salt, what would we flavor the seasons of our lives, Lady Dhukai?”

Awei sucked her teeth at the princess and turned away.

“I assume you have urgent news for me?” Yulori said, looking over her shoulder at the guards. “You two can go,” he said, “And not a word of this to anyone.” The men nodded and walked back into the house.

“You should go back inside as well, princess.” Yulori turned to Shumaiyuki and looked at her as she hovered in place.

“Don’t worry about me, Lord Aiyo, I am quite comfortable here. Chua, please go ahead, tell us why you have returned days late, and empty-handed,” Shumaiyuki looked straight at Awei as she spoke.

“You understand my business is with the lord of the house,” Aiwei said, and took a step back, out of range of the princess’s stick.

"I have news, and it is not at all good," she continued. "First of all, the imposter is on the march. We have lookouts positioned and are ready to burn down any road we suspect she will use. But the reason I came empty-handed is to inform you that she is being helped by the crown prince himself. My men watched them escape Gah temple two days ago, disguised as vagrants."

The words remained suspended in the air between them. Shumaiyuki's face relaxed, and her eyes brightened. Her uncle, on the other hand, looked grave.

"Rilkian?" asked Yulori.

"Why would the crown prince want to disguise himself as a vagrant and help the imposter?" Awei asked.

"Because he has been bewitched by her," he replied, barely containing his anger. "If she thinks she can escape us disguised as a peasant, then she is even more foolish than we thought. But how much does Rilkian already know?" Yulori spoke very slowly and carefully.

Shumaiyuki looked at her uncle as her serene face turned into a solemn visage.

"If this is true, then what are we to do?"

"We must maintain the elaborate deception I am sure the empress has already put into play," he said. "The Imperial House wouldn't dare admit the crown prince is missing. She would see to that. Awei, you must find them before Prince Rilkian comes to any harm. By now, anyone could have seen and recognized him. We must contain the situation."

"My men lost track of them when they entered the city," Awei continued, "However, they did run into Aiyo men disguised as bandits at the river. They were disposing of the body of a fallen comrade." A smile played on Awei's face. "Oh, they tried to deny their clan affiliation, but we Inouei have a way of loosening tongues."

Yulori looked at her smile, and then at Shumaiyuki. Shumaiyuki sat up with a start, nodding her head sideways once.

"Am I to understand you've harmed Ayio men?" she asked. "We will surely conduct an inquiry over this."

Awei smiled. She had the habit of pushing her bosom a little higher when she was being insincere.

"Of course not," she replied with a gleam in her eyes, "I would ever lay a finger on one of yours, my lady, but unfortunately we were well into torturing them before we found out their true affiliation with your house. You could imagine my shock that the House Aiyo would risk sending assassins after the crown prince, in the capital no less." All the pleasantness that had been in Awei's voice was now gone.

"This is valuable information," she continued in a narrowing and steady tone. "And so little is spoken of it, even at the court."

A grin played on Yulori's face as he reached into his purse. "At least one of our houses retains their dignity." He pulled out a couple of gold coins which he tossed to her, and then chuckled. Awei's smile returned to her face,Yulori's didn't.

"Keep it close to the chest, Awei," he said, "Now where are our men?"

Awei's smile vanished. "They are outside with my men at the gate."

"Bring them in," Yulori ordered, "This is a matter best taken care of in private."

"They were careless and very confused," Awei teased.

Yulori looked over to Shumaiyuki and gave a sigh. "Thank you! That is all we need to know. Lady Chua."

"As you wish," Awei said and clicked her fingers, and within seconds, the two guards appeared behind her from within the castle. The three moved past Shumaiyuki's floating bed and bowed to Yulori. Yulori pursed his lips, nodding back.

Shumaiyuki nodded. “Come uncle, let us continue this conversation over tea, it looks like rain,” she said as she floated back towards the veranda. She could feel his penetrating eyes on her back.

“What have you done?” he asked, in a hushed tone. Shumaiyuki chuckled.

“Nothing, uncle. I have done nothing. How could I have done anything?” she replied, turning her head to look at him.

“I leave for a few days, and you send out your spies! I am not impressed!” he said, looking ahead. “Please slow down.” He struggled to keep up with her as she sped away. The chase ended at her grand room.

“I am sorry, uncle. I was distracted by a sudden sense of foreboding,” she drifted over to the back dais and landed softly on it. It was one of the most extravagant rooms in all of Odahni, a warm and welcoming place filled with classical beauty. Yulori plopped himself down on the floor and slapped it with an open palm. Shumaiyuki immediately lifted from the ground again and hovered in place.

“Did you send assassins to Domotedai? What were you thinking?” he said, looking up at her from the floor.

“I thought it best I took action where you had not the will. Why rely on Chua when our own network of spies and assassins has no rival?”

“Because having assassins is illegal, Shumai!”

“Oh, please. All houses of note have them. And if they don’t, then they should. Now I fear if the crown prince is seduced by that woman, it will make things worse within the empire. I do not know, I just do not know,” she replied in a weary tone.

“You have crossed a red line with me, damn it! Are you trying to drive us into war with the Imperial Dynasty?” Yulori said in a very low voice. Shumaiyuki looked down on her uncle, the corners of her lips turning upwards.

"But why would I do that? I don't want to fight with anyone," she said very softly, mimicking his quiet tone.

"Again, I ask you, are you trying to drive us into war with the Anele? I don't know what you were thinking, Shumaiyuki!" Yulori exclaimed.

"Red line! Why are you even back in Odahni so soon? Weren't you just in the capital?"

Yulori shot up from the floor and slowly walked towards the floating girl.

"No, I was here in Kue, making arrangements to ensnare the imposter. I depart for Nyongoyuchi tonight, but I have been reading. I read all the dispatches, the letters, and intelligence reports. It all means nothing if you send out assassins behind my back," he said.

"The fate of the empire now depends on the life of one woman, and that's you, Shumaiyuki! If the imposter somehow survives another day, she will surely be captured before she even gets to petition the emperor. If we do things your way, we will be at war within a month. Our clan's survival is in my hands. You have caused the needless death of one of our men! How many more will we bury because of you?"

Shumaiyuki leaned over the edge of the lounge and peered at him intensely.

"Would you rather have imperial soldiers ravage our lands and burn our people's homes?" Yulori continued his rant. "Would you rather see our warriors slaughtered?" he asked.

"I would rather see our people released from imperial tyranny, and the Aiyo hold its rightful place on its throne. Do you have no honor, uncle? Do you have no feelings for what is best for our people?"

Yulori looked up at her, his face expressionless. "I have more honor than you know. I will give you this," he said. "There is only one family in the entire empire that could stand against us," he paused and stared directly into her eyes. "I will not let the Anele harm the Aiyo.

You are not to act without my knowledge." He turned to walk away.

"Where are you going?" Shumaiyuki asked. "Am I to just sit here quietly while the scandal brews? The crown prince has gone missing! Surely that concerns the house of his future bride. I shall depart for Nyongoyuchi with you and confront Phule myself."

"You will do no such thing!" said Yulori. "Your place is here. We cannot afford any harm to befall the Aiyo!"

"I will not allow it, uncle. I will fight my way out of here if I must," she said, floating up above the dais.

"The capital is several days' journey from here. You won't get far with your speed," he said.

"You will not! You will not make fun of me!" she screamed.

"Just do as you are told," he said, turning to leave, paused, and looked back laughing. "You are just a girl, Shumai. Too damned ambitious for your own good."

"You speak as if I were still your prisoner, uncle."

Yulori's mouth dropped open. "You are named as the Imperial bride and should not step foot in the capital before the official ceremony."

"It's not as though it is the law, now is it?"

"It is tradition. And that is law enough for me!"

"Oh, how I wish Grandfather was allowed out of house arrest. We need a real man to sit as the lord of our clan again, but I guess I will do it for now." Shumaiyuki held her head in her hands.

"Eunuchs have larger testicles than you, uncle." Shumaiyuki had several more words she wanted to say, but Yulori had no patience.

"Shumaiyuki! This is a delicate time! I have steered you within reach of the crown! The Gjwoan ceremony is only three months away! Do not let your pride snatch victory from the jaws of defeat," he turned to walk away.

"Yuyuki is here, damn it!" slamming her bamboo stick against her the frame of her floating couch. "What bride am I to be if she exists to challenge me? And what are you doing about it? Nothing! Nothing but allowing her to make menace! And Aunt Yumeiko, she won't even see me!" she screamed and floated past his retreating figure, blocking him from leaving the room.

"But the Tabaiken are loyal to me, uncle! Me! A girl! Our troops! Our houses! They see your fecklessness! Your weakness, and they weep at my feet lamenting the erosion of our illustrious name under your stewardship!"

Yulori stared at her floating form and crossed his arms over his chest. "I have every ounce of support for you, Shumaiyuki. Of course, I have. But you must stay in your place, girl! You have a use! Spread your legs and produce an heir! Don't you ever forget it!"

Shumaiyuki's eyes darkened as she moved to face Yulori. "I will do as I see best, uncle," she replied with a low voice. And then, "Bastard!" she swung the stick at his face and upper body.

Her cry of rage echoed through the room. Yulori saw the gleam of light off the spiraling bamboo and reflexively raised his arm to block it.

"Not while my eyes see you! I shall not forget this day!" she screamed, beating him.

"Your ambition will ruin our house, not I!" Yulori seized hold of the stick but then had trouble maintaining his grip due to her commendable strength.

"How did you become such a monster, Shumai?"

"Monster?" Shumaiyuki floated back and then charged him, screaming, "Perhaps when you and the empress conspired to replace me with that bitch! Or when you locked me away in a tower for years! Yes, uncle! I do think that is when I became a monster. Now what is your excuse?"

Yulori tripped backwards and ran as she furiously continued swinging the stick.

"You who know nothing of swordplay! Do you really think you can protect this house with your silver tongue? The men look to me for leadership, not you!" she continued. "It was I, a cripple - that's right, uncle; I know what you call me behind my back - who visited the troops at the battle of Thafsar, not you!"

Yulori timed it just right and quickly yanked the stick away from her, throwing it across the room, where it struck a silently weeping Rebecca, about twenty feet away.

The clunk of the stick hitting her drove her to collapse onto the floor, grasping her back.

Shumaiyuki grimaced as she twisted the lounge around and floated over to her. "How dare you assault my pet!" she breathed rapidly, shocked. "I just had her hair done."

"Your pet?" Yulori uttered in disbelief. "Your pet? It is a girl thing."

"Its… her name is Lady Ribiki, and she knows all sorts of things you don't!" Shumaiyuki began stroking Rebecca's back.

"Don't worry Riri, everything is fine. Pay him no attention. Leave now! See how you've upset my Riri!

"You are on house arrest from this moment forth," said Yulori, furiously breathing. "If you continue to misbehave, I will have it taken away from you and thrown in the dungeons!" With that, he turned and stormed out of the room.

Shumayuki reached and turned the dial for the speaker box on –

"Are you hurt, Riri?" she whispered her voice gentle as she stroked the poor girl as if she were a shelter cat.

"I'm not your pet!" Rebecca stammered in garbled Brenhi.

"I feed you, clothe you, and you entertain me with your vast knowledge. Is this not the duty of a pet?"

"I'm a human," Rebecca sighed.

"Oh, but Yulori has put me in a foul mood. Do those dances from your show that so delights me!"

"But my back still…"

"The dance, Riri!" Shumaiyuki demanded, slamming her stick against the floor.

Perilous At Best

The way to the Raven's temple wasn't so much a dangerous trek as it was an annoying and wet one. Everywhere Emily turned, it was gloomy. Dull mountains on one side, a dense forest of thistles and brambles on the other, with just a thin path of withered grass to walk on; she feared her and Ary's horse might topple over.

It rained heavily throughout the night – the kind of rain that soaked into the soul and weighed down one's spirit. The next day brought dark skies, heat, and humidity. Emily felt like her skin was baking under her clothes, and a torturous wind whipped her face with dust and grime, despite the protection of her hooded cloak.

Setogi said they had only a few hours more of traveling to do, yet the dense and oppressive forest of thorns and weeds seemed to continue on and on, endlessly. Emily thought surely there must have been a mistake in the route they had taken. Perhaps they would have to retrace their steps.

She wasn't sure if she should be sad or rejoice as she looked up at a very small gap between the forest and the mountains where the clouds gathered like a swarm of flies. She welcomed the cooling drops once they began to fall again.

The rain started properly a few minutes later, thrashing down on their heads with enough force that it felt like being pelted with fine pebbles; its ferocity was unexpected.

For quite a while, they trudged on in the storm, becoming increasingly soaked and so hot Emily thought she could feel her own fat oozing out of her pores.

The torrential rains flooded their paths, forcing them off their main track. The stony mountainsides' runoff gushed forth like an engorged river. Thankfully, though, Setogi found a way around the raging stream.

"It must be monsoon season," was all Emily could think as she rode and watched the weather change around her. The temperate rain gave way to warm and sultry gusts. The forest was saturated and dark. Suddenly, she wished to see the hot sun again.

Then, after many hours of hiking, walking, and riding –

"This is it," announced Setogi. He made a gesture towards a gaping hole in the mountain. An odd greenish-blue mist wafted lazily through the tunnel and swirled around, causing the tree branches around the entrance to appear like waving, gnarly tentacles. Emily couldn't help but feel apprehensive at the sight.

They rode forth, slowly, into the passage. The walls of the cave were a dull gray sheen. Everything was gray. The atmosphere was damp and fuzzy but not as creepy as Emily had anticipated. Though they had been trekking in the heat and rain, the passage was delightfully cool. The mist was actually soothing as it seeped around them. It was like stepping into a giant hug.

The group emerged from the tunnel onto a riverbank across from an open plain of forest, stretching far into the horizon. Setogi pointed out the dilapidated two-story 'Temple of the Raven' in the near distance.

Anything but a temple, it looked like a wounded beast slowly dying amongst the trees. They crossed the river over a rickety bridge and rode up the path towards the structure. As they got closer, Emily could see it was made of what looked like old, rusty metal that had a dull, tarnished gray to it.

There was a large porch with a thick glass dome to one side of the first floor. The dome was cracked and peeling, its shards of glass scattered across the porch. It looked like the roof had been caved in during a violent storm and was now covered in mud-colored tarps. The windows and shutters had been damaged as well, probably by past torrential rains.

The entire place was in ruins, Emily thought. She looked to the second floor. The walls were cracked and padded with moss, windows were boarded up, and paint was peeling off. It looked like the building was about to collapse.

Her first thought was that it was abandoned, but the sight of a group of men hanging outside seemed to indicate otherwise. A raven came swooping by the cracked dome and landed on the railing of the porch. It took flight again and circled twice.

The bird flew over to the group, landing on Setogi's shoulder. It pecked at his ear and swiped a strand of hair from his sideburn; he smiled.

"Tell White Eyes…"

"The Laughing Lark is here to see him!" Arymaitei cut in. The raven looked her over, then cawed.

"I'm his boss, you little shite," Arymaitei plucked a damp strand of her own hair from her head and held it up. "Here! Take it, and let White Eyes know the Laughing Lark is here!"

The raven cawed again and then flew away, keeping Setogi's hair instead. The group finally made it to the porch and dismounted. Emily could hear a jig coming from inside as people shuffled in and out of the entrance. Arymaitei leapt down from her saddle with her men close behind. Setogi turned to Emily, motioning for her to come with him as he dismounted from his horse. The raven circled overhead and landed on a branch nearby, cawing. Moving timidly, Emily followed behind and walked through the front doors of the inn.

Under the dome, Emily saw a crowd of men walking around the perimeter, laughing, drinking, and dancing atop their feet. Many were helping others to the bar where they gulped and guzzled down frothy beers. Women were dancing, and the music was lively. Couples threw each other around and swung and spun, leaping into the air and catching each other. The place was like a monastery, a whore's mansion, and a party all rolled into one.

Emily saw and felt the palpable madness in the room. There was a fierce hunger and passion whirling through and boiling beneath the surface that surprised her. She took a step forward, letting all of it wash over her. Glehson patted her on the shoulder.

"Something you don't see every day, huh? Everyone has a festive demeanor."

"I didn't expect it to be like this at all. Especially from how it looks outside."

"How are you feeling?"

“Sore, but I’ll manage. You?”

“A little tuckered out but feeling a second wind coming on. I’m heading to the bar,” Glehson took her hand. “And you?”

“She’s had enough to drink,” said Setogi, turning around and looking at Emily sternly. For her part, Emily passed on the offer, but not before telling Setogi to mind his business.

“Zatrik, Bisui, you lads each circle and watch the room. Yazgiroh, Koe, you two hang around the bar and keep an ear out,” Arymaitei ordered her men. “I can already feel hungry eyes on us,” she said, and then walked across the busy room to a set of stairs.

Setogi and Emily followed behind her, and they took the stairs up to the second floor. He told Emily that was where White Eyes would be.

She asked why they were walking up to him instead of him greeting them.

“Because we are the ones showing up to his place with our hands out,” said Arymaitei.

They reached the top of the steps. “Right then, come along, shall we?” she said. Setogi stepped forward past her and knocked on the door to the first room they came to. Behind him, Arymaitei attempted to budge him out of the way but failed.

The door opened. Despite the amount of noise and activity outside, the room was quiet and still. A heavy man sat at a beachwood desk of sorts, head bowed, breathing softly and steadily, seemingly disinterested in everything around him.

He wore a burgundy velvet waistcoat and a black robe that could easily moonlight as a tent. His face was round and unshaven, with large jowls, a pug nose, and small eyes that were nearly always scrunched shut. He seemed asleep, with one hand resting on his stomach, wider and rounder than most. His other hand held a long cord attached to the inner doorknob.

“Wakey wakey…” said Arymaitei in a cheerful voice. White Eyes slowly took his hand from his stomach, setting the tether free from the door, and opened his eyes. Red pupils, to Emily’s disappointment. He looked over at her and then at Setogi with a stony expression. He let out a small groan,

“Bloody Laughing Lark.”

“Hello, White Eyes. I’m sorry to intrude on you like this,” said Setogi.

“Oh! It’s quite alright, no harm, no foul. You come in and have a drink but leave the troublemaker at the door.”

“I’d rather join. Hehe,” said Arymaitei, putting her hands in the air and waltzing over to the table. She pulled out a chair and sat. Then with a twirl, she turned it around, sat on its edge, and set her feet on the table.

“By the way, this place could really use some spring cleaning. At least hose down that mosh pit of musk you got going on downstairs.”

“Ah, but you are mistaken! My place is top-notch and the envy of this town,” said White Eyes with a menacing gaze and sucking his teeth. Arymaitei frowned with her nose scrunched up.

“Of course. We are known for having a fine establishment,” said White Eyes, turning to Emily and Setogi. Setogi nodded to Emily and then ushered her over to a stool by the table. Emily kept her eyes on White Eyes, who was staring intently at her with his beady little red ones.

“Please tell me you haven’t kidnapped the Golden Swan,” he turned to Arymaitei, who was still hanging off the chair, but now swinging her legs back and forth.

“Are you mad? Look again and see how your eyes deceive you.”

“Of course, of course not. But the resemblance is uncanny even looking as rough as this one does.”

"If she were an Aiyo princess, how much would you pay for her? I'm willing to make a deal," Arymaitei continued.

Emily gulped and tried not to stare.

"Ha ha ha ha, no. I wouldn't dare. Her appearance would put my health at risk. Though I would pay many a gold graloon for her. She is quite beautiful, ha ha ha ha ha."

Emily narrowed her eyes at him as she scooted the stool back away from the table.

"Right then," said White Eyes to Setogi. "I have your hair. What's this all about?"

"What is it about?" Arymaitei interrupted, "It's about the job you fetched Seita for. Everything with that witch has gone sideways just like I said it would, you bulbous pork!"

"I was talking to the lad. He is fully capable of speaking for himself," said White Eyes, shooting Arymaitei a cross look while leaning back in his chair. "I told you about barging into my establishment with your shite, Lark. Keep it up and…"

"Save your goddamned threats and just stop trying to poach my guys!"

"Do I have to have you dragged out of here like last time, Lark?"

Arymaitei laughed loud and hard, "If you want to watch me break more of your goons' arms! Sure!"

"Enough, Ary," said Seitogi, stepping forward, "We are looking for Maishae. Her cabin was ransacked, and she's gone missing. We thought maybe one of your ravens might have seen something."

"I've heard things," said White Eyes, slowly twiddling his fingers beneath his chin. "But it ain't going to come cheap. And judging by the number of Merry-Larks turning up here looking for side work," here he gleefully glared at Arymaitei, "I hardly think you could foot the bill."

"Where is the witch?" Arymaitei slammed her fist on the table.

"Yep. Rumor is your Dhukai is virtually bankrupt," said White Eyes, pointing at Setogi. "Used to be a rule of thumb. Never do business with a man who answers to a woman."

"This is a misunderstanding," said Setogi as Emily gritted her teeth and looked at Arymaitei.

Arymaitei looked at her for a moment, pursed her lips, and looked back at White Eyes,

"I'm a woman, and his boss for that matter," cocking her head to one side. "You have some nerve to say women are useless!"

"What! I would never say such a thing," said White Eyes, putting one finger to his chin.

"But everyone knows your little Dhukai's expenses are through the roof. You can barely feed your men. You don't even have an imperial seal."

"Ehh. I hate to break up the bullfight, but I wish to speak with White Eyes alone," said Seitogi.

"But Seita! I'm about to find out where she is!" Arymaitei whined. "You're undermining me, damn it!"

"You're a nuisance, Ary!"

"Are you going to help me question him or what?" Arymaitei curled her lip.

"But…" said Seitogi.

"White Eyes! Do you, or do you not have info on the missing witch?" said Arymaitei, clenching her teeth.

White Eyes sighed, "I can't give you any information. You don't show proper respect."

"I'm warning you, White Eyes. You know how I can get." Arymaitei tightened her fist and sternly looked at him in his red irises, "I swear I will break something! Starting with your jaw!"

“Ehh…just a minute,” said Seitogi, “Just ignore her, White Eyes. I will figure the money out; just give me some time,” he said.

White Eyes looked over at Seitogi and then back at Arymaitei, “It’ll cost you extra since she’s involved.”

“I can cover any expenses you need,” Glehson appeared at the entrance holding a mug of ale.

Arymaitei shook the table by dropping her chair back onto its four legs with a loud thud.

“C’mon then, pull up a seat and join us,” she said.

“Who is this fellow you’ve turned up with?” asked White Eyes, looking at Setogi through a cloudy expression as he sat back in his chair.

Arymaitei answered before Seitogi could get a word out, “His name is Glehson. He’s a herb trader and associate of mine. Why? Are you jealous that I have rich friends?”

“Looks like a boy with hands too soft to handle you, Lark.” White Eyes grinned.

“Not to worry. I know my share of labor,” said Glehson, stepping into the room and siding up to Arymaitei.

“His money is good, but not needed,” said Seitogi. “Besides, I’m calling in a favor.”

White Eyes wiped his brow with the back of a rough-looking, thick-fingered hand, “That serious, huh?” he said, “Uhh…alright. But don’t make me regret this. I deal with Dhukai out of necessity, not charity.” He scratched at his stubble. “I’ll send my birds out tonight. I’ll have your information by the morning, midday at the latest,” he said after a long, hard look at Arymaitei.

Arymaitei nodded, “Sounds good. You’ll be covering our overnight stay, ale, and meals as well.”

“Put the money up front, Lark. I’ll get your information, but you need to pay for your own room and board.”

"We'll cover that then," said Seitogi, "I'll check back with you before dawn."

"Right then," White Eyes said, "Let's see if I can find you your witch."

***

"I don't understand how this works," Emily said to Arymaitei as they walked back down to the ground floor. "How are his birds going to find out the whereabouts of this witch?"

Arymaitei began to lead them to the bar. She stopped and turned around,

"His 'birds' apparently are always in flight, watching everyone in every place. They share information with each other and then report back to him. He supposedly has some psychic connection with them. It's all bullshit if you ask me, but he does tend to come through on what you want to know most of the time."

"Regardless," Seitogi said, looking at Arymaitei and making a fist, "if he doesn't have what we need to know by tomorrow, we've lost out on a lot of time."

Reaching the bar, Arymaitei ordered a pitcher of ale as Seitogi laid down silver on the wooden surface and ordered food for everyone.

"So, what do you think White Eyes is up to?" asked Emily.

"His only concerns are money," said Arymaitei.

"And that is all we have to go on at the moment," said Seitogi. "For now, it is enough. Let's just eat and get some sleep. And you," turning to Glehson, "your voice gives away your class. It's better if you play mute in the company of others."

"I can speak just fine, thank you," replied Glehson as he sipped his drink. Arymaitei watched him with a smirk.

"Don't be upset," Seitogi said, "I'm only saying it for your own good."

Glehson went to take a sip of his drink and set it back down on the bar, the cup rattling on its surface. He walked away, and Arymaitei bellowed with laughter. Emily chased after him as Seitogi groaned.

"Go easy on him, lover boy. He is a very useful idiot," said Arymaitei as she turned back to Seitogi.

"I'm inclined to agree with you on that one."

Emily caught up with Glehson outside the inn, out back where a crowd of twenty or more men were sitting on log stumps around a large fire pit. There was a live deer thrashing amongst the flames.

It made a horrifying grunting noise as it burned and kicked its legs. The crowd of men clapped and cheered.

Glehson scowled at two men as they walked by, staring them down as though he were itching for a fight. Emily began to turn back to the inn, deciding to give him space, but he walked closer and put his arm around her shoulder.

"Don't just stand there watching. Come and sit with me," said Glehson.

"I think I'll just stay for a minute, then I'll head back inside," said Emily, looking around at the other men and the thrashing deer.

"Don't mind them. They are playing a game. Whoever is hit with a burning ember from the deer's kicking loses his money and is out of the circle. The last man standing wins the pot." He pulled her towards the fire, the dancing light reflecting off Emily's eyes, causing them to glow emerald.

"I think it's disgusting and totally inhumane. Oh, the poor thing."

"I agree. It's a game once popular with the soldiers, but the emperor outlawed it."

"As he should have," said Emily.

"I don't think Seitogi likes me very much," he said.

Emily looked up at him with a broad smile. "No, I'm sure he likes you just fine, Glehson. He will get used to you, don't worry."

"I'm not worried. I'm annoyed."

"He doesn't have it out for you. You must know that. Right?"

"I know, but I do think he has an attraction for you, and that is the issue at hand, isn't it?"

"What do you mean?" She felt her face redden, and her hair fell in her eyes.

"You know what I mean. I've seen the way he looks at you, Emily."

"I'm sorry, I don't know what you mean at all." She nervously picked little bits of ash from the fire out of her hair. "I'm not interested in him."

"He wants you. The way he looks at you. It's obvious. It's not like he even tries to hide it."

Emily stared at the fire. A leaf from above fell down and caught ablaze with a sizzle. "I don't think Seitogi wants me," she answered in a quiet tone of voice.

"Emily…" He took a step toward her and pulled at her hand. She bit her bottom lip, and he let go.

"They approach," Emily said, her eyes warningly directed toward the inn. Seitogi and Arymaitei were walking towards them, carrying two trays of fish and chips with mugs of beer.

"We can talk about this later."

"Of course," he said with a smile. They followed Seitogi and Arymaitei over to a few tables and sat down to join them for the meal.

"I could eat a horse," Emily said with a hint of forced cheeriness in her voice. Seitogi nodded and handed her a plate. He grabbed another and passed it to Glehson.

Arymaitei nodded at Emily and sat down next to her with Seitogi, distributing their meal. They ate and drank in silence. Once the meal was finished, Arymaitei stood up and yawned.

"I'm going to go get a few hours of sleep before I pass out," she said. "Glehson, can you show me to my room?"

"Um…sure," he seemed unsure but got up to follow her. Seitogi watched as they weaved through the crowd and smiled, glad she was gone for the moment.

Emily watched as he gathered up their plates and put them back on the tray. She stood up and leaned over to help. Her hand brushed against his, and he went flush, almost dropping the tray.

Emily looked at him blankly as he stood up. He looked away and cleared his throat.

"Umm… I, uh… I don't think…" He squinted his eyes, blinking in embarrassment. "I'll just go dispose of this. Be right back." He took the tray and walked off in the direction of the inn.

"What an odd man, so alpha-shy," Emily said to herself as she smiled.

In the end, Emily followed Seitogi up to their room where Arymaitei was already snoring loudly, arms and legs spread akimbo on a lumpy mattress. Glehson was laid back on his cot, staring at the ceiling. The four Merry-Larks were nowhere to be seen. She and Glehson spoke a little, but she eventually yielded and drifted off to an exhausting sleep.

Emily awoke the next morning to Glehson gently tapping her shoulder. Many thoughts filled her mind as she recalled the previous night. Glehson stood at the foot of the cot, smiling toward her. He was wearing the same clothes he wore the night before.

"Morning, Glehs."

"Good morning," he said. "They are meeting with the bird man now and want us to get the horses ready and wait out front." He handed her a small ball of pounded yam and a cup of tea.

“Ok. Let’s go,” said Emily. She was energized but not well-rested. She was more anxious to get back on the road and away from the prying eyes of the inn’s residents. She was fairly certain they were already being watched despite the early hour of the day.

They moved slowly to the front of the building where the horses were, and the Merry-Lark men were talking and laughing with each other while having their breakfast with beer.

“Listen, Emily, it might not be anything, but I thought I should at least tell you.” Glehson drew near. His face was flushed with urgency.

“Last night on the way to our room, Arymaitei was approached by one of White Eyes’ men. She left with him and was gone for several minutes before she returned. She came in and went right to bed; however… I can’t help but feel something’s afoot.”

“Thanks for telling me. We should keep this between us for now. As you said it might be nothing. Let’s speak no more on the matter until we must.”

They moved the rest of the way to the horses, greeted the men, and began fitting the steeds. It took almost no time for the two of them to get the horses ready. Soon, Seitogi and Arymaitei emerged from the inn.

Arymaitei looked at Emily for a moment as if she were about to share something but held back as she looked away.

“Morning, Arymaitei, Seitogi. How did it go?” Emily asked as they made their way over to them.

“Well enough. You ready then?” said Arymaitei, and then to her men, “According to the birdman’s ravens, the witch is hiding out in Bashi.”

“That’s Carp territory,” said Yazgiroh.

“Bashi!” said Glehson, Emily could sense his alarm and regarded her sister.

"Where is Bashi? Why would the witch be hiding there?" she asked.

"Bashi is Behra's black market capital. A cesspool of organized crime made up of about a dozen or so separate settlements floating out in the Adehshi sea. According to White Eyes's ravens, she has taken refuge in Adishe temple. People often seek asylum there as the warrior monks offer protection for those who can pay."

"I have heard the Adehshi monks are essentially Dhukai draped in religious robes, but thugs and criminals, just the same," said Glehson.

"You have a point there," Arymaitei agreed and looked at Seitogi.

"It's mainly ports and factories. The people there know how to keep to themselves. And yes, it also has a lot of illegal trade going through. But it's nothing we can't handle," he said.

"I beg to differ. The princess shouldn't be taken anywhere near such a place. I've heard stories about the Adehshi Monks. They are not going to just turn the witch over to us! I'm not sure what we've gotten ourselves into, but I don't know if it will be worth it," said Glehson.

"No one asked you to come along so save your complaints," said Seitogi. Glehson looked shocked and took several steps back.

"That's not a cool thing to say," said Emily. Seitogi looked a little annoyed but realized he had to keep his cool.

"Bashi Intermediate. It is the closest of the various settlements, about a two-day ride." Opening a map, he spread it out to display the different trails.

"White Eyes said they have just begun their carnival season and that it would be full of tourists. So, we should be able to easily blend in with the out-of-towners."

"Hmmm," said Arymaitei, looking over the map and tracing her finger over the route drawn by White Eyes. "It's not very close, and I don't like the idea of traveling on horseback through these mountains. Particularly Aarub Canyon, Komori, you know."

"The Komori are currently in hibernation and shouldn't give us any problems. Plus, it's the only direct pass aside from scaling the cliffs with our horses in tow."

"I guess we don't really have a workaround. But we'll have to stay sharp."

As the group began to mount their horses, Seitogi pulled Arymaitei aside.

"Don't you think it would be better if Enoshi and I went on alone? Are you sure you want to enter Carp territory?"

"Why? Bashi doesn't fall under Carp jurisdiction."

"But we have to travel through Mingtao first. And your adventures there last year are still the talk of gossip."

"I don't expect we'd run into any of the Flying Carps along the way. Besides, Gailen's quarrel is with my father, not me."

"And what about Nog..?"

"Don't!" she placed her finger to his lips. "Let's move out."

The eight of them departed the Ravens Temple, with Emily electing to ride with Glehson this time around. They hit the road just as the sun completed its morning climb. After the first fifteen minutes, Emily could tell the trip was going to be rough.

The snaking path that led into the mountain pass was well-worn by the countless number of wagon wheels and horses' hooves that had passed over it before. They spent the morning riding mostly with Seitogi at the lead.

Emily's jaw dropped as they passed under a massive wall of overhanging branches. Trees as high as a multistory complex forged a tunnel that eventually opened out onto a small plateau above a valley. At the opposite end of the plateau, there was a large circular opening in the trees. The tunnel ended with another path that led off into the grassland below. Seitogi nodded in its direction.

"There," he said.

The light reflected off a small trickle of a stream winding its way down through the valley. The smell of pine and dirt was strong as they trotted across the open expanse.

It was then that Glehson rode up to Seitogi and shared his nagging suspicion that they were being followed and how twice he had spied a raven in the air.

Seitogi looked up to the sky, "White Eyes keeps a tab on everything. It wouldn't surprise me," then pushed his horse on. Emily looked behind them, concerned.

The eight riders were soon at the stream, and all dismounted to take a drink. They waded into the cold water; it was cool but not troubling. The horses lowered their heads and drank and drank. Glehson kept an eye on the sky. A raven was circling above.

Once they remounted the horses, they climbed up a narrow gully fed by the stream. The sunlight grew smaller and smaller until it completely disappeared. The sounds of the forest drowned in with the dark.

The green glow of the stream soon replaced daylight. Their path became more and narrower until there was barely a foot of clear space between their horses and the rocks on the bed. The path steadily ascended higher and higher. As they persisted with the climb, they eventually encountered a small ridge.

The eight of them stood and paused to gather their breath and listen. The wind was picking up. The trees seemed to shake. The sound of squawking, like a flock of crows, flew through the gap above and behind them. Seitogi guided them down and through it. The gap opened onto a canyon floor nestled between soaring cliffs pockmarked with large oval holes.

The Aarub Canyon passage was a strangely beautiful place. The floors of the canyon were littered with gems beneath a smooth black obsidian surface. Emily had never seen a place so beautiful.

"Wow," she said as Seitogi dismounted and walked to a rock and sat down.

"Let's eat before we walk through. This is Komori country, so we have to be on guard."

He took his pack of yam from the saddle and started gnawing at it. Emily and the others followed his lead. Their stomachs were rumbling too.

But Arymaitei seemed agitated and paced back and forth, exploring the surrounding rock faces with her eyes.

"Why is she so restless," Emily whispered to Seitogi.

"I'm sure she's wary of the Komori. They make their nest in the holes in the caverns above us. But we can't reach our destination without passing through their territory," he said as he watched Arymaitei pace.

"Is it a good idea to take a break in Komori territory?" Glehson said.

Emily became alarmed with his words and looked to Seitogi as though expecting an explanation. Seitogi smiled and turned his head to face Arymaitei, who was still pacing. He gave her a reassuring look, and she stopped. Seitogi stood,

"Remember, it's their hibernating season. There would only be one or two around to protect the others as they sleep. We're at the bottom of the canyon and pose no danger, so we should be fine."

"I don't like it all the same," said Arymaitei. "Yazgiroh, Zatrik. I want you two to ready your bows and ride at our flank as soon as we are done eating."

"Certainly, Lady Lark," the two men bowed and began tearing through their yam cake.

"It's alright, Ary. Take a load off," Seitogi said, gesturing toward the rock. She hesitated, and then hopped over and sat. Seitogi returned to his spot and continued to eat.

"It's alright," he said again. "They are not going to attack us."

"Famous last words," said Emily.

They finished eating and replaced the packs on their horses. They were standing and fully reloaded when they heard a loud squawking amplified by the acoustics of the canyon walls. The horses reared on their back legs and jerked, almost knocking Seitogi off his feet.

Emily and Glehson took a few steps back. Seitogi stood with his hand on his blade and waited. Arymaitei drew her blades, Yazgiroh, Zatrik, and the other Merry-Lark men drew their bows towards the sky.

There was a loud rustling from above, and then a giant falcon-like bird, the size of two water buffalo, descended from the gap overhead. It tucked in its legs and opened its massive wings, swooping down directly at Seitogi. Six razor-sharp talons extended below its body like the missiles of a jet fighter. It shrieked loudly as it struck the ground. Seitogi leapt back, barely avoiding its attack.

The giant bird pulled back its wings and hunched down, ready to strike again. Seitogi dashed back beyond its range, but his horse wasn't as lucky as it tried to run off. The bird darted in with a quick slice of its beak at the panicking beast's underbelly.

The horse's entrails spilled out onto the ground, and it slumped over, dead.

Seitogi drew his sword and held it out in front of him. He kept his eyes on the bird. The bird was snarling and screeching as it stepped over the dead horse. Its bloody beak was emitting a low bellowing sound. The four Merry-Lark men moved in together and unleashed a volley of arrows as the bird advanced.

The creature spun its body around to face them and arched its wings as they reloaded. It screeched at them and grabbed the dead horse with its beak, flinging its lifeless body in their direction. The men ducked out of the way, letting the beast slam into the ground near them.

The creature hunched over and continued to screech. Its pale-colored skin illuminated in the dimming light. The men fired a few more rounds at its neck, but it didn't seem to faze it at all.

Seitogi made use of the opportunity and went in for an attack, slashing with his blade. The bird lowered its head and charged him, he smoothly dodged its bunt and cut into it with his sword. The creature squealed in pain and rubbed its beak against Seitogi's cheek.

Seitogi swung his blade again, cutting deep into the creature's wing, trying to sever the appendage. It screeched louder and flew up high in the air, out of reach from his sword. The men quickly reloaded their bows and looked around for any other threats.

Koe and Seitogi looked at each other, their faces stained with blood.

"Glehson, take Emily and head for the end of the canyon into the forest!" he called back, "Yazgiroh, Koe, ride with them. Protect the princess!" They responded with nods and all mounted their horses, with Emily and Glehson on their steed.

Another shriek echoed through the canyon as Emily watched the Komori spread its enormous wingspan, almost twenty feet from wingtip to wingtip. The bird came in on another attack. This time it wasn't a swooping attack from its back as it had done before, but from its side.

Yazgiroh turned his steed as fast as he could and thrust out his blade, hitting the Komori in its left wing. The giant bird screeched in pain and fell off to the side, crashing to the ground, its severed left wing lay several feet behind it.

The creature screeched and swung its head around, watching the riders in front of her as they galloped away. Emily looked back in horror as the Komori regained its footing and charged at them, trying to pounce on her.

Glehson gripped the reins of his steed with both hands and screamed out, "Faster! Come on! Faster!" urging the horse to race for the far end of the canyon.

Arymaitei bolted behind them, swinging her blades with slashes, swipes, and outthrusts.

The wingless Komori turned around on her and took a swipe at her with its beak. She dodged the attack and hopped as it came in for another attack. The creature shrieked loudly in her face and forced her to duck, but her horse bolted out and away from them, leaving her to fight alone.

She narrowly avoided the swipe of the creature's beak and used the opportunity to slash her blade against its pale neck. She stabbed the bird through the throat and cut clean through to its beak.

A second bird descended, reached for her, and missed. Arymaitei brought her two short swords up and crossed them in front of her. The bird dived towards her, but she quickly dodged it, cutting both swords across the creature's chest as she passed beneath it.

The bird screeched and retreated, backing off to the top of the canyon. It came in for a second strike and Arymaitei drew blood, nipping one of its legs. It shrieked and held up its beak like a knife and slashed at her face.

She staggered backward and fell, rolled to the side, and stabbed it in the underbelly. The bird grabbed at her leg and Arymaitei lashed out and stabbed it in the neck, dousing herself in its blood.

It released her and fell to its side. She jumped up and sliced off its head to ensure it didn't get back up.

She looked up and saw two more creatures racing toward her from the sky and cursed out loud.

"I think we've awakened them!" said Seitogi, running towards her. He skidded to a halt in front of Arymaitei and Zatrik. Bisui came galloping up behind him.

"Koe, Yaz, Enoshi, and Glehson are nearing the far end of the canyon. Go protect them!" shouted Seitogi.

The birds flapped their wings furiously as they flew along the canyon bottom. One of them spun in midair, extended its wings, and soared upwards, emerging at the top of the canyon and then dived back down at a blurring speed.

Bisui launched a dozen arrows as it dove. The arrows darted off the end of the creature's wing and pinged off the canyon walls. The creature screeched and banked, angling back toward him. Bisui fired at the bird, and it flapped back, using its wings to speed away, wings damaged to the point where they were almost deflated and useless.

Seitogi and Zatrik ran forward, their swords a blur, fending off the third bird. They thrust and slashed and spun, keeping the creature at a distance. Seitogi's sword came up, and he struck at the Komori and missed; it dove at him but slammed into the rock wall instead.

Seitogi seized the opportunity and swung his sword back and forth repeatedly, hacking away at the beast in continual strikes, making a furrow in the rock beneath it and churning up pebbles.

Emily and Glehson were just feet away from a small opening in the rock. Behind them, she saw another Komori dropping like a stone into the canyon and coming after them. It slammed into their horse with the force of a train. The Komori sent the poor thing careening into the wall headfirst, snapping its neck while both Emily and Glehson were thrown to the ground.

Emily could only watch in horror as the Komori screeched to a stop, no longer in pursuit. It turned and stared at her, then leapt forward and landed on her chest, pinning her to the ground.

She gasped as she felt its weight, its claws wrapping around her waist. She kicked and wailed in pain, squirming around as she tried to break free.

Glehson charged and threw himself onto the downed bird's back and sunk his dagger deep into its neck. It batted its wings and began to flutter up in the air. He let out a curse as he lifted his blade and stabbed again. The Komori screeched in pain and turned around, its beak stabbing down at him.

Then it turned and landed on Emily. Her terrified eyes looked up at it squirming around on her chest. Some strength returned to her, and she slammed her elbow backward into the creature's flabby chest. The Komori fell back and released her.

She rolled forward and looked up to see Seitogi riding with Bisui, and Arymaitei with Zatrik. Emily picked herself up and ran, keeping up with them. As they galloped past, Arymaitei reached out and grabbed her arm and pulled her up onto their steed.

The Komori roared and swung its beak at them again. Emily twisted and dodged, falling to the ground and rolling. The Komori missed and turned up to them. The bird leapt back up, and when it came down, it swung its wings and struck like a hammer upon Bisui, sending him flying several feet into a wall of rock. The bird was fifty feet off the ground, swooping down onto them. Emily and Seitogi went for the beast while Arymaitei mounted her horse.

"Got it," Seitogi said.

Arymaitei spurred and shot under the bird, slashing her swords along its belly. Its pained screech echoed throughout the canyon as it pulled back and closed its massive wings around Arymaitei and her steed. Arymaitei hit the ground and rolled out from under it, and then the bird soared upward.

Seitogi watched as it flew out over the canyon and away, a ribbon of blood trailing from its wound like a holiday streamer, with Arymaitei's horse, kicking and neighing in its claws.

Arymaitei dropped her swords and ran over to Bisui, helping him sit up. He was alive.

"Wow, I think there's a hole in my chest," he said, rubbing his chest and wincing.

She rolled him onto his back and saw that he was right; his chest had a large open wound that gushed blood. Arymaitei wrapped her torn cloak around his chest in an attempt to slow the bleeding.

"My… side…" he muttered.

"It's okay, Bisui, it's okay," Arymaitei said, trying to reassure him. "I'm going to get you help."

"Arymaitei," Seitogi said, coming up beside her, "I'm sorry, but he's as good as dead."

"No, he isn't!" Arymaitei said. She grabbed Seitogi's collar and spun him around, glaring into his eyes.

"He's right, boss," said Bisui. "I'm a goner."

"No! There must be something we can do," Arymaitei said. "A healer, do we have a healer?"

"We don't have a healer, Arymaitei," said Seitogi. "You know that."

Yazgiroh stepped forward and towered over the three of them. "We can't stop the bleeding, boss," he said. "You know what we need to do."

"I think… you… should… go… to… the… mountains," Bisui said, and then he spat a mouthful of blood onto the ground. "Call… a breeze… Antiren." And then his eyes went blank.

Arymaitei gasped and dropped to the ground, "Bisui!" she said, "It can't be!"

"Antiren. She is a girl he loved back in Meriwell," Yazgiroh said, "We must burn his body, boss."

"It is the only way," said Seitogi.

Arymaitei nodded, reaching down and pulling Bisui's arms across his chest. Yazgiroh and Seitogi lifted him up and then laid him down flat. They placed his equipment onto a pile, and then Seitogi pulled a leather pouch from his robe and sprinkled a handful of glitter-like powder over him.

Arymaitei watched him with her head bowed. She glanced over at her two captains and smiled sadly at them. Seitogi replaced the bag and brought out two small flint stones, striking them against one another until they sparked. All it took was one spark to ignite the body into a full blaze of green-blue fire.

Bile rose in Emily's stomach as smoke filled the air. She coughed and looked away as the fast-acting substance burned fiercely. She had never seen a funeral ceremony before. For a moment, she wondered if she had the fortitude to not pass out.

"Arymaitei," Seitogi murmured.

"Yes," she said, taking his hand in hers and giving a weak smile.

"I'm sorry. For everything."

"It was nothing. So don't say that. He wouldn't want you to feel bad."

"Had I not got involved with the witch, none of this would have happened."

"I know," she said.

It took half an hour for the incendiary agent to completely disentigrate the body. Yazgiroh collected Bisui's ashes in the severed hood of the dead man's cloak. He dropped it into his saddlebags and then turned to Arymaitei. "We will hand them over to his mother when we get back."

"That's fine. I'd like to pay my respects to her." She looked around, all but one of their horses were dead.

"What about the horses?" she asked. "How will we ride out of here?"

"We walk," Seitogi replied, taking out a map. He unfolded the crumpled parchment on the glassy black canyon floor and traced a path with his finger. "We should reach Aarub before nightfall. Once there, we can tend to our wounds and purchase new horses. After that, we'll take this route to the Baraga River. If we cross by early morning, we can make it to Bashi by midday."

They quickly left the canyon. There was a sad calmness in the air as they marched down the mountain track, with Arymaitei and Emily on the remaining horse. Seitogi and Yazgiroh took the lead on foot, and Glehson, Koe, and Zatrik brought up the rear. They soon entered a forest and walked and rode along as a misty fog rose from the ground and blanketed them. The sun was setting as they emerged onto a small clearing.

"There," Seitogi said. "Aarub is just a few miles out. You can see the tall buildings just beyond the tree line."

They were just starting to feel hopeful when they crossed the clearing and came over the top of a hill, where they encountered bandits blocking the road. The bandits wore distinctive animal masks and bore swords and bows.

"This is not good," Arymaitei, caked in dry Komori blood, put her hand on her blades. "This is not good at all."

Seitogi, using Bisui's bow, took an arrow from his quiver and swiftly loaded it. "Ambush!" he whispered.

"Whatever you do, don't hold back!" Yazgiroh said as he took out his spear and twirled it as fast as he could. The four bandits spread out, ready to pounce.

"Why should you block our way?" asked Arymaitei. "There is no toll to enter Aarub."

"Hold there. You are my brothers," said one of the bandits, a massive pikeman with a bull's mask. "But we will let you pass, as long as you leave us your weapons, the horse, and, of course, the women." The bandit lowered his pike, and two others strung their bows.

“Give over our weapons and comrades?” Seitogi said. “What sort of madness are you getting at?”

The bandits’ bowmen took aim. “I had a hunch you would say that” he said, and then he nodded to his pikemen.

The pikeman struck as the bowmen released. Seitogi deflected an arrow, and Arymaitei deflected the other.

“Arymaitei,” Seitogi shouted. “Take Emily and go. I’ll hold them off!”

“What? No!”

“Go!” Seitogi yelled.

“Seita!” She cried.

“GO!” he demanded.

Koe and Zatrik ran toward the bandits, attacking with spear and dagger. Glehson also ran forward with Bisu’s piked hammer. The bandits released another volley of arrows, but Yazgiroh deflected them with his whirling spear.

“Seita,” Emily shouted.

“Go!” he said.

Arymaitei forced herself back and then glided away. She and the horse burst into a sprint down the hill. The bandits gave chase, but she was soon out of sight behind the tree line. Emily couldn’t help but feel they were leaving Seitogi and Glehson the same way she had left Rebecca and Darren.

The massive pikeman charged toward Seitogi. The weight of his massive blade and the force of his swings were too much for him. Zatrik tried to strike his spear into the pikeman’s side, but the pikeman deflected it with his shield.

Instead, the pikeman struck him with his blade and sent him crashing to the ground.

The pikeman then turned on Glehson and Yazgiroh. He struck Yazgiroh across the face and then sliced at Glehson's head. The two of them backed off. Glehson charged again with the large double-sided hammer, but the pikeman ran low and then jumped high, his spear gliding through the air. Yazgiroh stepped to his side and with one swing struck him right in the chest. Yazgiroh pulled back, but the pikeman still had fight left.

Seitogi caught an arrow aimed for him and ran ahead in a zigzag pattern. He leapt to his left, and a second arrow sped past him. He twisted around and ran into a patch of dense trees and came back around in a crescent moon pattern, catching the bowman from behind and pushing the arrow deep into the man's neck until it broke through from the other side.

The bandit fell to his knees, having inhaled his own blood. Seitogi then deftly rose to his feet and caught the other bowman with a kick to the jaw followed by a knee to the neck, crushing the man's windpipe. He pulled out his sword and pierced him through the throat, turning just in time to block the pikeman's spear.

Seitogi deflected the spear with his blade and, with a gliding lunge at the left side of the pikeman's chest, slid his sword through the material of the bandit's cloak.

Almost instantly, he drew his blade to the right side of the pikeman's breast, paused, and then slid it up to the neck, catching the large bull mask as he pressed upwards.

The pikeman fell over, his soul escaping his lifeless body. Seitogi walked back over to Yazgiroh and Glehson.

"Well, this is rather unpleasant," Yazgiroh said, catching his breath while still looking around. "I have never seen men fight so pointlessly for nothing more than our weapons."

"And the women, good sir," Glehson said. "They also wanted the women."

"Trust me, they want no part of Lady Lark, boy," Yazgiroh laughed.

"It looks like trouble is following us around, wherever we go," said Seitogi. "Will they be the only obstacles we must face in these lands?"

"I think so, at least this go-round," Glehson replied.

Seitogi breathed a sigh of relief. They heard the sound of horses coming in fast. Seitogi whipped around, sword in the air. Arymaitei and Emily arrived, Arymaitei laughing.

"Everybody in one piece?" she asked.

"Why are you laughing!?" Seitogi said with a smile. "They almost killed us!"

"Well, I thought it was funny, you protecting the girls and all," Arymaitei said.

"They wanted us dead," said Seitogi.

"There's no telling how many more of them are around," said Zatrik.

"We need backup," Yazgiroh said.

"I don't like this, I don't like this at all," Arymaitei said.

"Zatrik, Yazgiroh, and I will circle around. If we encounter any trouble, we will deal with it," Arymaitei said, dismounting and motioning for Glehson to take the reins from her. "We will meet you at the bottom of the hill."

The group broke ranks and took a few steps away so as not to attract any more unwanted attention. Emily could still hear faint cries in the night. Her eyes grew heavy, and the dark clouds hung low with a gloom, threatening rain. She nestled into their horse, embracing the creature for its warmth.

The comforting earthy scent of the horse's mane surrounded Emily as Glehson sat behind her, guiding the animal with the reins. She was relieved not to be separated from him as the thought of it made her heart race. They arrived in Aarub as night was falling.

The slums of Aarub were worse than anything Emily had imagined. Large shacks enclosed in rough wooden frames with cloth coverings served as homes for the poor. Other abodes were in more decent shape but not entirely well off.

The streets were more crowded than she had expected, and the shops were lined up with an item for every need and a need for everyone. Seitogi spotted a small tavern, and it seemed the better of the two choices, so he led them in.

By the looks on their faces and their wavering eyes, the tavern keeper knew these guys were looking for something and wanted to get something from them too.

"Keep your voices low," Seitogi whispered. "Glehson, remember you are mute."

"And keep your eyes open," said Arymaitei. "This place probably has more rats than people."

A skinny child pushed himself out from the other side of the bar. He was covered in dirt, and he had a runny nose. "Bring the drinks," he said, holding up a tray of warm mugs of beer. "Compliments of the house."

"What is this?" said Arymaitei, sniffing the contents of her mug and sliding it back over to the boy. "It smells like piss."

"Calm down, miss," the boy said, eyeing her. "It's the only thing this tavern serves. It tastes fine," he said.

She lifted her mug to her mouth, and pulled it away, her face twisted in disgust. "Yuck!" she said. "It tastes like piss!"

"It does not. It tastes pretty good," said Seitogi, lying. He handed the boy a silver coin, enough for three or four trays of beer.

"Tell your master we will need two horses. See that it happens quickly, and I have another one waiting for you as well."

"Yes, sir," he said. The boy glanced over at Glehson and giggled, then skipped back over to the bar.

The man at the bar grabbed the silver coin, jug in hand. “This is good stuff,” he said. “It is not often we get such beautiful women here either.” The boy told him of Seitogi’s request, and the man invited the crew over to sit while he sent the boy off to the local stables.

“I think we are in trouble,” said Yazgiroh.

“As opposed to the last time we were in trouble?” said Seitogi.

“Well, yes, but…” Yazgiroh looked over at the rest of the group and then back at Seitogi, as if seeking advice on whether or not to continue.

“You may as well,” Seitogi started.

“Not ordinary trouble, that is for sure,” said Yazgiroh. “Lots of eyes on us.”

“Well, Ary is giving ‘Carey,’ all drenched in blood after all!” Emily whispered.

“Don’t worry,” said Seitogi. “We can handle this.”

Arymaitei believed they were being watched too. “Carp’s men,” Yazgiroh leaned over and whispered in her ear. She searched the room with her eyes and saw the two men he was referring to.

“What are they doing so far out here?” she wondered and tapped Seitogi on the shoulder. “Looks like we might have to go fishing,” she said.

After several minutes had passed, the stable man returned with the two horses. “Horses are taken care of,” he said. Seitogi took out two silver coins, handed them to the man, and pulled him aside to negotiate.

“They recognize me,” Arymaitei whispered. “I can feel it.”

“They don’t seem willing to look in our direction,” said Yazgiroh, “which means they are watching our every move.”

Arymaitei glanced over at the two men, one with a long sword, the other with a spiked mace. Both stood tall with strong stature.

“What are Carp men?” Emily asked.

“The Flying Carps are a rival Dhukai of the Taisehsai, and our father’s enemy. We Merry-Larks have no particular fight with them, but I don’t like running into them nonetheless.”

“Everything is set. We need to get to the stables and set out; it’s getting late.” Seitogi reappeared and followed the stable man out of the pub.

As they left the tavern, Emily noticed a large hooded man watching them venture up the street. He tried to conceal himself in the shadows, but she felt his gaze.

She thought perhaps she was being paranoid due to their encounter with the bandits and that if she noticed him, surely Seitogi had too.

As they traveled out of the city, Arymaitei kept her eye out for trouble, concerned that those Carp men from the pub might be following them. Along the way, they encountered a few townspeople who either turned up their noses at them or begged for help. Emily was anxious to be clear of the place.

They continued to head straight out of the city, eventually running into a shrub-laden path that led them to a large forest area. The trees grew very close together, and Arymaitei found herself wary of the place. The group traveled on for some time.

A bit further, they came across a small clearing. Arymaitei noticed a patch of trampled grass and held up her fist signaling for them to stop.

“It’s getting colder out here,” she said. “Let’s rest for a bit. Seitogi, you get a fire going. I’ll take the lads and secure our perimeter.”

“I’ll leave it to you then,” answered Seitogi.

They all dismounted, and Arymaitei took off into the forest with Yazgiroh, Koe, and Zatrik setting off in different directions than she. The dark, the cold, and the eerie quiet were setting in.

Emily started to feel a bit uncomfortable. Her body ached and felt like it was falling apart. She didn't feel well at all.

She came up next to the remains of a dry old stump and sat. "Isn't it better that we stay together in case we are attacked again?" she asked Seitogi.

"Ary's trying to prevent that from happening right now," Seitogi ignited a small blaze of ragged, dry sticks and they sat around it. "Someone has been following us since we left town."

"Oh no! Are you sure?" Emily asked. The fire crackled and gleamed in the darkness. "Perhaps they're hiding in the trees."

"Perhaps," Seitogi replied as he gazed into the fire.

In a sudden moment, the distant clang of metal upon metal could be heard.

"Is that what I think it is?" Glehson stood.

"We have company," said Seitogi with a sigh.

"Then we should go," Emily cried, as she stood up. Seitogi never moved, he simply stared into the fire and poked at it with a long stick.

The clang of metal continued to echo in the forest, growing steadily louder. Glehson wrapped his arms around her, and she clung to him.

"I hope no one else gets killed because of me," she said, her voice quivering.

"There's no need to worry," Glehson said. "We'll take care of it." He kissed her on the forehead and gently gave her a hand squeeze.

"We'll go over to the horses and wait until they are out of sight. Then we can make our move."

"You will stay put and let us do our job," said Seitogi with a glare. "What's that?"

"To my right, ten degrees north!" Arymaitei called from some unseen place, then from her men. "Eight degrees southeast," and "West! South of me by five," - "Northeast aim third and left!"

Seitogi quickly donned a black leather mitt and dipped it into the flames, releasing a flurry of burning orange darts in the directions he was instructed. His mastery of heated spikes was startling. A number of screams and guttural cries echoed around them as six figures emerged from the dark thicket, their clothes in various states of combustion, running towards Seitogi.

Seitogi crouched and swept his leg through the fire, sending projectiles of flaming tinder directly at his attackers, striking the three closest figures. Arymaitei, now in plain sight, took advantage of the situation and defeated the nearest attacker – a man trying to extinguish the flames on his clothing – before proceeding to attack another.

Her men emerged from the nearby woods to apprehend the remaining attackers.

"Yield! I yield to you now!" screamed the one Arymaitei was harassing with a knee to the abdomen and blade to his neck. He put his hands above his head as she knelt on his chest. Koe and Zatrik also had people down, struggling on the ground.

"Well look who we have here, Seita," Arymaitei pressed down harder on the boy's chest, patches of his clothes smoldering.

"Nogitunde Tomon. It's been a while since we last crossed paths. Why are you and your Carps following us?" Sheathing her blade, she stood and offered him her hand.

"You know him?" Emily asked, recognizing him as the hooded figure back in Aarub.

"I've known him," Arymaitei batted her eyes. "Why so far from home, handsome?"

"It's none of your business why I'm here, Lark! You and your friends are trespassing on prohibited territory!" The dark-haired boy with a thin mustache above his lip stood with his chest puffed out and made eye contact with everyone.

Arymaitei smiled and rubbed her shoulder up against his. "You're just mad I put you on your back again," and then to her men, "It's not the first time!" she winked. Nogitunde pushed her away with a pouty gesture.

"None of the Taisehsai can come over the Mingtoa border without being stopped."

"You know very well I left the Taisehsai. I have nothing to do with them aside from antagonizing them for my pleasure."

"The boy is always at Yienguoi-Jin's side," one of the Carp men pointed out Seitogi.

"He is my spy, which is why he is here with us now, and not with them."

"And just who is us?" Nogitunde walked around Arymaitei, suspicious. She attempted to obscure Emily and Glehson, both trying and failing to look inconspicuous.

"They are friends of a friend. Now why are you here, really? Please enlighten me." Arymaitei quickly matched his movement and stood again in front of him.

Nogitunde licked his lips and whistled, his eyes turning up to the trees. Suddenly, hundreds of torchlights melted the darkness, surrounding them. Arymaitei clenched her fist.

"So, we've been ambushed?"

"Uh… yeah." Nogitunde turned his dark eyes to the torches moving in and surrounding them. "Let's see you talk your way out of this one, Ary."

"Nice job, lads!" she barked at her men.

"We only counted five, eight tops," Yazgiroh countered but was silenced with a glare.

Arymaitei gave a wicked smile and laughed. "We will be taking them out slowly," she scoffed, "Four to one, not that difficult for these kinds of odds."

"Weapons down!" a great booming voice reverberated through the air, its owner a tall broad man draped in a flowing cloak who stepped from the darkness. Arymaitei gave her men a cautionary glare, and all weapons in her and their possessions were dropped to the ground.

The imposing man gave Seitogi a questioning look, and the boy, after a moment of consideration, relented and threw his last hidden blade down among his comrades.

"You let that girl beat you again, boy!" The broad man strode up and looked down at Nogitunde, a foot shorter than him.

"Father, I…" Nogitunde felt the hot flash of pain; saw white light, and his feet lifted from the ground as the blow from the back of his father's massive hand sent him flying several feet away. He looked down on Arymaitei with unkind eyes.

"What is the meaning of this, Lark? I told you Taisehsai never to enter my territory!" the elder man growled.

Arymaitei bowed deep, "My apologies, Sir Gailen, for not informing you earlier about our movements. We thought Mingtoa was far enough from the grounds your Dhukai claims."

"So, I should believe you when you disobeyed my orders and trespassed on my land?"

"Apologies again." She quickly bowed again, "But my father's quarrel with you has nothing to do with us, Merry-Lar…grurgg!" Gailen's hand clamped around her neck and lifted her from the ground as though she were a feather. Her face reddened as she struggled.

"Careful with your tongue, little girl! You are not my equal!" he growled.

"No!" Emily screamed and ran to assist, but found her feet stuck in place when the man's fire agate eyes fell upon hers. Arymaitei's eyes bulged from the pressure, and she began to spew dark bile from her mouth.

“Arymaitei!” Nogitunde sprang at Gailen from where he lay. A temporary release of pressure gave Arymaitei enough time to wriggle free and scramble away, spitting up the contents of her stomach that stained her mouth and throat.

“Father, that’s enough! The Laughing Lark is not our enemy!”

Nogitunde took a deep breath as he stepped in front of Gailen, who stared at him menacingly.

“She still has you smitten, I see. Pathetic!”

He downed the boy with a single blow to his stomach, stepped over him, and mumbled,

“I have much to do, boy. Do not get in my way again.” Marking Emily and Glehson with his eyes, he tossed Arymaitei a waterskin. “Clean yourself, Lark. I grow weary of your scent.”

He towered over Emily and looked at her with curiosity in his eye. She felt her heart pounding faster. He then looked at Glehson, his eyes widening even more.

“Ahahaha!” He laughed. “What a pleasant surprise. To what do I owe the pleasure of your visit?” his voice dripping with sarcasm.

Glehson took a step back, unsure of what to say to the monster in front of them, but managed,

“You must have mistaken me for someone else, sir,” a hint of disquiet in his voice. Gailen stared at him, his brows raised, and then slowly settled on a flat stare.

“Round them up, boys!” he said and walked away as Emily scurried over to Arymaitei and helped her sit up.

“Why didn’t you do anything?” Emily glared at Seitogi.

“There was nothing Seita could’ve done,” said Arymaitei, her voice raspy. “We’re in a bad situation now.” She grabbed the skin of water that Emily offered her and took several gulps, wiping her mouth.

Yuyu & Ary

Yuyuki sat wrapped in a heavy wool cloak, her tiny body rattled by the dips and uneven surface of the ground as Yienguoi-Jin pulled her through the snow on a wooden sleigh. Despite her fur-lined attire, she still felt the cold, and it annoyed her to no end. At least, she was pretty sure she would be warm soon.

Yienguoi-Jin had told her that once they reached Smitemae, there would be a hot meal and a warm bed waiting for her. Assuming all went well, they would have just a few more miles to go before they arrived.

She pulled the cloak a little tighter, thinking about how glad she was that her father had come to rescue her from Odahni. Life there had become exceptionally unpleasant after discovering her sister, Princess Shumaiyuki, sequestered in the tower's hidden wing.

After the discovery, the castle split into factions of sorts and sunk into internal political intrigues. Shumaiyuki had her supporters from former adherents of her father. Yuyuki had the support of Yulori, though it would eventually weaken his standing as clan leader with its elders.

She often longed for those free-roaming days back in Daiye village with Seitogi, and even cherished the little time she spent with the man in the demon mask. Yienguoi-Jin stopped suddenly, looking back at her. She gave him an uncertain look.

"Something wrong?" she asked.

Yienguoi-Jin just shook his head and said, "I just wanted to look at your beautiful face again, my love." Yuyuki giggled at the compliment. How could a man wearing a demon's mask be so sentimental?

He took her hand and held it for a moment, brushing a snowflake from her eyelashes. Oh, how much she looked like his beloved Ameiki, he thought. Then he resumed pulling her through the falling snow, looking ahead with a serene expression in his eyes.

The sky was low over the infinite flat white horizon, covered by a canopy of deep blue and purple, which melted into darker grays as the day turned to night. Somewhere in the distance, the high peaks of the Shweivord Cliffs reared out into the wind like a mighty sentinel against the coming darkness.

"How much further is it to Smitemae?" Yuyuki tried to keep her voice level, despite fatigue dampening it. Yienguoi-Jin looked down at her and paused for a moment.

"Just a little farther, my precious," he said before continuing.

Yuyuki sighed, leaning back against the curved railing and letting her eyes drift shut. She was exhausted. They had been traveling on foot for seven days already, and nothing but the changing of the stars had marked their passage.

She'd barely slept since the night they stole away from Odahni; she couldn't even recall the last time she'd actually slept peacefully since meeting Shumaiyuki.

It was pitch black now, and there was nobody out to see their arrival. The next thing she knew, the sleigh was slowing. Suddenly awake, her eyes widened as the out-of-the-way destination ahead came into view.

The sky was outlined by a coal-black mountain range, in contrast to the white snow-covered trees, which seemed to stretch away into forever. Yienguoi-Jin needed no torchlight as he knew this path like the back of his hand. The passage led them through dark, winding tunnels deep into the mountainside until there was a soft glow, and they emerged into a massive cavern.

It was a deep natural well, girding the whole area with high stone walls and huge iron gates, like a collar around a dog's neck. They pulled up to the entrance, and Yienguoi-Jin looked over at her.

"We're here," his voice was soft. He removed his mask, and though hideously scarred, the look he gave her was full of love – the look of love she had been missing since leaving Daiye village and the Abete family.

"Welcome to Smitemae," he announced. "Remain on the sleigh." He then began unloading their bags.

Yuyuki looked around in amazement, clutching her swan hairpin.

"What time is it?" she asked.

"Second half of the fox," he said, "I think."

Yuyuki sighed again. She was tired from the long journey and from the life she'd left behind. She was tired of running, tired of pretending to be somebody she wasn't. But, most of all, she was tired of not being a part of Yienguoi-Jin's life.

She watched listlessly as he unpacked their things from the back of the sleigh and began unloading them. Suddenly, the massive door creaked open, and a woman came rushing out followed by three men. She was as tall as he and wore a long copper overcoat.

"Ah," she greeted him in a joyful voice, "I thought for certain you had gotten lost in the snow. I'm so happy to see you!" She turned back to the men, "Take our lord's belongings inside and drop them off in our apartment."

She looked over at Yuyuki and gave a short bow.

"And who might you be?" she asked. Yuyuki returned the bow shyly.

"Why, she's my daughter," Yienguoi-Jin replied. The woman's eyes flared up with interest. She looked mystified for a moment, then she burst out laughing.

"Oh, someone finally got a sense of humor!" she cried, relieved, and she gave a warm smile. "Ah," she said, "What noble's child have you kidnapped? How much is her ransom?"

"Awei," Yienguoi-Jin warned her with just a look, and her laughter ceased. She looked over at Yuyuki and studied her face for a moment.

"Ah, I see," she said, and slapped Yienguoi-Jin so hard across the face that he dropped his mask to the ground. For a moment, the air was silent. Yienguoi-Jin rubbed his face then grabbed her arms.

"You are a disgrace," she told him. "You dare seed another womb and go against the laws our kind has upheld for a thousand years!"

"What are you talking about?!" he demanded. "What laws of Dhukai would a lady of luxury like you know?" He was shouting, his eyes flashing red, not in anger but in confusion. Nonetheless, it frightened Yuyuki just the same.

Awei yanked herself away from his grip.

"That's what I thought anyway!"

"Well then, I could say the same for you, lord majesty." She turned away, walking back inside. "Come, girl. My name is Awei. Apparently, I am your new mother and, unfortunately, your depraved father's wife."

She and Yienguoi-Jin erupted into an argument about morals and a mother's honor as Yuyuki followed behind them. They walked down a narrow corridor, lit dimly by torches, until they came to another door. She ushered them through, and inside it was warm, lit by several blazing furnaces and bustling with activity.

As they walked inside, Yuyuki was struck by the chaos of the chamber. Chattering, shouting, laughing, and cursing carried on all at once. She was greeted by an array of fantastical faces, from which a very familiar voice came to her ears.

"Enoshi!"

"Seita!" Yuyuki cried, running to him and throwing herself into his arms. Seitogi hugged her close and pushed her away a moment later, laughing and holding her at arm's length.

"Enoshi!" he looked at her, holding back tears in his eyes. "You've grown so much!"

"You look older too, Seita," she said, laughing.

"It's almost been three years since the Aiyo took you away," he guessed. Yuyuki nodded.

Seitogi patted the top of her head, "And you haven't changed a bit." The two hugged again. It was then that Yuyuki noticed the frowning little girl standing just behind him.

She looked familiar, but Yuyuki didn't know why.

"And who is this?" she asked. Seitogi turned as the girl boldly stepped forward and pushed past him, petulantly asking,

"Who are you to be so familiar with my Seita?"

"I'm Shumai…" She thought back to the girl in the tower, the real Shumaiyuki, and instead introduced herself as Yuyuki. The girl twisted her face into a grimace and then,

"No! You are Yuyu from now on! Come, Seita, let's go play," grabbing Seitogi by the hand and pulling him along with her. "You can come along too, Yuyu!"

Yuyuki stood shocked, then looked over at Seitogi, who had a curious smile on his face.

"Mouse! You are being rude to your sister. Now give her a proper greeting," the tall gap-toothed woman glided across the room and placed her hand on the little sprite's shoulder and shoved her forward.

"My sister?" Yuyuki jumped back in fright and looked at her father, bewildered. "What do you mean?" she asked.

"My name is Arymaitei," the ruddy girl quickly bowed at the waist. "You can call me Ary if you like. Now come, Seita." The girl stomped away, pulling Seitogi in tow, but he stood in place, causing her to stumble forward. Yuyuki looked at her father, confused.

Yienguoi-Jin just laughed, "We'll talk later. For now, go take a meal with Seitogi and Ary." He said and gave her and Seitogi a soft push forward. She and Seitogi ambled off, and then he turned to his wife. "I suppose I have some explaining to do."

“Always something with you,” Awei muttered.

He hesitated, “Take note of the age difference, my wife. Her birth predates Ary’s. I have not broken our vows.”

“But you’ve kept your secrets all the same,” Awei nodded and began walking away. “I’ll leave you to explain it to our daughter,” she said. Yienguoi-Jin sighed and then turned to Arymaitei and said,

“Listen, Ary… I—”

“Always something with you, Dad,” she threw him a look of disgust and then ran off to catch up with Seitogi and her new sister.

The next day, Yuyuki walked with Seitogi, Arymaitei trailing behind them. As they walked, they giggled and scolded her for her moody antics.

“Slow down, you two, slow down,” she cried. “I’m tired of following after you!”

Seitogi began to quicken his pace with Yuyuki encouraging, “Go, Seita!” and to Arymaitei, “Hurry up, you!”

The two laughed alongside each other. Arymaitei picked up her pace with desperate determination, trying to catch up with them. Seitogi stopped at a small flower garden that had sprouted from the side of a large rock and plucked a small purple flower from its stem and placed it in Yuyuki’s hair.

“What is it, Seita?!” Arymaitei stopped walking. “Why don’t you pick one for me too? Have I done something wrong?”

“No, of course not, Ary,” he said, patting her on top of the head before taking Yuyuki’s hand and walking on. She leaned her head against Seitogi’s shoulder to Arymaitei’s dismay.

“What about me?” she asked. “Don’t tell me you have forgotten about me already!”

“Far from it, Ary, but I haven’t seen Enoshi in years, so stop complaining,” he said.

"Are you kidding?! When do you ever spend time with me?!" she asked as she caught up to them and slipped her arm around his waist.

"Ary..." he began, but she glared up at him and pulled him along very forcefully for a child.

Yuyuki thought it was funny, though. She leaned her head against his shoulder, saying, "It's fine, Ary. We can all walk together."

As the weeks went on, Yuyuki, Arymaitei, and Seitogi became an inseparable trio. They showed her all the fun and hidden places of the mega fortress while introducing her to everyone they came across. Her day would begin with following Yienguoi-Jin and Seitogi and Ary to where the men trained in a twisty maze-like structure made of stone, wood, and rope. There, she trained as though she were one of them, though clumsy in her efforts.

Yienguoi-Jin instructed the two girls in various skills, including using a dagger, crossbow, longbow, and spear, as well as throwing, grappling, swimming, and running.

Yuyuki excelled in all of these disciplines, as if she had received prior training, while Arymaitei was particularly skilled in swimming.

One day, while Yienguoi-Jin and Yuyuki were off training, Arymaitei overheard her mother complaining to Belfast about Yuyuki's sudden appearance. Her curiosity piqued, the child hid in stealth and listened intently.

"All of Yienguoi's mistakes are of his own making," she said weakly.

"You try his patience," Belfast replied.

"I don't see how he could have any reason for complaining about me. Have I not been a loyal partner all these years? If the Aiyo finds out he has brought the Pearl Swan here, we are all dead, or it's war at the very least!"

"But she is his child!"

"She belongs to the Aiyo, as do all who carry their blood in their veins. He has kidnapped her. Do you not think the men will speak of this amongst themselves? He has put the entire Taisehsai in jeopardy to fulfill his own selfish needs. For all Yienguoi-Jin's faults, it's his Aiyo manipulation that threatens us all!"

"The Aiyo wouldn't dare move against us. We are the emperor's favored Dhukai, and our numbers are vast."

"Not so vast as to ward off the entirety of Aiyo's Tabaikin."

Arymaitei crept away and ran to the raised stone plateau where she trained daily and clambered up a hand-chiseled stairwell that led to the giant stone's apex. Eventually, she reached the top, to find Seitogi and her father watching Yuyuki run through lines.

"Dad!" she called and ran over to him. "What are you doing?" she asked.

"Her form is impeccable," the demon muttered to himself, "almost as if…"

"As if what, Dad?" Arymaitei asked.

"I see what you mean," said Seitogi, "She's far more advanced than she should be. She knows basic light-foot as well."

"Her martial skill is beyond her years," said Yienguoi-Jin, "Colossal and yet, it flows through her like water. Something is strange here."

"Is it because she's the Pearl Swan?" Arymaitei asked. Yienguoi-Jin stiffened and stared down at his daughter, seemingly only then noticing her presence.

"Where have you heard that name?" he asked.

"What's the Pearl Swan? You said that the other day," she said innocently.

"No, girl," Yienguoi-Jin said sternly. "You lie." He looked at Seitogi for a moment, as if about to speak, but he stopped himself, thinking better of it.

"Never repeat what you have said here today. To anyone!" he said. "I have to go talk with Awei," he said, grabbing Seitogi's arm. "Watch the girls for now. I'll be back later."

He left Arymaitei frozen like ice. Seitogi looked at her questioningly.

"What's the matter, Ary?" he said.

"The Pearl Swan," she said softly.

"What is that?" he asked.

She could feel her heartbeat in her chest. Tears welled into her eyes. "Leave, Seita," she said. "Leave me alone!" and ran off, leaving Seitogi looking after her, confused.

The next morning, Arymaitei and Yuyuki were sitting on the ground underneath a tree playing Tajine, a card game that involved players playing a mixed hand of people and animals against the other in their opponent's hand and capturing them.

"What's this Pearl Swan thing?!" Ary asked, clearly distressed about her mother and Belfast's words the previous day. "I don't understand."

"It's nothing," said Yuyuki. "Tell me something about you."

"There is little to know."

"Don't lie to me," Yuyuki asked.

"What is the Pearl Swan?" she asked again. "It means something. I heard my mother say it yesterday, and my father seemed upset when I mentioned it to him. It was like he was ashamed. Does it mean you are really an Aiyo princess?"

"Why ask if you already know?" snapped Yuyuki.

"So you are? A princess?"

"Not anymore. And I am happier for it. It would be nice to talk about other things. What about you, Ary?"

"No wonder you act so stuck up. I guess it's because you're an Aiyo," said Ary as she laid down a card displaying a fire-spouting griffin.

Yuyuki still laid an armored maiden atop the card.

"You are right. It's not something to be proud of, being an Aiyo. I am sorry you are so jealous," Yuyuki smiled. "I win," and stood up, saying, "I'm going back inside."

Arymaitei stood up as well. "No, don't go. Please don't leave me. I'm sorry."

Yuyuki turned to face her, and Ary began to cry. "I'm sorry, Yuyuki. Please don't be mad."

The two stood staring at each other for a few seconds before Yuyuki laughed.

"It's alright, Ary. I'm glad you asked. I'm not stuck up though. It's just hard to talk about. I would also like to talk about other things as well."

Arymaitei smiled. "Well…I'm an only child, and my mother and father argue and kiss all the time."

Yuyuki looked over at her with sad eyes. "My mother died when I was a baby, so I'm an only child too," she said.

"I want to show you more of the village. Can we go together?" Arymaitei asked.

"Father said I'm not allowed," said Yuyuki.

"I'm sorry, but you'll soon realize dad is an idiot. Come with me. You don't want to stay here, do you? You'll get sick of this place soon enough."

"Okay," Yuyuki said, still unsure, but the two girls ran off towards the Taisehsai village hidden amongst the mountains. They crept silently through the valley, avoiding the guards armed with crossbows.

"Old Nukei," Arymaitei pointed out, "the leader of the guards. He's a real tattletale." They moved stealthily through a jagged crag.

Yuyuki could see the tops of a citadel, with a giant black and green banner surmounting the tower.

"And that's the Grand Shrine," she said.

They continued on, jumping from stone to stone until they moved past the tower, hidden behind crooked rock faces. The girls talked about their lives, and soon the nine and seven-year-olds felt like they were the only people in the world.

An hour later, the girls reached the gates to Taisehsai village.

"I can't believe we made it," Yuyuki said. "There is so much to see. I've never been allowed outside Odahni, and father wouldn't allow me to sightsee on our way to Smitemae."

They walked into the village, following the torrent of adults, kids, and old people who were slowly making their way towards the market square. They danced and giggled as they strolled through the crudely paved streets of Taisehsai.

"How long have you lived here?" Yuyuki asked.

"My whole life, silly," Arymaitei said. "I am a Dhukai by birth."

Ary pointed out buildings and sights to Yuyuki as they passed. They came across a large square full of roughly fashioned buildings, leaning at odd angles. In the middle was an old man sitting on a high-backed chair.

"That's Rinske. He sits there all day and complains about dad. He doesn't think he is worthy of the mask," said Ary. The girls stopped in front of a series of rickety shops built of rudimentary stone hewn from the mountainside.

Many proprietors knew Arymaitei and asked about her new friend. People watched them curiously, pointing and whispering as they passed. Ary talked to every shopkeeper they passed until they reached the market square.

The square was packed. A congregation of people had created a dense central area with the stalls and booths of various vendors. Arymaitei and Yuyuki made their way through the crowd, stopping to pet animals and buying snacks. As they were making their way through the crowd, Yuyuki suddenly heard someone shout.

"That's her!"

After a few moments, Yuyuki turned to see Rinske pointing at her. Had he been following them? Yuyuki quickly pulled Arymaitei away, moving through the crowd of people.

"That there is an abomination! An abomination! The witch's spawn!" the man shouted. Yuyuki, still holding onto Arymaitei's hand, began to run.

The two girls dodged the crowd, moving up and down the larger stalls. They ran through the streets of Taisehsai back through its gates until they were back on the trail that would take them back higher into the mountains of Smitemae proper.

Yuyuki was exhausted by the time they stopped running. "I don't understand. Why would the old man hate me so much?" Yuyuki asked again.

"Mother says Rinske is one of those stupid people who fear things they don't understand," said Arymaitei. "Don't worry, you can't take anything he says seriously. He'll leave you alone once we tell dad."

Yuyuki leaned against a boulder and sighed. "I really hope that's true."

"Forget about it," said Arymaitei. "Hey, let's climb up to the top and watch the sunset."

The two girls continued on their way up the rocky trail, competing for speed on the way up. Yuyuki was faster, and she easily outran Arymaitei. The two girls stopped to rest at the top of the cliff overlooking Kue Province, both panting from the run.

Snow was light, but the wind blew in all directions, causing Yuyuki's and Arymaitei's hair to dance and swirl and lift up their cloaks. They stood in silence for a moment. Arymaitei spoke first.

"So, Yuyu, is it really true that the swan princesses of Aiyo can fly?" she asked.

Yuyuki chuckled. "Maybe. But it's supposed to be a secret."

Arymaitei held up her little finger. "I promise to keep a secret, even if Yuyu tells me."

Yuyuki laughed. "Fine. I promise to show you one day. Hey, where are you going?"

"If we climb up to the overhang, we will have a better view," said Arymaitei. "Come on! Follow me!"

The two girls climbed to the very top of the high, craggy peak and sat down in the snow. They watched the sunset in silence.

"It's so beautiful," said Yuyuki, reaching out to the sky, a vibrant shade of orange and purple. "It's almost like I could touch the sun."

"How do you do it?" asked Arymaitei. She leaned her head against Yuyuki's. "You're a swan princess of Aiyo. How do you fly?"

The orange tinge in the sky had vanished almost completely, and the deep starry twinkling of an evening twilight had begun to settle over Smitemae. Yuyuki remained silent, unsure of what to say. Arymaitei walked over and looked out over the edge down into the foggy abyss that was the base of the mountainous mega fortress.

"I don't think you're really an Aiyo princess at all," she pouted, kicking snow. "And I bet you can't really fly. Otherwise, you would have shown me. I can't wait to tell Seitogi what a fake you are!"

"What!?" Yuyuki struggled to her feet, face red. "What do you know, you little brat? I am a princess! It's in my family history; it's recorded in the books I've been reading. I can fly, and I can read. I bet you can't even read!"

"Do it then! Show me! Fly! Or are you too scared!"

Yuyuki's temper flared, and the girl stomped over to the edge of the cliff, leaving a lingering vapor trail in her wake.

"Fine!" she huffed. "I'm going to show you a real princess's power!"

She took a step closer to the edge; another step would be into empty air and certain death. She looked down the precipice, and a slight drop in blood pressure made the girl feel lightheaded.

It was at that moment that Arymaitei crept behind Yuyuki with a nervous, but evil gleam in her eye and pushed outward just as her sister took a step backward, causing Ary to stumble and fall straight into the open space beyond the edge. Yuyuki's stomach flipped, then her body twisted, and she bent at an odd angle grabbing her sister's hand mid-scream. Arymaitei hung suspended over the drop, shouting for help as Yuyuki held tight onto her hand.

"Don't panic, I have you. I won't let you go, I promise!" Yuyuki reassured her.

The volatile wind and snow swung Arymaitei back and forth like a pendulum, and Yuyuki could feel her grip beginning to slip as Arymaitei screamed with panic. Yuyuki reached with her other hand and slowly, carefully grabbed her sister's cloak, pulling painstakingly slowly as she had no true anchor to keep from going over herself.

The howling wind was tremendous and Arymaitei clung on tightly as Yuyuki pulled her back to safety. The two sat huddled together on the plateau, close to tears and shivering, while the wind grew fiercer, swirling around them and getting stronger by the second.

Yuyuki pulled her fingers into Ary's cloak around her and kept a tight grip on her sister as Arymaitei sobbed. "I'm sorry! I'm sorry!" she cried into Yuyuki's lap.

"Shh," Yuyuki urged as the two pulled up their hoods. "I know you're scared, but you tripped, it was just a mistake."

Arymaitei looked into Yuyuki's eyes, realizing she hadn't caught on that she meant to push her to her death, and the overwhelming guilt she felt caused tears to fall from her eyes anew. She looked up at the sky and realized what a terrible mistake she had made. She felt awful. "I'm sorry! I'm sorry!" she repeated.

The wind whipped the two girls, stronger and stronger by the second, blow after blow after blow as they made their way down the mountain safely away from the ledge and back to the fortress.

"What happened?" asked Awei, noticing their bedraggled state as they walked to their rooms. "You girls okay? Mouse?" She followed them to the stairs.

"We're fine mum," said Arymaitei.

"It's a long story," said Yuyuki. "We had an…incident."

Awei nodded, urging them on before walking to the stairs. "You know your father's going to be pissed you took your sister into town. Of course, I know. It is my job to know," she said. "Tomorrow when he returns, I'll tell him what he needs to hear. I'll handle it. You girls eat and get some rest. You've obviously had a long day."

Later that night, Arymaitei stood in Yuyuki's doorway as she slept, tears still in her eyes. "I'm sorry I…I didn't mean to."

***

Several days later, Arymaitei and Yuyuki sat outside on the doorstep to the fortress with their father, as Awei told him about their jaunt into town. Yuyuki was admonished, and Arymaitei was ordered to apologize for disobeying a direct order.

"I'm sorry, father," Arymaitei pouted.

"What am I to do with you two?" he sighed. "I'm surprised at both your behaviors, my princesses. Especially you, Yuyuki. I expect more as you are older."

"It won't happen again, father," she said, tears welling up.

Arymaitei looked over at her sister and rolled her eyes. "Oh, you don't have to cry. It's just Dad. He's always carrying on about something," she whispered loudly.

"Don't undermine your father!" said Awei. "And stay in your place."

She looked over to see that Yuyuki was smirking. Arymaitei shrugged and grabbed Yuyuki's hand, walking over to the doorway and clearing her throat.

"Well, Awei, we're heading down to town again today. Should we take our swords?"

Awei shot her a look that could pierce bone. "Call me Mum, you little cow! Oh, I should beat you!" Awei turned to Yienguoi-Jin. "Aren't you going to say something? You're her father! Beat her then."

Yuyuki bit her lip, trying to suppress a smile. She thought her sister was a brat, but a brave one to call such an intimidating woman by her first name.

"Wait a minute. I have a better idea," said Yienguoi-Jin. "You girls come with me now," scratching his beard in thought. "Grab your things. I'm sending you to clean all the pissers under Crebs supervision."

The two princesses' eyes grew wide, "Eww dad! No way! Gross!"

Awei looked on and laughed, "Heh. What a fitting punishment."

And with that, Yienguoi-Jin called two guards to escort them. But Arymaitei stuck her tongue out and hurriedly pulled Yuyuki along with her, running down the mountain path.

"Stop it!" Yuyuki shouted.

"Damn you Mouse! Get back here dammit!" Awei yelled.

"What did I do but show her around!" Arymaitei called back. "It's not fair!" She spun around and they continued to run.

"We're shit parents, aren't we?" Awei sighed to Yienguoi-Jin, eliciting laughter from the guards.

Ary laughed as they ran, letting go of Yuyuki's hand, leaving her sister behind and vanishing into the mountainside. Yuyuki sighed and followed, running after Arymaitei deeper into the rocky wilderness.

She walked on a downward path, winding her way through the harsh rocky landscape.

"Ary! Where are you? Come out from hiding or I'm going back!" she called out, scanning the terrain. Arymaitei finally appeared from a hidden crevice, her dark eyes narrowed.

"I'm right here. Don't be such a baby," she said. The wind howled, raising her hair and fluttering her cloak.

"Where were you?" Yuyuki complained, puffing. She stomped forward to catch up with her sister, kicking rocks out of her way.

The two adventured all morning, happily chatting and enjoying the scenery. They saw an abandoned nest high in a tree, a message inscribed in an ancient language, and a small iced-over stream.

They stopped for lunch in the shade of a crevice in the cliff wall. Arymaitei pulled dried strips of meat from her satchel and passed a piece to Yuyuki. Afternoon bled into evening and Yuyuki found her arm aching from a day of climbing and running.

"Okay, I want to go back," she said, "We've been out all day and I'm exhausted!"

Arymaitei smiled, "How boring." She stood up, stretching her arms above her head, then tucking them behind her back.

"He's still going to make us clean the pissers," she said.

"It's getting dark," said Yuyuki.

“So what if it’s getting dark? It will still be sunny again tomorrow.”

“What do you want to be when you grow up?” asked Yuyuki as she watched her sister draw figures in the snow with a stick.

“I want to lead my own Dhukai,” Arymaitei said, looking up.

Yuyuki smiled. “You’re very brave. I’m sure you would be a great Hakurumi,” she said.

“Since you are a princess, are you going to marry a prince?”

“I’ll just be an ordinary girl from now on,” Yuyuki said, a hint of sadness in her voice.

“You are the daughter of Yienguoi-Jin and the Bronze Swan of Aiyo!” a woman’s voice came from the rapidly diminishing dusk that made the girls jump. “You are anything but normal, child.”

The girls took a step back as she emerged from the encroaching darkness.

“Who goes there?” Arymaitei stood in front of Yuyuki, looking up at the shrouded figure and took a fighting stance.

“Oh my, such a brave girl,” the woman said, smiling behind the black hood of her cloak. She coughed several times and wavered a bit, as though she were ill.

“Show yourself or be considered a coward!” Arymaitei twirled a dagger in her hand.

“Where’d you get a knife?” asked Yuyuki.

“Does it matter? I am a Dhukai by birth and always ready for a fight!” answered Arymaitei.

“Step aside and be gone,” the bent over woman ambled from behind a boulder shrouded in the deepening wintry light. Her arms and legs, though wrapped in rags, were slightly muscular but still much stronger than an ordinary octogenarian. Her long hair was overgrown and wild, like wind-whipped fire.

"My business is not with you. I've come for the Pearl Swan."

"Oh no! It's the old witch Maishae!" said Arymaitei. "Dad warned me about you! You'd best get lost or I'm going to stab you in the leg!"

"Please have some compassion for me," Maishae coughed and spat out a ball of phlegm.

Yuyuki stepped forward, looking down at the woman, who was no taller than her.

"What could a witch possibly want with me?"

Maishae's eyes squinted to see the princess better. She had the look of an old lady beat down in life at every turn. Toothless, frail-looking, she had rheumy black eyes and a wrinkled grin.

"It's quite simple, my dear. You belong to me! Now come along. I'm taking you back to the pocket. Don't be difficult."

"The pocket? I'm afraid I can't go with you," Yuyuki said, backing up and pulling Arymaitei with her.

"We'll see about that," Maishae sauntered closer with an exaggerated hunch and laid a large pouch down on the rock. She pulled out a long black rope, a thorn whip, a large sickle, and a curved dagger. All the weapons excited a distant sense of familiarity in Yuyuki, but so did the witch. She felt like she'd met Maishae before, in a different time and place. Fought her before, even.

Yuyuki continued to back away, her eyes alive and searching, watching Maishae with an intense focus. She felt a new kind of energy flowing through her, eyes glowing, hair swirling, as the witch walked towards her holding the rope and repeating for her not to be difficult.

"Ary, I'm scared," Yuyuki whispered.

"Try to stay calm, I won't let her hurt you!" Arymaitei jumped forward with her weapon in hand.

"If you want to take Yuyuki, then you must go through me!"

"Such a brave Dhukai girl. It's too bad you have to die now." Maishae smiled darkly, her eyes squinting with a look of utmost hate.

Arymaitei lunged at her, but Maishae knocked her aside with an arm that felt like a metal bar. She slipped on the ice and fell to the ground. Maishae delivered her a sharp kick to the ribs and laughed.

Yuyuki cursed the old woman and threw a rock at her as Maishae seemed to glide over the snow, advancing towards her.

"You are my property!"

"I am no such thing to you!" Yuyuki cried and flung another rock, causing Maishae to stumble. Suddenly unsure of herself, the witch regained her posture in a huff.

Yuyuki glared at her, whose own eyes reflected a mixture of impressed awe. Yuyuki's hands moved on their own accord, rapidly picking up stone and ice alike and using the projectiles as a feint/strike as she rushed forward.

Her legs felt lighter than air, and she felt a strange euphoria as she made contact with the ground. Each step was filled with a raw, new energy. Maishae was suddenly forced to retreat backward. She dropped her rope and cried out as she fell to the ground.

"Come now child! As you can see I am a bit under the weather and in no mood for a tussle!" Maishae jumped back to her feet. Yuyuki wasn't afraid; her fear was her fuel for anger. Why? What was happening? How could this witch even know who she was?

Suddenly, Yuyuki felt something gnaw at her consciousness, something vaguely remembered. She could feel it inside her, scratching at her, almost like a loose tooth trying to come out. And then,

"The rain! You…you locked me outside in the rain!"

"Enough!" Maishae shrieked, "I order you to come along with me now!" The witch's eyes were wild, her face vicious, and she waved her arms in a circular pattern and then pushed out with her palms.

Yuyuki felt like she had been hit with an invisible force that winded her. Her body was convulsing; her mind was fading. She was losing grip on reality. She fell to the ground, losing consciousness.

"Yah!," cried out Arymaitei, her eyes wide. Maishae grabbed the girl's arm, stopping the momentum of the dagger strike, but it was a feint. Arymaitei rolled back and slammed her foot into the old woman's rib cage.

Maishae yelped, letting her go as Arymaitei danced away. Maishae wobbled, hardly phased, and laughed.

"How amusing! I remember training your Papa. Do you think I'd allow a child to beat me?" She jumped back, seemingly injured. Then Yuyuki jumped on her back. Maishae stumbled forward and fell face-first into the snow.

"Come on, Ary!" Yuyuki got back up and started to run. She saw Maishae trying to stand, blood trickling from her crushed nose. She almost got back up, but fell again when Arymaitei leaped into the air and delivered a forceful kick to the jaw.

"It's over," Arymaitei said, "We'll defeat you and your friends anytime." Arymaitei jumped up, striking the air with a fist. Maishae groaned as Arymaitei jumped onto her back, spun the knife around in her hand, and struck down, aiming for the nape of the old woman's neck.

Maishae spun around with blinding speed and slapped the girl across the face. Arymaitei felt the intense sting spread across her cheek to her whole skull as she landed at Yuyuki's feet. However, she flipped back up, ready to launch herself forward but felt a strange burning spreading from her chest to her throat.

Her face was bright red, and she held her hand to her abdomen, feeling as though she were going to be sick. Maishae cursed and charged forward. Yuyuki grabbed Arymaitei's hand and dragged the girl along with her as she barreled through the snow. Both stumbled several times navigating the rocky terrain.

"Never! I will not let you get away!" Maishae was quickly gaining ground on them. Yuyuki's face was contorted with rage, her body felt like a block of ice, and her head ached from the race.

As the snow pelted down on her, she felt her chest constrict, and her vision began to blur. Everything around her was hazy, and her heavy breathing whistled in her ears. Arymaitei struggled to keep up with her, but Yuyuki refused to slow down. They both were approaching the end of their strength!

“You’ll have to tear me limb from limb to stop me,” Maishae followed, twirling her rope around like a horse wrangler.

“Hold onto me, Ary! I’m going to run fast so you’ll have to hang on with all your strength!” Yuyuki took Arymaitei up in her arms, lifting the girl from the ground and carrying her as she ran.

“But she’s gaining on us!” Arymaitei cried back.

“We’ve come this far; there’s no stopping us now!” Yuyuki responded and flew down the mountain like she was on skis, her legs moving so fast she was afraid to look down for fear of tripping.

She sprinted until they reached the bottom of the climb where her chest could take no more. She bent her knees and skidded to a halt, falling forward, dropping Arymaitei in the process.

“Why are you stopping? Are we okay?”

“I think so. We’re both still alive…” Yuyuki answered, panting.

She helped Arymaitei to her feet and leaned against the icy wall. She felt so tired, her body heavy, and her eyes were watery. She slumped to the ground, her arms falling to her side.

“What happened?” Arymaitei asked. “Where did the witch go?” looking behind her.

Breathing hard, Yuyuki pitched forward and emptied the contents of her stomach, disturbing the pure white of the snow with brownish-orange vomit. She closed her eyes and saw herself in an open field surrounded by hundreds of Maishaes and screamed. Arymaitei rushed over to help her and patted her on her back.

"Why would she say I belonged to her?" Yuyuki asked and began to cry uncontrollably. Arymaitei threw her arms around her, crying too.

"I won't ever let her take you, Yuyu! I promise! I'll always protect you from that witch."

"Do you really promise?" Yuyuki collapsed her face into her sister's lap, her eyes closed and her head pounding.

"I promise. Always," Arymaitei said, casting a cautious eye back up the mountain pass.

The Old Flame

Dowahg Gailen stared at the parchment in his hand. The scroll's ink had run. Irked, he tossed it aside and looked at the other one. Idly, he traced his finger over the characters inscribed on the sheet. His brow furrowed as he looked at the back of the scroll, then back down again. He sighed and rubbed his chin with a hand and bit his lip thoughtfully.

"What do you think of it, m'lord?" Ralavar Zefrey's voice broke into his musings.

Gailen's head jerked up and he glared at his advisor. A doughy, gray-skinned man with crooked teeth and full body alopecia. "Think of what?" he snapped.

Ralavar swallowed, nodded, and bowed. Gailen threw his head back and rubbed his eyes with the back of his hand. Then he looked at the small table in front of him, surrounded by his most trusted retainers. His expression was grim.

"Mmmm," he muttered. "It looks like White Eyes has played us for fools. To claim he didn't know the boy was the crown prince is ridiculous. Now he's stuck him with us. Will it not appear we kidnapped the emperor's heir?" he asked.

"Yes, m'lord," Ralavar crossed his arms and slowly shook his head from side to side. "Our spies have confirmed the crown prince has gone missing from the palace, though we cannot be certain the boy we have captured is he."

However, should he prove to be, then yes, White Eyes has put us in quite the predicament?"

"We aren't even certain he really is the crown prince," said Gailen, "We are just going by your word, boy, and you are known for your tall tales."

"But it is true, my lord!" Nogi protested from near the hut's door, his face still sore from his father's slap. "That boy is the future emperor. I saw him at the spring festival last year just after he won the fencing competition. I knew him at once. It is the same boy!"

"May I speak, my lord?" asked a handsome man with dark eyes and thick sideburns.

"Speak, Roten, what have you?" he asked.

"I have spoken to one of Chua's men. He rumors that in reality the girl is an Aiyo princess. The Golden Swan's secret twin, but born with a tail! If the Golden Swan is offering Awei 10 million ohn for her. Why not ransom her directly to the Aiyo ourselves and double the fee?"

"Impossible!" said Ralavar, "The Golden Swan has no tail twin! The girl looks nothing like her. I have never heard of such madness!"

"As if you have ever laid eyes on the Golden Swan!" countered Roten.

"Neither have you!"

"Enough bickering," Gailen frowned.

Roten bowed and then continued, "My lord, the presence of the heir should be all the proof we need that something is foul! He and The Golden Swan are to be married in a matter of months. Yet he is gallivanting across the country with an Aiyo lookalike!"

"That may be the case, old friend," said Ralavar, "But we cannot ransom a member of the royal family to his own house! We would be inviting the wrath of the imperial army."

"If the girl is Aiyo and she is with the heir," Roten again, "The Golden Swan would pay a high price for her. Since White Eyes has stuck us with the prince, I say we cut him out of his share. Negotiate 30 million ohn for the girl and the prince. Plus, we'd be one-upping Chua!"

"But Awei and her daughter are enemies and run rival Dhukais! Chua wouldn't pay a copper for her freedom."

"A ruse they employ to confuse the Taisehsai and other Dhukai Guilds. But I know better of It." said Roten.

Gailen sighed as his advisors continued to argue the matter, but at last, he simply said, “Send out three sparrows! One to Chua. Tell her her daughter has trespassed into Carp territory, so a price must be paid in coin or blood.”

“Very good, m’lord,” said Ralavar, bowing.

“The second one to Odhani. Address it to Lord Yulori. Tell them we have the Aiyo girl along with the Taisehsai boy. Let him make an offer. If she truly is their blood and a possible challenge for The Golden Swan, then House Aiyo wins either way. Word it somewhere along those lines.”

Roten cleared his throat, “It is common knowledge that Princess Shumaiyuki really runs Odhani. It is she whom we should address the sparrow. Thus, she will be in our debt after helping her procure her rival and her prince. Once she becomes empress, she will elevate our Dhukai.”

“That may be a dangerous move, m’lord,” Ralavar cut his eyes at Roten. “If we send the prince to the Aiyo, it may be looked at as though we were profiting off his life. It’s best if we escort him back to Nyongoyuchi. As the Taisehsai are the emperor’s preferred Dhukai, wouldn’t it put us in good standing with the imperial house?”

“Do you truly suggest we turn him back over and expect a pat on the head?” Roten was aghast. “The Aiyo have the Taibaiken armies. If we gain influence with Princess Shumaiyuki, she could then influence the emperor to recognize us as the imperial house Dhukai. It could be a win for all of us.”

“I don’t give a damn about the politics of House Aiyo! Address it to whomever you must! I just want the highest price for both!” Gailen threw up his hands.

The two advisors continued to argue, but Gailen wasn’t finished. “Send the third sparrow to Lord Sowaos’ office and tell him that we have the prince,” he stated. “I understand he is the prince’s closest advisor and is a man of his word.”

Nogitunde slipped out of the room as the arguing continued. He was still burning inside from the humiliation suffered at Gailen's hand. And to strike him in front of Ary, too. Despite the fact he was Gailen's son, he had grown to dislike his father vey much. Yet, he somehow still craved his approval.

He walked out into the humid air and let the warm, light rain wash over him. The sky was crowded with gray clouds stretching far into the distance, casting their long shadows over his face. He felt as if his soul was weighed down, as though he had spent his life buried deep in the ground. But he also felt a budding courage to climb out from the dirt. Walking aimlessly, he came to a halt and looked up. He was standing outside a poor-looking holding cell, a windowless 10x15 wood and iron box on the outskirts of the camp.

"I guess it's too late to turn back now." He looked over both shoulders. "I'm sorry I didn't come sooner." He opened the door and walked into the dark room. As his eyes adjusted to the dim light, he made out two decrepit cages.

In the first cage, Emily sat curled up, knees to chest, slowly rocking back and forth. Arymaitei lay next to her snoring with her mouth wide open and a trail of snot coming from her left nostril. Nogitunde struck a flint and lit a torch. Emily saw his face and gasped.

"You!" She immediately shook Arymaitei awake, saying, "Hey, your idiot boyfriend is here."

"What do you want?" Arymaitei yawned as she turned over, burying her head in Emily's lap, but to her chagrin, she was pushed away just as quickly.

"I don't have time for this." She leapt to her feet. Even in the dim light, Nogi could make out her face drenched in sweat, hair plastered against her forehead. Her damp robe was dyed red from the Kimori's blood, as were her arms and legs.

"What do you want?" She asked again, anger flashing in her eyes. "You come here for a last goodbye before I die?"

"How are you holding up?" he asked.

Arymaitei didn't answer at first, but just looked around and then said, "What do you think, asshole? We've been packed in here like sardines for hours!"

"I'm sorry about that. Father's orders, but I was against it from the start." He took a deep breath, "I'm going to get you guys out of here."

"You? And just how are you going to do that? And why? You never cared before; what makes now different?"

"I know I didn't treat you like I should have in the past, Ary, but I can at least make it up to you by helping you now. Besides, I'm going to need your help too." He looked down at his feet. She wasn't sure how to respond.

Nogitunde took a key from his robe and unlocked the door to her cage.

"Come with me. We need to talk."

She hesitated a moment before stepping out of the cage.

"What about the rest of us?" asked Emily.

"Just stay put for now. We're leaving soon. Just be patient."

"You know we have no intention of trusting you, right?" Seitogi asked from the second cage.

"I said just stay put," Nogitunde repeated. "I will get you out of here, don't you worry."

"You could at least cut our bands as a show of good faith," Seitogi lifted his leather-bound wrist.

"I must speak with Ary first. Come along, Lark." Nogitunde turned and walked out of the cell as Arymaitei shuffled out behind him with a slight limp.

"Are you okay, Nogitunde? What's up?" she asked as they entered the fresh air.

“Me? I’m fine. I just have to get out of here.” He said as he looked over his shoulder and smiled.

She immediately asked what he meant, but he shushed her and brought a finger to his lips as he led her behind him. He walked out into the rain and pulled his hood up over his head.

They walked quickly, and within minutes they were back at his own tent. He pulled the curtain and looked inside to make sure they were clear and motioned for her to go in first. Arymaitei went in as quickly as she could, and he followed.

There was a lantern hanging that provided a bit of light. When he made sure the curtain was pulled closed, he picked it up and walked over to her.

“Okay, Nogi, what’s this all about? And can you cut these damned binds already!”

“What? You’re angry that I’m helping you?” he asked.

“I am,” she replied, “leaving me to rot in there like that.”

He raised the lantern and stared into her eyes, “I’m sorry. I was trying to warn you before my father showed up, but you were too busy being an ass!”

“What?” she asked.

“Yeah! I was trying to protect you. But you wanted to show off.”

“Protect me? If you intended to warn or protect me, your old man would have never gotten his hands around my neck!”

“I’m sorry about that, Ary, but you know I care.”

“Care? What more do you want from me, Nogi? My heart? Because you won’t get that. Not after the games you played on me! Plus, I have Seita to consider.”

“Seita? That long-faced boy,” he paused, “Have you told him you love him yet?” He handed her a towel and jar of astringent.

"As if that should matter to you. I care about him, that's all."

"When you broke it off with me, you told me it was because you loved him."

"You misunderstood. He's like my brother, you idiot! I meant brotherly love."Arymaitei wet the cloth and began wiping herself down.

"Horse shit. You said you loved him," he lowered the lantern, "What do I have to do?"

"Get us all out of here! Only then can we talk about ourselves. Now, what was that warning you gave us about?" She undressed and continued to freshen up.

"White Eyes has betrayed you and enlisted my father to take the Aiyo girl from you."

"Huh?"

"Don't play dumb, Ary. The bounty for the girl is 10 million ohn. We can split it and live away from all this mess," He said. "Either way, your measly Dhukai wouldn't be able to bring in that kind of money in a decade."

"Wha…What bounty? White Eyes? I don't even know what you are talking about," she replied.

"Yes, you do," he said as he handed her a black canvas jumpsuit. "Don't bullshit me, Ary. You didn't ride out this far facing the perils you have to be charitable. Even if she is your sister."

"True," she said, "Charity is not my forte. But I wouldn't betray Yuyu just to make a few coins either."

"A few coins," he said as he moved even closer, "That bounty's worth 10 million ohn. The two of us could retire on that. Split it with me, and I will get you out of here."

She slapped his hand away. "Not on your life, lover-boy! I would rather rot in here than share my spoils…eh, betray, my…" But she stopped, almost like she had become mentally paralyzed.

“Heh? What was that? Your spoils?” he asked.

“No…” she said as if to herself.

“I know you, Ary. When we were together, you said you wanted out of the Dhukai business, right? You wanted to escape to Dreesh and live a life of peace and luxury. Let’s do it together.”

“Don’t you dare! At least not now,” she said, “That was when I foolishly believed you meant something to me. But you are nothing but wet wax, wicking every candle but mine! I loathe you! You must know that!”

“Useless drama as a smokescreen, Ary. You’re wasting time. Now I’m risking everything for you! You must know that!”

“I don’t know what you think you know! But you know nothing.”

“I know you were attacked by a flock of Komori not too long ago.” Nogitunde’s grin widened.

“So! You’ve been following us. Big deal,” She replied in a pouty tone.

“I know several days ago you received a raven from White Eyes warning you that your mother was on her way to Meriwell to take back the girl she lost in the forest days before. I know he proposed you split the profit instead, and that you agreed to cut Chua out of the deal.”

“Foolish conjecture.”

“I know you lied about the witch being holed up in Bashi because Bashi is where the exchange with the Aiyo emissaries will take place, and your precious Seita would’ve never agreed to help if he knew that. How am I doing?”

“What?!” she shouted. “That’s a lie…it’s not true! How could you know? You are bluffing; this is just a trick,” fumbling as she buttoned up her suit

"Dunno, Lark. I think I'm really on point. It's not like you to betray your friends, but I'm sure you have your reasons," he said.

"I'm not a coward!" She snapped. "I wouldn't betray my sister or Seita."

"I advise you to listen to my proposal, Lark," Nogitunde said. "Otherwise, I might just have to march back over there and let your team in on how you and White Eyes were working together the whole time."

"Idiot! Why would I do that?" Ary said and crossed her arms, turning away. Nogitunde knew she was cracking.

"So, so crafty. That's what I love about you."

"Excuse me?"

"Do you think it's a coincidence the Flying Carps just happened upon you?"

"I…"

"It's because White Eyes alerted my father to your movements directly after you set out for Bashi. We were here to capture you, Lark. Apparently, White Eyes didn't trust you would hold up your end of the bargain and deliver his cut of the money."

"Sonofabitch!"

"All we had to do was wait for you guys to show up."

"I should have known not to trust that bastard!"

"You shouldn't have, but luckily you have me here to set things right," He answered with a smirk on his face.

Arymaitei glared back at him and shook her head, "No, no Nogitunde. I am not going to negotiate with you."

"God damn it, Ary! Why not!"

"Because… you know me, Nogi. I never do stupid things. And relying on you would be stupid."

“Then you admit it,” Nogitunde sneered.

“I… I… no…” she started to walk away.

“Tell me what I need to hear, Lark. Or Seitogi and the rest will hear it from me. I bet your own men aren’t even in on it. Bet they’d be really pissed to learn they lost a brother to the Komori due to your scheming.”

“Bisui wasn’t supposed to die!” Ary whirled around and slammed her fists against his chest. “That wasn’t supposed to happen! I didn’t anticipate the Komori.”

“Just as I thought,” he wrapped his arms around her and pulled her close. “What are you doing, Lark? I thought you loved Seitogi, but now you are delivering him into the hands of those who wish him harm.”

“How can’t I expect you to ever understand how a woman feels?” she asked as she freed herself and took a step back. But then she committed a fatal error in judgment and reached out, placing her hand on his chest again.

“I know. I could understand how a woman feels… but I know how I still feel.” He reached out and forcibly pulled her back into his embrace, her cheek against his chest.

“You must think I’m some kind of monster to turn on them both like this, but they betrayed me first!” Arymaitei closed her eyes and wrapped her arms around him. “Everything at Smitemae was fine until she came along. Suddenly everyone was wrapped around her fingers. Dad, Seita. I tried with him over the years. I gave so much of myself, but for what? For him to drop me and go off visiting different realms to rescue her!”

Arymaitei looked pleadingly into his eyes, “She was out of our lives! And just as suddenly, she’s back! And just as suddenly, he’s out of mine. I warned him not to take that witch’s job, but he wouldn’t listen. And now he’s killed many of my mother’s men. I can’t save him. I’ve steeled my heart as I should have a long time ago. My only regret is losing Bisui; that wasn’t planned. But to know White Eyes betrayed me to the Carps… That is a mistake that will be paid for in blood.”

Nogitunde lowered his head and put his hand on her shoulder. “Lark,” he said. “Forget about White Eyes.”

“Look at me,” she replied. “Look me in the eyes. I am going to slit that bastard’s throat.”

“Forget all of this. Let’s go to Dreesh. You and I. Like you dreamed of.”

“I don’t remember you being part of that dream,” she said softly and tried to pull away.

“I’m sorry for how I was, Ary. I’m sorry,” he said again.

“Don’t be,” she said as she closed her eyes.

He breathed in and held his breath, “To have you in my arms again… it feels like coming home,” he whispered.

“I missed you,” Ary grimaced and swallowed as the words left her lips.

“I missed you too,” he said as he looked down and to the side, not sure if he should kiss her or not. “Do we have a deal, Ary?” he asked softly.

“Fine. Seventy-thirty split, and I won’t promise you Dreesh.”

“Not good enough,” he said. “But it’ll do for now. Let’s go get the others and make our way to Bashi before my father catches on.” He grabbed a cloak and handed it to her.

After they made their way back to the prison cell, Nogitunde freed everyone of their binds and addressed them all.

“I know you consider me the enemy at the moment, but now I have your lives in my hands, and I am bound by my word to Ary to help you escape. All I ask from you is your trust.”

The prisoners all looked at each other and then back at him.

"What about my armor?" asked Seitogi as he dusted off his arms.

"In my father's tent, where he is gathered with his men. Consider it gone."

"Consider it our payment out of here!" snapped Arymaitei. "Now let's go."

Nogitunde nodded, "Ready?" as he held his hand out to help Emily to her feet.

"Ready!" Seitogi confirmed with a frown.

The party ducked outside into the woods. They stealthily made their way through the forest. As they neared the swamp, Nogitunde noticed a sudden change in his surroundings, the sound of birds and that of a bird cawing could be heard in the distance. The party froze as they felt eyes on them.

"White Eyes," said Seitogi.

The raven in question landed on a log right in front of them and cawed. Arymaitei strode forward with her dagger in hand.

"Could it be one of his birds? Why would it be here?" she said with a quizzical look on her face.

"What did you do?" Seitogi said, stepping forward. "Nothing about this sits right, Ary."

"What do you mean, Seita? Are you accusing me?"

"Hmm, something's up," Emily whispered to Glehson.

"Why are you here, White Eyes?" Nogitunde asked.

"Surely we should be asking what you are doing here," Seitogi said, getting in his face.

"Perhaps you should explain yourself," Nogitunde said. "Before I put my sword to your throat."

"Seitogi, stop," Emily said. "He's here to help us, right? He asked for our trust. We should hear him out."

"So, he says," said Seitogi. "And maybe he's the enemy." He looked over at Arymaitei. "Maybe you are her spy. What do you say, Ary?" he asked, holding his hand out to the bird, which took several hops backward on the log.

"You're just jealous, Seitogi! Admit it," Ary said in her defense.

"What would Seita have to be jealous of?" asked Emily. "That you have a bird following your every move?"

"He's jealous because he knows Nogi sets me aflame in a way he never could."

"Would! Never would," Seitogi corrected. "It's because White Eyes is spying on us."

"Why would White Eyes be spying on us? His birds are always flying about gathering information. Is it so strange to see one here?" asked Arymaitei.

"It's because who knows what he's doing!" Seitogi said with anger in his voice. "He's spying on us!"

"Seita, Ary is right," Emily said, attempting to quell the rising tension. "It could be spying, but it could also be here for something else. Whatever the case, Bashi is ahead. We must hurry."

"We were heading to the river so we could cross over to Bashi," Nogitunde said, not taking his eyes from the bird. "How are we supposed to do that with a sky raven following us?"

"Of course, we won't be able to escape its eye," said Yazgiroh. "So, we might as well just move along."

"Alright, let's move out," said Nogitunde as he turned around and began walking, prompting Glehson and Emily to follow, but Seitogi stayed put.

"Seita, we can't outrun it," Arymaitei said. "So let's just go do what we came here to do."

"I put my trust in you, Ary. No matter what, I always have. Don't make me regret it."

"Seita, I…" She wanted to tell him she still loved him. That she just didn't know how to, but instead, she said, "You won't." And then she turned away from him and began to follow Nogitunde.

The sky raven looked around with its large black eyes and then cawed as it flew over the swamp. "Bashi ahead. We must hurry," it said in its high-pitched voice, over and over again.

Broken Bonds

The group made it to the river before sundown, with the raven always overhead. The water was deeper than back in the swamp, and some strange things resided there. They debated wading across or walking the extra five miles to the nearest bridge. In the end, Seitogi suspected Gailen would have all bridge crossings watched, and so wading waist-deep across the river was their best plan.

After a long pause, Arymaitei spoke up, saying, “Maybe we should wait until the morning to cross?”

“It’s imperative we go now,” said Seitogi. “We would most likely be caught in the daylight and not make it to Bashi alive.”

“I agree,” added Nogitunde. “We’re too exposed to stay here and rest.”

Arymaitei nodded. “Fine. Seitogi, you first. Then Yazgiroh, Glehson, Emily, and me. Koe, you two make up the rear.” Her eyes scanned the group. “Everyone is to help each other in case something goes wrong.”

“Alright,” said Yazgiroh. “I’ll be right behind you, Seitogi…”

Lightning started to dash across the sky, and Emily shivered. “Well, if we’re going to cross, we’d better do it now,” she said, “Or we’ll be stuck here until morning.”

Arymaitei looked worried, as did everyone else. “Alright then. Let’s go!”

They made it over slowly, as the swift current pushed them forward. They matched their stride to the ebb and flow of the river, watching each other carefully. The final ten yards to shore took all their concentration, but they managed to make it to the other side before long. The raven landed on a tree and watched them intently before flying up and away once they were on dry land again.

Arymaitei and her men continued to scout ahead. She quietly crept over the ground, being careful not to disturb any branches or leave footprints. Glehson and the rest of the group followed soon after, in the same way.

They traveled on through the forest for another hour before they began trudging up an incline. The higher they climbed, the thinner the forest became, and with considerable effort, they reached the top of the rise with Arymaitei ahead of the rest.

The horizon was bathed in violet indigos as early evening set in. They stepped out onto a grassy clearing overlooking a rocky coastline with natural land bridges leading from the beach to an offshore colony of several small islands, all interconnected with narrow man-made passages.

Emily counted twelve pods, all of which had signs of light industrialization. Her view of the archipelago stretched as far as she could see, and in the distance, she noted several ships of varying types floating on the water.

"This is it," she said. "It's amazing. I've never seen anything like it."

"Yes," replied Arymaitei. "This is Bashi. Now we just need to get down there." The group took a few minutes to recoup their energy and surveyed the channels of land that would take them to Bashi Intermediate, the entry point to the other colonies.

"See the bridge there," Arymaitei said, pointing to the base of the rock on which they stood. "It looks the sturdiest of the bunch."

"It looks pretty thin. We will probably have to walk single file just to be safe," said Seitogi. "It's going to be a rough climb down. Might take some time. We should get going."

Seitogi led the way. The downward hike was a difficult jaunt of rugged terrain and loose muck. Occasionally someone lost their footing, but no injuries were incurred. It took them a good hour before they reached the beach and collapsed onto the sand.

They didn't rest for long before eventually tackling crossing the open water. The bridge swayed and creaked alarmingly, but it was thick wood, first hammered and then nailed together for durability. It had lasted for several years, although no one knew how much longer it would hold up.

Across the bridge, they reached an abandoned looking guard post. They were all surprised to enter the village unmolested, perhaps due to its carnival season. The villagers were full of energy as the streets bustled with festivities, many residents celebrating in costume.

"It looks like Mardi Gras!" Emily said.

"It's a holiday for all of their citizens," Yazgiroh said. "A celebration of their so-called independence from the empire."

"Bashi and its citizens are still subjects of the emperor," said Glehson reflexively. "No matter what flag they erect, or what laws they invoke."

The group continued on, headed toward the center of town. As the village continued to expand, the crowds grew larger. It was like a hive of energy; streets filled with decorations and running fountains everywhere.

They made it to the town's center, where Arymaitei spoke to a man who pointed them in the direction of lodgings. Upon entering the house, they encountered a friendly woman dressed in a colorful frock.

She welcomed them warmly, giving each a big hug, leaving smudges of powder and rouge on their cloaks.

"Come in and get yourselves settled!" She walked them through a wide foyer, chatting gaily about the festivities and led them to a second-floor room. After collecting the night's rent, she floated away on a wave of blown kisses and well wishes.

"This room isn't so bad. At least they have a private gjo with hot water and a meal for the night. Why don't we go get cleaned up? We have a long day ahead of us tomorrow."

"We don't have until tomorrow." Seitogi shook his head. "We need to infiltrate Adehshi Temple tonight."

"Are you mad?" asked Nogitunde, "Adehshi is heavily fortified and even more heavily guarded."

Emily spoke up, "Maybe we could persuade the monks to help us? We can't go up against them with just eight people."

"No. Five people," said Arymaitei. "You and Glehson would only get in the way, and Nogi mustn't be involved either."

"Do you expect me to come all this way and just sit on my ass?" said Emily.

"You don't have a choice, Enoshi. You need to stay here and ensure our mission isn't hindered," said Seitogi, "But leaving you two alone with him is a non-starter," he motioned to Nogitunde.

"Do you really think you could hold your own against the Adehshi monks?" Nogitunde scoffed. "We're talking about hundreds of armed men of the cloth."

"True," said Seitogi, "but I have a plan for that."

Nogitunde crossed his arms and looked away with a sullen frown. "Well, I don't mind tagging along," he said. "I'm sure I'll enjoy kicking back and watching those guys make minced meat of you all."

"Yuyu and Glehson will remain behind. We will advance our mission as planned. With or without you, Nogi, stay or go. Whatever you choose is up to you."

Nogitunde glared at Arymaitei and Seitogi. "It's your bloody burial then." He left, slamming the door behind him.

Arymaitei turned and seated herself at a small, disc-shaped table. "Well," she said, "I propose we eat and get some rest at least. Particularly since Seita is in such a rush to get to the temple."

"I still feel we should all stick together," said Emily. "What if you fall into a trap or something?"

"Don't worry, Enoshi. Arymatei and I are used to maneuvering these types of situations. We can handle ourselves," said Seitogi.

"What does that even mean?"

"Just trust us, Yuyu," Arymaitei said.

"Goddamnit! How many times do I have to tell you to stop calling me that? You know it annoys me."

Arymaitei sighed, patting her on the back. "I apologize, princess."

Emily huffed and stomped out of the room onto a terrace. From there, she could see the vast expanse of Bashi. The twelve islands had many ports that opened out onto the sea. She observed men busy loading and unloading throngs of cargo.

"Goddamned Arymaitei," Emily thought. The girl could be so petty, but how was she able to so easily push her buttons? The fact that her younger sister appeared somewhat older, more mature, and was clearly far more experienced than she was only made her feel more insecure.

"Bashi is the main source of illegal trade between the mainland and the distant colonies of the empire," said Glehson, joining her. "And as such, they probably traffic all the black market goods that pass between here and the capital as well."

They took a seat on a bench before an empty fire pit, watching the din of the festivities. "It will be a long night," said Emily. "I'll admit, I'm tired of all of this. I'm tired of being terrified. All this death is surrounding us. It's just too much to handle."

"I know it's been hard for you seeing people cut to pieces right before your eyes. I'm sorry you have to witness such things. Berah can sometimes be a violent place," Glehson said.

Emily's eyes filled with tears, "It's like feudal Japan or something. People just kill without thought. And he, Seitogi. He brought me to this hell hole against my will."

Glehson smiled as he reached out and put a hand on her wrist. "I'm so sorry. It seems we have similar misfortunes of duty. You see, I am the second-born son. I was not meant to be crown prince. It's a burden I wish to be free of."

Emily nodded as she looked out over the islands. "This place is fucking depressing; it doesn't matter your status. To be born into exalted roles is not the fairy tale one would think."

"In this world, there is no peace," said Glehson. "For me, the only difference is that I'm allowed some illusion of control over my suffering because of our lineage."

"No, it's more than that." Emily sort of breathed out the words as though they were a dying gasp and stroked his smooth cheek with a delicate hand. "I can feel it. You're different from them. You're noble. You share my sorrows. You're trying to do the right thing."

Glehson smiled and rose from his seat, "Despite our pain, we have to remain strong, Emily. Right now, neither of us can appear weak. They are depending on us too."

"They are depending on us?" Emily stood next to him, "What in the hell can I do? I'm totally useless! I can't fight, I can't spy. I have no idea of the layout of the land because, um, well, I'm not from around here. And people are chasing me, trying to kill me!" Her eyes were large, and her pupils were wide.

"I thought my life sucked back on Earth, but in truth it was just kinda boring. Sure, I was poor… ha! Senior year! And oh my god, I was dating Darren Toliver. I mean, buyer beware, but still, he's like the second hottest guy in school. Not that I cared about that sort of thing, but it was nice to have, wasn't it? It wasn't this! I didn't want this!"

Glehson pulled her into his embrace as she wept; her body trembled. "You have me. And so I finally have something to fight for. I will defend you to my last breath."

Emily was struck silent.

"I know it's difficult to find strength when your world has been turned upside down, but just know you are not alone. Everyone is risking life and limb to help get you back home," his voice was a soothing whisper that felt to her like a second warm embrace.

"I'm not so sure about that. I think the only reason my sister is helping me is because she doesn't want me around Seitogi. She thinks I might have some sort of weird feelings for him.

Like she totally went out of her way to give me the impression they slept with each other back at her compound. And I'm like, girl, you're barely fifteen, or at least she should be."

"I can assure you, Seitogi slept in the same room as I when we arrived at Meriwell."

"It doesn't matter to me. I mean, we knew each other a long time ago, sort of like siblings, but believe me, I have no interest in someone like him.

I mean, my god, he kills people with no remorse. I could never be with someone like that."

"I couldn't imagine you would have such intentions towards him," said Glehson. "He does seem kind-hearted, at least where you are concerned, but he lacks refinement in all other ways."

"You're the only one here who understands me, Gleh." Emily looked up into his eyes. She blushed and pushed out against his chest. Her face moved towards his, and his towards hers.

"I…" she began but was interrupted by the creaking of the terrace's floorboard. Looking up with a start, Seitogi stood in the entranceway, his jaw clenched tight, and his eyes downcast.

"We are going down to the dining hall. You both should join us and eat," Seitogi said, though his expression betrayed a hidden discomfort he refused to acknowledge.

"How long have you been standing there?" Emily asked.

"Long enough," his face grew darker, "We should eat."

Emily's eyes widened, "I-I'm not really-"

"It's high time you eat something. I will not have you falling ill," he stated, his tone leaving no room for argument.

As he took her wrist, Emily was infuriated. For whatever reason, Seitogi seemed angry with her, and she suddenly wanted to get away from him.

"I can walk on my own!" Emily said, pulling away from his grip. "What's gotten into you? I'm not hungry, and I don't need you to escort me anywhere."

Glehson stepped in between them, placing a hand on Seitogi's chest to prevent him from advancing towards Emily. "I think it's clear the princess does not desire your company, sir."

"I wish not to quarrel over the matter, nor further upset you, Seitogi, but you should have a care with how you handle Lady Aiyo," Glehson said.

"It's fine, Glehson," Emily said with a defiant smile, "I'll take my meal with you."

"It's been settled then. I will accompany the princess to the dining hall," said Glehson.

"Fine, Enoshi," Seitogi said, his face dark with anger, "You go with him then," before storming off down the hall, his eyes glaring daggers.

Rolling her eyes and shrugging, Emily said, "I knew he'd be mad…that's what happens when you eavesdrop."

Glehson's face was a mask of chivalry that only the wealthy who have rarely engaged in life-or-death battles are entitled to. Despite living in the real world, he fully expected to emerge unscathed from their adventure. A life of privilege had numbed him to the reality of the situation at hand.

The dining hall was an empty, vaulted space supported by wooden arches and pillars. Narrow and dimly lit, its walls were covered with carvings, portraits, and statuary of Bashi's greatest figures. The smell of spilled wine and stale air made Emily's stomach churn.

They sat at a long wooden table, eating in strained silence. The food was good, though; hearty fish stew and cassava flatbread with gobs of salted butter that left Emily feeling warmly satiated.

She was not pleased, however, to be sitting under the weight of Seitogi's stare. She tried to ignore him, but he looked as if she had injured him terribly, which was unbearable.

"Do you mind?" she snapped, but he remained silent as she looked into his eyes. "Whatever…I'm tired," said Emily, throwing her napkin down on the table. She rose quickly and stomped out of the room and down the hall, fuming as she held back tears.

She couldn't help but feel that Seitogi was unfairly upset with her over her attraction to Glehson. Worse, her attraction to the prince left her feeling as though she had, in some way, betrayed Seitogi. And she still had unresolved issues with Darren, who, for all she knew, was dead.

She ran her fingers through her hair, letting it fall to her face. "Really, really stupid, Emily," she said to herself. "Why couldn't you have just stayed with Darren? I would have been hanging out with him at lunch, and none of this would've ever happened." She sighed and tossed her head.

"But, oh god. Why did I have to meet Gleh? He's so gorgeous." Sighing, she placed a hand on her cheek, "Oh, I wish you were here right now, Beck." Was she ashamed of her feelings for Glehson? He made her feel weak yet somehow stronger and more confident than ever.

"What kind of monster am I? My focus should only be on Beck and Darren. But instead, I'm out here walking around like death, pretending to be alive." She leaned her head against the wall, a tear escaping her eye.

Emily heard footsteps down the hall, and then Glehson entered the room. Her look softened when she saw him. He approached her cautiously and placed his hand on her shoulder.

"Are you alright?" his voice tender and filled with concern.

"Y-yeah…" she said, wiping her eyes, "I'm fine."

"I understand that Seitogi was rather hostile back there. I apologize."

“It’s fine…” she said, holding back tears, “I think I’ll just go to the room for now, if that’s alright…”

“Yes, of course,” he said, keeping his hand on her shoulder.

They stood there in silence for only a moment. Even though it was just a simple touch, Emily felt her face grow warm. Glehson leaned in close to her.

“I want to be there for you, Emily. Please let me.”

Emily looked into his eyes, and she realized they were just like hers: deep, sad, and clouded with a grief she could not explain. She threw her arms around him and let the tears flow.

“I’m sorry,” she sobbed into his chest, “I’m so sorry you’re mixed up in all of this.”

Glehson held her close, his arms wrapping tightly around her. “It’s alright,” he said, his voice thick with emotion, “It’s alright.”

***

Arymaitei walked down the hall, cloaked and hooded. She carried herself with a rigid posture, her head held high, and her lips set in a grim frown. She emerged from the doors of the inn onto the crowded street.

Men and women in colorful, outlandish dresses passed by her, singing and playing music, drinking, and dancing. She watched a man juggle flaming clubs. There were fire-breathers, knife throwers, and acrobats. She quickly lost herself in the crowd of color and chaos, as she circled and weaved through the streets.

She turned down a winding cobblestone road, her cloak billowing behind her. Another turn and there was Nogitunde, sitting on a bench with a girl on his lap.

He looked up and smiled at Arymaitei. She felt herself turn to stone and stared at him indifferently. He ushered the girl away and beckoned Arymaitei over next to him. He gave her a guilty stare and then pecked her on the cheek.

"I was hoping you'd come," he said, his voice a little nervous, "We need to come up with a plan for making the exchange."

Arymaitei, still glaring, said, "Yes, it's fine with me, though you seem to be busy enjoying yourself." Her voice crisp and hollow.

"What? The girl? She gave me a hug and I caught a whiff of her perfume. She stepped closer and I was…ah, distracted. Next thing I know she's trying to climb onto me. I pushed her off when she offered her price.."

"Oh really?" said Arymaitei, "Well, I don't care how much she was going to charge you! I'm just here to get what I want." She paused, "I can't wrap my head around the fact that you'd be willing to entertain such a vile creature."

Nogitunde glanced downwards from Arymaitei's critical eye. He stood up, his cloak falling around him.

"You know I don't mean anything by it," he said, his voice quiet. He turned and looked at Arymaitei directly. "You believe I'd actually do something so despicable? Wow Ary, do you know nothing about me."

"I know more than enough about you, Nogitunde. So get over yourself!" her voice was cold and harsh. "I'm in a difficult position here and you're holding me back. You could at least not complicate things. I have a great deal more to lose."

Nogitunde stared down at his feet, his expression reflecting defeat and embarrassment. "What would you have of me? Have I not already offered you my heart?"

"You mean what you offer to people at parties?" said Arymaitei, fixing her eyes on a group of young girls chasing each other in the playful chaos.

"But I am nothing without you," said Nogitunde, his voice filled with sorrow. "I'll do anything for you. It is you I have wanted, you I dream of." He paused, and she averted his gaze. "And you know it."

Arymaitei looked at him blankly. She remained silent, waiting for him to continue.

"Forgive me," he said. "I ought not to be so forward."

Arymaitei watched as he paced, his shoulders hunched and his head down. She let out a small sigh and closed her hands into fists. She stood up.

"You wrong me, Ary," he said, looking away.

"Rumor has it you took the honor of both Grundsion's daughters in the same night and made it to the pub to tell the tale before the midnight hour."

"Rumors and nothing more than that," said Nogitunde, squirming under her glare. "Okay, it happened. But that is the past. Is that why you broke up with me and have been avoiding me all this time?"

"I don't know why I put up with you," said Arymaitei.

"You are afraid of losing something rare and perfect," said Nogitunde, taking her hand. His voice caught. "And I fear losing you again."

Arymaitei stood still, feeling his hand clasped tightly to hers. "So, what are we to do?" he said.

"Find somewhere quiet to talk and discuss the exchange," she looked around at the throngs of people on the streets. "And not talk about us."

"Sounds like a plan," he replied.

He left the bench and walked towards the market square. Arymaitei followed, lost in her own thoughts.

"It wasn't real…was it?" she said, breaking the silence. Nogitunde looked at her over his shoulder, his face puzzled.

"What we had," she added. "Not real. Was it?"

"It was all real. We were just really good at pretending it wasn't?"

Arymaitei felt her heart beating harder and faster. Her arms prickled and itched. She glanced at Nogitunde, then away.

"You're not having second thoughts, are you?" he asked nervously. He stopped and turned to her. "I want you to be mine."

"I want you to be mine too," she whispered, but he didn't hear her over the festivities.

They continued walking until they came to a quiet alleyway. The cobblestones here were uneven, rising and falling, making for a bumpy walk.

"This should do," said Nogitunde.

He held his hand out to Arymaitei. She placed her hand in his and let him lead her into the alley. The stone walls were close and high. The only sources of light were the street lanterns half-buried in the cobbles.

"We can talk better here. No one's going to bother us."

Arymaitei stayed silent, watching him. He crossed his arms, pinching his elbows and resting them on his ribs.

"I'm not sure what I'm supposed to say now. I want to say I love you, but I know how hasty and rash that would be. I don't want to disappoint you again."

"We are here to talk business and business only, Nogi," Arymaitei snapped. They were close to each other, within reach. She didn't dare move closer.

"O.k. First and foremost, we have to keep your long-faced boy distracted," he said. "I will hire some of the local thugs as fodder for his blade while I double back to the inn and steal away with the girl and make the exchange with the Aiyo."

Arymaitei thought for a moment, her brow furrowing and her eyes glazing over. "And am I to trust you would return for me with all of that money? You surely think I'm a fool."

"It must appear to Seitogi we are ambushed," Nogitunde insisted. Arymaitei shook her head.

"I'm not so trusting, Nogi. I have seen your heart; I know its darkness."

"And I've seen yours too! Dark as coal from the mines at Smitemae!"

Arymaitei reached out and slapped him across the face. "You know nothing of what I have seen! Nothing of what I have to take the blame for! Why should I trust you?"

"Because I love you!" he said.

Arymaitei placed her hand over her heart; the other clenched into a fist, and brought it up to her mouth, biting her knuckle. She looked down.

"What are we to do?" she asked quietly.

"Take the money and run. Start a new life together. A life without the fear of spies, constant threats, and fear of being killed."

Arymaitei looked up, her expression silent and stern. Her heart was beating wildly. He looked at her for a moment, then reached out and took her shoulders into his hands.

"I will protect you. I will stay with you and guard you with my life. These hands I give you for the taking," he said, clasping his hands together.

"Oh, please stop with the poetics, Nogi."

"This isn't about money for me. This is about love," he said. "I don't want the money." He took her hand and pulled her close until she was flush with his body, his face inches from hers. She pushed him away.

"Is this how you want it, Ary?" he breathed.

Arymaitei tightened her hands into fists and pressed them against his chest. "I want to believe you, Nogitunde, I do. More than anyone I know. I want to. I want to trust you."

"Then trust me," he said, his voice gentle and smooth. He ducked his head and brushed his lips against hers. Her breath hitched and shc put her hands on his chest again.

"Trust me." They kissed. She gave him a small smile, hesitantly, and stepped closer. They kissed again.

"Listen," Arymaitei said, once again all business. "You will hire your hands and watch the inn from afar. Follow us when we leave for Adehshi Monastery and attack us.

I will escape and return to the inn and take Yuyuki to the Aiyo myself. Once the exchange is made, I will charter a boat at Gulf Port and wait for you."

Nogitunde laughed bitterly. "I don't think Seitogi would be stupid enough to fall for that one."

"I'm not sure if you mean me or Seita when you say that."

Nogitunde ran his fingers through his hair. "Don't leave me out in the cold, Lark."

"My word is my bond. Do we agree on the plan?"

Nogitunde took a step back, looking at her for a moment before he answered, "I guess we do, but it's not going to be as easy as you make it sound."

"I've dealt with worse challenges," she shrugged. She glanced at the sky, a spilled inkwell with stars that looked down on her like a thousand cold, accusing eyes. Silence fell between them. The crowded streets echoed faintly as people sang, laughed, and danced.

"We should go before they start wondering where I am. Be quick, hire some roughs to do your bidding," she said, turning to leave the alley.

"Wait," he said, gripping her wrist. She turned, and he looked at her sadly. "I'm sorry I disappointed you before, Ary. I took us for granted. I didn't mean to."

Arymaitei wasn't sure how to reply. Suddenly, she really didn't want to go. "I forgive you, Nogi. I do." He nodded and looked down at their clasped hands. He pulled her closer, wrapping her in his arms.

"I love you."

Arymaitei looked up at him, "Nogitunde, I… I can't believe how much you mean to me."

He rested his forehead against hers and said, "Maybe one day you will. We will have a rich life together, Ary!" Nogitunde gave her one last peck on the lips, and then disappeared into the crowd.

"A life together. How naive does he think I am?" Arymaitei whispered as a group of revelers stumbled between her and her path.

***

Seitogi returned to the inn, muttering to himself. He entered the common room and sat in one of the large wooden chairs. They were carved in the shape of human feet and a little uncomfortable. He watched the door and listened for a while.

He could hear noises coming from the tavern next door and the occasional footfall of other lodgers thumping down the hall. He had heard what he needed to hear back in the alley and now; he needed to be alone to decide his next move.

He knew he and Emily were in grave danger. What he had overheard was devastating to say the least, but he had suspected as much, though it was perhaps even worse than he'd imagined. There was no way he could trust that anyone would help them; he didn't even know who to trust.

He cracked his knuckles and stood up. He had come to a decision. He had to be prepared. He took out two short blades from beneath his robe and hid them in his sleeves.

He went to their room. Emily was lying in bed, sleeping, a tiny, framed body with a little mop of hair. He watched her for a moment before he quietly crept over to shake her awake.

"Enoshi," he whispered in her ear.

She sat up and massaged her neck with a stiff hand. He could see the fear on her face and put his finger to her lips, signaling for quiet. They crept out onto the outside terrace that wrapped around the inn.

Seitogi leaned against the railing and closed his eyes. Emily thought he looked tired and stressed. She walked over to him and cleared her throat. "Okay. So what is this all about?"

"Arymaitei," he said.

"She's a piece of work, I'll give you that," Emily said matter-of-factly.

"That's one way of putting it," he said, lowering his head. "She has taken everything she has built and is throwing it away."

"What is that supposed to mean?"

"It means she'll do what she wants, when she wants, and how she wants," he said, looking up at her.

"She's passionate about something, or someone, that's for sure," Emily smiled sympathetically.

Seitogi frowned, looking like a confused child. "I'm sorry?"

"Nogitunde, silly. I think she, and he, must have some unresolved feelings for each other. My god, it's obvious," she smiled.

Seitogi's confusion deepened. "Of course, they have feelings. That's obvious," he said. "They've been on and off for a while now. That's not what I'm talking about."

"But emotions and feelings are a lot more complex than people think, is all I was saying," Emily said.

"Whoa! Don't tell me you're jealous?" Her eyes widened, and she playfully nudged him in the gut.

"What? No! No, I am not! Why would I be jealous?" he said.

"Mmm," Emily said in a sweet voice. "You sure you're not jealous?" she continued to laugh.

"She and White Eyes lied to us, Enoshi!" Seitogi said definitively. "The witch is not at Adehshi Temple, but the Aiyo are here in Bashi. Do you know what that means for us?" he asked, raising his head.

"Of course, I know what it means, Seitogi! No, wait… I just don't know if you know what it means."

Seitogi rolled his eyes. "It means she has been planning on turning you over to the Aiyo all along," he said, pointing at Emily.

"I don't know about that…" Emily said. "She wouldn't."

"No, Enoshi, she has tricked us all. She has tricked me," he said, slamming his fist against the rail. "She has tricked me!"

"She can be crazy though," Emily said. "But she isn't that cold, Seitogi. She cares too much. She cares for you." Emily placed a hand on his forearm.

"Seitogi, I'm still your friend, right?" she asked.

"What kind of a question is that? Of course!" he looked disgusted.

"I don't think Ary would do us like that," she said. "I think she cares for you too much to betray you, Seitogi."

"I listened to her with my own ears. She means to have your head as a gift to the Aiyo and serve mine to her mother," he said. "We have to leave immediately. I have no idea if Yaz and the others are in on it too."

"But you don't know that" Emily said. "Aiyo or not, she will not betray me. Not like that." She gripped the railing tightly. "Think about it, Seitogi. It's something you just can't come back from."

"You were not there, Enoshi, and you did not hear it. She…" he started, turning to look at her before lowering his voice, "She approaches," he whispered.

"Do not confront her just yet, Seita. Be smart." She walked closer. "Please!" She reached for his shoulder, but he turned away.

"I know what you think has transpired, but I'm telling you, Ary cares enough to make up for the mistakes she has made," she walked around to face him. "Just trust me."

Seitogi turned away and looked out at the ports. "I know what is at stake. I do. And I know what I want from her, but…but I can't, Enoshi," he said. "I can't."

"You have to," Emily said, wrapping her arms around him. He turned to look over his shoulder. "Come on, Seitogi," she said and led him back into the room.

Arymaitei entered just as they did. Behind her, Yazagorih, Koe, and Zatrik followed in close order. She looked as Emily and Seitogi entered from the terrace and felt a bitter jealousy she thought she had left back in childhood.

Emily cracked a smile at her, and she flushed with guilt. The two women looked at each other, communicating some unspoken message. Arymaitei knew that she couldn't hide the truth for long.

"Looks like you two made up!" she said with forced cheeriness and a wink. "We leave for Adehshi within the hour."

"Let us be ready," Seitogi said, with a coldness she was not accustomed to.

"Of course," she said. "How are you feeling, Yuyu?"

"I am well enough," Emily smiled. Arymaitei watched them stand side-by-side like reunited lovers, close, quiet, and comfortable with one another. She suddenly felt isolated and alone. Was it selfish of her to choose Nogitunde? To let go of her relationship with Seitogi? To betray him? To betray Emily? She sighed, reflecting on how it would devastate her Merry-Larks.

A small part of her wanted to change her mind, but she had come too far. “I’m sorry, Seitogi,” she thought.

Glehson woke and stretched. He turned his head lazily, “Are we ready to go?” he asked. “What is the plan?”

“Same as before. You and Enoshi will remain here where you are safe,” Seitogi answered. “The rest of our party, including myself, will continue to Adehshi.”

“What do you intend to do once you are there?” Glehson raised an eyebrow at him.

“I will confront her,” he said, looking at Arymaitei and then back to the prince.

“How are you going to do that exactly?”

Seitogi stood up. “By force. By whatever means it takes to get what I want,” his voice trembling.

“Seitogi…” said Emily.

“I am aware of what I’m doing. Let us go down and plan in the common room,” he walked out. Arymaitei looked at Emily and gave her a grave frown. She followed Seitogi and the others from the room.

“What was that all about?” Glehson turned to Emily.

“Nothing. It’s nothing.”

“Please don’t keep me in the dark, Emily.”

“Oh Gleh, come on now. It’s not worth worrying about.” She tried to look reassuring. “Things will be fine. Don’t worry.”

In the common room, Nogitunde was waiting for them next to a map of the city. He nodded at them without saying a word.

“Ok,” Seitogi said as he closed the door. “It’s good you’re here. We are going to need you after all.”

“Understood,” Nogitunde said. “Now, what’s the plan?”

“Observe!” Seitogi addressed them. “We have a clear shot coming from the north, across the river here into Adehshi’s plaza. My plan is simple, if not optimistic. We will pair up and split into three groups. Under the guise of drunken revelers, Yaz and Koe will cause a disruption at the temples entrance.

As security comes to flush them from the area, we will rush through and enter the monastery,” he said, consulting Yazgiroh and Koe with a meaningful glance. “Once inside, Ary and I will head for the guest chambers.” He looked to Arymaitei, who shook her head in disagreement.

“And how are we supposed to do that? We’ve no map of its interior.”

“I’ve made a copy of an old expedition report.” Seitogi handed her a tattered-looking page.

“This is the worst map I’ve ever seen,” she said, placing it on the table for his companions to see.

“Where did you get this?” Nogitunde asked, while the others chimed in with inquiries of their own.

Seitogi held up a hand to stifle the clamoring from the others. “Once inside, we’ll pin the doors shut and barricade ourselves in,” he said. “Our method of escape lies in the witch herself. She has a powerful looking glass by which she can spirit people away,” he looked directly at Arymaitei and Nogitunde.

“This we will use to our advantage. I will force her to confess her intent, using the element of surprise and the use of force, if necessary,” he said this last part with a sly grin. Arymaitei just stared at him. He turned to her, “What do you think?” he asked.

Arymaitei looked over at Nogitunde, “It isn’t without risk, but I can acquiesce,” she gave him a faint smile, “for now.”

“Excellent,” Seitogi nodded. “If everyone is ready? Let us go then!”

The group, divided into three teams, with Seitogi, Zatrik, and Yaz partnering with Arymaitei, Nogitunde, and Koe. Emily and Glehson watched from a window as they set off and moved swiftly down the road, heading towards Adehshi.

When she could no longer see them, Emily faced Glehson with urgency, "We have to leave immediately," she said. "We won't be safe here at all."

"Leave! Why?" he asked.

"Ary is going to come after us," she said, looking down at the floor. "We have to leave now, Gleh," her voice shaking.

"'Ary?" he cocked his head to the side. "What is this all about? I'am confused."

"Seitogi will meet us later at the Lush Sanctum." Her voice hurried; she held up a folded sheet of paper with a crudely drawn map from the inn to the tavern. "He gave me directions, see."

"This seems like an awful lot of trouble," he said, rising slowly.

"Look, you're the one who said you didn't want to be kept in the dark earlier. Well, I'm trying to shed some light on the situation! We are in an awful lot of trouble," she said. "I'll explain along the way!"

"Very well then. I'm ready when you are."

She put the paper away in her hoodie's papoose and they escaped the room, shimmying their way down the back terrace onto the street.

"Let's go then," she said and turned, walking fast towards the direction of the Lush Sanctum indicated on the map.

Arymaitei and Seitogi walked through the streets on the city's outskirts towards Adehshi. She looked at the moon already halfway into the eastern horizon. And then her eyes fell on him. Why was he acting so sullen? Seitogi turned his head towards her, his gaze piercing.

Clenching her teeth until it hurt, her face began to flush red. She suppressed a shudder and turned her away from him, facing forward. The thought of him and Emily holding each other came and went.

She shuddered again and suppressed the urge to turn around and throw herself into his arms and confess on the spot. If she did that, his image of her would shatter. "My love, my life," she thought, "what have I done?"

They walked quickly through the streets, Seitogi anticipating Nogitunde's appearance at any moment. Whenever he thought about it, he became sick. His heart turned cold and icy, tainted with rage. How could she do this? How could she just abandon him?

"Ary, think of me!" Yet, his thoughts only blurred, wrapped itself into a knot of confusion upon confusion.

He shook his head from side to side, trying to contain his anger, and walked faster. Arymaitei followed him.

"You seem vexed, Seita," she said. "Perhaps we can talk about it."

He turned and stared at her directly. "Sorry, I'm just a little anxious, wondering when Nogi's hired swords will attack," he said.

Arymaitei froze, not saying a word, a stunned expression on her face. She looked at the ground, her mouth agape. She wanted to provide an explanation but did not want to bear the burden of having to explain why she had done what she had done.

"You followed me earlier," she managed to say, raising her head and looking back at him with fiery eyes.

They stopped in the middle of the street. The alley remained empty except for the two of them. Yet she spoke to him in a whisper, but the rage was clear in her face and in her voice.

"I should have known it," she said. "You and Yuyu were acting suspicious earlier when I returned to the inn." Her voice rose higher. "It's always about Yuyuki with you!"

She jabbed his chest with a finger. "And I hope she's worth it." With suspended breath, she waited for his answer, hands digging into her clothes.

She saw the rage in his face, and his eyes squinted into thin shafts. "Don't you dare blame me or Enoshi for your two-faced actions," his voice trembled. He was livid.

"You know very well you are responsible for betraying us! You and your carp," he raised a finger and pointed at her, "You're in too deep, Ary, and it will destroy us. Now that you have chosen to run away with Nogi, I will act on my own accord and protect Enoshi from any harm you two might inflict on her."

"Why is she so special to you?" she clenched her fists. "She carries with her the witch's curse! Our family, Seita…Everything was fine until she showed up! Awei and Dad were together! You were everything, Seitog!"

"We were all a family until she came along, and everything went to shit!" she yelled. "She is evil, and she will destroy us if we don't get rid of her!" Her words came as a bitter, guttural grunting wail. She clenched her fists tighter and turned away from him.

"She is your sister!" he yelled, the rage boiling up inside him. "She is your blood!"

"She is a witch, Seitogi! Don't you see it?" She turned and faced him. "And she is worth a fortune! Enough that we can leave this place and live a life of comfort." Her expression softened as her voice got softer. "Forget about her, Seita. Come with me to Dreesh. Away from the wretchedness of this land."

Seitogi gripped his fingers into a fist and stood silent. What could he say? His eyes flicked up towards the star-filled sky.

He took a deep breath and replied,

"So, is it me or Nogitunde, Ary? Did you not promise him the same?"

"Nogi has a use, nothing more. If not for him, we'd all be in Gailen's custody still!"

"If not for you, we would have never entered the Flying Carp's territory! You knew from the very beginning the wizened woman wasn't at Adehshi! You just didn't know White Eyes had sold you out to the Carps."

He began walking, leaving her in the middle of the street fuming. He had been through so much in the past few days, and he did not have the energy or will to continue this conversation. Not now. Not tonight.

"I'm so sorry," he said. "There's nothing left for me here. I'm leaving… you've broken my heart," his brow furrowed, his eyes filled with tears.

"Your heart! How pathetic can you be, Seita! She hasn't even aged properly and is now my junior! Are you so lovestruck by that idiot girl? Even when she flaunts her scandalous affair with the crown prince right before your very eyes!"

"I trusted you with all my heart, Ary!" he said. "Enoshi still believes in you! And you betrayed us!"

"No!" she screamed. "No! I trusted you! And you left me to go and bring her back! And in doing so, killed several of my mother's men. Did you not think there would be a price to pay for that?"

She walked behind him, her fists clenched. "You fool, I thought you could see reason, but you're blind to anything but her." She sped past him, and then swung around to face him, her expression stony.

"What will you do now?" she asked. "Are you going to try to run away with her again like you did when we were kids?" She smiled and shook her head. "I won't let you leave with her. Not a second time."

"You're unbelievable, you know that. Why deny that this is all about money for you? I'm taking Enoshi back to Daiye. I will figure it out once there."

"Your father won't allow you to step foot in Daiye village. And even if he did, the Golden Swan would have the whole place burned to the ground before sunrise.

Do you really want all that innocent blood on your hands? Think about it, Seitogi! She's always been nothing but trouble."

Her words stung, his heart boiled with anger.

"Don't you ever speak about Daiye! Don't you dare mention Enoshi as well," he snarled. "She's more a sister to me than you could ever be, and I would die for her. You think a little fortune is worth that?" He strode away, his hand balled up into a tight fist that caused the veins in his forearms to bulge.

Arymaitei ran after him and grabbed his shoulder, turning him around to face her.

"Listen to reason, Seitogi. You don't know what you're doing." Her eyes were glossy, tears flowing down her face. She searched for the right words, desperate to change his mind.

"That's enough!" he said. "I have had it with you," he pointed his finger at her chest. "Your choices have consequences. You let your hatred and your jealousy of Enoshi blind you and make you reckless."

"Seitogi." She clasped both hands around his arm. "I just want what's best for all of us."

He searched her eyes, his anger and resentment evident, "Some choices have consequences, Ary," he said, coming to terms with his decision. "Even when they are difficult."

"Seita."

"Goodbye, Ary." He stepped back from her and started walking away. "In case you are going to try anything ridiculous, I gave Enoshi my oath to protect her life." He clenched his fist and turned about.

Arymaitei stood for a moment, her expression cold. She was about to speak when they heard movement and the sound of footsteps in the alley.

A group of twenty or so rough-looking men were advancing down the tight passage. They looked like they had seen hard times; their ragged clothing and poor hygiene were evident.

“Well, gents! It looks like we just witnessed a bad breakup,” the man Seitogi took to be their leader had a menacing growl and was larger than the rest, dressed in leather armor. His face was badly scarred, and he glared at them from beneath a pointed steel helmet. He held a large, curved blade in his right hand and a spear in his left.

“Nogi really scraped the bottom of the barrel to gather this lot,” Seitogi said in a low whisper. “What do you want?” he called out, addressing scarface.

“What do I want? Your head, of course, or any part of your body will do really,” he spat on the ground.

“Oh, I see,” Seitogi’s voice was flat. “If you want to settle this the hard way, then you have found the right guy,” he cracked his knuckles and tensed his muscles, his eyes narrowing.

“It won’t take all of us to bring your head back,” said Scarface. “We have orders to chop you into little pieces.”

With that, he jumped at Seitogi, slicing at him with the blade as he landed. Seitogi managed to evade the attack and swung his arm back, catching the man on the chin with a solid fist. Scarface’s head snapped up, and he fell back, but he managed to spin around and come up with his spear. Seitogi leapt back and unsheathed his twin blades.

The two men circled each other, their eyes locked. The tip of Scarface’s spear was dipped towards the ground, his hand tightening around the shaft. Seitogi furrowed his brow as he readied himself, his eyes darting to and fro.

Scarface charged at Seitogi, swinging the spear in a wide arc. Seitogi leapt back, barely managing to avoid the attack. The force of Scarface’s landing shook the alley walls, and bricks and mortar fell to the ground. Scarface’s face was contorted in pain, and blood spilled from his lip. Somehow in his quick movements, Seitogi landed a blow.

Seitogi's gaze grew fierce. "We'll see who crumbles first," he snarled and raced towards Scarface with blades at the ready. He launched a flurry of lightning-fast strikes, the blades aimed at Scarface's head. The man fought back, parrying Seitogi's blades with precise thrusts from his spear. However, he struggled to keep pace with Scitogi's relentless assault.

They took a few steps back from one another to readjust their positions. Seitogi's face was a mask of concentration, his eyes dilated. His posture was low, and he held his blades forward.

In a sudden movement, he lunged forward, his feet heavy against the ground, and rushed towards Scarface, his swords yielding a swift slash. Scarface was a fraction slower to respond and screamed in panic.

"Attack! Inside out! Inside out!" As he fell to the ground, he swung his spear wildly.

Seitogi deflected the pole with his blade, but his balance was shunted. He somersaulted, rotating in midair with a slice against the back of Scarface's neck. Scarface toppled down with a scream, his face contorted in agony.

Seitogi landed deftly on his feet, his blades extended. Scarface's face was a twisted mask of pain. He was slowly bleeding from his neck, lying on the ground, flailing.

Seitogi's gaze grew intense as he found himself surrounded by ten warriors wielding spears. Some of them trembled with fear, while others gritted their teeth in anger, but all of them were glaring at Seitogi with animosity. He stiffened and braced for their attack, staring defiantly at the men surrounding him.

"If you want to try and fight, fine – then fight me!" he yelled in a loud voice, his eyes struggling to stay focused.

"Didn't you hear the boss? Kill him!" one of the spearmen shouted to his comrades.

In an instant, several spear points hurtled towards him. Seitogi barely had time to leap backwards and fend off the attack. The men around him rushed forward, shouting, but Seitogi expertly countered each strike with a rapid series of defensive thrust. They attempted to trap him in a small circle.

He was barely able to keep up with the rapidity of their attacks, his eyes darting around. He breathed hard through his mouth. He knew he had to take out his attackers before he became overwhelmed by their numbers. He linked together his dual blades and moved fluidly, as though it was one big sword. He parried and deflected as he tried to keep them at bay.

Some of the spears were deflected by the powerful swings of his blades; others were cleanly sliced. Seitogi lunged forward and struck the ground with his swords, sending a shower of red dust into the air that enveloped everything within reach.

He swiftly moved within the cloud of red dust, using his heightened senses to locate the remaining spearmen. He raised his heavy swords above his head and swung them with precision, cutting down six more opponents in just a matter of seconds. The effort took its toll on his arms, but he pressed on, accompanied by the piercing screams echoing throughout the alley.

"Why, Ary? Why did you do this?" Seitogi stood in the center of the alley, surrounded by fallen opponents. He held his swords at chest level, his face slick with sweat and blood. His eyes were wide and darting around, searching for a way out of the dangerous situation. He took a deep breath, trying to steady himself. He knew he needed to escape quickly, or he would meet the same fate as the men lying at his feet.

He swiftly moved forward, his blades swaying back and forth like a fan, creating a gap in their formation. He watched for an opportunity and, as soon as one presented itself, he lunged forward with incredible speed, his eyes still dilated. He swung his blades in a wide arc, his feet firmly planted on the ground.

Seitogi advanced, expertly wielding his blades to take down each opponent. The men surrounding him either backed away or crumpled to the ground, injured, and gasping for breath.

Seitogi stood tall, his weapons at the ready, his expression menacing. One of the men let out a scream, “Demon! Demon!” before dropping his spear and running down the alley. Seitogi quickly retrieved the man’s spear and chased after him, plunging it into his back and causing him to collapse. Blood flowed from the wound as the man lay motionless on the ground.

The remaining spearmen were in chaos. Seitogi’s gaze became clear as he surveyed the situation. Some were running away down the alley, while others were brandishing their weapons in fury, their faces contorted in anger. A few were still in a daze.

Seitogi backed away, holding his weapons aloft, his eyes fixed on the opponents. He was close to the alley’s entrance when suddenly, a spear struck him in the thigh, sinking deep into his flesh. He stumbled and attempted to crawl away. Nogitunde appeared from the shadows, seething with rage.

“Where is the girl?” he growled through gritted teeth.

Seitogi grimaced as he struggled to stand. The pain was intense, but he was determined not to let it defeat him. He focused all his energy on dulling the pain, making it bearable. With a fierce growl, he yanked the spear from his thigh, ignoring the gush of blood that followed.

Despite being covered in the blood of his fallen enemies, his vision was clear. He fixed his gaze on Nogitunde, his expression stoic and unreadable, before launching himself forward with a guttural howl.

Seitogi and Nogitunde clashed in the alley, their weapons clanging against each other in a fierce bout. Seitogi was quick and agile, dodging Nogitunde’s attacks and retaliating with swift strikes of his own. Nogitunde, however, was determined and relentless, not backing down from the fight.

Just when it seemed like Nogitunde had the upper hand, Seitogi moved with lightning speed. He kneed Nogitunde in the stomach, causing him to double over in pain, and pushed him away. Nogitunde stumbled and fell to the ground, looking pale and shaken.

Seitogi stood over him, his weapons in hand, his face expressionless. A raven circled overhead, its caw echoing through the alley. Seitogi's eyes were clouded as he looked up at the sky, barely registering the pain from his wounds. The men in the alley were intimidated by Seitogi's strength and none dared approach now that their benefactor was defeated.

Seitogi hovered over Nogitunde, the tip of one of his blades pressing against his neck. Nogitunde's eyes flickered and closed, his face contorted in a grimace. But Seitogi did not slay him. Instead he delivered two thin cuts on both his cheeks.

"Every time you look at these scars I leave you with, remember Arymaitei, your beloved, and how she sent you to meet your certain death at my hands."

Seitogi turned and limped down the alley, with the remaining opponents clearing a path for him. He exited without a backward glance and merged into the throngs of revelers, disappearing into the crowd.

The blood of his foes dripped down his face, and the wound in his leg pulsed with pain. He took a deep breath and clenched his jaw, scanning his surroundings. The blood covering his eyes made it difficult to see clearly, but he pressed on, determined to reach Emily.

He made his way down the street, avoiding eye contact and trying to blend in with the crowds. Some people glanced at him with curiosity, taking in his pale complexion, blood-soaked clothing, and dilated eyes, but no one stopped to offer help. With each step, the pain grew more intense, but he pushed through, repeating her name, "Enoshi."

Blood on the Docks

Emily and Glehson sat in a corner of the Lush Sanctum, cloaked in the shadow of a small alcove. The tavern was located in a dark area of the town, usually not very busy, but tonight it was crowded with townspeople and tourists alike. There was a band playing a lively tune, and the sounds of laughter and piping voices filled the air.

Emily was sick with nervousness and looked rather pale. Glehson sat next to her, his arm around her, in an attempt to offer comfort.

"He should be here by now," Emily said. She was looking towards the door, anxious to see Seitogi. But for all she knew, Nogitunde's ambush was successful. Just the thought of it devastated her.

"He'll come," she said, vigorously shaking her leg as she gazed into Glehson's eyes. "He has to. He's strong and fast, and he knows how to fight. He has to come."

"Of course he will," Glehson said, smiling at her. Emily looked away, her eyes darkened, and she looked to the tavern's entrance. Glehson saw the fear on her face. He didn't know what more he could say to reassure her.

"Perhaps I will go get us something to drink and some food?" Glehson announced. He had to do something to break the awkward silence between them. Emily nodded, focused on the entrance again. She was worried sick, they both were.

Glehson left Emily and walked towards the bar. The tavern was busy, the band was swinging their bows to their heart's content, and the atmosphere was lively. People were dancing, eating, and drinking. He ordered plantain fritters and waited. The barman was an elderly man with almost pure white hair and a beard to fit. He was smiling but worn out looking. He had heavy lines on his face, lines that said he'd seen it all and and was tired of seeing it.

"I'm afraid it'll take a while. The place is very busy tonight," the barman said.

“Not to worry, I’ll wait. Thank you.” Glehson stood back, taken aback by how crowded the place was. He was about to ask the barman how many people there were when he felt a hand grab his arm.

“It’s good to see you again, His Grace,” Glehson felt his heart jump as Arymaitei squeezed his arm tighter.

“Where, pray, is my dear sister?” Her voice was light in his ear but cut above the noise of the tavern. Glehson swallowed; he was dazed. The look on Arymaitei’s face was malicious. His arm hurt; she squeezed it with such force. People were beginning to stare at them.

“I really don’t want to make a scene, and time is of the essence. So, I’ll make this short. Where is Yuyuki?”

“What Arymaitei? Are you going to kill me? That would be treason,” Glehson tried to pull out of her grip, but she held tight.

“To be sure, handsome. Your royal title will not protect you from my blade.”

“That’s enough, Arymaitei! What in the hell did you do to Seita?”

Arymaitei slowly turned around to face an angry Emily and smirked.

“Seitogi was weak,” she said flatly, “He’s not fit to stand by my side.” Yet she didn’t sound pleased as she spoke. Her hand went to her sword pommel; she was visibly ready to draw. Emily didn’t move away; she was determined not to be intimidated. Finally, Arymaitei smiled and released her grip on Glehson and said,

“We have an appointment to keep. Come along.”

“I’m not going anywhere with you!” Emily spat, her fear and anger reaching a boiling point. Arymaitei stepped back, still smiling, and raised her hand to Emily’s cheek. Emily flinched and took a step back. Arymaitei laughed, grabbing Glehson again.

"All I have to do is announce the crown prince's presence, and every man, woman, and child in this place will tear him to pieces! Haven't you heard? The Imperial House isn't liked much in these parts. Now come!" She motioned Emily to follow as she dragged Glehson along with her.

"All right, give us a minute!" Glehson dug in his heels and gave the pub's patrons a nervous once-over. He looked into Emily's eyes and found there terror and the shock of betrayal. The lines in her face, the veins on her forehead; this was bad.

Arymaitei pulled Glehson out of the tavern into the ongoing festivities. There were men, women, and children walking so freely in the streets. All gleeful and happy. They carried no fear. No expectant gazes. The only ones that couldn't hide their fear were Emily and Glehson.

Arymaitei led them to a nearby stable. Glehson felt numb, his mind racing as he tried to figure out how to escape. He wanted to run, but he knew they were at Arymaitei's mercy. He purposely tripped and fell to buy them some time. But she pulled him along.

As they entered the stable, Arymaitei took his dagger from his waist and bound his hands, clapping his shoulder, and asking him not to take it personally.

Emily stood frozen, unable to move. "You said you'd always protect me from the witch," she said.

"I promised I'd protect you from the witch. Not the Aiyo. You belong with them anyway. They're your family. You destroyed mine, so I'll let them destroy you. Only seems fair."

Emily stared at Arymaitei as if she were a ghost. Glehson watched in complete shock as she strode over to the door and quickly poked her head out.

"Who are you waiting for?" asked Glehson. "Is Nogitunde in on this too?"

"To a point, but his role is finished." Arymaitei answered as she kept her eyes on the door. "I sent a raven to White Eyes and reworked our arrangement. We're awaiting our transport now."

“Impossible! You hadn’t the time, nor chance without someone seeing something,” said Glehson.

“I never really trusted White Eyes, as should anyone in our line of work, and so put in place a contingency plan should he betray me. No need to keep you in the dark, boy. So, here we wait. As for Nogi. Well, he was always expendable.”

“Stop this at once!” Emily burst out. “You can’t do this!”

“Do what?” Arymaitei asked.

“What?” shouted Emily. “You know what! I have to stop you.”

“My dear sister, you can’t stop me. You’re not fit to fight.” Arymaitei said. “Look at you; you’re basically a little girl.”

“I’m older than you, dammit!”

“You were. Once. But whatever that witch did to you stunted your growth. You’ve no hips or breasts. It’s a wonder the boy has an eye for you.”

“Leave his eyes out of this, miss male gaze! How long have you been plotting this? Why?”

“Plotting? I have been planning my vengeance since you disappeared all those years ago. Let us not forget how you treated me. You were a spoiled, arrogant girl!” Arymaitei said as she turned her back to Emily.

A horse-drawn cart with a round canopy pulled up outside of the stable. The middle-aged driver gave a loud whistle. Arymaitei turned and smiled.

“It’s time to go; now don’t be troublesome.”

“Wait, who is that guy? Can you trust him?” Glehson asked as Arymaitei ushered him out onto the road and laughed.

“Of course, I can trust him.”

She forced them both into the cab, and at her urging, the driver set off. The bright colors and festive sounds of the streets faded away.

They drove further and further into the outskirts of town. It was plainly obvious the driver was headed for the docks.

"We'll be there shortly," Arymaitei sat back, relaxed.

Emily tried to force her to make eye contact, but Arymaitei stubbornly refused to look in her direction. She ignored Emily and looked out the carb's window instead.

"Don't you feel the least bit ashamed for being such a backstabber?" asked Emily. "For making an enemy out of your only sister?"

Aryimaitei's eyes widened; she turned to Emily and smiled, "Backstabber? No. I am not that. You try running a house full of men when there's barely any grain in the cupboard. No, I'm tired of it. I'd be a fool to pass up this opportunity. Plus, I finally get to ruin your life like you did mine."

"My life was ruined from birth, you selfish cow! It wasn't me who made you like this!" Emily shouted.

Arymaitei laughed. "Selfish cow? Well, if there is one thing I'm good at, it's looking out for me," she said and then turned back to the window.

Emily was shocked at her sister's cavalier attitude; she looked at Glehson, and he shook his head.

"You can't reason with her, Emily. This has been her plan all along."

"I swear I'll make you pay for this," said Emily as tears fell from her eyes.

Arymaitei giggled, smiling. "Say what you want, Yuyu. You've had this coming for years."

Emily was about to say something when the cart lurched to a stop outside of a large pier. The driver opened the cart door and offered a low bow. Arymaitei drew back and placed her hand on her sword hilt, but the lanky man quickly held up his hands in submission.

"Reyer, what are you doing here? What happened to my driver?"

"Now, now. None of that, Miss Ary." said her mother's captain.

Reyer reached forward, but Arymaitei snarled and kicked outwardly, landing a blow on his chest, knocking him to the ground. She jumped out of the carriage onto the creaky, splintery dock and stood over him but was distracted by a familiar voice.

"Mouse! Behave yourself!" Arymaitei turned to see Awei, a raven on her shoulder, talking with Aiyo Yulori, only he was disguised, dressed in typical Dhukai gear with the lower half of his face covered. Behind them, several men were loading a nondescript barge with what appeared to be bales of hay.

"The Bakau," Arymaitei muttered to herself, eyeing the ship.

"Mouse," Awei waved her over, "I'm assuming you have my prize with you."

"Chua?" Arymaitei walked over, "Didn't expect to see you here. Nor did I expect Lord Aiyo."

Aiyo Yulori cut his eyes at the girl and then settled them back on Awei, who rolled hers.

"The girl, Arymaitei," she said.

"Yes, of course. The girl," said Arymaitei, turning to Yulori. "I am here to collect the bounty on her head, Lord Aiyo."

"You mean the money being loaded onto The Bakau," Awei nudged her chin in the direction of her barge. "It's thirteen bloody million ohn, my dear. What were you going to carry it all off in? A sack slung over your shoulder?" she laughed.

"Perhaps she was expecting a check," Aiyo Yulori sniggered.

Arymaitei placed her hands on her hips and waited until they were done laughing. "Actually, Mother, you lost her, and she came to me. Therefore, you've no claim to her or my fortune."

"Mouse, my dear, you are smarter than this," said Awei.

"Apparently not, because I'm not giving her up unless I… Did you say thirteen million?" Arymaitei asked as she realized the magnitude of the prize on Emily's head.

Aiyo Yulori brushed a bit of dust from his shoulder, "I believe that is what your mother said."

"White Eyes. Dirty bastard!" Arymaitei said as she sheathed her blade and walked away. She did not look back. She walked back over to the carriage and motioned for Emily, who reluctantly followed her. Arymaitei placed a hand on the hilt of her sword.

"Well, Yuyu, I wanted to have a little fun, and I have, but now I must deliver you to your new master."

"Kick rocks and chew glass, you rotten piece of shi…" Reyer placed his hand over her mouth, but Emily was quick to react and bit down on two of his fingers.

With a curse, he pulled his hand back and raised it, ready to slap her. Yet even though she was breathless from the effort she'd just made; Emily was swift enough to skirt under the incoming blow.

Aiyo Yulori and Awei shared an awkward stare, and Reyer quickly recovered and grabbed Emily by the back of the neck and shoved her towards them.

"But what am I going to do with this one?" Arymaitei cleared her throat and pulled Glehson from the cart and patted him on the top of the head.

"I could keep him if you'd like, but then who would inherit the country?" she said.

"Such an uncouth girl," tutted Aiyo Yulori, "But she has a point." He tossed her a bag of coins which landed to the side of the dock. "Come along, cousin. Auntie Yumeiko is worried sick over you," he said.

"I'm not afraid of you, Lord Aiyo," said Glehson. "In fact, if you harm one hair on Emily's head…"

"Emily, you say," Aiyo Yulori smiled beneath his mask. "This girl is but one part of a larger plot to deceive the Imperial House. I wouldn't place my bets on her, Your Grace. She is an imposter whom Phule has used to deceive you too."

"Imposter? Deceived me? Shows how much you know, Lord Aiyo." Glehson began to explain the last few days and Emily's part in it all. Aiyo Yulori was uninterested in hearing any of it and turned away.

"Let's go," Awei said, taking Emily by the arm and pulling her along toward the Bakau.

"Wait, Awei!" shouted Emily. "Aren't you aware of what they are going to do to me?"

"It's the punishment of your birth that awaits you. It's nothing to do with me."

"I suppose you blame me for breaking you and Yienguoi-Jin up as well."

"You misunderstand me, child," Awei said as she pulled Emily up the side of the barge and onto its gangplank. "This isn't at all personal in the least."

"Then let me go!" Emily spat.

"If I let you go now," Awei said coldly, "Then I would've lost several of my brothers for naught."

The two women climbed aboard, and Awei turned to a man standing near the rail, dressed in a gray and black hemp jumper, and said, "Take care of this one."

Emily felt her world caving in on her. How was this fair? This punishment of her birth. She had to escape, even if it meant jumping into the ocean and drowning herself. Her face turned red with rage as she backed away, feeling energy build up in her. Deep in her mind, she heard the words of her grandmother,

"Strike, child!"

Without a second thought, Emily crouched down and struck upwards with a flattened palm that caught Awei in the throat.

Awei's eyes bulged as she gasped for air, and Emily turned on her heel while swinging her leg, nimbly catching the older warrior in the side of the jaw with a stiff foot.

Awei stumbled up and tried catching hold of Emily, but Emily stepped back and kicked her in the chest, knocking her off the gangplank and into the water. All eyes fell on her as she stood there, breathing heavily and glaring at them on the dock.

"See how she has the eyes of a demon." Aiyo Yulori scowled, pulling his sword from its sheath and pointed it at Emily. "Detain her!"

The men on the dock began to surge forward, but Arymaitei stepped forward, placing herself between them and the gangplank.

"Hold it! Hold it! Hold! Lay one finger on my bounty and lose your life!" she said when she felt a swoosh of air overhead.

Emily had leapt over her and landed on the dock with a flurry of precise kicks and punches that sent men flying in all directions. Arymaitei's eyes widened, and she instinctively stepped back, bracing for a potential attack.

But Emily ignored her, running past her uncle and grabbing Glehson's hand.

"Run!" she screamed, pulling him along with her. Aiyo Yulori's head spun around in amazement to see Glehson clutching Emily's hand as they dashed away. Arymaitei sucked in a sharp breath.

"You're letting her run? Give me the bounty for her head, and I'll catch her," Arymaitei shouted behind him.

"Stay in your place, little girl. Then you have nothing to lose," Aiyo Yulori said, stiffening the sword in front of him.

"Your loss," Arymaitei said, tightening her grip on the edge of her sword, "But I'll still take that purse." She cut the mooring ropes of the Bakau and blew him a kiss goodbye. Arymaitei leapt up as the vessel pulled away from the dock and gracefully landed on the deck. She easily fought her way to the bridge, harassing the helmsman with the tip of her sword at his neck.

"It's been a while, Douyo, nice to see you again," she said, "Now make for the sea, and I'll let you live" she taunted as the barge slowly lumbered out into the bay. Suddenly, the barge's starboard side was peppered with flaming arrows as archers on the shore reloaded their bows.

"Spears!" Dowahg Gailen's gruff voice carried over the howling wind from the dock to the barge.

Arymaitei grimaced, "Steer away from the dock this instant, or I'll have you hanging from the mast," poking the helmsman Douyo with the tip of her blade. Awei pulled herself from the water onto the dock, only to be met with the sight of no less than a hundred flying carp men marching towards her with shields up and spears forward.

"What is the meaning of this, Dowahg?" Awei raised her hands and glared at the man. "Are you going to attack a fellow Dhukai unprovoked?"

"Attacking without a single provocation is not the general way I do things, Chua. But we have been provoked and will defend ourselves," Dowahg shouted back.

"Defend yourselves from what? When has my Inouei ever crossed you?"

"The Aiyo girl, Chua!" he demanded. "Dead or alive, she is our prize."

"Damned nuisance, that one. But her prize is well worth the effort all the same," Awei cursed.

"I take it you refuse to comply then!" growled Dowahg.

"Go ahead, attack if you must! But don't begrudge me later, for your losses will be great!" Fully drenched, she whistled loudly, and throngs of her own men appeared from the bowels of the Bakau and flooded onto its deck, many of them archers as well.

Arymaitei quickly swung her head back and forth as the men surrounded the bridge and noted the grin on the helmsman's face. Defeated, she sighed, tossing her blade to the floor.

"Nice to see you come to your senses, Miss Ary."

"Oh, toss off, why don't you!" Arymaitei angrily crossed her arms.

"Emily, slow down!" Glehson was struggling to keep pace with her, but it was no good as Emily currently had only one thing on her mind: getting them to safety. She pulled him by the rope binding his wrist and turned around a corner, entering a chaotic maze of stacked cargo containers.

Aiyo's men were not far behind. Emily pulled Glehson into an unlit passageway beside one of the containers and hid in the shadows.

"We need a way out," she panted. Glehson held up his bound hands and cleared his throat.

"Oh, sorry!" she hurriedly cut his binds and tossed the ropes aside.

"What was that back there?" Glehson asked as he rubbed his wrists.

"What? What was what?"

"You! You fought better than a Dhukai! You were amazing," Glehson said.

“I got a bit angry,” Emily breathlessly spoke as she looked into his eyes. “Tbh I can’t explain it myself, but man, am I sore. I feel like I just crunched a month of Pilates in five minutes.”

“What should we do now?” Glehson asked. “Yulori’s men won’t stop coming. We can’t allow them to catch you.”

“Then we have to take them down before that happens,” Emily said. “I have a potential plan, but it is kind of dangerous. Together we may be able to do it,” she said as Glehson pulled her close.

“Alright then,” he said, holding her tight. “What do you have in mind?”

“It’s the horse,” said Emily. “If we can double back and get the horse from that cart, we can ride out of here.”

“There is no way for us to reach it unscathed,” said Glehson. “Those men would be waiting for us at the other end.”

“Yes, but think about it,” she said as she looked at him with a smile. “They won’t be expecting it.” Glehson raised a skeptical eyebrow. “It will buy us some time, at the least,” she said.

Glehson opened his mouth to answer when his words were drowned out by the sound of a high-pitched hunting horn.

“What was that?” asked Emily, looking out of their hiding spot. Glehson looked out the other side and then back to her,

“The Carps and Inouei are fighting. We are going to have to run for it. This way,” he said, pointing back the way they came.

Emily nodded, and they stepped out and sprinted. They reached the edge of their hiding spot and found the path lined with slabs of timber that could act as cover for their escape to the other end of the dock.

“How do we get to the horse?” Glehson asked.

“Above!” Emily shouted as three men dived down from overhead. Emily managed to duck and roll and sliced one of the man’s ankle tendons as he landed, but the other two blocked her and Glehson’s path forward. She tried to strike at both simultaneously, but the men were deft in their blade craft and managed to stay just out of range.

They darted forward and jumped backward, drawing her out until she lost her footing and fell. Her head snapped back when one of the men’s boots came down on her shoulder. To her left, more men turned the bend around the crates, and more were converging behind them.

Emily quickly grabbed the belt of one of her assailants and yanked him forward onto her blade, regaining her footing. She used his body as a shield as she pressed forward, hacking his comrade in the neck, dislodging his head.

“Come on!” she cried out, and they sprung across the tall piles of timber.

Glehson darted and dodged as Emily held her blade and slashed at both Aiyo and Inouei attackers alike. In her mind’s eye, she saw her grandmother practicing some form of martial arts in a beautiful garden as she followed along at the old woman’s side.

A flash of light blinded her, followed by an intense pain to her right jaw. She dropped to her knees and then forward onto her belly, but moved just in time to dodge the second blow. Raising her blade over her shoulder, she stabbed through the stomach of the man attempting to stomp her with his boot. Flipped onto her back, she pushed until the hilt butted against his gut.

While still at an awkward angle, she blocked an incoming spear and quickly rolled over onto her belly and rose to her knees.

As she pushed the man away, he spun his knife out of its sheath and dug in deep into her right thigh. She screamed, and in one swift movement, sliced off his arm below the elbow.

Glehson was surrounded by several Aiyo men threateningly dangling ropes and cuffs. Emily ran over to help him, but a Carp man blocked her way; the sword he was holding almost took her eye out.

"We are meant to take you alive, girl!" he said, with the blade to her face. Emily ducked, pressed forward, but two more attackers emerged from behind the timber. Using everything she could, she kicked, spun, and slashed, killing her assailant as the other two fell on her.

Her blade was a blur of movement. Despite being winded, she did not intend to lose and ferociously defended against their attack.

"Bind her," a voice called out.

"We've subdued the prince!" said another.

Emily stepped back to assess the situation. Glehson was being dragged off by two men, his wrists bound once again. Panicking from the sheer number of waiting men and the pain from her leg, she leaned against a container for support.

An Aiyo man grabbed her wrist, pushed her against the side of the container with his chest, and leaned into her back with his knee.

"You dare to strike down Tabaiken! You will pay that debt with your own slow death."

"Go to hell, coward!" she said, wincing with pain. "When I am empress, yours will be the first head put to the pike!"

However, the man did not reply, so she tried again. "I am the future empress, that man is my husband. Now let us go, and the emperor will pardon you all!"

To her surprise, the men laughed. "I do not know of any girl raised as a princess who would speak like you."

"My name is Emily," she said, reaching out with her left hand to grab the blade of another one of her would-be captors. She used her knees to push off the container and push the man back. She spun around and put the sword through his breast.

"Emily goddamned Heart is my name!"

"Enoshi!"

Seitogi's voice reverberated throughout the air. He stood above them atop the containers and looked down with a menacing glare. His leg was bandaged, and he held a spear in each hand.

"I have no quarrel with the Aiyo," he said, pointing a spear at Emily; the arm beneath his sleeve was blue and swollen. "But an attack on my family is an attack on me!" he yelled as he jumped down.

The Aiyo men gave space as he took up Emily's flank and twirled both spears in a butterfly pattern. A brave Aiyo man decided to be the first to attack, and Seitogi ducked below his strike and drove his spear upwards through the man's armpit.

The man shrieked and pulled backward to escape the blade, but Seitogi's spear was longer. He then drove back the rest of the Aiyo and Carp men as he stepped over their discarded, blood-stained bodies.

He kicked aside the man who had held Emily pinned and pointed to the blade still stuck in his chest.

"You did that?"

Emily nodded yes, and then threw her arms around him, crying as he asked how.

"I don't know, Seita," she cried, "Something's wrong with me. I keep remembering my grandmother's training, but…" she trailed off, looking off into nothingness, and quietly said, "Kill craft. Yes, that's what she called it. Kill craft. But Seitogi, my grandma… Dolores never taught me martial arts. We did Tai chi with the old folks in the park, sometimes, but that was all. I'm so confused."

"You're delirious and you're hurt," Seitogi softly touched the gash on her thigh; he stopped and stared at it for a second. How queer that they were injured in the same exact place, though his was far more serious.

“Seita… what is it?” Emily spoke over her sniffles, “Oh no, you’re hurt too.”

Tears rolled from his eyes as he wrapped a strip of cloth around her wound. “I’m not long for this world, Enoshi. I’m sorry for letting you down.”

Emily reached out and stroked his smooth cheek with a clammy hand. “Please don’t talk like that, Seita. We are going to survive this. We mustn’t give up.”

“I… I love you. I will always know that no matter what happens,” he gasped weakly as Emily looked up and behind his shoulder; she froze, petrified.

“Atem,” she whispered.

Seitogi turned to see the man emerging from behind the tall piles of timber. He was tall and built like an ox, with prodigious shoulders and back muscles. He slowly strutted forward, a bamboo staff resting on his shoulder.

“Princess.” He recognized Emily and bowed low with his hand at his waist. “It is a pleasure to see you well after all these years.”

“I’m bleeding out, Enoshi,” Seitogi spoke quickly now, his dull eyes staring into hers. “I’m so sorry for bringing you here and ruining your life.”

He looked over his shoulder, noticing the other man was taking care to allow him more time to mend her injured leg. He felt his chest tighten, and then Emily pulled him close.

“We have to run. He is Huasau Atem, Odahni’s man-at-arms,” she whispered.

“I am well aware of him,” said Seitogi. “Listen, Enoshi, I’ll hold them off. Run!” Seitogi was moving with great amounts of effort and pain as he spoke.

A group of men formed behind Atem; more crowded the tops of the containers above them, quiet and waiting. Seitogi knew they had arrived to deliver them both to their deaths.

"You are outnumbered, boy," said Atem, "And you are too weak to run. But I will allow you a courtesy. Disembowel yourself now, or I will slowly skin you alive. Ask the princess about me. She knows."

Seitogi looked Emily in thc eyes. She hesitated and then whispered, "One night I snuck out of my room and happened upon him in the yard skinning a thief alive." She looked away and closed her eyes. "I saw him at the height of his fury, covered in blood and cursing the man. Please. Please run!" she begged.

Seitogi reverted to a calmer state, clear-eyed he took a deep breath. His lips curled into a grin,

"Enoshi," he said with a soft chuckle. "Let him think I'm terrified. I'm not." He then looked Atem in the eye, "I am not going to go easy on you, or allow you to take Enoshi anywhere."

"Enough." Atem yelled dismissively, and then raised his staff. Seitogi touched the hilt of his sword and looked at Emily. "Be quick and use the mirror."

Seitogi again looked up into the royal guards' faces as Emily clumsily fetched the mirror from her hoodie.

"Enoshi. Run!"

She nodded, not brave enough to speak as she began running to the edge of the container. Seitogi simultaneously confronted Atem head-on. Atem immediately lashed out with his staff; Seitogi was prepared and moved aside. The two became a blur of movement.

"Catch her! I will handle this boy!" Atem yelled, glancing over his shoulder as Emily moved just past the cover of the containers. She was followed by the Aiyo men, chasing her down the narrow alleyways created by the stacked containers.

Seitogi's counterattack was blocked for a second time. He attempted to dislodge the staff, but Atem held it with an iron grip and used its length to push him back. Seitogi took the chance to hit Atem in the ribs, but the man was taller and faster.

Seitogi gritted his teeth and pushed through his pain. He struck out and performed a quick flip over Atem, and in an upwards ricochet pattern, he pushed off the enormous wooden crates with his feet, and danced his way up and over the edge of the containers until he settled on one at the top.

Still grasping the staff with both hands, Atem followed and nimbly ascended the enormous stacks of containers. He could see the light of the sky approaching and grinned widely.

In what felt like just a few seconds, Atem landed hard on top of the container and breathed heavily, twirling his staff.

Seitogi gripped his sword and rushed forward to attack as Atem gained his footing. Even with his blood loss, Seitogi felt a surge of energy as he jumped up, vaulted into the air, and slammed into the man-at-arms.

The two clashed in midair, cursing and swinging. Seitogi's attack was blocked by Atem's staff. They tried to force each other back to their respective platform's edge; a twenty-foot drop waited.

Atem's flurry of swipes caused Seitogi to pause and retreat several feet. The man-at-arms took the moment to jump forward and harass the boy with the tip of the staff. There was a calm rage in his eyes as he raised the staff over his head and brought it down, aiming for the boy's head. Seitogi twisted and rolled to the side as the staff smashed through the wooden container.

Atem pursued him with another powerful strike, which Seitogi clumsily was able to block. They fought each other with Seitogi giving all that was left in him, pausing occasionally to catch his breath. Suddenly he staggered back, clutching his side and groaned.

He had been pierced with an arrow from behind, its point jutting forth from his lower right abdomen. His color drained, as did the last of his strength.

Another arrow shrieked through the air and tore into his torso. He gasped and pulled it out just as another struck his back shoulder and brought him to his knees.

He looked over the top of the plateau of cargo containers. Archers were perched all around, firing at him. Atem charged forward; staff high. Seitogi again leaned and dodged, barely getting out of the way of the staff as it broke the wood beneath his feet.

Seitogi dropped his sword; it clanged on the deck below. Atem didn't stop there, his movements piercing the air as he relentlessly swung his staff. Seitogi hobbled away. Using his good leg, he jumped and landed on an adjacent stack of cargo containers, rolling to his side.

Atem was quick and landed next to him, bringing the staff down on him, but Seitogi jumped again, avoiding the blow, and bounced off the containers as he fell to the ground. Staggering to stand, he finally collapsed as more arrows hit him in the chest and back.

"Enough!" Atem waved a massive hand, and the archers lowered their bows. He leaned over the edge and looked down at Seitogi's body.

Seitogi was breathing heavily, bleeding out, seemingly delirious. Atem jumped down to the pavement and stood over him, frowning,

"They've ruined you, boy. Too many holes in your body to have fun skinning you now."

Seitogi clamored to his hands and knees, blood dripping from his nose and eyes. He looked up at Atem and smiled, and with one last quick movement, flung an exploding smoke bomb into the man's face, causing Atem to shriek in pain as the smoke burned and engulfed him.

Seitogi slowly rose to his feet and limped forward as Atem continued to cough. Atem shook his head like a wet dog and blindly chased after Seitogi, who cleared the complex of containers and made a desperate run across the dock, through the melee of fighting Inouei and Carps Dhukai.

He tossed out several more smoke bombs as he blindly ran, becoming lost in the thick fog. Surrounded by the chaos and screams of battle. Arrows tore into the ground next to him as he made gut-wrenching efforts to escape them.

He knew Atem was somewhere amongst the smoke in pursuit. The sheer breadth of the dock prevented him from ducking down and staying out of sight. He knew the danger another confrontation posed. His strength was draining, and the smoke was burning his eyes and filling his lungs.

He finally reached the end of the dock and stumbled forward, falling into the agitated waters. He inhaled and choked due to his collapsed lung. What little time he had left in the world of the living was quickly fading; he called for Enoshi as he thrashed about.

The water filled his lungs, his agony was immense. The way his chest pounded as he flailed trying to swim, trying to escape. But the many arrows jutting from his body prevented him from doing so. Enoshi, he gagged, calling out her name as gravity pulled him downwards.

Atem finally made it to the end of the dock and spat out a wad of blood as he watched Seitogi sinking below the surface. He gripped the staff and used its flat end to push down on the top of his head to be certain the boy was properly drowned.

Satisfied with his kill, albeit not his preferred "live skinning", Atem's eyes suddenly bulged, and he let fly a wail of pain as a sword burst from his chest. He staggered back and groaned, covering his face in shock.

"Yuyuki!" Atem turned and dropped the staff, gurgling in pain as he fell forward and gasped for air. He spat blood and groaned as he rolled over onto his back. Emily stood over him, panting heavily, still holding the bloody sword.

He looked down at his chest and saw the unbearable wound. He stared up at Emily.

"You…" but he could barely speak. Emily stood rigid, ready to strike again. He laid his head back.

“I know,” he said. “…I know.” He tried to breathe. “I know…”

She raised the sword over her head, aiming to strike down, but Atem shot up and grasped her wrist and held it.

“If I die, princess, so does Darren.” He groaned.

A tear streamed down her cheek. “Damn you!” She kicked him aside and ran to dive after Seitogi, but Atem caught her by the ankle and pulled her back.

“Sei-” She began but stopped herself.

“The boy is already dead,” Atem choked out the words, as she scowled at him.

“Let me go,” she looked him in the eyes, “Please. I can save him!”

“It’s too late, princess.”

She swung her hand with force, striking him and causing him to release her grip and fall to the ground. Emily lifted the sword, ready to deliver the final blow, but he grabbed her wrist, stopping her from striking.

“It’s finished, my lady.”

She surveyed her surroundings and saw that several Aiyo warriors were approaching from the dock, and archers had her in their crosshairs.

With a heavy sigh, she lowered her arm and let the sword drop from her hand. Exhausted from the struggle, she knelt down and pounded her fist on the wooden planks.

“I’m sorry, Seitogi,” she cried, struggling to breathe. “I’m so sorry,” she said again, almost inaudibly. And then took up her sword and erupted to her feet, running towards the men.

“No one is going to take me alive!” she screamed.

Atem tried to stand but slid back down, awash in his own blood. The dock moaned and creaked as the Aiyo men ran forward in an organized formation with their blades aimed. They met Emily head-on, clanging metal, and screaming as the battle erupted.

Emily swiped and sliced and thrust her sword; she fought with newfound strength. She leapt and flipped over the group, spinning and kicking along the way.

She landed behind them and slashed her sword; one man fell as she passed. She turned and jumped and kicked again, but the Aiyo men no longer fought as a group; they were now running towards her separately.

She was outnumbered, alone, and more men were forcing their way down the pier. They began to encircle her. She had to run, and so she backpedaled as the Aiyo men advanced and surrounded her. They all raised their swords, ready to strike.

"Yuyuki!" It was Aiyo Yulori's voice thundering over the noise. The Aiyo men paused, many had bows aimed, their swords pointed and ready to slash.

"This is over!" he shouted. "Throw down your arms, girl!" he commanded. The Aiyo men continued to surround Emily, with steely eyes.

"Do it!" he commanded again. Emily could barely stand; she was gasping for breath, but she still stood and met his eyes with hate in hers.

"You're going to die for this!" she screamed, chest heaving.

"Not yet, princess," he laughed and looked at his men and commanded, "Beat her!"

The circle of Aiyo men came forward. Emily braced herself and struck out with her blade, but the swipes and strokes of her sword were weak and had little effect.

The Aiyo men began to close the circle. One lunged in and yanked the sword, trying to wrest it from her hands. She was trying to defend herself, but her arms were shaking, and her eyes were beginning to water.

Emily could no longer defend herself. He pulled the sword away from her and kicked her square in the chest, causing her to stagger back and fall to the ground. She cursed them as the men gathered around her, but there were too many. They all fell into stomping her like they were stamping out a fire.

"No! Stop it!" Emily cried out, buried in countless, thumping leathery boots forcing her to collide against the splintery, rusted, wooden docks. She cried out for help; she called out to her grandmother in pain. She screamed again and again.

Unable to stand by and watch any longer, Arymaitei jumped from the deck of the Bakau, landed on the dock, and ran forward, swinging her blade.

"No, you don't," said Awei, catching her by cloaks hood, stopping her in her tracks. Arymaitei tried pulling away, but her mother's grip was too firm.

"They're killing my bounty!" Arymaitei cried, still pulling away, but Awei looked her in the eyes and gave a coy smile.

"Your bounty, silly mouse," she said. "You're not going to collect any bounty by getting yourself killed."

Aiyo Yulori marched over to Awei. "Where have you been?" he asked.

She pointed over her shoulder, in the direction of the ongoing clash between her Dhukai and the Carps. Yulori took a deep breath and looked down.

"Oh well, this thing is going to take longer than expected." He looked on as the rival Dhukais continued to fight and turned back to Awei.

"Seems like I'm going to have to take some of my men and clean up your mess with the Carps," he said.

He flung a flare high into the air, which ignited and illuminated the night sky with a white blue. This was followed by the blaring of a horn from a ship further out at sea, its port side crowded with archers aiming flaming arrows at the dock.

Aiyo Yulori gave Awei a final glare before he focused on Dowag, "Retreat with your men now, Gailen, or find that you have started a war with the House Aiyo. A war you can't possibly win."

"Am I not to be compensated? My men have bled here, many lay dead on this pier alone." Gailen pointed to the dead behind him, some Carps and a few Inouei.

"Relent now, and you will be duly compensated. The blood on this dock should be the only blood spilled tonight."

Dowag shrugged. Aiyo Yulori nodded and looked behind him, a smile emerging on his face. Atem still lived, barely, as he was carried over by three of his subordinates.

"You let a girl beat you," Yulori patted the hardly conscious man on the shoulder. "I'll have to remedy that." He whistled, and men nearby sprang to action.

"Take him aboard the Garlanza. If he dies, you will join him soon after." He turned away from his falling man-at-arms and shouted out orders for his men to pick up the corpses of the slain, and to the men surrounding Emily, he simply stated, "That's enough," as he walked away.

"You can't just go! I brought her to you! What about my pay?" said Arymaitei, finally breaking out of her mother's restraint. Aiyo Yulori stopped and turned to her with an alarmed expression; it appeared he was surprised she had spoken at all.

"Chua! Control your dog, lest I leash her."

"Come away from her, child," said Awei, attempting to comfort her, but Arymaitei slapped her hand away.

"You pigs! You don't know what I went through to bring her here! I lost one of my men, damn it!"

"Such arrogant words, girl," Yulori sneered. "But I will spare you. We've had enough violence for one night." With a dismissive flick of his wrist, Yulori tossed her a coin and walked away, chuckling to himself.

He stood over Emily's battered body and kicked it. "Clean up this mess. Get it over to the Garlanza."

Two men came over and lifted Emily as she moaned. Her lips, eyes, and face were swollen, bruised, and bloodied. She coughed up blood and made a horrid wheezing sound that suggested she struggled to breathe, but -

"One day I'm going to kill all of you," she wailed, and then caught a glimpse of Arymaitei as they carried her away to a waiting rowboat, one of several moored to the dock.

"You let them kill Seita, Ary! He's dead because of you!"

Arymaitei turned her face away, too ashamed to confront Emily's eyes.

Yulori scoffed, "Dive for the boy! I want his head," he ordered two of his men.

"Seitogi, I didn't mean…" Arymaitei said, backing away. Awei grabbed her again, this time by the chin and held her head still,

"Open your eyes, child. What's done is done. I know you feel bad about your pet but offending The Aiyo isn't going to help."

Arymaitei stopped resisting and opened her eyes, letting a small tear fall. Yulori reached her, his chest and stature big and imposing. He folded his arms,

"It sounds like you've had quite the change of heart, Lady Lark."

"I haven't, but I didn't intend on Seita or Yuyuki dying."

"Yuyuki is a witch. And as soon as we are out to sea, I will have her thrown in the ocean where she belongs." Yulori reached for Arymaitei's cheek, and she covered her face with her hands.

"But try to think rationally here. Be thankful I'm sparing your life and not throwing you in with her."

Emily watched them, seething with anger as the men bound her arms and legs. She looked back at the countless bodies littering the dock.

"This war will not end at sea," she thought. "This war will not end on land. This war will end when you Aiyo and Dhukai are dead and gone."

Emily felt a boot on her shoulder, and she was roughly lifted off of the ground by some of the Aiyo men and tossed into the well of the rowboat. She tried to say something, but her swollen tongue just gestured around loudly. She grew cold and slipped into darkness.

Victory Bittersweet

I have a report! The urgency in the Aiyo vassal's voice was mirrored by his rushed demeanor as he ran in and knelt with bowed head.

"What is the meaning of this?" Aiyo Shumaiyuki's eyes were blazing with anger as she exploded. "Can you not see that I am teaching my pet to speak as the civilized do?"

"Please don't call me your pet," Rebecca said, leaning towards the speaking box. Shumaiyuki balked at the request and found her temperature rising.

"Well! Why have you not yet learned our speech? I've taught you over a period of days? I expect an answer!"

"You can't learn a whole other language in a week or two! It takes time. And, you don't teach. You just yell and hit me with your stick!"

Shumaiyuki waved a hand, indicating a want for silence, and then focused back on the kneeling vassal.

"What matter is so important you saw fit to interrupt me?"

"The Lord has returned! Rumored to be in his possession is the scalp of the imposter!" the vassal pressed his forehead to the floor, his voice riddled with enthusiasm. Shumaiyuki narrowed her eyes.

"What are you saying?"

"Lord Aiyo has returned with her majesty's enemy's scalp, my lady," he said.

"Are you saying she is dead?" Shumaiyuki's lounge lifted from the ground and hovered in place; she placed her hand over her heart and shot Rebecca a quick, guilty glance. Rebecca, for her part, placed both her hands over her mouth to stop herself from screaming as she listened to the box's translation.

"The Lord returned with Yuyuki's scalp?" Shumaiyuki said in a hushed tone.

“Yes!” said the vassal, looking very proud of himself.

“And where is he now?” She asked, staring at Rebecca.

“He is en route here from the shipyard.”

“He was to bring her to me alive!” Shumaiyuki flung her head back and let out a chilling roar. “Damn him,” she hissed as she struck the floor with her stick.

Rebecca stood, her chest heaving as tears rolled down her face, “You killed her!” she cried, pointing a finger at Shumaiyuki. “You killed her!”

“I did not kill her!” shrieked Shumaiyuki.

“Obinari! Subdue her!” Obánā Te-tae, seated in a far corner of the ornate room, pointed a rigid finger at Rebecca as she stood and bobbled over to the princess, fearing her “pet” would attack her.

“I did not kill her!” Shumaiyuki repeated, only now there was no ferocity in her defense, for her sense of guilt was ripe, regardless of who struck the killing blow.

“You had my best friend murdered! I will never forgive you!” Rebecca screamed and fel to her knees, sobbing.

“It’s not true! I wanted to question her at least and…”

“You wanted Emily dead! You said so yourself! So don’t pretend you’re not happy!”

“I did want her dead. In the beginning, maybe,” said Shumaiyuki, “But after watching your videos and looking at all your photos. With all that you have told me about your friendship. Well, she seemed a likable enough person. I think perhaps I might’ve exiled her after a thorough interrogation.”

“Exile? Emily didn’t deserve any of this!” said Rebecca. “She was the nicest person I ever met. She was the only one who spoke to me in fourth grade, and she never let anyone bully me!” Rebecca’s voice rose to fill the room.

"And even though she was always taller and prettier than me, she still befriended me when no one else would. She was my best friend, my only friend!"

"And see! There you have it," said Shumaiyuki, "I wouldn't have taken her head. I would have simply had her imprisoned and allowed you a visit from time to time. Why I might have even visited her myself... oh, take your hands off of her Obánā!"

"But princess, it has spoken out of turn! Not to mention it raised its voice to you!" said the old woman, slowly removing her hands from around Rebecca's neck.

"She is in mourning!" Shumaiyuki put an emphasis on the word 'SHE' and waved Rebecca over. "She has suffered a great loss, and we all should show empathy," she glared threateningly at all her ladies in waiting, who shrank back and bowed in compliance.

Rebecca bent over, laid her head on the floor, and covered her face with her hands. She began to wail. "The Lord enters!" came the call of another vassal, followed by the heavy footsteps of leather boots on the polished wood.

Shumaiyuki adjusted her robes and sat up in her lounge. Obánā and the other ladies in waiting formed a circle around Rebecca and bowed as Aiyo Yulori made his entrance. He carried with him a linen bundle, the Tri-leaf crest emblazoned on the cloth. He ignored the bowing women as he walked in and stood before Shumaiyuki.

"I have a gift for you, Shumai."

"You killed her!" Rebecca screamed.

"Calm yourself, child," said Te-tae as Yulori pulled back the cloth to reveal what appeared at first, a dirty wig, but soon became obvious to everyone was freshly cut hair.

"I thought this would be a more suitable gift than to simply return her body; it will serve you as a trophy and remembrance of your fight and victory." Yulori threw the hair on the floor.

Rebecca looked down at the damp, bloody mane; the once dappled shine of its strands was gone. She looked up at Yulori, her hands covering her mouth.

"My lord," said Shumaiyuki. "I apologize for my pet's behavior. I should have known she would become upset after learning of the untimely death of her friend. I will ensure she behaves accordingly in the future."

Shumaiyuki looked down at Rebecca, who was sniffling into her hands. *"I'm so sorry, Ribiki,"* she thought, and picked up the mop of Emily's hair from the floor.

"Why are you dressed in the garb of a Dhukai? And why did you feel the need to kill her before questioning?" She asked pointedly, adding, "It's not like you, uncle, to personally get your hands dirty!"

Rebecca slowly lifted her head, her eyes red and swollen from her weeping. Yulori avoided looking at her.

"There was nothing to ask her. Her very presence was a danger, and now that danger is no more. I would have thought you'd be pleased."

"I would have been pleased had I had a chance to weigh judgment! Do you not think it has occurred to me she may have been nothing more than a pawn in this game you and the empress decided to play with our lives?"

"Why are you never satisfied?" Yulori raised his voice. "I had hoped you would grow weary of this power play with me, yet here you are, trying to undermine me again!"

"I assure you, Lord Yulori, I am ever eager to reign as your empress, and so you must take care," Shumaiyuki leaned forward and whispered. "You will never win against me!"

"The crown prince was also taken into custody. I have sent notice to the empress and await her instructions."

“Rilkian is here! In Odahni?” Shumayuki’s hands went to her chest, and she began to fan herself. “I am delighted beyond words!” she said with a gleeful smile.

“You are not to see him, Shumai. Not before the engagement ceremony.” Yulori warned her.

“But I must see him!” She said, “You know how long it has been since we last met. I’ve been counting down the days to the ceremony in my head. It can’t be soon enough for me.”

“You will not see him until the day of your union. Imperial tradition dictates it so! I am not to be disobeyed.”

“I don’t want to argue with you about this,” said Shumaiyuki. She rewrapped the hair in the stained linen. Yulori took the bundle and slung it over his shoulder.

“We shall speak more about this later.”

“What? Why do we need to talk? Rilkian and I are to be husband and wife!”

“The arrangements were made well before you were old enough to understand what marriage is.” Yulori’s voice trailed behind him as he left the room, his boots thumped loudly on the wooden veranda.

* * *

Rilkian sat alone in a dreary compartment, barely illuminated by a small amount of sunlight that showed through two slits for windows that were barred. The space was not intended for hosting guests and had a low, wooden table set atop its polished floor. A washbasin and a porcelain waste bowl sat in one corner; a lumpy futon sat discarded in another.

“Damn you, Yulori. You’ve dishonored me,” Rilkian sat at the table and banged his fist against its surface. His features were twisted with rage as he muttered to himself. It was only through a great effort of will that he managed not to scream out loud.

He was usually stoic and composed, owing to his royal upbringing, but he was deeply grieving. He sat in silence, lost in thought, until the tears started to stream down his face.

The future he had dreamed of for himself and Emily, a future without the constraints of royalty, was now gone with her. He wept uncontrollably, but soon realized he couldn't let others see him in such a state. He needed to regain his composure.

A few moments passed before he finally collected himself. He looked up at the gold metallic ceiling and emitted a long exhale. It was then that he could hear voices conversing from outside the door just at the end of the compartment.

He calmly stood and walked to the door, not knowing who he was going to face. He stood still, a hint of a plan beginning to form. The door opened, and he was greeted with a bowing Te-Tae.

"If you will, Your Grace," she pointed him down the hallway. "Come with me."

Te-Tae strode away from the room with Rilkian behind her. She stopped when they reached a set of double doors and pushed them open; the prince followed her in. They entered a large room ripe with the scent of jasmine. A warm evening breeze flowed through.

Several maidens were preparing his bath, pouring large vases of hot water, and adding herbs and oils to a steaming circular tub. Te-Tae gestured for him to take a seat on a pillow near it. Then she shuffled off.

The prince sat in front of the bath, taking in the rising steam and the aroma of jasmine and eucalyptus. The scents were soothing to his nerves, helping to calm his beating heart. A maid approached and assisted him in removing his soiled tunic, and another came to help him stand so that he could remove his pants. Throughout the process, the maids maintained a respectful demeanor, keeping their eyes respectfully downcast.

Once fully undressed, they poured two buckets of cold water over the top of his head, and then helped him into the tub. He sat in the ceramic well, and then lay back, savoring the soothing feeling of hot water melting the soreness away. He closed his eyes and let his mind empty. All the while, three more servants washed him from head to toe. With his head relaxed against the lip of the tub, it wasn't long before he felt himself dozing off.

"My dear," Shumaiyuki's soft voice whispered in his ear, causing a shiver to run down his spine. He quickly sat up and opened his eyes to see her hovering above him, stretched out on her floating couch. Her sea-green eyes focused on his wet, bare chest. She blushed and patted her finely constructed chestnut bun.

"Your Grace. You truly are a sight to behold." She batted her eyes and covered her mouth with her fan.

"Princess Shumaiyuki," he said, surprised at her presence. He was even more surprised that she was referring to him as 'My dear'. "What are you doing here?"

"Did you not want me to come?" she replied, blushing even more. Without responding, he climbed out of the bath and stood before her. Her eyes drank in the full sight of him, forcing her to fan herself anew.

"It has been ages, princess. Are you well?" he snapped his fingers at the maids in a dismissive manner and they immediately jumped to toweling him off.

"I am fine, my love," she said, smiling. "It is good to see you again. Wonderful, in fact!"

"This is far from a happy reunion. Please forgive my rudeness on this occasion," he said with a slight trace of anger in his voice. "But I must ask you, was it you who ordered Emily to be killed?"

"Rilkian," she sighed. "It saddens me that you would be so cynical. For I have no involvement in such vile matters. Oh, but I have missed you and simply wanted to bond with you some. But if you must know, I had hoped to work on building a relationship of sorts between Emily and I." Her voice was soft and sad, and she touched beneath her glazed eyes with a lacy kerchief.

"Well, I am worn out. I do need to rest," he responded, turning away from her. A maid wrapped him in an ivory robe. He then reclined on a long, elegant cushion near the tub. He was annoyed at how sincere Shumaiyuki seemed to be.

He felt that he was supposed to be angry with her. Instead, confusion about her feelings for him was overshadowing that instinct.

She sighed and landed next to him on her lounge. "Rilkian," she said.

"Rilkian, please. Don't be upset with me. I had a change of heart. Uncle manipulated me…my feelings. I didn't want Yuyuki to die."

"You said you wanted to bond with me," he responded coldly. "Then be honest with me."

Shumaiyuki shook her head, holding back tears. "What do you want from me? I can tell you are angry with me," her voice choked. She tried to embrace him, but he held her at arm's length.

"Please understand. I am not my uncle. I am not evil like he is. He is trying to control my mind and I-"

"I want the truth! Why did Emily have to die? To what end?" his voice rose despite himself.

"I want you to forgive me," she finally broke. "Please! Please, I am sorry. I love you." She reached out and pressed her hand against his heart. He felt his anger dissolve into emptiness. Shumaiyuki leaned in from her lounge and clung to him like a lost child, crying softly. He sat still, uncertain of what to say or do.

"Then why? Why did you kill her?" he asked quietly. Anger mixed with misery at her emotional display. Shumaiyuki's startled eyes looked into his, and then she slowly turned away.

"Rilkian, Rilkian," she whispered into the air. Her tears flowed freely, and her shoulders shook. He watched her in silence, unsure of what to say. Several long seconds passed. Finally, he pulled her close and held her loosely in his arms. She leaned over from her lounge and wrapped her arms around his waist.

"It's okay," he whispered, though he knew things weren't, he knew he was in a bad situation. Shumaiyuki slowly pulled herself from his embrace and sat back.

"You've been taught about The Collapse?"

He nodded. "Of course, I have. It was the country's only civil war." Bits and pieces of the stories he was taught flashed through his mind. "Why do you mention it?"

Shumaiyuki nodded in acknowledgment, and continued,

"In reality, the Collapse was caused by political and economic chaos. The nobles of the empire fought amongst themselves, and the common people rioted throughout the land and fought against royal authority."

"And what has this to do with Emily? Or Lord Aiyo?"

"The Aiyo are bitter, you must know that! Our lord. My grandfather has been humiliated and remains imprisoned in the palace to this day. My uncle fans the flames of war of which only our marriage could douse." She looked up into his dark, cold eyes. "I am the only thing that holds him back!"

"What nonsense is this? Do you really want to know the truth?" Rilkian asked with a cold, hard voice. "The empress herself arranged for Emily and I to meet. She does not intend for you and I to exchange vows!"

"Are you really so arrogant and dull?" Shumaiyuki scoffed. "The empress is in league with grandfather. She too, is thirsty for an Aiyo takeover of the crown," her eyes fell to the floor.

"This is madness!"

"The emperor ignores her! He has imprisoned her twin brother! He has humiliated her clan at every turn. Of course, she wants the impos… Yuyuki to marry you. Someone ignorant of our ways. Someone she can easily control as she clearly controls you."

"An interesting theory, but that would mean Lord Aiyo was in league with her. Yet they are clearly adversaries in this adventure."

“That is because they came to a disagreement. The empress plans on disposing of the emperor and returning grandfather to his post here as Lord Aiyo. Whereas Yulori prefers to keep the title for himself. Hence the rift. Have you really no nose for intrigue? Do you even have personal spies report to you?”

“What need would I have for spies? Or intrigue for that matter?”

“Having both at your disposal would have surely kept you from falling into your enemies’ hands, and make no mistake about it, Lord Grace. Aiyo Yulori is your enemy. The only thing that stays his hand from harming you is the thought of retaliation from the imperial army.”

“Why would you tell me all of this?” he asked, bewildered.

“I am telling you this because we are being manipulated by all of them - the empress, grandfather, and uncle. They are playing games with people’s lives, and it sickens me. Ask yourself, did the emperor know of auntie’s plans to marry you to Yuyuki? Or did she mean to pass her off as me while I rotted away imprisoned in this very tower?” Shumaiyuki’s voice trembled with emotion.

Rilkian’s face softened, afraid of what she might say next. “What do you mean, ‘rot away’?” he asked.

Shumaiyuki held her head in her hands, breathing deeply. “My uncle and your mother wished for me to live out the rest of my life in this tower. As a child, I became ill, and so they replaced me with Yuyuki, Emily. They gave her my name and locked me and all of my maids away in this very tower. I dwelled here for years, a prisoner with only murals of Domotedai to serve as my outside.”

“My mother wouldn’t have…I have seen no evidence to support such an outrageous lie,” Rilkian said, frustrated. He stared at the floor, searching for words.

“Do you really mean to say the empress is capable of such cruelty? Why would she punish you? Why deceive the emperor with an imposter?”

"It was because I lost the ability to walk without the aid of a crutch for a number of years. There is no place in the imperial family for those with disabilities. You of all people should know that, seeing how your own brother was exiled. That too, was a piece of the empress's handiwork."

"What? My mother had Jeil exiled? That is absolutely absurd! Why would she do such a thing?"

"You would have to ask the empress. But I dare say his being born blind may have had something to do with it."

"It was my father who had his mother exiled for plotting the very thing you accuse my mother of!" His voice was a low growl, and he clenched his hands into fists. "Why are you trying to ruin my life?"

There was a long silence before Shumaiyuki looked at him again, her eyes narrow and incisive. "Your anger betrays your tongue, my love. You know what I say is true."

Rilkian's heart was hammering in his chest, and his face was flushed. He turned away quickly, feeling her eyes on him. How could someone with such an innocent face be so well-versed in political intrigue? He was actually impressed with her savviness, but he didn't know how to process those feelings along with the loss of Emily. He stood and paced the floor, running his hand across his forehead.

"I ask you to forgive my anger. This is all very upsetting," he said.

"I am sorry to be the bearer of bad news," replied Shumaiyuki, her eyes both sad and alluring.

He looked at her, sensing her body language. "Perhaps we were both being played," he said softly.

A thin smile crept upon her sad, tear-stained face. She wiped her eyes with her hands, trying to collect herself. "Perhaps we were," she said.

“I should return to my chamber,” he said, moving toward the door. Shumaiyuki followed him.

“Please, do not leave. I wanted to. I wanted you to tell me about her,” she said.

He hesitated, looking at her, and then quite suddenly he leaned forward and pressed his lips against hers. It was a quick kiss, without game or heat. He pulled away to gauge her reaction. She didn’t speak or move.

“That is what Emily meant to me,” he said. “That is all you need to know about her.”

“I am sorry, I just…” She wiped her eyes on her sleeve. “I am sorry, but why me?”

She attempted a smile, but her face fell into tears. “We should speak about this in the morning,” she sobbed and quickly floated out of the room followed by her maids. Rilkian turned and huffed out into the hallway and walked back to his own chamber.

He was confronted the moment he entered, “Lord Aiyo,” he said.

“You should remain in your accommodations for the time being. You will be returned to the capital first thing in the morning,” said Yulori, closing the door behind him. “It is for your own protection.”

“You mean to hold the crown prince prisoner?” his voice was filled with anger, frustration, and fear, and he let out a guttural cry. With his emotions all over the place, he cried out, “What is happening here? Why did you kill Emily, damn it!”

Yulori withheld a smirk and closed the door, locking it. He walked away whistling to himself as Rilkian cursed,

“Tell me what is going on! I’ve been deceived a number of times! Yulori, knave, bastard!” He collapsed on the floor, thinking, *“If Mother is arranging my return under stealth, then all that Shumaiyuki says may very well be true.”* He stared at the ceiling.

Maybe Shumaiyuki was in on it too. Maybe she lied to him. Maybe he was wrong about everything.

"I don't know what to think anymore," he whispered, seeing both Emily and Seitogi in his mind's eye.

* * *

Rebecca's eyes were bloodshot as she timidly approached the figure in dull robes standing across the courtyard under a dark sky. Her sobbing had subsided, and she tried to steady her emotions.

"Hey Beck! How you been? Everything okay?" asked Darren with a hint of concern in his voice. He opened his arms, offering a hug, but she held back. He pulled back his hood, wiping his brow.

"Hey," she said, her voice quivering. She looked about, nervously, and then sobbed, "They cut off Emily's head. She's dead, Darren! They killed her!"

Darren froze and averted his eyes. "Did you hear me? Mr. Yulori brought us her scalp. He tossed it on the floor right in front of me."

"Listen, Beck! Emily wasn't who we thought she was! I mean, fuck man! It's because of her I got hurt and we got stuck here in the first place!"

"What the hell, Darren! They've killed her!"

"Yeah, Rebecca! And what about all the people she's killed! Huh? You think that shit that went down with the cops was just a fluke? It wasn't. My benefactor is fighting to survive as we speak because of her."

"Your benefactor?"

"Yes, Mr. Atem. Emily almost killed him. I've spent the better part of the day tending to his wounds. You should see what she did to him."

"He's a fucking maniac who skins people alive for a living. My god, what kind of idiot are you? None of these people here are our benefactors! We are their prisoners, Darren, nothing more, nothing less!"

"I'm nobody's prisoner. Mr. Atem fixed my arm, see…I can still barely use it, but he made sure I didn't lose it! And he's letting me train in swordsmanship and learn Bernhi! I'm damn near his personal attendant."

"Jesus, Darren! We've barely been here a month, and you already have Stockholm syndrome? Think about it! Now that Emily is dead, so are our chances of ever returning home!"

"Look, Beck. We have to play ball here. Adjust to the situation. Right now, I serve Mr. Atem and clean the Tabaiken's equipment and armor. I get to train with the new recruits. Of course, I'm of no use now because of my arm, but once it fully heals, he'll consider me for the Tabaiken. I'm not going to screw all that up over Emily."

"What the fuck, Darren! He killed her, and you're fanboying out!"

"It was Lord Yulori who killed her! Not Atem! I'm just saying if we want to keep our heads, you need to chill and stop making a fuss about this," he said, backing away.

"So, you knew she was dead?"

"Does it even matter now? They say she was a witch, you know! That's the only way she could've taken Atem down. It's her fault we are here in the first place." As he continued to retreat, he narrowed his eyes and stared directly into hers,

"I wish I could've gotten my hands on her myself. Her and her little blue-haired freak! And I will get my hands on him, and when I do, I'm going to slice him limb from limb and watch him bleed out till he's dead. So, no! I'm in no rush to get back."

"What? Now you're a killer too?"

"Cut the shit, Beck! We're stuck here forever. Get with the assignment or die!" He turned and stiffly walked away.

"Emily was right about you, Tolliver! You're a selfish jerk and a coward!" she yelled. Yet after he had gone, she sank down onto a stone bench and let her tears fall.

Shumaiyuki, concealed in the darkness, observed the entire interaction before emerging from her hiding place and floating down beside the bench. She tenderly tried to wipe away Rebecca's tears, but Rebecca rejected her gesture by striking her hand away.

"Leave me alone!"

"I understand you may hate me," Shumaiyuki said. Rebecca looked up at her, only understanding the words 'you' and 'me.'

"But know that I loathe watching you mourn." She floated off.

"Mourn me? Why should I grieve for you?" Rebecca asked, surprised. Her mastery of the language caught Shumaiyuki's attention.

"That was good, Ribiki. I understood you perfectly."

* * *

Aiyo Yulori itched beneath the hemp jumper he still wore from his jaunt to Bashi. Damp with sweat though the night was cool, he looked down the long winding stairway that sank beneath the depths of Odahni's foundation and sighed.

"You have to be smart about this," he thought. The only sounds were his hollow footfalls and the hiss of a natural gas torch he carried as he picked up his pace and wound his way down the steps carved out of a chalky gray stone.

As he drew in breath after breath, the walls seemed to blend into each other, drawing him deeper and deeper into the underworld. Once he reached the bottom of the stairs, he continued down a stone corridor that seemed to stretch on forever.

His boots were covered in the fine grit of the chalky stone, and he moved carefully so that he wouldn't take a spill on its uneven flooring.

"Better to be safe than sorry," Yulori tested the ground with his foot. He continued on in that manner for a short while longer before he turned his head ever so slightly, just enough to check that the corridor behind him was still empty and that no one was following.

Slowly, he reached down and slipped open the latch that led to a massive metal gate, leading into a series of cavernous rooms that held dank holding cells.

The brightness of the torchlight dropped slightly just before he reached the room he sought. It was the last chamber.

It wasn't a very large space, no bigger than a small pantry really. He lit two small torches set into metal sconces and proceeded to the middle of the cell where Emily lay on the cold floor, her wrist bound by a rusted chain that hung from the ceiling.

She was a sad sight to see.

Her clothes were nothing but tattered rags about her waist, ripped chinos, and a torn hoodie. Around her neck was a thick leather collar, rope bound her ankles, and her shaved head was caked in dry blood from several cuts on her scalp. One eye was swollen closed, and her nose was obviously broken. The skin around her left earlobe was a deep purple.

Yulori raised her chin so that she could look at him. "No need to worry, you'll be fine here," he said. "You see, even in this state, you still serve a purpose," he added, chewing on his bottom lip.

"No!" She said, weakly struggling against the chain.

"In the end, though, I really don't see the need for you to die. In fact, you may prove most useful, as your sister can be quite difficult. I may need you to replace her yet."

Yulori paused, checked the door one last time, and then pulled on the chain, hoisting Emily up from the floor into a standing position, but the metal slipped from his hands, and he had to catch her from falling. He lifted her into his arms and laid her back down on the grimy floor.

"Get off of me!" She yelped and attempted to kick at him with her legs, but they barely responded to her mental commands.

"Why do you hate me so much?" she mumbled miserably. Yulori looked down into her one good eye with a cold stare.

"If not for you, my precious sister Ameiki would still be alive. You must understand, we came into this world together. I almost died in the womb, and she held on to me. She pulled me into this world, and you took her from me."

"You, you're my mother's twin?"

He grunted as he bent down over her and forced her to face him. "I don't hate you; I pity you," he said. Emily drew in a sharp breath and spit a wad of bloody saliva directly into his eye.

"Vile bitch!" Yulori recoiled, standing up to wipe at his eye with the rough Dhukai hemp sleeve, irritating it even more. A sinister grimace spread across his face, "I could have beheaded you! But I choose not to. Perhaps a few days soaking in your own piss will humble you, princess."

Emily stared back at him, her eye filled with anger and defiance and spit at him again. Without hesitation, Yulori lunged towards her, grabbing her by the arms and shaking her violently. An object fell from her clothes and clattered to the ground.

It was the witch's mirror, no bigger than the palm of her hand. Yulori picked it up and examined it closely, wondering what possible use it could have for her. As he examined the mirror's intricately carved metal casing, he sneered in disdain.

"Another one of your Arth trinkets," he muttered, tossing it carelessly to the ground. But his derision turned to surprise when the glass did not shatter upon impact. Intrigued, he picked up the mirror from the floor and turned it over in his hands.

The glass was like no other he had ever seen. He was astonished as the pristine surface remained unscathed, not even a scratch to mar its perfect reflection.

“I will hold on to this,” he said to himself, tucking the mirror into his jumper pocket. He turned to leave. “You must remember,” he said. “Your life and future are in my hands.” He closed the cell door securely behind him, locking her.

“You monster!” Emily yelled after him as he disappeared up the stairway. Her words turned to a hoarse whisper as she lay on the cold stone and wept. She felt empty of life and was desperate to purge her stomach. Her broken body was racked with dry heaves as her stomach clenched and released.

She closed her eye and remembered the feeling of the wind in her hair and the smell of warm summer days. Dear god, her hair. The bastard had taken it all off with a dull blade. She cursed him again, for she had never been in the type of pain she was in now.

Her fingers were numb with cold. Her body was covered in goosebumps; she shivered uncontrollably. A wave of nausea washed over her. Her body ached, and her head spun. Tears fell freely down her scoured cheeks. She laid her shorn head against the stone floor and closed her eyes to rest.

The Prince with Black Teeth

The slap stung Rilkian's face as its sound echoed throughout the room. He stared directly into the empress's furious eyes as she raised her hand and slapped him again. As promised, Yulori had delivered him back to the capital, five days on the road under heavy guard.

"Did it even occur to you that you could have easily been killed? You are the emperor's heir! What more scandals will befall the imperial house because of your recklessness?" Aiyo Yumeiko stroked her sore hand and paced back and forth, fuming.

"Sit down." She pointed at a pillow. "I want to speak with you." Her tone softened, and she sat on a pillow opposite him. She folded her hands at her waist, her eyes held a serious gaze.

"I want you to listen to me very carefully. You must never forget my words." She paused and looked into his sullen face, and her voice took on a tone of reverence. "You are my first responsibility."

She continued, "It is your duty as the emperor's heir to avoid danger and scandal. As such, you court ruin when one's path has been laid out for him. Learn to respect others." She stood and took several small steps.

"And learn to respect yourself." She turned away and looked out of a window, sighing. "You must grow into a man, Rilkian. I will be forever disappointed if you do not."

"And what say you about Princess Emily? Are you going to let Yulori get away with killing her?"

"I will raise the matter with him when the time is right."

"When?" he demanded.

Aiyo Yumeiko shook her head and frowned. "That is not something I intend on discussing with you."

"What is it that you are keeping from me?"

“I do not approve of what you did, Rilkian. Perhaps the princess would still be alive had you not involved yourself.” She paused. “Nor do I approve of your questioning me as though I were your peer.”

Rilkian dropped his head, and after a moment, he stood and walked over and joined her at the window.

“I cannot help but wonder if the Golden Swan was empress, if she would handle things differently,” he said.

“Enough, Rilkian. I am saddened by this. I am disappointed. I do not wish to be further offended by your tongue.” She sighed and turned to leave. “I have much to think about.”

“As do I, mother,” he said, instantly regretting the quip. He knew well enough to keep his thoughts to himself.

He looked down at the city of Domotedai as it glittered under the night sky like diamonds atop black sand. Beneath the luster of night, the city was just as alive as it was during the day. Bright colors and the sounds of laughter poured from the inns and restaurants.

“Can we preserve this fragile peace any better than the adults, Shumaiyuki?” he asked, looking out to the stars.

***

Aiyo Yumeiko rushed hurriedly through one of the palace’s many gardens to a separate building behind the main structure. She paused for a moment and straightened her white robes as well as her composure, and then approached the single-story structure with an elegant gait.

“I need to speak with the emperor,” she said to the guards who stood at the building’s main door. Both men bowed, but one spoke up.

“I apologize, lord lady, but is it possible you to return at a later time? The emperor is deep in meditation.”

“I will not come back later,” she said. “It cannot wait. My apologies as I did not inform the emperor of my intent to visit. But I must see him immediately!”

“My apologies to the empress,” he said.

“Is he well?” she asked.

“The emperor is in good health,” said the other guard. “He has taken to the salt rest of late.”

“Oh, I despise small talk! Make way for your empress!” Aiyo Yumeiko forced the two guards aside and opened the door.

“I need to see the emperor!” she called out into the vestibule. Her voice echoed the same request as the answer. “Oh, how I loathe this place.”

As she entered the room, she was disappointed to find that no one was there to greet her. She glanced around, taking in the tapestry on the wall, a majestic mountain range with a lion perched atop a rock. Frustrated, she walked further into the room until she reached the doors to the emperor’s Palladium Maze.

After pausing for a moment to gather her nerves, she tentatively stepped inside. The passage was dimly lit, with walls, floors, and ceilings made of gleaming silver that seemed to stretch on endlessly. Yumeiko’s reflection was cast back at her in every direction, creating the disorienting illusion of being trapped in a funhouse. Despite the surroundings, she pressed on, determined to reach her destination.

As she journeyed on, the smooth surfaces around her seemed to blend together and become indistinguishable. The walls curved and twisted in ways that made it hard to keep her balance, or at least that’s what it felt like. Nevertheless, each step she took landed perfectly flat.

She continued to walk through the winding paths and straight lines, her gaze fixed on the way ahead. Despite the seemingly endless nature of the maze, it remained shrouded in shadows. Even the echoes of her footsteps died away in the eerie blue-gray gloom.

The silence became oppressive, and eventually, Yumeiko clapped her hands in an attempt to break the stillness.

"Is anyone here?" she called out.

"You know you have a country to run, don't you!" she yelled out into the hall of reflection. "We are on the brink of two wars and what are you doing but resting your nerves! Come out here and talk to me, dammit! Rie-Saehyun!" she pleaded and wrung her hands together, but only the echo of her voice returned.

"Stubborn fool!" she yelled out. "I need to speak with you." The darkness of her reflections stared back at her in silence.

The empress lost track of time, but soon found herself out of breath and thoroughly lost. She cursed herself for embarking on the adventure and tapped her fingers against her lips as she tried and failed to understand the maze's twists and turns. But she held on and continued forward as much as she could.

"Hello?" she asked. "Is anyone here?" she called out. Defeated, she reached into the sleeve of her robe and took out a tiny bell tied to a colorful piece of string and shook it several times.

She listened as it echoed throughout the maze, but the eerie silence continued.

She sighed and summoned the words, "I must rest a moment." But she almost let out a scream as she looked up to see one of the guards she had met out front standing before her.

"Oh, my apologies, Your Majesty," he bowed. "I did not mean to startle you."

Yumeiko returned the bow, "I was hoping to find the emperor. Do you know where he might be?"

"No, I've not seen him for two days, empress," he said. "The Palladium is very large though."

"I am fully aware of its size," she said. "But might he be at its center tea room? Lead me there and you will be rewarded with a new bride!"

“I thank you, Your Majesty, but I am already married, and with a child on the way,” he said proudly.

“And she will desire you no more once the babe is born and her jewel shattered asunder. Take a new…younger maiden. One trained by my very hand. She will warm your bed for years to come!”

“Forgive me, majesty, but our love is secure.”

Yumeiko furrowed her brow, “Send away this harlot you call a wife. I am certain she has been seeded by another man. For the child cannot be yours. Let her, and her bastard enter the Jyoshi Sisterhood with shaved heads. There they can contemplate the error of their births.”

“Please, Your Majesty, the exit is this way.”

The guard’s gaze lingered for a moment on Yumeiko’s high-collared robe and golden corselet, unsure of where else to look. He followed her gaze up to her beautiful face and flinched his eyes away. He knew that it was not his place to stare at the empress.

“Do you find me beautiful, young man?”

“Please, Your Grace, I…”

“Hmm?” she asked, “Do you expect me to believe you were just impressed with my attire?”

“No, Your Majesty, I…” he said.

“How dare you insult me. Is this what the emperor has taught you?” she asked, stepping backward, and waving her hands as if to shoo away a fly, “Is this what you are teaching your guard?” She bellowed in her loudest voice. “To disrespect their empress as though she were a peasant tramp!”

“Oh, please, empress,” he said, backing away from her. “I meant no disrespect. I’ve never seen anyone more commendable than Your Majesty.” Sweat trickled down his brow, having to lie to her.

"Fool," she yelled. "My guards just may have to visit your wife and her cuckold fetus before the night is done!"

"Your Grace," he said. "I did not mean to be disrespectful."

"Take me from this infuriating place at once!" she screamed as she lunged forward.

"Oh, of course, empress, right this way." He held his hand out and walked quickly before her, deftly navigating the mirrored tunnels towards the exit. She followed closely behind him, not looking down, but instead glaring at his back as he walked. Soon, they exited the maze back into its wider atrium, where they were met by a waiting messenger.

"Here you are, empress," the guard said. "Please excuse me." He returned to his post outside the door, looking as though he had seen a ghost.

"What is it?" Yumeiko asked the kneeling woman, "Is it important?"

"Yes, empress! Imperial Prince Rijeil has returned from Seizhone and awaits an audience with the emperor!" the messenger announced.

"Jeil?" Yumeiko covered the lower half of her face with her sleeve. "Have him seated in the Arbor room. I will see him in the emperor's stead."

"Yes, empress." The messenger bowed and ran out of the building towards the palace.

Yumeiko walked and turned to stare at her blue reflection in the dim silvery light. "Why is Jeil here now?" she asked herself.

She looked up and touched her reflection in the mirror. She stared at it for a long time, thinking to herself.

"It cannot be that he seeks his father's advice," she said. "So why is he back?" She closed one eye and looked at her reflection, narrowing her gaze. "And why?" she asked, "Why would he appear now?"

* * *

Nestled among lush greenery, the arbor room was a picture of luxury with its gleaming glass and wood furnishings. Upon entering the ancient wooden chamber, one was immediately enveloped by a sense of nature's embrace. The room's large windows were open, inviting in the refreshing evening breeze and the sweet songs of nocturnal birds.

Rijeil had always thought it a truly magical and peaceful place. Dimly lit, a single clay pit in the floor blazed with amber light. He sat cross-legged on a pillow in the center of the room, his eyes closed in peaceful contemplation. The warm glow of the light seemed to envelop him, casting a soothing spell over the entire space.

"Your presence here is unexpected," Yumeiko's voice steady and measured as she entered the room. She approached cautiously, her gaze fixed on him as if he were a potential threat.

As she drew closer, she called out to him, "Can you hear me?" Rijeil opened his eyes and gazed up at her, causing her to recoil in surprise at the intensity she felt from him through his visors.

Yet, it was clear that he was fully present and aware of his surroundings.

"Her majesty," Rijeil said, pitching forward and bowing deeply with his forehead touching the floor. "I humbly beg your forgiveness for my unexpected arrival." His words were laced with respect and humility, indicating his awareness of his own lack of protocol in showing up unannounced.

The situation was uncomfortable, to say the least. Yumeiko was taken aback by Rijeil's sudden appearance, and it was clear that she was still processing the shock. He bore a striking resemblance to Rilkian, with a lighter complexion and a taller, muscular build. His hair was styled in a wooly blue top knot, and he wore rustic metal goggles with blackout lenses that obscured his eyes from view. He grinned, revealing a set of perfectly aligned black teeth. Two thin strands of hair extended from above his lips, completing the unusual but striking appearance.

He was adorned in a series of vibrant robes that flowed elegantly around his arms and torso, with glimpses of his hidden body armor peeking through in strategic places. The overall effect was one of regal splendor and fierce determination.

"Your foul stench offends my nostrils. I would have preferred you bathed first," Yumeiko said as she sat across from him.

"I ask your forgiveness as I traveled on a straight run with no stops at any inns to refresh."

To say he spoke formally was an understatement. Every word out of his mouth was a finely honed blade of politeness. The longer he spoke, the more she noted the peculiar way his intonation and consonance differed from that of his fellow countrymen.

"I have an urgent message from King Zhon for the emperor," he said, holding out an envelope. "I must see the emperor and deliver this letter at once."

"What is it?" she asked, reaching for the letter, but he held it back. "A message from King Zhon?" she asked. "I am the emperor this evening. Give it to me."

"It's for the emperor's eyes only, Your Grace," he said, giving her a warm smile.

"Give it to me!" she insisted, holding both hands out for the envelope. "I am acting in the emperor's stead!" she growled.

"I apologize, but it is not my place to deliver this message to anyone but the emperor," he bowed.

"You may keep your apology," she said as she stared at him. "So much like your mother."

"My mother?" he asked, placing the letter back into his robe.

"Excuse me, Your Grace," the same vassal who announced the prince knelt and bowed at the room's entrance. "The emperor has summoned Prince Rijeil to an audience."

“Has he now?” Yumeiko replied, standing. She looked around the room at the prince in confusion, exhaled and closed her eyes. “Will the humiliations never cease?”

“Prince Rijeil, please come with me,” the messenger said, leading him away. Through his goggles, Yumeiko appeared as a static-laced, infrared monochrome of bright greenish-gray tones.

“Your Grace,” he bowed deeply, excusing himself.

“Of course,” Yumeiko sat and glared at him. She slapped her fan against the floor the moment he was out of sight, rushed away from the room, and marched through the halls without a care in the world, passing guards without so much as a second look or remark. At last, she couldn’t take it anymore and let loose a flood of tears. After a few minutes, she composed herself and continued down the hall, coming upon a large circular door where the lone guard dropped to his knees, bowing in greeting.

“Hokushiro, isn’t it?” She came closer, and the guard bowed lower.

“Yes, my empress,” his words muffled slightly.

She sighed, “I am not here to reprimand you, Hokushiro.”

“I apologize, my empress. I know better.”

“Nonsense, I just came here to see Lord Ai…my brother.”

She stepped inside, following the guard’s directions, though she knew the layout well enough. She entered a walled-off garden and stood before a large weeping cherry tree, picking one of its fruits before slowly making her way around a winding path to the manor’s door. Two maids came out to greet her and quickly bowed.

“Lord Teiyulori is expecting you,” they said together.

Lord Aiyo Teiyulori was seated on a lavish gold futon, pulling marijuana smoke from a hose attached to a water chalice, surrounded by a large set of books. He was a handsome man with a silver-streaked black top-knot and goatee. His hazel eyes and a pale, curvaceous face added to his youthful appearance.

His tied obi was decorated with gold stitching, while his kimono underneath was crimson red, embroidered with different patterns and sewn with the softest silk.

"Greetings, empress," he said, "Unless you have come to chastise me." He raised his eyebrows and quickly rose to his feet.

"At the least, my brother, I have not," she said. "Bring wine. A lot of it!" She ordered the maid.

"Please sit, let us talk," he set down the chalice tube and proceeded to retake his seat. She sat across from him and took the hose from the floor.

"I see you've been drinking already."

"Ah-ah, no chastising, dear sister of mine," he smiled, exciting the fine wrinkles in his face. "It's a good way to get a dose of inspiration. Now tell me what is on your mind."

"It's bloody Saehyun!" she sucked her teeth and then pulled from the challis's hose.

"Oh! Your husband again? What is our emperor, who prefers to be a priest, up to that makes you so upset?" He leaned in and accepted the hose back and smiled.

"He is acting rather irrationally," she said.

"He has always been that way."

"But it has gotten worse recently. I have not seen him in over a month. Yet he summons Rijeil to an audience."

"Jeil?"

"Yes, he arrived earlier this evening. Don't your palace spies tell you anything? What is their use if you are so late on the news?"

"I have my own methods of knowing things," he smiled smugly.

"He comes bearing a letter from Zhon himself," she noted.

“King Zhon? Since when is Jeil his messenger?”

“He has taken the boy under his wing to irk us. Such a petty man this Zhon is. And another thing…” she scrutinized her brother.

“All I receive is harsh silence. What would have happened to this government if not for my guidance? Yet Saehyun leaves me powerless.”

“It is the never-ending world of politics,” he sighed.

“I am ever-weary of his politics,” she raised her eyebrows at him.

“You don’t know what the emperor’s intentions are.”

“He suspects me.”

“Of what?”

“Of seeking to overthrow him, of course.”

“Your frequent visits to me don’t help you in that respect.”

“If not for me, you would sit here and rot in loneliness.”

“No. I have a healthy supply of maidens to warm my nights and heat my day.”

“They are here to wipe you, not warm you, Teiyu!”

He leaned back, “What would he gain by such a banal accusation?”

“He hasn’t outright accused me, but it’s the inference.”

“Do you think he will act on it?”

“He is the emperor; he can do whatever he pleases.”

She groaned, “We argued when we last spoke. Well, I argued. He just sat there pretending to meditate. He should just abdicate to Rilkian.”

“Are you serious?”

"He is the crown prince, after all."

"You have not mentioned that to the emperor, have you?"

"Not directly, but the implication was clear."

"Careful, sister! Your ambition could cost you your head."

"My ambition made me your empress. Don't you forget it."

"That cuttlefish between your thighs made you empress. Don't forget it!"

"You're disgusting!"

He laughed, "I know, the absolute worst!"

Yumeiko and Teiyulori erupted into laughter, their faces contorting with amusement. Teiyu, as Yumeiko affectionately referred to him since they were children, was the only one who could bring out the lighthearted side of the empress. The sight of her laughing was a rare occasion indeed.

"We just need a little more time," she said. "Once the wedding occurs and the houses of Anele and Seizhon are united, we can make our move."

Lord Teiyulori nodded. He understood her position, but he would never have dared to be so bold as to take it upon himself to challenge the Aneles. The woman before him was far from the shy child she once was.

"Until then, it's best to keep the emperor in line," she said, pulling the hose away and rubbing her face with her hand in frustration.

"And what of my granddaughter? Tell me about her."

"She's the spitting image of Ameiki, a bit rough around the edges, but she can be molded into her proper place."

"Aren't you worried that the Aneles will see right through our ruse?"

"Not at all. As I said, she's the spitting image of Ameiki, even more so than Shumai."

"But how will we teach her to play her role?"

"I'm leaving that up to Yulori. He currently has her imprisoned in Odahni, teaching her humility."

"Oh, Yui, what have you done?"

"She was terribly obstinate. It was she who enticed Rilkian to run away with her. I felt she had to be broken. Otherwise, all our plans would have been for naught."

"Your plans, Yumeiko! Imprisoning the girl was never part of your plans before. Perhaps it's not fair to force a crown upon her head. Shumaiyuki is more than capable of taking up the mantle. The elders are keen on her, and she has the loyalty of our Tabaiken guard, whereas they only tolerate Yulori. And now you've tasked him with torturing the poor girl!"

"Shumaiyuki is much too ambitious and would never heed my guidance," Yumeiko replied.

"You mean allow you to rule through her," Lord Teiyulori said with a laugh.

"Hush, you. And your son is not torturing Yuyuki. Granted, she was a little roughed up when captured, but as of now, she is just being administered basic starvation tactics, periodic beatings, and a denial of hygiene. Another two weeks should fix her just fine."

"You are an absolute monster," Lord Teiyulori whistled.

"Whose side are you on, anyway?" Yumeiko demanded.

"The side that would free me from my captivity and return me as head of my house. Do you think your lap dog Yulori is going to step down when the time comes?"

"He certainly will. Once Yuyuki is broken, healed, and married to Rilkian, Yulori will be promoted as Rilkian's chief of staff and take over Garner House."

"The boy is Aiyo Yui," Lord Teiyulori corrected her.

"A boy no more, Yulori is a man. I only hope he doesn't make the same mistakes his father did."

"Careful now," the old man sat up and rubbed his back with a heavy groan. "I believe it is time for my medicine." He rang a bell to summon the servants.

Lord Teiyulori half laughed, "And what of your other plans with the wayward clansmen?"

"Yulori should have no trouble bringing them in line."

"I certainly hope you are correct, sister. But I would advise you not to act too hastily. Saehyun likes his mazes and getting yourself stuck in one is a sure way to die a very, very slow death."

"One thing at a time," she smiled as the servants entered with trays of sweets and wine. Yuemeiko arched an eyebrow. "You took bloody long enough!" she scolded.

"Ignore the empress, girls!" Lord Teiyulori laughed. "She's all bark with dull teeth."

"I am sorry, my lady," the girls bowed.

"Humpf," Yumeiko huffed. "Nothing worse than a serving wench who can't read the mood."

Lord Teiyulori chuckled. "No, I wouldn't say so. Especially the ones who keep me in my prime."

"You disgust me," Yumeiko sipped from her saucer.

"Don't I know," he bowed.

Tears Of Resolve

Rebecca sat isolated on an upper balcony of Odahni, overlooking meticulously maintained green spaces and perfectly carved hedges. She hated it all - the rigid order, the stagnant atmosphere, the heavy, dull manners of the people who lived there, and the lack of freedom and anonymity.

Leaning on the balustrade, she stared off into the distance. Above her, the gray sky threatened rain. She picked up her tea cup and twirled it between her fingers. "So this is my life now," she murmured. "I wish Emily was here."

She lowered herself to the floor, crossing her legs, and let out a sigh. Across the floor, toward the door, she heard a low humming noise and felt her body tense. It was the all-too-familiar sound of Shumaiyuki's floating couch- a sound she had come to fear in the five weeks since their arrival. She pushed herself to her feet and began to walk away from the balcony.

"You know," she said as the Aiyo princess entered the adjoining room on her floating couch. "I wish you'd just get it over with and kill me too." However, she spoke in English, so her words were gibberish to Shumaiyuki, but her emotional trauma was evident in her demeanor.

"I have given you several days to mourn," the princess said, and then realizing she hadn't activated the box, did so and repeated her statement. "You have my word that no harm will come to you."

"What is your word supposed to mean to me? I'm alone now, a slave. No, a pet to a sociopath who floats around on a fancy sofa."

"Sociopath?"

"No! Sociopath! It means you're crazy! Cruel. You don't care about the feelings of others and feel everyone is beneath you!"

"I assure you—"

"It doesn't matter," Rebecca cut her off. "Just behead me already."

"I was about to say, I assure you I do care about the feelings of others. And while it is true, most people are beneath me. It is not so much a curse on them, as it is a privilege of my position by birth. But have you forgotten your place so soon?" She raised her stick.

"Oh, go to hell with your goddamned stick!" Rebecca crossed her arms. "If you didn't always have that jerk-off Obinari lurking in the background, I'd've taken it from you and beat you with it long ago."

Shumaiyuki turned to Obinari and sent him away, turning back to Rebecca she said, "And now what then? You've no guard to fear. Show me this fierceness you possess."

"I don't know what to do anymore." Rebecca sat down. "I wish we never came here."

A pause indicated Shumaiyuki's confusion. She coughed, stiffened up and said, "I'm sorry you…don't like it here."

"How could you expect me to?"

"So, I take it you don't intend on beating me with my own stick then?" she subtly lowered her hand and Obinari, crouching outside the room, withdrew the blow gun he had poked through the door.

"We both know I don't have it in me!" Rebecca sighed, deflated, "Emily was the one to take on bullies, not me."

"I did not want to be cruel to her. We were set against each other from the very start."

"I understand," said Rebecca, "But no one made you try to kill her when you were children. That was all you! Wasn't it?"

"I couldn't possibly know what you mean," said Shumaiyuki.

"In the tower. You're the girl from the tower aren't you? You walked with a cane under your arm."

Shumaiyuki's hand shook as did her eyes, "How could you possibly know that?"

“Emily told me about it. She thought it was just a crazy dream. But here we are. You’ve always had it in for her.”

Shumaiyuki impatiently tapped her stick on the floor waiting for the box to fully translate. She did not like what she heard and her face became cross.

“What could you possibly know!” Her lounge slowly lifted from the floor, menacingly, but Rebecca only shrugged at the implied threat.

“At least she’s at peace now, free of your torment,” Rebecca furrowed her eyebrows and turned away. “But it’s not over! Not for me. I don’t know how much more I can take from you. I wish you’d just hang me or behead me now!”

“No, no, hanging one is so inelegant. Now, while beheadings may initially sound far too messy. It is tradition to first slit the throat, just so, and let the blood spill forth into a bowl before the full chop. It avoids unnecessary splatter.”

“How could you be so cold!” Rebecca yelled at the top of her lungs. She placed her hands over her ears and ran away back towards the balcony.

Shumaiyuki was stunned. She sat up in her lounge, clapped and said, “As if I could behead you. You are far too valuable.”

“Bullshit! I’m just some exotic pet to you. And soon enough you’ll become bored of me, and then what? Maybe you’ll lock me up in a tower too!”

“I am not a monster!” Shumaiyuki’s voice slightly raised before she regained her composure. “What could you possibly know to judge me?” she pounded her fist on the floor and her lounge shot up towards the ceiling. “I was locked away against my will!” she said, her voice full of emotion. “They twisted my mind. Obánā told me Yuyuki was evil and I believed her.” She sat stoically and quiet for a moment before adding, “I do not wish to discuss the matter anymore, and you should take care not to mention it again.”

“You’re insane!”

"Return to your chambers now, or I'll have you whipped!"

"Sure, I'll go then," Rebecca said and turned and headed towards the door. "But, you know, one day you're going to have to cry about it with someone," she said, and then, "Um, these are my chambers, so…"

Shumaiyuki's eyes rested on the translator box as Rebecca spoke to her. And then, in a crisp voice, she said, "Stay then! But I do not wish to endure further discussion on the topic."

"You could always leave," said Rebecca.

"I do not wish to be alone," Shumaiyuki stared ahead, past the balcony and into the gray sky, without appearing to shift her gaze. Rebecca walked over and sat down on the floor next to the lounge. They remained silent until finally, Shumaiyuki said, "It devastated me to know that there was a girl merely downstairs living my life."

Shumaiyuki's eyes had a distant look, as if she was reliving her past. "To know she was freely able to do as she chose, and I was locked away to suffer in perpetual loneliness. It should be understandable that I would attack her in a fit of rage. I was a child, and she was so beautiful that day, wearing my robes. Something inside me just broke. I'm sorry."

Rebecca's face relaxed somewhat, and in a quiet voice said, "You were young, alone, and desperate. I can understand that." She leaned back onto her elbows and sighed, "I also understand that it wasn't really Emily's fault."

Shumaiyuki said nothing but stayed looking ahead as if looking at something past the balcony.

"How old were you when you were locked away?"

"I was six. When my paralysis from the cheriba bite subsided, I could barely walk and was considered an embarrassment to the family. So, I was locked away to not display the clan's vulnerability. I wanted to die. I spent years alone with my maids. All because of…"

"Greed!" said Rebecca.

“Mhm. Perhaps. But I did not understand the situation then.”

“But what about your parents? Why did they allow you to be locked away?”

“Their tragedy broke our house. Its repercussions have been far-reaching for the country, and their spirits haunt Odahni day and night.”

“I’m so sorry,” said Rebecca.

“Mhm,” Shumaiyuki’s eyes shifted back to the box and she said, “My father was Anele Ril Sahyuh, the emperor’s younger brother. He took my mother’s life right in front of me when I was an infant. He’s one of the reasons my uncle and I fight so often. The fool actually blames me in some sense for what happened to my mother due to the fact that she fell by my father’s hand. The official line is that my father died in a tragic hunting accident. But grandfather beheaded him as he should have.”

“Jesus! That sounds terrible,” said Rebecca, trying to think of something comforting to say.

Shumaiyuki took a deep breath and put her hands on either side of her legs, as if she was about to do stretching exercises.

“When I was thirteen, I was given a sloth as a present from my uncle. As a joke of course, because I moved about so slowly with my crutch,” she laughed condescendingly.

“I loved her, though she was a bit of a pest. I named her Mee. Mee was my first real friend. She was everything to me.” She paused and Rebecca waited for her to continue.

Shumaiyuki looked down and fiddled with her fingers when she wasn’t talking. “I…I know I’m rambling on,” she said, with no trace of apology in her voice. “I just thought that you…”

“It’s ok. I know it must be hard for you to share, but I’m glad I can listen,” Rebecca said.

"Mee died several years ago. I only had her for a few, but inside I was inconsolable. I wouldn't let them see me cry though, not even my Obánā."

Then Shumaiyuki bit her lip to stifle her tears and said, "I've no proof, but the day after she died, I heard from one of the servants that my uncle had fed Mee poison. But it's clear now he was always deriving some weird, sick joy from the fact that I was in pain."

"Oh no," Rebecca said.

"And what's worse," Shumaiyuki continued. "No one believes me!"

"I believe you," Rebecca said.

"Even though you just said I was insane a minute ago?" Shumaiyuki said in a flat voice.

"People say things when they are upset. And I am pretty pissed right now, but I believe you because hearing your story, I know you're telling the truth." She shrugged. "I can't describe how I know that, but I just do."

Shumaiyuki gazed into the box for a long moment. Then she said in a voice far more reserved than her normal way of speaking, "If only people had the same amount of faith in me as you do."

Rebecca raised her eyebrows.

"You are so…" Rebecca paused, trying to think of some innocent thing to say.

Then Shumaiyuki said, "Thank you."

"For what?"

"For being honest."

A single tear rolled from her eye down her cheek and left a line of wetness in its wake.

"You tell me the truth and you tell me about your emotions, about your past," Rebecca said. "And now that I've heard it, I can understand you a little better."

"Ribiki, I never mean to hurt you."

"Then don't. I'm really glad you've opened up to me. But I could do without you swinging that stick around all the time. It hurts."

Shumaiyuki's smile seemed forced, and she said, "Am I to apologize…to you?"

"I somehow don't see apologies as being in your wheelhouse."

"Well, with your help, I'm sure I'll be able to use it just a little more wisely."

"You're welcome," said Rebecca. Then she looked at the floor. "But I've some reason to be afraid."

Shumaiyuki's enigmatic look was replaced with a grim one. "Is it my uncle?"

"He beheaded Emily." Rebecca said. "Forgive me, but I don't trust him."

"It's understandable," Shumaiyuki said. "But I need you to understand that I could never hurt you. Nor will I allow another to lay hands upon you."

"And I'm grateful for it." Rebecca said with a worn smile. "I get seriously anxious when I see that," she said, looking at Shumaiyuki's stick.

"Mhm," Shumaiyuki said. "And I suppose that is my fault too?"

"You do the math."

"I am unfamiliar with the terminology, but I shall withhold my strikes unless necessary."

"Thank you…I guess?" Rebecca said. She looked at the speaker box and said, "I don't know why, but whenever I'm around that thing, I swear it's like some form of modern technology I'm looking at, not magic at play. It's the same with your lounge. It makes a noise when it hovers, like there are micro-machines at work. I mean, we don't even have technology like that in my world."

She waved at the box. "I mean, look how sophisticated it is. The marquetry on the front is beautifully done despite the splintery wood," she said. "Meaning it looks basic, but it's obviously machine-made. Just how did you come to have a floating bed?"

"It was a gift from my grandfather, made especially for me by the witch, Maishae."

"The witch again," said Rebecca, very carefully and quietly. "There's something really strange about that woman. And her creations," using air quotes.

"Strange maybe," said Shumaiyuki. "But they are very different from the technologies you brought with you from your world. Did I say it right?"

"Yes, that was the correct pronunciation," said Rebecca. "But see, that is just the point. My phone and both my tablet's batteries died a few days after I arrived here. Yet I can't figure out what's powering this box, or your lounge. Therein lies the mystery. Like maybe it wasn't magic that brought us here at all, but a wormhole of some sort."

Rebecca noticed Shumaiyuki's face had gone blank. "I'm sorry. You don't understand half of the crap I'm talking about and I don't have the proper terms to explain in your language."

Shumaiyuki's face broke into a soft smile. "I understand. And I think I'm right in saying I don't know everything. But maybe you shouldn't stop thinking about it if it intrigues you so."

"There is no way to know what technology this is. Obviously I have no way to confirm what I thought of, but I think it's wrong to dismiss it as magic," Rebecca replied.

“And what’s so wrong about magic? The people believe it is a true principle.”

“Well, I wouldn’t know what’s so special about magic, but I can’t accept that the people believe in it as a plausible answer. I mean my world would have you locked up if they thought you were a witch.”

“The people here tell stories about magic as a way to explain random inexplicable events. It suggests there are things which are so wondrous and strange that one is not fit to understand them,” Shumaiyuki said.

“And do you believe in magic?” Rebecca asked with a worried expression.

“No, I don’t,” Shumaiyuki said.

“It’s probably better not to,” Rebecca said with as serious a face as she could make.

Shumaiyuki put her hand on Rebecca’s knee and spoke. “Not everything in this strange world is bad.”

“What was that?” Rebecca exclaimed in a high voice; her cheeks flushed with warmth.

“I don’t know. This world is odd compared to your carefree world.” Shumaiyuki looked away and said, in a plain tone. With a forced smile, she added, “But it is also full of wonder.”

Rebecca cleared her throat. “Maybe. But there are so many things I don’t understand.”

“There are things here that make me uneasy too. Hence, I must become emperor and change things for the better.”

“Don’t you mean empress?”

“I said what I said.”

Shumaiyuki lifted her chin. "There are people here who look down on me because I am a woman. I will force them to see that women are the future. Once I'm established as emperor, I'm sure all women's lives will be better."

"I guess. I think it would be good for women to have more power." Rebecca felt a twinge of sadness as Shumaiyuki's eyes filled with pride.

"Emily was kind of a feminist too," she murmured.

"What was that?"

"Oh, nothing," Rebecca said.

"Yuyuki. Emily was a large part of your life, Ribiki. I feel like she still is and will always be," said Shumaiyuki with a sincere look.

"She was," said Rebecca, casting a sad expression.

Shumaiyuki nodded and said, "It's okay to feel that something is missing. But you must also look ahead, to a future where you find happiness."

"How can I possibly find happiness here?"

"Adapt." Shumaiyuki floated up and hovered towards the door. "Well then, I shall leave you to your mourning."

"Thank you, my lady," Rebecca bowed.

"Call me Shumai, but only in private. I am, my lady, before others," Shumaiyuki said with a smile and floated out of the room, closely followed by Obinari.

A Mad Descent

Is this for real or is it just another dream? *(Just another dream)* Is this for real or is it just another dream? *(Just another dream)...*

The siren's voice carried throughout the tightly packed Lower East Side club, driven by a heavy bass and snatching dance beat. Emily's eyes glittered as her head and body jerked to the music. She twirled around, her wet, bleached blond hair moving with her, and vigorously shook her hips while grinding into Glehson, moving in rhythmic patterns.

The club was packed with scantily clad college students partying hard. Indie and alternative beats worked the crowd, the DJ leading folks into a sweaty free-for-all as she spun. The heady mixture of music, booze, and hormones had everyone in frenzy.

Seitogi kept a watchful eye on her from a distance. Ignoring his stare, Emily turned to face Glehson, awash in his own sweat, and stuck her tongue into his mouth, exciting a passionate kiss. Seitogi self-consciously took a step back, trying to look away yet still remain in control.

The music and lights in the club abruptly ceased, and Emily found herself struggling to keep her balance. She coughed and felt dizzy, her knees started to buckle beneath her. Seitogi rushed over and supported her, lifting her away from the crowded dance floor.

"We need to get you medical attention!" Seitogi shouted as he quickly carried Emily towards the exit. Glehson followed closely behind, shouting out, "Don't leave me, Eleanor! I won't be able to survive without you!"

Suddenly, Emily's eyes snapped open, and she shrieked, "Eleanor! Who in the world is Eleanor?" She then sprang from Seitogi's arms and started attacking the partygoers, who had now transformed into police officers.

Her movements were wild and frenzied, fueled by a mixture of adrenaline and confusion. She swung her arms and kicked her legs, taking down one officer after another with a surprising amount of strength and skill.

Rebecca stood behind the DJ booth; she called out over the microphone to Emily, urging her to stop struggling with the police officers or risk getting arrested. However, just as suddenly as the fight had begun, the world around her disappeared, leaving her alone in the darkness.

Emily awoke with a jolt, realizing that the events of the club had been nothing but a dream. Her eyes felt heavy and were crusted over with sleep. As she coughed, a deep, raspy sound echoed in her chest, and she expelled a thick wad of mucus onto the floor. The air was thick with the unpleasant odors of urine and her own unwashed body, and she felt weak and disoriented.

Emily's thoughts were a jumbled mess as she tried to make sense of the events that had landed her in chains. The thick, noxious air weighed heavily on her chest, making it difficult for her to breathe. The sweat that dripped from her brow and into her eyes obscured her vision, making it challenging for her to take in the full extent of the dimly lit cell she was confined within.

The oppressive silence of her surroundings weighed heavily on her as she lay in her cell, struggling to shake off the fear that gripped her. Her mind churned with memories she dared not confront, fueling her determination to stay awake. Despite her efforts, she soon found herself succumbing to the lure of sleep. But in her dreams, she was plagued by terrors beyond her control. Her heart ached with pain, and she felt as though her soul was tearing apart at the seams. The haunting words echoed in her mind, "You are not me!" seemed to leave a permanent stain on her very being.

Emily's eyes fluttered open, and she gradually became aware of her surroundings. Feeling groggy and somewhat sick, she noticed a woman dressed in a crisp, white nurse's uniform standing before her.

"It's time for your training, Princess," the nurse said, guiding Emily, dressed only in a patient gown, out of the hospital room and onto a veranda overlooking a well-manicured lawn. The sky was dark and overcast, with clouds that seemed ready to release a downpour of rain.

The sound of distant thunder echoed in the air, and the trees swayed in the stiff breeze, their branches rustling against the wind.

The nurse, now resembling Dolores Heart, led Emily to a set of six polished steppingstones. Dressed in a stiff kimono with her gray hair tied in a neat bun, she brandished a stick and barked out instructions.

"Again! You will continue until you get it right!" she shouted, striking Emily in the shins.

Emily tried again, focusing all of her might, but was struck with the stick once more. Undeterred, she swung her silver hairpin through the air and concentrated.

"Please grow! Please..." she thought, just as the sky opened up, and heavy rain began to fall. The cold water soaked into her clothes and ran down her back, causing her to shiver as her hair wilted, strands sticking to her face.

"Focus!" the old woman barked as she struck Yuyuki's shins with her stick. "You need to master these movements if you want the hairpin to transform into a proper staff."

Determination was written all over Yuyuki's face as she repeated the intricate movements over and over again, despite the repeated blows from the stick. She repeated the words, "Please grow, please grow," as she willed the hairpin to transform. The rain poured down on her, drenching her clothes and hair, but she didn't let it distract her.

She was determined to master her training and prove herself to her grandmother. After several more attempts, exhausted and in pain, Yuyuki dropped her arms and let out a cry of frustration as she once again failed to complete the movement correctly.

"I can't do it, grandmother," she said, panting for breath. "It hurts my head to even try! I'm sorry, but can we please stop for now?" she pleaded.

But the old woman was unrelenting. "You will not stop until you have successfully summoned the staff as I have shown you. As future empress, your duty is not just to bear an heir, but also to protect the emperor. You must become proficient in both weapons and hand-to-hand combat.

This is the duty of all empresses. And you, Yuyuki, will be no exception," she said firmly, punctuating her words with another swift strike of her bamboo cane

"Once more," the old woman commanded, and Yuyuki started the routine anew. However, her movements were unsteady and awkward. Frustrated, the elder snatched the hairpin from the girl and twirled it around her fingers until she held it by its base. With a flick of her wrist, she pointed the tip towards the sky. The metal hairpin seamlessly elongated and transformed first into a rapier, before continuing to grow into a six-foot staff with a sharpened point.

"Look, child!" the old woman said as she effortlessly transformed the hairpin into a staff and back again. "You must practice until you can do this with ease," she handed Yuyuki the hairpin as it transformed back into its original form. "Try again," she ordered, turning and walking back towards the house, her kimono drenched from the rain.

Yuyuki's tears flowed freely as she struggled to control her shaking arms. The weight of her rain-soaked robe and the chill from the storm made it difficult for her to concentrate. Despite her efforts, she failed repeatedly, causing her frustration to boil over.

"You will stay out here in the rain until you can do it correctly," her grandmother declared sternly before slamming the screen door shut behind her.

Yuyuki dropped the hairpin and ran after her grandmother, banging on the door until her knuckles bled and her voice became hoarse from shouting, but there was no answer. She ran through the storm to the back of the house and tried again.

"Let me in!" she yelled, but after several moments of silence, she gave up and returned to the yard. Exhausted, she fell to her knees, feeling defeated, helpless, and alone.

"Please grow," she muttered through her tears as she picked up the hairpin from the grass.

Yuyuki's fingers twirled the hairpin with renewed confidence and determination. This time, the metal elongated and transformed into a long, sturdy staff. She held it with ease, but its shape only lasted a few fleeting moments before it reverted to its original form.

"I did it!" she exclaimed, exhilarated by her progress. Undeterred by the relentless rain, she continued her training, her movements becoming smoother and more fluid with each repetition.

As the storm finally passed and night fell, the stars and moon cast a soft, silvery light across the landscape. Yuyuki was filled with a sense of pride and fulfillment. She had mastered the art of summoning, and she could feel a newfound power stirring within her.

Suddenly, she was whisked away from the yard and found herself standing next to a smartly dressed woman waiting for the traffic light to turn green.

"You have the potential to be much more than just a mere witch," the sophisticated woman spoke to Emily as they waited for the pedestrian signal to change. "We've been keeping an eye on you, Emily Heart, and we believe you would be perfect for our latest venture in the city."

Emily was taken aback. "Excuse me? My name is not Emily. It's Yuyuki, Aiyo Yuyuki!" she exclaimed, slamming her hands on the glossy desk. The modeling agent, seated across from her, simply smiled and replied, "You are whoever we say you are, dear. You have no say in the matter."

Feeling overwhelmed and frustrated, Yuyuki stood up from her seat and bolted out of the office, sprinting down a bustling 5th Avenue. The agent chased after her, laughing all the while. As she turned a corner, she ran straight into Seitogi, sending them both tumbling to the ground.

"Seitogi get up! Let's get out of here," she said.

As Yuyuki and Seitogi ran down the crowded street, a violent tremor shook the ground and a horde of identical Dolores Hearts emerged from a crack in the pavement, calling out to Yuyuki and pursuing them while recklessly pushing pedestrians out of their way.

“Seitogi, you shouldn’t be here,” Yuyuki cried out as they ran. “I’m sorry for getting you caught up in this craziness. I was contracted for a modeling job by a woman named Dolores, but I never expected this to happen.”

“I don’t want you to go, Yuyuki, but I’ll understand if you have to,” Seitogi replied, running alongside her.

“Don’t be ridiculous,” Yuyuki retorted as they reached a car and quickly got inside.

However, Shidia Moffit, was in the driver’s seat and said –

“The fairy tale is a lie,” she wore a white nurse’s uniform. “You’re not a princess, you’re a witch. And Seitogi is not your prince.”

Yuyuki sat across from Aiyo Yulori, admiring the modern design of his downtown office. “I’m impressed with your space,” she commented.

Yulori smiled. “I can make any dream a reality,” he said, standing up and locking the door. “Let me explain how my company operates. We offer two services: the finest suitors for any and all Hearts on the market, and you, as the biggest Heart of all, you are no exception.”

With that, he reached for metal cuffs and locked them onto her wrists and ankles. Yuyuki’s heart sank as she was lifted over Yulori’s shoulder like a heavy sack, unable to fight back against his strong grip.

“But, as you already know, the market is already oversaturated,” he explained as he carried Emily down a long, winding stone corridor. “That’s where my second business comes into play. I fashion your soul into a ghost and upload it to the cloud.”

“Yeah, I guess I understand,” Emily said weakly. “Ghosts don’t feel pain, especially in the dungeons under the castle.”

“Exactly,” Yulori agreed. “They may experience emotions like joy and hate, but these feelings are transmitted digitally through a non-invasive implant in the ear.”

He opened a cell door and gently placed Emily on the cold floor. "Don't worry, Yuyuki, I'll make sure you receive the best care," he said as he left the cell, his footsteps echoed down the hallway.

"What? Wait…!" Emily called out, waking up from her slumber of mottled dreams. She heard a strange gurgling sound. She felt a chill run down her spine as she realized she was not alone. The sound came again, and it was a ghastly cough.

Her eyes strained to adjust to the darkness, and she could just make out the silhouette of a small, frail figure.

"Hello?" she called out, trying to stand, but her efforts was in vain. The only response she received was another hacking cough.

The shadowy figure fumbled through their clothes, muttering to themselves before triumphantly declaring, "Found it!" There was a scratching sound, like a match being struck, and the cell was suddenly illuminated by the bright, hissing fire of an emergency flare. The intense cherry-red flame shot towards the ceiling, forcing Emily to shield her eyes from the brightness. As her eyes adjusted, the figure's silhouette became clearer as they stood, holding the flare aloft.

The petite woman slightly hunched and with a wrinkled, bird-like face, was anything but ordinary. With a silver topknot, she approached Emily with a warm smile, her eyes lighting up with excitement. "Ahh, so it is you!" she exclaimed, breaking into a joyful dance.

Gripping Emily's wrist with surprising strength, the old woman declared, "Come, little one. I've been searching for you for over a month now. We must hasten, child! Hasten!"

But Emily pulled back, her heart racing with fear as the woman produced a mirror from the depths of her robes. Emily gasped, taking in the sight before her.

"Grandma!"

"Ho! What was that dear?"

"It's really you, grandma!" Emily cried out in joy as she hobbled forward on her knees and threw her bound arms around the old woman's neck. The woman struggled to free herself, but Emily held on tightly.

"How did you find me?" she asked, tears streaming down her face.

"It took me some time to navigate through Odahni Castle, but I'm here now," the woman replied. However, something about Dolores's voice was different from what Emily remembered. It was higher pitched and had a distinct accent that made her uneasy. The fear that this was just another one of her hallucinations crept into her mind.

"Step back, child! You reek like a horse that's fallen into a pile of manure!"

"Are you Dolores Heart or not?" Emily demanded.

"I am a wizened woman, but some call me a witch, a scientist, an old miser, but never Dolores Heart. You may call me Maishae."

"Maishae?" Emily asked. "But why do you look so much like my grandmother? I mean, you look a lot worse for wear, but…"

"That is my name, child," Maishae replied. "As for my resemblance to Dolores, you must be referring to that ignorant hefer Pheptae."

"Pheptae?"

"A former servant of mine, and a backstabbing traitor to be sure!" said the old woman, "But she is not your grandmother, dear."

"Oh god," Emily groaned, "You're the one in my dreams. You're the cruel one who locked me outside in the rain. What kind of monster locks a child out in a thunderstorm?"

The old woman's eyes lit up with recognition. "Well, there you have it! You do remember me!" she exclaimed, a hint of pride in her voice.

“It’s true, isn’t it?” Emily exclaimed; her voice filled with wonder. “Even when I fought Chua back in Bashi, it was your voice that I heard in my head, guiding my movements.”

“I admit, pretending to be your grandmother, Aiyo, was a necessary deception. And as for being mean to you, that’s a matter of perspective. But that’s not the issue at hand. Let’s get you out of this hole.”

“A necessary deception,” repeated Emily, feeling both shocked and betrayed. “I was a child? I trusted you!”

“Calm yourself, young one,” Maishae said, reaching out a hand to help Emily to her feet. “I did what I had to do to ensure your survival and to hone your skills. You have come a long way, and now it is time to leave this place and face the challenges ahead.” Maishae’s words were firm and unyielding, and Emily could hear the determination in her voice.

“I remember now! It was you! Ary and I fought you when you tried to kidnap me from Smitmae! Just what do you want from me anyway? Who the hell are you?”

“I already told you I am Maishae! Now come along, child.” She took hold of Emily’s wrist again, but Emily aggressively pulled her hands free and hopped back, falling onto the floor.

“I’m not going anywhere with a weirdo like you.”

“So you prefer your cell?” Maishae’s face lit up ominously as Emily tried to push her away with her crusted feet, but Maishae was quick and pounced on the girl’s chest, driving Emily back hard against the stone.

She held up the mirror, and Emily’s eyes widened as she saw a blue sky illuminated across its smooth surface.

“You have another mirror?” Emily gasped as she gazed upon the image in the mirror, a world so different from the one she was trapped in. She could see the blue sky, the clouds, and the trees. It was all so vivid; it seemed as though she could reach out and touch it.

“Another mirror, yes,” Maishae said as she held the mirror steady, “one that leads to a world beyond this one. But to reach it, you must come with me.”

Emily’s mind raced as she considered the woman’s words. She had been trapped in this cell for what felt like an eternity, and the thought of finally escaping was almost too much to bear. But something about Maishae’s mannerisms and the way she spoke made her wary.

“Why should I trust you?” Emily asked, looking up at the woman’s wrinkled face.

“Because you have no other choice,” Maishae simply replied. “Stay here and rot or come with me and flourish. You had a mirror too. You took the other from the boy Seitogi, did you not? Where is it?”

“Yulori. Aiyo Yulori took it from me. But it stopped working anyway.”

“The mirrors are infinite, child. They do not stop working. Now come along with me, and I can remind you all about them.”

“Remind me? Look, I don’t know what ‘deus ex machina’ bullshit this is but leave me out of it unless you’re taking me back home to Earth and my real grandmother!”

“I already told you that the thieving bitch is not your grandmother. Now don’t be difficult, or I will have to be forceful.” She focused on the mirror - “time is of the essence. We have to get you back into shape, don’t we?” Maishae wrapped her scaly hand around Emily’s bone-thin wrist.

“Ow! You’re hurting me!”

“Oh, snuff.”

“Let go of me, you old git!”

“Hush, child. We’re already here.”

Emily opened her eyes and was greeted by a breathtaking sight. The sky was a brilliant blue, dotted with white clouds. The sun shone down, warming her skin with its rays. The air was fresh and crisp, filling her lungs with its purity. Despite being bound by chains, she was lying in a field of lush green grass, surrounded by the beauty of nature. The cell that she had been trapped in beneath Odahni Castle was nowhere in sight.

Maishae

The wind chime filled the nursery with a charming tinkling sound. The room was sparsely decorated, with a plain cradle next to a small table with a box lamp on top, and two sitting pillows haphazardly placed on the floor.

A thin, frail woman landed quietly on the tatami-covered floor and made her way to the crib where a newborn baby slept peacefully.

"Yuyuki," the woman whispered as she gently stroked the sleeping baby's cheek. "There you are my precious darling."

The room was quiet except for the sound of the wind chime and a light wind blowing outside the window. The woman lifted Yuyuki out of the crib and held her close. The newborn awakened and gazed into the old woman's face. The toothless smile on the child's face only served to deepen the lines around the woman's grandmotherly eyes.

"Finally, you're here, my dear. You came out just perfect. Oh, look at you. You're nothing like the Others. I have so much to teach you about us."

Maishae held up a small mirror so that it captured their reflections and said, "See, Yuyuki, there are many doors in life, and it is up to us to choose which ones we walk through." She gestured to the mirror with her pointed chin and said, "This mirror is also a door, and it can open us up to many worlds. Take a look."

Yuyuki cooed and simply stared with her new eyes, fascinated by the light reflecting off the shiny glass.

"See, child, mirrors can be used to trick others and even the person looking into them. But they can also be used to show us the truth." Maishae raised the mirror again and focused on their reflections, but her concentration was interrupted by a horrified scream. A maid had entered the room.

In a swift motion, Maishae threw a small pellet to the floor, and it instantly turned into a cloud of smoke that filled the room. When the smoke cleared, Yuyuki was back in her crib, and Maishae was gone. The maid collapsed onto the door frame, overwhelmed by what she had witnessed.

A minute later, several guards entered the room, ready for a fight with their swords drawn. The last man to enter, a stocky, rough-looking fellow with a handsome face, rushed over to the crib and picked up Yuyuki in his arms.

"What did you see?" Duke Sahyuh demanded. The maid, still in shock, just shook her head and wept. He gestured to two of the guards and said, "Useless. Take her to the miser and have him give her a sedative."

The Duke glanced around the room. "Damned Yienguoi-Jin! It's not enough for him that he's dishonored my wife. He dares to come and claim his bastard as well!"

He began pacing the floor. "The rest of you, surround and search the castle. Bring me word that the demon is out of the house."

The Duke placed the tiny squawking baby back in her crib and glared down at her, saying, "I won't let Ameiki or Yienguoi-Jin have you, demon child. Somehow, I feel you will ruin both Houses Anele and Aiyo." And with that, he stormed out of the room, leaving a solo guard at the entrance to the nursery.

The guard glanced down the hall with a knowing expression, muttering curses under his breath.

"This is not going to be easy," the guard thought as his body began to dissolve into countless particles of light until only Maishae's tiny figure remained.

"Sahyuh may think he has you, but he doesn't know what he's in for with me around. I'll teach you how to use our power," she said with a smile to herself. Yuyuki's cries quieted as she drifted off into a peaceful sleep.

The old woman held her tightly in her arms and gazed out the window for the last time. "Soon my dear, you will be mine forever."

Maishae held her mirror and looked at herself. In its reflection, she saw her own image fade away as she walked into an open meadow. The nursery disappeared behind her, and she was standing under a brilliant summer sky.

The warmth of the sun and the roughness of the grass beneath her feet awakened her senses. Maishae was suddenly overwhelmed with a longing for her homeland. The places and people she used to know seemed so long ago. She looked down into the mirror and saw the nursery again and teared up. Triumphantly, she looked at the countryside around her, "It's time for me to share the news." She began walking through the field and up towards a single-story property that resembled a series of interconnected ranch houses surrounded by lush gardens. Each step brought flashbacks from her past into her mind.

"After all these years, I am finally going home." As she approached the gates of the property, her hands began to shake, and she had to catch herself before she fell.

The woman who awaited her at the gate walked out to meet her, "Pheptae!" Maishae grinned, taking the identical woman's hands into her own. "Eleanor has been born healthy and strong."

"Congratulations, my lady. Will you be having tea?"

"Huh? What…No, you old fool; we must prepare this place for the princess. I will be bringing her here soon when she is strong enough!"

"Delightful, my lady! I will have the others get right to it, but you really should have your tea."

"Oh, very well, but I will have to instruct them on the baby proofing; otherwise, they'll do it all wrong, as they do with everything else. Shame none of them turned out with half your wit." Pheptae bowed and led the old woman into the house.

Weeks later, Maishae stared into the mirror looking down at Duke Sahyuh's Nyongoyuchi estate, filled with bustling activity. She held her hand out and waved at the scene below her, and the nursery came into view.

"Come, Yuyuki, it is time to pick up where we left off." She walked directly into the nursery. The room was bare of all furnishings and looked like it hadn't been touched in months.

"Humph!" Maishae looked around. "Perhaps Sahyuh had her moved to another part of the castle." She turned and began to pace back and forth. "He did say he wouldn't let Ameiki or Yienguoi-Jin have her. But he wouldn't have hurt the child?" she wondered as her heart sank.

"Oh my, but he would have!" she thought as she ran out of the room and straight to the lord's chambers. It was a long trek, but the woman was in too much of a hurry to notice the distance.

"Hold it right there!" a guard yelled as she jogged up towards the room's double doors. She jumped into the air brandishing a short sword and slit his throat. She landed before his body hit the floor and slid open the screen doors and screamed, "Where is she?"

A regal, handsome man with fine set wrinkles and graying hair drew his sword with lightning speed, knocking the weapon from her hand with the butt of its hilt. He then put her in a chokehold and lifted her off her feet.

Maishae fought with all her might, but the man was in excellent physical shape. She bucked him off and fell to the ground. The man delivered a kick that sent her flying back into the wall.

"I am Lord Aiyo Teiyulori of House Aiyo! Have you no respect for the laws of our forefathers? Name yourself before announcing battle!" Blood streamed from his nose, and one of his eyes was already swollen. He realized with horrified glee that she had landed several blows and put up his hands and chuckled, "Impressive, my lady, you've excellent training for a wizened woman."

Maishae climbed to her feet and rushed forward. They exchanged several kicks and punches.

"Peace woman! What is your quarrel?" Lord Teiyulori demanded.

Maishae backed herself into a corner of the room, "Where is Princess Yuyuki?"

She was out of breath but was still able to hold the man off. Lord Teiyulori stared at the old woman, the hardened lines in his face softened at the mention of the baby's name.

"That is precisely what I am here to investigate," he said. Several of his men crowded the doorway, but he held up his hand to halt their advance. They reluctantly lowered their weapons. "Leave us," he commanded. The men saluted and filed out.

"What business do you have with my granddaughter?" he asked.

"I am her benefactor," said Maishae. "You can consider me her fairy godmother of sorts."

Lord Teiyulori remained unmoved, "I'll repeat: what business does a dirty old, wizened woman have with my granddaughter?" He roared with wrath and lunged toward the woman. Maishae blocked his swing and delivered a heel kick to his ribs. She produced a dagger from her sleeve and landed several blows against his blade, but he kept blocking and driving her back. She stumbled, and he lunged forward once more, placing the tip of his sword at her throat.

There was a knock at the door. "Enter," he said without moving from his spot. An Aiyo soldier stepped into the room with a young maid in front of him who immediately shrieked at the sight of Maishae. "My lord!" The man drew his blade and ran to Teiyulori's side. The distraction was enough for Maishae to retrieve her mirror and quickly disappear, then reappear behind the maid.

"You're coming with me!" she snarled as she dragged the girl with her into the mirror.

Moments later, they were transported. The maid fell to her knees and emptied the contents of her stomach onto the grassy field, then looked up at the world around her in confusion.

Maishae grabbed her by the collar. "Quit being sick, we have no time to waste."

The maid looked at Maishae with a startled look on her face. "You're the one I saw trying to kidnap the princess, aren't you?" she asked, wiping her mouth with the sleeve of her uniform.

"Not a witch! A wizened woman, and I was not trying to kidnap the princess, you dolt."

"Well then what are we doing here?"

Maishae rolled her eyes. "I can cross into other realms, and I have brought you here because I obviously need your help!"

The girl's mouth dropped. "But what do you need from me?"

"Come along, we'll talk over tea," Maishae led the girl into the gardens that surrounded her home. "I need to know what Duke Sahyuh has been up to, and I need you to tell me what he's done with the princess."

"Why should I tell you anything?" the girl cried out.

Maishae shook her head. "It is not my place to tell you my motives; that is for me alone to know and for you to agree to."

The young maid looked at Maishae suspiciously. "I don't like the look of you… but." Maishae grinned and replied, "Neither do I. That is why I must find Yuyuki." After some hustle and bustle, the two sat in a decorative tea room sipping from delicate cups and talking in hushed whispers.

"Are you really just a wizened woman?" asked the maid.

"You have obviously not heard of the Great Maishae, healer of all?" Maishae took up a flamboyant pose. "The truth is, I'm quite famous. But that is beside the point; I need to find Yuyuki."

"Well…" began the maid. "It is somewhat your fault she was sent away."

"My fault?" Maishae's face went white with shock.

"I told his lordship what I saw, but he insisted it must have been Yienguoi-Jin of the Taisehsai who," here the girl's eyes went wide, "he said fathered the princess."

"He's completely delusional." Maishae shook her head and took a sip from her tea. "And so, then what?" she asked the girl.

“After that day, she was gone. One of the older servants told another girl his lordship had her sent into the service of prayer with the Jyoshi.”

“The Jyoshi sisterhood…” muttered Maishae. “Seriously?”

“Yes, and our lady Ameiki is always locked in her room. Sometimes I can hear her crying. I don’t know why he took the child away.”

“I cannot believe this,” Maishae said aloud. “And why was Lord Aiyo there today in the duke’s chambers?” She stood and began pacing back and forth across the room. “He must have been talking to the duke on the matter.”

“The duke is currently away, so my mistress called for her father to come and hopefully find the princess.”

“In the meantime,” Maishae replied. “I need you to tell me everything you have heard of the duke’s activities in the last few days.”

Hours later, Maishae sat on her veranda gazing up at the stars. Her body was stiff in the cool autumn breeze.

“She is alive,” she whispered with a slight smile. Tears streamed down her face. She was afraid that Duke Sahyuh had killed Yuyuki and regretted not taking her the day she was born.

Now it was a simple matter of her visiting the local nunneries to see if the princess was being held there. If so, she would take her away from them. “Nuns, of course,” she growled. “I’m sure they will take in a little old lady like me.”

“Um, Ms. Maishae?” The Anele maid had been trying to get her attention as the wizened woman had seemed to have forgotten her presence.

“Yes, what is it?”

“Are you going to take me back soon?” the girl asked.

“Of course not,” Maishae looked over at her and raised an eyebrow.

The girl flushed and stared down at the floor. She gave a small sigh with a defeated look on her face.

* * *

Maishae searched for years but could find no trace of Yuyuki. The old woman, with a bent back and a wrinkled face covered in fine warts, had searched every nunnery in every town, city, and location within a hundred or so miles of the Duke’s palace.

She began to cry, holding her cracked old hands to her face. “I’m sorry, I’m so sorry,” she cried to herself. “After years of planning and so many failures, I finally had her, and I let her slip right through my hands. I’m such a fool.”

Later that day, it was by pure chance that Maishae came across a group of truffle hunters. They were a gentle, agile bunch, laughing and singing as they worked their way across the countryside. Several children were helping their families gather the precious delicacy, but Maishae only had her eye on one of them - a girl of about five.

All day, the old woman shadowed the villagers, observing the girl with interest. There was something about her, something familiar.

“It can’t be!” Maishae’s face straightened and her eyes narrowed as she approached the parents who were seated on the grass, eating their lunch. They eyed Maishae carefully.

“May I help you, madam?” asked the father of the little girl.

“Yes,” said Maishae. “By any chance, is that there with the blue-haired boy, your daughter?”

“Well, yes, that is our daughter,” the man replied cautiously.

“She is my daughter!” answered the mother as she studied their party crasher.

"You lie! She is mine! She belongs to me!" Maishae snarled, causing both parents to jump.

"Madam," said the mother in a shaky voice, rising. "Please do not do anything silly."

Maishae laughed now and looked at the girl. "Would you like to come with me? I'll take care of you," Maishae smiled.

"No!" the child said emphatically as she grabbed her mother's leg.

Maishae glared at the woman, "This child is no more the product of your womb than the sun is father to the moon!" The mother gasped, and the father looked at his daughter.

"Seitogi," he called the boy over. "Come take Enoshi," he pulled a dagger from his breast and held it aloft.

"I won't let you have her!" The man screamed as he lunged forward to stab Maishae.

"Gah!" Maishae dodged his attack. Drawing her own knife, she parried the blade.

"How did you come to have my Eleanor?" Maishae continued to challenge his attack. "Why did you take her from me?"

The man stared at the woman. "You don't know who Enoshi is! Stay away from us!"

"Yes," snapped Maishae. "I do know her! Better than you could ever know her!"

The man lunged again, stabbing at Maishae. She dodged and struck back, wounding him on his side after landing a vicious hit to his back. He howled in pain and went to attack again.

The old woman laughed as she dodged the attack, "I spared you a cut that time! Next one I will open you right up!…Gah!" she screamed as she stumbled for a moment, stunned.

The rest of the villagers had surrounded her and began to beat her with sticks and pickaxes.

"What are you doing!?" she cried and lunged out at the crowd. But the villagers only beat her more.

"Eleanor! Give her back!" She screamed as she struggled to get up, blood pouring down her face. She struggled to rise, wincing in pain. She grabbed the foot of one of the attackers.

"What have you done with her!?" Maishae raged, feeling the dagger slice into her hand. "Who took her?"

There was no answer. Everything seemed to be fading away. She could feel the warmth of her blood. The pain was loosening her grip on her mind. She could feel the darkness take her.

After a moment of abyss, Maishae opened her eyes and saw her own room. The Anele maid she had taken so long ago was leaning over her. She gave the girl a wan smile.

"You really must take better care of yourself, Lady Maishae."

"I'm fine, Cheedi… I'm fine," she said softly. "Ugh…" she looked around and gave a soft moan as she saw the bruising around her hand. "What happened?" She felt sick.

"You were attacked," Cheedi said, "by a gang of truffle hunters. You were injured quite badly."

"Truffle hunters?" Maishae answered as she tried to sit up.

"At least that is what you said when we found you lying out in the field." Cheedi replied before taking out a damp towel and putting it on her head. "We found you with bruises from your head to your feet. You were unconscious for several days."

"Days?" Maishae sniffed the air. "Did I say anything else?" She asked.

"Yes, Madam." Cheedi stared at her. "You told us you found Princess Yuyuki amongst them."

Maishae stared at her, "Yes," she sighed. "Yuyuki." She strained to talk. "She was with them, but…they…they…" Maishae fell silent as Cheedi applied more sheets to her forehead.

"It was my fault the princess was exiled from her rightful place as future empress. It is up to me to figure out a way to get her back in."

"Madam!" Cheedi insisted. "You should rest!"

Maishae smiled a lopsided smile as she looked up, "Let us see. The only one who truly stands in my way is the duke's heir, Princess Shumaiyuki."

"But," Cheedi began.

"But what?" Maishae replied, staring at the servant.

"Well…she's just a little girl," Cheedi struggled with her resolve, then finally. "I won't believe that you would hurt a child. That would make you no better than the duke!"

"Hah! Foolish girl, I'm far worse than Suhyuh could ever have imagined being. You've been my hostage for years now and you haven't figured that out?"

"I've rather enjoyed my time here. Had you sent me back, the duke would have surely had me beheaded. Plus, Pheptae and the others have taught me how to read, and about all sorts of math.

They have shown me my value is more than someone who should dance and cook."

"Fool! The others are a bunch of idiots! It's a wonder they don't have you reading backwards!"

"You really should treat them kinder. They are quite lovely and never grumpy like you."

"They're trifling," Maishae replied as she drifted off to sleep, "Anyway, I will figure a way to remove Shumaiyuki without killing her if that would make you happy."

"Hmph." Cheedi pulled up the sheets again. "That would be lovely."

* * *

The swaying wind chime in the window filled the air with a haunting melody. The room was lavishly decorated and furnished. In one corner sat a large, comfortable-looking bed, and in the other corner, a rocking chair. There was a large chest at one end of the room and a full-sized porcelain tub in another. The room had three windows and a wardrobe, all wide and well-made.

Maishae gazed in awe. It was not only well-furnished but also well-cared for, and rarely did she see any palace as beautiful as Odahni Castle. Shumaiyuki's room stood out as an exception.

Maishae took a slow, deep breath and let it out as she quietly landed on the tatami-covered floor and bobbed over to the extravagant bed where the princess slept.

"Shumaiyuki," she whispered as she stroked the sleeping girl's cheek. "You must forgive me for what I am about to do, princess," she said. "I promise it is for the best."

She reached into her robe and fumbled about until she found a large syringe. She quickly thrust it into the princess's spine.

"I'm so sorry, child, but life can be a cruel, untamable beast. And tonight, it has chosen you for its meal."

The girl screamed in agony, writhing on the bed before slowly flopping back onto the silken covers. Maishae sprang from the window onto a nearby tree as several maids entered the chambers. She hurried through the tree limbs, making sure not to be seen.

The next morning, Odahni Castle was in a frenzy.

"My princess! My princess!" screamed Obánā Ta-tae as she ran into the throne room and threw herself before Aiyo Yulori.

"The princess can't move a single limb, my lord! She has not spoken a word, and she may die at any time!" her voice broke into a sobbing wail.

"You must find whoever did this!" he ordered the older maid. "Be thorough!"

"We found these in her bed," the maid said as she handed over a folded sheet of paper holding several little red insects.

A puzzled look crossed Yulori's face. "Cheriba bugs? But how?"

"Yes, my lord," the older maid replied as she bowed her head.

"Immediately! Find out who brought them into this castle!" Aiyo Yulori ordered.

"I already did, Lord Aiyo," the harridan replied. "Two of the younger girls allowed the princess to wander past the gate and pick flowers from the wild. We think the cheribas must have clung to her robes."

Aiyo Yulori's face turned red as he struggled to keep his growing anger at bay. "I want those girls beheaded and send for our Mizer!"

"No, my lord," the Obánā replied.

"What do you mean no?" Aiyo Yulori bellowed. "You are not permitted to disobey me!"

"Yes, my lord, but they are just girls. Yes, they should be punished, but…"

"They may have ruined Aiyo's future and the royal engagement! I will deal with them personally!"

Huasau Atem came to his defense,"It's alright, my lord. Let me deal with them."

Aiyo Yulori stopped and turned to look at his man at arms.

"No, that is no proper punishment. I will do it! All of it!"

"As you wish, my lord."

Aiyo Yulori stormed into his private chambers, just off the throne room, and locked himself in. He paced and cursed under his breath.

"Shumaiyuki. She will never be tall or beautiful without movement in her limbs. She'll be useless to me and our house." His pacing grew faster and harder.

***

Aiyo Yulori walked back to Shumaiyuki's room. The mizer had arrived and was sitting by the princess's bedside. Judging from the old man's expression, the prognosis didn't look good. He turned to Aiyo Yulori and slowly shook his head, as if to say there was nothing he could do.

"You don't understand old man! It will be disastrous for us if she is unable to move about. You must fix her!"

"Lord Aiyo," the mizer replied, "I fear it is beyond my power to help. Cheriba bites are rare. It's been thirty years or more since I've seen one. I have a few powders to help with the pain and fever, but I am afraid there is nothing I can do about her paralysis."

Aiyo Yulori stomped his foot. "It's not your fault, my old friend, I know that. It must be a curse of some kind. We should send for my father's witch. Perhaps she can help."

"I would advise against it, my lord. I would not let that woman within a foot of this castle."

"But she is a powerful mizer too, you must admit," Aiyo Yulori asked.

"Yes, she is, my lord, but she is still a woman."

Aiyo Yulori stared in shock at the old man for a moment and then smiled a little. "Oh, you are right. I guess we can wait. We will leave her in your capable hands."

The old man bowed his head in thanks. "Yes, my lord. Em, my lord if I may." The old man indicated he wanted to speak in private, and so Yulori had the room cleared.

"What is it?"

"As you know, my lord, I have delivered all Aiyo births since the time of your grandfather. I delivered you into this world."

"And what of it?"

"I also delivered Princess Yuyuki at Bhurl Manor. Oh, a beauty she was. A face one does not forget."

"Out with it, old mizer! I have to plan contingencies to ensure an Aiyo lead future!"

"That is precisely what I have in mind. The Aiyo's future," the Mizer's eyes twinkled in a way that disturbed and delighted Yulori all at once, for he had never known the gentle man to have a scheming bone in his body.

"If Princess Shumaiyuki's body is rendered useless, then she will be unable to carry out her duties as a future partner to the emperor."

"It is a damnable situation indeed," Yulori agreed.

"But it doesn't have to be. Recently, while out charitably providing my services in Daiye village, I encountered a girl no more than a year older than our Shumaiyuki."

"You are beginning to annoy me."

"It was Yuyuki, my lord! As I said, I never forget a face, let alone one that I brought into this world. She lives among the villagers as a daughter of the Abete family. She is the spitting image of…" here he pointed to Shumayuki, her breathing shallow, and her brow drenched with sweat.

"Yuyuki, alive?"

"Procure her. Bring her to Odahni and begin her training."

"Bring her back from Daiye?"

"Yes, my lord. Let Yuyuki become Shumaiyuki. That is the only way the line of Aiyo imperial succession will survive."

“Yes, now that is a clever idea,” Yulori declared. “Perhaps the perfect antidote. If the girl really favors Shumai, she is the blood of Aiyo.” He seemed to have made his decision. “I will retrieve the girl personally. You are to speak of this to no one.”

“Yes, my lord.”

“What of our Shumaiyuki? There are ways and means to this matter.”

“Don’t worry, my lord. She will be well cared for until she is back to her usual self.”

“Good. You are dismissed.”

“Yes, my lord.” The old man turned and shuffled out of the room, the edge of his gown trailing behind him.

As the mizer hurried back to his chambers, sweat poured from his brow. Finally, alone in the room, he let out a deep sigh as his body disintegrated into a cloud of sparkling light. Maishae slumped to the floor, taking several long breaths to calm her racing heart.

“A body’s not meant to wear a holographic shroud for so long,” she said to the hunched over body of the old Aiyo mizer lying next to her. A stream of blood flowed from his slit throat, a grim reminder of how far she would go to attain her goal.

“Trust me, honey,” she continued, “That cad Yulori was more than likely going to have you murdered before nightfall anyway.”

She stood and stretched, trying to get the kinks out of her spine. “Alright,” she said and took out her mirror. “I’m off then.”

She checked her reflection for a moment and then began to concentrate. Colors danced about as her form began to shift. A few seconds later, she stood outside her home in the pocket.

The Pocket

Maishae knelt and removed the leather cuff around Emily's neck. She cut the cords that bound her ankles, then helped her to her feet. They walked through an exceptionally manicured garden with towering, oversized flowers and exotic plants, their perfumed scent filling the air.

"Where on Earth are we?" she asked, stunned, and then drew back in disgust. "Whoa! You're a worse sight in the daylight."

"You're one to speak," the old woman gave her a once-over.

Emily looked over herself and wrinkled her nose. Outside in the fresh fragrant air of sweet grass, she fully noticed her horrid smell. Her chinos were stained with a mix of blood, urine, mud, and soot, and her hoodie's original color was barely perceptible, as it was now torn at the shoulder and papoose.

"You were saying?"

"Touché," Emily frowned. A silence fell between them. Emily sniffed her hoodie and turned her head to the side. Maishae was walking slowly, seemingly lost, but Emily saw that she had a beatific smile on her face.

"Why do you look like an extra crispy version of my grandmother?"

"Saucy girl," said Maishae and gave her a pinch.

"Ouch! Keep your hands to yourself."

"Then don't be rude. I've taught you better than that."

"Are you going to unlock these handcuffs anytime soon?"

"Goodness, you are full of questions, aren't you?"

"Well, are you?"

"Hold still or you'll get burned." Maishae had Emily hold out her hands and took out a small cylindrical device that reminded Emily of a Bic lighter.

A thin blue laser shot out of its tip and easily cut through the heavy, metal cuffs. After several moments of hissing smoke, the heavy cuffs fell to the grass with a loud clink.

"Was that a laser?"

"Quiet girl. I am gathering my thoughts."

As they approached the main house, Emily noticed several servants in ordinary khaki-colored uniforms tending to the flowers and plants. Two lay on the grass, smoking cigarettes, dressed in plain frocks and aprons.

Emily stopped walking and stared at them, astonished. They all looked like Maishae. Granted, there were some small differences, height being the main one she could immediately identify, but other than that, they were all identical.

"I'm sure there's a sensible explanation for all of that?"

"Who? What are you carrying on about?"

"There's like thirty of you running around here!" Emily sighed. "It's like a cult of you."

"Oh! Those are the others; ignore them. They're a bunch of halfwits if ever there were."

"That's it? That's all you're going to say about them?"

"What else do you want me to say?"

"Well, if they're a bunch of idiots, what does that make you?"

"Listen, girl, I won't be insulted. I saved your ass! You should be grateful! Cheedi! Cheedi, we are home!" she yelled out in her croaky voice.

Cheedi strode from the house and offered both Emily and Maishae a courteous bow. "Welcome home, Lady Maishae. It has been a while. It is good to see you are well."

Cheedi nodded to Maishae, then turned to Emily. “And you are? Hello!” She gave a friendly smile, her eyes crinkling. “I am Cheedi, chief of the estate.”

“My name is Emily. Emily Heart. Hey, why does everybody here look the same except you?”

“She is Princess Yuyuki!” said Maishae, “Uncouth and foul as any spoiled brat would be!”

“Spoiled! I’ve been chained up in a cave for I don’t know, weeks! Months!”

“Cheedi, it would be best if you ignore our friend’s rude tone. She has been through some tough times.” She turned to address Emily, “You look wretched and smell even worse. We will talk later once you have settled in.”

“Where is this place even?”

“Cheedi, I have important business to attend to and will be away for another spell. Don’t allow her to make any menace while I am gone.”

“Of course, my lady.”

“Bathe her in milk and honey twice a day; make sure she soaks at least an hour in both. She’ll need a hot Dit-da-jow soak for her scars and sore muscles alike. And she’ll need plenty of body and scalp massages. We’ve got to get that hair growing back quicker. See that she is kept fed.” She looked back at Emily, “We need to fatten you up a bit,” she said, and then abruptly walked away.

“But wait! Where are you going? We just got here! You can’t just leave me by myself…er, with them. No offense to you, Cheedi.”

“I have to take my other mirror back from Lord Aiyo, amongst other things.” Maishae said as her body faded away into the vision in her mirror. Cheedi smiled a kind smile and softly clapped her hands together. Two of the other assistants stopped working and came up to Emily’s side.

“Don’t you worry, young mistress,” said one of the servants.

"We'll have you nice and plump before ol' mistress returns," said the other. It was unnerving; both sounded exactly like Maishae.

"What are you people?"

"We are us!" they spoke in unison and began pushing Emily towards the house.

"I'm not going anywhere with you two! Just go away!"

The two servants looked at each other and frowned, then both gently took her by an arm and dragged her to the main house. Cheedi looked at her sympathetically.

"Is something wrong?" she asked.

"Oh, nothing! Just freaked out is all!" Emily said angrily.

"There is no need to be embarrassed. It is quite normal to be frightened in new surroundings; all of us have felt it. Our home is your home, no matter what. Come inside."

Cheedi held the door open, and the others ushered Emily inside. The moment she stepped in, she felt a wave of relief wash over her. The house was dimly lit. The air was mild and sweet with incense. The walls were wood-paneled and warm from the sun.

Emily noticed large abalone shells held the incense. There were statues of Buddha everywhere. On the left side of the hall were two wooden doors. The twin women led her up the stairs, into a large room. It was a bathing room where a tiled tub sunk into the floor. One of the women walked over and turned on its faucet. It soon gushed forth with hot water.

"Young mistress, soak for a while, then let us scrub your bones clean" firmly stated one servant.

"My name is Ehhh…" stammered Emily. "Wait a minute! You guys have plumbing! And running hot water?"

"It doesn't matter, Young Mistress," said the other. "Come, lie in the bath. You should be clean before you soak in milk and honey."

"Ok. I know I'm stinky!" she huffed. "I just figured, living in a cave for so long, I didn't even think about what I smelled like."

The woman just chuckled, which annoyed Emily. "Leave me for a moment. I'll call you when I'm ready."

The servants left, closing the door behind them. Emily stripped down and stepped into the hot water. She reached up with both hands and cried out as sudden pain ran through her. She reached down to cover one breast.

"Damnit!" She was covered with sores, nasty scabs almost all the way around her body. She held her right forearm gently and cried out again; it was covered with red, angry welts. She looked at her legs, her thighs, her buttocks—all were bruised and covered in scars.

The more she looked at herself, the angrier she became. The more she thought of all the bad things she had been through since leaving Earth, the angrier she became.

A half-hour later, she climbed out of the tub and carefully toweled off, avoiding her wounds so as not to agitate them. She looked in the mirror and gasped. The towel was covered with blood. She had forgotten about the wounds on her neck.

"Damn, I really am a mess," she cursed.

Emily washed her face and walked out past the two servants who had escorted her to the bath. She addressed them.

"Mhmm. I'm ready for my milk and honey soak. Also, have a meal ready for me immediately afterward. I'm famished."

After a hearty soak and massage, Emily was both physically and emotionally tired, but she was warm and clean and felt secure for the first time in a long time. About ten of the servants excitedly twittered about, fussing over her short mop of hair and choosing which silks she should wear.

She couldn't be upset with them, as they all seemed to adore her in equal measure. When she was finally dressed, she wore a thick, pure white tunic on top of flowing blue and gold embroidered robes. The others held up mirrors in front of her, showing her the most flattering angles.

Her hair was slicked up into a beautiful, complex braid secured with a swan hairpin and silver coins woven through the intricate designs. Her face was powdered, and her lips were berry red, along with dark kohl rimming her eyes. She felt beautiful.

"You look stunning! Wonderful, young mistress," said one of the servants.

"I'm so happy you're here, young mistress," said another, touching Emily's hand gently.

Emily followed along down a long hall, passing several rooms, but there was one door that caught her attention. It was made from black wood, lathed on both sides, with a pattern carved in relief into the wood that resembled the rings in a tree.

Emily couldn't tell if the markings were carved or painted. Looking at them, she remembered studying the design in the past. She tried to follow the pattern and count off the rings, but it was too hard; there were a lot of them, and they overlapped one another, and some were missing. She couldn't keep track. She recalled this image from her childhood. It perplexed her as a child, and it still did now.

Emily slid the door open, peering out, her curiosity now piqued. She stepped out onto a veranda that led to an open courtyard garden with a tiny bridge over a lily pond. At the center of the courtyard, a set of six polished stone steps was carved out of the ground.

Emily exhaled and drew the swan hairpin forth. She jumped from the veranda, turning in the air in a rapid twist and landing squarely on the polished stone, maintaining her balance on her pointed foot. The servants cheered in unison. Joy and awe were painted on their faces.

“I remember this place,” Emily smiled. She pointed the tip of the hairpin towards the sky and then nimbly skipped from stone to stone, jumping up onto each step and landing on the grass in a cat-like crouch.

The others whooped and hollered, applauding and marveling at Emily’s prowess. Emily stood, shaking out her arms, feeling accomplished but also very tired.

But she pushed on, spacing her feet shoulder-width apart, legs slightly bent at the knees. She thrust the hairpin forward and willed it to grow, and it answered, extending several feet until it was the length of an actual sword.

Emily smiled and went through the same steps she had been taught as a child that were stored deep in her muscle memory. In a blur, she went through a set of twirls and kicks and into a roll, leaping to her feet and backpedaling, doing a cartwheel and repeating. The more she moved and thrust and jumped, the more excited the crowd of Maishaes became.

“Ok. That’s enough for one day,” said Cheedi, stepping down onto the grass and walking over to Emily. “You should really eat, my lady.”

Emily nodded, rubbing her stomach, and smiled. “Yes, please have a meal brought here.” Cheedi bowed and immediately scampered off in a flurry with several others behind her.

Emily sat down on the veranda and sighed, feeling tired but happy as several servants made a fuss by fanning and dabbing her off with towels. Several minutes later, others brought her a meal of grilled fish, greens, and rice with several slices of various fruits, and a large steaming bowl of some kind of stew.

Emily rarely had the chance to eat fresh fish, and the taste was unlike anything she had ever had. The rice was soft and fluffy, the greens mixed and seasoned with sweet chili and a little salt; she could taste the sweet yet hot spice. She devoured the meal and ordered more.

“My lady, I don’t think you should eat anymore,” said Cheedi.

“I’ll be fine. This is so good, I don’t mind being a little full,” Emily smiled.

***

The others were early risers, coming and going from the main house fastidiously. Always rushing about and preparing for the day.

Emily was fascinated by all the activity and enjoyed watching them hustle about, seemingly in no particular hurry, but somehow always getting the work done.

She often joined them as they gathered in an open field and practiced a form of what Emily thought was very much like the Tai Chi she used to watch the old people doing in the park near her home back on Earth.

Her days were filled with the same routines of Dit-da-dow soaks, milk and honey soaks, long massages, and training to regain her strength. Soon, she noticed her body beginning to heal and muscle mass return.

“How are the scars, my lady?” asked Cheedi.

“I see progress,” Emily blushed. “It’s not perfect, but they’re healing. There’re lots of mental scars that won’t go away though. Not yet anyway.”

Cheedi nodded sadly. “I was once a servant in the House of Anele Suhyuh. I know far too well what it means to carry mental scars. Lady Maishae saved me,” Cheedi said, looking down.

“Is that why you serve her?”

“Yes. It is my honor to serve her. I would have done anything to be here serving Princess Yuyuki too, and now I can.” Cheedi bowed, smiling.

***

A few weeks passed, and the weather turned cooler as the sky began to thicken. It was a pleasant coolness, but at night, a chill set in, with a wind that blew away the heat. Emily could not sleep after laying awake trying to do so for over an hour. She finally left her room and sat out on the veranda, staring out into the night sky watching the glow of the moon.

The moon was full, a flat, dazzling disk; it reminded Emily of a mirror.

"The mirrors," she whispered to herself. "Maishae."

Emily closed her eyes and remembered sitting with Maishae as a child. The old woman sat behind her but held the mirror up in front of them so that it caught both their reflections.

"Don't concentrate on our reflections, but the wall that lies behind us. Look deeper into the mirror and now imagine the wall becoming a golden meadow beneath a warm pink sky. Concentrate on the wall. See it become the meadow."

"Ah! I see!" said Yuyuki.

"Good! Now accept that it is real. Just as real as the room we are sitting in now."

Yuyuki relaxed her shoulders and breathed slower as the wall behind them seemed to fade away and become that of a golden meadow beneath a pink sky. They were sitting on soft grass now. She could smell moist, salty air as though a sea were nearby, and she could feel the warmth of a setting sun on her back.

"Wow, grandmother! We are here!"

"Very good, Yuyuki. Now, take us back."

"But can't we stay? It's so pretty!"

"In due time. Now focus on the sky in the mirror and see my chambers."

This time, the image came much easier for Yuyuki, but before they could be transported back, Maishae reached out and placed the tip of her finger on the mirror and held the image of her chambers in place.

"Now I want you to see the garden outside of my chambers. Imagine the pond, see the bridge."

Yuyuki began to see it in her mind's eye. Maishae slowly moved her finger horizontally across the mirror, moving the image of her inner chambers along with it - until the full image of the garden came into view. Seconds later, they were sitting in the garden. Yuyuki jumped up with excitement, turned around, and hugged her grandmother. The old woman beamed with pride.

Emily walked back into her bedroom, sighing, "Why was she bringing me here? And why pretend to be Grandmother Aiyo?"

She crawled back into bed, burying herself under its covers. "And what are those mirrors?" she wondered. "I don't know what the old bat is up to, but I want out. And it seems the only way to get out of this place and back to Earth is to get ahold of one of them. I have to get one of her mirrors!" she thought, and finally drifted off to sleep.

A Reunion

Emily woke earlier than the others and decided to go out into the garden and pull weeds, one of their many morning chores. She had pulled a few when she heard a voice that shook her to her very core.

"Emily? Is it really you?"

She waited a moment and then turned slowly to look in his direction. And there stood a young man in linen robes, with long blue hair that fell in a braid down his back. A long moment of utter stillness passed before she was able to speak.

"Seitogi?"

His dark eyes smiled, "Is it really you, Emily? I can't believe it! You're here in The Pocket!"

"Seitogi. It's you! You're alive! I was so heartbroken." She felt the aching in her chest and ran to him, throwing her arms around his neck and hugging him close. He held her tightly, tears of joy streaming down his face.

"I thought you were dead."

"Wow Emily. I thought the same of you."

Finally, she pulled away and looked into his eyes. There was a great sadness there, beneath the tears.

"Abete Seitogi," she said. "Why are you here? How are you even alive?"

"I was pulled from the water by the witch," Seitogi said, his voice low. "Come, we must walk. There is much that needs to be said, and no time to lose."

He turned, and they walked side by side across the garden and through a low archway in the wall. Finally, Emily could stand it no longer.

"Where are we going, Seitogi?" she asked.

“Somewhere we can talk without the others hearing us.” They continued, in silence, until they reached a patch of forest that lay adjacent to the property.

“But where have you been? I arrived weeks ago!”

“I’ve been here close to half a year now. Trying to find my way back to Behra. Walking in circles for months. I ran out of provisions; that’s the only reason I came back today. Otherwise, I live out in the wild.”

“I suspected I was trapped here,” said Emily. “But I didn’t want to raise suspicions by asking.”

“I can’t say for certain that we are either,” said Seitogi. “How did you arrive here? What happened after I died?”

“I was captured by the Aiyo and held prisoner in their dungeon until Maishae rescued me and brought me here.”

Seitogi’s eyes misted over, and he put a hand on her shoulder. “Emily, I’m so sorry. I failed to protect you.”

“You mustn’t. I should be the one apologizing. I was horrible to you, Seita. I’m so sorry; I hope you can forgive me. I have no excuse for behaving the way I did towards you.” Emily took his hands into hers and squeezed softly.

“No. No, Emily, you have every reason in the world to hate me. It’s like you said. I took you from your peaceful life and brought you into all this suffering. My one job was protecting you from the Aiyo.”

“But it was my own fault! I should have listened to you in the first place…you called me Emily!”

“But it’s who you are, isn’t it? I apologize for refusing to see it before…for refusing to see you, Emily.”

“I get it now, Seita,” Emily’s voice grew quiet as she stared into his watering eyes. “I know you meant well. In fact, you’ve wanted nothing but the best for me ever since we were children.

It was always you by my side until they took me back to Odahni and changed me."

"Emily," Seitogi stared into her eyes, just as moist as his own.

She reached up and brushed a single tear from his cheek. In that moment, all she wanted was to hold and reassure him that everything would work out for the best in the end. But before she knew what was happening, she drew him in and softly placed her lips on his.

The feel of his warm lips was overwhelming, causing her to swoon. Seitogi smiled, pleased that she was feeling the same way he had been for so long.

"I shouldn't have done that," she said, pulling back, now afraid she had done something terribly wrong.

"Yes, you should, if my dreams were right. Come, I need to show you something."

They walked together through the dense forest in silence, deep in thought, now and then stopping to pick some wild mushrooms. Soon they came upon a makeshift hut that was fashioned from branches, mud, and bark.

Seitogi led her to the front of the hut, where a pile of dead branches were stacked next to a fire pit.

"This is where I live," he said, and motioned her to sit down on a stump. Emily sat and watched Seitogi arrange the branches in the pit and set them ablaze with a flint stone. The wood crackled and blazed brightly.

"I'll be right back, Emily." Seitogi disappeared inside the hut once the fire was burning; Emily could hear him moving things around. He returned from inside the hut with a dented kettle and a loaf of stale bread. He broke the loaf in half and tossed one half to Emily.

Emily picked at the loaf with her fingers and watched the fire grow. In the meantime, Seitogi filled the kettle with water from a small brook; he came back and placed it carefully over the fire.

“I never thought I would see you again,” Emily said.

“I was afraid to even hope for such a thing,” Seitogi sat next to her.

“There are so many things I want to ask you.”

“Like?” Seitogi asked.

“Like, how did you get pulled out of the water? How did she know to find you?”

“No idea. But when I came to, there was a group of the others mending my wounds. I remember very little of that. But they were all kind to me. Even when I eventually tried to escape, they stopped me for my own good.”

“It’s a good thing they did,” Emily said.

“They are nice enough. Never felt a sense of danger from them, but they still make me uneasy because they all look like her.”

“I know, it’s weird! One of them lived in my world as my grandmother, Dolores Heart. Turns out she was the former head of staff for this place. On the other hand, Maishae also pretended to be my Aiyo grandmother before even sending me to Earth.”

“Grandmother?”

“Yeah, I know. Sounds bonkers, right? But I have all these memories of her training me in martial arts, weapons. All this esoteric stuff. I initially thought it all took place at Odahni, but now I realize that she was bringing me here the whole time. I even remember the others. They always doted on me and were always kinder than she. Apparently, I’m their young mistress.”

“Forgive me for saying it, but that all sounds very bizarre,” said Seitogi. “Perhaps Dou Dadachi was correct.”

“The priest?” Emily asked, unsure.

"He was terribly suspicious of the wizened woman's intentions towards you. I told him what she told me, that you were in grave danger from the Aiyo, which turned out to be true, but well, I can't help but feel she might have had ulterior motives the whole time. I was just so focused on getting you back I didn't see it."

The two grew quiet. Each contemplating the strangeness of their situation. The fire crackled in the silence as Emily consumed her half of the loaf by dipping it in the tea, and Seitogi sat beside her, lost in thought.

"I've wandered around here for weeks," she said. "I never wanted to ask Cheedi, or admit that I was a prisoner, but now I am scared of not knowing what my purpose for being here is."

Seitogi thought for a moment, "I don't claim to have all the answers for you. But I can assure you that there is nothing for you to be afraid of. I won't fail again."

Emily nodded, unsure if she actually believed his words, but knowing she could not go on as she had done for the past weeks. When they returned, Cheedi was there to greet them at the door. She gasped and held her hands to her mouth.

"My, well if it isn't Sir Abete," she said in her delicate, squeak of a voice.

Seitogi burst out laughing, "You are always so formal, Cheedi," he said.

Emily glanced over at him, then at Cheedi and grinned. Emily's hand on Seitogi's shoulder made Cheedi's face bloom into a rosy blush. Cheedi cleared her throat and bowed.

"I do apologize. Breakfast has been prepared for the princess. Please stay and eat with us, Sir Abete."

"I would love to," Seitogi said.

Emily and Seitogi spent the following weeks training and reacquainting themselves with one another. Their memories were a bit foggy, but that didn't stop them from becoming friends again.

During their morning runs, Emily told Seitogi about Earth and high school life. Seitogi thought it sounded strange; Earth had elements similar to his world, but the technology included things that had no place being in the natural world. Throughout their runs, Seitogi found himself daydreaming about Emily. He was amused by her seriousness but intrigued by her forward nature as well.

One morning he woke early and walked over to the others' sleeping dorms.

"Good morning," he said as he entered.

"Morning, boss," said an other, who was sitting toward the center of the room around a table. "I see you are up early; I was just making some tea."

Seitogi worked his way over to the table. "I will be needing to borrow a few of you later on today if that is okay."

"sounds good," said the other as she poured him a cup.

Later that day, he and Emily stood in an open clearing when he turned to her and said, "I'm thinking of adding a little twist to our training today."

"What might that be, Sir Abete?" she asked.

Seitogi blushed, "Instead of taking on one opponent at a time, when we train, we will be engaging many at once."

"How do we do that?" Emily asked.

Seitogi whistled twice. The loudness startled Emily.

"What is it?"

"The others," he said, pointing. Four of the others walked towards them from the house, each carrying a metal staff. One, her face lined with age, carried a staff with a long blade upon it.

Emily gasped. "I've never seen them look so fierce."

Seitogi smiled. "I trained with them a bit while recovering. They may be imps, but they are as skilled as any Dhukai I've known."

"Scary," Emily grabbed her hairpin and sank into a defensive stance as it grew into a six-foot staff.

"I don't think I'll ever get used to seeing that," he joked.

"Are you ready, princess?"

"I've been a punching bag for long enough." she said.

"It's time to hit back!"

The first other attacked with a hard jab to Seitogi's abdomen. He blocked it and threw a jab of his own at the same time. The second other struck; Seitogi deflected and threw a right hook. The others backed off and circled around them, twirling their staffs.

They went in for the attack. Emily found herself double-teamed. Seitogi too found himself attacked from both sides. He was thrown, quickly recovered and swung wildly at the duo, managing to land a twisting kick to one of the others.

Emily blocked another strike, but had her legs swept from under her with an other's staff. She managed to retain her balance by leaning into her own staff, but a blow to the kidney stung. The others looked on at her, amused.

"Hey, that's a pretty damned hard hit!" she shouted.

"Forgive us, but the young mistress must always be prepared!" shouted the others in unison.

They twirled their staffs, and this time their strikes were lightning fast. They struck from all sides, and Emily found she was growing dizzy from the flurry of assaults. She backpedaled. The others fell into a four-way dance, slowly circling her.

She managed to lean on an old willow tree and caught her breath.

"Enough," she said. "Give me a moment to rest." Seitogi was breathing hard, and his face was red from his fight.

"I told you they were skilled," he said as he took a water skin from his pack.

The others huddled. "Aye, you're right," said the one with the blade. "We've bored her enough with this routine."

"Bored!" said Emily, "You damn near killed me."

The others glanced at the ground. "The young mistress needs more training," they said in unison. "But you have improved greatly," all four again.

"Others!" Emily rolled her eyes. A satisfied grin crept across Seitogi's face. "You think this is funny, don't you?" she asked him.

"You were amazing," he said.

"Amazing," the four Maishaes said again, in unison.

***

"I'm not sure of what I'm doing, but I'm sure I'm doing it right," Emily said yawing. It was towards the end of her third week with Seitogi.

Both sat out front of the estate on a colorful mat, woven by the others from stringy tree bark.

"It will all come together," said Seitogi. He pulled out a pocket watch and looked through the lens, mimicking the act of reading time by opening and closing its lid.

"Where did you get that?" Emily asked.

"I found it in the forest a while back. I believe it's some sort of compass, but its directions are all off. Probably why I can't find a way to at least neighboring land."

"No, it's not a compass!" said Emily, "It's one of those old school Winston Churchill watches! There would usually be a chain attached to it. Here, let me see it," she said as she reached for it.

He handed it to her. The watch denoted military time marks, and its hands were frozen at 13:13.

"Holy crap, look, it's made in England," she said as she inspected it in turn. "This is crazy! Why would this be here?"

Emily stood and began to pace, "Something's wrong here, or wrong with me. I don't know… I don't know if any of this is real. Like maybe I've died, and all of this is like purgatory, eternally taunting my soul or something!"

"I don't know what any of that means, Emily, but…"

"No, Seita! You don't understand. If I'm not dead, then I have to at least be locked away somewhere in an insane asylum!" she began to weep.

"I'm here for you. You're going to be okay. I promise." Seitogi took Emily's hands.

"But what am I going to do?" Emily's eyes widened. "I want to go home. I want my old life back!"

Seitogi nodded, unsure of what to say. He slowly reached for her and drew her into a hug. "I'm so sorry to put you through this. I'll help you get back."

"How can I get back Seita? My mother's dead. My father is a demon. I'm sorry. I don't know what I'm saying. I keep getting confused, lost. Sometimes I don't know who I am."

"It's okay," he said, trying to comfort her. He stroked her back, as he brushed away her tears. "It is going to be alright."

"I'm sorry, I'm like totally bugging out on you," Emily seemed embarrassed, "I must be suffering from a little PTSD from being imprisoned for so long. Whatever. I'm sorry."

"It's okay, you don't have to apologize."

"You should go. I'm a mess right now." Emily said.

"No. I don't want to. I don't want to leave you all alone like this."

They sat back down on the mat, in silence.

"A while ago, you said Master Abete disowned you, and exiled you from Daiye. Why?" Emily whispered. "I remember you two being very close."

"One day, Aiyo Yulori and his soldiers appeared in our village. He demanded my father turn you over to him. Lord Aiyo threatened to burn the village down if he refused. I took you and tried to escape, but he chased us down and snatched you from my arms. I managed to pull him off of his horse and grab you, but we were surrounded."

"Lord Aiyo ordered my father to behead me. Otherwise, everyone would've been slaughtered, all because of me. My father begged him to show us mercy, and then the Lord struck me with his riding crop, here," Seitogi rubbed a small scar in the middle of his forehead, "He told my father I was to be exiled. I had just turned twelve. After that, I had nowhere to go, so I went to Master Yienguoi-Jin, and he took me in."

"How did you come to know my father?" Emily asked.

"It was a few months before the Aiyo took you. During the winter some local bandits attempted to kidnap you. I killed them all but Master Yienguoi-Jin stepped in and took you. I followed him back to his lair. I waited for night to fall and snuck inside and rescued you. Master Yienguoi-Jin caught us as we were leaving, and we fought, but he was just playing with me. In the end, he cited my bravery and allowed me to return with you to Daiye. But he promised he'd always keep an eye on us. Master Yienguoi-Jin is a wise man. He's very powerful. I owe him my life. I will forever be in his debt whether he cares or not."

"Oh, spit out the Kool-Aid, Seita, he's a douchebag."

"That doesn't sound very nice."

"Oh, it isn't, but it's apt. I don't care that he's my dad, or rather the sperm donor who helped fertilize me."

Seitogi looked blank, and Emily stifled a laugh, "Jeez, Seita, you're like twenty-two, twenty-three. Don't you know anything about how a baby is made?"

Seitogi appeared outwardly confused, "Well, let's not go into detail," he said.

"Oh, someone's blushing, I can tell." Emily smiled.

The two of them continued talking for the remainder of the afternoon, enjoying the peace and quiet. Afterwards, they went to join the others and Cheedi for dinner. It was a simple meal noodles, a meat sauce, and hard-boiled eggs in vinegar. Emily added a few vegetables to the mix, making a salad.

Seitogi was relieved that she seemed more like herself again. After dinner, Cheedi served what was left of the plum wine. Soon after, the others started to conk out, their energy drained by the long day's work. Emily and Seitogi were among the last still talking.

There were still a few blinks of light in the sky, but the moon was near its zenith, so Seitogi and Emily sat on the steps together. They could connect so well here. There was no one to bother them or get in their way. Emily leaned her head against Seitogi's shoulder. He put his arm around her.

"My feelings for you are so strong. I wish there was something I could say," he thought.

"Well, you two look nice and cozy," said Maishae. Emily immediately sprang up and looked around. She had not heard or seen Maishae approach, but there she was, standing in front of them. Where the others seemed well-fed and healthy, she appeared dry and withered.

"Maishae, how long…"

"Long enough," the old wizened woman chuckled, "I have a present for you." Maishae reached behind her and grabbed a dirty, knotted cloth from her back. She placed it in Emily's hands.

Emily unfolded the cloth. It was a white and green kimono with a pale tan pattern covering it. Emily glanced up at Maishae with a quizzical look.

"That belonged to my grandmother when she was a young woman," beamed Maishae.

"She was very beautiful and even more powerful. She told me it would bring luck and happiness to the wearer." Maishae looked into the distance. "And now it will do the same for you," she looked Emily in the eye, "but it means more."

"Maishae, I… I'm…"

"It is time to move on to greater things, my dear," Maishae cut her off.

"Where have you been?" Emily demanded. "It's been almost three months!"

"Not in Berahni. Time acts differently depending on where I am."

"Well at least tell us what you've been up to."

"I had to retrieve my special little trinket you let Lord Aiyo take from you. I stole it back!" she took the mirror from her robe and held it up for Emily to see.

"Now I have my set again!" the old woman turned and raised an eyebrow. "Eh, Seitogi, I see you came back. I thought you had had your fill of this place. You should have seen how he wailed and tore at his hair when he thought you were dead. Oh, the moaning and self-loathing. It was quite entertaining."

"She may make fun, but I suffered greatly thinking you were dead."

"See that then!" said Maishae, "Isn't he precious? And such a handsome face."

She squeezed his bicep, "He's strong too. You've seen it for yourself," she then squeezed his crotch, "And virile! Unspoiled. For he has yet to spill his seed! Not even for Arymaitei, huh…"

"Oh my god, you're horrible!" exclaimed Emily, covering her face, blushing.

"Keep your hands to yourself, you!" Seitogi used an elbow to push the old woman away.

Maishae burst out laughing, "Oh, shy boy! How could you not just love him," she leapt up, pinching both his cheeks.

"Stop teasing him," Emily said, reaching over and separating the two.

"Won't you two join me inside for tea?" Maishae turned and hobbled away. Emily looked at Seitogi and smiled before getting up to follow her into the house.

"This ought to be interesting," he said, getting up to join her.

Minutes later, the three were seated around a tea table in Maishae's chambers, a thin cloud of mist and steam curling around their drinks. "Okay, so I have at least four questions right off the bat," Emily said, "The first being. Just where in the hell are we?"

"We are in a pocket dimension of my making… well, my finding to be more accurate," replied Maishae. Emily detected a little bit of pride in her voice. She picked up the mirror and stared at her reflection, "And is it this mirror, that is the gateway to this dimension?"

"And countless others."

"But how come Seitogi couldn't get it to work?"

"Oh! Because he's not the best listener. I specifically told him he needed you to activate the mirror for the return trip."

Maishae reached over the small, lacquered table and tugged at Seitogi's ear. He winced. "This," she said as if he were a stubborn child. "This wouldn't have become so complicated if you had better comprehension skills."

"I did what I thought was best. Don't try and blame this on me."

Emily dared a try, staring at the background of the room in her reflection and gasping; it was slowly changing into open blue sky.

She was becoming transfixed as the sounds in the room became muffled and distant, and suddenly it was all gone as Maishae snatched away the mirror.

"Careful, girl. If you don't know where you are looking for, you'll end up getting lost. It might take me years to find you again!"

"It felt so weird. I was beginning to hear seagulls, I think. It's absolutely fascinating."

"Indeed, and dangerous too," Maishae nodded. "Which is exactly why you are here. I have so much to teach you."

"Teach me?"

"Yes. No rush, of course, but we mustn't dally about either. Nyongoyuchi is abuzz with the royal engagement! I must prepare us, for we will be crashing the festivities! Or rather I will, but that is neither here nor there. The less time lost before our arrival, the better."

"Excuse me," said Emily.

"We will discuss it in the morning. You look quite exhausted."

"I am," Emily nodded. "Seitogi, will you escort me back to my room, please?"

"Heh', eh, no funny business, huh," Maishae said. "I don't want you to ruin my body any more than you already have."

Seitogi held Emily's hand as Maishae watched them go. The old woman sighed and looked out the window to the night sky.

"It's time for me to move on from this," she said quietly to herself.

***

"She is really starting to freak me out," Emily said once they hit the hall. "I'm afraid to go to sleep. I'll wake up with her standing over me."

"She can be very strange."

"Really strange."

"Let's discuss this in the morning. I'll come wake you up. We need to talk anyway."

"No, let's talk now. Come inside," Emily pulled Seitogi into her room and ushered him out onto its veranda.

They stood there silent for several moments looking up at the stars when Seitogi began massaging her neck.

"What?" He said, his cheeks warming.

"Don't you try anything weird," Emily leaned into the warmth of his touch as he kneaded away her aches.

"I think I can get us out of here if I could get ahold of one of those mirrors," she said. "I may even be able to get us back to Earth. Or at least I think so."

"So, you were planning on leaving?"

"I have to. I don't feel particularly safe here. I mean, Maishae's giving me real Gingerbread Hag from Hansel and Gretel vibes, you know what I'm saying."

"I'm afraid I don't, but would you mind if I were to come with you?"

"Of course, you are coming too. We just have to rescue Rebecca and Darren first. I'll snag a few jewels to sell over in the diamond district back home, and we'll be sitting pretty in a condo in the city in no time."

"Sounds nice," he hugged her close, and they stared out into the sky in silence when Emily noticed a star. It was brighter than the rest and appeared to twinkle with alternating green and red lights.

"Hey, Seitogi. Look at that up there." Emily pointed; he followed her long finger to the twinkling in the sky. "Have you ever seen a star like that in the skies of Behra?"

"Can't say that I have," Seitogi stared hard at the light. "It looks as though it is…alive?"

"I know where I've seen a star like that before! Over the city! That, my friend, is a satellite!"

"Is that good? Not good?"

"It's not magic, that's for damn sure, and Maishae's no witch!" Emily walked back into the room and grabbed her Earth clothes, mended, washed and folded into a bundle.

"Do me a favor. Hold on to these and meet me back at your camp in half an hour."

"Where are you going?" Seitogi asked as she stuffed her belongings into a bag.

"I'm not waiting! I'm getting that mirror tonight!" Emily said, tossing him the bag and throwing the door open. "It's time to find my story's end and stop this nonsense!" she said as she stormed out of her room and marched back towards Maishae's chambers.

Eleanor Celeste

Emily marched into Maishae's chambers, fists clenched, anger simmering in her veins. She found the old woman putting away her tea utensils. The wizened woman didn't seem to notice her at first. Emily's eyes looked about for one of the others or Cheedi. She wanted to be sure she was alone with the old witch before she went on the attack.

"Back in the dungeon when you rescued me, you said you were a scientist. You weren't just speaking figuratively, were you? There is a satellite floating overhead! And Seitogi has a pocket watch made in the United Kingdom. Just what is all of this?"

"You are so excited, my dear, and shouldn't be. But I understand your confusion," said Maishae in a calm manner.

"Do you?"

"Just be patient. All will be set right in the end."

"End of what? Dammit, stop being so vague!" Emily's patience was wearing thin. What was this old woman planning to do? It all seemed impossible, a woman living in a remote valley a satellite passes every night. It all seemed like lunacy.

"Sit child, and listen," she said to Emily as she sat down in front of her.

At length, Emily took a seat, arms folded, and Maishae began to tell her story.

"We are one in the same, you and I, aren't we? We were always too curious for our own good."

"What do you mean, we?"

"At one time, well, a very long time ago. Or one could say a long time from now. We, you, and I, were once called Eleanor Celeste, a rather prominent physicist from Earth, year 2133."

Emily wore a blank expression, Maishae continued -

"We worked for BP-CAST," she paused and waited for a sign of recognition from Emily, but her expression remained unchanged.

"The Bronson-Pinfold Center for Advanced Science and Technology. We were on the team that helped develop the fading mirrors alongside our senior research physicist. Dr. Eihn Pinfold." She leaned over and took up an ornate box housing the two mirrors and ran her hand over them.

"Back then, Eleanor was the youngest member of the team. We were considered a prodigy of sorts." She winked.

She took out a locket from around her neck and offered it to Emily. When Emily opened it, she saw a picture of a woman who looked similar enough to herself, albeit differed in complexion and height. The woman was dressed in a white lab coat and wore her blondish hair shoulder length and had large glasses. Standing next to her was a handsome man who appeared to be serious and scholarly.

"There we are with Dr. Pinfold," Emily could detect a sense of pride in the old woman's voice.

"I had such deep admiration for him," she said, reminiscing. "He was the lead for our team at BP-CAST and the son of the company's founders. Despite his family's legacy, he was brilliant in his own right, kind, and deeply intelligent.

However, one day our lab was breached by armed men. They started shooting everyone. All of my colleagues were being killed. In a moment of desperation, I grabbed three of the experimental mirrors and used one to escape. It was a risky move, but I felt it was my only chance to survive."

"OK, pause," Emily raised her hand.

"You are telling me this was you. A woman who almost looks exactly like me?" she was pointing to the photograph. Her heart began racing, and she desperately felt a need to laugh but suppressed it. She had to keep her mind on the goal of gaining a mirror, no matter what the crazy old bat told her.

Lies, that's what they were, she told herself. It was terrible nonsense, and so she smiled.

"But how exactly do they work?"

"The mirrors are equipped with some of the most advanced technology you'll ever see. At the heart of it all is the Bronson-Pinfold neural interface, which is able to read and interpret your thoughts and visualizations."

"OK, but how?"

"The way it works is, as you focus your thoughts and visualizations on where you want to go, the neural interface takes that information and turns it into complex algorithms. Those algorithms then modulate the light reflecting off the mirror's surface, creating a resonant frequency that opens a stable wormhole through space-time. The neural interface is so precise that it can extract information about your desired destination from your thoughts and use that information to calibrate the portal to the correct location. Once the portal takes shape in the mirror's reflection, you simply step through the mirror's surface and into the other dimension."

"Really, all of that from a mirror?" Emily sounded skeptical. "Sounds like a bunch of Star Trek mumbo-jumbo you ask me."

. "Do you find it so hard to believe that all of this could be achieved through a mirror?" Maishae's voice grew stern as she spoke to Emily.

" I used them, yes, to escape a brutal death. But what I found on the other side was a harsh reality. The atmosphere of that place was unbearable, and it took a toll on my body. I had to keep jumping from one world to another until I finally found a safe haven. But by the time I arrived here, I had aged significantly due to all the time I spent hopping through dimensions."

"And what about Behra? You just happened upon it too?"

Maishae averted her gaze to the open veranda overlooking the garden.

"It's a bit of both. Our father was a Japanese theoretical physicist, and our mother came from a prominent physics family in Nigeria. Growing up, we frequently visited both countries and were fascinated by their rich cultural histories.

I believe our subconscious combined elements from both cultures and guided us to Behra. That's how impactful the mirrors can be."

"Hold on a minute," Emily interjected, clapping her hands. "Are you saying that Behra is just a product of your imagination?"

"No, not exactly," Maishae corrected her. "Behra didn't originate from our imagination. Its houses, politics, and wars were already in existence before we arrived. Our subconscious thoughts and imaginings simply shaped its form and appearance, but it was always here waiting to be found. Do you follow?"

For the sake of convenience, Emily nodded her head, even though she didn't fully grasp the concept.

"Child, let me explain. Our travels through the mirrors are based on probability. That's the reason I used them to flee from danger."

"I see," said Emily, "That's why Berahni has elements of Japanese and Nigerian culture. But hold on, I remember you bringing me here when I lived with the Aiyo?"

"Yes, I would come at night when you were asleep and bring you into the pocket. One hour in Behra can be several hours or even a day here, so no one would notice your absence."

"But why?"

"I needed you to have a refined upbringing in a powerful house. I can wield a certain amount of influence in Behra, but I've had my eye on the imperial crown for quite some time now. And so house Aiyo was the easiest route. However, Duke Suhyuh threw a monkey wrench in my plans and exiled you to death. But when I did find you again, the only way to get you back in Odahni was to sideline Shumayuki. I engineered her a floating chaise lounge later, out of guilt, but sacrifices…"

"What! It was you?" Emily stood now, shocked.

"Shush child. Let me continue."

Emily listened intently but could barely keep in her anger; it felt like the old woman was doing all of this to torment her.

"And so I was able to engineer your way back into Odahni as the heir's bride-to-be. But then that damned Yienguoi-Jin got in the way and kidnapped you away to Smitemae. Bastard that he was. Luckily, I was able to woo Chua with a considerable bribe to turn you back over to me during the summer festival."

"Awei! Wow!"

"But the very night I got you back, I was betrayed by my own right hand. I had no idea Pheptae had figured out how to use the mirrors. It was she who took you away to Earth. She knew I could no longer traverse different worlds in this body. It would've killed me. You see, the pocket exists within the dimensional realm of Behra, whereas Earth is another world completely with its own planetary system."

"Why! Why would she kidnap me right after you had done so?"

"We had a disagreement on the course of your upbringing. And for the record, I didn't kidnap you."

"And why was she able to travel between worlds and not you? You're twins, right? And even me. Why didn't I grow all old and shriveled with all the times you brought me here as a child?"

"Because I had already taken the hit for us."

"Meaning?"

"It took me years to figure it out, but you see, one has to calibrate themselves to the mirrors before just using them willy-nilly. I didn't do that. With the duress I was under when our lab was attacked. I didn't have time to."

"That didn't answer a thing!"

"You just aren't listening, child. I believe it is too hard for you to accept the obvious?" Maishae waited for a response, received none, and then continued.

"I wanted myself back. Not to live out my days as this haggard old troll. So I began cloning myself with plans to raise a new me from birth, and then simply upload my mind to the body when she was mature enough. But my cloning chamber malfunctioned during the first run, and it spit out over three hundred copies of me as I am now."

"The others," Emily covered her mouth in shock.

"Simple things they were. None possessed my brilliance. Pheptae was the smartest of the bunch, but still a dolt by my standards. However, I thought it wouldn't have been ethical to destroy them."

"Because mind swapping an innocent person isn't?"

"It's a common practice in 2133… not mind swapping, but uploading a backup of yourself to a biological clone if you can afford it. Anyway, I tried hundreds of times, but kept getting the same results."

"Hold on here! Are you suggesting that I'm your clone?"

"My first successful one!"

"But I'm Yienguoi-Jin's daughter…" Emily's voice went high. *"Careful now,"* she told herself. *"Calm down. Remember you want the mirrors."*

"The mistake was that I was cloning myself from my own DNA. To get the proper distribution of growth genes, I still needed a host sperm and a host egg. So I took Yanguit's semen while he lay injured in my lair, and I retrieved several of Ameiki's eggs while she slept, and made the mix. All the embryos died save you, and so I impregnated Ameiki, again as she slept. That was after Yienguoi-Jin had lain with her of course, so they are in fact your parents. But at the end of it all. You are me… or shall soon be."

"You're not lobotomizing me! Oh my god, the thought of being any part of you is gross!"

"There is no lobotomy involved. The technology is very sound."

"I don't care about that! Ever since I came to this place, people have been telling me what I am, and what I'm not! But you're the grandmother of them all! You literally want to possess me!"

"Saucy girl. I've successfully transferred copies of myself to several of the others; those I had to destroy of course, as they thought they were me."

"You're a monster! It's gruesome!"

"Now you sound just like Pheptae did that night, with all her carrying on about letting you live your own life. Now stop fussing. You wouldn't even be alive if not for me! You are my property. That is my body!"

"So, what will happen to me? Emily Heart?"

"What? Don't worry about her, dear. Emily is just a construct of your mind. When you are me, I will finally be me again, and she'll be gone."

"It's not my fault that you turned old early! I'm not going to just let you erase me!"

"Well, you've obviously had a hard enough time being you. I'd think you'd be happy to become someone so brilliant as I."

"I knew I couldn't trust you."

"Oh, don't be upset. What would you rather be, weak and inefficient as you are now? When I found you, you were gaunt and frail."

"I have spent the last few months locked in a dark cell eating mush, lady! What's your excuse? You dried up old prune. I refuse your offer!"

"Well, it's not an offer! And to be frank, you belong to me because you are me. Admit it, you can feel me coursing through your veins even as we speak. Now I've gone through considerable trouble to get you here, so don't be difficult."

The sounds of a scuffle outside the room could be heard intermingled with the thump of heavy footsteps.

“What’s that?” Maishae stood wide-eyed at the door.

Emily looked over to the door. “What’s going on?” she asked.

The door slid open, and two others marched in, restraining Seitogi. “Caught him eavesdropping on you, o’l mistress.”

“My guards did well.” She leaned onto the table again and took a deep breath.

“Seitogi, my boy, tell me. What exactly is a clone?”

“Um… I don’t know, but if it upsets Emily.”

Emily stood and angrily pushed past the guards. “I’m going back to my room.”

Seitogi shook off the others and followed her.

“Alert the medical team,” Maishae turned to the others. “I want to do the procedure tonight.”

Emily grabbed Seitogi’s hand and pulled him along with her out of the house and into the garden. As they approached a corner patch, she stopped.

“Why didn’t you wait for me back at your camp like we planned?”

“I was worried. Hey, what was all that stuff she was saying back there?”

“It’s too hard… soul-shattering to explain now. I just know we have to get out of here now!” She pulled a mirror from her robe just as an alarm began to sound. Seitogi pointed to two others on the roof blowing long tubular horns.

“This way,” he grabbed Emily’s hand and ran across the garden to a small thicket of trees.

“Can you get that thing working?” he asked as they ran.

"My heart is pounding," Emily said. "I have to concentrate!" She held up the mirror. "I know how to do this."

"You crafty girl!" Maishae stepped out of a portal in front of them, with a line of others behind her brandishing various weapons.

"You have something that belongs to me, dear."

"You're wrong." Emily held up the small mirror. "This belongs to me."

"But you are me… the new me, but me!" Maishae countered.

"I say that you are the old, inferior me instead."

"Very well. Subdue them."

A large other with a scythe-like weapon stepped forward.

"Any of you who does not accept my mistress' offer will be destroyed."

"No, you fool! I didn't say destroy them," Maishae chided. "I need them both alive!"

"Both!" said Emily.

"Take her." Maishae commanded.

The others attacked as a group. Seitogi jumped in front of Emily brandishing his dagger. The scythe wielder showed him the business end of her blade. She slashed at Seitogi, hitting him with the flat side, sending him flying into the thicket of trees.

"Seitogi!" Emily took off through the brush after him.

"Get the boy too!" Maishae yelled.

Seitogi regained his footing and performed a series of cartwheels and spins to keep his attacker off balance, all the while drawing back and striking at their legs.

The scythe wielder advanced on him and aimed for a stab. Seitogi grabbed her wrist and pulled her in close.

He then gave her a strong headbutt, which knocked the scythe from her hands. his momentum carried the two of them into the thicket, still fighting.

Emily ran into the thicket, slicing and hacking at branches as she ran. The air was filled with the sounds of multiple strikes, and the impact of Seitogi's knife against wood.

"Seitogi!" Emily called. "Seitogi!"

She pushed past a branch and stumbled into the underbrush. She looked up to see the large other lying on the ground. Seitogi was standing next to her, his blade wet with blood.

"Hurry!" he said, "get behind me."

Emily looked over to see two more charging toward them. Seitogi raised his dagger and jumped in, slicing once at the first one, then hacking at the second. He then turned and sliced twice at the final attacker in one fluid motion. The three of them toppled together.

Seitogi reached down to help Emily up, but she was staring into the mirror intently. She imagined, of all people, Aiyo Yumeiko. She stared at the fuzzy room that became clearer by the second and nodded.

"Come on." She grabbed Seitogi's hand and jumped forward. They had entered the portal and on the other side, Emily ended up tumbling out onto the floor of a sparsely furnished, but luxurious room. She watched from the corner of her eye as Seitogi followed suit, landing in a crouch on the soft tatami beside her.

The Pearl Swan

"Ghost! Ghost! Ghost!" The loud cries echoed through the empty room as the maid dropped her wash basin, spilling its contents on the floor, and fled through the open door.

"There's a ghost in the temple!" She screamed, running down the oaken corridor as her fellow servants emerged from their rooms to see what the commotion was.

Emily grabbed Seitogi's hands and said, "Get out of sight for now. I'll see if I can find the empress."

"I'll keep my eye on you." Seitogi said. "If anything happens, run." He added as he climbed out of the window.

Emily nodded and hurried to the door, running head-on into a tall man dressed in what she took to be mud cloth adorned armor. Emily stepped back and covered the lower half of her face with her sleeve, like she had seen a thousand times in various Chinese soap operas, and feigned shyness.

"I'm sorry to disturb you. I was meditating in the next room when I heard a scream… it's you," Rijeil dropped to one knee and took Emily's hand into his, looking into her eyes, his hidden behind his gun-metal goggles with their blackout lenses.

He smiled, displaying his polished, black teeth. Emily felt her cheeks warm; something about him sent an odd sensation through her, and she found herself intrigued.

"Oh, forgive me, princess. I am Anele Rijeil Yunsae, firstborn to emperor Behrani, and Envoy Seizhon. I've been sent by your grandfather to both confirm Jebah Nami's reports that you lived and to deliver you this letter."

He reached beneath his breastplate, under his mud cloth tunic, and produced a narrow, flat rectangular piece of paper sealed with wax. Emily looked over it but quickly placed the letter in the breast of her robe at the sound of approaching footsteps.

Three guards entered the room with their curved sabers drawn, and the young servant crying behind them. They looked around, flustered.

“Find what is the matter!” the taller guard yelled, stepping closer. Emily moved out of the way as they all jumped to block the doorway and close ranks.

“It’s alright. She is with me,” said Jeil, waving them away as he looked over the guards.

“Sorry for frightening you,” Emily said, smiling at the young maid. “I got lost!”

“My apologies, my lady. Please be careful.” The black-haired beauty bowed, as did the guards, and then withdrew.

Jeil sighed and grew serious, “Princess, if you will,” he led her out of the room to the main corridor.

“You seem to know me, but I don’t know you,” she said.

He stopped and turned to her, “Yes, your Obánā wrote extensively about you to his majesty Zhon.”

“Oh!” She touched his shoulder, “And how is my grandfather? We’ve never actually met.”

“He is as strong as ever.” He smiled as they began to walk.

“Well then,” she replied, glancing at his armor, “If he sent you, you must be really important to him. Despite your being a prince of Behra?” She asked.

“Apologies, princess, but I’m not all that important.” He smiled. “King Zhon took my mother and me in after she was exiled by the emperor.” He added. She looked at him, confused.

“He banished her?” Emily asked.

Jeil nodded. “In his eyes, it was either banishing my mother or beheading her. It’s somewhat complicated.”

He showed her into the room he had been meditating in. It was beautiful. Old furniture and book-lined walls, with a large window overlooking the grounds complete with a small ornamental pond and weeping willow. She looked out the window and saw the bright lights of Domotedai under a star-filled, indigo sky.

"Ah! Are we in Gah Temple?" she asked.

"We are." He seemed surprised by the question. "This is its Chrysanthemum Room. Won't you have a seat?" he added, motioning to a pillow.

She sat down on the overstuffed red cusion and felt her heart flutter as she watched him remove his 'Mud-Cloth' tunic and chest armor and set them aside. He sat down across from her.

"Where are my manners?" he said, smiling. "I don't think I ever asked you what you wished to be called?"

"My name is Emily if that is alright with you." She said, blushing and covering her smile with her sleeve. Being in his presence suddenly made her feel warm and flushed. He shook his head, amused by her.

"Emily." He repeated, slowly sounding out each syllable, and smiled. "I really do like that. It's a very unique name."

"Thank you. But it's super basic, where I come from," she replied.

"I pray you can forgive my forwardness," he said. "I've been requesting an audience with you for months, but I was told you didn't wish to see me."

Emily felt the heat rush to her cheeks again. "Oh," she said, "I didn't know… I never meant to offend you."

"No, no, no. That is not the case, Emily," He smiled. "It is just, I'm sure you understand. It is not my place to pry."

"I apologize," She said, "I only meant. I just didn't think you would want to see me," she lied, "I'm afraid I can be terribly shy."

"Emily, I assure you that is not the case! I am only afraid I might be imposing upon you," he said.

She smiled, "Trust me, you're not."

They regarded each other, she with a smile and he with a smile and raised eyebrows. The room fell silent, punctuated only by the soft whispers of the fire of the lamps. Emily fidgeted uncomfortably. Jeil reached across the table and took her small, soft hand into his own large, warm one. Emily felt her cheeks heat with a slight flutter, and he smiled.

She suddenly felt self-conscious. "I'm sorry about your mother," she said,

"Thank you," he replied, still smiling.

"So, what happened exactly? If you don't mind my asking?" she asked. "Why was she exiled?"

"It's a long story," Jeil said and laughed. "But essentially the accusations against her were never truly proven, but there were whispers. Talk of her bewitching the emperor with sorcery. There were many things," He added.

"Like what?" Emily asked.

"She was accused of conspiring against the empress with the wizened woman who fashioned my visors. You see, I was born blind and thus, unable to fulfill my duties as heir, but my mother would not accept that fate. Instead, she searched high and low for cures. I understand at one point she had a line of mizers trailing out of the palace," Jeil said, "None but the wizened woman was able to help me, one rumored to be a witch."

"Maishae," Emily said, with a small shudder.

"Indeed. I am surprised you know of her."

"I'm wondering if she's the reason you're blind," Emily said.

"I should think not. In fact, it was her inventiveness that has allowed me even partial vision. I do not believe hers is the hand of sorcery if that's what you were suggesting."

Emily flushed beet red. "Oh no! I swear I'm not poking fun at you!" she said, holding up her hands. "I do not know why I just said that" she murmured.

"It's fine," he said.

"So, my mother presented me to the emperor, but the empress refused to accept me, and instead declared me diseased, and unfit to rule. My mother became enraged, and it was then the hatred grew," he added.

"The empress found a feather intertwined in the strings of the emperor's lute, for which she accused my mother of casting a spell on him. From then on, the rumors spread that my mother and the witch were conspiring to overthrow the empire."

"But I never believed any of it. My mother would never use sorcery for such a thing. I've since learned that most of it was the empress's doing."

"Wow!" Emily said, astonished.

"After much pleading, she was exiled for conspiracy along with the wizened woman. My mother and I were branded traitors and were forsaken by our family," He finished.

Emily felt bad for him. "They disowned you?"

"They did."

"Why would you tell me all of this? I mean we just met."

"I just want you to have a transparent understanding of the types of people you are dealing with here."

A silent wave of understanding washed over Emily. He leaned across the table and gently caressed her cheek with the back of his hand.

“Your grandfather longs to meet you,” he said. The edges of his visor reflected the warm glow of the room as he moved his face closer to hers.

“If you would. The letter?” he asked, his voice deepening. Emily’s heart raced, and she felt short of breath.

“What…” she trailed off, feeling hot. “Oh, hahaha, yes! The letter,” she said.

He took the folded piece of parchment from her and broke the wax seal; his expression clearly changed when he glanced over its contents. He placed the parchment on the table where she could view it, but the words in front of her were foreign, just a collection of black, squiggly lines, small boxes, and large circles.

Confused, Emily picked it up and very slowly looked over its contents.

“I’m so sorry. But could you read it for me? I promise I’m not illiterate or anything.”

“It’s quite alright. Chonda is a difficult language to read if you haven’t studied it,” he replied, and opened his mouth to read, when a banging on the door cut him off.

Emily jumped and almost dropped the letter, turning to the door and nervously grabbing a handful of the pillow under her.

Jeil stood up and yelled, “Who is it!?”

“Unlock the door this instant!” Emily heard a woman’s voice shouting, and Jeil’s face darkened as he moved to undo the latch, but not before whispering,

“The empress.”

Emily scrunched up the letter in a panic and stuffed it into her robe. Jeil opened the door, revealing Yumeiko in all her grandeur, flanked by two armed guards. The room suddenly felt very small, and Emily shrank down into the pillow, self-conscious of being caught alone with a prince, whose name was not Rilkian.

Jeil moved closer to Yumeiko, who, with a dismissive flick of her wrist, motioned for him to sit. He sat, crossing his legs, and gave Emily a cautious look. Emily slowly bowed her head, shrinking in on herself.

"Your maj-empress, it's so good to… Hi!" was the best she could manage.

Yumeiko was silent and stared at Emily. Emily didn't dare look up; she felt very small in front of her grand aunt.

"Ayah, princess. We missed you at tea this afternoon," Yumeiko said, forcing a smile. "I was worried about you."

"I…," Emily paused, not feigning astonishment. "I had to go for a fitting for the ball. I'm very sorry." Emily played along. Jeil gave an interested frown. Yumeiko watched him expectantly.

"Oh, that is quite alright. I understand." Yumeiko stretched out her hand and touched her niece's shoulder.

"Well, let us away and take tea in my apartments, for there is much to discuss concerning the coming engagement ceremony. Would you not agree, my dear?" She said, looking past Emily but directly at her.

"Yes. I mean, yes, Ma'am. I would like some tea," Emily said, half-heartedly standing up.

The guards, who had been quietly standing behind Yumeiko, stepped forward.

"It was a shame we couldn't get to know each other better," Emily said, turning to face Jeil.

"I understand we should have tea together too, soon," he bowed.

"Yes. Bye," Emily said, with a wave.

With Yumeiko in the lead, Emily found herself sandwiched between the royal guards as they escorted her down the temple halls and couldn't help but feel she was once again a prisoner.

When they finally arrived at the palace, the guards continued to escort Emily the whole way to Yumeiko's apartments, making it clear she wasn't to be offered any freedoms.

"Please, you mustn't frown so, dear. We are desperately happy to have you back," Yumeiko gushed, pulling her niece into an embrace. "I hope you have forgiven us since we last met. Tradition dictates a certain coldness when wearing the crown," she said, simpering, as Emily wriggled closer to the seating area and perched herself atop a cushion.

"Rikillian has told me how he was able to learn so much about you on your little adventure. He was quite distraught when you took your leave of him," Yumeiko said with a light smile.

Emily felt her face grow hot, "I…I don't! I didn't exactly take my leave," she spoke in a calm, but direct manner.

Tea was brought in by a maid and a meal was set on the table for her. Emily ate without much appetite. Yumeiko, who sat across from her, nibbled delicately on a dainty fruit tart, chatting about the doings of court and making cheerful small talk about the upcoming festivities.

When tea was finished and they were alone, Yumeiko said, voice firm, "Dear, you must understand that you are very lucky to have survived your ordeal in Bashi."

Emily's eyes flicked up to Yumeiko. The empress touched her lips with her thumb as she took a sip of tea. "Of course, Rilkian told me all about what happened. Oh, don't fret, dear. You are safe now."

Emily remained silent.

"You are a lucky young woman and have been given the privilege to marry a prince of our empire. I know this must all be a lot, and you have yet to fully understand the situation."

"Did you also know that Yulori kept me hostage in the underbelly of Odahni for months? And that he tortured me?" Emily said, her voice shaking.

Yumeiko's eyes widened, "I've heard of no such thing," she said, barely audible.

"I was able to eventually escape. But the damage has been done," Emily whispered.

Yumeiko put her hand to her mouth, shock written across her face, "Dear… you don't really mean that, do you?" she said, shifting in her seat. "Yulori is a man, perhaps too proud for his own good, but if what you say is…"

"Sadistic!" Emily said, "He is a man who obviously enjoys hurting women."

Yumeiko raised her hand, as if attempting to stop a fall.

"I think my life as an Aiyo princess ended in that dungeon," Emily said, braver now that she had said her piece.

Yumeiko's eyes flashed, and she raised her hand but didn't lash out. "If what you say is true, then you would be wise to marry Rilkian," she said, dabbing the side of her mouth with a napkin.

Her lips curled up into her false smile, and she picked up her fan and opened it with a flick of her wrist. "As empress in waiting, no man will ever again have the power to overcome you, and you can use your power to exact revenge!"

Emily's face drained of color, and she stared. The empress showed no signs of having considered what she had just said.

"Revenge? I'm not going to marry Rilkian so that I can get revenge!" she said indignantly.

"Oh no! Of course not," Yumeiko said, wheezing. "You have misunderstood me. I simply meant it is your best means to leave Yulori… disappointed."

Emily's head jerked up in alarm.

"Men, my dear, are like dogs. The only reason they turn their heads is to find fault. Yulori is no different. Oh, I'm so very sorry I've upset you. I should not have said anything,"

Yumeiko said, just before placing a hand on her head and heaving. "I'm feeling so ill at the thought he would harm you that I forgot my tongue."

"It…it's okay," Emily said, her eyes damp.

"However," Yumeiko said in a fainting voice, "one must be discreet in one's disclosures of capital abuse. You are the granddaughter of Zhon. If he were to hear these things about Yulori, it would surely end in war between our countries."

Yumeiko sighed and fanned herself, "And you are Behrani's future. Who else have you confided this information to?"

"I have no friends here, and I have told no one about this," Emily said, lowering her eyes. "I was so afraid. I couldn't tell anyone."

"And you should not tell another soul for the time being, particularly Rijeil. He is here for one purpose and one purpose only, to fan the flames of war between Behrani and Seizhone. He covets the emperor's crown and openly flaunts Zhon's backing. You'd be better off and stay away from that boy."

"Boy?" said Emily, "He's friggin' built like a rock!"

"It is imperative that you distance yourself from him and remain quiet. He will dance a different tune in front of you, but in the end, he is nothing but a snake."

"A snake?" Emily said, half laughing, "Well, if he is, then I'll be sure to keep really, really quiet."

"I suppose that is exactly what you should do," Yumeiko said, feebly. The empress shook her head, "I'm so very sorry. But I just want you to have an easier go at it than I did. I thought you and Rilkian felt something for one another. He is quite enamored with you."

"But don't you love the emperor?"

"The emperor was my consolation gift," Yumeiko frowned, cradling her hand to her chest, eyes downcast.

"I was originally meant to wed his older brother, Anele Ril Saehthun. Oh, he was a man to die for. He was so tall his head touched the sky, and his shoulders so wide, he could carry the whole world on them. And his face. Oh, his face was so beautiful, I would just-" Yumeiko sighed, lost in thought.

Emily gave a skeptical look.

"He was to become emperor after the death of their father, Emperor Hasejiel. But as fate would have it, he was thrown from his horse, and died when he hit the ground."

"That's very sad," Emily said, with keen interest.

Yumeiko fanned her face. "I was devastated. Their mother, Empress Seberah, informed my parents that I would take Saehyun's hand instead. Saehyun, a man who had devoted his life to the priesthood, had no desire to marry or join politics as a crown prince."

"That sounds pretty rough."

"They forced him to become heir. He had no say in the matter, but I still couldn't stand him. Humph, a soft, unappealing man if ever there were one. Oh, to gaze upon him, one might as well have gazed upon a blank sheet of paper left out in the rain."

"Ouch."

"He was a frail, clean-shaven man when we met. I was disgusted. Why, my Saehthun had a flowing beard, and eyebrows so full and lush, no man could compare. Yet, he was beautiful and kind," Yumeiko cooed, before snapping her fan shut.

"I'm sure the emperor has some good qualities," Emily offered, "Gleh-, Rilkian turned out alright."

"He barely knows the crown prince. I married him strictly out of duty." Yumeiko took a sip of tea, nostrils flaring.

"I refused him my touch, you know? They wanted an heir, but I was a stubborn girl, all of us Aiyo women are. And so his courtiers presented him with Saowahn. Sao was only a year younger than me, prettier by some accounts."

"She birthed him Rijeil, but as you have seen, the boy was blind, thus disqualified from the crown. It was then that my mother pressured me to lay with him, before Sao had a chance to give him another son. As I said before, I swallowed my pride and performed my duty. Rilkian was born healthy and became crown prince. All was well."

"Until?" Emily urged.

"The wizened woman interfered by fashioning the boy seeing goggles with hopes of challenging Rilkian's birthright. But the emperor ruled against it, stating the boy would be an embarrassment to the empire.

Saowhan and Maishae gave it one more try, but the girl's schemes were thwarted."

"It seems we have a complicated family history," Emily said.

Yumeiko swiped at a wisp of hair. "You children are my legacy. Rilkian is my only hope of a son to carry on the Aiyo name with a daughter of our blood. Even now Rijeil has decided to stay for the official ceremony representing your grandfather. You have shown up at the right time as the official engagement ceremony is only two days away."

"Two days?" Emily said. "But what about Shumaiyuki?"

"What of her?" Yumeiko said. "With what you have told me of Yulori, I am certain she was privy to his activities, and will be held accountable, as will he."

Emily nodded.

"Do not worry." The empress started fanning herself again. "I have given my blessing to your union with my son. In two days, you shall be well on your way to being a married woman and a future empress!"

"But I, I…" Emily stumbled for words. "I don't know how to be an empress."

"Oh, I know, my dear," Yumeiko said, waving her fan, "That is what you have me for."

A House Divided

The Aiyo residence in Domotedai was an opulent home that was adorned in the luxurious style typical of the upper class. The three-story house featured a clay-tiled roof and a finely crafted structure. The doors were made of dark oak and added to the grandeur of the mansion.

Of the twelve-room house, the master suite was occupied by Aiyo Shumaiyuki and not the clan's lord and master, Aiyo Yulori. Shumaiyuki held enough sway within the family and was in a strong enough position to lay the claim.

That hadn't always been the case. She had to put up with years of struggle against Yulori and now was on the cusp of outranking him, as empress. Power, position, and prestige were all things she now enjoyed, thanks to her strong standing within their clan.

But in the end, none of it really mattered to Shumaiyuki if she couldn't walk freely, unhindered by a weak leg and an unreliable limp. She wanted to be treated with respect and be able to meet her people without feeling embarrassed or ashamed of her disability, a word she had come to learn from Rebecca, and didn't particularly care for.

When she finally became empress, she would be a focal point of many people's admiration, fear, and hate. At the very least, she felt the presentation was important. For she would be emulating the great emperors and empresses of Behrani's past!

Carefully placing one foot in front of the other, she walked down a straight line of ribbon stretched across the polished oak floor. Slowly, with as much dignity as she could muster, she made her way towards Rebecca who stood on the other side of the chamber cheering her on.

Halfway through the exercise, Shumaiyuki stopped suddenly to catch her breath, turning her head to look at the nearby window. The screen was partially open, allowing her to feel the sunshine and soft wind on her frowning face.

"I need to rest a moment, RiRi," she whined, her growing frustration evident. Hopping on one leg, she grabbed her walking stick, and limped over to her lounge. No sooner had she settled onto its bed, before she moaned loudly and rolled over onto her side.

Rebecca walked over and laid a hand on her hip and began massaging her leg.

"The ceremony is in two days," she said, her red hair traditionally styled into a tight bun. "Do you think you'll be able to hop on one foot?"

Shumaiyuki rolled onto her stomach and Rebecca began massaging her foot with both hands.

"I know that!" she snapped, "but I'm tired. This walking is draining me! I feel like I can't move after an hour. My leg must be numb by now."

"Don't give up! You've made a lot of progress these past few months," said Rebecca, holding her enthused tone. "If you keep at it, you will be physically capable of not only walking but joining your prince in a dance as well!"

"I told you I am not dancing!" said Shumaiyuki. "How am I supposed to look my people in the eye if I am like this?"

"You can't! And that is why you should get up and keep walking. Practice those dance moves and give your people something to talk about. I can help you with that," said Rebecca, "But you've got to want it bad enough too."

"I'm done. Now let me rest."

"Look. I understand why you're so frustrated. We've been training day and night. I know I've been pushing you to your limit. But I can't help it though. I'm a perfectionist sometimes," she reached down and pulled Shumayuki back to her feet in one big heave.

"So, what do you say, are you game for another round?"

Shumaiyuki moaned and shook her off, “No. I’m going to the bathhouse to soak.”

“We have a lot riding on you being able to walk on your own by the time the ceremonies come around.”

Shumaiyuki held up her walking stick and thumped it on the ground repeatedly and lost her balance. As she fell, while holding onto the stick, Rebecca leapt to her side and caught her in a hug.

Their faces nestled close together, and Shumaiyuki’s breathing slowed, but her heart rate ascended. Rebecca looked into her eyes with a passionate, caring expression that made her face warm.

“I… such impudence,” Shumaiyuki frowned. “I could have you beaten.”

“You know, you’re not half as scary as you try to appear to be,” said Rebecca, a teasing smile on her face. “So do your worst, princess, but first, you’re going to get off your ass and continue practicing.”

“You’ve been so bossy lately Lady Ribiki!” blushed Shumaiyuki, arms wrapped around Rebecca’s sides. “But I can strip you of the title just as easily as when I granted it.”

“I must be doing something right,” said Rebecca as she helped her back to her feet. “Now, let’s have another go at it.”

“I mean… I can’t! I can’t walk across that dais. I’ll do something stupid, and I’ll embarrass the Aiyo. I don’t expect you to understand.”

“From what I see, you are the de facto leader of the Aiyo clan. For as long as you are standing, everyone will look to you for answers. So, drop the scary act and concentrate!”

“But am I not a woman? Humph… scary. I am surrounded by incompetent men, men far less capable than I. Yet and still, these men get to decide my fate, my uncle, my grandfather, the emperor himself. So, I must be fierce and unflinching! Over the top! Cruel even if I am to compete and prevail. My needs demand that I be scary.”

"But it's an act!" said Rebecca. "The floaty couch, the stick. I've seen another side of you these past couple of months! People would respect, not fear you, if you weren't floating around beating everyone within sight."

"I am to be the future empress! She must have grace in her steps! Not a monstrous lurch like mine," her voice lowered as did her head.

"It's hardly a monstrous lurch," Rebecca helped her settle back onto the lounge. "And if it's already decided you are to be empress, it shouldn't matter."

"That's not the point," Shumaiyuki closed her eyes and covered her face with her hands. "It's humiliating to walk in such an obscene fashion."

"You're playing hard for the sympathy card here, honey." Rebecca rolled her eyes.

"How dare you insult me! Hold your tongue or I shall have it plucked from your mouth!"

"Go for it! I'm the only one who talks to you anyway!" Rebecca snapped. Shumaiyuki's face trembled, and she lowered her hands.

"I am very weak in the knees," Shumaiyuki said, pulling her knees to her chest. Rebecca moved behind her and wrapped her arms around her.

"It's simple. If you don't want to do it for the people, then do it for yourself. You know I've got your back."

Shumaiyuki swallowed back a lump that had formed in her throat.

"What if I fall on my face after I can't stand anymore? Or encounter some other humiliation? I know you believe, Riri. But I just can't do it." She placed her hand on Rebecca's. "I don't want to disappoint myself."

Rebecca squeezed Shumaiyuki's hand, "Believe me, if you fell on your face, I'd pick you up before anyone even noticed."

Shumaiyuki looked up sharply, a flutter passed across her heart, "Why you… you…"

"Now, let's try this again. You will stand here, like this." Rebecca's hand gripped her shoulder. "And place your left foot there."

Shumaiyuki slowly lifted her foot and set it down. She removed her hand from the lounge, and it fell with a thump to the ground.

"Now set up your free leg and heel here." Rebecca placed her foot down and demonstrated. She then pushed Shumaiyuki's foot into its proper place.

"And finally, your right foot goes here." Shumaiyuki teetered in place but didn't lose her balance.

"Good," said Rebecca. "Now go for a walk."

Shumaiyuki took a step forward when Obinari ran into the room out of breath and fell to his knees.

"Your Highness!" he called. "I have a report!"

"Obinari, I'm busy," she said.

"It's of the utmost urgency," Obinari said. "The imposter lives and is residing in Nyongoyuchi Palace as a guest of the empress!"

"Impossible!" Shumaiyuki shrieked and stood straight, severing Rebecca's grasp. "The imposter is dead. We saw her scalp!"

"I was told by one of Lord Aiyo's spies," Obinari said, "he said he saw her with the empress with his own eyes."

"Emily, is alive…?" Rebecca whispered.

Shumaiyuki closed her eyes. "Give me a moment," she said, and her head fell. Rebecca breathed in sharply and gripped onto her shoulder for support and then addressed Obinari.

"Where is this spy?" Rebecca asked, "My lady wishes to hear from him now!"

"I apologize, Lady Ribiki, but that would be impossible as their identity cannot be revealed." Obinari bowed his head and prepared for a scolding.

Ever since Rebecca's promotion to first lady in waiting for the Golden Swan, she had become nearly as hard of a taskmaster as Shumaiyuki.

"That is not good enough, Obi!"

"Please don't call me Ob…"

"You cannot deliver such perilous news and expect our lady to just casually accept it! What proof does this informant have of the imposter's identity?" her voice was stern and direct as she spoke. "We only seek the truth, Obi, for it is a crime to doubt our lady." Her hands massaged Shumaiyuki's shoulders.

"That was never my intention!" Obinari said louder than he intended.

"My lady," Rebecca said, running her hand up and down Shumaiyuki's back. "Why don't we get some fresh air? You will feel better."

Shumaiyuki brushed her hands aside and emitted an odd whistle Rebecca had never heard before. This was followed by the soft fluttering of a cloak, and suddenly there was what appeared to be a Dhukai, draped all in black, kneeling on the terrace just outside the chamber.

"Mistress Swan," said the kneeling woman, her face obscured in the shadows cast by her cloak's hood.

"Teje!" Shumaiyuki said in what Rebecca could only read as a sinister tone.

"Yes," Teje said, bowing low.

"Confirm what Obinari says regarding the imposter. Also, alert my contact in the Palladium Maze and tell them I'm calling in their debt."

"Yes, Mistress Swan," she said, bowing and darting off as quickly as she arrived.

"How does Teje come and go unseen?" Rebecca said, staring blankly.

Shumaiyuki shrugged. "You only see the tip of the iceberg when it comes to me, Riri. Many do my bidding in the shadows, and my bidding is never made public. Teje has been with me for years. Always in the shadows, watching. Another gift from grandfather." And then, "I do not need an audience with Yulori's spy!" she said, glaring at Obinari.

"No, Your Highness," he said, bowing. Shumaiyuki's lounge began to lift off the ground, a low hum accompanied its ascent.

"I shall go directly to the one who laid claim to her murder instead," she said as she floated out of the room. Rebecca took her left flank, and Obinari caught up and marched to her right.

* * *

"My lord, the Golden Swan requests an audience," the attendant reported hesitantly.

Yulori's foot was tapping rapidly on the floor as he sat at his desk, his expression one of fear and apprehension. The attendant retreated to a corner, keeping a watchful eye on him.

"Why now?" Yulori muttered, his voice filled with frustration.

"She is with Lady Ribiki and her man-at-arms," the attendant said, "and she is not happy."

"When is she ever happy?" Yulori glanced over his shoulder. He supposed it might be a good time to change. He began fiddling with his robes. "Go. Tell them to come in," he said.

Yulori stood from his desk as Rebecca and Obinari walked in and bowed. Yulori bowed back and then forced a cheerful demeanor.

"Ah, Lady Ribiki. It is always an honor to receive the famed Red Lotus. Will you be blessing us with a preview of your upcoming performance?" he asked sarcastically. Rebecca sensed his inflections and forced a polite smile.

"It's good to see you, my lord."

"I've received a troubling report, uncle," Shumaiyuki spoke, floating in her lounge, "It seems that one of your spies has verified that the imposter is still alive."

Yulori's eyes went wide. Shumaiyuki continued,

"And we were led to believe that you were the one to strike the killing blow."

"How dare you speak of such a thing!" Yulori snarled. "I am the lord of this house! I shall not be questioned by the likes of you!"

"How dare you lie to me!" Shumaiyuki slammed down her stick on the floor and tore into Yulori.

"You worthless worm! How could you? How could you have lied to me? And now what, with the engagement just two days away!" She floated towards the desk, waving the stick in the air.

Rebecca stepped between them, calming Shumaiyuki with a glance,

"My lady. Now is not the time to quarrel. We have to be calm and collected in this matter. Your Highness, please show the proper respect for our lord."

Shumaiyuki turned away from Yulori but didn't let go of her anger. She slowly dropped her stick as she settled down.

"Proper respect? Surely you jest, Lady Ribiki. Does one respect the ants who ruin one's picnic? I think not!"

She looked over her shoulder at Yulori, who crossed his arms and stared daggers at his niece. He then turned his attention back to Rebecca,

"Lady Ribiki…" Yulori's voice was slightly raspy as he spoke. "I do not understand why my niece even bothers with a low-born dolt such as yourself. Nor do I understand how she has been able to seduce half the clan to work against me. But when it's all said and done, your head will rest on a pike right next to hers."

"Dare you threaten the Golden Swan!" Obinari took to his feet, his hand on his blade. Rebecca placed her hand on Obinari's shoulder and shot him a withering look.

"You forget who is your lord, Obinari."

Yulori raised his hand and clenched his fist. He narrowed his eyes on Obinari.

"You forget this place." His voice was deadly as a series of eight narrow slots opened along the upper perimeter of the wall behind him. Loaded bows poked out of each one, ready to unleash a volley of arrows.

Yulori glared at Shumaiyuki, "Now, as I was saying," he said. "You are unpredictable, niece. A savage, really. Oh yes, you are perfumed and powdered, but you are your father's daughter. You are not worthy of this house, let alone the crown."

Shumaiyuki turned and stared at Yulori with a cold look in her eyes. "Do you intend on assassinating me here and now, uncle? As if a coward like you could pull off such a feat. You wouldn't even dare."

"I would not risk the safety of this house. Even for you," Yulori said. "And so, yes. Princess Yuyuki is alive and well.

The empress and I have spent the past several months training her to become the crown prince's bride. And in two days, it will be her, not you, who will be named as so."

"Hah, fool. The emperor wouldn't allow the scandal to ensue, should such a move be made at this late junction in the game."

"Oh, but he will, dear niece, when he learns you have been secretly raising an army to displace him," Yulori told her, "and let me assure you, the emperor will know about all your plans. He will be meeting with me tomorrow. I have my spies everywhere, Shumai. Did you not think I wouldn't find out about all the secretive troop movements and regiments you placed throughout the capital? You will be branded a traitor and beheaded along with your co-conspirators."

Shumaiyuki was speechless. Rebecca moved to her side, knowing that she needed support.

"Lord Yulori. Is this true?" she asked.

"Utterly," he answered. "Now please. I have much to do today. Please leave my office."

Rebecca held her hand to her mouth and turned away from Yulori. He shot her a withering look.

"There is no way Emily would have gone this long without letting me know she was alive," Rebecca said.

"Quite on the contrary, Lady Ribiki. It was the princess herself who made it her foremost duty to keep it a secret. Princess Yuyuki is a very capable woman. She has devoted herself to the study of stealth, deception, and warfare…" Yulori said with a coy smile.

"That's what she told you! But it's not true. I know Emily. She would have told me she was alive."

"You lying monster! The Golden Swan will not bow down to you!" Shumaiyuki floated high until she was on level with the hidden archers and deftly released a dozen razor-sharp spikes at them. The spikes found their way through the slots and slammed into their intended targets, splattering blood from the upper wall. Screams could be heard from inside as Shumaiyuki glared down on Yulori, and then descended from the ceiling.

"I will not forgive this, Uncle. I will not forget it. I will not let it pass."

“Good. I see that we understand each other,” Yulori said with a raised eyebrow. Shumaiyuki lifted the chaise and floated out of the room.

The moment he was alone, Yulori ran the back of his hand against his mouth and wiped the wet sheen of sweat from his brow. He looked over to his attendant, who was trembling in the corner, looking up at the blood-drenched slots in horror.

“Stop shaking in your pants and have this mess cleaned up.”

“Yes, Lord Yulori,” the attendant bowed and left.

Yulori chuckled morbidly, “So now it begins,” he said. He paced the office and looked out the window. A feeling of dread invaded his body and heart. He rubbed his hand across his chest and eyes, “Shumaiyuki,” he mumbled.

* * *

“Oh my god, you killed them! You just killed them in cold blood!” Rebecca said breathlessly as she kept up with Shumaiyuki’s couch. It was moving faster than she had ever seen before, from one end of the mansion to the other, weaving around corners, down hallways, and through archways with reckless abandon.

Shumaiyuki was in no mood to talk, but Rebecca pressed.

“If it’s true. If the emperor is meeting with Yulori tomorrow, then it means we’re done for. Then all our plans, everything you worked for!”

“Obinari. Send word to General Nathum immediately. Tell him to stand by to march on the capital at my orders.” Shumaiyuki said. Obinari closed his eyes and nodded, then ran ahead of them and disappeared around a corner.

“You know you can’t take on the Imperial army, right?” cried Rebecca as they came upon Shumaiyuki’s chambers. “You know that you have to have more than one plan. You can’t go in with guns blazing.”

Shumaiyuki laughed, “Oh, you are right; I have one more plan.” She floated higher in the air, and then dropped down and through the door to her chambers.

“What? What plan?” Rebecca shouted after her.

“Riri! Calm yourself!” Shumaiyuki said curtly.

“I can’t calm myself! You just murdered, I don’t know, seven, eight people! I didn’t even know you were capable of that!” Rebecca said as she collapsed on the floor.

“Of course, we are all capable of it.” Shumaiyuki said as she landed her couch on the floor. “But it is best to do so with honor. Do you understand?”

“Y-yes, ma’am.”

“Good.” Shumaiyuki said. “Now. I don’t have much time. I have to look appropriate when I visit the palace for an audience with the emperor. I will see that he declares uncle a traitor tomorrow.”

“B-but Shumaiyuki. Yulori is meeting with the emperor tomorrow.”

“Yes. Which is why I am meeting him tonight.” Shumaiyuki said.

“I’m sorry I misunderstood. I thought you just sent Obinari to warn the troops.”

“Yes, I did, didn’t I,” said Shumaiyuki with a wide grin. “Only General Nathum is under the impression he, and all the Aiyo troops dispersed throughout and around the capital, are fighting on behalf of Lord Aiyo. I’m excellent at forging my uncle’s handwriting. All of his missives come through me, after all.”

Rebecca pushed herself up from the ground. “So, you mean to say you have set him up?” she said.

“I’m not familiar with the terminology, but I’ll allow it,” Shumaiyuki said with her signature pointed smile.

"But how can you get a meeting with the emperor on such short notice?" Rebecca asked.

Shumaiyuki laughed. It was such a beautiful sound that, for a second, Rebecca was completely enthralled.

"Oh, dear Riri. I always have contingencies in place. Remember, iceberg. You only see what I allow you to see. In truth, my uncle is correct. I am a savage, an Anele by birth. But for my mother's feckless disregard of her duties, my father would not have refused me his name. I will right that wrong and take the throne. Even if I have to spill a sea of blood to do so."

"Then you have set the emperor up too," Rebecca said.

"Good. Now you are catching up," said Shumaiyuki.

* * *

"A bird from Yulori?" Aiyo Yumeiko received the small, tightly wound scroll from her aide. "And a falcon at that. One of his favorites?"

"Yes, he calls this one by the name Peora," the aide said.

"See that it is fed a morsel," said Yumeiko. "Now leave me." She took a deep breath. "I need to rest for a bit."

The aide bowed. "Of course, Highness." The door closed slowly behind her.

"I'm going to make you pay for losing her, Yulori," she said, unrolling the scroll. She read through it quickly. "The fool wants me to facilitate a meeting with the emperor." She threw the scroll to the ground. "I think not. No telling what you are up to, nephew," she sighed. She stood and walked to the window.

"Of course, setting you up would be an excellent way to get rid of you." She laughed for a moment. She took a deep breath and smoothed her robe. "I can't allow you to implicate me. I'll have to put you down myself."

She walked over to her desk and sat down. She opened a drawer and retrieved a scroll that was bound by a green ribbon. With quick and precise movements, she wrote on the scroll. After she finished writing, she blew on the ink to let it dry. She then rolled up the scroll and added a final line on the outside before sealing it with a drop of wax.

She stood and put the scroll in her pocket. She left her chambers and called for the aide, and they made their way to the flier posts. She saw a large falcon and carried the scroll to it.

“I swear you get bigger every time I see you, Peora,” she said as she tied the scroll around the bird’s leg. “Go. Fly back to your master,” she said, clasping the bird’s beak. “Make sure you don’t get shot down, or I will hold you personally responsible.” The bird screeched slightly as she released it into the air.

She watched as it circled twice before flying higher and higher. “Go to him,” she said as the bird disappeared from sight. She turned to the servant. “Let’s make haste.”

The Rivals

Emily woke early the next morning as the light was just starting to seep through the rice paper screens. She sat up, tossing the duvet aside. "Can't sleep," she whispered. "I have to find Beck."

She got out of bed and padded around the chamber, and several maids entered and bowed.

"Good morning, my lady," the head maid greeted her with a smile. "We've brought everything you need to get ready for the day."

She gestured to the girls behind her, who were holding a kimono, slippers, makeup, and accessories. The other maids gathered around a small dressing table in the corner of the room, eager to assist. Emily let out a sigh and rolled her eyes, clearly not thrilled about the preparations.

After being dressed by the maids in heavy silk robes, having her face painted and hair coiled, Emily was left feeling frustrated. The restrictive robes made it difficult for her to move freely, and she felt a pang of hunger. With a sigh, she left the room and made her way down the corridor. As she stepped into the atrium, she encountered two servants, one of whom timidly raised a hand.

"My lady."

"Yes?"

"Someone will be along soon to escort you to take a meal with the empress." The maid looked at her with uncertainty.

"Oh! Of course, but that won't be for a while yet, right? The sun has just barely risen."

"Hecho Heeba. As of now, the empress has not risen. She tends to rise late in the morning and take her meal in her chambers. However, her order was to be awakened when you awoke," the maid bowed her head again.

"Ah! Of course! Well, in that case, how about I just go out and sit on the terrace and wait?"

Emily returned to her room cursing under her breath. “She wants to keep an eye on me. It feels like I’m trapped in Maishae’s pocket dimension all over again.” She spun in a full circle on the spot for a moment and sighed. “I’m so ready to leave this place. Grams always said, ‘Treat one thing differently, and all else becomes different as well.’ I never knew what she meant, yet I’m reminded of it now.”

Emily sat in the middle of the room, slouched and sulking. It was then that she noticed a dingy bundle neatly tucked on the bottom of a shelf. She looked up and realized that it was her old clothes, folded and tied with a ribbon.

She reached up and untied the ribbon and held it up to herself. “Seitogi.” She smiled and felt reassured. “Now, when did he put them here?” She asked.

She put them under the bed and then waited on the terrace. Time passed, and Emily was about to get up and check to see if the empress was actually awake, when suddenly the maid from earlier appeared at the door and bowed.

“Please, I have been sent to escort you to the empress,” the maid said.

“Finally.” Emily stifled a yawn. “Lead on, my lady. Just point me in the right direction.”

The maid smiled and bowed down once again.

Empress Yumeiko sat on a long pillow of silk, surrounded by several maidens, noble daughters, perhaps, thought Emily, definitely not the help. The sight of them all sitting there cooing and talking reminded Emily of the painting of the Last Supper.

The empress was draped in rich red and peach silk embroidered with a swarming mass of pinion and bamboo leaves, the symbol for good fortune. She wore two braids, one on either side of her head, held fast by thin golden threads and ovals of silver.

Her sun-kissed tone and her golden hazel eyes were a clear and unblemished. She sat before a long table overflowing with extravagant fruits and delicate sweet cakes, cassava porridge, and sliced roast meats of all sorts. All of it was laid on small plates and bowls with a golden rim.

"Ah, here she is," Yumeiko smiled and rose to her feet as the maidens all remained seated and bowed, all enthusiastically calling Hecho-Hiba.

"Come in, my lady," Yumeiko waved Emily over. She gestured for Emily to take the seat directly across from her. "I trust you slept well?"

Emily smiled nervously, she bowed, "Yes, Your Majesty. Thank you."

The empress nodded once, and the other ladies continued talking. There was an almost palpable energy of otherness hanging in the air, which radiated through Emily. It was an odd stress where she felt like she didn't quite belong, yet she felt honored and apart at the same time.

The breakfast, or meal, as they called it, lasted for what seemed hours. There was a constant quiet hum of conversation that filled Emily with anxiety. At the end of the meal, it felt like she was finally getting a break from the tone of sharp politeness as the maidens filtered out of the room, bowing before her.

Then the maids all stood around the empress, bowing and curtsying. The empress herself simply smiled and waved them away.

"Please, my lady," Emily began once they were alone. "I have an errand I must attend to."

The empress waved her hand, and Emily felt relieved all at once. "Of course, of course," she said. "You should be on your way."

The empress stood and smiled a smile that gave Emily an uneasy chill down her spine.

Emily bowed and prepared to leave. As she turned to go the empress called after her,

"Though it is a mystery what errand one needs to personally see to when one has plenty of servants to handle such trifles?"

Emily stopped in her tracks and turned to face the empress. "I apologize, Your Majesty, but I am used to handling such common affairs."

The empress laughed and gestured for Emily to go. "I suppose I need not be so strict," she said. "Oh, how you young people are always on the move."

Emily bowed. "Thank you, Your Majesty. I shall be on my way, then," she smiled politely, wondering if the empress was making a joke or if she should be worried.

Emily hurried along the corridors, trying to calm her frazzled nerves. She finally found herself outside the front gates of Yumeiko's apartments. Once through, she ran to the great palace square, drenched in the smell of summer flowers.

She was in search of the stables but became lost, and so crossed the square and entered a grand gazeebo surrounded by glass doors and walls. The floor was tiled in black and white checkers. On the ceiling was a painting of the sun and moon above a great tree.

"Princess."

Emily, so caught up in the painting, jumped at the sound of Jeil's voice. She turned to see him standing behind her, bare-chested and sweating, a wooden sword in one hand and a staff in the other.

"Princess. I heard you were enjoying the company of the empress and her ladies-in-waiting." Emily's eyes darted to his chiseled chest and then quickly away.

"I see you've been working out. Um, sorry. Exercising."

"Yes, sparring." Jeil handed the wooden sword to a servant. Emily noticed two other shirtless men on the far end of the courtyard packing away their sparring weapons as well.

“I prefer to spar in the morning before I take my meal,” he said, drying his sweat with a towel.

Jeil excused himself and walked into a small room, where he shrugged on a fitted vest and shirt. He looked out of the open doorway to see a greenish grey, night vision rendering of Emily rife with static lines and distortion. He blushed, and then walked back into the gazeebo.

“What brings you out?” he asked.

“The stables?” Emily answered. “I am looking for the stables. I need a horse.”

Jeil looked confused. Emily’s voice never rose above a whisper, “I must ride into town and visit the Aiyo residence,” she said.

Jeil laughed. “You are jesting,” and then he stared into her eyes with intent. “With all due respect, princess, I am fully aware that the Aiyo are your enemies. Emily, it would be certain death for you to deliver yourself into their arms.”

Emily’s eyes widened, but she did not flinch. “I wouldn’t ever know what you meant by that, Lord Jeil.”

Jeil’s face turned into an unmistakable look of dissappointment.

“I suppose you think it a matter of honor to continue the farce, but I will not allow it if it means putting yourself in danger, especially when the empress is using you to challenge the legitimacy of the Golden Swan. You must be smart when navigating the courts of chaos.”

“I wish I was,” Emily replied. “But look, the Aiyo are holding friends of mine hostage. I’m going to negotiate their release; I just need a horse. Will you be so kind as to help me?”

Jeil looked at her, his brow furrowed. “A hostage situation. That sounds quite serious, Emily.”

Emily nodded. “That’s because it is very serious.”

“Should you not seek the help of the emperor? He is the one with the power to make and break true injustice.”

Emily clenched her teeth. “Since you already know the empress’s plans, then you would also know I am no better than a hostage here in the palace myself. How am I to approach the emperor?”

“I see. Will you tell me more?” he asked. “Perhaps we can find another solution. One that does not include such a drastic and dangerous course of action.”

“I wish you’d tell me more,” said Emily. “Starting with how did you know I was meant to replace Shumaiyuki?”

“Nami’s letters. She wrote to His Highness Zhon and divulged the entirety of the scandal. It is precisely why I was sent here to protect and collect you, on the king’s orders. Your safety is my top priority. I hold no particular obligations to the emperor.”

“Why didn’t you tell me this yesterday?” Emily gasped.

“We had only just met, Emily. The empress came before I could really say anything about my true purpose in her presence.”

“And my grandfather wants me to go live in Seizhone?”

“That is what he writes in his letter. He invites you to serve at his side as his last living blood heir. Upon his death, you will become Queen Zhon.”

Emily stumbled back into the doorway.

“Queen! Me? Surely, I have some aunt, uncle, or cousin who can fulfill that role?”

“Aside from Minister Djowobb, you are the king’s closest blood descendant.”

Emily frowned, "I can't be Queen. I've found a way to get back home, to my world. The real world. And once I get my friends back. We are leaving this place, and never coming back."

"That is not an option." Jeil replied. "If it means risking your life to confront the Aiyo."

"I'm sorry but I don't take orders from you or my grandfather and I won't abandon my friends."

Jeil smiled. "You could ask your betrothed, if you truly are fond of him..."

"I have no betrothed," Emily sighed, "Rillz almost died several times because of me. I couldn't bear to face him" she moaned at the thought, and then, "Why? Has he asked about me?"

"The crown prince and I are not very close. He tends to keep me at arms length." Jeil replied. "But, perhaps it would be prudent to seek his counsel still. At the very least he could order emissaries to visit the Aiyo compound and inquire about your friends on your behalf."

Jeil's smile grew larger displaying his polished black teeth, "I understand my brother has been depressed for quite some time now and rarely leaves his apartments. I'm sure a visit from an old friend would cheer him up."

"Your very sweet Jeil to be so concerned about him," Emily said, "Could you possibly show me the way to his room?"

After navigating multiple turns and levels of the palace, they arrived at the steps of the white stone gate that made the entrance to the crown prince's palace quarters.

"Well, this is far enough I suppose." said Jeil.

He whistled loudly and was almost immediately answered with the appearance of a short, slim man with a bushy, beaver-like face, due mainly to large buck teeth. He enthusiastically took Jeil's hands into his own.

"My word if it isn't the young master. I heard you were in the palace but missed to see you."

"Dear Braun, it's been an eternity. This is Princess..."

"I'm Emily Heart, nice to meet you." Emily offered her hand, but the man took a step back instead.

"I'm here to see Rilkian. Is he in?"

Braun bowed and nodded to another servant quietly standing behind him, "Go alert the master that he has a guest!" and with that the servant bowed, scurried off and was gone.

He then turned and looked back at Jeil, "How fares the lady Sao? She is in good health, yes?"

"Mother is well," replied Jeil, "She is happy about her new arrangements."

Braun's eyes widened for a moment, as he looked at Emily, then back at Jeil,

"That is wonderful news, I just wish I could get a chance to visit her myself," he laughed.

Emily felt awkward as the small man began to steal glances at her while he nervously clasped his hands together.

"You see my lady. Before I was in the service of the crown prince, I worked in the house of Lady Sao. I was her personal servant, and I was there when Prince Jeil was born." and then he smiled. "I held little master Jeil in my arms," he boasted.

"Braun and I were very close when I was a boy," Jeil replied.

Emily tapped her foot. "That's nice. So Rilkian is here is he?"

"Indeed he is" Braun said, his voice dropping an octave lower. "His Highness has kept to himself for quite some time now."

"Why is that?" asked Emily.

"He came back from the Aiyo castle quite distraught. We all thought he would pull out of it. It's been a horrifying state of affairs."

"Enough with you gossiping Braun," Rilkian stepped from inside the gate and then took several steps back.

"Emily!" he cried, "I just received word less than an hour ago that you were here in the palace, but I...I just couldn't believe it." Rilkian looked pale, and his eyes were puffy and red.

"Howdy stranger, long time no see," Emily winked and leaned in placing a kiss on both his cheeks.

"Oh my!" exclaimed Braun.

"It's ok Braun. It's an Arth custom." Rilkian laughed and then to Jeil.

"Lord Shepthi," he bowed curtly.

"His Grace," Jeil smiled, offering a bow. "The princess wished to see you, thus I escorted her here to your apartments. I hope you don't mind."

"I don't really know how to move about the palace. Jeil's been a great help," added Emily, hoping to lessen some of the tension in the air. She sensed the heat coming from Rilkian more so than Rijeil.

"It was very kind of him," Rilkian told Emily. She noticed he wouldn't even look at Jeil as he spoke. "Please princess," he stepped aside and motioned for her to step through the ornately carved circular doors of the gate.

"Oh! Thank you, and Jeil?"

"I'm certain Lord Shepthi has other business to attend to."

"I do," said Jeil, bowing. "I will take my leave then. It was wonderful seeing you again Emily."

"I will see you later," Emily bowed, "And thank you."

Rilkian closed the gate and turned, "Come, I'll show you to the parlor. A servant will be along shortly to serve us."

Emily followed close behind as Rilkian walked quickly across a green lawn.

"I am speechless. I never thought I would see you again." He showed her over to a low, round table atop a wooden platform.

Behind it stood a small, two-story manor surrounded by lush gardens and circular walls covered in maze like ringlets of ivy. The entirety of the enclosed space was lit from above by sunlight filtering in through a giant octagonal pane of glass.

"I just don't know what to say." Rilkian said. "I thought Yulori had you killed."

Emily tried reassuring him by putting a hand on his shoulder. "I was able to escape him and take some time to heal. I'm here to rescue my friends."

"Have you no idea what has become of them?" Rilkian helped her lower herself to sit on her pillow, as her garments made it a near-impossible endeavor alone.

"Your friend Rebecca is one of the most famous women in all of Behra."

"I don't understand, famous how?"

"She is called Lady Ribiki now and serves as a personal attendant to Shumaiyuki. But she is more widely known for her Red Lotus dance. Her performances of it have become popular during the current party season. She is due to perform it tomorrow night during the engagement ceremony."

"What!" Emily was shocked by the new revelation. "Red Lotus dance? She was always so clumsy."

"I have not seen it myself, but the empress seems to be quite impressed with it, as well as her red hair! It's all you hear the ladies talking about."

"No one mentioned it during breakfast." Emily bit down on her thumbnail. "I'm sorry; I must ask you a question." Emily rubbed both hands hard down her face and then turned to Rilkian.

"Can you help me free her and Darren? I'm sure Shumaiyuki is forcing her to do this Red Lotus bit and dance for her."

Rilkian's face flushed beneath the surface of his pale skin, and he ran his hand through his hair. "I am afraid my political situation has changed, and I cannot simply order such an action without repercussions."

Emily felt the bottom drop out of her stomach. "Then I must go to them myself."

"It's not possible." Rilkian said. A servant brought them tea and cakes, however, the tea sat untouched by Emily.

"I'm so sick of tea. I need a real cup of joe. At this point, I'd even take it black with no sugar," she said.

"My apologies." Rilkian reached out and placed his hand on her shoulder. "I cannot allow it. You're too valuable for me to lose you again." Rilkian helped himself to a cup of tea and placed it back on the table.

"I understand," she replied. Emily's mind raced. "You are to be engaged to Shumaiyuki tomorrow. You mustn't worry about me."

"But now that you are here, we can change that! I say we approach the emperor with the truth of your lineage. I know that you are against an arranged marriage, Emily, but if we were wed, it would unite both Behrani and Seizhone and stop a madwoman from one day becoming empress. I know that we only met again this morning, but I care for you deeply, Emily, and would never let anyone, especially the Aiyo, hurt you again."

"Rilkian. I don't know what to say."

"Say yes, Emily. Say you will marry me. Together we can turn this world around. I've thought so much about your words on women being right."

"You mean women's rights," Emily smiled, fanning herself with her hand.

"Yes. As emperor, I could issue a decree allowing women to be educated and even own property."

"What? Wait, women don't even receive education here? How did I miss that one?"

"Peasant women generally don't. Most noble and royal women receive some. But together we can change that."

"Listen, Rillz—"

"Rillz?"

"I am so flattered you'd want to marry me. God knows you are gorgeous and intelligent. Well, you're just an overall great guy. But, well, for one, it just wouldn't work. We are both far too young to be even thinking about marriage. I mean, we have years of personal growth ahead of us. And while I appreciate you recognize the inequalities women face; those are changes you can implement yourself without being married to me!"

"But I want to be married to you. Marriage is my only duty. That and producing a male heir."

"No, you don't want to marry me. You just think you do because you've been conditioned to. And while, I guess I sort of care for you too, I don't belong here."

"But—"

"Besides. When we last met, you said you wanted to ghost this place and go to Earth too. Well, I know how to get back now. You are more than welcome to join the trip, but I can't stay here, Rilkian. I want to get back to my real life."

"You've discovered the path home?"

"Yes, I have. My plan was to go to the Aiyo residences and escape with Beck and Darren before we could be caught. But now, I'm thinking I'll do it tomorrow during the ceremony," a mild sense of guilt came and went for not mentioning Seitogi would be accompanying them on the trip back to Earth too.

"But you only just returned," taking her hands into his.

“Rilkian, my friends are being held hostage, and it’s my fault. I have to save them. I have a duty too.”

Rilkian remained silent and just stared into her eyes, his puffy from months of crying, but still stark and beautiful. Emily felt a flutter in her chest. She had forgotten how it was to be around her runaway prince. His hands were so soft and comforting, nothing like Seitogi’s rough, thick hands. Hands she had come to enjoy holding during their many walkabouts in the gardens of Maishae’s pocket.

“Oh no! Why am I thinking about Seita right now? It’s not like I’m cheating on him or something. Jeez, get it together, Emily. He’s like a brother to you, not a boyfriend. God, I hope he’s not out there hidden in the trees watching us.” Emily’s face flushed.

She was just about to say something when Rilkian stood up and began to pace. She sat paralyzed as her fingers twirled a lock of hair in her hand.

“Emily.” He stopped pacing and knelt before her. “Are you sure you want to leave?”

“I have to. Even if I was born here in Behra, I miss my home, my world. Even my grand-me…me? Look, everything I know is back on Earth.”

“Arth.”

“E-R. Earth,” she corrected.

“Very well then. How will we get there?”

“You mean you still want to come?”

“I do! I never wanted to be emperor. Other people make every decision for you. It’s why the emperor stays hidden in the Palladium Maze. He hates it too.”

“Well, this is our ticket home.” Emily pulled the mirror from her sleeve and held it up for Rilkian to inspect.

“I don’t understand.”

"I'll show you," Emily shuffled around until she sat behind him and held the mirror up so that it caught both their reflections. She focused on the surrounding garden and sought the room that she held in her mind's eye.

Seconds later, they were sitting in the Chrysanthemum room in Gah Temple, sending the same maid from the day before screaming, "GHOST!" again.

Rilkian jumped up amazed. "How did you do that!"

"I don't know. But I can do it again. And again. We'll just have to wait for the ceremony tomorrow." Emily took his hand, and they ran from the room, laughing.

"See, I practiced a lot last night. I wasn't able to find Earth, but I'm certain I will have it by tomorrow. I have no choice."

"So, you have magical powers too, Emily?"

"Hah, it's not magic. Magic isn't real."

"Of course, it is."

"You'll see when we get to Earth. This," holding up the mirror, "is a function of something we on Earth call technology. Your wizened woman is a fraud. Magic isn't real. Science and technology are."

"How could you know what a wizened can do?"

"I know because technology works in my world. And, well, magic doesn't. Like I could never go back to what I was before this had happened. And I don't plan to."

"I'm honored to be along for the adventure. I…I've dreamt of this moment. Getting away from this awful place and what it has become. I want to see Earth too. I want to see the sky, mountains, and forests." Rilkian was smiling, but tears crested in his eyes.

"Well, then let's go." Emily pulled his hand softly and held up the mirror again with their reflections in it. Seconds later, Rilkian heard a sharp intake of breath that made him jump.

He looked around to see that they were back in his apartment's garden. Yumeiko stood as still as a statue, her hand covering her mouth, her eyes wide as saucers. Next to her, Madame Nanda shrieked and ran to Rilkian's side.

"They've seen us!" Rilkian shouted in his mind.

"Mother! Obánā!" he cried out as he avoided his nursemaid's embrace and walked over to the empress. "What brings you two by? I thought you'd be preparing for tomorrow."

Rilkian then turned toward Emily and took her hand, pressing his forehead against her hand.

"Lady Aiyo was just checking in on me as we have not seen each other for quite a spell."

"I hope you were well," Yumeiko said, displaying a fake sweet smile, trying to make light of the situation even though she was dying for an explanation for what she had just seen.

"I came to personally inform you that the princess had returned to us. But I see you two have already reunited, and how lovely that is. Is it not, Madame Nanda?"

"It is splendid indeed, Your Grace."

Emily and Rilkian remained quiet, both too stunned to say anything.

"I am pleased to see you two making such wonderful friends again," Yumeiko continued.

"Mother, this isn't really a good time."

"You are right, my son. The Lady Aiyo and I were just leaving." Yumeiko slipped her arm around Emily's and gracefully walked/tugged her out of the garden, leaving her son looking after them both, not saying a word, as Madame Nanda held him by the arm like a warden ready to return a prisoner to his cell.

Yumeiko continued smiling until she was out of earshot. "What did you just do?"

"Nothing!" Emily said, attempting and failing to detangle herself from Yumeiko's arm.

"Tell me now! I saw you two appear out of thin air."

"So, she did see us." Emily forced a smile. "Oh, that? It was a trick of the light, Your Ladyship."

"I don't believe for a second that is all there is to it." Yumeiko eyed Emily up, leering into her soul.

"Well…it's not possible to really explain it to you. But it has nothing to do with magic or witchcraft."

"You are a sly thing, aren't you?" Yumeiko grinned. "A girl after my own heart. I like you. But I won't allow anyone or anything to harm Rilkian."

"Me…hurt him?" Emily cried out. "What could I do to hurt him? I adore Rillz."

"Let us hope so, my dear. As you can see, his Obánā, Madame Nanda, is very protective of him as well and is an expert in kill craft. Now, if you don't need anything else, I must continue preparations."

"Of course, Your Ladyship. You must be very busy." Emily bowed to Yumeiko. "I'll see you again this evening for the fitting as planned."

"It is 'I will,' my dear. You are a princess of Aiyo. You will speak as we do," Yumeiko curtsied back and walked away, her face a stoic, bitter mask of determination.

Emily wasn't sure what to make of all that had just occurred, but it did not please her. However, she had much bigger problems to solve. She returned to her apartment.

"The Red Lotus," she said to herself. "I will get to the bottom of this."

***

Some hours later, Emily found herself back in Yumeiko's apartments, surrounded by twittering maidens who were all giggling and gossiping as they dressed her. She did not have a care as all her thoughts were centered on the ceremony she would be a part of. She had to keep her cool.

Aiyo Yumeiko sat fanning herself at her dressing table, watching with a proud, motherly expression on her face.

"I wore that very same gown during my ceremony of engagement to Saehthun," she said, her eyes closing as she recalled a fond memory. "He was so handsome that day." She smiled.

A servant tapped Yumeiko on the shoulder and whispered something in her ear that made her face contort into a look of horror, then settle into a sullen expression.

"Ladies, please excuse us for a moment. All of you!" The maidens bowed and left the room, leaving Emily and Yumeiko alone.

"We may have a problem," Yumeiko said.

"What is it?" Emily asked.

"It seems the emperor granted The Golden Swan a secret audience last night."

"Oh," Emily thought frantically. "Shumaiyuki! She was here?"

"Yes," Yumeiko's voice was low, her expression showing worry. "Apparently, she was disguised as one of the maidens. I need to speak with him."

"What can I do?" Emily asked, worried. "I'll go with you."

"I'm afraid not," Yumeiko said. "You are to stay here under guard in my apartments. Assassins might be about." She glanced around the room before looking back at Emily. "They want to kill you. And I must prevent that from happening."

"I understand, my lady. I'll stay here. I will be fine," Emily nodded encouragingly.

“That is good. Relax and make merry with my ladies while I investigate.”

“If you say so, my lady,” Emily nodded.

“Good,” Yumeiko nodded in agreement. “Now I must go. I will tell you what I find.”

“Yes, of course. If you need anything, let me know,” Emily bowed. “I’ll stay alert.”

“Very well.” Yumeiko spoke with a calm tone and left the room, the quick moment of silence left in her wake was quickly filled with the chatter of the maidens filling the air, as they filtered back into the room.

Emily stood there, thinking of what to say, she could not help growing a little nervous. She sat down on a pillow and allowed the maidens to do her hair with beading. But she could not relax.

“I just have to survive tomorrow night,” she told herself, over and over. “*Somehow I will survive.”*

The Red Lotus

The next day, the buzz of activity filled the air as everyone worked to prepare for the arrival of the guests. The palace was a hub of commotion, with workmen putting the final touches on the camps that would house the large army of people expected to arrive that evening. The sound of construction echoed throughout the palace grounds as servants bustled about, completing their tasks. Meanwhile, guards at the large iron gates were busy deciding who was allowed in and who was not, ensuring the security of the palace and its inhabitants.

The arriving people were, of course, mainly dignitaries representing the more influential families of the empire. As Yumeiko acted as a sort of czar, she made a habit of meeting often with the empire's various bureaucrats and heads of the influential families. While meeting with Yumeiko, many bureaucrats often had the chance to give their input on how the empire should move in the coming year.

And of course, the heads of the families and those below them gained insight into the empire's policy. Any citizen who was a member of a family recognized and accepted by the empire received a yearly stipend when Yumeiko held a meeting with the heads of these families, ensuring their loyalty to House Anele.

The engagement was being held in the enormous hall of the palace, and as the sun began to set, it started to fill with several hundred people ready to pay homage to and celebrate the future of the empire. The smaller tables and seating had been swept aside to make room for a long central table that ran down the length of the hall. On the north side of the hall, a small receiving line was formed where Yumeiko and a glum looking Rilkian sat to meet and greet several important guests.

Emily watched all this happening from behind a screen, hidden inside a small palanquin-shaped box positioned behind and to the far right of the empress. She was dressed up in elaborate garments, with her hair adorned with flowers and beads of many colors.

She scanned the hall, watching the constant flow of people entering, chattering with subdued excitement. The women wore elegant and costly gowns and adorned themselves with jewels. The men, whom she had previously thought of as rustic and uncouth, transformed into men of the world, men of refinement and power.

All these people, who are so important in the empire, while that jerk sits there amongst them like he's so great. Her father sat in what appeared to be a state of deep meditation. Next to him were Phule and the Sowao delegation.

She was genuinely impressed by the grandeur of the event, and in no way used to being in the epicenter of the class elite, even though her presence was veiled within the elaborately adorned box. The entire occasion felt surreal to her, offering a glimpse into a completely foreign world that she had never encountered before.

However, this was a world she only partially comprehended, and she realized she would never fully comprehend it.

It was almost time for the ceremony to begin. Finally, the Aiyo delegation, led by Aiyo Yulori, entered the hall. He was followed by Shumaiyuki, who floated through the door on her lounge, hidden behind a curtained canopy attached to it. Rebecca and Obinari made up her rear. Behind them were the senior Aiyo leadership followed by a bevy of servants and aides. There was no sight of Darren, though.

Emily came to attention, watching as a representative of the imperial house escorted Shumaiyuki to the south side of the hall where a box very similar to Emily's sat. Rebecca helped her step inside, then she and Obinari sat on either side of it.

Emily was taken aback by the sudden noise that rang out as the emperor and his retinue entered the hall. Several hundred people stood, and many began to cheer. The emperor was dressed in a white robe, with sleeves that were long and reached down to his feet. Over this, he wore a heavily embroidered red silk robe that reached the floor.

Emily squinted through the screen, trying to get a glimpse of him. With the shaved head of a priest, she thought he was as regal as could be, and he brought life to the room as he made his way down the receiving line before he sat next to Yumeiko and Rilkian.

The empress was greeted by the emperor, and conversation followed briefly, then the ceremony began. For the first hour, the party sat together and chatted about inconsequential details over wine while various dancers and performers entertained them with their art. It was all very interesting, and the empress seemed particularly impressed.

Emily looked down at the mirror and stared into it, her eyes fixated on her own reflection. She looked oddly beautiful in her alien robes and makeup. Her image was slowly replaced with that of Rebecca, and then suddenly, she was sitting behind her.

Obinari jumped at her sudden appearance as she tapped Rebecca on the shoulder.

"What is it, you fool?" whispered Shumaiyuki, too annoyed to look up and see what the sudden commotion was.

"It's Emily," said Rebecca as she turned to regard her. A brief look of fear flickered in Rebecca's eyes, as Obinari moved in, then hesitated.

"Stay back! I'm a powerful witch! You see what I can do. Come any closer and I'll turn you into a frog!" Emily smiled, holding up the mirror as though it were a weapon.

"She cannot turn you into a frog, you bloody fool!" Shumaiyuki spoke in a rushed whisper. "Apprehend her!"

Emily stared back down at the mirror with an uncertain smile on her face and then pulled Rebecca through with her. In a flash, they were sitting on the grass lawn of Rilkian's apartments. They were surrounded by the gardens and walls that were inlaid throughout the grounds.

"What is going on?" asked Rebecca as she stood up and brushed herself off. She looked exquisite in a gorgeous red gown with a gold obi.

"Why did you bring me here, Emily? How are we even here?"

"Why, hello! It's great to see you too, Beck," said Emily, somewhat taken aback. "I brought us here because I'm going to take us home."

"Home?"

"Yes, home. Back to Earth, away from this crazy place," Emily said with a glimmer of hope in her eyes. "My god, I'm so happy to see you again, Beck!" She moved in for a hug, but Rebecca stepped back.

"Hold on, wait. What are we doing here? I don't get it," Rebecca said, shocked by their surroundings.

"We're in the prince's quarters now," Emily informed Rebecca as she took her hand. "All we have to do is grab Darren, and we can leave this place immediately." However, as she attempted to lead the way, Rebecca swiftly pulled away her hand.

"Emily! Slow down! Darren is back at Odahni, and I don't understand how you managed to bring us here. But you need to take me back now!" Rebecca was visibly upset. Emily turned back with a look of determination.

"What do you mean, take you back?"

"You heard me. Take me back to the ceremony!"

"Beck. Like, aren't you happy to see me?" asked Emily with a hint of pleading in her voice.

"Of course, I am! I thought you were dead. We all did." Rebecca relented as she went over and took Emily in her arms. "I'm just so glad you're alive."

They hugged, and small tears formed in Rebecca's eyes. They held each other for a moment and smiled.

"Don't make me cry," Rebecca whispered. "I don't want my mascara to run."

“Girl, you look amazing! I was scared out of my mind knowing you were being held by the Aiyo. I thought for sure you might’ve been hurt,” said Emily as she released Rebecca.

“I’m fine… really. I’m okay.”

“We can talk about this some other time.” Emily nodded, and with a bright smile, she turned and walked into one of the garden archways.

“Hey! Where are you going?” Rebecca called after her.

“Come on, we have to hurry. I want to grab Darren and get out of here,” Emily said as she took out the mirror.

“I don’t want to see Darren!” said Rebecca, “And I don’t want to go back to Earth!”

“…What?” Emily froze.

“There are too many things I need to do here!” Rebecca continued. “I figured I would never see you again, so I thought I would make a life for myself here. And I have.”

“Are you kidding me? You’re the prisoner of a powerful family, and you’re saying you want to stay here?” Emily looked on quizzically.

“Do I look like a prisoner?” asked Rebecca defensively. “I have a special place in this culture, and I will not be forced to go back, to what? A mediocre life? Emily, I will not go back. I like my status with the Aiyo. It’s better than what I could ever have hoped to have on Earth. I’m not going to let this life slip out of my grasp, so don’t even think about it. And besides… I don’t believe you really want to go back to Earth either. Look at you dressed in ceremonial robes. Aren’t you here to really challenge Shumai?”

“Shumai? You mean my sister? What does she have to do with anything? I have no interest in her or her crown! I’m trying to get as far away from the Aiyo as I possibly can!” Emily seemed perplexed by Rebecca’s reaction. “I came here to take us home!”

"Save it, Emily! Yulori told us all about what you and the empress have planned. And it's a real shame because if you got to know Shumai, you might actually like her. I think you all could learn to love each other and forgive what happened in the past."

"What the…? What, do you have a crush on her or something? Oh my god! You do, don't you?" Emily's eyes widened as the sneer on her face betrayed the shock in her mind.

"What? No! I mean we're close, I guess, but… Whatever! I just don't think you can hate someone just because they tried to kill you when you both were kids! And besides, I'm thankful to her. She's put her trust in me as a close advisor, and she is teaching me how to navigate the politics of this place."

Emily mulled this over for a few moments, then shook her head.

"Beck? These people are dangerous. I've watched them murder in cold blood. They beat me and held me for months in Odahni's dungeons. Believe me, Shumaiyuki is using you. Probably to get to me!"

"You don't even know her! How she's been manipulated, used, and humiliated. And for what? So that she can have someone else come in and take her place? That's messed up! And as for Shumai, she's my friend. We may have had our differences, but she doesn't deserve to be maligned by you!"

Emily rolled her eyes in disdain. "You fell for her sob story? Or did you fall for her? Beck! I've met that girl!"

"You've met a child who was locked away in a tower! I don't know how else to describe it," Rebecca said as her eyes welled up with tears.

"Don't cry," said Emily, sounding almost condescending.

"Don't take that tone with me, Emily! I'm not a child, and this is my choice. Now take me back, damn it! Tonight is my national debut as the Red Lotus, and I'm not going to let you ruin it!"

"I'm not taking you anywhere but back to your family! I have no choice but to take you by force!" Emily replied, raising her voice as she stepped towards Rebecca.

A flurry of thoughts ran through Rebecca's mind. She didn't have time to work through a bunch of emotions and decisions. She had to make a quick choice. Her decision was to consider a good old-fashioned escape.

"Get out of my way!" Rebecca said as she lunged for Emily. Her eyes squinted, and with a dark menace, she came at Emily, and the two girls collided as they tumbled and tangled with each other onto the plush lawn.

"Rebecca, stop! What is wrong with you?" Emily grunted. They were exchanging soft punches as they rolled across the lawn—furious and labored as they struggled under the inescapable weight of their ceremonial attire.

Emily overpowered Rebecca, suddenly wrenching an arm free, and initiated an arm-bar on her. Rebecca's face slowly twisted and contorted in a tremendous show of force as she used her brute might to pull her arm free. Once her arm was free, she then kicked Emily off of her and stood up as Emily slowly stood.

"Leave me alone and take me back!" Rebecca shouted. She was breathing heavily while she took several backward steps.

Emily stepped forward and locked eyes with her. "So this is all about power and position for you, Beck? Is that it? You get seduced by the Aiyo and all you want to do is what? Advance a political career? What about when they came for Marie Antoinette's head? What do you think is going to happen to you, Beck?"

"You're one to talk, Emily," Rebecca said between breaths.

"Look, I don't know what the hell Yulori told you, but believe me, it's a lie."

"You do not know me, Emily. I've always been your charitable plus one, the nerdy sidekick, and you can't stand to see me stepping into myself. Shumaiyuki sees me. She understands love, loyalty, and friendship."

“Oh, please! Don’t even try that. I know what this is really about!” Emily shouted.

“Really? Go on, what is this really about?”

“This is about you using Shumaiyuki to make yourself feel important. You’re always looking for validation, and now you’ve found it in her,” Emily shot back.

Rebecca’s face became flushed, and there was a deep sense of anger in her eyes. “You’re wrong!” she said, averting her gaze…, “You just think it’s all about you all the time, Emily! Sometimes you can be so self-absorbed. Well, I’m all about me now!”

“Is that all it is?” A vein popped up on Emily’s forehead. “Cause I can’t go back to Earth without you?”

“Well, then I suggest you start looking for real estate here, Emily. Because I am not going anywhere with you!” Rebecca shouted.

Emily’s face reddened and her eyes narrowed as she took several steps forward. “Fine! If that’s how you want to play it. I hope you find a home with the Aiyo. In the end, you’ll end up dead!”

“Says the girl that had Yulori fake her own death so that she could practice being queen,” Rebecca retorted as a sly smirk overtook her lips. “Poor Emily, you see your plan won’t work! Everyone is gathered for Shumai, not you!”

“Idiot! Rilkian proposed to me yesterday! All I have to say is yes, and I’m your next empress! Furthermore, my grandfather has offered me the position of Queen Seizhone! I don’t want either position because I’m not some power-hungry asshole! I just want a return to something normal.”

“Well, this is my new normal, Emily. I wish you’d respect it.” Rebecca’s face was flushed with anger as she stood her ground.

“Beck, don’t do this!” Emily shouted at her.

“Please take me back, Emily. This is a very important night for me, and my lady, Princess Shumaiyuki. If you really have no interest in marrying the crown prince, then just step aside, go where you want, and leave us alone!”

“How am I suddenly the bad guy in all of this?”

“You just up out of nowhere showing off your new powers, telling people what to do. Who the hell do you think you are? Maybe you are the bad guy, Emily, maybe you are a witch just like they said you are.”

Emily was taken aback as she considered Rebecca’s statement. The thought came to her that she was Maishae, and Maishae was her.

But Emily couldn’t help feeling a twinge of guilt, as if none of this was her fault, but rather it was Eleanor’s. Eleanor was the one who was the witch.

“Take me back, damn it!” Rebecca was screaming, as she took Emily by her shoulders and shook her out of her haze.

“I’m going to miss my whole performance because of you! You selfish…oh.”

Suddenly they were standing next to Shumaiyuki’s box in the grand hall, only now it was surrounded by several Aiyo servants and soldiers who all gasped and took a step back at the girls’ sudden appearance.

“Have it your way, Beck! But the second you’re done with your stupid dance; we are out of here!”

Emily disappeared just as quickly as she had come.

“How long were we gone?” Rebecca turned to Obinari.

“Long enough!” Shumaiyuki’s voice came from the box. “What did she want?”

Rebecca looked at the small crowd that had gathered around the box.

"I… I think perhaps that is a discussion better held for later, my lady," she said, looking back into the box nervously.

"Tell me," Shumaiyuki said sternly.

Rebecca pursed her lips, trying not to look nervous. "She just wanted to talk about… the party," she said lightly.

"What about it?"

"Oh, nothing, she was just saying that the guests are all gathered for you… and not her," she said.

Shumaiyuki looked down into the room at the crowd. "I see," she said, "You are lying."

Rebecca gave a small smile and then spoke to the Tabaiken soldiers, "As you can see, we are in good condition here. You may proceed with your tasks elsewhere."

The soldiers respectfully bowed and went back to their original positions.

Shumaiyuki turned to look at Rebecca through the wooden lattice work screen.

"Ribiki… Are you lying to me?"

"No… I just didn't want to worry you…" Rebecca said softly.

"So, she is here, and with the powers of a witch no less," Shumaiyuki said uneasily.

Rebecca nodded. "she said she has a way to return me, us to our world and wanted me to leave with her, but I refused. My place is here by your side, my lady."

Shumaiyuki smiled, then laughed in a slightly harsher tone. "She is doing this to get to me, isn't she? Do you know where she is now?"

Rebecca looked away from Shumaiyuki and shook her head. "I suspect she was inside the box behind the empress. I don't know where she might have gotten to now.

I told her Darren is back at Odahni. Perhaps she is trying to convince him to join her." Rebecca lied, haunted by Emily's last words to her.

"That is a possibility, but I do not think it is true," Shumaiyuki looked out at the vast open space of the room, watching the dancers and musician performers.

"Especially when all of the action is here," she said, looking over at the crowd of people. "No, Ribiki, I am certain she is here for me. She probably still blames me for that unfortunate incident when we were children. I can understand her anger, but I cannot allow her to take you from this world."

Rebecca leaned closer to the box and whispered, "She told me Yulori is lying about them working together. She has no interest in marrying the prince or becoming empress. She just wants to go home. I really don't think she is our main concern as much as he is."

Shumaiyuki nodded. "Do you think she's telling the truth, Ribiki? It seems a little too convenient."

"She could have just as easily whisked you away instead of me," said Rebecca, "So I'm inclined to believe her."

"I suppose so," said Shumaiyuki. "But that is not all that bothers me," she said, watching Yulori traverse the room, shaking hands with other guests. He bowed to the emperor and empress, who were upon a small platform. He then came directly to the box and bowed before Shumaiyuki.

"My lady, the Anele would like for your pet to perform for them. I am to give you this," he pushed a small scroll towards the screen.

"Obinari," Shumaiyuki said; Obinari came to her side and took the scroll and pushed it through one of the many small openings.

Shumaiyuki read silently. "Very well, uncle, please show Lady Ribiki the way."

"Yes, my lady." He glared at Rebecca with a sly smile upon his lips. "If you would be so kind as to follow me," he said.

“Yes, of course, my lord,” Rebecca said as she bowed to the screen.

He led Rebecca to a room where another box sat, only it was highly decorated with colorful carved peacocks and peonies. A large green curtain was pulled across the front side, which Yulori moved aside so that she could enter.

“Enjoy your last dance, Lady Ribiki,” he said with a bow as he left the room, shutting the door behind him. Two servants, dressed in scarlet jumpsuits, began to wheel the box out after him.

Once back in the hall, large mirrors placed in front of fire-lit urns acted as stage lights, and Rebecca was blinded by the sudden brightness. Four musicians sat on each corner of the center platform, playing traditional music of their native lands.

Yulori opened the curtain as the musicians finished their music.

“This is a very special performance given to only a very select few,” he bellowed. “It is a performance that will be remembered by generations to come. Now, I give you a special treat! A mystical maiden from the fire realm whose speed and grace will surely delight you. I give you the pinnacle of Aiyo entertainment; I present Lady Ribiki! The Red Lotus!”

Rebecca gracefully glided onto the stage, her delicate steps echoing the sound of a hollow drum accompanied by the soothing melody of a Biwa and flute. She wore traditional robes, her hair styled in a sleek and sophisticated updo, adorned with delicate hairpins and fresh flowers. As the music began, she gracefully lifted her arms, her movements slow and controlled. Her fingers gently fluttered, as if they were the wings of a butterfly, her hips swaying in perfect time with the rhythm of the music.

The Red Lotus dance was a mesmerizing blend of fluid movements and still poses, each one executed with precision and poise. Rebecca’s every step was a statement of grace and beauty, her every gesture a symbol of the elegant and refined culture of the feudal land.

Her facial expressions were controlled and subtle, her eyes downcast, adding to the air of mystery surrounding her.

Shumaiyuki watched the performance with a racing heart. Her Ribiki was a stunning sight. Initially, she may have viewed her as a pet, but they had since formed a friendship. She wouldn't let the witch Emily take her away.

Across the hall, Emily rolled her eyes and let out a sarcastic remark from behind her screen, "This is ridiculous! She's copying that dance from that actress on Love in the Time of Ming!" She then spoke up over the music, "She's basically just ripping off a TV show!"

Yumeiko's eyebrows furrowed, and she shot a scowl at the box, but her gaze was soon drawn back to the excitement of the magnificent performance. As the music crescendoed, Rebecca's movements became more and more energetic, her body flowing like water. She twirled and spun, her robes billowing out behind her, the colors of the fabric blending with the colors of the stage. The audience was captivated, their eyes fixed on her every move, as she danced with an ethereal grace that seemed to transcend time and place.

She twirled in a fluid motion, her limbs flowing seamlessly as she lifted one leg and wrapped it around the other in a stunning display of balance. Her landing was graceful, with one foot pointed elegantly to the ground. She bowed deeply to the applause of the audience.

Yulori descended to the floor and gave a bow to Rebecca, before offering his hand to her.

"The Red Lotus!" He exclaimed joyfully. "May I be honored with the opportunity to introduce you to the Aenele?"

Rebecca gazed into his eyes and asked, "Do I have a say in the matter, my lord?"

"Of course, you don't," He lowered his voice. "I would stay in my place if I were you. After tonight, you won't have my niece to protect you. But I can." He pulled her along with him, waving as groups of nearby elites bowed to her enthusiastically.

As they approached the royal dais, Yulori bowed to the emperor and empress.

"She is Lady Ribiki, Your Grace," he turned to Rebecca and bowed.

"My lady, you were magnificent," said the emperor in a soothing voice. "Your performance was just magnificent. I believe we must have a scroll written about this dance. It will survive the test of time." He said, pulling a lacquered box off a nearby table. "Please accept this humble gift as a gesture of our gratitude for blessing us with such delight."

"Oh, my lord," she said as she bowed, accepting the box, "I am beyond honored by Your Grace."

The empress looked at her husband in surprise but then stood up and clapped her hands together as if catching an idea.

"The emperor is correct! We must have a scroll written of this dance. It would be a shame not to preserve such a masterpiece."

"I agree with Your Grace." Yulori said, holding her gaze for a second longer than she liked.

"Let us all join in the spirit of dance," she said, ignoring her nephew, "This celebration of unity is also a ball. Please, take to the floor and make merry with this wonderful occasion."

The emperor smiled and clapped his hands in agreement. Yulori stood and pulled Rebecca close to him, "Lady Ribiki, would you honor me with a dance?" he asked, holding her hand tightly.

"I don't much like to dance with men who threaten my life, my lord," she whispered, looking away coyly.

He leaned into her, "And yet you like it just the same."

"How do you know what I like, my lord?" she said, tilting her head as he pulled her along to join the growing crowd of couples performing a waltz-like two-step.

He pulled her close, held her hand, and pleaded, "Please continue to hate me. I find it makes me want you in ways I hadn't considered."

Rebecca looked him in the eye and calmly said, “I don’t hate you, my lord. Your megalomaniacal behavior intrigues me.”

“I’m extremely good at manipulating people. I take great pride in it,” he said quickly. He then spun her around for a second or two and then pulled her back so close that their faces almost touched.

“Surely you have a man that intrigues you. You’re an exceptional woman,” he whispered, holding her waist. “Though I doubt you can do better than me.”

“I don’t want to do better than you,” she said with a sly smile. “I don’t want to do you, at all.”

“Careful now,” he warned. “You never want to provoke the lord of the house you’ve aligned yourself with,” he said with a laugh.

“Hm,” she replied, glancing away, “I should fear for my life were I to provoke a monster like you, but I do not.” She stepped back, slightly. He pulled her close to him, looked down on her, and said,

“You are a remarkable woman, Lady Ribiki.”

“My lord, what has come over you? You dishonor your wife and children!”

“Perhaps. But this night, I find your dance has aroused in me a certain… possessiveness.”

“You’re the lord of a house. Have you no shame?”

“Of course, I do, but since I am, as you say, a monster. Why not enjoy chasing the damsel through the forest, as a monster does,” he said, placing her arm around his shoulder, “And when you decide to run, I’ll be close behind.”

“I don’t appreciate the way you speak to me, my lord,” she said with a frown. “I’m not a thing, I’m a person. You need to remember that.”

“You are an it, yet an exceptional one, and that is why I want you in such a way.”

"You just told me to enjoy my last dance! I can't be yours because you're going to kill me! Right?" she said angrily.

"That was before I saw your core value, my lady," he said calmly. "I see why my niece keeps you around. The novelty of your presence has considerably upped her political capital with the families as a whole."

"Oh," she shot back, "and what is my core value?"

He spun her around again, "Those big blue eyes so full of dignity. That bright smile is so full of wonder. You are a captivating woman, Lady Ribiki," he said, slowly spinning her around and then pulling her closer. "The people cannot keep their eyes off you. Look at how they stare. I hear women are even dying their hair to emulate yours."

"You know who else is staring? Your wife."

"Even she desires your red hair."

"Big deal. I'm finally the popular girl on campus!"

"You are popular. I know Shumaiyuki better than she knows herself, Rebecca. How far do you think you will go before she becomes jealous of all the attention you are getting?"

"What!" Rebecca said angrily. "She is my friend!"

Yulori placed one hand on the small of her back,

"People like us don't have friends. We have people we want to use for our own purposes."

"Enough," she said, pulling away. "I'm tired of your games and lies. I spoke with Emily, and she said you put her in a dungeon."

"You lie and are no good at it," he said, looking her in the eyes. "How could you have possibly spoken with her?"

"What do you want from me, my lord?" she said with a frown, looking down at his hand on her waist.

"I want three things from you," he said in a quiet, deliberate voice, "First, I want you to stay here in the capital with me. Second, I want you to deny her lies when the emperor confronts her treachery, and third and most importantly, I want you to watch. You will be witnesses as I crush my enemies like grapes under my foot."

"The scandal will be unreal when the truth comes out about you," Rebecca said bravely but nervously.

"I doubt it. Shumai will be executed for treason against the empire; why should you die with her when the very power of your presence assures your ascension by my side?"

"I will suffer her fate even knowing it will cost me my life because I believe in her."

"Sacrifice is the cost of the weak with barely a concept of the greater good," he said, turning to face the emperor and empress. A queer look on his face quickly turned to one of horror.

"Oh no," he whispered, "she's here."

Rebecca followed his eyes to see Emily hastily emerge from her box behind the royals and begin to walk towards them. Rilkian quickly stood and sidled up to her, took her hand, and pulled her to the dance floor before she got too far. The volume of the tones in the ballroom dropped considerably as the crowd backed away from the scene in front of them to watch the drama unfold.

"What are you doing?" Emily hissed.

"What are you doing? You're going to get yourself killed!"

He took her in his arms as the music played. They waltzed a few turns around the room and didn't speak until they were out of the spotlight. He let her hand go and leaned into her.

"Your intentions are good, but rash. I know you want to save your friends, but Rebecca is under The Aiyo's protection now and will not die."

"None of us will ever be safe if we stay here," she said.

"You cannot win against them alone."

"I've already won. Now I just have to collect my prize," Emily looked at Rebecca, the redhead watching them with her mouth agape.

"Please let me keep you safe," Rilkian said, and kissed her deeply. The shock that went throughout the room was palpable as people milled around them, unsure what to make of what was happening.

"Get off of me!" she said forcefully, her anger overcoming her shock. Rilkian slowly backed away and quickly whispered,

"I fear for your life, Emily. Now that we have kissed before the families, we must be wed."

"Never," she said, balling her hands into fists.

"If you love me, you will do this."

She thought for a moment, and her anger seemed to fade away. "I care for you, Rillz, I swear I do, but love… oh Jeil!"

Jeil stepped between them and pushed Rilkian away from Emily, "You dishonor our lady, brother."

The crowd moved back, and a stunned silence fell over the room as he slowly turned and glared at Rilkian. The tension between the brothers was unmistakable.

"You will not touch her," Rilkian said quietly.

"Brother, a word," Jeil looked around the room and saw that people were watching them.

"She is my bride. You will not touch her," he repeated, his voice dropping to a growl.

"I did not wish to interfere, but our lady was clearly distressed!" Jeil said with a sad look. "I do not wish to quarrel."

Rilkian's eyes flashed, and his hands balled into fists. "Get out of my way, Rijeil."

"You cast yourself into the depths, brother," he said without moving. "See how all eyes bear witness to your reckless abandonment of protocol."

"Do not challenge me!" Rilkian said, pushing between them and taking Emily's hand.

"We leave for Arth!"

"Not after what you just pulled!" said Emily, "Kissing me out of the blue like that."

"I merely showed you what you've been feeling, and you felt it!" he said as his voice got louder. "It's no different than how you make me feel! What has changed?"

Emily winced as she felt the anger radiating from him. "That's different! You just said I had to marry you! Like you are planning on staying here after all."

"I am planning on going wherever you go," Rilkian said, calming down. "I only kissed you to break off the official engagement to her!" He pointed across the room. Shumaiyuki was floating towards them, glaring murderously.

Emily stiffened as she looked at the girl who once tried to kill her. They were almost identical, something which Emily had forgotten.

"I have a feeling things are about to get ugly," Emily said as the crowd parted, making a path for Shumaiyuki's lounge.

"Seize the witch!" Shumaiyuki yelled over the crowd. "She is a witch and has enchanted the crown prince!" Several Aiyo guards trotted behind the lounge as Shumaiyuki waved a gold scepter wildly.

Emily gazed at the crowd's reaction; first, someone gasped, then whispers ran through, and then everyone's eyes widened. It was like someone had dropped a bucket of ice water over the whole party. They parted in a wave and allowed many Aiyo guards to advance.

Minister Djowobb moved to stand, but a steady hand and raised eyebrow from Phule held him back.

“This is a damned nightmare,” he said to Phule in a low voice.

“Perhaps, maybe not. I’m interested in seeing the end result.” Phule shrugged.

The crowd was shocked, their eyes flicking between the twin princesses as Shumaiyuki stepped off her lounge and stood. She had a tinge of recognition in her eyes as she slowly approached Emily.

Her guards formed a semicircle around herself, Emily, and the rival princes. She stopped within arm’s reach of Emily.

“Shumaiyuki,” Emily said in a low voice, sparing no emotion for the girl standing before her.

Zohri

As Emily was escorted by the emperor's Drizen guard to the royal dais, she found herself unsure of how to react. She was torn between expressing defiance and trying to appeal to his compassion. Her thoughts and feelings were in turmoil. She didn't know whether it would be best to stand proudly and glare at him or to appear submissive and beg for mercy.

The emperor stared at her, frowning and stroking his bare chin, while she took the opportunity to assess his face as well. He remained silent, his gaze alternating between Emily and Shumaiyuki.

Surrounding them, the room was filled with a group of intimidating Drizen knights, all of whom were large men. They were all dressed in identical black armor and seemed to be watching Emily intently as she looked between them and the emperor.

The emperor leaned forward and turned his gaze back to Shumaiyuki. She bowed her head slightly and spoke.

"Your Highness, I fear these circumstances call for imprisonment or death."

"Hmm, indeed, Lady Aiyo, but this girl is not an imposter. She is your sister. You failed to mention that!" The emperor replied, glancing out into the crowd and smirking. He raised his hand to quiet the room and then turned his attention back to Emily.

"You are first born to Lady Oeki, am I right?"

"Yes, Your Grace. I am," Emily answered.

After pausing to look at her for a moment, he replied, "Oeki was one of the most wonderful people I have ever known. I deeply regret giving her to my brother, but she did bring shame upon herself in the way you were conceived." He glanced over at Phule's group, noting that Djowobb was nowhere to be seen, before returning his attention to Emily.

Emily turned pale as a shiver ran down her spine. She felt the impact of his words as if he had spoken them with physical force.

After staring at her for a moment, he took a deep breath and looked over at his wife.

"Did you know about this?" He asked her.

"Of course I did," Yumeiko replied, covering her mouth with her fan. "Why ask what you already know?"

"Hmph. I suppose I do, Yumeiko," he said, leaning back on his pillow. He looked at Emily again and then leaned forward. "Come here, girl," he said, motioning for her to move closer. Emily stepped forward, causing the standing Shumaiyuki to startle slightly.

"What should we do with you, young lady?" he asked Emily. But before she could respond, he called out, "Rilkian!"

The crown prince stepped forward and bowed, "Your Grace."

"What do you think we should do, boy? Two princesses, essentially with the same face. What does your heart say?"

Emily heard Shumaiyuki mutter something under her breath as she took a step forward,

"She is an imposter, Your Highness. Working with Aiyo Yulori to try to take my place!"

"You speak out of turn!" Yumeiko stood up and pointed accusingly.

"You are in on it too, auntie, and I won't tolerate it!"

"Auntie! How dare you! I am your empress. Lower your eyes and show me respect!"

Shumaiyuki seemed unfazed and stood her ground. "Your Highness, I must insist that you take this woman into custody," she said, bowing again.

"Tell me, young lady. What is it that you want?" The emperor asked softly, his demeanor calm as he spoke.

“Are you really not going to address this? This shortfoots disrespect!” Yumeiko turned to her husband. “Your Highness, this child is…”

He waved his hand, and Yumeiko stared at him, her mouth half open. He looked over at Emily and motioned for her to continue.

“I…I want to go home,” Emily said. She looked over at Rebecca, feeling afraid and alone, unsure of what was going to happen to her.

“I want to go back to my real home on Earth. I want to return to my small, one-bedroom apartment that I share with my grandma, who, believe it or not, made her own sleeping bed in the crawl space because she’s so small. I want to go back to my underperforming high school with its anti-theft gates covering all the windows. I want to watch the old people in the park do Tai Chi again. I want to go home with my best friend.”

Emily took a deep breath and said, “I want…I want my life back.”

The emperor looked at her for a moment, his eyes steady and unamused. Emily tried to stop herself from crying, knowing she needed to be strong. But the more she thought about everything that had happened and the people who had died, the worse she felt. She just wanted to go back to the life she had before.

“You are home, my dear,” the emperor said. He looked over at Yumeiko and then back at Emily. “While I understand your desire, princess, I cannot allow war to consume the land. That would be a crime too great and unforgivable.”

“What? Why would there be war?”

“Your grandfather, Zhon, is threatening to attack our lands and has positioned his troops on our borders. I cannot allow this when all he is asking for is the return of his kin. We will not let Zohara soldiers defile our land.”

“But Your Highness, you cannot undo their union…” Yumeiko started. “It was her! She was betrothed to the crown prince when they were children, not the Golden Swan.

We were there! I swear on this." She tore off the yellow sash with a red ribbon around her waist and dropped it on the floor. She took a deep breath and continued, "Your Highness..."

"You will speak no longer," he glared at Yumeiko, speaking just loud enough for her, Emily, and Shumaiyuki to hear. She bowed her head, her face contorting with contempt for the man she had never wanted to marry.

Emily looked at the yellow sash on the floor and then at the emperor. "I want to go home," she said.

He ignored her, his face serious, and addressed his son. "Rilkian!"

"Yes, Your Highness."

"You will marry the Golden Swan, as per my decree," the emperor ordered. "Zohri will be returned to her grandfather, where she will become Queen Zhon with Rijeil as her Prince Consort."

Shumaiyuki smiled and then burst into uncontrolled laughter. Emily looked at her, trying to understand what was happening.

Jeil stepped forward and bowed, smiling as the hall was filled with gasps, screams, and even cheers from nobles and high-born alike.

"What are you saying? Who is Zohri?" Emily asked. "And what does it mean to be a prince consort?"

"Zohri is the name of your grandfather's mother, and the name he has given you," Jeil explained. "Being a prince consort means that we are to be married. You as the ruling monarch of Zhon, and I as your champion."

"What the fuck!" Emily exclaimed.

"It was in your grandfather's letter. Unfortunately, I wasn't able to finish reading it to you earlier..." Jeil said.

"Cut the crap, Jeil! You knew this all along and didn't say anything?" Emily accused.

"Princess Zohri, I..." Jeil started.

“Don’t call me Zohri! The last thing I need is another name,” Emily interrupted, turning to face Rebecca. She had to raise her voice over Shumaiyuki’s laughter.

“Hey! Did you know about this?” Emily asked.

“No, Zohri. I assure you none of us did,” Shumaiyuki replied, settling back down in her lounge.

Emily looked at Jeil, fuming. “What about you? When were you planning on telling me about this, huh?”

“Princess, please don’t be upset,” Jeil said, looking at her apologetically.

Emily felt like smashing his face in. The more she thought about it, the angrier she became. She could feel the tears rolling down her cheeks, leaving trails of dark mascara down her packed foundation. Someone hugged her, and she realized it was Rebecca.

“I’m sorry, Emily, but maybe this is for the best,” Rebecca said.

“Will someone explain to me what’s going on?” Emily demanded. She pushed Rebecca off of her so hard that the girl went crashing into Shumaiyuki’s lounge and landed hard on the floor.

“Jeil! Explain it to me!” Emily demanded.

“Silence!” The emperor said, his voice echoing across the hall. Everyone melted and bowed as he spoke. He stood and waved his hand, and instantly Emily was surrounded by his Drizen guard.

“You will return to your apartments and await the conclusion of this evening’s celebration. Take her,” he ordered.

“I’m not going anywhere without a fight!” Emily protested, standing her ground.

“Princess Zohri, please allow us to escort you,” the Drizen knight said, his voice impassive but his right-hand hovering near his sword.

Emily stepped back and reached into her robe, pulling out her keyring. She glared at the Drizen and said, “This is going to burn.” as three more stepped forward and held their swords at the ready. Emily quickly maneuvered a small metal tube attached to the keyring and sprayed a stream of pepper spray, creating a cloudy mist that stung the eyes of anyone in the immediate vicinity, including the emperor.

Using the confusion and temporary blindness of the Drizen, Emily tried to run but tripped on her heavy robes. She fell and felt someone’s arms grab her and pull her up. She turned her head and saw the demon mask of Yienguoi-Jin.

“Are you alright, child?” The demon looked down at her, and Emily slowly realized who he was.

“Father?” She stood up, feeling his arms wrap around her. She started to cry.

A voice in her head said, Now is not the time for tears, but for escape.

“This way, run,” he whispered.

The emperor’s voice boomed, “Capture them! She must not escape!”

The cry of the Drizen filled the air, and the sound of their boots striking the floor resonated through the hall like a beating heart. Yienguoi-Jin found his and Emily’s way blocked as Drizen fighters surrounded them. As he looked up, his eyes glowing red, he spoke in a commanding voice, “Stand aside!” The Drizen retreated, but kept their swords pointed at him.

“That man is Yienguoi-Jin!” Shumaiyuki yelled. “Kill him and you’ll become famous!”

Emily turned to her right, where Shumaiyuki stood with a look of anger and shock on her face. But Emily’s focus was on Rebecca. She broke free from her father’s grip and ran across the hall, grabbing her best friend’s hand.

“We’re leaving now!” she exclaimed.

"Stay back!" Shumaiyuki swung her gold, swan-tipped scepter at Emily's wrist, using it to push them apart. Emily recoiled, feeling the searing pain in her arm, and grabbed the swan pin from her hair. She aimed the sharp end at Shumaiyuki and watched as it grew in size, piercing through the floating cushion.

Shumaiyuki countered by swinging her scepter, knocking the staff loose, and then launching a hard punch at Emily. Both were around the same size, but Shumaiyuki was very strong.

As Emily stumbled backwards, cursing the restrictive nature of her robes, Shumaiyuki chased after her, unleashing a barrage of punches and two charging strikes with her scepter.

Emily managed to roll out of the way of the strikes and pushed herself off the ground, swinging her staff at Shumaiyuki. The fox demon floated out of the way by rapidly raising her lounge higher, but then swooped back down immediately.

Emily ducked another swipe from the scepter and charged forward, spinning her staff in a full arc and forcing Shumaiyuki into a defensive posture. With a short hop and well-timed right hook, Emily knocked Shumaiyuki off her lounge and she crashed to the floor, landing on her back.

Yienguoi-Jin was occupied with fighting the Drizen, his strength and fearlessness making him a formidable opponent.

He swung his dagger with such force that it tore through their armor, but the Drizen pressed their advantage and closed in, surrounding him.

The massive knights attacked from all sides, but Yienguoi-Jin leaned back and avoided their swipes, then launched himself in a flying kick towards the emperor. Another group of the emperor's guard rushed in to stop him, leaping from the walls and landing in front of the emperor along with his Drizen. Yienguoi-Jin's thrashing legs wrapped around one bodyguard and he forced him to the ground.

Emily's heart pounded in her chest and her breathing became heavy as she backed away from Shumaiyuki. She stumbled and fell backwards, tripping over a spectator trying to escape the melee.

She tumbled into one of the emperor's bodyguards and scrambled to grab her staff, using the pommel to break free. She used the momentum to roll out of the way of Shumaiyuki's follow-up attack.

As they backed away from each other, Emily prepared to defend herself against Shumaiyuki's next attack. The scepter seemed to have a life of its own, as if it were determined to pierce right through her. She danced backwards and held her staff between herself and Shumaiyuki.

"You won't escape! How dare you ruin my festival!" Shumaiyuki lunged forward and struck. Emily tried to move out of the way, but the razor-sharp wings of the scepter's swan pummel cut through her robe and sliced her skin just above her breast.

"This is no contest," Shumaiyuki laughed as she struck again, smashing her staff into Emily's chest as Emily retreated.

"Please, I don't want to hurt you!" Emily gasped, stumbling back and struggling to keep her staff in the air.

Shumaiyuki charged at Emily once more, screaming, "You'll have to kill me first!"

The entire hall had become a battleground, with Yienguoi-Jin still fighting the Drizen, outpacing them five to one. Aiyo soldiers trying to reach Shumaiyuki grappled with soldiers from other clans.

Nobles ran about the room in excitement and panic, trying to get to safety and rescue their wives and daughters. But above it all, the shrill wail of a familiar voice echoed through the hall:

"Give me back my body!"

Emily froze as a portal opened above her. Shumaiyuki's eyes widened in shock.

"What is it?" Jeil rushed to Emily's side and held her as Maishae landed on the floor, a long metal halberd in her hand. Behind her, no fewer than two hundred of her others emerged from the portal, wielding swords, spears, and maces. They all made a beeline for Emily and Shumaiyuki.

"It's time for us to settle this!" Maishae bellowed. "Attack! Attack!"

Emily stood, blood dripping from her lip, her robe torn, and her hair in tatters. She glanced to her side, where Yienguoi-Jin was fighting Drizen and others alike, smiled, and licked her lips.

"So be it," Emily said as her staff spun in her hands and her hair whipped back. With a quick twirl, she lashed out at Maishae. Maishae blocked the feint and, with a jab of her halberd, sent Emily flying into the center of the crowded hall.

As the imperial family was rushed out of the hall, Jeil jumped into the fray, his long sword finding its mark deep in one of Maishae's others. Maishae leapt into the air, her halberd crackling and sparking as she swung towards them.

Emily caught the halberd with her staff and pushed it aside. Maishae landed and swiveled in one smooth motion, meeting Emily with a furious slash of her blade. Emily ducked the heavy swipe and launched a wild counter-swipe, catching the old woman in the chest.

Maishae stumbled and fell to the ground, gasping for air as she stared in shock at the ferocity of Emily's attack. Emily pressed forward, delivering a powerful blow to another of her opponents. With every swing of her staff, another one of Maishae's group was sent to their demise, their cries and war cries filling the hall.

Suddenly, Shumaiyuki tried to impale Emily with her scepter, but Emily managed to duck and counterattack, causing Shumaiyuki to stumble. Emily's hair and staff flew around her as she charged forward and, with a quick movement, knocked Shumaiyuki to the ground. She straddled the girl, sitting on her chest and gazing into her eyes.

"I was holding back on you earlier for Beck's sake," Emily declared, her voice full of determination, "but now I'm going to…" She was unable to finish her statement as Obinari caught her off guard with a swift kick that sent her tumbling to the ground. He pounced on her, his sword swinging down towards her.

Emily, determined not to be defeated, quickly rose to her knees, and began to back away from Obinari with lightning speed.

He licked his lips hungrily, clearly eager for the kill, and charged towards her blindly. Emily sprang to her feet and took a step back, her staff held at the ready as she defended herself.

As Obinari approached, Emily gracefully launched herself into the air with a flip, landing just in time to catch the hilt of his long sword with a strike of her own. She delivered a powerful kick to his back and spun her staff around, using it to force the sword from his hand.

Shumaiyuki, undeterred, made another sudden attack on Emily from behind. But Emily was quick to respond, stepping to the side and striking the scepter with her staff, sending it flying out of Shumaiyuki's grasp. Spinning her staff around, Emily slashed at Shumaiyuki's chest; blood sprayed from her broken nose as she ducked and rolled to avoid the blow.

With a quick glance and a swift movement, Shumaiyuki threw several small, spiked metal balls towards Emily, forcing her to retreat and deflect them with her staff. One of the balls caught Emily in the shoulder, causing her to cry out.

Weakened by the blow, she stumbled backwards, her staff falling to her side as blood spurted from her wound. She watched as Shumaiyuki crawled towards her, a look of determination on her face.

Emily raised her staff and snapped it with a sharp crack. She spun around and delivered a powerful blow to the side of Shumaiyuki's head, knocking her unconscious. The Golden Swan collapsed to the floor, with Obinari abandoning his attack to protect her from further harm.

Emily stood with her staff over her shoulder, surveying the fray as the sound of battle engulfed her. The Drizen and Aiyo soldiers were locked in a fierce battle, while Maishae and her allies seemed to be everywhere at once.

Emily's eyes landed on Yienguoi-Jin, who was covered in blood, much of it belonging to Drizen. He stood over one of the fallen knights, his long sword stuck deep in the chest of the defeated foe.

"Dad," Emily called out, hurrying over to him. "Are you okay?"

Yienguoi-Jin shook his head and sighed. "Let's just get this finished," he muttered, pulling out his blade. Maishae leapt forward, frowning, and shouted, "Get out of my body! It's mine, mine, mine!" Emily charged forward as well, moving faster than she thought possible.

Maishae struck Emily, and the blow sent her stumbling backward, causing her to fall to the ground. But Emily quickly pushed herself back up and, with a grimace, raised her staff. Maishae's staff swung through the air, trying to hit Emily's head.

With a wide swing, the witch raised her halberd and stabbed it forward. Emily's body twisted and swayed with the attack, allowing the blade to pass by her.

Maishae gasped for air as Emily's staff hit her in the abdomen, stunning her. In turn, Emily was surrounded by a group of others as she and Yienguoi-Jin became trapped.

She managed to strike one of the others, despite her bleeding shoulder, but she knew she wouldn't be able to hold out much longer. Yienguoi-Jin glanced at her, then turned back to the others and charged forward, blade raised, cutting down their vanguard. Emily watched as he dispatched one of their captains.

Emily swung around to meet the next wave of Drizen soldiers approaching her. She was wild-eyed and used her staff to balance herself. She took a deep breath, picked up the staff, and swung it through the air, unleashing powerful attack after attack.

The Drizen soldiers around her fell, some mortally wounded, and others simply struck down as Emily continued her relentless assault. An other disrupted her onslaught by slamming into her, causing Emily to stumble and fall to the ground, landing on her back. She tried to recover but felt winded and filled with pain as she held her stomach.

A horn sounded, signaling the arrival of more imperial soldiers who rushed into the hall. Emily struggled to her feet and braced her staff, just in time to deflect the blow from a sword.

Emily avoided the blade and struck back repeatedly, her force knocking the man back. But she couldn't hold him at bay.

Maishae regained her footing and readied her halberd. "Don't you dare, Maisha," Yienguoi-Jin shouted as he rushed towards Emily. Maishae turned to him and swung her halberd down, but Yienguoi-Jin deflected the blow with his sword.

"No, Yienguoi-Jin, no! You don't understand!" Maishae screamed. He resisted the halberd, with gritted teeth and made a lunge at her.

Emily raised her staff into the air but was unable to stop her opponent's blow. The force of it knocked Emily off her feet, and she was flung into the side of the wall. She fell and lay nearly unconscious on the ground. Her mouth tasted of blood, and she coughed as she tried to move.

The imperial soldiers advanced on her, ready to strike, only to be stopped by a roaring Seitogi as he barreled into them. His blades set loose sprays of blood as he hacked at the them. He knocked down another one of their soldiers and was cut by a sword on his right arm. He stabbed the man through the heart and then snatched Emily's hand, dragging her to her feet.

"Get her out of here; I'll hold them off," Yienguoi-Jin said, dashing towards the Drizen imperial soldiers.

Seitogi threw his arm around Emily and held her to his chest. "Hold on to me tight," he whispered in her ear, dropping his blade and picking her up.

"I don't need you to rescue me," Emily barely managed as they plunged into the sea of bodies, pushing against everyone and everything.

Seitogi held her tightly, his face nuzzling her hair. Emily's eyes were closed, her trembling figure crushed against his rock-hard chest. His eyes were trained on the exit; it seemed an eternity before they reached it and broke through.

The moon was full, the air was cooling, but it was overshadowed by the stinging pain of her wounds. Emily opened her eyes to see Seitogi carrying her up a flight of stairs; several others were in pursuit.

“Seitogi, where are you taking me?” Emily managed to ask, her breathing heavy and her vision blurred.

“Away from here,” Seitogi replied, his voice gentle in her ear. “Away from here.”

“We have to go back for Beck!”

“You are hurt and bleeding, Emily.”

“I just can’t leave her here. I couldn’t live with myself.”

Seitogi sighed and nodded, “Alright, I will go back for her! But let me get you somewhere safe first.” Emily nodded yes. Seitogi took another flight of steps and pushed open a door with his foot.

“Can you use your mirror to hide somewhere?” he asked, carrying her into the room and setting her down.

“I can, but what about you?” Emily asked.

“I’ll return for Beck. Once I have her, we’ll meet you in the city where I met you and the crown prince the night you were attacked. You can find it in the mirror, can’t you?”

Emily nodded and concentrated again, this time with the mirror. She saw the dark alleyway Seitogi had rescued her and Glehson in all those months back.

“Yes! I can see it!”

“Then go there and hide yourself. I will bring your friend, I promise!”

“But…”

“I’ll find my way back to you, Emily, no matter what.”

Seitogi bowed to her and turned to leave, but Emily pulled him back, causing him to spin into her arms, and in one quick moment pulled his face down to hers and kissed him passionately. Seitogi straightened, pulling her up with him to the tips of her toes.

He held her around her waist and leaned into the kiss fearlessly.

"You'd better go." Emily forced a weak smile. He stroked her cheek and then left the room in a rush.

Once he was gone, she sat back and let the pain settle; her heart was filled with a sadness she had never felt.

She dragged herself to a corner of the room and stared into her mirror. The mirror showed her a teary-eyed image: a mess of smeared makeup with several wounds on her face. Emily dabbed at her face with her sleeve to clear the blood. She breathed in deeply, set the mirror down, and closed her eyes.

Maishae burst into the tiny room and cursed as she moved up to knock the mirror away from Emily. Emily raised the mirror up to defend herself.

"Don't, or I'll smash it."

Maishae paused and laughed, spitting. "The fading mirror won't easily be destroyed, little girl!"

Emily raised her arm and blocked another blow, but Maishae dropped her halberd, dodged a weak punch, and slammed her fist into Emily's jaw. Emily buckled; her head hit hard against the wall, and she slid down it, bleeding.

Maishae dropped to her knees next to Emily.

"Time to go, little girl. We have to get you back to the pocket!" Maishae dragged Emily up and slung her over her shoulder. She picked up the mirror and peered inside it.

"You can't do this, Maisha." Emily cried; her vision completely blurred from the blow.

"Of course, I can. You are my property."

Emily reached out and grabbed her sleeve, screaming, but Maishae slapped her hand away.

"I'm just taking you somewhere safe to perform the procedure." Maishae shouted for the others to follow.

As several others began to crowd the room, Maishae cursed and tripped. Emily saw an opening; using every ounce of strength to push herself off the floor, she pitched forward and flipped over Maishae's shoulder, snatching the mirror out of her hand as she did. Emily landed in front of the broken door, blood oozing from her mouth as she grinned and burst through the opening.

She ran head-on down the elevated loggia, kicking and swatting away others like so many flies. She blindly turned down a corridor and ran until her heart felt as though it were going to burst out of her chest.

She took a moment to catch her breath and concentrated on the mirror. She thought of Earth, its people, its cities, its nature. She sought out her town in her mind's eye, her grandmother; it somehow didn't matter that Dolores was Pheptae, who herself was a clone.

Suddenly, a shock of pain surged through Emily's skull as Maishae struck her in the head with the ball of a cane.

"I'm tired of playing nice with you," said Maishae, jumping from a portal above Emily, and stood over her, breathing hard too.

The pain was excruciating as Emily staggered forward and slammed onto the floor. Maishae grabbed her by her hair and held up her mirror. Emily struggled to her feet, but Maishae was too strong, and soon she had Emily sitting down on the floor again and brought the mirror down in front of them.

With an animalistic growl, Emily leaned forward and bit down on Maishae's ear, ripping off a large chunk of flesh and spitting it to the side. Maishae howled and struck out with her cane, the blow hitting Emily with such force that she went flying backward.

Emily groaned and somehow rose to her feet, holding up her mirror. In a daze, she focused on the cool glass, and a small, faraway ghostly image of Delores faded in and out of view. Emily drew a deep breath; the pain in her head was disorienting.

She reminisced about her grandmother, recalling their times spent shopping in local markets, cooking meals in their small apartment, and binge-watching shows together. Despite Delores's true identity as Pheptae, Emily missed her deeply. She pictured her seated in a place that seemed like an office, appearing frightened and anxious.

The mental image slowly grew more vivid, as though it were unfolding on a projected screen. She concentrated on the vision until it wholly engulfed her. Maishae's anguished cries of "No!" receded into a faint reverberation as Emily's presence gradually faded into oblivion.

Emily stumbled into the cramped room, brushing past two somber-looking men in cheap suits. Her tired and battered body gave way as she collapsed onto the desk where Delores was sitting.

Her grandmother shrieked as Emily tumbled into her lap, sending both of them crashing to the floor. In the ensuing chaos, one man's badge slipped from his grasp, while the other drew his firearm and struggled to maintain his grip.

Delores knew she only had a few seconds before the detectives regained their composure and pounced on her and Emily. In a moment of desperation, she grabbed the mirror from Emily's hand and focused her attention on it.

The surface of the mirror flickered, and Delores saw an image of a beach flash across it - blue sky, sand, and seagulls. She heard one of the detectives shout in bewilderment,

"What the hell is that?"

The brief distraction caused her to lose her grip on the image. Suddenly, she and Emily were enveloped by a searing wind filled with grains of sand, and Delores felt the burning sand beneath her. The sun hung low in the sky, casting its scorching rays down on them.

Looking around, Delores saw They had been transported to a scorching desert, a never-ending sea of sand, with no trace of an ocean in sight.

The End

Cast

Emily Heart

Aiyo Yuyuki, the Pearl Swan / Abete Enoshi / Aiyo Shumaiyuki / Zohn Gjei Zohri

Our protagonist

∞

Dolores Heart - Emily's grandmother

Rebecca Shaw - Emily's best friend

Abete Seitogi - Emily's adoptive brother

Shidia Moffit - A high school frenemy

Darren Toliver - Emily's boyfriend

Dwykhin Reyer - Squad leader for the Inouei Dhukai

Awei Chua - Leader of the Inouei Dhukai

Aiyo Shumaiyuki - Princess of House Aiyo, known as the Golden Swan

Aiyo Yulori - Lord of House Aiyo and uncle to Yuyuki and Shumaiyuki.

Rihtzkaya Inashata - Lord of House Rihtzkaya

Huasau Atem - Odahni Castle's man at arms

Dou Dodachi - Former head priest for the imperial House Anele

Yienguoi-Jin / Minister Djowobb / Zhon Yeingui Yeit

Father to Emily / Leader of the Taisehsai Dhukai / A finance minister with House Sowao / 1st Prince of House Zhon

∞

Sowao Dobein Phule - Lord of House Sowao and finance minister for the imperial court.

Daewon Iogwoei - Former leader of the Taisehsai Dhukai

Maishae - A wizened woman often referred to as "The Witch"

Tian Vhel Zao - A Taisesai Dhukai

Belfast Mannerling - A Taisesai Dhukai

Hun Yoosnom - Former leader of the Taisehsai Dhukai

Te-Tae - Shumaiyuki's nursemaid and personal attendant.

Reyj Obinari - Shumaiyuki's personal guardsman

Nami / Namai - Emily's former nursemaid

Ohna - A servant in House Sowao

Gléhson - A stable hand in House Sowao

Madame Nanda - An Imperial attendant

Kem - An imperial scribe

Aiyo Yumeiko - Empress of Behrani and Emily's Great Aunt

Anele Yunyu Rilkian - Crown Prince of Behrani

The Laughing Lark, Chua Arymaitei - Leader of the Merry-Larks Dhukai, sister to Emily

Zatrik / Bisui / Yazgiroh and Koenia - Merry-Larks

White Eyes - A former imperial spy turned Whisperer who uses his ravens to gather valuable information throughout Behra.

Dowahg Tomon Nogitunde - Heir to the Flying Carps Dhukai. Arymaitei's ex boyfriend.

Dowahg Gailen - Leader of the Flying Carps Dhukai and father to Nogi.

Ralavar Zefrey - A Carps Dhukai and advisor to Gailen

Jutha Roten - A Carps Dhukai and advisor to Gailen

Anele Yunsae Rijeil - First Berahnian Crown Prince. Older brother to Rilkian

Aiyo Teiyulori - Former lord of House Aiyo, Yulori's father, Yumeiko's twin

Anele Riju Sahyuh - The Emperor's brother, father to Shumaiyuki

Pheptae - Maishae's head of grounds and housekeeping

Cheedi – Anele maid serving in Maishae's house

Abete Syinta - Magistrate of Daiye village and father to Seitogi

Abete Demai - Mother to Seitogi

Teje Thalmeida - Personal spy to Shumaiyuki

Anele Ril Saehyun - Emperor of Berahni

Aiyo Oekei Ameiki – Princess of House Aiyo, known as the Bronze Swan and mother to Yuyuki and Shumaiyuki

Post

Emily coughed and choked as she was suddenly dragged back into the light and found herself spitting up a mouthful of water. She put up her hands in defense as another splash hit her in the face. She blinked several times and focused on a grinning, handsome face.

It was the face of a young man, his dusty brown hair whipped in the searing breeze and his soft gray eyes seemed kind. She struggled to sit upright, but he was quick to assist her and she clasped on to his strong arms as he lifted her into a sitting position.

"Please, drink more," he said as he gently placed the spout of the wooden canteen to her cracked lips. "Don't worry. We will help you." He cradled her, "May I ask your name?"

Emily turned her head and nodded. "Zoh...Zohri."

"Ok. Hello Zohri, I'm Bouen."

"Beau?" she whispered.

"I'm sorry, it's Bouen. My name is Thaijon Bouen, of Kathunobi village. You're lucky to be alive. How long have you been stranded out here?"

"I don't know. I'm sorry" Emily's eyes filled with tears, overcome with emotion.

"Please don't apologize. We found an old woman unconscious about half a mile from here. Were you together?"

"I, I don't know. I can't remember." Emily tried to focus her eyes but couldn't. Her body ached, she was bleeding from several wounds, and her chest throbbed. She was having difficulty trying to keep her breath.

"Where are you?" she said, softly. She strained to look at him, and then her head rolled to her side and fell limp. Her eyes fluttered shut and her world became dark and silent as she lost consciousness.

∞

Emily will return in

BTM 2: Zohri Kathunobi

About The Author

Leihei Emigli, a New York City-based author, initially started his career as a visual artist before transitioning into writing. Through his unique storytelling style, he skillfully translates the visions of his artwork, resulting in vivid imagery and rich descriptions. Emigli's passion for the arts shines through in his writing, which is celebrated for its creativity and originality. In his spare time, he enjoys delving into the city's dynamic arts scene.

Made in the USA
Middletown, DE
13 May 2023